Orwell and Politics

Animal Farm *in the Context of Essays, Reviews and Letters*
Selected from The Complete Works of George Orwell

Edited by Peter Davison
Introduction by Timothy Garton Ash

PENGUIN BOOKS

PENGUIN BOOKS

Published by the Penguin Group
Penguin Books Ltd, 80 Strand, London WC2R 0RL, England
Penguin Putnam Inc., 375 Hudson Street, New York, New York 10014, USA
Penguin Books Australia Ltd, 250 Camberwell Road, Camberwell, Victoria 3124, Australia
Penguin Books Canada Ltd, 10 Alcorn Avenue, Toronto, Ontario, Canada M4V 3B2
Penguin Books India (P) Ltd, 11 Community Centre, Panchsheel Park, New Delhi – 110 017, India
Penguin Books (NZ) Ltd, Cnr Rosedale and Airborne Roads, Albany, Auckland, New Zealand
Penguin Books (South Africa) (Pty) Ltd, 24 Sturdee Avenue, Rosebank 2196, South Africa

Penguin Books Ltd, Registered Offices: 80 Strand, London WC2R 0RL, England

www.penguin.com

This collection first published 2001
011

The texts in this collection are taken from *The Complete Works of George Orwell*, published by
Martin Secker & Warburg Ltd (vols. 1–9 1986, vols. 10–20 1998). *Animal Farm* previously
published in Penguin Books 1951 and 1989. Some material previously published in different form,
in *The Collected Essays, Journalism and Letters of George Orwell, Vols. 1–4*, in Penguin Books 1970

Animal Farm copyright © 1945 by Eric Blair
Other material copyright © the Estate of the late Sonia Brownell Orwell, 1998
Introduction copyright © Timothy Garton Ash, 2001
This selection, headnotes, footnotes and the Note on the Text of *Animal Farm*
copyright © Peter Davison, 2001
All rights reserved

The moral rights of the editor and of the author of the Introduction have been asserted

Set in 10/12.5 pt Monotype Columbus
Typeset by Rowland Phototypesetting Ltd, Bury St Edmunds, Suffolk
Printed in England by Clays Ltd, St Ives plc

www.greenpenguin.co.uk

MIX
Paper from
responsible sources
FSC
www.fsc.org
FSC™ C018179

Penguin Books is committed to a sustainable
future for our business, our readers and our planet.
This book is made from Forest Stewardship
Council™ certified paper.

ALWAYS LEARNING   **PEARSON**

Contents

Introduction

Why should we still read Orwell on politics? Until 1989, the answer was plain. He was the writer who captured the essence of totalitarianism. All over Communist-ruled Europe, people would show me their dog-eared, samizdat copies of *Animal Farm* or *Nineteen Eighty-Four* and ask, 'How did he know?'

Yet the world of *Nineteen Eighty-Four* ended in 1989. Orwellian regimes persisted in a few remote countries, such as North Korea, and Communism survived in an attenuated form in China. But the three dragons against which George Orwell fought his good fight – European and especially British Imperialism; Fascism, whether Italian, German or Spanish; and Communism, not to be confused with the democratic socialism in which Orwell himself believed – these three were all either dead or mortally weakened. Forty years after his own painful and early death, Orwell had won.

What need, then, of Orwell? One answer is that we should read him because of his historical impact. For George Orwell was the most influential political writer of the twentieth century. This is a bold claim, but who else would compete? Among novelists, perhaps Alexander Solzhenitsyn or Albert Camus; among playwrights, Bertolt Brecht. Or would it be a philosopher, such as Karl Popper, Friedrich von Hayek, Raymond Aron or Hannah Arendt? Or the novelist, playwright and philosopher Jean-Paul Sartre, whom Orwell privately called 'a bag of wind'? Take them one by one, and you will find that each made an impact more limited in duration or geographical scope than did this short-lived, old-fashioned, English man of letters.

Worldwide familiarity with the word 'Orwellian' is proof of that influence. 'Orwellian' is used as a pejorative adjective, to evoke totalitarian terror, the falsification of history by state-organized lying, and, more loosely, any unpleasant example of repression or manipulation. It is used as a noun, to describe an admirer and conscious follower of his work. Occasionally, it is deployed as a complimentary adjective, to mean something like 'displaying outspoken intellectual honesty, like Orwell'. Very few other writers have garnered this double tribute of becoming both adjective and noun.

Everywhere that people lived under totalitarian dictatorships, they felt he was one of them. The Russian poet Natalya Gorbanyevskaya once told me that Orwell was an East European. In fact, he was a very English writer who never went anywhere near Eastern Europe. His knowledge of the Communist world was largely derived from reading. As you can see from the book reviews reprinted in this volume, he drew heavily and directly on other people's reports from Soviet Russia.

Three personal experiences had transformed his understanding. First, as a British imperial policeman for five formative years in Burma he was himself the servant of an oppressive, though not a totalitarian, regime. By the time he resigned, he had acquired a lifelong hatred of Imperialism but also a deep insight into the psychology of the oppressor, displayed already in two classic early essays, 'A Hanging' and 'Shooting an Elephant'. (There is a rather obvious irony in the fact that post-colonial Burma is, at this writing, one of the world's few remaining Orwellian regimes.) Then he went to live among the 'down-and-outs' in England and in Paris. So he knew at first hand the humiliating unfreedom that comes from poverty.

Finally, there was the Spanish Civil War. Spain, for Orwell, meant the experience of fighting Fascism and getting a bullet through his throat. But still more important was the revelation of Russian-led Communist terror and duplicity, as he and his comrades in the heterodox Marxist POUM militia were hunted through the streets of Barcelona by the Communists who were supposed to be their allies. Of the Russian agent in Barcelona, charged with defaming the POUM as Trotskyist Francoist traitors, he writes, in *Homage to Catalonia*, 'It was the first time that I had seen a person whose profession was telling lies – unless one counts journalists.' The tail sting is typical black humour. It also reflects his disgust at the way the whole left-wing press in Britain was falsifying events that he had seen with his own eyes.

As he says in his 1946 essay 'Why I Write': after Spain he knew where he stood. He had earlier adopted the pen-name George Orwell, rather than his own Eric Blair, but it was after Spain that he really became Orwell. Every line of his writing was now to have a political purpose. Imperialism and Fascism would remain major targets of his generous anger. But the first enemy would be the blindness or intellectual dishonesty of those in the West who supported or condoned Stalinist Communism – ever more so, after the Soviet Union became the West's ally in the war against Hitler. And so he sat down to write a Swiftian satire on Stalinist Russia, with the Communists as the pigs in a farm run by the animals. 'Willingness to criticise Russia and Stalin,' he wrote in August 1944, 'is *the* test of intellectual honesty.'

The rejection of *Animal Farm* by several British publishers, because they did not want to criticize Britain's heroic wartime ally, showed what he was up against. When it was finally published in Britain in 1945, and then in the United States in 1946, the book was a political event, helping to open the eyes of the English-speaking West to the true nature of the Soviet regime. One might call this the Orwell effect. (France had to wait thirty years for its 'Solzhenitsyn effect'.) *Nineteen Eighty-Four*, with its more generalized dystopia, became another defining Cold War text. Not accidentally, the first use of the phrase 'Cold War' recorded in the *Oxford English Dictionary* comes from an article by Orwell.

In short, he was more memorably and influentially right than anyone, and sooner, about the single greatest political menace of the second half of the twentieth century, as well as seeing off the two largest horrors of the first half. But those monsters are dead, or on their last legs. To say 'read him because he mattered a lot in the past' will hardly attract new readers to these volumes, in the way that my generation was irresistibly drawn to the earlier Penguin four-set of his *Collected Essays, Journalism and Letters*, published in 1970.

Fortunately, there is a more compelling answer to the question why we should read Orwell in the twenty-first century. This is that he remains an exemplar of political writing. Both meanings of 'exemplar' are required. He is a model of how to do it well, but he is also an example – a deliberate, self-conscious and self-critical instance – of how difficult it is.

In 'Why I Write', he says that his purpose, after Spain, was to 'make political writing into an art'. At the heart of this volume is the work in which he most completely succeeded. *Animal Farm* is much more finely formed as a piece of literature than *Nineteen Eighty-Four,* which is marred by melodrama, *longeurs* and scratchy drafting by a dying man. In his 'little fairy story', artistic form and political content are perfectly matched – partly because they are so grotesquely mismatched. What could be further apart than Stalinist Moscow and an English country farmyard?

Orwell's prosecraft was hard learned. One of his earlier efforts earned the friendly criticism that he wrote 'like a cow with a musket'. Here he writes beautifully, about things he really knows. He cared passionately for the English countryside, and lived there in the late 1930s, keeping a village shop, a goat and a notebook. *Animal Farm* overflows from its first pages with lovingly observed physical detail of country life. But then, from the mouth of the pig Major, there erupts a perfect parody of a Communist speech: the fruit of many hours Orwell had spent poring over the political pamphlets he collected. Only he would have this peculiar combination of expertises. Only Orwell would know both how to milk a goat and how to skewer a revisionist.

The twists and turns of his animal regime closely follow the decay of the Russian revolution into tyranny. There is no ambiguity here: the pig Napoleon is Stalin, the pig Snowball is Trotsky. As Peter Davison points out, at the last minute Orwell even changed a detail in Napoleon's favour, after being told by a Polish survivor of the gulag that Stalin did, after all, inspire his people by remaining in Moscow during the German advance. His earlier novels are often poorly plotted. Here, history provides the perfect plot.

And there is his humour, an underrated part of Orwell's sandpapery charm. (Soon after he was shot through the neck in Spain, his commanding officer perceptively reported: 'Breathing absolutely regular. Sense of humour untouched.') When the animals have taken over the farm, 'some hams hanging in the kitchen were taken out for burial'. The morning after the pigs' first bout of whisky-drinking, Orwell has the propagandist Squealer come out to report to the other animals that 'Comrade Napoleon was dying'. Anyone who remembers their first hangover will know how he felt. And, finally, there is that perfect one-liner, at once comic and deeply serious: 'All Animals Are Equal, But Some Animals Are More Equal Than Others.'

In the end, *Animal Farm* far transcends its original occasion. It becomes a satire on the central comi-tragedy of politics altogether – that is, always and everywhere, the comi-tragedy of corruption by power. This ability to move from the particular to the universal also characterizes his essays: the other genre in which he wrote best about politics. His great essays, such as 'Notes on Nationalism', 'Benefit of Clergy' and 'Politics and the English Language', all share this quality. Even the shorter articles suddenly shine with sentences like this: 'It is a most encouraging thing to hear a human voice when fifty thousand gramophones are playing the same tune.'

What he abhors, perhaps more even than violence or tyranny, is dishonesty. Marching up and down the frontier between literature and politics, like a sentry for morality, he can spot a double standard at five hundred yards in bad light. Does a Tory MP demand freedom for Poland while remaining silent about India? Sentry Orwell fires off a quick round.

Orwell the moralist is fascinated by the pursuit not merely of truth, but of the most complicated and difficult truths. It starts already with the early 'Shooting an Elephant', where he confidently asserts that the British empire is dying but immediately adds that it is 'a great deal better than the younger empires that are going to supplant it'. Dissecting the work of Salvador Dali, he points out that 'what is morally degraded can be aesthetically right'. Then, characteristically, he goes one further and insists that we should be able to say, 'This is a good book or a good picture, and it ought to be burned by the public hangman.' At times, he seems to take an almost masochistic delight in confronting uncomfortable truths.

Not that his own political judgement was always good. Far from it. His vivacious and perceptive wife Eileen wrote to his sister that he retained 'an extraordinary political simplicity'. There are striking misjudgements here. It is startling to find him, early on, repeating the Communist line that 'fascism and capitalism are at bottom the same thing'. He opposed fighting Hitler until well into 1939, only to reverse his position. In *The Lion and the Unicorn*, his wartime tract on 'Socialism and the English Genius', he proposes that nationalization of 'land, mines, railways, banks and major industries'. So far as I can see, he never clearly acknowledged a link between private property and individual liberty. In this respect, at least, he was a socialist of his time.

Orwell was a very English writer, and we think of understatement as a very English quality. But his speciality is outrageous overstatement: 'No real revolutionary has ever been an internationalist', 'All left-wing parties in the highly industrialised countries are at bottom a sham', 'A humanitarian is always a hypocrite'. As V. S. Pritchett observed, in reviewing *The Lion and the Unicorn*, he 'is capable of exaggerating with the simplicity and innocence of a savage'. But that is what satirists do. Evelyn Waugh, from the other end of the political spectrum, did the same. (The great English curmudgeons of Left and Right had a wary but genuine mutual respect.) So this weakness of his non-fiction is one of the great strengths of his fiction.

Both his life and his work are case studies in the demands of political engagement. In 'Writers and Leviathan' he describes the political writer's dilemma: 'seeing the need of engaging in politics while also seeing what a dirty, degrading business it is'. After briefly being a member of the Independent Labour Party, he concludes that 'a writer can only remain honest if he keeps free of party labels'. That key-word 'honest' again. But he plans and becomes vice-chairman of a non-party organization called the Freedom Defence Committee, defending freedom against Imperialism and Fascism, of course, but now, above all, against Communism.

In this connection, a word is due about the already notorious list of crypto-communists and fellow-travellers, which he is popularly thought to have handed over to the British secret service. ('Socialist icon who became an informer', trumpeted the *Daily Telegraph* when 'breaking' the story on its front page in 1998.) The true facts are summarized at the end of this volume. Orwell kept a pale-blue notebook in which he noted names and details of suspected Communist agents or sympathizers. One should say at once that the content of this notebook is disquieting, with its sharp judgements – 'almost certainly agent of some kind', 'decayed liberal', 'appeaser only' – and especially its national/racial annotations: 'Jewish?' (Charlie Chaplin) or 'English Jew' (Tom Driberg) as well as 'Polish', 'Jugo-Slav', 'Anglo-American', and so on. There is something unsettling – a touch of the old imperial policeman – about a writer who could have lunch with a friend like the poet Stephen Spender and then go home to note: 'Sentimental sympathiser, & very unreliable. Easily influenced. Tendency towards homosexuality.'

However, two very important things need to be said in explanation. First, there was a cold war on. There were Soviet agents and sympathizers about, and they were influential. The most telling example is the man Orwell had down as 'Almost certainly agent of some kind'. His name was Peter Smollett. During the Second World War he was the head of the Russian section in the Ministry of Information, and it was on his advice that *Animal Farm* was rejected by Jonathan Cape. We now know that Smollett was indeed a Soviet spy.

Second, Orwell did not give this notebook to the British secret service. He gave a list of some thirty-five names drawn from it to the Information Research Department, a semi-secret branch of the Foreign Office which specialized in getting writers on the democratic Left to counter the then highly organized Soviet Communist propaganda offensive. Absurdly, the British government has not declassified this list and any letter that accompanied it. So we still do not know exactly what Orwell did. But from the available evidence it is quite clear that Orwell was not putting some British thought police onto these people's tails. All he was doing, in effect, was to say: 'Don't use these people for anti-Communist propaganda because they are probably Communists or Communist sympathizers!'

A dying man, but still in complete command of his faculties, Orwell judged this to be a morally defensible act for a writer in a period of intense political struggle, just as he had earlier judged that it was proper for a politically engaged writer to take up arms against Franco. I think he was right. You may think he was wrong. Either way, he exemplifies for us – he is that exemplar of – the dilemmas of the political writer.

Finally, of course, Orwell's list, and Orwell's life, are much less important than the work. It matters, to be sure, that there is no flagrant contradiction between the work and the life – as there often is with political intellectuals. The Orwellian voice, placing honesty and single standards above everything, would be diminished. But what endures is the work.

If I had to name a single quality that makes Orwell still essential reading in the twenty-first century, it would be his insight into the use and abuse of language. If you have time to read only one essay in this book, please read 'Politics and the English Language'. This brilliantly sums up the central Orwellian argument that the corruption of language is an essential part of oppressive or exploitative politics. 'The defence of the indefensible' is sustained by a battery of euphemisms, verbal false limbs, prefabricated phrases, and all the other paraphernalia of deceit that he pinpoints and parodies.

The extreme, totalitarian version that he satirized as 'Newspeak' is less often encountered these days, except in countries like Burma or North Korea. But the obsession of democratically elected governments, especially in Britain and America, with media management and 'spin' is today one of the main obstacles to understanding what is being done in our name. There are also distortions that come from within the press, radio and television themselves, partly because of hidden ideological bias but increasingly because of fierce commercial competition and the relentless need to 'entertain'.

Read Orwell, and you will know that something nasty *must* be hidden behind the euphemistic, Latinate phrase used by NATO spokespersons during the Kosovo war: 'collateral damage'. (It means innocent civilians killed.) Read Orwell, and you will smell a rat whenever you find a British newspaper or politician once again churning out a prefabricated phrase such as 'Brussels' inexorable march to a European superstate'.

He does not just equip us to detect this semantic abuse. He also suggests how writers can fight back. For the abusers of power are, after all, using our weapons: words. In 'Politics and the English Language' he even gives some simple stylistic rules for honest and effective political writing. (Hard-won wisdom, for he had worked a heavy passage to such clarity.) He compares good English prose to a clean window-pane. Through these windows, citizens can see what their rulers are really up to. So political writers should be the window-cleaners of freedom.

Orwell both tells and shows us how to do it. That is why we need him still, because Orwell's work is never done.

Timothy Garton Ash
Oxford, December 2000

Editorial Note

In the main, the items reproduced here are given in the chronological order in which they were written or published. However, the order of events is sometimes better represented by not following this practice. It will be obvious, from dates and item numbers, where the chronological order has not been followed. Letters are typewritten unless stated otherwise. The titles used for Orwell's essays and articles are not always his own but this distinction is not noted unless there is a special reason to do so.

All the items are drawn from *The Complete Works of George Orwell*, edited by Peter Davison, assisted by Ian Angus and Sheila Davison (Secker & Warburg, 1998). Some explanatory headnotes and many footnotes have been added, amplified and modified. The *Complete Works* did not provide biographical notes of authors of books reviewed but, for this selection, these have been added if the author had a link with Orwell or if they might illuminate the context of Orwell's review. Item numbers from the original edition are given in italics within square parentheses, and a list of volumes in which these items can be found is given in the Further Reading.

Where the text was in some way obscure, the original edition does not modify but marks the word or passage with a superior degree sign (°); in most instances such passages have been silently corrected in this edition but in a few instances the degree sign has been retained, for example, where one of Orwell's idiosyncratic spellings occurs: e.g., 'agressive' or 'adress'.

References to items in the *Complete Works* are generally given by volume, forward slash and item number in italic: e.g.: XV/*1953*; page references to *CW* are given similarly except that the page number is in

roman: XII/387; page references to this present volume are given as 'p. 57';
references are also made to the companion three volumes: *Orwell in Spain*,
Orwell and the Second Nation and *Orwell's England*. References to *Animal
Farm* are given to this edition by page and, within square brackets, by the
CW volume number (VIII) and page (the page numbers in *CW* and
Penguin Twentieth-Century Classics are identical for the text): e.g., p. 7
[VIII/239].

The following works are designated by abbreviated forms:

Complete Works and *CW*: *The Complete Works of George Orwell*, edited by
Peter Davison assisted by Ian Angus and Sheila Davison, 20 vols.
(1998); volume numbers are given in roman numerals, I to XX.
Vols. X–XX of a second, enlarged and amended, edition are being
published in paperback from September 2000.

CEJL: *The Collected Essays, Journalism and Letters of George Orwell*, edited by
Sonia Orwell and Ian Angus, 4 vols. (1968; paperback, 1970)

Crick: Bernard Crick, *George Orwell: A Life* (1980; 3rd edn, 1992)

A Literary Life: P. Davison, *George Orwell: A Literary Life* (1996)

Orwell Remembered: Audrey Coppard and Bernard Crick, eds., *Orwell
Remembered* (1984)

Remembering Orwell: Stephen Wadhams, ed., *Remembering Orwell* (1984)

S&A, *Unknown Orwell*: Peter Stansky and William Abrahams, *The Unknown
Orwell* (1972)

S&A, *Transformation*: Peter Stansky and William Abrahams, *Orwell: The
Transformation* (1979)

Shelden: Michael Shelden, *Orwell: The Authorised Biography* (1991)

The Thirties: Malcolm Muggeridge, *The Thirties* (1940; 1971); reviewed by
Orwell, XII/615

Thomas: Hugh Thomas, *The Spanish Civil War* (revd edn, 1977; Penguin
1979)

A selection of articles and reviews in the *Complete Works* which are not
included in this selection and a fuller reading list is given in Further
Reading.

Peter Davison,
De Montfort University, Leicester

Acknowledgements

George Orwell's (Eric Blair's) work is the copyright of the Estate of the late Sonia Brownell Orwell. Most of the documents in this edition are held by the Orwell Archive (founded by Sonia Orwell in 1960) at University College London. Gratitude is expressed to the Archive, and particularly to its Archivist, Gill Furlong, for the help given the editor. Thanks are also gratefully extended to the Henry W. and Albert A. Berg Collection, The New York Public Library, Astor, Lennox and Tilden Foundations, for permission to reproduce the conclusion to Orwell's letter to John Middleton Murry, 5 August 1944; and to Yale University Library, Manuscripts and Archives, for permission to reproduce the extract from Orwell's letter to Dwight Macdonald, 5 December 1946.

'How a Nation Is Exploited: The British Empire in Burma'
Le Progrès Civique, 4 May 1929

*George Orwell[1] served in the Indian Imperial Police in Burma from 1922
until 1927. He returned to England on leave on 12 July 1927 and, having
left his ship in Marseilles and travelled home through France, arrived back
in England in August. While on holiday with his family in Cornwall in
September he decided not to return to Burma. His resignation took effect from
1 January 1928 and entailed the loss of almost £140 (approximately £5,500
in today's values). By the time he left Burma he was earning £696 a year
(roughly £28,000 today),[2] to which were added bonuses for learning
Hindi, Burmese and Shaw-Karen. He would only earn approaching this
much again in the next fourteen years when he joined the BBC in 1941
(£640). It is likely, from what we know of clothes he had made for him on
his return (see* A Literary Life, 36) *and the style in which he lived for most
of his time in Paris, that he had saved a fair amount of his pay. During the
rest of his leave he rented a cheap room in the Portobello Road in Notting
Hill, London W11. He began to make expeditions to the East End of London
in the autumn of 1927. In the spring of 1928, Orwell went to Paris and
took a room at 6 rue du Pot de Fer in the Fifth Arrondissement, a
working-class district near Monge Métro station. He set himself to becoming
a writer and had a modest success in getting articles into small-circulation,
left-wing journals. He also wrote either one or two novels and a number of
short stories, none of which survive. The article reproduced here, 'How a
Nation Is Exploited: The British Empire in Burma' (translated from the
French version by Janet Percival and Ian Willison), is one of a number he
wrote which were published by* Le Progrès Civique *in 1928 and 1929.
The journal also published his articles on unemployment, tramps and
beggars, two of which are reprinted in companion volumes in this series,*
Orwell and the Dispossessed *and* Orwell's England. *For each he was*

*paid 225 francs (about £1.80 – some £70 at today's values). He also wrote
articles on John Galsworthy and on censorship in England which were
published by French journals. They, with an article on 'A Farthing Newspaper' published in England (and reproduced in* Orwell and the Dispossessed*), are an epitome of the interests he would pursue as an essayist:
social and political issues, literature, popular culture and imperialism. The*
Complete Works *prints all the articles, with their French originals. The
very short paragraphs are not typical of Orwell. Orwell wrote in English
(in a version that has not survived) and the French translator, Raoul Nicole,
is almost certainly responsible for breaking Orwell's prose into short bites. It
is possible that the divisions marked by line breaks represent Orwell's original
paragraphing.*

Burma lies between India and China. Ethnologically it belongs to Indo-
China.

It is three times the size of England and Wales, with a population of
about fourteen million, of whom roughly nine million are Burmese.

The rest is made up of countless Mongol tribes who have emigrated at
various periods from the steppes of Central Asia, and Indians who have
arrived since the English occupation.

The Burmese are Buddhists; the tribesmen worship various pagan
gods.

To be able to talk in their own language to the people of such diverse
origins living in Burma, you would need to know a hundred and twenty
different languages and dialects.

This country, the population of which is one-tenth as dense as that of
England, is one of the richest in the world. It abounds in natural resources
which are only just beginning to be exploited.

Its forests are full of timber trees, an ideal source of first-class building
materials.

There are tin, tungsten, jade and rubies, and these are the least of its
mineral resources.

At this moment it produces five per cent of the world's petroleum, and
its reserves are far from exhausted.

But the greatest source of wealth – and that which feeds between
eighty and ninety per cent of the population – is the paddy-fields.

Rice is grown everywhere in the basin of the Irawaddy, which flows through Burma from north to south.

In the south, in the huge delta where the Irawaddy brings down tons of alluvial mud every year, the soil is immensely fertile.

The harvests, which are remarkable in both quality and quantity, enable Burma to export rice to India, Europe, even to America.

Moreover, variations in temperature are less frequent and sharp than in India.

Thanks to abundant rainfall, especially in the south, drought is unknown, and the heat is never excessive. The climate as a whole can thus be considered one of the healthiest to be found in the tropics.

If we add that the Burmese countryside is exceptionally beautiful, with broad rivers, high mountains, eternally green forests, brightly coloured flowers, exotic fruits, the phrase 'earthly paradise' naturally springs to mind.

So it is hardly surprising that the English tried for a long time to gain possession of it.

In 1820 they seized a vast expanse of territory. This operation was repeated in 1852, and finally in 1882 the Union Jack flew over almost all the country.[3]

Certain mountainous districts in the north, inhabited by small savage tribes, had until recently escaped the clutches of the British, but it is more and more likely that they will meet the same fate as the rest of the country, thanks to the process euphemistically known as 'peaceful penetration', which means, in plain English, 'peaceful annexation'.

In this article I do not seek to praise or blame this manifestation of British imperialism; let us simply note it is a logical result of any imperialist policy.

It will be much more profitable to examine the good and bad sides of British administration in Burma from an economic and a political standpoint.

Let us turn first to politics.

The government of all the Indian provinces under the control of the British Empire is of necessity despotic, because only the threat of force can subdue a population of several million subjects.

But this despotism is latent. It hides behind a mask of democracy.

The great maxim of the English in governing an oriental race is 'never get something done by a European when an Oriental can do it'. In other words, supreme power remains with the British authorities, but the minor civil servants who have to carry out day-to-day administration and who must come into contact with the people in the course of their duties are recruited locally.

In Burma, for example, the lower grade magistrates, all policemen up to the rank of inspector, members of the postal service, government employees, village elders etc. are Burmese.

Recently, to appease public opinion and put a stop to nationalist agitation which was beginning to cause concern, it was even decided to accept the candidature of educated natives for several important posts.

The system of employing natives as civil servants has three advantages.

First, natives will accept lower salaries than Europeans.

Secondly, they have a better idea of the workings of their fellow countrymen's minds, and this helps them to settle legal disputes more easily.

Thirdly, it is to their own advantage to show their loyalty to a government which provides their livelihood.

And so peace is maintained by ensuring the close collaboration of the educated or semi-educated classes, where discontent might otherwise produce rebel leaders.

Nevertheless the British control the country. Of course, Burma, like each of the Indian provinces, has a parliament – always the show of democracy – but in reality its parliament has very little power.

Nothing of any consequence lies within its jurisdiction. Most of the members are puppets of the government, which is not above using them to nip in the bud any Bill which seems untimely.

In addition, each province has a Governor, appointed by the English, who has at his disposal a veto just as absolute as that of the President of the United States to oppose any proposal which displeases him.

Yet although the British government is, as we have shown, essentially despotic, it is by no means unpopular.

The English are building roads and canals – in their own interest, of course, but the Burmese benefit from them – they set up hospitals, open schools, and see to the maintenance of law and order.

And after all, the Burmese are mere peasants, occupied in cultivating the land. They have not yet reached that stage of intellectual development which makes for nationalists.

Their village is their universe, and as long as they are left in peace to cultivate their fields, they do not care whether their masters are black or white.

A proof of this political apathy on the part of the people of Burma is the fact that the only British military forces in the country are two English infantry battalions and around ten battalions of Indian infantry and mounted police.

Thus twelve thousand armed men, mostly Indians, are enough to subdue a population of fourteen million.

The most dangerous enemies of the government are the young men of the educated classes. If these classes were more numerous and were *really* educated, they could perhaps raise the revolutionary banner. But they are not.

The reason is firstly that, as we have seen, the majority of the Burmese are peasants.

Secondly, the British government is at pains to give the people only summary instruction, which is almost useless, merely sufficient to produce messengers, low-grade civil servants, petty lawyers' clerks and other white-collar workers.

Care is taken to avoid technical and industrial training. This rule, observed throughout India, aims to stop India from becoming an industrial country capable of competing with England.

It is true to say that in general, any really educated Burmese was educated in England, and belongs as a result to the small class of the well-to-do.

So, because there are no educated classes, public opinion, which could press for rebellion against England, is non-existent.

Let us now consider the economic question. Here again we find the Burmese in general too ignorant to have a clear understanding of the way in which they are being treated and, as a result, too ignorant to show the least resentment.

Besides, for the moment they have not suffered much economic damage.

It is true that the British seized the mines and the oil wells. It is true that they control timber production. It is true that all sorts of middlemen, brokers, millers, exporters, have made colossal fortunes from rice without the producer – that is the peasant – getting a thing out of it.

It is also true that the get-rich-quick businessmen who made their pile from rice, petrol etc. are not contributing as they should be to the well-being of the country, and that their money, instead of swelling local revenues in the form of taxes, is sent abroad to be spent in England.

If we are honest, it is true that the British are robbing and pilfering Burma quite shamelessly.

But we must stress that the Burmese hardly notice it *for the moment*. Their country is so rich, their population so scattered, their needs, like those of all Orientals, so slight that they are not conscious of being exploited.

The peasant cultivating his patch of ground lives more or less as his ancestors did in Marco Polo's day. If he wishes, he can buy virgin land for a reasonable price.

He certainly leads an arduous existence, but he is on the whole free from care.

Hunger and unemployment are for him meaningless words. There is work and food for everyone. Why worry needlessly?

But, and this is the important point, the Burmese will begin to suffer when a large part of the richness of their country has declined.

Although Burma has developed to a certain extent since the war, already the peasant there is poorer than he was twenty years ago.

He is beginning to feel the weight of land taxation, for which he is not compensated by the increased yield of his harvests.

The worker's wages have not kept up with the cost of living.

The reason is that the British government has allowed free entry into Burma for veritable hordes of Indians, who, coming from a land where they were literally dying of hunger, work for next to nothing and are, as a result, fearsome rivals for the Burmese.

Add to this a rapid rise in population growth – at the last census the population registered an increase of ten million in ten years – it is easy to see that sooner or later, as happens in all overpopulated countries, the

Burmese will be dispossessed of their lands, reduced to a state of semi-slavery in the service of capitalism, and will have to endure unemployment into the bargain.

They will then discover what they hardly suspect today, that the oil wells, the mines, the milling industry, the sale and cultivation of rice are all controlled by the British.

They will also realise their own industrial incompetence in a world where industry dominates.

British politics in Burma is the same as in India.

Industrially speaking, India was deliberately kept in ignorance.

She only produces basic necessities, made by hand. The Indians would be incapable, for example, of making a motor-car, a rifle, a clock, an electric-light bulb etc. They would be incapable of building or sailing an ocean-going vessel.

At the same time they have learnt in their dealings with Westerners to depend on certain machine-made articles. So the products of English factories find an important outlet in a country incapable of manufacturing them herself.

Foreign competition is prevented by an insuperable barrier of prohibitive customs tariffs. And so the English factory-owners, with nothing to fear, control the markets absolutely and reap exorbitant profits.

We said that the Burmese have not yet suffered too much, but this is because they have remained, on the whole, an agricultural nation.

Yet for them as for all Orientals, contact with Europeans has created the demand, unknown to their fathers, for the products of modern industry. As a result, the British are stealing from Burma in two ways:

In the first place, they pillage her natural resources; secondly, they grant themselves the exclusive right to sell her the manufactured products she now needs.

And the Burmese are thus drawn into the system of industrial capitalism, without any hope of becoming capitalist industrialists themselves.

Moreover the Burmese, like all the other peoples of India, remain under the rule of the British Empire for purely military considerations. For they are in effect incapable of building ships, manufacturing guns or any other arms necessary for modern warfare, and, as things now stand, if the

English were to give up India, it would only result in a change of master. The country would simply be invaded and exploited by some other Power.

British domination in India rests essentially on exchanging military protection for a commercial monopoly, but, as we have tried to show, the bargain is to the advantage of the English whose control reaches into every domain.

To sum up, if Burma derives some incidental benefit from the English, she must pay dearly for it.

Up till now the English have refrained from oppressing the native people too much because there has been no need. The Burmese are still at the beginning of a period of transition which will transform them from agricultural peasants to workers in the service of the manufacturing industries.

Their situation could be compared with that of any people of eighteenth-century Europe, apart from the fact that the capital, construction materials, knowledge and power necessary for their commerce and industry belong exclusively to foreigners.

So they are under the protection of a despotism which defends them for its own ends, but which would abandon them without hesitation if they ceased to be of use.

Their relationship with the British Empire is that of slave and master.

Is the master good or bad? That is not the question; let us simply say that his control is despotic and, to put it plainly, self-interested.

Even though the Burmese have not had much cause for complaint up till now, the day will come when the riches of their country will be insufficient for a population which is constantly growing.

Then they will be able to appreciate how capitalism shows its gratitude to those to whom it owes its existence.

E.-A. BLAIR

1. The pen-name 'George Orwell' was first used in January 1933 for *Down and Out in Paris and London*. It was not regularly used for reviews and articles until December 1936. Unless the pen-name is used, the form given here for articles and essays is that found in the original publication – E. A. Blair, E.-A. Blair, Eric Blair, E. A. B., or E. B. For much of his time at

the BBC (1941–3) Orwell was known as Eric Blair. In correspondence, he tended to sign himself, and be addressed, as Eric or George depending upon whether the correspondent originally knew him as Eric or George. Occasionally, if a secretary typed a letter for him, he would sign Eric Blair over a typed George Orwell.

2. Very roughly, prices in the 1930s can be multiplied by forty, and in the 1940s by thirty-five, to give an approximate contemporary equivalent. It must be realized that inflation has not affected everything to the same degree. In Orwell's lifetime the coinage had not been metricated. There were twelve pennies to a shilling and twenty shillings (so 240 pennies) to one pound sterling; halfpennies and farthings, as well as threepenny bits (much sought after at Christmas to put into Christmas puddings), were current. So: 1p = 2.4 old pennies.

3. Burma was annexed by the British following the Anglo-Burmese Wars of 1824–6, 1852 and 1885. It was at first ruled as part of India but in 1936 there was a strike by university students of the Thakin Movement led by U Nu and Aung San, and in 1937 Burma was ruled independently of India. This led to fears that Burma would not share in reforms proposed for India. From 1942 to 1945 it was occupied by the Japanese and the scene of fierce battles. In July 1947, Aung San and members of his Cabinet were assassinated. However, Burma became independent on 4 January 1948. It now calls itself Myanmar and has for some years been under military rule. In 1999 it was possible to buy pirated copies of *Burmese Days* in Rangoon for 600 Kyats (about £1.30), photocopied (with cover) from the Penguin Twentieth-Century Classics edition, 1989.

[108]

'A Hanging'
The Adelphi, *August 1931; reprinted in the* New Savoy, *1946*

> *Although 'A Hanging' and 'Shooting an Elephant' were not written as specifically 'political' essays, they have important political implications. They may be considered as precursors of what Orwell described as his aim in 'Why I Write' (reprinted in this volume), 'to make political writing into an art'. Orwell referred to 'the obscene fact' of hanging in 'As I Please', 61 (XVIII/3115) when discussing the public hanging of three Germans on 19 December 1943. They had been found guilty of atrocities in the first war-crimes trial at Kharkov; a Ukrainian was also hanged. Four paragraphs were reprinted under the heading 'Hanging To-day' in The Plebs, June 1947, as part of the (successful) campaign to end the death sentence by hanging in the UK. In The Road to Wigan Pier, Orwell wrote, 'I watched a man hanged once' (136–7). For 'Shooting an Elephant', see below.*

It was in Burma, a sodden morning of the rains. A sickly light, like yellow tinfoil, was slanting over the high walls into the jail yard. We were waiting outside the condemned cells, a row of sheds fronted with double bars, like small animal cages. Each cell measured about ten feet by ten and was quite bare within except for a plank bed and a pot for drinking water. In some of them brown silent men were squatting at the inner bars, with their blankets draped round them. These were the condemned men, due to be hanged within the next week or two.

One prisoner had been brought out of his cell. He was a Hindu, a puny wisp of a man, with a shaven head and vague liquid eyes. He had a thick, sprouting moustache, absurdly too big for his body, rather like the moustache of a comic man on the films. Six tall Indian warders were guarding him and getting him ready for the gallows. Two of them stood by with rifles and fixed bayonets, while the others handcuffed him, passed a chain through his handcuffs and fixed it to their belts, and lashed his arms tight to his sides. They crowded very close about him, with their hands always on him in a careful, caressing grip, as though all the while feeling him to make sure he was there. It was like men handling a fish which is still alive and may jump back into the water. But he stood quite unresisting, yielding his arms limply to the ropes, as though he hardly noticed what was happening.

Eight o'clock struck and a bugle call, desolately thin in the wet air, floated from the distant barracks. The superintendent of the jail, who was standing apart from the rest of us, moodily prodding the gravel with his stick, raised his head at the sound. He was an army doctor, with a grey toothbrush moustache and a gruff voice. 'For God's sake hurry up, Francis,' he said irritably. 'The man ought to have been dead by this time. Aren't you ready yet?'

Francis, the head jailer, a fat Dravidian in a white drill suit and gold spectacles, waved his black hand. 'Yes sir, yes sir,' he bubbled. 'All iss satisfactorily prepared. The hangman iss waiting. We shall proceed.'

'Well, quick march, then. The prisoners can't get their breakfast till this job's over.'

We set out for the gallows. Two warders marched on either side of the prisoner, with their rifles at the slope; two others marched close against him, gripping him by arm and shoulder, as though at once pushing and supporting him. The rest of us, magistrates and the like, followed behind. Suddenly, when we had gone ten yards, the procession stopped short without any order or warning. A dreadful thing had happened – a dog, come goodness knows whence, had appeared in the yard. It came bounding among us with a loud volley of barks, and leapt round us wagging its whole body, wild with glee at finding so many human beings together. It was a large woolly dog, half Airedale, half pariah. For a moment it pranced round us, and then, before anyone could stop it, it had made a dash for the prisoner, and jumping up tried to lick his face. Everyone stood aghast, too taken aback even to grab at the dog.

'Who let that bloody brute in here?' said the superintendent angrily. 'Catch it, someone!'

A warder, detached from the escort, charged clumsily after the dog, but it danced and gambolled just out of his reach, taking everything as part of the game. A young Eurasian jailer picked up a handful of gravel and tried to stone the dog away, but it dodged the stones and came after us again. Its yaps echoed from the jail walls. The prisoner, in the grasp of the two warders, looked on incuriously, as though this was another formality of the hanging. It was several minutes before someone managed to catch the dog. Then we put my handkerchief through its collar and moved off once more, with the dog still straining and whimpering.

It was about forty yards to the gallows. I watched the bare brown back of the prisoner marching in front of me. He walked clumsily with his bound arms, but quite steadily, with that bobbing gait of the Indian who never straightens his knees. At each step his muscles slid neatly into place, the lock of hair on his scalp danced up and down, his feet printed themselves on the wet gravel. And once, in spite of the men who gripped him by each shoulder, he stepped slightly aside to avoid a puddle on the path.

It is curious, but till that moment I had never realised what it means to destroy a healthy, conscious man. When I saw the prisoner step aside to avoid the puddle, I saw the mystery, the unspeakable wrongness, of cutting a life short when it is in full tide. This man was not dying, he was alive just as we were alive. All the organs of his body were working – bowels digesting food, skin renewing itself, nails growing, tissues forming – all toiling away in solemn foolery. His nails would still be growing when he stood on the drop, when he was falling through the air with a tenth-of-a-second to live. His eyes saw the yellow gravel and the grey walls, and his brain still remembered, foresaw, reasoned – reasoned even about puddles. He and we were a party of men walking together, seeing, hearing, feeling, understanding the same world; and in two minutes, with a sudden snap, one of us would be gone – one mind less, one world less.

The gallows stood in a small yard, separate from the main grounds of the prison, and overgrown with tall prickly weeds. It was a brick erection like three sides of a shed, with planking on top, and above that two beams and a crossbar with the rope dangling. The hangman, a grey-haired convict in the white uniform of the prison, was waiting beside his machine. He greeted us with a servile crouch as we entered. At a word from Francis the two warders, gripping the prisoner more closely than ever, half led half pushed him to the gallows and helped him clumsily up the ladder. Then the hangman climbed up and fixed the rope round the prisoner's neck.

We stood waiting, five yards away. The warders had formed in a rough circle round the gallows. And then, when the noose was fixed, the prisoner began crying out on his god. It was a high, reiterated cry of 'Ram! Ram! Ram! Ram!'[1] not urgent and fearful like a prayer or a cry for help, but steady, rhythmical, almost like the tolling of a bell. The dog answered the sound with a whine. The hangman, still standing on the gallows, produced a small cotton bag like a flour bag and drew it down over the prisoner's face. But the sound, muffled by the cloth, still persisted, over and over again: 'Ram! Ram! Ram! Ram! Ram!'

The hangman climbed down and stood ready, holding the lever. Minutes seemed to pass. The steady, muffled crying from the prisoner went on and on, 'Ram! Ram! Ram!' never faltering for an instant. The superintendent, his head on his chest, was slowly poking the ground with his stick; perhaps he was counting the cries, allowing the prisoner a fixed number – fifty, perhaps, or a hundred. Everyone had changed colour. The Indians had gone grey like bad coffee, and one or two of the bayonets were wavering. We looked at the lashed, hooded man on the drop, and listened to his cries – each cry another second of life; the same thought was in all our minds: oh, kill him quickly, get it over, stop that abominable noise!

Suddenly the superintendent made up his mind. Throwing up his head he made a swift motion with his stick, 'Chalo!' he shouted almost fiercely.

There was a clanking noise, and then dead silence. The prisoner had vanished, and the rope was twisting on itself. I let go of the dog, and it galloped immediately to the back of the gallows; but when it got there it stopped short, barked, and then retreated into a corner of the yard, where it stood among the weeds, looking timorously out at us. We went round the gallows to inspect the prisoner's body. He was dangling with his toes pointed straight downwards, very slowly revolving, as dead as a stone.

The superintendent reached out with his stick and poked the bare brown body; it oscillated slightly. '*He's* all right,' said the superintendent. He backed out from under the gallows, and blew out a deep breath. The moody look had gone out of his face quite suddenly. He glanced at his wrist-watch. 'Eight minutes past eight. Well, that's all for this morning, thank God.'

The warders unfixed bayonets and marched away. The dog, sobered and conscious of having misbehaved itself, slipped after them. We walked out of the gallows yard, past the condemned cells with their waiting prisoners, into the big central yard of the prison. The convicts, under the command of warders armed with lathis, were already receiving their breakfast. They squatted in long rows, each man holding a tin pannikin, while two warders with buckets marched round ladling out rice; it seemed quite a homely, jolly scene, after the hanging. An enormous relief had come upon us now that the job was done. One felt an impulse to sing, to break into a run, to snigger. All at once everyone began chattering gaily.

The Eurasian boy walking beside me nodded towards the way we had come, with a knowing smile: 'Do you know, sir, our friend (he meant the dead man), when he heard his appeal had been dismissed, he pissed on the floor of his cell. From fright. – Kindly take one of my cigarettes, sir. Do you not admire my new silver case, sir? From the boxwalah, two rupees eight annas. Classy European style.'

Several people laughed – at what, nobody seemed certain.

Francis was walking by the superintendent, talking garrulously: 'Well, sir, all hass passed off with the utmost satisfactoriness. It wass all finished – flick! like that. It iss not always so – oah, no! I have known cases where the doctor wass obliged to go beneath the gallows and pull the prissoner's legs to ensure decease. Most disagreeable!'

'Wriggling about, eh? That's bad,' said the superintendent.

'Ach, sir, it iss worse when they become refractory! One man, I recall, clung to the bars of hiss cage when we went to take him out. You will scarcely credit, sir, that it took six warders to dislodge him, three pulling at each leg. We reasoned with him. "My dear fellow," we said, "think of all the pain and trouble you are causing to us!" But no, he would not listen! Ach, he wass very troublesome!'

I found that I was laughing quite loudly. Everyone was laughing. Even the superintendent grinned in a tolerant way. 'You'd better all come out and have a drink,' he said quite genially. 'I've got a bottle of whisky in the car. We could do with it.'

We went through the big double gates of the prison, into the road. 'Pulling at his legs!' exclaimed a Burmese magistrate suddenly, and burst into a loud chuckling. We all began laughing again. At that moment Francis' anecdote seemed extraordinarily funny. We all had a drink together, native and European alike, quite amicably. The dead man was a hundred yards away.

ERIC A. BLAIR

1. Ram: Hindu god, said to have been born at Ayodhya, Uttar Pradesh. A Muslim temple was built on the site in the fifteenth century. This was torn down in 1992 by Hindus. In the ensuing violence hundreds of people were killed.

[308]

Review of The Fate of the Middle Classes by Alec Brown
The Adelphi, May 1936

It is interesting and rather depressing to see such a complex thing as the English class-system expounded by an orthodox Communist. It is like watching somebody carve a roast duck with a chopper. Mr. Brown, resolutely ignoring everything except economic status, lumps into the middle class the entire block of the population between the dividend-drawers on the one hand and the wage-slaves on the other. The lawyer, the publican, the retail grocer, the clergyman, the smallholder and the village cobbler are all, it seems, 'middle class', and Mr. Brown discusses now this type, now that, as though there were no serious distinction between them except the size of their incomes. It is a method of classification about as useful as dividing the population into bald men and hairy men.

In reality the most important fact about the English class-system is that it is *not* entirely explicable in terms of money. The money-relationship on which the Communist rightly insists is interpenetrated by a sort of spurious caste-system. There is no aristocracy in England and in the last resort money will buy anything; yet the aristocratic tradition persists and people are willing to act on it. Hence the fact that every manufacturer or stockbroker who has made his pile sets up an alibi as a country gentleman; hence also the fact that a man with £3 a week who can pronounce his aitches regards himself – and is regarded by other people, to some extent – as the superior of a man with £10 a week who can't. This last fact is enormously important, for it is because of this that the aitch-pronouncing section of the population tend to side with their natural enemies and against the working class, even when they grasp the economic side of the question fairly clearly. The statement that 'every ideology is a reflection of economic circumstances' explains a good deal, but it does not explain the strange and sometimes heroic snobbishness that is found in the English middle classes.

The best thing in this book is the explanation – repeated rather too often – of the change that has come over British capitalism since it ceased to export goods and began to export capital. The writing, as in Mr. Brown's other books,[1] is vigorous but slipshod, and there are some exaggerations which might have been avoided. For instance, it is absurd to say that 'a quarter of our population is definitely starving', unless by 'definitely starving' you merely mean underfed. The analysis of Mr. H. G. Wells, chosen as a typical middle-class writer, is brilliantly done, but, once again, it fails to take account of the stratifications within the middle class itself.

1. In his diary for 23 March 1936 (see *296*), Orwell wrote, 'I have glanced at Brown's novel [*Daughters of Albion*]. It is b———s.' He reviewed *The Fate of the Middle Classes* also, anonymously, in *New English Weekly* (see *307*).

[319]

Review of Indian Mosaic *by Mark Channing*
The Listener, *15 July 1936*

For an average Englishman in India the basic fact, more important even than loneliness or the heat of the sun, is the strangeness of the scenery. In the beginning the foreign landscape bores him, later he hates it, in the end he comes to love it, but it is never quite out of his consciousness and all his beliefs are in a mysterious way affected by it. Mr. Channing knows this, and throughout his story – for it is in a loose sense a story, a history of his 'spiritual pilgrimage' towards Hinduism – he keeps the physical scene before one's eyes.

Mr. Channing is, or was, an officer of the Indian Army. Probably it was fortunate for him that he was in the Supply and Transport Corps and not in an ordinary regiment, for it allowed him to travel widely and to get away from the atmosphere of the barracks and the European clubs. It is interesting to watch his development from a thoughtless youngster contemptuous of 'natives' and chiefly interested in shooting, into a humble student of Persian literature and Hindu philosophy. One of the paradoxes of India is that the Englishman usually gets on better with the Moslem than the Hindu and yet never entirely escapes the appeal of Hinduism as a creed. But as a rule his response to it is unconscious – a mere pantheistic tinge in his thoughts – whereas Mr. Channing has studied Yoga at the feet of a guru and believes that we have far more to learn from India than she from us. He does not, however, believe India to be capable of self-government, and his book ends with a queerly naïve mixture of mystical reverence and Kiplingesque imperialism.

To enjoy this book one need not share Mr. Channing's beliefs or take too seriously his accounts of magical happenings. There is a geographical element in all belief – saying what seem profound truths in India have a way of seeming enormous platitudes in England, and *vice versa*. Perhaps the fundamental difference is that beneath a tropical sun individuality seems less distinct and the loss of it less important. But even those with no interest in Hinduism will value this book for its vivid pictures of camps, forests and bazaars, saints, soldiers and animals – pictures which at first seem arbitrarily selected but in the end fall into a coherent and sometimes beautiful pattern.[1]

1. This review, Orwell's first for *The Listener* – for which he was paid £1 11s 6d – is not signed. It appears in a section entitled 'The Listener's Book Chronicle'. *The Listener*, published by the British Broadcasting Corporation, first appeared on 16 January 1929. Its literary editor from 1935 to 1959 was J. R. Ackerley (1896–1967).

[326]

'Shooting an Elephant'
New Writing, 2, Autumn 1936

It is impossible to know whether Orwell, when writing 'Shooting an Elephant', had in mind the end of the British Empire, but the elephant's death may be so interpreted. There was for a long time much dispute as to whether Orwell did shoot an elephant, but Orwell's letters to John Lehmann leading up to publication of the essay suggested he did. He wrote: 'It all came back to me very vividly the other day' and 'the incident had stuck in my mind' (X/312 and 317). Moreover, the reminiscences of George Stuart, one of Orwell's colleagues in Burma, make it plain that Orwell did shoot an elephant ('Burma, 1922–1927', Orwell Archive, UCL). When a message was brought to the club in Moulmein one Sunday morning, Orwell 'went off in his old Ford to pick up a rifle and went in search of the elephant which was causing great damage on a semi main road and causing danger to life and limb and he shot this elephant'. He was very nonchalant about the whole affair, according to Stuart, but got into serious trouble because the elephant was valuable and because of 'the influence these big firms had over the government'. As a result, Orwell was transferred to Katha. The chief of the police service, Colonel Welbourne, was particularly angry and made a point of denigrating Orwell, saying, for example, that he was a disgrace to Eton: 'Everyone was disgusted with the way he ran Blair down.'

Curiously, more doubt might have been cast on Orwell having shot the elephant had a little news item in the Rangoon Gazette *for 22 March 1926 been noticed:*

Major E. C. Kenny, subdivisional officer, Yamethin, when on tour in the Tatkon township on 16th March 1926, came across a rogue elephant feeding in a plantain grove at Dayouk-ku village 5 miles east of Tatkon and brought it down to the delight of the villagers. The elephant had killed a villager and caused great havoc to the

plantations. It is not known whether or not this is the elephant proclaimed by the
Bombay Burma Trading Corporation.

Similarities with 'Shooting an Elephant' will be apparent. Kenny, however,
was not penalized; indeed, on 13 September 1926, the Rangoon Gazette
announced that he was to become Deputy Commissioner of the Pakokku
District.

See Jeffrey Meyers, A Reader's Guide to George Orwell, *71–3;*
Crick, *165–6, 301–2, 583, 586–9;* A Literary Life, *46–7; SℰA,*
Transformation, *159–61; Shelden, 115, 117–18.*

In Moulmein, in Lower Burma, I was hated by large numbers of people –
the only time in my life that I have been important enough for this to
happen to me. I was subdivisional police officer of the town, and in an
aimless, petty kind of way anti-European feeling was very bitter. No one
had the guts to raise a riot, but if a European woman went through the
bazaars alone somebody would probably spit betel juice over her dress.
As a police officer I was an obvious target and was baited whenever it
seemed safe to do so. When a nimble Burman tripped me up on the
football field and the referee (another Burman) looked the other way, the
crowd yelled with hideous laughter. This happened more than once. In
the end the sneering yellow faces of young men that met me everywhere,
the insults hooted after me when I was at a safe distance, got badly on
my nerves. The young Buddhist priests were the worst of all. There were
several thousands of them in the town and none of them seemed to have
anything to do except stand on street corners and jeer at Europeans.

All this was perplexing and upsetting. For at that time I had already
made up my mind that imperialism was an evil thing and the sooner I
chucked up my job and got out of it the better. Theoretically – and
secretly, of course – I was all for the Burmese and all against their
oppressors, the British. As for the job I was doing, I hated it more bitterly
than I can perhaps make clear. In a job like that you see the dirty work
of Empire at close quarters. The wretched prisoners huddling in the
stinking cages of the lock-ups, the grey, cowed faces of the long-term
convicts, the scarred buttocks of the men who had been flogged with
bamboos – all these oppressed me with an intolerable sense of guilt. But

I could get nothing into perspective. I was young and ill-educated and I had had to think out my problems in the utter silence that is imposed on every Englishman in the East. I did not even know that the British Empire is dying, still less did I know that it is a great deal better than the younger empires that are going to supplant it. All I knew was that I was stuck between my hatred of the empire I served and my rage against the evil-spirited little beasts who tried to make my job impossible. With one part of my mind I thought of the British Raj as an unbreakable tyranny, as something clamped down, *in saecula saeculorum*,[1] upon the will of prostrate peoples; with another part I thought that the greatest joy in the world would be to drive a bayonet into a Buddhist priest's guts. Feelings like these are the normal by-products of imperialism; ask any Anglo-Indian official, if you can catch him off duty.

One day something happened which in a roundabout way was enlightening. It was a tiny incident in itself, but it gave me a better glimpse than I had had before of the real nature of imperialism – the real motives for which despotic governments act. Early one morning the sub-inspector at a police station the other end of the town rang me up on the phone and said that an elephant was ravaging the bazaar. Would I please come and do something about it? I did not know what I could do, but I wanted to see what was happening and I got on to a pony and started out. I took my rifle, an old .44 Winchester and much too small to kill an elephant, but I thought the noise might be useful *in terrorem*.[2] Various Burmans stopped me on the way and told me about the elephant's doings. It was not, of course, a wild elephant, but a tame one which had gone 'must'.[3] It had been chained up as tame elephants always are when their attack of 'must' is due, but on the previous night it had broken its chain and escaped. Its mahout, the only person who could manage it when it was in that state, had set out in pursuit, but he had taken the wrong direction and was now twelve hours' journey away, and in the morning the elephant had suddenly reappeared in the town. The Burmese population had no weapons and were quite helpless against it. It had already destroyed somebody's bamboo hut, killed a cow and raided some fruit-stalls and devoured the stock; also it had met the municipal rubbish van, and, when the driver jumped out and took to his heels, had turned the van over and inflicted violences upon it.

The Burmese sub-inspector and some Indian constables were waiting for me in the quarter where the elephant had been seen. It was a very poor quarter, a labyrinth of squalid bamboo huts, thatched with palm-leaf, winding all over a steep hillside. I remember that it was a cloudy stuffy morning at the beginning of the rains. We began questioning the people as to where the elephant had gone, and, as usual, failed to get any definite information. That is invariably the case in the East; a story always sounds clear enough at a distance, but the nearer you get to the scene of events the vaguer it becomes. Some of the people said that the elephant had gone in one direction, some said that he had gone in another, some professed not even to have heard of any elephant. I had almost made up my mind that the whole story was a pack of lies, when we heard yells a little distance away. There was a loud, scandalized cry of 'Go away, child! Go away this instant!' and an old woman with a switch in her hand came round the corner of a hut, violently shooing away a crowd of naked children. Some more women followed, clicking their tongues and exclaiming; evidently there was something there that the children ought not to have seen. I rounded the hut and saw a man's dead body sprawling in the mud. He was an Indian, a black Dravidian coolie, almost naked, and he could not have been dead many minutes. The people said that the elephant had come suddenly upon him round the corner of the hut, caught him with its trunk, put its foot on his back and ground him into the earth. This was the rainy season and the ground was soft, and his face had scored a trench a foot deep and a couple of yards long. He was lying on his belly with arms crucified and head sharply twisted to one side. His face was coated with mud, the eyes wide open, the teeth bared and grinning with an expression of unendurable agony. (Never tell me, by the way, that the dead look peaceful. Most of the corpses I have seen looked devilish.) The friction of the great beast's foot had stripped the skin from his back as neatly as one skins a rabbit. As soon as I saw the dead man I sent an orderly to a friend's house nearby to borrow an elephant rifle. I had already sent back the pony, not wanting it to go mad with fright and throw me if it smelled the elephant.

The orderly came back in a few minutes with a rifle and five cartridges, and meanwhile some Burmans had arrived and told us that the elephant was in the paddy fields below, only a few hundred yards away. As I started forward practically the whole population of the quarter flocked out of the houses and followed me. They had seen the rifle and were all shouting excitedly that I was going to shoot the elephant. They had not shown much interest in the elephant when he was merely ravaging their homes, but it was different now that he was going to be shot. It was a bit of fun to them, as it would be to an English crowd; besides, they wanted the meat. It made me vaguely uneasy. I had no intention of shooting the elephant – I had merely sent for the rifle to defend myself if necessary – and it is always unnerving to have a crowd following you. I marched down the hill, looking and feeling a fool, with the rifle over my shoulder and an ever-growing army of people jostling at my heels. At the bottom, when you got away from the huts, there was a metalled road and beyond that a miry waste of paddy fields a thousand yards across, not yet ploughed but soggy from the first rains and dotted with coarse grass. The elephant was standing eighty yards from the road, his left side towards us. He took not the slightest notice of the crowd's approach. He was tearing up bunches of grass, beating them against his knees to clean them and stuffing them into his mouth.

I had halted on the road. As soon as I saw the elephant I knew with perfect certainty that I ought not to shoot him. It is a serious matter to shoot a working elephant – it is comparable to destroying a huge and costly piece of machinery – and obviously one ought not to do it if it can possibly be avoided. And at that distance, peacefully eating, the elephant looked no more dangerous than a cow. I thought then and I think now that his attack of 'must' was already passing off; in which case he would merely wander harmlessly about until the mahout came back and caught him. Moreover, I did not in the least want to shoot him. I decided that I would watch him for a little while to make sure that he did not turn savage again, and then go home.

But at that moment I glanced round at the crowd that had followed me. It was an immense crowd, two thousand at the least and growing every minute. It blocked the road for a long distance on either side. I looked at the sea of yellow faces above the garish clothes – faces all happy and excited over this bit of fun, all certain that the elephant was going to be shot. They were watching me as they would watch a conjuror about to perform a trick. They did not like me, but with the magical rifle in my hands I was momentarily worth watching. And suddenly I realized that I should have to shoot the elephant after all. The people expected it of me and I had got to do it; I could feel their two thousand wills pressing me forward, irresistibly. And it was at this moment, as I stood there with the rifle in my hands, that I first grasped the hollowness, the futility of the white man's dominion in the East. Here was I, the white man with his gun, standing in front of the unarmed native crowd – seemingly the leading actor of the piece; but in reality I was only an absurd puppet pushed to and fro by the will of those yellow faces behind. I perceived in this moment that when the white man turns tyrant it is his own freedom that he destroys. He becomes a sort of hollow, posing dummy, the conventionalized figure of a sahib. For it is the condition of his rule that he shall spend his life in trying to impress the 'natives', and so in every crisis he has got to do what the 'natives' expect of him. He wears a mask, and his face grows to fit it. I had got to shoot the elephant. I had committed myself to doing it when I sent for the rifle. A sahib has got to act like a sahib; he has got to appear resolute, to know his own mind and do definite things. To come all that way, rifle in hand, with two thousand people marching at my heels, and then to trail feebly away, having done nothing – no, that was impossible. The crowd would laugh at me. And my whole life, every white man's life in the East, was one long struggle not to be laughed at.

But I did not want to shoot the elephant. I watched him beating his bunch of grass against his knees, with that preoccupied grandmotherly air that elephants have. It seemed to me that it would be murder to shoot him. At that age I was not squeamish about killing animals, but I had never shot an elephant and never wanted to. (Somehow it always seems worse to kill a *large* animal.) Besides, there was the beast's owner to be considered. Alive, the elephant was worth at least a hundred pounds; dead, he would only be worth the value of his tusks – five pounds, possibly. But I had got to act quickly. I turned to some experienced-looking Burmans who had been there when we arrived, and asked them how the elephant had been behaving. They all said the same thing: he took no notice of you if you left him alone, but he might charge if you went too close to him.

It was perfectly clear to me what I ought to do. I ought to walk up to within, say, twenty-five yards of the elephant and test his behaviour. If he charged I could shoot, if he took no notice of me it would be safe to leave him until the mahout came back. But also I knew that I was going to do no such thing. I was a poor shot with a rifle[4] and the ground was soft mud into which one would sink at every step. If the elephant charged and I missed him, I should have about as much chance as a toad under a steam-roller. But even then I was not thinking particularly of my own skin, only of the watchful yellow faces behind. For at that moment, with the crowd watching me, I was not afraid in the ordinary sense, as I would have been if I had been alone. A white man mustn't be frightened in front of 'natives'; and so, in general, he isn't frightened. The sole thought in my mind was that if anything went wrong those two thousand Burmans would see me pursued, caught, trampled on and reduced to a grinning corpse like that Indian up the hill. And if that happened it was quite probable that some of them would laugh. That would never do. There was only one alternative. I shoved the cartridges into the magazine and lay down on the road to get a better aim.

The crowd grew very still, and a deep, low, happy sigh, as of people who see the theatre curtain go up at last, breathed from innumerable throats. They were going to have their bit of fun after all. The rifle was a beautiful German thing with cross-hair sights. I did not then know that in shooting an elephant one should shoot to cut an imaginary bar running from ear-hole to ear-hole. I ought therefore, as the elephant was sideways on, to have aimed straight at his ear-hole; actually I aimed several inches in front of this, thinking the brain would be further forward.

When I pulled the trigger I did not hear the bang or feel the kick – one never does when a shot goes home – but I heard the devilish roar of glee that went up from the crowd. In that instant, in too short a time, one would have thought, even for the bullet to get there, a mysterious, terrible change had come over the elephant. He neither stirred nor fell, but every line of his body had altered. He looked suddenly stricken, shrunken, immensely old, as though the frightful impact of the bullet had paralysed him without knocking him down. At last, after what seemed a long time – it might have been five seconds, I dare say – he sagged flabbily to his knees. His mouth slobbered. An enormous senility seemed to have settled upon him. One could have imagined him thousands of years old. I fired again into the same spot. At the second shot he did not collapse but climbed with desperate slowness to his feet and stood weakly upright, with legs sagging and head drooping. I fired a third time. That was the shot that did for him. You could see the agony of it jolt his whole body and knock the last remnant of strength from his legs. But in falling he seemed for a moment to rise, for as his hind legs collapsed beneath him he seemed to tower upwards like a huge rock toppling, his trunk reaching skyward like a tree. He trumpeted, for the first and only time. And then down he came, his belly towards me, with a crash that seemed to shake the ground even where I lay.

I got up. The Burmans were already racing past me across the mud. It was obvious that the elephant would never rise again, but he was not dead. He was breathing very rhythmically with long rattling gasps, his great mound of a side painfully rising and falling. His mouth was wide open – I could see far down into caverns of pale pink throat. I waited a long time for him to die, but his breathing did not weaken. Finally I fired my two remaining shots into the spot where I thought his heart must be. The thick blood welled out of him like red velvet, but still he did not die. His body did not even jerk when the shots hit him, the tortured breathing continued without a pause. He was dying, very slowly and in great agony, but in some world remote from me where not even a bullet could damage him further. I felt that I had got to put an end to that dreadful noise. It seemed dreadful to see the great beast lying there, powerless to move and yet powerless to die, and not even to be able to finish him. I sent back for my small rifle and poured shot after shot into his heart and down his throat. They seemed to make no impression. The tortured gasps continued as steadily as the ticking of a clock.

In the end I could not stand it any longer and went away. I heard later that it took him half an hour to die. Burmans were arriving with *dahs*[5] and baskets even before I left, and I was told they had stripped his body almost to the bones by the afternoon.

Afterwards, of course, there were endless discussions about the shooting of the elephant. The owner was furious, but he was only an Indian and could do nothing. Besides, legally I had done the right thing, for a mad elephant has to be killed, like a mad dog, if its owner fails to control it. Among the Europeans opinion was divided. The older men said I was right, the younger men said it was a damn shame to shoot an elephant for killing a coolie, because an elephant was worth more than any damn Coringhee coolie. And afterwards I was very glad that the coolie had been killed; it put me legally in the right and it gave me a sufficient pretext for shooting the elephant. I often wondered whether any of the others grasped that I had done it solely to avoid looking a fool.

1. *in saecula saeculorum*: from one generation unto another – for ever (Latin)

2. *in terrorem*: as a warning (Latin).

3. 'must': a state of frenzy from the Hindi for 'intoxicated'.

4. Typical of Orwell's self-depreciation and for the sake of the story; he was an excellent shot.

5. *dahs*: short swords or long knives (Burmese).

---

[428]

Review of Workers' Front *by Fenner Brockway*[1]
New English Weekly, *17 February 1938*

For the past year or two every Socialist, whether he likes it or not, has been involved in the savage controversy that rages over the policy of the Popular Front. Hateful in every way as this controversy has become, it raises questions that are too important to be ignored, not merely by Socialists but also by those who are outside or even hostile to the whole Socialist movement.

Mr. Brockway's book is written from the standpoint that it is now usual to denounce as 'Trotskyist'. His plea is that a Popular Front (*i.e.* a line-up of capitalist and proletarian for the ostensible purpose of opposing Fascism)[2] is simply an alliance of enemies and must always, in the long run, have the effect of fixing the capitalist class more firmly in the saddle. There is very little doubt that this is true, and a short time ago few people would have bothered to deny it. Until about 1933 any Socialist, or any anti-Socialist in an unbuttoned moment, would have told you that the whole history of class-collaboration (and 'Popular Front', or 'People's Front', is only a polite name for this) is summed up in the limerick about the young lady of Niger.[3] But unfortunately the menacing rise of Hitler has made it very difficult to view the situation objectively. Rubber truncheons and castor oil have scared people of the most diverse kinds into forgetting that Fascism and capitalism are at bottom the same thing. Hence the Popular Front – an unholy alliance between the robbers and the robbed. In England the Popular Front is as yet only an idea, but it has already produced the nauseous spectacle of bishops, Communists, cocoa-magnates, publishers, duchesses and Labour M.P.s marching arm in arm to the tune of 'Rule Britannia' and all tensing their muscles for a rush to the bomb-proof shelter when and if their policy begins to take effect.

Against all this Mr. Brockway urges that Fascism can only be combatted by attacking capitalism in its non-Fascist as well as its Fascist forms; and that therefore the only real enemy Fascism has to face is the class that does not benefit from capitalism, *i.e.*, the working class. It is a pity that he tends to use the expression 'working class' in a rather narrow and restricted sense, being, like nearly all Socialist writers, too much dominated by the concept of a 'proletarian' as a manual labourer. In all western countries there now exists a huge middle class whose interests are identical with those of the proletariat but which is quite unaware of this fact and usually sides with its capitalist enemy in moments of crisis. There is no doubt that this is partly due to the tactlessness of Socialist propaganda. Perhaps the best thing one can wish the Socialist movement at this moment is that it should shed some of its nineteenth-century phraseology.

Much of Mr. Brockway's book is taken up in criticising the tactics of the Communist Party – necessarily so, because the whole manoeuvre of the Popular Front is bound up with the Franco-Russian alliance and the volte-face performed by the Comintern in the past few years. Underlying this is a much larger question, always more or less present when the Popular Front is discussed, though it is seldom brought into the foreground. This is the question of the huge though inscrutable changes that are occurring in the U.S.S.R. As the destinies of all of us are involved here, directly or indirectly, this book, written from what is at the moment the most unpopular angle, ought not to be neglected even by those who are hostile to its main implications.

1. Fenner Brockway (1888–1988; Lord Brockway, 1964), General Secretary of the Independent Labour Party (ILP), 1928, 1933–9, and its representative in Spain when Orwell was fighting there. He was a devoted worker for many causes, particularly the peace movement.

He resigned from the ILP in 1946 and rejoined the Labour Party, which he represented in Parliament, 1950–64.

2. The Popular Front was a (sometimes loose) alliance of Communists, Socialists and other left-inclined parties and individuals. It was fostered by the Communist International in 1935 and was seen by many (including Orwell) as a Communist-front organization. In France, a Popular Front government under Léon Blum took power in 1936–7 and briefly in 1938. The Front made less headway in England and the Nazi–Soviet Pact of 23 August 1939 virtually destroyed its fortunes, though they revived somewhat after the Germans invaded the Soviet Union on 22 June 1941.

3. There was a young lady from Niger [or Riga]/Who went for a ride on a tiger./They returned from the ride / With the lady inside / And a smile on the face of the tiger.

[429]

Anonymous review[1] *of* Trials in Burma *by Maurice Collis*
The Listener, *9 March 1938*

This is an unpretentious book, but it brings out with unusual clearness the dilemma that faces every official in an empire like our own. Mr. Collis[2] was District Magistrate of Rangoon in the troubled period round about 1930. He had to try cases which were a great deal in the public eye, and he soon discovered the practical impossibility of keeping to the letter of the law and pleasing European opinion at the same time. Finally, for having sentenced a British Army officer to three months' imprisonment for criminal negligence in driving a car, he was reprimanded and hurriedly transferred to another post. For the same offence a native would have been imprisoned as a matter of course.

The truth is that every British magistrate in India is in a false position when he has to try a case in which European and native interests clash. In theory he is administering an impartial system of justice; in practice he is part of a huge machine which exists to protect British interests, and he has often got to choose between sacrificing his integrity and damaging his career. Nevertheless, owing to the exceptionally high traditions of the Indian Civil Service, the law in India is administered far more fairly than might be expected – and, incidentally, far too fairly to please the business community. Mr. Collis grasps the essential situation clearly enough; he recognises that the Burman has profited very little from the huge wealth that has been extracted from his country, and that the hopeless rebellion of 1931 had genuine grievances behind it. But he is also a good imperialist and it was precisely his concern for the good name of English justice that got him into hot water with his fellow-countrymen on more than one occasion.

In 1930 he had to try Sen Gupta, one of the leaders of the Congress Party and at that time Mayor of Calcutta, who had paid a flying visit to Rangoon and made a seditious speech. The account of the trial makes curious reading – an Indian crowd roaring outside, Mr. Collis wondering whether he would be knocked on the head the next moment, and the prisoner sitting in the dock reading a newspaper to make it clear that he did not recognise the jurisdiction of an English court. Mr. Collis' sentence was ten days' imprisonment – a wise sentence, for it deprived Sen Gupta of a chance of martyrdom. Afterwards the two men were able to meet privately and talk the affair over. The description of the Indian and the Englishman meeting in perfect amity, each fully aware of the other's motives, each regarding the other as an honourable man and yet, in the last resort, as an enemy, is strangely moving and makes one wish that politics nearer home could be conducted in an equally decent spirit.

1. As with all reviews published anonymously in *The Listener*, attribution to Orwell has been made from the journal's records.

2. Maurice Collis (1889–1973), author, biographer and art critic (for *Time and Tide* and the *Observer*, 1942–7). His books were not restricted to Burma and the East. His biographies include those on Ma Saw, Queen of Burma (*She was a Queen*, 1937), *Marco Polo* (1950), *The Discovery of L. S. Lowry* (1951), *Nancy Astor* (1960), *Stanley Spencer* (1962) and *Somerville and Ross* (1968). He also published poetry, paintings and drawings under the pseudonym 'Alva'. His *Trials in Burma* is a revealing parallel to Orwell's *Burmese Days* (1934).

[446]

To the Editor, New English Weekly
26 May 1938

On 14 April, A. Romney Green had published, in New English Weekly, *an article on Aldous Huxley, in the series Delinquent Stars. He said that Huxley was 'the arch-exponent of . . . [the] philosophy of "meaninglessness" which was so convenient, as he frankly admits, in its emancipation of their sexual appetites'; and he accused him of taking 'the intolerably smug and absolutely fatal view of his brother pacifists that the abolition of war must precede other social reforms'. Green grouped with Huxley, as 'delinquent stars' and 'false prophets', C. E. M. Joad, Siegfried Sassoon, Osbert Sitwell 'and the rest of our pacifist philosophers and literati', and he made sarcastic reference to Huxley's* Ends and Means: An Inquiry into the Nature of Ideals and the Methods Employed for Their Realization *(1937).*

Two weeks later, B. J. Boothroyd defended Huxley's position against what he called Green's 'ill-considered attack' on the author of 'this brilliant and inspiring book', an attack 'ill-mannered and ridiculously inapplicable to such a man' as Huxley. On 12 May, J. S. Collis (1900–1984) accused Boothroyd of being himself ill-mannered, showing the 'insolent complacency of a man incapable of grappling with a new idea'. In the same issue, Green said he felt no need to retract anything he had written except for a passing and 'too hasty reference to the Everyman' editions; he had exaggerated the number of misprints he claimed to have found in the Everyman Huxley. At this stage, Orwell joined the debate.

ENDS AND MEANS

Sir, – May I suggest the following considerations to your correspondent, Mr. Romney Green?

(1) He says: '(pacifist) theories are just sufficiently plausible to put to rest the consciences of those well-to-do intellectuals who are rather worried by the social problem but who, if war can otherwise be averted, don't really want to see it solved. It is these people who have the pacifist stars on all their drawing-room tables, and who, since nothing can be done about the social problem till war is abolished, may clearly feel quite justified in doing nothing about it.'

Is anything of this kind happening? Is it really pacifist literature that we see on every drawing-room table – is it not, on the contrary, so-called 'anti-fascist' literature? Pacifism is so far from being fashionable, or acceptable to the possessing class, that all the big daily newspapers unite to boycott all news of pacifist activities. Virtually the whole of the left-wing intelligentsia, via their mouthpieces in the *News Chronicle*, the *New Statesman, Reynolds*,[1] etc., are clamouring for a Popular Front Government as a prelude to war against Germany. It is true that they are usually too mealy-mouthed to say openly that they wish for war, but that is what they mean, and in private they will often admit that war is 'inevitable', by which they mean desirable.

(2) He also says: 'I seriously doubt either the intelligence or the sincerity of anyone who goes about England with his eyes open . . . and who . . . professes to think that nothing can be done about the social problem until war is abolished.'

The implication is that pacifism is somehow being used, or could be used, as an excuse for blocking social reform. Once again, where is this happening, and how could it happen? In every country except those which are definitely outside the war-orbit, the supposed necessity to prepare for war is being systematically used to prevent every kind of social advance. It goes without saying that this happens in the Fascist countries, but 'guns before butter'[2] also rules in the democracies. We have seen how, in the space of two years, the French working class have been swindled out of every advantage they won in 1936,[3] and always by means of the same catchword – 'All Frenchmen must unite against Hitler'. The truth is that any real advance, let alone any genuinely revolutionary change, can only begin when the mass of the people definitely refuse capitalist-imperialist war and thus make it clear to their rulers that a war-policy is not practicable. So long as they show themselves willing to fight 'in defence of democracy', or 'against Fascism', or for any other flyblown slogan, the same trick will be played upon them again and again: 'You can't have a rise in wages *now*, because we have got to prepare for war. Guns before butter!'

Meanwhile there is considerable possibility of producing an effective anti-war movement in England. It is a question of mobilising the dislike of war that undoubtedly exists in ordinary decent people, as opposed to the hack-journalists and the pansy left. The fact that a book like Mr. Huxley's contains a certain amount of self-righteousness (we are all self-righteous in different ways), and is written too much from the stand-point of a middle-class intellectual, is beside the point. Anyone who helps to put peace on the map is doing useful work. The real enemies of the working class are not those who talk to them in a too highbrow manner; they are those who try to trick them into identifying their interests with those of their exploiters, and into forgetting what every manual worker inwardly knows – that modern war is a racket.

> *A. Romney Green replied in the issue of 16 June. He reiterated that war was inevitable; that Britain's supremacy as an imperial power 'might very well be challenged by less fortunate races even if we were putting our Empire to reasonably good use'; that if we couldn't have butter and guns it was better to have guns, but 'our victory in the terrific struggle which lies ahead of us depends upon our discovering before it is too late that a people whose gunmaking leaves them still with vast reservoirs of unemployed labour and ill-developed natural resources might have butter also'.*

1. The *News Chronicle* was founded as the *Clerkenwell News and General Advertiser* in 1855 and became the *Daily Chronicle* in 1872. It amalgamated with the *Daily News* (founded 1846) in 1930 as *News Chronicle*. It was loosely associated with the policies of the Liberal Party. The *New Statesman* was founded in 1913 and incorporated the *Nation and Athenaeum* in 1931. It was (and is) on the political left. Orwell contributed more than twenty items to it. *Reynold's News* (often spelt *Reynolds's*) ran from 1851 to 1944. It was Labour inclined. In 1944 it amalgamated with and then was subsumed in the *Sunday Citizen* until 1967.

2. 'Guns before butter' stems from a broadcast made in 1936 by Hermann Göring (1893–1946), head of the German air force and of the Four Year Plan: 'Guns will make us powerful; butter will only make us fat.' It puts memorably a policy outlined in a secret memorandum to Hitler of 3 May 1935 by Dr Hjalmar Schacht (1877–1970), German Minister of Economics, 1934–7: 'The accomplishment of the armament programme with speed and in quantity is *the* problem of German politics, and everything else should be subordinated to this purpose, as long as the main purpose is not imperilled by neglecting all other questions' (Alan Bullock, *Hitler: A Study in Tyranny*, 1952; revd Pelican edn, 1962, 356). Schacht resigned because he thought economic and social questions were being ridden over roughshod.

3. The Popular Front government led by the Socialist Léon Blum, which was elected in June 1936, had enacted a series of reforms which benefited working men and women.

---

[451]

Review of Assignment in Utopia *by Eugene Lyons*
New English Weekly, *9 June 1938*

To get the full sense of our ignorance as to what is really happening in the U.S.S.R., it is worth trying to translate the most sensational Russian event of the past two years, the Trotskyist trials, into English terms. Make the necessary adjustments, let Left be Right and Right be Left, and you get something like this:

Mr. Winston Churchill, now in exile in Portugal, is plotting to overthrow the British Empire and establish Communism in England. By the use of unlimited Russian money he has succeeded in building up a huge Churchillite organisation which includes members of Parliament, factory managers, Roman Catholic bishops and practically the whole of the Primrose League. Almost every day some dastardly act of sabotage is laid bare – sometimes a plot to blow up the House of Lords, sometimes an outbreak of foot and mouth disease in the Royal racing-stables. Eighty per cent of the Beefeaters at the Tower are discovered to be agents of the Comintern. A high official of the Post Office admits brazenly to having embezzled postal orders to the tune of £5,000,000, and also to having committed *lèse majesté* by drawing moustaches on postage stamps. Lord Nuffield, after a 7-hour interrogation by Mr. Norman Birkett, confesses that ever since 1920 he has been fomenting strikes in his own factories. Casual half-inch paras in every issue of the newspapers announce that fifty more Churchillite sheep-stealers have been shot in Westmorland or that the proprietress of a village shop in the Cotswolds has been transported to Australia for sucking the bullseyes and putting them back in the bottle. And meanwhile the Churchillites (or Churchillite-Harmsworthites as they are called after Lord Rothermere's execution) never cease from proclaiming that it is *they* who are the real defenders of Capitalism and that Chamberlain and the rest of his gang are no more than a set of Bolsheviks in disguise.

Anyone who has followed the Russian trials knows that this is scarcely a parody. The question arises, could anything like this happen in England? Obviously it could not. From our point of view the whole thing is not merely incredible as a genuine conspiracy, it is next door to incredible as a frame-up. It is simply a dark mystery, of which the only seizable fact – sinister enough in its way – is that Communists over here regard it as a good advertisement for Communism.

Meanwhile the truth about Stalin's régime, if we could only get hold of it, is of the first importance. Is it Socialism, or is it a peculiarly vicious form of state-capitalism? All the political controversies that have made life hideous for two years past really circle round this question, though for several reasons it is seldom brought into the foreground. It is difficult to go [to] Russia, once there it is impossible to make adequate investigations, and all one's ideas on the subject have to be drawn from books which are so fulsomely 'for' or so venomously 'against' that the prejudice stinks a mile away. Mr. Lyons's book is definitely in the 'against' class, but he gives the impression of being much more reliable than most. It is obvious from his manner of writing that he is not a vulgar propagandist, and he was in Russia a long time (1928–34) as correspondent for the United Press Agency, having been sent there on Communist recommendation. Like many others who have gone to Russia full of hope he was gradually disillusioned, and unlike some others he finally decided to tell the truth about it. It is an unfortunate fact that any hostile criticism of the present Russian régime is liable to be taken as propaganda *against Socialism*; all Socialists are aware of this, and it does not make for honest discussion.

The years that Mr. Lyons spent in Russia were years of appalling hardship, culminating in the Ukraine famine of 1933,[1] in which a number estimated at not less than three million people starved to death. Now, no doubt, after the success of the Second Five Year Plan,[2] the physical conditions have improved, but there seems no reason for thinking that the social atmosphere is greatly different. The system that Mr. Lyons describes does not seem to be very different from Fascism. All real power is concentrated in the hands of two or three million people, the town proletariat, theoretically the heirs of the revolution, having been robbed even of the elementary right to strike; more recently, by the introduction of the internal passport system, they have been reduced to a status resembling serfdom.[3] The G.P.U.[4] are everywhere, everyone lives in constant terror of denunciation, freedom of speech and of the press are obliterated to an extent we can hardly imagine. There are periodical waves of terror, sometimes the 'liquidation' of kulaks[5] or Nepmen,[6] sometimes some monstrous state trial at which people who have been in prison for months or years are suddenly dragged forth to make incredible confessions, while their children publish articles in the newspapers saying 'I repudiate my father as a Trotskyist serpent'. Meanwhile the invisible Stalin is worshipped in terms that would have made Nero blush. This – at great length and in much detail – is the picture Mr. Lyons presents, and I do not believe he has misrepresented the facts. He does, however, show signs of being embittered by his experiences, and I think he probably exaggerates the amount of discontent prevailing among the Russians themselves.

He once succeeded in interviewing Stalin, and found him human, simple and likeable. It is worth noticing that H. G. Wells said the same thing,[7] and it is a fact that Stalin, at any rate on the cinematograph, has a likeable face. Is it not also recorded that Al Capone was the best of husbands and fathers, and that Joseph Smith (of Brides in the Bath fame) was sincerely loved by the first of his seven wives and always returned to her between murders?

1. In 1932–3 as part of the Soviet plan for the collectivization of agriculture, all food in the Ukraine was requisitioned and no new supplies were admitted. The result was the deaths of seven million people: genocide by state-organized famine. This horrendous terror passed virtually unnoticed outside the USSR. In his 'Notes on Nationalism', 1945, Orwell pointed out that 'Huge events like the Ukraine famine of 1933' had 'escaped the attention of the majority of English Russophiles' (see p. 363). In 1941 he referred to the famine as one of the 'hideous controversies' that had 'simply passed over the average newspaper-reader's head' (see London Letter of 17 August, below), and he again wrote of it in 1949, in one of his last articles, 'Reflections on Gandhi' (see below).

2. Lyons's account of the 'Five Year Plan in Four Years' and his recording of the formula used to express that, $2 + 2 = 5$, directly influenced Orwell's writing of *Nineteen Eighty-Four* (although this formula is to be found at least as early as the mid-eighteenth century, in Sterne's *Tristram Shandy*, a copy of which Orwell had in his possession, and in Dostoevski's *Notes from Underground*, 1864).

3. Under the tsars, serfs needed internal passports to leave their villages to take up seasonal work elsewhere.

4. GPU: Soviet security and intelligence service. Originally the Cheka, December 1917 to February 1922, when it was incorporated in the NKVD (the People's Commissariat for Internal Affairs); from July 1923 to July 1934 it was known as the OGPU and was then again incorporated in the NKVD. It had various other manifestations and from March 1954 to December 1991 was known as the KGB

5. Kulaks were rich peasants (often taken to be exploiters) and were systematically eliminated by the Soviets.

6. Food shortages and a harsh regime led to a series of strikes, supported by the sailors at the Kronstadt naval base in Petrograd in 1921. Leon Trotsky (1879–1940 – when he was assassinated) and Mikhail Tukhachevsky (1893–1937 – when he was executed) put down the rebellion. However, a milder regime, the 'New Economic Policy', permitting a measure of private enterprise on a small scale, was established. Some people manipulated the new system and came to be known as Nepmen. Orwell was very conscious of 'Kronstadt': see below, pp. 230–31.

7. See *Stalin–Wells Talk: The Verbatim Record, and a Discussion* by G. Bernard Shaw, H. G. Wells, J. M. Keynes, Ernst Toller and others (1934).

[457]

'Why I Join the I.L.P.'

New Leader, *24 June 1938*

Orwell's membership card for the Independent Labour Party' was issued on
13 June 1938. This article was given a position of prominence, running
parallel to the leader, or editorial, and on the same page as details of the
journal's editorial offices and the name of the editor, Fenner Brockway. See
Crick, 364–5.

Perhaps it will be frankest to approach it first of all from the personal angle.

I am a writer. The impulse of every writer is to 'keep out of politics'. What he wants is to be left alone so that he can go on writing books in peace. But unfortunately it is becoming obvious that this ideal is no more practicable than that of the petty shopkeeper who hopes to preserve his independence in the teeth of the chain-stores.

To begin with, the era of free speech is closing down. The freedom of the Press in Britain was always something of a fake, because in the last resort, money controls opinion; still, so long as the legal right to say what you like exists, there are always loopholes for an unorthodox writer. For some years past I have managed to make the Capitalist class pay me several pounds a week for writing books against Capitalism. But I do not delude myself that this state of affairs is going to last for ever. We have seen what has happened to the freedom of the Press in Italy and Germany, and it will happen here sooner or later. The time is coming – not next year, perhaps not for ten or twenty years, but it is coming – when every writer will have the choice of being silenced altogether or of producing the dope that a privileged minority demands.

I have got to struggle against that, just as I have got to struggle against castor oil, rubber truncheons and concentration-camps. And the only régime which, in the long run, will dare to permit freedom of speech is a Socialist régime. If Fascism triumphs I am finished as a writer – that is to say, finished in my only effective capacity. That of itself would be a sufficient reason for joining a Socialist party.

I have put the personal aspect first, but obviously it is not the only one.

It is not possible for any thinking person to live in such a society as our own without wanting to change it. For perhaps ten years past I have had some grasp of the real nature of Capitalist society. I have seen British Imperialism at work in Burma, and I have seen something of the effects of poverty and unemployment in Britain. In so far as I have struggled against the system, it has been mainly of writing books which I hoped would influence the reading public. I shall continue to do that, of course, but at a moment like the present writing books is not enough. The tempo of events is quickening; the dangers which once seemed a generation distant are staring us in the face. One has got to be actively a Socialist, not merely sympathetic to Socialism, or one plays into the hands of our always-active enemies.

Why the I.L.P. more than another?

Because the I.L.P. is the only British party – at any rate the only one large enough to be worth considering – which aims at anything I should regard as Socialism.

I do not mean that I have lost all faith in the Labour Party. My most earnest hope is that the Labour Party will win a clear majority in the next General Election. But we know what the history of the Labour Party has been, and we know the terrible temptation of the present moment – the temptation to fling every principle overboard in order to prepare for an Imperialist war. It is vitally necessary that there should be in existence some body of people who can be depended on, even in face of persecution, not to compromise their Socialist principles.

I believe that the I.L.P. is the only party which, as a party, is likely to take the right line either against Imperialist war or against Fascism when this appears in its British form. And meanwhile the I.L.P. is not backed by any monied interest, and is systematically libelled from several quarters. Obviously it needs all the help it can get, including any help I can give it myself.

Finally, I was with the I.L.P. contingent in Spain. I never pretended, then or since, to agree in every detail with the policy the P.O.U.M.[2] put forward and the I.L.P. supported, but the general course of events has borne it out. The things I saw in Spain brought home to me the fatal danger of mere negative 'anti-Fascism'. Once I had grasped the essentials of the situation in Spain I realised that the I.L.P. was the only British party I felt like joining – and also the only party I could join with at least the certainty that I would never be led up the garden path in the name of Capitalist democracy.

1. The Independent Labour Party (ILP) was founded in 1893 by Keir Hardie (1856–1915). The Labour Party was formed by the ILP and trade unions in 1900. The ILP disaffiliated from the Labour Party in 1932 and the two parties were separately represented in the House of Commons. Orwell resigned from the ILP shortly after the outbreak of the Second World War because of its pacifist stance. Keir Hardie was the first Socialist to be elected a Member of Parliament (1892). He led the Labour Party in the House of Commons, 1906–15. Crick (255) gives a useful 'character sketch' of the ILP; it was, he wrote, 'a striking mixture of optimism and pessimism, of heavens and of hells . . . [it] appealed to Left-wing activists in the existing British Labour movement, still picking itself up slowly after its betrayal by Ramsay MacDonald'.

2. The POUM was the Partido Obrero de Unificación Marxista, a revolutionary, anti-Stalinist Communist party, which Orwell joined to fight the Nationalist rebels under Franco. It was targeted to be eliminated by its supposed allies, the Communists, at the behest of the USSR. See *Orwell in Spain* in this series.

[485]

Review of The Communist International *by Franz Borkenau*[1]
New English Weekly, *22 September 1938*

When Dr. Borkenau's *The Spanish Cockpit* appeared the Spanish War was about a year old and the book dealt only with the events of the first six or seven months. Nevertheless it remains the best book on the subject, and what is more, it is a book different in *kind* from nearly all that have appeared on either side. As soon as one opened it one was aware that here at last, amid the shrieking horde of propagandists, was a grown-up person, a man capable of writing dispassionately even when he knew the facts. It is unfortunate that political books nowadays are almost invariably written either by fools or by ignoramuses. If a writer on a political subject manages to preserve a detached attitude, it is nearly always because he does not know what he is talking about. To understand a political movement one has got to be involved in it, and as soon as one is involved one becomes a propagandist. Dr. Borkenau, however, apart from his intellectual gifts, is in the very unusual position of having been for eight years a member of the German Communist Party and for some time an official of the Comintern, and of having finally reverted to a belief in liberalism and democracy. This is a development about as uncommon as being converted from Catholicism to Protestantism, but a sociologist could hardly have a better background.

In the twenty-years' history of the Comintern Dr. Borkenau traces three more or less separate periods. In the first period, the immediate post-war years, there is a genuine revolutionary ferment in Europe, and in consequence the Comintern is an organisation sincerely aiming at world revolution and not entirely under Russian influence. In the second phase it becomes an instrument in Stalin's struggles first against the Trotsky-Zinoviev group, later against the Bukharin-Rykov group. In the third phase, the one we are in now, it becomes more or less openly an instrument of Russian foreign policy. Meanwhile there are the alternate swings of Comintern policy to 'left' and 'right'. As Dr. Borkenau points out, the earlier changes were comparatively insignificant, the more recent ones catastrophic. The swing-over in Communist policy that took place between 1934 and 1936 was in fact so extraordinary that the general public has as yet failed to grasp it. In the 'ultra-left' phase of 1928–34, the 'social fascist' phase, revolutionary purity was so pure that every labour leader was declared to be in capitalist pay, the Russian sabotage trials 'proved' that M. Blum and other leaders of the Second International were plotting the invasion of Russia, and anyone who advocated a united front of Socialists and Communists was denounced as a traitor, Trotskyist, mad dog, hyena and all the other items in the Communist vocabulary. Social democracy was declared to be the real enemy of the working class, Fascism was dismissed as something utterly without importance, and this insane theory was kept up even *after* Hitler had come to power. But then came German rearmament and the Franco-Russian pact. Almost overnight Communist policy in the non-Fascist countries swung round to the Popular Front and 'defence of democracy', and anyone who cavilled at lining up with Liberals and Catholics was once again a traitor, Trotskyist, mad dog, hyena and so forth. Of course such changes of policy are only possible because every Communist party outside the U.S.S.R. gets a new membership every few years. Whether there will be another corresponding swing to the 'left' seems doubtful. Dr. Borkenau thinks that Stalin may ultimately be compelled to dissolve the Comintern as the price of a secure alliance with the western democracies. On the other hand it is worth remembering that the rulers of the democracies, so called, are not fools, they are aware that Communist agitation even in its 'left' phases is not a serious danger, and they may prefer to keep in being an organisation which plays almost invariably into their hands.

In so far as it aims – and it still professes rather vaguely to aim – at world revolution, the Comintern has been a complete failure. Nevertheless it has done an immense amount of mischief and has been, in Dr. Borkenau's opinion, one of the chief causes of the growth of Fascism. In every Communist party only about five per cent of the membership – that is to say, a framework of party officials – remains constant; but in each phase of policy there pass through the party some thousands or tens of thousands of people who emerge having learnt nothing save a contempt for demo-cratic methods. They do not emerge with a belief in Socialism, but they do emerge with a belief in violence and double-crossing. Consequently when the critical moment comes they are at the mercy of the man who really specialises in violence and double-crossing, in other words, the Fascist.

Dr. Borkenau thinks that the root cause of the vagaries of Comintern policy is the fact that revolution as Marx and Lenin predicted it and as it happened, more or less, in Russia, is not thinkable in the advanced western countries, at any rate at present. Here I believe he is right. Where I part company from him is when he says that for the western democracies the choice lies between Fascism and an orderly reconstruction through the co-operation of all classes. I do not believe in the second possibility, because I do not believe that a man with £50,000 a year and a man with fifteen shillings a week either can, or will, co-operate. The nature of their relationship is, quite simply, that the one is robbing the other, and there is no reason to think that the robber will suddenly turn over a new leaf. It would seem, therefore, that if the problems of western capitalism are to be solved, it will have to be through a third alternative, a movement which is genuinely revolutionary, *i.e.*, willing to make drastic changes and to use violence if necessary, but which does not lose touch, as Communism and Fascism have done, with the essential values of democracy. Such a thing is by no means unthinkable. The germs of such a movement exist in numerous countries, and they are capable of growing. At any rate, if they don't, there is no real exit from the pigsty we are in.

This is a profoundly interesting book. I have not enough specialised knowledge to judge its accuracy, but I think it is safe to say that it is as little coloured by prejudice as a book on a controversial subject can be. Probably the best way to test its value as a historical work would be to watch its reception in the Communist press – on the principle of 'the worse the better', I need hardly say. I hope that Dr. Borkenau will not only go on writing, but that he will find imitators. It is a most encouraging thing to hear a human voice when fifty thousand gramophones are playing the same tune.

1. Dr Franz Borkenau (1900–1957), Austrian sociologist and political writer. He was born in Vienna and died in Zurich. From 1921 to 1929 he was a member of the German Communist Party. His *Zur Soziologie des Faschismus* was published in Tübingen in 1933, the year he emigrated because of the coming to power of the Nazi Party. Orwell greatly admired him from the time he reviewed his *The Spanish Cockpit* in 1937 (see *Orwell in Spain* in this series). On 6 April 1949 he recommended Borkenau to the Information Research Department of the Foreign Office as one of those who could be relied upon to write articles for them (XX/3590B).

---

[487]

Extract from letter from Eileen Blair to Marjorie Dakin[1]
27 September 1938   *Handwritten*

Orwell suffered a tubercular lesion in one lung on 8 March 1938. He was a patient at Preston Hall Sanatorium at Aylesford, Kent, from 15 March to 1 September 1938. It was thought, erroneously as it proved, that Orwell's health might improve if he spent the winter in North Africa. An anonymous gift of £300 from the novelist L. H. Myers (which Orwell accepted as a loan and later repaid) enabled Orwell and his wife, Eileen, to travel to Marrakesh. While there he wrote Coming Up for Air *(1939). See Crick, 368–70, 419–20; Shelden, 316–19, 324–5; A Literary Life, 111–12, 129.*

Chez Mme Vellat, rue Edmond Doutte, Medina, Marrakesh,
French Morocco

I was rather cheered to hear about Humphrey's dugout.[2] Eric has been on
the point of constructing one for two years, though the plans received
rather a check after he did construct one in Spain & it fell down on his &
his companions' heads two days later, not under any kind of bombardment
but just from the force of gravity. But the dugout has generally been by
way of light relief; his specialities are concentration camps & the famine.
He buried some potatoes against the famine & they might have been very
useful if they hadn't gone mouldy at once. To my surprise he does intend
to stay here whatever happens. In theory this seems too reasonable &
even comfortable to be in character; in practice perhaps it wouldn't be so
comfortable. Anyway I am thankful we got here. If we'd been in England
I suppose he must have been in jail by now & I've had the most solemn
warnings against this from all the doctors though they don't tell me how
I could prevent it. Whatever the solution I do still desperately hope that
there won't be war, which I'm sure would be much worse for the Czechs.
After all political oppression, though it gets so much publicity, can make
miserable only a small proportion of a whole nation because a political
régime, especially a dictatorship, has to be popular. We keep seeing &
being exasperated by pictures of London crowds 'demonstrating' when
we don't know what they're demonstrating for, & there are occasional
references to 'extremists' who are arrested but whether the extremists are
Communists demonstrating against Chamberlain's moderation or Fascists
or socialists or pacifists we don't know. Eric, who retains an extraordinary
political simplicity in spite of everything, wants to hear what he calls the
voice of the people. He thinks this might stop a war, but I'm sure that the
voice would only say that it didn't want a war but of course would have to
fight if the Government declared war. It's very odd to feel that Chamberlain
is our only hope, but I do believe he doesn't want war either at the moment
& certainly the man has courage.[3] But it's fantastic & horrifying to think
that you may all be trying on gas masks at this moment.[4]

1. Marjorie Dakin was Orwell's elder sister (1898–1946). She married Humphrey Dakin
(1896–1970) in July 1920. Humphrey was a civil servant working for the National Savings
Committee. When Orwell was researching for *The Road to Wigan Pier* he stayed with the

Dakins at their home at Headingly, Leeds, on two occasions for about ten days in total in order to get some writing done and to be cared for by his sister. Humphrey resented this and there was tension between the two men. See 'The Brother-in-Law Strikes Back', *Orwell Remembered*, 127–30. Two of their children, Henry and Lucy, stayed with Orwell on Jura in 1947 and were involved in the wreck of Orwell's small boat in the Corryvreckan Whirlpool between Jura and Scarba (see XIX/*3257*). As Henry Dakin told the editor in 1998, Orwell seemed completely unphased by their being stranded on a small rocky islet, hoping for rescue. He was far more interested in the puffins and said to Henry, 'I must write an article about puffins one day.' Unfortunately, he died before he could do so.

2. An air-raid shelter dug into the back garden. Such a shelter – not much more than a corrugated steel shell covered by earth – was introduced in November 1938 by Sir John Anderson, and was named after him. Over two million were erected, or dug out. They were free to those earning £250 a year or less and cost £7 for those earning more. Though subjected to a fair amount of ridicule, they did probably save lives.

3. Early in September 1938, Sudeten Germans, led by Konrad Henlein (1898–1945 – by suicide), organized rallies demanding the reunification of Czech border areas with Germany. By 14 September, the Czech government had declared martial law in the Sudetenland and the French had reinforced the Maginot Line, and on 26 September mobilization of the Royal Navy was ordered. The French and British governments urged the Czechs to accede to German demands, but on 23 September the Czech government ordered general mobilization, and war seemed inevitable. The day after Eileen wrote, Hitler called a conference of the Czechs, French and British, and the British Prime Minister Neville Chamberlain (1869–1940) flew to Munich to attend. For the sake of a short breathing space, the Czechs were forced to accept German demands, and annexation of the Sudetenland began on 1 October. Poland seized the opportunity to take over Czech Silesia. For the light it casts on Chamberlain's much criticized statement in a radio broadcast on 1 October that he believed 'it is peace in our time . . . peace with honour', Eileen's comment is particularly telling. His stance was probably that of most British citizens, including many who were, with hindsight, to criticize him. Thus, J. L. Garvin (1868–1947), right-wing editor of the *Observer*, on New Year's Day 1939, argued that 'Mr. Chamberlain was a thousand times right in saving the world's peace at Munich even at the price exacted' (quoted by Robert Kee, *The World We Left Behind*, 1984, 8).

4. Gas masks were distributed in late September 1938.

[489A]

Manifesto: If War Comes, We Shall Resist
New Leader, *30 September 1938*

This manifesto, printed in the New Leader, *the paper of the ILP, on 30 September 1938, was signed by 149 people, forty-eight of whose names were printed. Orwell was listed among 'Authors', the others being Vera Brittain (see 2473, n. 1)*, Havelock Ellis, Laurence Housman, C. E. M. Joad and Ethel Mannin. *Five MPs signed:* James Maxton, H. G. McGhee, Alfred Salter, Campbell Stephen and Cecil H. Wilson. *Among others listed were* Frank Horrabin, Fenner Brockway, Fred. W. Jowett *(Treasurer, ILP),* J. H. Hudson *(Chairman, Parliamentary Pacifist Group),* Tom Stephenson *(Cumberland Miners),* H. A. Moody *(Chairman, League of Coloured Peoples),* George Padmore *(Chairman, International African Service Bureau),* C. H. Norman *and* J. S. Rowntree. *See* P. J. Thwaites, 'The Independent Labour Party, 1938–1950', *unpublished Ph.D. thesis (London University, 1976).*

The European crisis has arisen from larger issues than those which centre on Czechoslovakia. Should war break out, now or later, Czechoslovakia or some other country (like Belgium in 1914) would provide only the incidental occasion for it.

The danger of war arises from the injustices of the Treaties which concluded the last war and the imperialist economic rivalries which they embodied. The danger will remain, even though war be avoided now.

The threat of war will continue until world supplies are made available to all peoples on a basis of co-operation and social justice.

By its policy of economic imperialism during recent years the British Government has aggravated the evils of world distribution, and thereby has a heavy responsibility for the present crisis.

We repudiate, therefore, all appeals to the people to support a war which would, in fact, maintain and extend imperialist possessions and interests, whatever the incidental occasion.

For the democratic countries which resort to war the immediate result would be the destruction of the liberties of the people and the imposition of totalitarian regimes.

If war comes, it will be our duty to resist, and to organise such opposition as will hasten the end of that war, not by Treaties which represent the triumph of one imperialism over another, and which would only sow the seeds of future wars, but by the building of a new world order based on fellowship and justice.

[492]

Extract from letter from Marjorie Dakin to Eileen Blair and Orwell

3 October 1938

166 St Michael's Hill, Bristol

As you will have gathered there has been complete wind-up about war, everybody thought it had really come this time, as indeed it may yet. All preparations are being pushed on just the same. I took the children down to get their gas masks the other day, not that I have much faith in them, but still it is the correct thing to do. I have heard that the A.R.P. is a farce so far, if there was a really bad bombing raid, there would be practically nobody who knew what to do.[1] I also heard that all the warning that Bristol would get would be four minutes, and London only 25 seconds, but I don't know if this is true.[2] If it is it hardly seems worth while to do anything, as I don't see myself getting the children into gas masks and shelter in four minutes. Humph[3] has been transferred pro. tem. into the Ministry of Transport, and has been sent off to Salisbury, but I imagine he will be back quite soon now. As far as he could make out all the high officials in London (in transport) moved out in a body to the south of England with their wives and families. The head man took over the Truro district. Humph as the only outsider was given Salisbury, it being the most dangerous place.

Everything here was perfectly calm, no meetings of any kind. All the parks and gardens have been dug up into shelters, and England is swept clean of corrugated iron and sand bags. I believe the grocers have done a roaring trade, 'better than Christmas'. I didn't go in for a food hoarding myself, except to buy a sack of potatoes, which the grocer offered me.

Devon and Cornwall are simply packed, there is not a house or rooms to be had for love or money, people who went up to London on Friday said it was practically empty, Hyde Park and Kensington Gardens have miles of trenches in them. The bill has now to be paid.

I hope Chamberlain rounds off the thing properly, and offers to give back Germany her mandated colonies, also tries to do something about removing tariffs. Otherwise I think we shall have everything to be ashamed of, in saving our skins at the expense of the Czechs. But I bet he won't. It looks as if poor France has had a kick in the pants, to be vulgar, agreements being signed without reference to her. Personally I think there is going to be a most awful row over the whole thing, when the hysteria has died down a bit. One school of thought says that we shall not be ready for war for another two years and that the Govt. will do anything to put it off till then,[4] others, that now that the great ones of the earth realise that it is really going to be a 'free for all' and that [it] is not just a case of 'giving' one's son it puts a different complexion on things.

I think if there is another war, I shall have Humph in a lunatic asylum in two twos,[5] his nerves are in an awful state, I was really quite glad when he went off to Salisbury poor dear, as he was adding to the horrors of the situation very considerably and of course the children[6] didn't care two hoots, and were enjoying the whole thing. Hen went round and really had his fill of looking at searchlights and machine guns, and Jane was perfectly indifferent, except that she hoped they wouldn't turn the Art School into a Hospital.

1. In January 1938 the government decreed that children be issued gas masks and in April 1938 the rest of the population be measured for them, many months before the Munich crisis.
2. It was not correct: there was invariably adequate time to seek shelter.
3. Marjorie's husband, Humphrey Dakin; see p. 41, n. 1, above.
4. This was a reasonable approximation of the position.
5. In the 1930s this meant the brief time necessary to add dabs of rouge and powder to each cheek before dashing out. In the nineteenth century it referred to an over-rouged over-powdered street woman.
6. Marjorie and Humphrey Dakin had three children: Jane, born 1923; Henry, 1925; and Lucy, 1930.

[504]

To John Sceats
24 November 1938

Boîte Postale 48, Gueliz, Marrakesh, French Morocco

Dear Sceats,[1]

Thanks so much for your letter with the very useful information about insurance offices. I see that my chap will have to be a Representative and that I underrated his income a little. I've done quite a lot of work, but unfortunately after wasting no less than a fortnight doing articles for various papers fell slightly ill so that properly speaking I've done no work for 3 weeks. It's awful how the time flies by. What with all this illness I've decided to count 1938 as a blank year and sort of cross it off the calendar. But meanwhile the concentration camp looms ahead and there is so much one wants to do. I've got to the point now when I feel I could write a good novel if I had five years peace and quiet, but at present one might as well ask for five years in the moon.

This is on the whole rather a dull country. Some time after Xmas we want to go for a week into the Atlas mountains which are 50 or 100 miles from here and look rather exciting. Down here it's flat dried-up country rather like a huge allotment patch that's been let 'go back', and practically no trees except olives and palms. The poverty is something frightful, though of course it's always a little more bearable for people in a hot climate. The people have tiny patches of ground which they cultivate with implements which would have been out of date in the days of Moses. One can get a sort of idea of the prevailing hunger by the fact that in the whole country there are practically no wild animals, everything edible being eaten by human beings. I don't know how it would compare with the poorer parts of India, but Burma would seem like a paradise compared to it, so far as standard of living goes. The French are evidently squeezing the country pretty ruthlessly. They absorb most of the fertile land as well as the minerals, and the taxes seem fairly heavy considering the poverty of the people. On the surface their administration looks better than ours and certainly rouses less animosity in the subject race, because they have very little colour-prejudice. But I think underneath it is much the same. So far as I can judge there is no anti-French movement of any size among the Arabs, and if there were one it would almost certainly be nationalist rather than Socialist, as the great majority of the people are at the feudal stage and the French, I fancy, intend them to remain so. I can't tell anything about the extent of the local Socialist movement, because [it] has for some time only existed illegally. I asked the I.L.P. to get the French Socialist party to put me in touch with any Socialist movement existing here, if only because I could thus learn more about local conditions, but they haven't done so, perhaps because it's too dangerous. The local French, though they're quite different from the British population in India, mostly petty traders and even manual workers, are stuffily conservative and mildly pro-Fascist. I wrote two articles on local conditions for the *Quarterly*[2] which I hope they'll print as they were I think not too incorrect and subtly Trotskyist. I hope by the way that *Controversy*[3] has not succumbed. It would be a disaster if it did, and still more if the *N.L.*[4] had to turn into a monthly. As to *Controversy* I'm sure the sale could be worked up with a little energy and a certain willingness to distribute back numbers, and I'll do what I can in my nearest town when I get back.

Have you heard any rumours about the General Election? The only person I can make contact with here who might conceivably know something is the British consul, who thinks the Government are going to defer the election as long as possible and that attempts may also be made to resuscitate the old Liberal party. Personally I don't think anything can prevent Chamberlain winning unless there is some unforeseen scandal. Labour may win a few by-elections, but the general election will be fought in a completely different emotional atmosphere. The best one can hope is that it may teach Labour a lesson. I only get English papers rather intermittently and haven't seen the results of some of the by-elections. I see Labour won Dartford but gather the Conservatives won Oxford.[5]

Let me have a line some time to hear how things are going.

Yours

Eric Blair

1. John Sceats (b. 1912), an insurance agent who had written articles for the Socialist monthly, *Controversy*. Orwell admired these and invited him to meet him at Preston Hall Sanatorium, Aylesford, Kent, where he was recovering from illness. Orwell also wrote to him on 28 October 1938 to ask for details of the work of an insurance agent; he needed those for the character of George Bowling of *Coming Up for Air* (1939), which he wrote while in Marrakesh. Sceats and Orwell only met once, at Aylesford, shortly after the publication of *Homage to Catalonia*. In a letter to Malcolm Muggeridge, 24 April 1955, Sceats described their conversation: 'We talked chiefly of politics and philosophy. I remember he said he thought *Burmese Days* his best book (excluding, *sans dire*, the latest). At the time he was reading Kafka. Despite his recent association with POUM, he had already decided he was not a Marxist, and he was more than interested in the philosophy of Anarchism. As he saw things then, it was a matter of months before either Fascism or War landed him in the Concentration Camp (British); whatever the future held he could not believe it would allow him to go on writing. He was of course anti-Nazi, but could not (at the time) stomach the idea of an anti-German

war: in fact, talking to Max Plowman (who called in the afternoon) he implied he would join him in opposition to such a war with whatever underground measures might be appropriate . . . Indeed, it was Max who put the views of common sense.' Max Plowman (1883–1941) worked on *The Adelphi* from 1929 until his death and was instrumental in publishing Orwell's early articles. He had fought in the First World War (his reminiscences are given in *A Subaltern on the Somme*, 1927) and became an ardent pacifist; he was General Secretary of the Peace Pledge Union, 1937–8. Although Orwell was often harsh about pacifists, he remained a friend of Max's and continued a friendship with his widow, Dorothy.

2. The *Quarterly* probably refers to the *Political Quarterly* founded in 1930 by Kingsley Martin, William Robson and Leonard Woolf, with help from George Bernard Shaw. Bernard Crick, Orwell's biographer, joined the editorial board in 1966 and became successively joint editor, chairman and literary editor, until resigning from the board in 2000 when he became 'the same age as the journal'. Orwell was never published in *PQ*. Up until the outbreak of war in September 1939, he had only two articles published, neither of which was concerned with Morocco. His essay 'Marrakech' appeared in the Christmas 1939 issue of *New Writing*. The two articles mentioned in the letter, despite a thorough search, have not been found.

3. *Controversy* began life in 1932 as an internal party bulletin of the Independent Labour Party. From 1936, however, it became a journal in which a wide variety of left-wing views could be expressed. In 1939 it became *Left Forum* and then its name changed simply to *Left*. It ceased publication in May 1950. Its editor was Dr C. A. Smith, a London headmaster and later a lecturer for the University of London. Orwell wrote for it under all its titles.

4. *New Leader*, to which Orwell contributed 'Why I Join the I.L.P.' (reproduced above) and a review of Frank Jellinek's *The Civil War in Spain* (see *Orwell in Spain* in this series). Despite being hard-pressed for money, Orwell contributed 5s 7d to its appeal for funds; the average of the seventy-six contributions by groups and individuals was 6s 11d (XI/510A).

5. In its issue for 9 December 1938, *New Leader* reported what it described as 'Amazing Stories' of how Labour candidates had been 'ousted' at selection meetings for the constituencies of Bridgwater and Oxford by 'Independent Progressives'. At Bridgwater, the 'alleged Independent candidate' was introduced to the constituency by Sir Richard Acland. There was also intervention by 'the new political party, the Left Book Club'. At Oxford, academics were blamed for manipulating the selection of an Independent Progressive, even though that meant the Labour candidate withdrew and wealthy members of the Oxford Labour Party had to find £350 to meet the Liberal candidate's expenses when he also agreed to withdraw. The report concluded: 'These "intelligentsia" and their Left Book Clubs are the new instrument of the Communist Party.' This manoeuvring was to little effect, since the Conservative, Quintin Hogg (later, Lord Hailsham), took the seat.

[505]
To Charles Doran
26 November 1938

Boîte Postale 48, Gueliz, Marrakesh, French Morocco

Dear Charlie,[1]

Thanks so much for your letter with the copy of *Solidarity* and the too kind review of my book. I see from the front page of *Solidarity* that those bloody liars in the *News Chronicle* reported the result of the P.O.U.M. trial under the heading 'spies sentenced' thus giving the impression that the P.O.U.M. prisoners were sentenced for espionage. The *Observer* also did something of the kind, though more circumspectly, and the French press of this country, which is in the main pro-Franco, reported the act of accusation against the P.O.U.M., stated that it had been 'all proved' and then failed to report the verdict at all! I admit this kind of thing frightens me. It means that the most elementary respect for truthfulness is breaking down, not merely in the Communist and Fascist press, but in the bourgeois liberal press which still pays lip-service to the old traditions of journalism. It gives one the feeling that our civilization is going down into a sort of mist of lies where it will be impossible ever to find out the truth about anything. Meanwhile I've written to the I.L.P. asking them to send me a copy of the issue of *Solidaridad Obrera*[2] which reported the case, so that if necessary I can write to the press, that is to say such papers as would print my letter, stating quite clearly what the P.O.U.M. prisoners *were* sentenced for. I trust, however, that someone has already done so. It's difficult for me to get hold of foreign papers here, especially a paper like *Solidaridad Obrera*, which I couldn't get nearer than Gibraltar and there only with difficulty.

As perhaps you know I was told to spend the winter here for the sake of my lungs. We've been here nearly three months now and I think it has done me a certain amount of good. It is a tiresome country in some ways, but it is interesting to get a glimpse of French colonial methods and compare them with our own. I think as far as I can make out that the French are every bit as bad as ourselves, but somewhat better on the surface, partly owing to the fact that there is a large indigenous white population here, part of it proletarian or near-proletarian. For that reason it isn't quite possible to keep up the sort of white man's burden atmosphere that we do in India, and there is less colour-prejudice. But economically it is just the usual swindle for which empires exist. The poverty of most of the Arab population is frightful. As far as one can work it out, the average family seems to live at the rate of about a shilling a day, and of course most of the people are either peasants or petty craftsmen who have to work extremely hard by antiquated methods. At the same time, so far as one can judge, there is no anti-French movement on any scale. If one appeared it would I think be merely nationalist at the beginning, as the great majority of the people are still at the feudal stage and fairly strict Mahommedans. In some of the big towns such as Casablanca there is a proletariat, both white and coloured, and there the Socialist movement just exists. But as for the Arab Socialist parties, they were all suppressed some time ago. I feel reasonably sure that unless the working class (it really depends on them) in the democracies change their tactics within a year or two, the Arabs will be easy game for the Fascists. French opinion here is predominantly pro-Franco, and I should not be greatly surprised to see Morocco become the jumping-off place for some French version of Franco in the years to come.

I don't altogether know what to think about the crisis, Maxton[3] etc. I think Maxton put his foot in it by being too cordial to Chamberlain, and I also think it would be absurd to regard Chamberlain as really a peace-maker. I also quite agree with what anybody chooses to say about the way in which the Czechs have been let down. But I think we might face one or two facts. One is that almost anything is better than European war, which will lead not only to the slaughter of tens of millions but to an extension of Fascism. Certainly Chamberlain and Co. are preparing for war, and any other government that is likely to get in will also prepare for war; but meanwhile we have got perhaps two years' breathing space in which *may* be possible to provoke a real popular anti-war movement in England, in France and above all in the Fascist countries. If we can do that, to the point of making it clear that no government will go to war because its people won't follow, I think Hitler is done for. The other fact is that the Labour Party are doing themselves frightful harm by getting stamped in the public mind as the war party. In my opinion they can't now win the general election[4] unless something very unforeseen turns up. They will therefore be in the position of an opposition pushing the government in the direction in which it is already going. As such they might as well cease to exist, and in fact it wouldn't surprise me in the next year or two to see Attlee and Co. cave in and take office in some new version of a national government.[5] I admit that being anti-war probably plays Chamberlain's game for the next few months, but the point will soon come when the anti-wars, of all complexions, will have to resist the fascising° processes which war-preparation entails.

I hope things are prospering with you. After all the frightful waste of time due to being ill I got started on my novel, which I suppose will be ready to come out about April. Eileen sends love.

Yours
Eric Blair

P.S. [at top of letter] Thanks so much for your good offices about my Spanish book. That's what sells a book – getting asked for in libraries.

1. Charles Doran (1894–1974) served in the POUM with Orwell in Spain. He was born in Dublin and moved to Glasgow in 1915. He served in the First World War and then became active in Guy Aldred's Anti-Parliamentary Communist Federation. He joined the ILP in the early 1930s. He opposed World War II and joined a small anarchist group led by Willie MacDougall that engaged in anti-militarist and revolutionary socialist propaganda throughout the war. In 1983, Doran's widow, Bertha, told Dr James D. Young that her husband was impressed by Orwell's modesty and sincerity: 'I remember Charlie saying that Orwell was not an argumentative sort of person. Charlie might voice an opinion about something hoping to provoke Orwell into agreeing or disagreeing, but Orwell would just say, "You might be right, Doran!" Orwell at that time had not read Marx.' In the mid-1940s, Mrs Doran said, her husband classed Orwell as 'a rebel – not a revolutionary – who was dissatisfied with the Establishment, whilst remaining part of it'. See *Bulletin of the Society of Labour History*, 51, part 1 (April 1986), 15–17; for an earlier letter to Doran, see XI/*386*. Mrs Doran gave her husband's letters to Waverley Secondary School, Drumchapel, Glasgow in December 1974; the editor is grateful to her and the school for permission to reproduce this letter.
2. A Spanish Anarchist daily newspaper of the time.
3. James Maxton (1885–1946), ILP MP, 1922–46; Chairman of the ILP, 1926–31 and 1934–9. His official biography, *The Beloved Rebel* (1955), was written by his colleague, John McNair.
4. A largely Conservative government – with National Liberal and National Labour adherents – had assembled on 16 November 1935, with a majority of 247, for a maximum five-year term. Orwell is expecting a general election in 1939 or 1940, but because of the outbreak of war none was held until 1945.

5. With the fall of Neville Chamberlain's Conservative government and the appointment of Winston Churchill as Prime Minister in May 1940, Labour joined a genuinely national government, Clement Attlee becoming Deputy Prime Minister. The Labour Party was to win the 1945 General Election with a majority of 146, with Attlee as Prime Minister.

[507]

'Political Reflections on the Crisis'
The Adelphi, *December 1938*

In all the controversies over the Popular Front, the question least often debated has been whether such a combination could actually win an election.

It was obvious enough from the start that a Popular Front in England would be something quite different from the French Popular Front, which was brought into being by an *internal* Fascist threat. If it were formed it would be, more or less avowedly, for the purpose of war against Germany. What was the use of saying that collective security and so forth meant peace and not war? Nobody believed it. The point really under debate was whether left-wingers ought to support a war which meant bolstering up British imperialism. The advocates of the Popular Front shouted 'Stop Hitler!' and its opponents shouted 'No line-up with capitalists!'. But both seem to have taken it for granted that if a Popular Front were formed the British public would vote for it.

Then came the war crisis. What happened? It is too early to say with absolute certainty, but if the signs are worth anything the crisis revealed two things. One, that the British people will go to war if they are told to; the other, that they don't want war and will vote against any party which stamps itself as a war party. When Chamberlain came back from Munich he was not booed and execrated but greeted by miles of cheering people. And it does not greatly matter that afterwards, when all was safe, there was a certain revulsion, on the strength of which Labour may win a few by-elections. In the decisive moment the mass of the people swung over to Chamberlain's side, and if the General Election revives the spirit of the crisis, as in all probability it will, they will do the same again.[1] And yet for two years past the *News Chronicle*, the *Daily Worker*, *Reynold's*, the *New*

Statesman,[2] and the sponsors of the Left Book Club had been deluding themselves and part of their public that the entire British nation, barring a few old gentlemen in West End Clubs, wanted nothing better than a ten-million-dead war in defence of democracy.

Why was it possible for a mistake of such magnitude to be made? Mainly because a small body of noise-makers can for a while give the impression that they are more numerous than they are. The mass of the people are normally silent. They do not sign manifestoes, attend demonstrations, answer questionnaires or even join political parties. As a result it is very easy to mistake a handful of slogan-shouters for the entire nation. At first sight a membership of 50,000 for the Left Book Club *looks* enormous. But what is 50,000 in a population of 50,000,000? To get a real idea of the balance of forces one ought not to be watching those 5,000 people who are making a noise in the Albert Hall: one ought to be watching those 5,000,000 outside who are saying nothing, but who are quite possibly thinking, and who will cast their votes at the next election. It is just this that propaganda organisations such as the Left Book Club tend to prevent. Instead of trying to assess the state of public opinion they reiterate that they *are* public opinion, and they and a few people round them end by believing it.

The net result of Strachey[3] and Company's efforts has been to give a totally false estimate of what the English people were thinking, and to push the leaders of the Labour Party a little further on the road to war. In doing so they have gone some distance towards losing Labour the election.

II

So far as one can judge from the French Press, it seems clear that nobody in France, except the Communists and M. Kérillis,[4] seriously wished for war. I think events showed that the English people did not wish for war either; but it would be absurd to pretend that there was not in England an influential minority which wished very ardently for war and howled with disappointment when they did not get it. And by no means all of these people were Communists.

A type that seems to be comparatively rare in France is the war-hungry middle-class intellectual. Why should this type be commoner in one country than in the other? One can think of several subsidiary reasons, but the question can probably be answered satisfactorily with a single word: Conscription.

Compared with England, France is a democratic country, there are fewer privileges attaching to status, and military service is not at all easy to dodge. Nearly every adult Frenchman has done his service and has the harsh discipline of the French army well fixed in his memory. Unless he is over age or in an exceptionally sheltered position, war means to him something quite different from what it means to a middle-class Englishman. It means a notice on the wall, 'Mobilisation Générale', and three weeks later, if he is unlucky, a bullet in his guts. How can such a man go about irresponsibly declaring that 'we' ought to declare war on Germany, Japan and anyone else who happens to be handy? He is bound to regard war with a fairly realistic eye.

One could not possibly say the same of the English intelligentsia. Of all the left-wing journalists who declare day in and day out that if this, that and the other happens 'we' must fight, how many imagine that war will affect them personally? When war breaks out they will be doing what they are doing at present, writing propaganda articles. Moreover, they are well aware of this. The type of person who writes articles for the political Left has no feeling that 'war' means something in which he will actually get hurt. 'War' is something that happens on paper, a diplomatic manoeuvre, something which is of course very deplorable but is 'necessary' in order to destroy Fascism. His part in it is the pleasantly stimulating one of writing propaganda articles. Curiously enough, he may well be wrong. We do not yet know what a big-scale air-raid is like, and the next war may turn out to be very unpleasant even for journalists. But these people, who have been born into the monied intelligentsia and feel in their bones that they belong to a privileged class, are not really capable of foreseeing any such thing. War is something that happens on paper, and consequently they are able to decide that this or that war is 'necessary' with no more sense of personal danger than in deciding on a move at chess.

Our civilisation produces in increasing numbers two types, the gangster and the pansy. They never meet, but each is necessary to the other. Somebody in eastern Europe 'liquidates' a Trotskyist; somebody in Bloomsbury writes a justification of it. And it is, of course, precisely because of the utter softness and security of life in England that the yearning for bloodshed – bloodshed in the far distance – is so common among our intelligentsia. Mr. Auden can write about 'the acceptance of guilt for the necessary murder'[5] because he has never committed a murder, perhaps never had one of his friends murdered, possibly never even seen a murdered man's corpse. The presence of this utterly irresponsible intelligentsia, who 'took up' Roman Catholicism ten years ago, 'take up' Communism to-day and will 'take up' the English variant of Fascism a few years hence, is a special feature of the English situation. Their importance is that with their money, influence and literary facility they are able to dominate large sections of the Press.

III

Barring some unforeseen scandal or a really large disturbance inside the Conservative Party, Labour's chances of winning the General Election seem very small. If any kind of Popular Front is formed, its chances are probably less than those of Labour unaided. The best hope would seem to be that if Labour *is* defeated, the defeat may drive it back to its proper 'line'.

But the time-factor is all-important. The National Government is preparing for war. No doubt they will bluff, shuffle and make further concessions in order to buy a little more time – still, they are preparing for war. A few people cling to the belief that the Government's war preparations are all a sham or even that they are directed against Soviet Russia. This is mere wish-thinking. What really inspires it is the knowledge that when Chamberlain goes to war with Germany (in defence of democracy, of course) he will be doing what his opponents demand and thus taking the wind out of their sails. The attitude of the British governing class is probably summed up in the remark I overheard recently from one of the Gibraltar garrison: 'It's coming right enough. It's pretty clear Hitler's going to have Czechoslovakia. Much better let him have it. We shall be ready by 1941.' In fact, the difference between the warmongers of the right and the warmongers of the left is merely strategic.

The real question is *how soon* the Labour Party will start effectively opposing the Government's war plans. Suppose that war actually breaks out. Some of the more soft-boiled left-wing papers have recently been discussing the 'conditions' on which the Labour Party should 'support' the Government in case of war. As though any Government at war could permit its subjects to make 'conditions'! Once war has started the left-wing parties will have the choice of offering unconditional loyalty or being smashed. The only group large enough to be capable of resisting, and perhaps even of scaring the Government away from war, is the Labour Party. But if it does not begin soon it may never do so. Two years, even a year, of tacit acquiescence in preparation for war, and its power will have been broken.

When and if Labour loses the election, the cry will be raised that if we had had a Popular Front the election could have been won. This may obscure the issue for a long time, perhaps even for two years. Hence more Popular Frontism, more brandishing of fists and shouts for a 'firm line', more clamour for overwhelming armaments – in short, more pushing of the Government in the direction in which it is going. So long as Labour demands a 'firm line' which entails the risk of war, it cannot make any but a sham resistance to the fascising° process which war-preparation implies. What is the use of asking for a 'strong' foreign policy and at the same time pretending to oppose increased working hours, reduced wages, Press censorship and even conscription? The retort will always be the same: 'How can we keep Hitler in check if you obstruct rearmament?' War, and even war-preparation, can be used as an excuse for anything, and we may be sure the Government will make full use of its opportunities. In the end a perception of what is happening may drive the Labour Party back to its proper 'line'. But how soon will that end come?

On September 28th the National Council of Labour made one of the few sensible moves that were made during the whole war-crisis. It appealed over the radio to the German people to resist Hitler. The appeal did not go far enough, it was self-righteous in tone and contained no admission that British capitalism, like German Nazism, has its faults; but it did at least show some perception of the right method of approach. What hope is there of that method being followed up if the Labour Party continues much longer on the path of jingoism and imperialism? It may be that sooner or later the mere fact of being in opposition will drive the Labour Party back to an anti-militarist and anti-imperialist line. But it will have to be sooner and not later. If it continues much longer in its present anomalous position, its enemies will eat it up.

1. Orwell is expecting a general election in 1939 or 1940. The outbreak of war ensured this did not take place until 1945.

2. The *Daily Worker* ran from 1930 to 1966 when it was incorporated in the *Morning Star*. It was a Communist paper, backed secretly by Moscow. The government suspended it from 22 January 1941 to 6 September 1942.

3. John Strachey (1901–63), political theorist and Labour MP, 1929–31. He stood as a candidate for Sir Oswald Mosley's New Party in 1931 but shortly afterwards became caught up in the current enthusiasm for Communism. His *The Coming Struggle for Power* (1932) was an influential exercise in Marxism. He became Minister for Food, 1945–50, and Secretary of State for War, 1950–51, in the first two post-war Labour governments.

4. Henri de Kérillis was a journalist and right-wing French politician. When Germany reoccupied the Rhineland in March 1936, he published *Français! voici la guerre*: in effect, the war has started (Eugen Weber, *The Hollow Years: France in the 1930s*, 1995, 243). He was the only non-Communist member of the Chamber of Deputies to vote against the ratification of the Munich Agreement with Hitler in 1938.

5. Wystan Hugh Auden (1907–73), poet and critic, was associated in the thirties with Christopher Isherwood, Stephen Spender and Louis MacNeice. He left for America in January 1939 and became a US citizen in 1946. He was Professor of Poetry at Oxford University, 1956–61. Orwell attacked him for 'the conscious acceptance of guilt for the necessary murder' in 'Inside the Whale' (XII/600; see pp. 103–4). This line appears in the first edition of the poem, 'Spain' (May 1937). He later revised the line to read, 'The conscious acceptance of guilt in the fact of murder'. For a full account, see XII/114, n. 37.

---

[524]

Review of Russia under Soviet Rule *by N. de Basily*
New English Weekly, *12 January 1939*

Russia under Soviet Rule falls definitely into the 'anti' class of books on the U.S.S.R., but for once it is not Trotskyist. The author – an exile, of course – holds approximately the same opinions as Kerensky[1] and the others of the Provisional Government of 1917, with which he was associated in an official capacity. He is therefore attacking the Bolshevik experiment not from a Socialist but from a liberal-capitalist standpoint, rather as Gaetano Salvemini[2] attacks the Fascist experiment of Italy. His book might almost, in fact, be a companion-volume to *Under the Axe of Fascism*. In the last analysis it is doubtful whether any liberal criticism of a totalitarian system is really relevant; it is rather like accusing the Pope of being a bad

Protestant. However, as the dictators are generally dishonest enough to claim the liberal virtues on top of the totalitarian ones, they certainly lay themselves open to attacks of this kind.

The author, it should be noticed, though hostile to the Bolshevik régime, does not think that it is going to collapse in the near future. His main thesis is that it has functioned inefficiently and that the loss of liberty and enormous suffering which it has caused were largely unnecessary. The modernisation of industry and agriculture which Stalin has undertaken is, according to Mr. de Basily, simply a continuation of something that was already happening in pre-war Russia, and the rate of progress has actually been slowed down rather than advanced by the revolution. It is of course obvious that a statement of this kind cannot be finally proved or disproved. Even to begin to examine it is to sink into a bog of statistics – and incidentally this book contains more figures, mainly from Soviet sources, and longer footnotes than any book I have read for years. But it is worth being reminded that Russia was already being fairly rapidly modernised in the ten years or so preceding the revolution. It is now, perhaps, beginning to be possible to see the Russian revolution in some kind of historical perspective, and the hitherto-accepted version of a barbarous feudal country turning overnight into a sort of super-America is something that will probably have to be revised.

But is life – life for the ordinary person – any better in Russia than it was before? That is the thing that it seems almost impossible for an outsider to be certain about. Statistics, even when they are honestly presented (and how often does that happen nowadays?), are almost always misleading, because one never knows what factors they leave out of account. To give a crude illustration, it would be easy to show, by stating the figures for fuel-consumption and saying nothing about the temperature, that everyone in Central Africa is suffering from cold. Who does not know those Soviet statistics, published by Mr. Gollancz[3] and others, in which the curve of everything except mortality goes up and up and up? And how much do they really tell one? Mr. de Basily's statistics, naturally, point a different moral, but, without in the least questioning the accuracy of his figures, I would not infer too much from them. As far as the material side of life goes, all that seems to emerge fairly certainly is this: that the standard of living was rising during the N.E.P. period,[4] dropped during the period 1928–33, and is now rising again but is still low by western European standards. This is denied by Soviet apologists, but not very convincingly. The average wage in 1936 was only 225 roubles a month – the purchasing-power of the rouble being about threepence. Moreover, it is well-known that it is next door to impossible for a Soviet citizen, unless on some kind of official mission, to visit any foreign country – a silent admission that life is more comfortable elsewhere.

If Mr. de Basily were merely claiming that twenty years of Bolshevik rule had failed to raise the general standard of living, his criticism would be hardly worth making. After all, one could not reasonably expect an experiment on such a scale to work perfectly at the beginning. Economically the Bolsheviks have been far more successful than any outsider would have prophesied in 1918. But the intellectual, moral and political developments – the ever-tightening party dictatorship, the muzzled press, the purges, the oriental worship of Stalin – are a different matter. Mr. de Basily devotes a good many chapters to this. He is, nevertheless, comparatively optimistic, because, as a liberal, he takes it for granted that the 'spirit of freedom' is bound to revive sooner or later. He even believes that this is happening already:

The thirst for liberty, the notion of self-respect . . . all these features and characteristics of the old Russian élite are beginning to be appropriated by the intellectuals of to-day . . . The moment the Soviet élite opens its fight for emancipation of the human individual, the vast popular masses will be at its side.

But will they? The terrifying thing about the modern dictatorships is that they are something entirely unprecedented. Their end cannot be foreseen. In the past every tyranny was sooner or later overthrown, or at least resisted, because of 'human nature', which as a matter of course desired liberty. But we cannot be at all certain that 'human nature' is constant. It may be just as possible to produce a breed of men who do not wish for liberty as to produce a breed of hornless cows. The Inquisition failed, but then the Inquisition had not the resources of the modern state. The radio, press-censorship, standardised education and the secret police have altered everything. Mass-suggestion is a science of the last twenty years, and we do not yet know how successful it will be.

It is noticeable that Mr. de Basily does not attribute all the shortcomings of the present Russian régime to Stalin's personal wickedness. He thinks that they were inherent from the very start in the aims and nature of the Bolshevik party. It is probably a good thing for Lenin's reputation that he died so early. Trotsky, in exile, denounces the Russian dictatorship, but he is probably as much responsible for it as any man now living, and there is no certainty that as a dictator he would be preferable to Stalin, though undoubtedly he has a much more interesting mind. The essential act is the rejection of democracy – that is, of the underlying values of democracy; once you have decided upon that, Stalin – or at any rate something *like* Stalin – is already on the way. I believe this opinion is gaining ground, and I hope it will continue to do so. If even a few hundred thousand people can be got to grasp that it is useless to overthrow Tweedledum in order to set up Tweedledee, the talk of 'democracy versus Fascism' with which our ears are deafened may begin to mean something.

1. Aleksandr Kerensky (1881–1970), Socialist Premier of the Provisional Government of Russia, July–October 1917, fled to France, lived in Australia from 1940 and in the United States from 1946, where he died.

2. Gaetano Salvemini (1873–1957), historian of contemporary Italy, was forced to leave Italy in 1925 because of his attacks on Fascism. He taught at Harvard University, 1933–48, and became a US citizen in 1940.

3. Victor Gollancz (1893–1967; Kt., 1965) was educated at Oxford and taught at Repton for two years. There his introduction of a class on civics brought him into conflict with the headmaster, Dr Geoffrey Fisher (later Archbishop of Canterbury). He was sacked in 1918 and then worked on minimum-wage legislation and edited 'The World Today' series for Oxford University Press. In 1921 he joined Benn Brothers, chiefly publishers of trade journals. In October 1927 he established his own publishing house, issuing sixty-four books in his first year. He had been born into an orthodox Jewish family and was a member of the Labour Party but later described himself as a Christian Socialist. His best-known achievement was the formation of the Left Book Club in 1936; under this imprint Orwell's *The Road to Wigan Pier* was published in March 1937. Orwell and Gollancz fell out over the latter's refusal to publish *Homage to Catalonia* and *Animal Farm*, and Orwell's publisher became Martin Secker & Warburg. However, he and Gollancz continued to collaborate, notably on the alleviation of hunger in Europe after the 1939–45 war. See *Gollancz: The Story of a Publishing House, 1928–1978*, Sheila Hodges (1978).

4. New Economic Policy; see p. 34, n. 6, above.

[529]
Review of Communism and Man *by F. J. Sheed*
Peace News, *27 January 1939*

This book – a refutation of Marxian Socialism from the Catholic stand-point – is remarkable for being written in a good temper. Instead of employing the abusive misrepresentation which is now usual in all major controversies, it gives a fairer exposition of Marxism and Communism than most Marxists could be trusted to give of Catholicism. If it fails, or at any rate ends less interestingly than it begins, this is probably because the author is less ready to follow up his own intellectual implications than those of his opponents.

As he sees clearly enough, the radical difference between Christian and Communist lies in the question of personal immortality.[1] Either this life is a preparation for another, in which case the individual soul is all-important, or there is no life after death, in which case the individual is merely a replaceable cell in the general body. These two theories are quite irreconcilable, and the political and economic systems founded upon them are bound to be antagonistic.

What Mr. Sheed is not ready to admit, however, is that acceptance of the Catholic position implies a certain willingness to see the present injustices of society continue. He seems to claim that a truly Catholic society would contain all or most of what the Socialist is aiming at – which is a little too like 'having it both ways'.

Individual salvation implies liberty, which is always extended by Cath-olic writers to include the right to private property. But in the stage of industrial development which we have now reached, the right to private property means the right to exploit and torture millions of one's fellow-creatures. The Socialist would argue, therefore, that one can only defend private property if one is more or less indifferent to economic justice.

The Catholic's answer to this is not very satisfactory. It is not that the Church condones the injustices of Capitalism – quite the contrary. Mr. Sheed is quite right in pointing out that several Popes have denounced the Capitalist system very bitterly, and that Socialists usually ignore this. But at the same time the Church refuses the only solution that is likely to make any real difference. Private property is to remain, the employer-employee relationship is to remain, even the categories 'rich' and 'poor' are to remain – but there is to be justice and fair distribution. In other words, the rich man is not to be expropriated, he is merely to be told to behave himself.

(The Church) does not see men primarily as exploiters and exploited, with the exploiters as people whom it is her duty to overthrow . . . from her point of view the rich man as sinner is the object of her most loving care. Where others see a strong man in the pride of success, she sees a poor soul in danger of hell . . . Christ has told her that the souls of the rich are in special danger; and care for souls is her primary work.

The objection to this is that *in practice* it makes no difference. The rich man is called to repentance, but he never repents. In this matter Catholic capitalists do not seem to be perceptibly different from the others.

It is obvious that any economic system would work equitably if men could be trusted to behave themselves but long experience has shown that in matters of property only a tiny minority of men will behave any better than they are compelled to do. This does not mean that the Catholic attitude toward property is untenable, but it does mean that it is very difficult to square with economic justice. In practice, accepting the Catholic standpoint means accepting exploitation, poverty, famine, war and disease as part of the natural order of things.

It would seem, therefore, that if the Catholic Church is to regain its spiritual influence, it will have to define its position more boldly. Either it will have to modify its attitude toward private property, or it will have to say clearly that its kingdom is not of this world and that feeding bodies is of very small importance compared with saving souls.

In effect it does say something of the kind, but rather uneasily, because this is not the message that modern men want to hear. Consequently for some time past the Church has been in an anomalous position, symbolized by the fact the Pope almost simultaneously denounces the Capitalist system and confers decorations on General Franco.

Meanwhile this is an interesting book, written in a simple style and remarkably free from malice and cheap witticisms. If all Catholic apologists were like Mr. Sheed, the Church would have fewer enemies.[2]

1. *Peace News* printed 'immortality' as 'immorality', and also duplicated 'almost' in the last sentence of the penultimate paragraph.

2. This review attracted two letters printed in *Peace News*, 3 February 1939, one signed 'A Roman Catholic', the other from John Nibb [not identified]. Among points raised by what Nibb called an 'apt review' were that 'Catholics are not tied to a belief in the necessary permanence of indigence' and that, although the Catholic Church taught and upheld 'the lawfulness of private property', that right might be abrogated 'to avoid worse evils and in the interests of a whole people'. Indeed, some responsible Catholics, according to 'A Roman Catholic', advocated 'that ownership of the means of production should be in the hands of the workers (*all* workers, not simply the "proletarians")'. Referring to what he described as the anomaly Orwell saw in the Pope denouncing the evils of capitalism yet approving of Franco, Nibb said, 'most Catholics find it impossible to view the Spanish war as an episode caused by wicked militarists and capitalists attacking a beneficient government . . . the wrong people are suffering for the actions of other individuals, and . . . the religion of the Franco element seems to be as much nationalism (and even imperialism) as Christianity'.

[536]

To Herbert Read
5 March 1939

Boîte Postale 48, Gueliz, Marrakesh, French Morocco

Dear Read,[1]

Thanks so much for your letter. I am probably leaving this country about the 22nd or 23rd of March and should be in England by the end of the month. I shall probably be in London a few days and I'll try and arrange to come and see you. If I could help with *Revolt!*[2] I'd like to, though till I've seen what kind of paper it is to be I don't know whether I could be any use. The trouble is that if I am writing a book as I generally am I find it almost impossible to do any other creative work, but on the other hand I *like* doing reviews, if they would want anything in that line. If we could keep a leftwing but non-Stalinist review in existence (it's all a question of money, really) I believe a lot of people would be pleased. People aren't all fools, they must begin soon to see through this 'antifascist' racket. A thought that cheers me a lot is that each generation, which in literature means about ten years, is in revolt against the last, and just as the Audens etc. rose in revolt against the Squires and Drinkwaters,[3] there must be another gang about due to rise against the Audens.

About the press business. I quite agree that it's in a way absurd to start preparing for an underground campaign[4] unless you know who is going to campaign and what for, but the point is that if you don't make some preparations beforehand you will be helpless when you want to start, as you are sure to sooner or later. I cannot believe that the time when one can buy a printing press with no questions asked will last forever. To take an analogous case. When I was a kid you could walk into a bicycle-shop or ironmonger's and buy any firearm you pleased, short of a field gun, and it did not occur to most people that the Russian revolution and the Irish civil war would bring this state of affairs to an end. It will be the same with printing presses etc. As for the sort of thing we shall find ourselves doing, the way I see the situation is like this. The chances of Labour or any left combination winning the election are in my opinion nil, and in any case if they did get in I doubt whether they'd be better than or much different from the Chamberlain lot. We are therefore in either for war in the next two years, or for prolonged war-preparation, or possibly only for sham war-preparations designed to cover up other objects, but in any of these cases for a fascising° process leading to an authoritarian regime, ie. some kind of Austro-fascism. So long as the objective, real or pretended, is war against Germany, the greater part of the Left will associate themselves with the fascising° process, which will ultimately mean associating themselves with wage-reductions, suppression of free speech, brutalities in the colonies etc. Therefore the revolt against these things will have to be against the Left as well as the Right. The revolt will form itself into two sections, that of the dissident lefts like ourselves, and that of the fascists, this time the idealistic Hitler-fascists, in England more or less represented by Mosley. I don't know whether Mosley will have the sense and guts to stick out against war with Germany, he might decide to cash in on the patriotism business, but in that case someone else will take his place. If war leads to disaster and revolution, the official Left having already sold out and been identified in the public mind with the war-party, the fascists will have it all their own way unless there is in being some body of people who are both anti-war and anti-fascist. Actually there will be such people, probably very great numbers of them, but their being able to do anything will depend largely on their having some means of expression during the time when discontent is growing. I doubt whether there is much hope of saving England from fascism of one kind or another, but clearly one must put up a fight, and it seems silly to be silenced when one might be making a row merely because one had failed to take a few precautions beforehand. If we laid in printing presses etc. in some discreet place we could then cautiously go to work to get together a distributing agency, and we could then feel 'Well, if trouble does come we are ready.' On the other hand if it doesn't come I should be so pleased that I would not grudge a little wasted effort. As to money, I shall probably be completely penniless for the rest of this year unless something unexpected happens. Perhaps if we definitely decided on a course of action your friend Penrose[5] might put up something, and I think there are others who could be got to see the necessity. What about Bertrand Russell,[6] for instance? I suppose he has some money, and he would fall in with the idea fast enough if he could be persuaded that free speech is menaced.

When I get back I'll write or ring up and try and arrange to meet. If you're going to be in town about the beginning of April, or on the other hand going to be away or something, could you let me know? But better not write to the above as the letter might miss me. Write to: AT: 24 Croom's Hill, Greenwich SE. 10.[7]

Yours
Eric Blair

1. Herbert Read (1893–1968; Kt., 1953), poet, critic, educator and interpreter of modern art, particularly influential in the thirties and forties. He served in World War I and was awarded the DSO and MC. He was assistant keeper at the Victoria and Albert Museum, taught at Edinburgh University, and edited the *Burlington Magazine*, 1933–9. Among his major books were *Form in Modern Poetry* (1932), *Art Now* (1933), *Art and Society* (1936) and *Poetry and Anarchism* (1938; as *Anarchy and Order*, 1954). His *Education through Art* (1943) was an important influence after the war. He was the most prominent British intellectual to support Anarchism before World War II and was closely associated with Anarchism until he was knighted.
2. *Revolt!*, jointly edited by Vernon Richards (who took many photographs of Orwell and his son, Richard), ran for six issues from 11 February to 3 June 1939. It aimed to present the Spanish Civil War from an anti-Stalinist point of view.
3. John C. Squire (1884–1958; Kt., 1933), journalist, essayist, poet and literary editor of the *New Statesman*, 1913–19. He founded the *London Mercury*, which he edited 1919–34. He stood for Parliament for Labour in 1918 and for the Liberals in 1924, unsuccessfully on both occasions. He had a particular interest in architecture and was an early advocate of the appointment of a minister of fine arts. Among the many books he wrote and edited were *A Book of Women's Verse* (1921) and *The Comic Muse* (1925). John Drinkwater (1882–1937), poet,

playwright and essayist, was an object of scorn to Orwell. In *Keep the Aspidistra Flying* (138), Gordon Comstock sneeringly refers to him as *Sir* John Drinkwater, though he was not knighted.

4. In a letter to Read on 4 January 1939, Orwell wrote, 'I believe it is vitally necessary for those of us who intend to oppose the coming war to start organising for illegal anti-war activities.' He was keen to establish a secret, underground press (XI/522).

5. Roland Penrose (1900–1984; Kt., 1966) was a painter and writer who used his independent means to help many painters and artistic and left-wing projects.

6. Bertrand Russell, 3rd Earl Russell (1872–1970), noted philosopher and Nobel Prize winner, was a prominent advocate for peace, and wrote and campaigned vigorously for it. He supported World War II and advocated threatening the USSR with the atomic bomb at the start of the Cold War. Orwell reviewed his *Power: A New Social Analysis* (XI/520).

7. The home of Eileen's brother, Laurence (known as Eric in the family) O'Shaughnessy, and his wife, Gwen.

[552]

Review of Union Now *by Clarence K. Streit*
The Adelphi, *July 1939*

It is possible that this review salvages something from Orwell's pamphlet 'Socialism and War', which was not published and the manuscript of which has not survived. See XI/458, n. 1, and 506.

A dozen years ago anyone who had foretold the political line-up of to-day would have been looked on as a lunatic. And yet the truth is that the present situation – not in detail, of course, but in its main outlines – ought to have been predictable even in the golden age before Hitler. Something like it was bound to happen as soon as British security was seriously threatened.

In a prosperous country, above all in an imperialist country, left-wing politics are always partly humbug. There can be no real reconstruction that would not lead to at least a temporary drop in the English standard of life, which is another way of saying that the majority of left-wing politicians and publicists are people who earn their living by demanding something that they don't genuinely want. They are red-hot revolutionaries as long as all goes well, but every real emergency reveals instantly that they are shamming. One threat to the Suez Canal, and 'antifascism' and 'defence of British interests' are discovered to be identical.

It would be very shallow as well as unfair to suggest that there is *nothing* in what is now called 'antifascism' except a concern for British dividends. But it is a fact that the political obscenities of the past two years, the sort of monstrous harlequinade in which everyone is constantly bounding across the stage in a false nose – Quakers shouting for a bigger army, Communists waving union jacks, Winston Churchill posing as a democrat – would not have been possible without this guilty consciousness that we are all in the same boat. Much against their will the British governing class have been forced into the anti-Hitler position. It is still possible that they will find a way out of it, but they are arming in the obvious expectation of war and they will almost certainly fight when the point is reached at which the alternative would be to give away some of their own property instead of, as hitherto, other people's. And meanwhile the so-called opposition, instead of trying to stop the drift to war, are rushing ahead, preparing the ground and forestalling any possible criticism. So far as one can discover the English people are still extremely hostile to the idea of war, but in so far as they are becoming reconciled to it, it is not the militarists but the 'anti-militarists' of five years ago who are responsible. The Labour Party keeps up a pettifogging grizzle against conscription at the same time as its own propaganda makes any real struggle against conscription impossible. The Bren machine guns pour from the factories, books with titles like *Tanks in the Next War*, *Gas in the Next War*, etc., pour from the press, and the warriors of the *New Statesman* glose over the nature of the process by means of such phrases as 'Peace Bloc', 'Peace Front', 'Democratic Front', and, in general, by pretending that the world is an assemblage of sheep and goats, neatly partitioned off by national frontiers.

In this connection it is well worth having a look at Mr. Streit's much-discussed book, *Union Now*. Mr. Streit,[1] like the partisans of the 'Peace Bloc', wants the democracies to gang up against the dictatorships, but his book is outstanding for two reasons. To begin with he goes further than most of the others and offers a plan which, even if it is startling, is constructive. Secondly, in spite of a rather nineteen-twentyish American naivete, he has an essentially decent cast of mind. He genuinely loathes the thought of war, and he does not sink to the hypocrisy of pretending that any country which can be bought or bullied into the British orbit instantly becomes a democracy. His book therefore presents a kind of test case. In it you are seeing the sheep-and-goats theory at its *best*. If you can't accept it in that form you will certainly never accept it in the form handed out by the Left Book Club.

Briefly, what Mr. Streit suggests is that the democratic nations, starting with fifteen which he names, should voluntarily form themselves into a union – not a league or an alliance, but a union similar to the United States, with a common government, common money and complete internal free trade. The initial fifteen states are, of course, the U.S.A., France, Great Britain, the self-governing dominions of the British Empire, and the smaller European democracies, not including Czechoslovakia, which still existed when the book was written. Later, other states could be admitted to the Union when and if they 'proved themselves worthy'. It is implied all along that the state of peace and prosperity existing within the Union would be so enviable that everyone else would soon be pining to join it.

It is worth noticing that this scheme is not so visionary as it sounds. Of course it is not going to happen, nothing advocated by well-meaning literary men ever happens, and there are certain difficulties which Mr. Streit does not discuss; but it is of the order of things which *could* happen. Geographically the U.S.A. and the western European democracies are nearer to being a unit than, for instance, the British Empire. Most of their trade is with one another, they contain within their own territories everything they need, and Mr. Streit is probably right in claiming that their combined strength would be so great as to make any attack on them hopeless, even if the U.S.S.R. joined up with Germany. Why then does one see at a glance that this scheme has something wrong with it? What is there about it that smells – for it *does* smell, of course?

What it smells of, as usual, is hypocrisy and self-righteousness. Mr. Streit himself is not a hypocrite, but his vision is limited. Look again at his list of sheep and goats. No need to boggle at the goats (Germany, Italy and Japan), they are goats right enough, and billies at that. But look at the sheep! Perhaps the U.S.A. will pass inspection if one does not look too closely. But what about France? What about England? What about even Belgium and Holland? Like everyone of his school of thought, Mr. Streit has coolly lumped the huge British and French empires – in essence nothing but mechanisms for exploiting cheap coloured labour – under the heading of democracies!

Here and there in the book, though not often, there are references to the 'dependencies' of the democratic states. 'Dependencies' means subject races. It is explained that they are to go on being dependencies, that their resources are to be pooled among the states of the Union, and that their coloured inhabitants will lack the right to vote in Union affairs. Except where the tables of statistics bring it out, one would never for a moment guess what *numbers* of human beings are involved. India, for instance, which contains more inhabitants than the whole of the 'fifteen democracies' put together, gets just a page and a half in Mr. Streit's book, and that merely to explain that as India is not yet fit for self-government the *status quo* must continue. And here one begins to see what would really be happening if Mr. Streit's scheme were put into operation. The British and French empires, with their six hundred million disenfranchised human beings, would simply be receiving fresh police forces; the huge strength of the U.S.A. would be behind the robbery of India and Africa. Mr. Streit is letting cats out of bags, but *all* phrases like 'Peace Bloc', 'Peace Front', etc., contain some such implication; all imply a tightening-up of the existing structure. The unspoken clause is always 'not counting niggers'. For how can we make a 'firm stand' against Hitler if we are simultaneously weakening ourselves at home? In other words, how can we 'fight Fascism' except by bolstering up a far vaster injustice?

For of course it *is* vaster. What we always forget is that the overwhelming bulk of the British proletariat does not live in Britain, but in Asia and Africa. It is not in Hitler's power, for instance, to make a penny an hour a normal industrial wage; it is perfectly normal in India, and we are at great pains to keep it so. One gets some idea of the real relationship of England and India when one reflects that the *per capita* annual income in England is something over £80, and in India about £7. It is quite common for an Indian coolie's leg to be thinner than the average Englishman's arm. And there is nothing racial in this, for well-fed members of the same races are of normal physique; it is due to simple starvation. This is the system which we all live on and which we denounce when there seems to be no danger of its being altered. Of late, however, it has become the first duty of a 'good antifascist' to lie about it and help to keep it in being.

What real settlement, of the slightest value, can there be along these lines? What meaning would there be, even if it were successful, in bringing down Hitler's system in order to stabilise something that is far bigger and in its different way just as bad?

But apparently, for lack of any real opposition, this is going to be our objective. Mr. Streit's ingenious ideas will not be put into operation, but something resembling the 'Peace Bloc' proposals probably will. The British and Russian governments are still haggling, stalling and uttering muffled threats to change sides, but circumstances will probably drive them together. And what then? No doubt the alliance will stave off war for a year or two. Then Hitler's move will be to feel for a weak spot or an unguarded moment; then our move will be more armaments, more militarisation, more propaganda, more war-mindedness – and so on, at increasing speed. It is doubtful whether prolonged war-preparation is morally any better than war itself; there are even reasons for thinking that it may be slightly worse. Only two or three years of it, and we may sink almost unresisting into some local variant of austro-fascism. And perhaps a year or two later, in reaction against this, there will appear something we have never had in England yet – a real Fascist movement. And because it will have the guts to speak plainly it will gather into its ranks the very people who ought to be opposing it.

Further than that it is difficult to see. The downward slide is happening because nearly all the Socialist leaders, when it comes to the pinch, are merely His Majesty's Opposition, and nobody else knows how to mobilize the decency of the English people, which one meets with everywhere when one talks to human beings instead of reading newspapers. Nothing is likely to save us except the emergence within the next two years of a real mass party whose first pledges are to refuse war and to right imperial injustice. But if any such party exists at present, it is only as a possibility, in a few tiny germs lying here and there in unwatered soil.

1. Clarence K. Streit (1896–1986) was an American author and journalist – for the *New York Times*, 1925–39. This review/article, advocating the righting of imperial injustices, was originally published with the ironic title 'Not Counting Niggers'.

Extracts from Orwell's 'Diary of Events Leading Up to the War'

2 July–3 September 1939

Orwell's 'Diary of Events Leading Up to the War' is chiefly composed of extracts copied from newspapers from 2 July to 1 September 1939 (the day German tanks, cavalry and infantry invaded Poland), concluding with a summary dated 3 September, the day England and France declared war on Germany because it would not withdraw from Poland. The manuscript comprises fifty-five pages and is transcribed in full in CW, XI. These few extracts, mainly political, are designed to give no more than a flavour of what Orwell thought it worth recording. Orwell quotes forty-one sources for the 297 items. Of these, 138 (46.5%) are, perhaps surprisingly given its Conservative political stance, from the Daily Telegraph, *but then, as now, it has proved a good paper for news, and on checking against other newspapers of the time it was found often to be fuller and ahead of its rivals in recording events. When Orwell went to stay with the novelist L. H. Myers (1881– 1944), on 24 August, quotations from* The Times *and* News Chronicle *increase significantly and those from the* Telegraph *decrease. (Myers had, unknown to Orwell, funded the Orwells' stay in Marrakesh in the vain hope that that climate would improve Orwell's health.) The most interesting journal from which Orwell quotes is* Socialist Correspondence. *This is hard to come by (though there is a complete set in the New York Public Library). It was run by a group within the ILP known as 'the right-wing opposition' (though it was only to the right of a very left-wing party). Members were followers of Nikolai Bukharin (1888–1938). For a long note on* Socialist Correspondence, *see XI/362–3. For convenience, the extracts are here grouped together.*

[554]

2.7.39

Foreign & General

1. Poland states that Danzig[1] will be occupied if Danzig Senate declares for the Reich. [*Sunday Times*]

2. N.L.C.[2] of Labour Party broadcast in German in much the same terms as at September crisis. [*Observer*]

1. Danzig (now Gdansk, Poland), first mentioned some thousand years ago as part of Poland, has since been variously Polish and German (including Prussian). It was made a Free City by the Treaty of Versailles (1919), but became a focus of dispute between Poland and Germany, especially after the rise of the Nazis. This was the pretext for the German invasion of Poland that initiated World War II in 1939.

2. This is probably an error for NCL (National Council of Labour); see XI/556, 15.7.39, *Party Politics, 2*. The sense is elliptical, but seems to refer to an appeal to the German people under the heading 'Why kill each other?' made by the NCL. Summaries were broadcast by the BBC on the night of Saturday, 1 July 1939, in German, French, Italian, Portuguese and Spanish. The NCL also arranged broadcasts to German workers from secret radio stations on the Continent and distributed printed copies of the appeal through underground organizations.

---

[556]

9.7.39

Foreign & General

1. Madame Tabouis[1] considers chances of full Russian-French-British pact are now small & hints that Russians wish to regain position of Czarist Empire in the Baltic provinces. [*Sunday Dispatch*]

16.7.39

Foreign & General

1. 12,000 naval reservists to be called up July 31 for about 7 weeks. [*Sunday Times*]

2. General impression that Anglo-Russian pact is going to fall through. [*Sunday Times; Sunday Express*]

3. *Sunday Express* states that move to include Churchill[2] in Cabinet is really move to get rid of Chamberlain. [*Sunday Express*]

Social

1. No mention of dissentients among 30,000 militiamen called up yesterday. [No reference]

17.7.39

Foreign & General

2. Anglo-Russian pact only just makes front page of *D. Tel.* [*Daily Telegraph*]

Social

1. Definitely stated in *D. Tel.* that Saturday's militia draft (34,000 men) turned up with not one absentee (except cases of illness etc). [*Daily Telegraph*]

Party Politics

2. Serious trouble in I.L.P. on pacifist-revolutionary controversy & long statement from I.L.P.'ers (London group) published in *Socialist Correspondence*, which also takes other opportunities of attacking McGovern.[3] [*Socialist Correspondence*]

19.7.39

Foreign & General

1. Gov.t° advising all householders to lay in supply of non-perishable food. Leaflet on the subject to be issued shortly. [*Daily Telegraph*]

20.7.39

Foreign & General

1. Public Information Leaflet no. 3 (evacuation[4]) issued today. Never less than 4 searchlights visible at night from this village. [No reference]

2. News from Danzig seems to indicate that all there expect Danzig to fall into German hands in near future. [*Daily Telegraph*]

3. France said to be in favour of acceptance of Russian terms for Anglo-Russian pact, which have not been altered re. the Baltic States. [*Daily Telegraph*]

Social

1. One of the editors of *Humanité*[5] questioned by the Paris police with ref. to spy revelations, but no indication from report whether merely in advisory capacity or under suspicion of complicity. [*Daily Telegraph*]

2. Recent W.O.[6] regulation has forbidden army officers to resign their commissions & seemingly steps are being taken to prevent N.C.O.s buying out[7] from the service (present cost £35). [*Daily Telegraph*]

1. Geneviève Tabouis (Paris, 1892–1985) was a diplomatic and international journalist, foreign news editor of *L'Oeuvre* from 1932, and correspondent for the *Sunday Dispatch*. On 23 June 1940 that paper printed her account of her escape to England via Bordeaux after the fall of Paris. This began with a statement attributed to Hitler: 'The speech I am making to-day she knew yesterday.' She directed the weekly *Pour la Victoire*, in New York, 1941–5, and was noted for her uncanny gift for forecasting accurately the outcome of political events.
2. Winston Churchill (1874–1965), soldier, politician, journalist and author. He held high office in Liberal and Conservative governments over nearly half a century but in the thirties was excluded because of his vigorous opposition to appeasement of dictators: he was

branded a warmonger. He was the natural choice for prime minister after the fall of Norway following the German invasion in 1940. Despite his success as a war leader, he was not returned to office in 1945 but he did succeed in becoming prime minister of a peacetime government, 1951–5. He was knighted in 1953 and the same year won the Nobel Prize for Literature.

3. John McGovern (1887–1968), ILP MP, 1930–47, Labour MP, 1947–59. He led a hunger march from Glasgow to London in 1934.

4. Large numbers of children were dispersed from cities to country areas for safety from air attack. Many stayed in their adopted homes for the duration of the war.

5. Leading French Communist daily newspaper.

6. War Office.

7. A serviceman could, with permission, reduce the time he had agreed to serve at his enlistment by buying his release. The practice continues today.

---

[558]

21.7.39

Foreign & General

1. Polish official assassinated on Danzig frontier & consequent 'tension'.[1] [*Daily Telegraph*]

23.7.39

Foreign & General

3. Calling up of territorials & naval reservists suggests that danger moment will be first week in August. [*Sunday Times*]

Party Politics

4. Beaverbrook press now more openly against the Russian pact & for isolationism than for some months past. [No reference]

25.7.39

Social

1. Bill to deal with I.R.A. provides for power to prohibit entry of aliens, deportation of aliens, & compulsary registration of aliens. Also emergency power to Sup.ts of Police to search without warrant. Bill said to be for 2 years only. Not seriously opposed (passed 218–17.) [*Daily Telegraph*]

1. Witold Budziewicz, a Polish customs officer, was shot dead shortly after being challenged by a Danzig customs officer accompanied by two Nazis. At the time, it was not known who fired the shot. This was one of a number of incidents designed to increase tension in the area in order to provide Hitler with a pretext for intervention.

[560]

30.7.39

Foreign & General

1. Seems clear that Parliament will adjourn as usual with no previous arrangements for recall before October. [*Sunday Times*]

2. There are now 60,000 German troops (ie. including police, storm troopers etc.) in Danzig. [*Sunday Times*]

Social

2. I.R.A. suspects already being deported in fairly large numbers (about 20 hitherto). [*Sunday Times*; *Daily Telegraph*, 29.7.39]

1.8.39

Foreign & General

1. Military mission probably leaving for Moscow this week. Leader (Admiral Plunkett-Ernle-Erle-Drax[1]) took part in mission to Tsarist Russia just before Great War. [*Daily Telegraph*]

2.8.39

Foreign & General

1. Announced today that ration cards are already printed & ready. [*Daily Telegraph*]

Social

2. Appears that German Jewish refugees are settling in great numbers in certain parts of London, eg. Golders Green, & buying houses which they have plenty of money to do. [Private (C.W.)[2]]

1. Admiral Sir Reginald Plunkett-Ernle-Erle-Drax (1880–1967), Commander-in-Chief, The Nore, 1939–41, was accompanied by a representative of the Army and one of the Royal Air Force. Although a talented man, he was ill-briefed for this mission and was subjected to derision in Moscow, Voroshilov ridiculing his being a Knight Commander of the 'Bath'. He signed himself simply as 'Drax'.

2. Probably from Cyril Wright, who served with Orwell in Spain.

[562]

4.8.39

Foreign & General

1. French–Brit. military mission leaving tomorrow on slow liner which will take a week to reach Leningrad. *The Week*[1] suggests that the move is

not intended seriously. Quotations from Finnish papers & Swedish Foreign Minister's speech suggest that Baltic States are genuinely nervous. [*Daily Telegraph*; *Manchester Guardian Weekly*; *The Week*, 2.8.39]

6.8.39

Foreign & General

1. Purge of Sudeten[2] leaders taking place, evidently as result of Czech pressure & as prelude to milder methods. [*Sunday Times*]

2. Polish gov.t° evidently now ready to allow Russians to use Polish air bases. [*Sunday Times*]

7.8.39

Social

1. *Soc. Corresp.* repeats complaints about food etc. in militia camps with implication that the men are being treated rough more or less wilfully. [*Socialist Correspondence*]

2. 57 people reported shot in connection with recent political murders in Madrid (number of people murdered was apparently 3). [*Daily Telegraph*]

---

1. *The Week* was a private-circulation, ostensibly independent but pro-Communist newspaper edited by Claud Cockburn (pseud. Frank Pitcairn, 1904–81). It was published from 29 March 1933 to 15 January 1941, when it was suppressed by government order. A new series was allowed from October 1942, and it ran until December 1946. See his book *The Years of The Week* (1968), 262–4.

2. The Sudetenland, parts of Moravia and Bohemia incorporated into Czechoslovakia by the Treaty of Versailles, led by the Sudeten German Party, under Konrad Henlein, wanted to reunite with Germany. It was aided and abetted by Hitler. The Munich pact of 30 September 1938 required Czechoslovakia to cede the area to Germany by 10 October 1938.

12.8.39

Foreign & General

1. *M. G.* correspondent reports that German mobilization will be at full strength half way through August & that some attempt to terrorise Poland will be made. War stated to be likeliest issue (as also in yesterday's *Time & Tide*). The striking thing is the perfunctory air with which these statements are made in all papers, as though with an inner certainty that nothing of the kind can happen. [*Manchester Guardian Weekly*, 11.8.39; Orwell incorrectly dates this as 12.8.39]

22.8.39

Foreign & General

1. Officially stated in Berlin that Ribbentrop[1] flies to Moscow tomorrow to sign non-aggression pact with U.S.S.R. News later confirmed from Moscow by Tass Agency, in a way that seems to make it clear that pact will go through. Little comment in any of the papers, the news having evidently arrived in the small hours of this morning & the Russian confirmation only in time for the stop press. Reported suggestion from Washington that it may be a Russian manoeuvre (ie. to bring England & France to heel) but everyone else seems to take it at face-value. Shares on the whole have dropped. Germans still buying shellac etc. heavily. The military talks were still proceeding yesterday. [*Daily Telegraph*; *Daily Mail*; *News Chronicle*; *Daily Mirror*]

Social

1. Illegal radio, somewhat on the lines of German Freiheit movement's radio,[2] has been broadcasting anti-conscription propaganda. Secretary of P.P.U. (Rowntree?)* denies knowledge but does not dissociate himself from the talks. P.O. engineers state that they have tracked down location of radio to within a few houses & will soon run it to earth. Indication is that it takes at least some days to locate an illegal radio. [*Daily Telegraph*]

  * Palmer [Orwell's note].

24.8.39

Foreign & General

1. Russo-German Pact signed. Terms given in Berlin (File War etc.[3]) suggest close pact & no 'escape' clause. This evening's radio news gives confirmation in Moscow in same terms. Official statement from Moscow that 'enemies of both countries' have tried to drive Russia & Germany into enmity. Brit. Ambassador calls on Hitler & is told no action of ours can influence German decision. Japanese opinion evidently seriously angered by what amounts to German desertion of anti-Comintern pact, & Spanish (Franco) opinion evidently similarly affected. Rumania said to have declared neutrality. Chamberlain's speech as reported on wireless very strong & hardly seems to allow loophole for escape from aiding Poles.

  E. on visiting W.O.[4] today derived impression that war is almost certain. Police arrived this morning to arrange for billeting of soldiers.

Some people (foreigners) arrived in afternoon looking for rooms – the second lot in 3 days. In spite of careful listening, impossible in pubs etc. to overhear any spontaneous comment or sign of slightest interest in the situation, in spite of fact that almost everyone when questioned believes it will be war. [*The Times*; *Daily Telegraph*; *News Chronicle*; *Manchester Guardian*; *Daily Express*; *Daily Herald*; *Daily Mail*; *London Evening News*]

Social

1. Emergency Powers Act passed evidently without much trouble. Contains clauses allowing preventive arrest, search without warrant & trial in camera. But not industrial conscription as yet. [Wireless 6 pm][5]

2. Moscow airport was decorated with swastikas for Ribbentrop's arrival. *M. Guardian* adds that they were screened so as to hide them from the rest of Moscow. [*Manchester Guardian*]

Party Politics

1. C.P.[6] putting good face on Russo-German pact which is declared to be move for peace. Signature of Anglo-Soviet pact demanded as before. *D. Worker* does not print terms of pact but reprints portions of an earlier Russo-Polish pact containing an 'escape' clause, in order to convey impression that this pact must contain the same. [*Daily Worker*]

28.8.39

No clear indication of the meaning of the Russian-German pact as yet. Papers of left tendency continue to suggest that it does not amount to very much, but it seems to be generally taken for granted that Russia will supply Germany with raw materials, & possibly that there has been a large-scale bargain which amounts to handing Europe over to Germany & Asia to Russia. Molotov[7] is to make an announcement shortly. It is clear that the Russian explanation will be, at any rate at first, that the British were playing double & did not really wish for the Anglo-French-Russian pact. Public opinion in U.S.S.R. said to be still somewhat taken aback by the change of front, & ditto left wing opinion in the West. Left wing papers continue to blame Chamberlain while making some attempt to exonerate Stalin, but are clearly dismayed. In France there has evidently been a swing of opinion against the Communist Party, from which there are said to be large-scale resignations (*D. Tel.* repeating Reuter). *Humanité* has been temporarily suspended. The Anglo-French military mission is already returning.

Germany & Poland now more or less fully mobilised. France has called up several more classes of reservists.

1. Joachim von Ribbentrop (1893–1946) was German Minister of Foreign Affairs, 1938–45. He negotiated the Russo-German Non-Aggression Pact in 1939 with Molotov (see n. 7 below). He was hanged as a war criminal after being found guilty by the International Military Tribunal at Nuremberg.

2. In November 1939, 'German Freedom Radio' was reported to be still broadcasting appeals to Germans to liberate themselves from Hitler's regime.

3. Presumably a file Orwell kept on this subject. Possibly related to his reference 'File S.P. 1'.

4. Eileen was working at the War Office in the Censorship Department; see XVII/*2831*, final section.

5. National news was broadcast by BBC at 6 p.m.

6. Communist Party.

7. Vyacheslav Molotov (1890–1986) was President of the USSR's Council of People's Commissars, 1930–41, and Commissar of Foreign Affairs, 1939–49, 1953–6. He negotiated the Russo-German Non-Aggression Pact in August 1939, with Ribbentrop. He was later a delegate to the United Nations General Assembly.

---

[567]

31.8.39

Foreign & General

1. No definite news. Poland has called up more reserves but this does not yet amount to full mobilisation. German occupation of Slovakia continues & 300,000 men said to be now at strategic points on Polish frontier. Hitler has set up inner cabinet of 6 not including Ribbentrop.

16,000 children already evacuated from Paris. Evacuation of London children thought to be likely before long. No news one way or the other about ratification of Russo-German pact. Such slight indications as exist suggest pact will be ratified. German persecution of Jews said to be slightly diminished, anti-German film withdrawn from Soviet pavilion at New York world fair. Voroshilov[1] reported as stating that U.S.S.R. would supply Poland with arms. [*Daily Telegraph*; *News Chronicle*; *Daily Mirror*]

Social

1. Sir J. Anderson[2] requests the public not to buy extra stores of food & to conserve those they have, & states that there is no food shortage. [*Daily Telegraph*]

Party Politics

1. E's[3] report of speeches in Hyde Park suggests that Communist Party are taking more left wing line but not anxious to thrash out question of Russo-German pact.

1.9.39

Invasion of Poland began this morning. Warsaw bombed. General mobilisation proclaimed in England, ditto in France plus martial law. [Radio]

Foreign & General

1. Hitler's terms to Poland boil down to return of Danzig & plebiscite in the corridor,[4] to be held 1 year hence & based on 1918 census. There is some hanky panky about time the terms were presented, & as they were to be answered by night of 30.8.39.,[5] H.[6] claims that they are already refused. [*Daily Telegraph*]

2. Naval reservists and rest of army and R.A.F. reservists called up. Evacuation of children etc. begins today, involving 3 m. people & expected to take 3 days. [Radio; undated]

3. Russo-German pact ratified. Russian armed forces to be further increased. Voroshilov's speech taken as meaning that Russo-German alliance is not contemplated. [*Daily Express*]

4. Berlin report states Russian military mission is expected to arrive there shortly. [*Daily Telegraph*]

1. Kliment Voroshilov (1881–1969), Marshal of the Soviet Union, was People's Commissar for Defence, 1925–40, and President of the USSR, 1953–60. He was one of those responsible for organizing the defence of Leningrad during the 900-day siege, September 1941–January 1944.

2. John Anderson (1882–1958; Viscount, 1952) was an MP representing Scottish Universities, 1938–50. Appointed Lord Privy Seal by Chamberlain in November 1938, with special responsibility for manpower and civil defence, he was responsible for what came to be called the 'Anderson' air-raid shelter. At the outbreak of war, he was made Home Secretary and Minister of Home Security; later, Lord President of the Council, 1940–43, and Chancellor of the Exchequer, 1943–5. In *The Lion and the Unicorn*, Orwell remarked that it took 'the unnecessary suffering of scores of thousands of people in the East End [sheltering in Andersons] to get rid or partially rid of Sir John Anderson' (see below, p. 113). The shelters could be extremely uncomfortable and were prone to flooding. On 3 September 1940 Churchill wrote to Anderson to say that 'a great effort should be made to help people to drain their Anderson shelters, which reflect so much credit on your name . . .' (*The Second World War*, 1948, I, 313).

3. Eileen, Orwell's wife, then working at the Censorship Department of the War Office in Whitehall. See Crick, 382.

4. The Polish Corridor, which gave Poland an outlet to the Baltic Sea between 1919 and 1939; it separated East Prussia from the rest of Germany and, with Danzig, was a source of friction and an ostensible cause of the outbreak of war.

5. Orwell wrote the date as 30.9.39 by mistake.

6. Hitler.

[570]

3.9.39 (Greenwich[1]).

Have again been travelling etc. Shall close this diary to-day, & it will as it stands serve as a diary of events leading up to the war.

We have apparently been in a state of war since 11 am. this morning. No reply was received from the German gov.t° to the demand to evacuate Polish territory. The Italian gov.t° made some kind of last-minute appeal for a conference to settle differences peacefully, which made some of the papers as late as this morning show a faint doubt as to whether war would actually break out. Daladier[2] made grateful reference to the 'noble effort' of Italy which may be taken as meaning that Italy's neutrality is to be respected.

No definite news yet as to what military operations are actually taking place. The Germans have taken Danzig & are attacking the corridor from 4 points north & south. Otherwise only the usual claims & counterclaims about air-raids, number of aeroplanes shot down etc. From reports in *Sunday Express* & elsewhere it seems clear that the first attempted raid on Warsaw failed to get as far as the town itself. It is rumoured that there is already a British force in France. Bodies of troops with full kits constantly leaving from Waterloo, but not in enormous numbers at any one moment. Air-raid practice[3] this morning immediately after the proclamation of state of war. Seems to have gone off satisfactorily though believed by many people to be real raid. There are now great numbers of public air-raid shelters, though most of them will take another day or two to complete. Gas masks being handed out free, & the public appears to take them seriously. Voluntary fire-brigades etc. all active & look quite efficient. Police from now on wear steel helmets. No panic, on the other hand no enthusiasm, & in fact not much interest. Balloon barrage[4] completely covers London & would evidently make low-flying quite impossible. Black-out at nights fairly complete but they are instituting very stringent penalties for infringement. Evacuation involving 3 m. people (over 1 m. from London alone) going on rapidly. Train services somewhat disorganised in consequence.

Churchill & Eden[5] are coming into the cabinet. Labour are refusing office for the time being. Labour MPs. in the house make violent protestations of loyalty but tone of the left press very sour as they evidently realise the wind has been taken out of their sails. Controversy about the Russo-German pact continues to some extent. All the letters printed in *Reynold's* extol the pact but have shifted the emphasis from this being a 'peace move' to its being a self-protecting move by U.S.S.R. *Action*[6] of 2.9.39. still agitating against the war. No atrocity stories or violent propaganda posters as yet.

M. T. Act[7] extended to all men between 18–41. It is however clear that they do not as yet want large numbers of men but are passing the act in order to be able to pick on anyone they choose, & for purpose of later enforcing industrial conscription.

1. Eileen's brother lived at Greenwich; see end of Orwell's letter to Read, above and n. 7 thereto.

2. Édouard Daladier (1884–1970), Socialist Prime Minister of France, 1933, 1934 and 1938–40. He supported appeasement of Germany and signed the Munich Agreement with Chamberlain, Hitler and Mussolini, surrendering the Czech Sudetenland to Germany on 30 September 1938. For Churchill's account of Daladier's visit to London on 18 September to discuss Hitler's demands with Chamberlain, see *The Second World War*, 1948, I, 270–72. He was arrested when France fell to the Germans and was interned. After the war he was politically active until 1958.

3. The sound of the siren was a false alarm, caused by a small civil plane coming in to Shoreham (near Worthing) from France.

4. Part of the air defence system was provided by barrage balloons. These were flown, unmanned, at a height that made dive-bombing to a low level impracticable owing to the cables anchoring the balloons in position.

5. Anthony Eden (1897–1977; Earl of Avon, 1961), Conservative MP, was Foreign Secretary, 1935–8. He resigned in protest against Chamberlain's policy of appeasement. In 1940 he was Secretary of State for War, then Foreign Secretary in the War Cabinet, 1940–45. He was Prime Minister, 1955–7, but resigned again, as a result of Britain's disastrous involvement in the occupation of the Suez Canal Zone in 1956.

6. Journal of the British Union of Fascists.

7. Military Training Act.

[571]

Application to Enrol for War Service
9 September 1939

Orwell offered his services to help the war effort in some capacity on 9
September 1939, six days after war was declared. His letter has not been
traced, but it is referred to in a reply dated 8 December 1939 from the
Ministry of Labour and National Service (reference C.R.B. 1382). This
stated that his name had been entered in the section of the Central Register
dealing with authors and writers. It went on: 'This entry is regarded as
recording your readiness to accept, if invited to do so, suitable employment
in war time.' With the letter was sent a leaflet describing the significance of
the Central Register. The scheme was voluntary and designed to put suitably
qualified people in touch with those who could use their services for 'National
Defence'. Enrolment on the Register 'did not mean that any guarantee is
given that the services of a particular individual will be called upon by the
Government'.

[602]

Review of Mein Kampf *by Adolf Hitler, unabridged translation*
New English Weekly, *21 March 1940*

It is a sign of the speed at which events are moving that Hurst and
Blackett's unexpurgated edition of *Mein Kampf*, published only a year
ago,[1] is edited from a pro-Hitler angle. The obvious intention of the
translator's preface and notes is to tone down the book's ferocity and
present Hitler in as kindly a light as possible. For at that date Hitler was
still respectable. He had crushed the German labour movement, and for
that the property-owning classes were willing to forgive him almost
anything. Both Left and Right concurred in the very shallow notion that
National Socialism was merely a version of Conservatism.

Then suddenly it turned out that Hitler was not respectable after all.
As one result of this, Hurst and Blackett's edition was reissued in a new
jacket explaining that all profits would be devoted to the Red Cross.

Nevertheless, simply on the internal evidence of *Mein Kampf,* it is difficult to believe that any real change has taken place in Hitler's aims and opinions. When one compares his utterances of a year or so ago with those made fifteen years earlier, a thing that strikes one is the rigidity of his mind, the way in which his world-view *doesn't* develop. It is the fixed vision of a monomaniac, and not likely to be much affected by the temporary manoeuvres of power politics. Probably, in Hitler's own mind, the Russo-German pact represents no more than an alteration of time-table. The plan laid down in *Mein Kampf* was to smash Russia first, with the implied intention of smashing England afterwards. Now, as it has turned out, England has got to be dealt with first, because Russia was the more easily bribed of the two. But Russia's turn will come when England is out of the picture – that, no doubt, is how Hitler sees it. Whether it will turn out that way is of course a different question.

Suppose that Hitler's programme could be put into effect. What he envisages, a hundred years hence, is a continuous state of 250 million Germans with plenty of 'living room' (i.e., stretching to Afghanistan or thereabouts), a horrible brainless empire in which, essentially, nothing ever happens except the training of young men for war and the endless breeding of fresh cannon-fodder. How was it that he was able to put this monstrous vision across? It is easy to say that at one stage of his career he was financed by the heavy industrialists, who saw in him the man who would smash the Socialists and Communists. They would not have backed him, however, if he had not talked a great movement into existence already. Again, the situation in Germany, with its seven million unemployed, was obviously favourable for demagogues. But Hitler could not have succeeded against his many rivals if it had not been for the attraction of his own personality, which one can feel even in the clumsy writing of *Mein Kampf,* and which is no doubt overwhelming when one hears his speeches. I should like to put it on record that I have never been able to dislike Hitler. Ever since he came to power – till then, like nearly everyone, I had been deceived into thinking that he did not matter – I have reflected that I would certainly kill him if I could get within reach of him, but that I could feel no personal animosity. The fact is that there is something deeply appealing about him. One feels it again when one sees his photographs – and I recommend especially the photograph at the beginning of Hurst and Blackett's edition, which shows Hitler in his early Brownshirt days. It is a pathetic, doglike face, the face of a man suffering under intolerable wrongs. In a rather more manly way it reproduces the expression of innumerable pictures of Christ crucified, and there is little doubt that that is how Hitler sees himself. The initial, personal cause of his grievance against the universe can only be guessed at; but at any rate the grievance is there. He is the martyr, the victim, Prometheus chained to the rock, the self-sacrificing hero who fights single-handed against impossible odds. If he were killing a mouse he would know how to make it seem like a dragon. One feels, as with Napoleon, that he is fighting against destiny, that he *can't* win, and yet that he somehow deserves to. The attraction of such a pose is of course enormous; half the films that one sees turn upon some such theme.

Also he has grasped the falsity of the hedonistic attitude to life. Nearly all Western thought since the last war, certainly all 'progressive' thought, has assumed tacitly that human beings desire nothing beyond ease, security and avoidance of pain. In such a view of life there is no room, for instance, for patriotism and the military virtues. The Socialist who finds his children playing with soldiers is usually upset, but he is never able to think of a substitute for the tin soldiers; tin pacifists somehow won't do. Hitler, because in his own joyless mind he feels it with exceptional strength, knows that human beings *don't* only want comfort, safety, short working-hours, hygiene, birth-control and, in general, common sense; they also, at least intermittently, want struggle and self-sacrifice, not to mention drums, flags and loyalty-parades. However they may be as economic theories, Fascism and Nazism are psychologically far sounder than any hedonistic conception of life. The same is probably true of Stalin's militarised version of Socialism. All three of the great dictators have enhanced their power by imposing intolerable burdens on their peoples. Whereas Socialism, and even capitalism in a more grudging way, have said to people 'I offer you a good time', Hitler has said to them 'I offer you struggle, danger and death', and as a result a whole nation flings itself at his feet.[2] Perhaps later on they will get sick of it and change their minds, as at the end of the last war. After a few years of slaughter and starvation 'Greatest happiness of the greatest number'[3] is a good slogan, but at this moment 'Better an end with horror than a horror without end' is a winner. Now that we are

inferring what is really happening. The seeming possibilities were: i. That the French were really about to counterattack from the south. ii. That they hoped to do so but that the German bombers were making it impossible to concentrate an army. iii. That the forces in the north were confident of being able to hold on and it was thought better not to counterattack till the German attack had spent itself, or iv. that the position in the north was in reality hopeless and the forces there could only fight their way south, capitulate, be destroyed entirely or escape by sea, probably losing very heavily in the process. Now only the fourth alternative seems possible. The French communiqués speak of stabilising the line along the Somme and Aisne, as though the forces cut off in the north did not exist. Horrible though it is, I hope the B.E.F.[2] is cut to pieces sooner than capitulate.

People talk a little more of the war, but very little. As always hitherto, it is impossible to overhear any comments on it in pubs, etc. Last night, E.[3] and I went to the pub to hear the 9 o'c news. The barmaid was not going to have turned it on if we had not asked her, and to all appearances nobody listened . . .

29.5.40: . . . E. says the people in the Censorship Department where she works lump all 'red' papers together and look on the *Tribune*[4] as being in exactly the same class as the *Daily Worker*.[5] Recently when the *Daily Worker* and *Action*[6] were prohibited from export, one of her fellow-workers asked her, 'Do you know this paper, the *Daily Worker and Action?*' . . .

30.5.40: The B.E.F. are falling back on Dunkirk. Impossible not only to guess how many may get away, but how many are there. Last night a talk on the radio by a colonel who had come back from Belgium, which unfortunately I did not hear, but which from E's. account of it contained interpolations put in by the broadcaster himself to let the public know the army had been let down (a) by the French (not counterattacking), and (b) by the military authorities at home, by equipping them badly. No word anywhere in the press of recriminations against the French, and Duff-Cooper's[7] broadcast of two nights ago especially warned against this . . . Today's map looks as if the French contingent in Belgium are sacrificing themselves to let the B.E.F. get away.

Borkenau[8] says England is now definitely in the first stage of revolution . . .

1.6.40: Last night to Waterloo and Victoria to see whether I could get any news of [Eric].[9] Quite impossible, of course. The men who have been repatriated have orders not to speak to civilians and are in any case removed from the railway stations as promptly as possible. Actually I saw very few British soldiers, ie. from the B.E.F., but great numbers of Belgian or French refugees, a few Belgian or French soldiers, and some sailors, including a few naval men. The refugees seemed mostly middling people of the shop-keeper-clerk type, and were in quite good trim, with a certain amount of personal belongings. One family had a parrot in a huge cage. One refugee woman was crying, or nearly so, but most seemed only bewildered by the crowds and the general strangeness. A considerable crowd was watching at Victoria and had to be held back by the police to let the refugees and others get to the street. The refugees were greeted in silence but all sailors of any description enthusiastically cheered. A naval officer in a uniform that had been in the water and parts of a soldier's equipment hurried towards a bus, smiling and touching his tin hat to either side as the women shouted at him and clapped him on the shoulder.

Saw a company of Marines marching through the station to entrain for Chatham. Was amazed by their splendid physique and bearing, the tremendous stamp of boots and the superb carriage of the officers, all taking me back to 1914, when all soldiers seemed like giants to me.

This morning's papers claim variously four-fifths and three-quarters of the B.E.F. already removed. Photos, probably selected or faked, show the men in good trim with their equipment fairly intact.

6.6.40: Both Borkenau and I considered that Hitler was likely to make his next attack on France, not England, and as it turns out we were right. Borkenau considers that the Dunkirk business has proved once for all that aeroplanes cannot defeat warships if the latter have planes of their own. The figures given out were 6 destroyers and about 25 boats of other kinds lost in the evacuation of nearly 350,000 men. The number of men evacuated is presumably truthful, and even if one doubled the number of ships lost[10] it would not be a great loss for such a large undertaking, considering that the circumstances were about as favourable to the aeroplanes as they could well be.

Borkenau thinks Hitler's plan is to knock out France and demand the

French fleet as part of the peace terms. After that the invasion of England with sea-borne troops might be feasible . . .

15.6.40: . . . P.W.[11] related that Unity Mitford,[12] besides having tried to shoot herself while in Germany, is going to have a baby. Whereupon a little man with a creased face, whose name I forget, exclaimed, 'The Fuehrer wouldn't do such a thing!'

16.6.40: This morning's papers make it reasonably clear that at any rate until after the presidential election, the U.S.A. will not do anything, ie. will not declare war, which in fact is what matters. For if the U.S.A. is not actually in the war there will never be sufficient control of either business or labour to speed up production of armaments. In the last war this was the case even when the U.S.A. was a belligerent.

It is impossible even yet to decide what to do in the case of German conquest of England. The one thing I will not do is to clear out, at any rate not further than Ireland, supposing that to be feasible. If the fleet is intact and it appears that the war is to be continued from America and the Dominions, then one must remain alive if possible, if necessary in the concentration camp. If the U.S.A. is going to submit to conquest as well, there is nothing for it but to die fighting, but one must above all die *fighting* and have the satisfaction of killing somebody else first . . .

17.6.40: The French have surrendered. This could be foreseen from last night's broadcast and in fact should have been foreseeable when they failed to defend Paris, the one place where it might have been possible to stop the German tanks. Strategically all turns on the French fleet, of which there is no news yet . . .

Considerable excitement today over the French surrender, and people everywhere to be heard discussing it. Usual line, 'Thank God we've got a navy' . . .

Considerable throng at Canada House, where I went to make enquiries, as G.[13] contemplates sending her child to Canada. Apart from mothers, they are not allowing anyone between 16 and 60 to leave, evidently fearing a panic rush.

20.6.40: Went to the office of the [*New Statesman*][14] to see what line they are taking about home defence. C.,[15] who is now in reality the big noise there, was rather against the 'arm the people' line and said that its dangers outweighed its possible advantages. If a German invading force finds civilians armed it may commit such barbarities as will cow the people altogether and make everyone anxious to surrender. He said it was dangerous to count on ordinary people being courageous and instanced the case of some riot in Glasgow when a tank was driven round the town and everyone fled in the most cowardly way. The circumstances were different, however, because the people in that case were unarmed and, as always in internal strife, conscious of fighting with ropes round their necks . . . C. said that he thought Churchill, though a good man up to a point, was incapable of doing the necessary thing and turning this into a revolutionary war, and for that reason shielded Chamberlain and Co. and hesitated to bring the whole nation into the struggle. I don't of course think Churchill sees it in quite the same colours as we do, but I don't think he would jib at any step (eg. equalisation of incomes, independence for India) which he thought necessary for winning the war. Of course it's possible that today's secret session *may* achieve enough to get Chamberlain and Co. out for good. I asked C. what hope he thought there was of this, and he said none at all. But I remember that the day the British began to evacuate Namsos[16] I asked Bevan and Strauss,[17] who had just come from the House, what hope there was of this business unseating Chamberlain, and they also said none at all. Yet a week or so later the new government was formed.[18] . . .

A thought that occurred to me yesterday: how is it that England, with one of the smallest armies in the world, has so many retired colonels?

I notice that all the 'left' intellectuals I meet believe that Hitler if he gets here will take the trouble to shoot people like ourselves and will have very extensive lists of undesirables. C. says there is a move on foot to get our police records (no doubt we all have them) at Scotland Yard destroyed.[19] Some hope! The police are the very people who would go over to Hitler once they were certain he had won. Well, if only we can hold out for a few months, in a year's time we shall see red militia billeted in the Ritz, and it would not particularly surprise me to see Churchill or Lloyd George at the head of them.

Thinking always of my island in the Hebrides,[20] which I suppose I shall never possess nor even see. Compton Mackenzie says even now most of the islands are uninhabited (there are 500 of them, only 10 per cent inhabited at normal times), and most have water and a little cultivable land, and goats will live on them. According to R.H.,[21] a woman who rented an island in the Hebrides in order to avoid air raids was the first air raid casualty of the war, the R.A.F. dropping a bomb there by mistake. Good if true.

The first air raid of any consequence on Great Britain the night before last. Fourteen killed, seven German aeroplanes claimed shot down. The papers have photos of three wrecked German planes, so possibly the claim is true.

1. There were at this time three London evening papers: *Star, Evening News, Evening Standard*; only the last has survived; it is still published.

2. British Expeditionary Force, the troops in France at the time of that country's fall to the Germans.

3. Eileen, Orwell's wife. They did not have a radio (or telephone); to hear a radio news broadcast they had to visit a pub.

4. A Socialist weekly, then edited by Raymond Postgate (1896–1971), to which Orwell contributed many reviews and essays.

5. The Communist Party's daily newspaper in Britain.

6. The journal of the British Union of Fascists.

7. Alfred Duff Cooper (1890–1954; Viscount Norwich, 1952) was a Conservative politician, diplomat and author. After he resigned as First Lord of the Admiralty, through disagreement with Chamberlain over Munich, he became the figurehead of the patriotic Right. Churchill made him Minister of Information in May 1940.

8. Dr Franz Borkenau; see above for Orwell's review of his *The Communist International*, and n. 1 thereto for biographical details. Orwell reviewed his *The Totalitarian Enemy* on 4 May 1940 (XII/620).

9. 'Eric', abbreviated from his second name, was the name by which Eileen Blair's much-loved brother, Laurence Frederick O'Shaughnessy, was known. Orwell does not type his name in his diary, representing it by four short dashes. He was a distinguished chest and heart surgeon, having won four scholarships and studied medicine at Durham and in Berlin. He was Hunterian Professor at the Royal College of Surgeons, 1933–5. In 1937 he won the Hunter Medal Triennial Prize for research work in surgery of the thorax, and the following year he received an honorarium and certificate of honourable mention for a dissertation on surgery of the heart. He produced an adaptation of Sauerbruch's *Thoracic Surgery* (1937) and in 1939 collaborated with two others in work on pulmonary tuberculosis. He joined the Royal Army Medical Corps at the outbreak of war and was killed tending the wounded on the beaches of Dunkirk. He was by then a major and only thirty-six years old (from obituary in *The Times*, 8 June 1940). His wife, Gwen, was also a doctor. Her brother's death greatly affected Eileen; see Tosco Fyvel, *George Orwell: A Personal Memoir* (1982), 105–6, 136.

10. These figures were, in fact, correct. Although most of their equipment was lost, 198,000 British and 140,000 mainly French and Belgian soldiers were evacuated. Of the forty-one

naval vessels involved, six were sunk and nineteen damaged. About 220,000 servicemen were evacuated from ports in Normandy and Brittany.

11. Victor William (Peter) Watson (1908–56), a rich young man who, after much travel, decided, about 1939, to devote his life to the arts, was co-founder with his friend Cyril Connolly of the magazine *Horizon*, which he financed and also provided all the material for the art section. In 1948 he was one of the founders of the Institute of Contemporary Arts. He was always an admirer of Orwell's writing. *Horizon* ran for 121 numbers from January 1940 to January 1950. It was edited by Cyril Connolly and it maintained a remarkably high literary standard. See Michael Shelden, *Friends of Promise: Cyril Connolly and the World of 'Horizon'* (1989).

12. The Hon. Unity Valkyrie Mitford (1914–48), fourth daughter of the second Lord Redesdale, was, from 1934, when she first met Hitler, his admirer. In January 1940 she was brought back to England from Germany suffering from bullet wounds in the head. Thereafter she lived in retirement.

13. Gwen O'Shaughnessy, Eileen's sister-in-law. In the early stages of the war, there was a government-sponsored scheme to evacuate children to Canada and the United States. Gwen's son, Laurence, nineteen months old in June 1940, went to Canada on one of the last ships to take evacuees before the evacuee-ship *City of Benares* was sunk in the Atlantic.

14. *New Statesman* seems probable here.

15. Probably Richard Crossman (1907–74), scholar, intellectual, journalist and left-wing politician, who was assistant editor of the *New Statesman*, 1938–55, and editor, 1970–72. He was also a Labour MP, 1945–70; Minister of Housing and Local Government, 1964–66; and Minister of Health and Social Security, 1964–70.

16. The British 146th Infantry Brigade landed at Namsos, Norway, on the coast some 300 miles north of Oslo, on 16–17 April 1940. They withdrew 2–3 May. The last Allied forces left Norway on 9 June.

17. Aneurin (Nye) Bevan (1897–1960), a collier from Tredegar who represented Ebbw Vale as Labour MP from 1927 until his death. He was an impassioned orator, beloved of those on the left, disliked, even feared, by those on the right. As Minister of Health, 1945–50, he was responsible for the creation of the National Health Service. He resigned from the second Labour government in 1951 over disarmament, and was defeated when he stood for Leader of the party in 1955. As a director of *Tribune* he allowed Orwell complete freedom, even to oppose the policies of the Labour Party. G. R. Strauss (1901–93; Life Peer, 1979), Labour MP and director of *Tribune*. Expelled from the Labour Party 1939–40 for supporting the Popular Front (see review of *Workers' Front*, n. 2, p. 27, above).

18. Neville Chamberlain's government fell on 10 May 1940, and a coalition government under Winston Churchill was formed. Magnanimously, Churchill included Chamberlain in his Cabinet.

19. Possibly Richard Crossman (see n. 15 above) or Cyril Connolly. Inez Holden suggested Christopher Hollis or a man called Carter, unknown to Orwell's friends. Whether or not Orwell's name was on a police file is unknown. In 1938–9 he felt sure he would end up in a concentration camp (see XI/*443, 489, 527* and *528*). *Invasion 1940: The Nazi Invasion Plan for Britain* by SS General Walter Schellenberg (2000) does not include his name in the 'Special Search List GB' (*The Black Book*), though his publisher, Victor Gollancz, and Ruth Gollancz are listed (she being specifically associated in the list with the Left Book Club).

20. This is the first reference to Orwell's dream of living in the Hebrides, to be realized in 1945 when he rented Barnhill, on Jura. Compare Winston Smith's vision of 'the Golden Country' in *Nineteen Eighty-Four*, *CW*, IX/129–30; see also Orwell's review of *Priest Island*, 21 June 1940 (XII/640), the day following this diary entry.

21. Rayner Heppenstall (1911–81), novelist, critic, broadcaster and crime historian. He and Orwell shared a flat in 1935 and, despite coming to blows, they remained lifelong friends. He produced Orwell's adaptation of *Animal Farm* for radio in 1947 and his own version in 1957. His *Four Absentees* (1960) has reminiscences of Orwell; the relevant portions are reprinted in *Orwell Remembered*, 106–15.

[655]

Review of The Iron Heel *by Jack London;* When the Sleeper Wakes[1] *by H. G. Wells;* Brave New World *by Aldous Huxley;* The Secret of the League *by Ernest Bramah*

Tribune, *12 July 1940*

The reprinting of Jack London's *The Iron Heel* (Werner Laurie 5/–) brings within general reach a book which has been much sought after during the years of Fascist aggression. Like others of Jack London's books it has been widely read in Germany, and it has had the reputation of being an accurate forecast of the Coming of Hitler. In reality it is not that. It is merely a tale of capitalist oppression, and it was written at a time when various things that have made Fascism possible – for instance, the tremendous revival of nationalism – were not easy to foresee.

Where London did show special insight, however, was in realising that the transition to Socialism was not going to be automatic or even easy. The capitalist class was not going to 'perish of its own contradictions' like a flower dying at the end of the season. The capitalist class was quite clever enough to see what was happening, to sink its own differences and counter-attack against the workers; and the resulting struggle would be the most bloody and unscrupulous the world had ever seen.

It is worth comparing *The Iron Heel* with another imaginative novel of the future which was written somewhat earlier and to which it owes something, H. G. Wells' *When the Sleeper Wakes* (Collins, 2/6). By doing so one can see both London's limitations and also the advantage he enjoyed in not being, like Wells, a fully civilised man. As a book, *The Iron Heel* is hugely inferior. It is clumsily written, it shows no grasp of scientific possibilities, and the hero is the kind of human gramophone who is now disappearing even from Socialist tracts. But because of his own streak of savagery London could grasp something that Wells apparently could not, and that is that hedonistic societies do not endure.

Everyone who has ever read *When the Sleeper Wakes* remembers it. It is a vision of a glittering, sinister world in which society had hardened into a caste-system and the workers are permanently enslaved. It is also a world without purpose, in which the upper castes for whom the workers toil are completely soft, cynical and faithless. There is no consciousness of any object in life, nothing corresponding to the fervour of the revolutionary or the religious martyr.

In Aldous Huxley's *Brave New World* (Chatto & Windus, 4/–), a sort of post-war parody of the Wellsian Utopia, these tendencies are immensely exaggerated. Here the hedonistic principle is pushed to its utmost, the whole world has turned into a Riviera hotel. But though *Brave New World* was a brilliant caricature of the present (the present of 1930), it probably casts no light on the future. No society of that kind would last more than a couple of generations, because a ruling class which thought principally in terms of a 'good time' would soon lose its vitality. A ruling class has got to have a strict morality, a quasi-religious belief in itself, a *mystique*. London was aware of this, and though he describes the caste of plutocrats who rule the world for seven centuries as inhuman monsters, he does not describe them as idlers or sensualists. They can only maintain their position while they honestly believe that civilization depends on themselves alone, and therefore in a different way they are just as brave, able and devoted as the revolutionaries who oppose them.

In an intellectual way London accepted the conclusions of Marxism, and he imagined that the 'contradictions' of capitalism, the unconsumable surplus and so forth, would persist even after the capitalist class had organised themselves into a single corporate body. But temperamentally he was very different from the majority of Marxists. With his love of violence and physical strength, his belief in 'natural aristocracy', his animal-worship and exaltation of the primitive, he had in him what one might fairly call a Fascist strain. This probably helped him to understand just how the possessing class would behave when once they were seriously menaced.

It is just here that Marxian Socialists have usually fallen short. Their interpretation of history has been so mechanistic that they have failed to foresee dangers that were obvious to people who had never heard the name of Marx. It is sometimes urged against Marx that he failed to predict the rise of Fascism. I do not know whether he predicted it or not – at that date he could only have done so in very general terms – but it is at any rate certain that his followers failed to see any danger in Fascism until they themselves were at the gates of the concentration camp. A year or more *after* Hitler had risen to power official Marxism was still proclaiming that Hitler was of no importance and 'social-fascism' (*i.e.*, democracy) was the real enemy. London would probably not have made this mistake. His instincts would have warned him that Hitler was dangerous. He knew that economic laws do not operate in the same way as the law of gravity, that they can be held up for long periods by people who, like Hitler, believe in their own destiny.

The Iron Heel and *When the Sleeper Wakes* are both written from the popular standpoint. *Brave New World*, though primarily an attack on hedonism, is also by implication an attack on totalitarianism and caste rule. It is interesting to compare them with a less well-known Utopia which treats the class struggle from the upper or rather the middle-class point of view, Ernest Bramah's *The Secret of the League*.

The Secret of the League was written in 1907, when the growth of the Labour movement was beginning to terrify the middle class, who wrongly imagined that they were menaced from below and not from above. As a political forecast it is trivial, but it is of great interest for the light it casts on the mentality of the struggling middle class.

The author imagines a Labour Government coming into office with so huge a majority that it is impossible to dislodge them. They do not, however, introduce a full Socialist economy. They merely continue to operate capitalism for their own benefit by constantly raising wages, creating a huge army of bureaucrats and taxing the upper classes out of existence. The country is therefore 'going to the dogs' in the familiar manner; moreover in their foreign politics the Labour Government behave rather like the National Government between 1931 and 1939. Against this there arises a secret conspiracy of the middle and upper classes. The manner of their revolt is very ingenious, provided that one looks upon capitalism as something internal. It is the method of the consumers' strike. Over a period of two years the upper-class conspirators secretly hoard fuel-oil and convert coal-burning plant to oil-burning; then they suddenly boycott the principal British industry, the coal industry. The miners are faced with a situation in which they will be able to sell no coal for two years. There is vast unemployment and distress, ending in civil war, in which (thirty years before General Franco!) the upper classes receive foreign aid. After their victory they abolish the trade unions and institute a 'strong' non-parliamentary *régime* – in other words a *régime* that we should now describe as Fascist. The tone of the book is good-natured, as it could afford to be at that date, but the trend of thought is unmistakable.

Why should a decent and kindly writer like Ernest Bramah find the crushing of the proletariat a pleasant vision? It is simply the reaction of a struggling class which felt itself menaced not so much in its economic position as in its code of conduct and way of life. One can see the same purely social antagonism to the working class in an earlier writer of much greater calibre, George Gissing. Time and Hitler have taught the middle classes a great deal, and perhaps they will not again side with their oppressors against their natural allies. But whether they do so or not depends partly on how they are handled, and the stupidity of Socialist propaganda, with its constant baiting of the 'petty bourgeois', has a lot to answer for.

1. The full title is *When the Sleeper Wakes: A Story of the Years to Come* (1899). In the review it was mistakenly given as *The Sleeper Wakes*.

Review of The English Revolution: 1640, *edited by* Christopher Hill
New Statesman & Nation, *24 August 1940*

The imprint of Messrs. Lawrence and Wishart[1] upon a book on the English Civil War tells one in advance what its interpretation of the war is likely to be, and the main interest of reading it is to discover how crudely or how subtly the 'materialistic' method is applied. Obviously a Marxist version of the Civil War must represent it as a struggle between a rising capitalism and an obstructive feudalism, which in fact it was. But men will not die for things called capitalism or feudalism, and will die for things called liberty or loyalty, and to ignore one set of motives is as misleading as to ignore the others. This, however, is what the authors of this book do their best to do. Early in the first essay the familiar note is struck:

The fact that men spoke and wrote in religious language should not prevent us realising that there is a social content behind what are apparently purely theological ideas. Each class created and sought to impose the religious outlook best suited to its own needs and interests. But the real clash is between these class interests.

It is not, then, denied that the 'Puritan Revolution' was a religious as well as a political struggle; but it was more than that.

In the light of the first paragraph, it is not so easy to see what is meant by 'religious struggle' in the last sentence. But in that cocksure paragraph one can see the main weakness of Marxism, its failure to interpret human motives. Religion, morality, patriotism and so forth are invariably written off as 'superstructure', a sort of hypocritical cover-up for the pursuit of economic interests. If that were so, one might well ask why it is that the 'superstructure' has to exist. If no man is ever motivated by anything except class interests, why does every man constantly pretend that he is motivated by something else? Apparently because human beings can only put forth their full powers when they believe that they are *not* acting for economic ends. But this in itself is enough to suggest that 'superstructural' motives should be taken seriously. They may be causes as well as effects. As it is, a 'Marxist analysis' of any historical event tends to be a hurried snap-judgment based on the principle of *cui bono?*,[2] something rather like the 'realism' of the saloon-bar cynic who *always* assumes that the bishop is keeping a mistress and the trade-union leader is in the pay of the boss. Along these lines it is impossible to have an intuitive understanding of men's motives, and therefore impossible to predict their actions. It is easy now to debunk the English Civil War, but it must be admitted that during the past twenty years the predictions of the Marxists have usually been not only wrong but, so to speak, more sensationally wrong than those of much simpler people. The outstanding case was their failure to see in advance the danger of Fascism. Long *after* Hitler came to power official Marxism was declaring that Hitler was of no importance and could achieve nothing. On the other hand, people who had hardly heard of Marx but who knew the power of faith had seen Hitler coming years earlier.

The third essay in the book, by Mr. Edgell Rickword, is on Milton, who figures as 'the revolutionary intellectual'. This involves treating Milton as primarily a pamphleteer, and in an essay of 31 pages *Paradise Lost* and *Paradise Regained* only get between them a hurried mention of half a sentence. The most interesting essay of the three, by Miss Margaret James, is on the materialist interpretations of society which were already current in the mid-seventeenth century. The English Revolution, like some later ones, had its unsuccessful left-wing, men who were ahead of their time and were cast aside when they had helped the new ruling class into power. It is a pity that Miss James fails to make a comparison between the seventeenth-century situation and the one we are now in. A parallel undoubtedly exists, although from the official Marxist point of view the latter-day equivalents of the Diggers and Levellers happen to be unmentionable.

1. This firm published left-wing, often pro-Communist books.
2. Who gains by it? (Latin).

Extracts from London Letter [Current political situation], 3 January 1941
Partisan Review, *March–April 1941*

Orwell contributed fifteen 'London Letters' to the most influential of US left-wing journals, Partisan Review, *from January 1941 to early May 1946. Clement Greenberg,[1] on behalf of the editors, told Orwell on 9 December 1940 what they were seeking: 'what's happening under the surface in the way of politics? Among labor groups? What is the general mood, if there is such a thing, among writers, artists and intellectuals? What transmutations have their lives and their preoccupations suffered? You can be as gossipy as you please and refer to as many personalities as you like. The more the better.' Payment was to be $2.00 per printed page – $11.00 a letter (approximately £2.75 at the then rate of exchange, perhaps £90–100 at today's values). The Letters are given in full in* The Complete Works; *only a selection of political extracts is given in this volume.*

. . . as to the political situation, I think it is true to say that at the moment we are in the middle of a backwash which is not going to make very much ultimate difference. The reactionaries, which means roughly the people who read *The Times*, had a bad scare in the summer, but they saved themselves by the skin of their teeth, and they are now consolidating their position against the new crisis which is likely to arise in the spring. In the summer what amounted to a revolutionary situation existed in England, though there was no one to take advantage of it. After twenty years of being fed on sugar and water the nation had suddenly realised what its rulers were like, and there was a widespread readiness for sweeping economic and social changes, combined with absolute determination to prevent invasion. At that moment, I believe, the opportunity existed to isolate the monied class and swing the mass of the nation behind a policy in which resistance to Hitler and destruction of class-privilege were combined. Clement Greenberg's remark in his article in *Horizon* that the working class is the only class in England that seriously means to defeat Hitler, seems to me quite untrue. The bulk of the middle class are just as anti-Hitler as the working class, and their morale is probably more reliable. The fact which Socialists, especially when they are looking at the English scene from the outside, seldom seem to me to grasp, is that the patriotism of the middle classes is a thing to be made use of. The people who stand to attention during 'God Save the King' would readily transfer their loyalty to a Socialist régime, if they were handled with the minimum of tact. However, in the summer months no one saw the opportunity, the Labour leaders (with the possible exception of Bevin) allowed themselves to be made the tame cats of the Government, and when the invasion failed to come off and the air raids were less terrible than everyone had expected, the quasi-revolutionary mood ebbed away. At present the Right are counter-attacking. Margesson's[2] entry into the Cabinet – the nearest equivalent possible to bringing Chamberlain out of his grave – was a swift cash-in on Wavell's victory in Egypt.[3] The campaign in the Mediterranean is not finished, but events there have justified the Conservatives as against the Left and they can be expected to take advantage of it. It is not impossible that one or two leftish newspapers will be suppressed before long. Suppression of the *Daily Worker* is said to have been mooted already in the Cabinet. But this swing of the pendulum is not vitally important unless one believes, as I do not – and I doubt whether many people under fifty believe it either – that England can win the war without passing through revolution and go straight back to pre-1939 'normality', with 3 million unemployed, etc., etc.

But at present there does not effectively exist any policy between being patriotic in the 'King and Country' style and being pro-Hitler. If another wave of anti-capitalist feeling arrived it could at the moment only be canalised into defeatism. At the same time there is little sign of this in England, though the morale is probably worse in the industrial towns than elsewhere. In London, after four months of almost ceaseless bombing, morale is far better than a year ago when the war was stagnant. The only people who are overtly defeatist are Mosley's followers,[4] the Communists and the pacifists. The Communists still possess a footing in the factories and may some time stage a come-back by fomenting grievances about working-hours, etc. But they have difficulty in getting their working-class followers to accept a definitely pro-Hitler policy, and they had to pipe down during the desperate days in the summer. With the general public their influence is nil, as one can see by the votes in the by-elections, and the powerful hold they had on the press in the years 1935–9 has been completely broken. Mosley's Blackshirts have ceased to exist as a legal organisation, but they probably deserve to be taken more seriously than the Communists, if only because the tone of their propaganda is more acceptable to soldiers, sailors and airmen. No left-wing organisation in England has ever been able to gain a footing in the armed forces. The Fascists have, of course, tried to put the blame for both the war and the discomfort caused by the air-raids onto the Jews, and during the worst of the East End bombings they did succeed in raising a mutter of anti-Semitism, though only a faint one. The most interesting development on the anti-war front has been the interpenetration of the pacifist movement by Fascist ideas, especially anti-Semitism. After Dick Sheppard's death[5] British pacifism seems to have suffered a moral collapse; it has not produced any significant gesture nor even many martyrs, and only about 15 per cent of the membership of the Peace Pledge Union now appear to be active. But many of the surviving pacifists now spin a line of talk indistinguishable from that of the Blackshirts ('Stop this Jewish war' etc.), and the actual membership of the P.P.U.[6] and the British Union overlap to some extent. Put all together, the various pro-Hitler organisations can hardly number 150,000 members, and they are not likely to achieve much by their own efforts, but they might play an important part at a time when a government of the Pétain type was contemplating surrender. There is some reason to think that Hitler does not want Mosley's organisation to grow too strong. Lord Haw-Haw, the most effective of the English-language German broadcasters, has been identified with fair certainty as Joyce,[7] a member of the split-off Fascist party and a very bitter personal enemy of Mosley.

You ask also about the intellectual life of England, the various currents of thought in the literary world, etc. I think the dominating factors are these:

(a) The complete destruction, owing to the Russo-German pact, of the left-wing 'anti-fascist' orthodoxy of the past five years.

(b) The fact that physically fit people under 35 are mostly in the army, or expect soon to be so.

(c) The increase in book-consumption owing to the boredom of war, together with the unwillingness of publishers to risk money on unknown writers.

(d) The bombing (of which more presently – but I should say here that it is less terrifying and more of a nuisance than you perhaps imagine).

The Russo-German pact not only brought the Stalinists and near-Stalinists into the pro-Hitler position, but it also put an end to the game of 'I told you so' which the left-wing writers had been so profitably playing for five years past. 'Anti-fascism' as interpreted by the *News Chronicle*, the *New Statesman* and the Left Book Club had depended on the belief – I think it was also half-consciously a hope – that no British government would ever stand up to Hitler. When the Chamberlain government finally went to war it took the wind out of the leftwingers' sails by putting into effect the policy which they themselves had been demanding. In the few days before war was declared it was extremely amusing to watch the behaviour of orthodox Popular Front-ers, who were exclaiming dolefully 'It's going to be another Munich', although in fact it had been obvious for months past that war was inevitable. These people were in reality *hoping* for another Munich, which would allow them to continue with their Cassandra role without having to face the facts of modern war . . .

Personally I consider it all to the good that the confident war-mongering mood of the Popular Front period, with its lying propaganda and its horrible atmosphere of orthodoxy, has been destroyed. But it has left a sort of hole. Nobody knows what to think, nothing is being started. It is very difficult to imagine any new 'school' of literature arising at a moment when the youngish writers have had their universe punctured and the very young are either in the army or kept out of print by lack of paper. Moreover the economic foundations of literature are shifting, for the highbrow literary magazine, depending ultimately on leisured people who have been brought up in a minority culture, is becoming less and less possible. *Horizon* is a sort of modern democratised version of this (compare its general tone with that of the *Criterion* of ten years ago), and even *Horizon* keeps going only with difficulty.[8]

1. Clement Greenberg (1909–94), associate editor of *Partisan Review*, who had invited Orwell to contribute, had written 'An American View' of the progress of the war for *Horizon*, September 1940. An editorial comment in that issue, though almost certainly written by Cyril Connolly, shows Orwell's influence. From 1945 to 1947, Greenberg edited *Contemporary Jewish Record* (afterwards, *Commentary*), to which Orwell contributed three articles.

2. David R. Margesson (1890–1965; Viscount, 1942), Conservative MP, 1924–42; Government Chief Whip, 1931–40; loyal to each prime minister he served. Six months after Churchill became Prime Minister he was made Secretary for War.

3. Archibald Percival Wavell (1883–1950), became Field Marshal and first Earl Wavell. He was strikingly successful in the campaign in North Africa, December 1940 to February 1941, against greatly superior numbers of Italians, and for the first five months of 1941 in East Africa. He was not successful in Greece and Crete and against forces under Rommel's command in North Africa later in 1941. In 1942, Singapore, Malaya and Burma were lost by forces under his command. He was replaced and, in June 1943, appointed Viceroy of India. His poetry anthology, *Other Men's Flowers* (1944), was reviewed by Orwell (XVI/*2433*). Orwell concluded that review, 'This is not a perfect anthology, but it is quite good enough to make one feel a certain regret that the man who compiled it should be wasting his talents on the most thankless job in the world' – as Viceroy.

4. British Union of Fascists.

5. The Reverend Hugh Richard Lowrie ('Dick') Sheppard (1880–1937) was a prominent pacifist. A man of great integrity and charisma, he served as a chaplain in France in 1914 and then as Vicar of St Martin-in-the-Fields, 1914–27, and Dean of Canterbury, 1929–31. He was a chaplain to the King from 1935. In October 1934 he set in train a movement that led to the foundation of the Peace Pledge Union.

6. Peace Pledge Union.

7. William Joyce (1908–46), known as Lord Haw-Haw from his manner of speaking despite his being an American. Although he spent most of his life in England, he never acquired British nationality. He was a Fascist for whom Oswald Mosley's line was too mild. In August 1939 he went to Germany and in 1940 became a naturalized German. In his broadcasts to Britain he endeavoured to spread fear by forecasting which cities were about to be bombed. His frequent inaccuracies (notably his oft-reported sinking of the aircraft-carrier, *Ark Royal*, long before it was eventually sunk by two German submarines off Gibraltar on 14 November 1941, fortunately with the loss of only one man) led to his becoming a music-hall joke. He was hanged on 3 January 1946.

8. See note on Peter Watson, p. 92, n. 11, above.

---

[763]

The Lion and the Unicorn: Socialism and the English Genius

19 February 1941

This was the first of the Searchlight Book series, planned by Fredric Warburg, Tosco Fyvel[1] *and Orwell during the summer of 1940. Orwell was persuaded, rather against his will, to write the first book, in effect, a sixty-four-page pamphlet. The Lion and the Unicorn was published by Martin Secker & Warburg on 19 February 1941 at 2s 0d. Initially, 5,000 copies were*

printed but, in response to the booklet's success, the run was increased to
7,500 and then a second impression of 5,000 copies was ordered in March
1941. The first thousand copies of this edition were delivered in June 1941,
but, when Plymouth was bombed, the type, and that for Homage to
Catalonia, *was destroyed. Two chapters Orwell contributed to* The
Betrayal of the Left *(Gollancz, March 1941), 'Patriots and Revolution-*
aries' (originally 'Our Opportunity') and 'Fascism and Democracy', give, in
shorter form, some of Orwell's concerns expressed in The Lion and the
Unicorn. *For fuller details, and these chapters, see* CW, XII/737, 753 *and*
763. In the April 1941 issue of Left News, *Orwell replied to a long*
letter from Douglas Ede responding to 'Our Opportunity'. This asked
precisely how a 'Socialist Democracy' was to be built. Orwell's response,
'Will Freedom Die with Capitalism?', followed (see CW, XII/782). The
Lion and the Unicorn *has three sections. The first, 'England Your England',*
is reproduced in Orwell's England *in this series.*

PART II: SHOPKEEPERS AT WAR

I

I began this book to the tune of German bombs, and I begin this second
chapter in the added racket of the barrage. The yellow gun-flashes are
lighting the sky, the splinters are rattling on the house-tops, and London
Bridge is falling down, falling down, falling down. Anyone able to read
a map knows that we are in deadly danger. I do not mean that we are
beaten or need be beaten. Almost certainly the outcome depends on our
own will. But at this moment we are in the soup, full fathom five, and we
have been brought there by follies which we are still committing and
which will drown us altogether if we do not mend our ways quickly.

What this war has demonstrated is that private capitalism – that is, an
economic system in which land, factories, mines and transport are owned
privately and operated solely for profit – *does not work.* It cannot deliver
the goods. This fact had been known to millions of people for years past,
but nothing ever came of it, because there was no real urge from below
to alter the system, and those at the top had trained themselves to be
impenetrably stupid on just this point. Argument and propaganda got one

nowhere. The lords of property simply sat on their bottoms and proclaimed that all was for the best. Hitler's conquest of Europe, however, was a *physical* debunking of capitalism. War, for all its evil, is at any rate an unanswerable test of strength, like a try-your-grip machine. Great strength returns the penny, and there is no way of faking the result.

When the nautical screw was first invented, there was a controversy that lasted for years as to whether screw-steamers or paddle-steamers were better. The paddle-steamers, like all obsolete things, had their champions, who supported them by ingenious arguments. Finally, however, a distinguished admiral tied a screw-steamer and a paddle-steamer of equal horse-power stern to stern and set their engines running. That settled the question once and for all. And it was something similar that happened on the fields of Norway and of Flanders.[2] Once and for all it was proved that a planned economy is stronger than a planless one. But it is necessary here to give some kind of definition to those much-abused words, Socialism and Fascism.

Socialism is usually defined as 'common ownership of the means of production'. Crudely: the State, representing the whole nation, owns everything, and everyone is a State employee. This does *not* mean that people are stripped of private possessions such as clothes and furniture, but it *does* mean that all productive goods, such as land, mines, ships and machinery, are the property of the State. The State is the sole large-scale producer. It is not certain that Socialism is in all ways superior to capitalism, but it is certain that, unlike capitalism, it can solve the problems of production and consumption. At normal times a capitalist economy can never consume all that it produces, so that there is always a wasted surplus (wheat burned in furnaces, herrings dumped back into the sea, etc., etc.) and always unemployment. In time of war, on the other hand, it has difficulty in producing all that it needs, because nothing is produced unless someone sees his way to making a profit out of it. In a Socialist economy these problems do not exist. The State simply calculates what goods will be needed and does its best to produce them. Production is only limited by the amount of labour and raw materials. Money, for internal purposes, ceases to be a mysterious all-powerful thing and becomes a sort of coupon or ration-ticket, issued in sufficient quantities to buy up such consumption-goods as may be available at the moment.

However, it has become clear in the last few years that 'common ownership of the means of production' is not in itself a sufficient definition of Socialism. One must also add the following: approximate equality of incomes (it need be no more than approximate), political democracy, and abolition of all hereditary privilege, especially in education. These are simply the necessary safeguards against the reappearance of a class-system. Centralized ownership has very little meaning unless the mass of the people are living roughly upon an equal level, and have some kind of control over the government. 'The State' may come to mean no more than a self-elected political party, and oligarchy and privilege can return, based on power rather than on money.

But what then is Fascism?

Fascism, at any rate the German version, is a form of capitalism that borrows from Socialism just such features as will make it efficient for war purposes. Internally, Germany has a good deal in common with a Socialist state. Ownership has never been abolished, there are still capitalists and workers, and – this is the important point, and the real reason why rich men all over the world tend to sympathize with Fascism – generally speaking the same people are capitalists and the same people workers as before the Nazi revolution. But at the same time the State, which is simply the Nazi Party, is in control of everything. It controls investment, raw materials, rates of interest, working hours, wages. The factory-owner still owns his factory, but he is for practical purposes reduced to the status of a manager. Everyone is in effect a State employee, though the salaries vary very greatly. The mere *efficiency* of such a system, the elimination of waste and obstruction, is obvious. In seven years it has built up the most powerful war machine the world has ever seen.

But the idea underlying Fascism is irreconcilably different from that which underlies Socialism. Socialism aims, ultimately, at a world-state of free and equal human beings. It takes the equality of human rights for granted. Nazism assumes just the opposite. The driving force behind the Nazi movement is the belief in human *inequality*, the superiority of Germans to all other races, the right of Germany to rule the world. Outside the German Reich it does not recognize any obligations. Eminent Nazi professors have 'proved' over and over again that only Nordic man is fully human, have even mooted the idea that non-Nordic peoples (such as ourselves) can interbreed with gorillas! Therefore, while a species of war-Socialism exists within the German state, its attitude towards conquered nations is frankly that of an exploiter. The function of the Czechs, Poles, French, etc., is simply to produce such goods as Germany may need, and get in return just as little as will keep them from open rebellion. If we are conquered, our job will probably be to manufacture weapons for Hitler's forthcoming wars with Russia[3] and America. The Nazis aim, in effect, at setting up a kind of caste system, with four main castes corresponding rather closely to those of the Hindu religion. At the top comes the Nazi Party, second come the mass of the German people, third come the conquered European populations. Fourth and last are to come the coloured peoples, the 'semi-apes' as Hitler calls them, who are to be reduced quite openly to slavery.

However horrible this system may seem to us, *it works*. It works because it is a planned system geared to a definite purpose, world-conquest, and not allowing any private interest, either of capitalist or worker, to stand in its way. British capitalism does not work, because it is a competitive system in which private profit is and must be the main objective. It is a system in which all the forces are pulling in opposite directions and the interests of the individual are as often as not totally opposed to those of the State.

All through the critical years British capitalism, with its immense industrial plant and its unrivalled supply of skilled labour, was unequal to the strain of preparing for war. To prepare for war on the modern scale you have got to divert the greater part of your national income to armaments, which means cutting down on consumption goods. A bombing plane, for instance, is equivalent in price to fifty small motor cars, or eighty thousand pairs of silk stockings, or a million loaves of bread. Clearly you can't have *many* bombing planes without lowering the national standard of life. It is guns or butter, as Marshal Göring remarked.[4] But in Chamberlain's England the transition could not be made. The rich would not face the necessary taxation, and while the rich are still visibly rich it is not possible to tax the poor very heavily either. Moreover, so long as *profit* was the main object the manufacturer had no incentive to change over from consumption goods to armaments. A business-man's first duty is to his share-holders. Perhaps England needs tanks, but perhaps it pays better to manufacture motor cars. To prevent war material from reaching the enemy is common sense, but to sell in the highest market is a business duty. Right at the end of August 1939 the British dealers were tumbling over one another in their eagerness to sell Germany tin, rubber, copper and shellac – and this in the clear, certain knowledge that war was going to break out in a week or two. It was about as sensible as selling somebody a razor to cut your throat with. But it was 'good business'.

And now look at the results. After 1934 it was known that Germany was rearming. After 1936 everyone with eyes in his head knew that war was coming. After Munich it was merely a question of how soon the war would begin. In September 1939 war broke out. *Eight months later* it was discovered that, so far as equipment went, the British army was barely beyond the standard of 1918. We saw our soldiers fighting their way desperately to the coast, with one aeroplane against three, with rifles against tanks, with bayonets against tommy-guns. There were not even enough revolvers to supply all the officers. After a year of war the regular army was still short of 300,000 tin hats. There had even, previously, been a shortage of uniforms – this in one of the greatest woollen-producing countries in the world!

What had happened was that the whole monied class, unwilling to face a change in their way of life, had shut their eyes to the nature of Fascism and modern war. And false optimism was fed to the general public by the gutter press, which lives on its advertisements and is therefore interested in keeping trade conditions normal. Year after year the Beaverbrook press[5] assured us in huge headlines that THERE WILL BE NO WAR, and as late as the beginning of 1939 Lord Rothermere[6] was describing Hitler as 'a great gentleman'. And while England in the moment of disaster proved to be short of every war material except ships, it is not recorded that there was any shortage of motor cars, fur coats, gramophones, lipstick, chocolates or silk stockings. And dare anyone pretend that the same tug-of-war between private profit and public necessity is not still continuing? England fights for her life, but business must fight for profits. You can hardly open a newspaper without seeing the two contradictory processes happening side by side. On the very same page you will find the government urging you to save and the seller of some useless luxury urging you to spend. Lend to Defend, but Guinness is Good for You. Buy a Spitfire, but also buy Haig and Haig, Pond's Face Cream and Black Magic Chocolates.

But one thing gives hope – the visible swing in public opinion. If we can survive this war, the defeat in Flanders will turn out to have been one of the great turning-points in English history. In that spectacular disaster the working class, the middle class and even a section of the business community could see the utter rottenness of private capitalism. Before that the case against capitalism had never been *proved*. Russia, the only definitely Socialist country, was backward and far away. All criticism broke itself against the rat-trap faces of bankers and the brassy laughter of stockbrokers. Socialism? Ha! ha! ha! Where's the money to come from? Ha! ha! ha! The lords of property were firm in their seats, and they knew it. But after the French collapse there came something that could not be laughed away, something that neither cheque-books nor policemen were any use against – the bombing. Zweee – BOOM! What's that? Oh, only a bomb on the Stock Exchange. Zweee – BOOM! Another acre of somebody's valuable slum-property gone west. Hitler will at any rate go down in history as the man who made the City of London laugh on the wrong side of its face. For the first time in their lives the comfortable were uncomfortable, the professional optimists had to admit that there was something wrong. It was a great step forward. From that time onwards the ghastly job of trying to convince artificially stupefied people that a planned economy might be better than a free-for-all in which the worst man wins – that job will never be quite so ghastly again.

II

The difference between Socialism and capitalism is not primarily a difference of technique. One cannot simply change from one system to the other as one might install a new piece of machinery in a factory, and then carry on as before, with the same people in positions of control. Obviously there is also needed a complete shift of power. New blood, new men, new ideas – in the true sense of the word, a revolution.

I have spoken earlier of the soundness and homogeneity of England, the patriotism that runs like a connecting thread through almost all classes. After Dunkirk anyone who had eyes in his head could see this. But it is absurd to pretend that the promise of that moment has been fulfilled. Almost certainly the mass of the people are now ready for the vast changes that are necessary; but those changes have not even begun to happen.

England is a family with the wrong members in control. Almost entirely we are governed by the rich, and by people who step into positions of command by right of birth. Few if any of these people are consciously treacherous, some of them are not even fools, but as a class they are quite incapable of leading us to victory. They could not do it, even if their material interests did not constantly trip them up. As I pointed out earlier, they have been artificially stupefied. Quite apart from anything else, the rule of money sees to it that we shall be governed largely by the old – that is, by people utterly unable to grasp what age they are living in or what enemy they are fighting. Nothing was more desolating at the beginning of this war than the way in which the whole of the older generation conspired to pretend that it was the war of 1914–18 over again. All the old duds were back on the job, twenty years older, with the skull plainer in their faces. Ian Hay was cheering up the troops, Belloc was writing articles on strategy, Maurois doing broadcasts, Bairnsfather drawing cartoons.[7] It was like a tea-party of ghosts. And that state of affairs has barely altered. The shock of disaster brought a few able men like Bevin[8] to the front, but in general we are still commanded by people who managed to live through the years 1931–9 without even discovering that Hitler was dangerous. A generation of the unteachable is hanging upon us like a necklace of corpses.

As soon as one considers any problem of this war – and it does not matter whether it is the widest aspect of strategy or the tiniest detail of home organization – one sees that the necessary moves cannot be made while the social structure of England remains what it is. Inevitably, because of their position and upbringing, the ruling class are fighting for their own privileges, which cannot possibly be reconciled with the public interest. It is a mistake to imagine that war-aims, strategy, propaganda and industrial organization exist in watertight compartments. All are interconnected. Every strategic plan, every tactical method, even every weapon will bear the stamp of the social system that produced it. The British ruling class are fighting against Hitler, whom they have always regarded and whom some of them still regard as their protector against

Bolshevism. That does not mean that they will deliberately sell out; but it does mean that at every decisive moment they are likely to falter, pull their punches, do the wrong thing.

Until the Churchill government called some sort of halt to the process, they have done the wrong thing with an unerring instinct ever since 1931. They helped Franco to overthrow the Spanish government, although anyone not an imbecile could have told them that a Fascist Spain would be hostile to England. They fed Italy with war materials all through the winter of 1939–40, although it was obvious to the whole world that the Italians were going to attack us in the spring. For the sake of a few hundred thousand dividend-drawers they are turning India from an ally into an enemy. Moreover, so long as the monied classes remain in control, we cannot develop any but a *defensive* strategy. Every victory means a change in the *status quo*. How can we drive the Italians out of Abyssinia without rousing echoes among the coloured peoples of our own Empire? How can we even smash Hitler without the risk of bringing the German Socialists and Communists into power? The left-wingers who wail that 'this is a capitalist' war and that 'British Imperialism' is fighting for loot have got their heads screwed on backwards. The last thing the British monied class wish for is to acquire fresh territory. It would simply be an embarrassment. Their war-aim (both unattainable and unmentionable) is simply to hang on to what they have got.

Internally, England is still the rich man's Paradise. All talk of 'equality of sacrifice' is nonsense. At the same time as factory-workers are asked to put up with longer hours, advertisements for 'Butler. One in family, eight in staff' are appearing in the press. The bombed-out populations of the East End go hungry and homeless while wealthier victims simply step into their cars and flee to comfortable country houses. The Home Guard swells to a million men in a few weeks, and is deliberately organized from above in such a way that only people with private incomes can hold positions of command. Even the rationing system is so arranged that it hits the poor all the time, while people with over £2000 a year are practically unaffected by it. Everywhere privilege is squandering good will. In such circumstances even propaganda becomes almost impossible. As attempts to stir up patriotic feeling, the red posters issued by the Chamberlain government at the beginning of the war broke all depth-records. Yet they could not have been much other than they were, for how could Chamberlain and his followers take the risk of rousing strong popular feeling *against Fascism*? Anyone who was genuinely hostile to Fascism must also be opposed to Chamberlain himself, and to all the others who had helped Hitler into power. So also with external propaganda. In all Lord Halifax's speeches there is not one concrete proposal for which a single inhabitant of Europe would risk the top joint of his little finger. For what war-aim can Halifax,[9] or anyone like him, conceivably have, except to put the clock back to 1933?

It is only by revolution that the native genius of the English people can be set free. Revolution does not mean red flags and street fighting, it means a fundamental shift of power. Whether it happens with or without bloodshed is largely an accident of time and place. Nor does it mean the dictatorship of a single class. The people in England who grasp what changes are needed and are capable of carrying them through are not confined to any one class, though it is true that very few people with over £2000 a year are among them. What is wanted is a conscious open revolt by ordinary people against inefficiency, class privilege and the rule of the old. It is not primarily a question of change of government. British governments do, broadly speaking, represent the will of the people, and if we alter our structure from below we shall get the government we need. Ambassadors, generals, officials and colonial administrators who are senile or pro-Fascist are more dangerous than Cabinet ministers whose follies have to be committed in public. Right through our national life we have got to fight against privilege, against the notion that a half-witted public-schoolboy is better fitted for command than an intelligent mechanic. Although there are gifted and honest *individuals* among them, we have got to break the grip of the monied class as a whole. England has got to assume its real shape. The England that is only just beneath the surface, in the factories and the newspaper offices, in the aeroplanes and the submarines, has got to take charge of its own destiny.

In the short run, equality of sacrifice, 'war communism', is even more important than radical economic changes. It is very necessary that industry should be nationalized, but it is more urgently necessary that such monstrosities as butlers and 'private incomes' should disappear forthwith. Almost certainly the main reason why the Spanish Republic could keep up the fight for two and a half years against impossible odds was that there were no gross contrasts of wealth. The people suffered horribly, but they all suffered alike. When the private soldier had not a cigarette, the general had not one either. Given equality of sacrifice, the morale of a country like England would probably be unbreakable. But at present we have nothing to appeal to except traditional patriotism, which is deeper here than elsewhere, but is not necessarily bottomless. At some point or another you have got to deal with the man who says 'I should be no worse off under Hitler'. But what answer can you give him – that is, what answer that you can expect him to listen to – while common soldiers risk their lives for two and sixpence a day, and fat women ride about in Rolls-Royce cars, nursing Pekingeses?

It is quite likely that this war will last three years. It will mean cruel overwork, cold dull winters, uninteresting food, lack of amusements, prolonged bombing. It cannot but lower the general standard of living, because the essential act of war is to manufacture armaments instead of consumable goods. The working classes will have to suffer terrible things. And they *will* suffer them, almost indefinitely, provided that they know what they are fighting for. They are not cowards, and they are not even internationally-minded. They can stand all that the Spanish workers stood, and more. But they will want some kind of proof that a better life is ahead for themselves and their children. The one sure earnest of that is that when they are taxed and overworked they shall see that the rich are being hit even harder. And if the rich squeal audibly, so much the better.

We can bring these things about, if we really want to. It is not true that public opinion has no power in England. It never makes itself heard without achieving something; it has been responsible for most of the changes for the better during the past six months. But we have moved with glacier-like slowness, and we have learned only from disasters. It took the fall of Paris to get rid of Chamberlain and the unnecessary suffering of scores of thousands of people in the East End to get rid or partially rid of Sir John Anderson.[10] It is not worth losing a battle in order to bury a corpse. For we are fighting against swift evil intelligences, and time presses, and

> History to the defeated
> May say Alas but cannot help or pardon.[11]

III

During the last six months there has been much talk of 'the Fifth Column'.[12] From time to time obscure lunatics have been jailed for making speeches in favour of Hitler, and large numbers of German refugees have been interned, a thing which has almost certainly done us great harm in Europe. It is of course obvious that the idea of a large, organized army of Fifth Columnists suddenly appearing on the streets with weapons in their hands, as in Holland and Belgium, is ridiculous. Nevertheless a Fifth Column danger does exist. One can only consider it if one also considers in what way England might be defeated.

It does not seem probable that air bombing can settle a major war. England might well be invaded and conquered, but the invasion would be a dangerous gamble, and if it happened and failed it would probably leave us more united and less Blimp-ridden[13] than before. Moreover, if England were overrun by foreign troops the English people would know that they had been beaten and would continue the struggle. It is doubtful whether they could be held down permanently, or whether Hitler wishes to keep an army of a million men stationed in these islands. A government of ——, —— and —— (you can fill in the names) would suit him better. The English can probably not be bullied into surrender, but they might quite easily be bored, cajoled or cheated into it, provided that, as at Munich, they did not know that they were surrendering. It could happen most easily when the war seemed to be going well rather than badly. The threatening tone of so much of the German and Italian propaganda is a psychological mistake. It only gets home on intellectuals. With the general public the proper approach would be 'Let's call it a draw'. It is when a peace-offer along *those* lines is made that the pro-Fascists will raise their voices.

But who are the pro-Fascists? The idea of a Hitler victory appeals to the very rich, to the Communists, to Mosley's followers,[14] to the pacifists, and to certain sections among the Catholics. Also, if things went badly enough on the Home front, the whole of the poorer section of the working class might swing round to a position that was defeatist though not actively pro-Hitler.

In this motley list one can see the daring of German propaganda, its willingness to offer everything to everybody. But the various pro-Fascist forces are not consciously acting together, and they operate in different ways.

The Communists must certainly be regarded as pro-Hitler, and are bound to remain so unless Russian policy changes, but they have not very much influence. Mosley's Blackshirts, though now lying very low, are a more serious danger, because of the footing they probably possess in the armed forces. Still, even in its palmiest days Mosley's following can hardly have numbered 50,000. Pacifism is a psychological curiosity rather than a political movement. Some of the extremer pacifists, starting out with a complete renunciation of violence, have ended by warmly championing Hitler and even toying with anti-Semitism. This is interesting, but it is not important. 'Pure' pacifism, which is a by-product of naval power, can only appeal to people in very sheltered positions. Moreover, being negative and irresponsible, it does not inspire much devotion. Of the membership of the Peace Pledge Union, less than 15 per cent even pay their annual subscriptions. None of these bodies of people, pacifists, Communists or Blackshirts, could bring a large-scale stop-the-war movement into being by their own efforts. But they might help to make things very much easier for a treacherous government negotiating surrender. Like the French Communists, they might become the half-conscious agents of millionaires.

The real danger is from above. One ought not to pay any attention to Hitler's recent line of talk about being the friend of the poor man, the enemy of plutocracy, etc., etc. Hitler's real self is in *Mein Kampf*, and in his actions. He has never persecuted the rich, except when they were Jews or when they tried actively to oppose him. He stands for a centralized economy which robs the capitalist of most of his power but leaves the structure of society much as before. The State controls industry, but there are still rich and poor, masters and men. Therefore, as against genuine Socialism, the monied class have always been on his side. This was crystal clear at the time of the Spanish civil war, and clear again at the time when France surrendered. Hitler's puppet government are not working-men, but a gang of bankers, gaga generals and corrupt right-wing politicians.

That kind of spectacular, *conscious* treachery is less likely to succeed in England, indeed is far less likely even to be tried. Nevertheless, to many payers of super-tax this war is simply an insane family squabble which ought to be stopped at all costs. One need not doubt that a 'peace' movement is on foot somewhere in high places; probably a shadow Cabinet has already been formed. These people will get their chance not in the moment of defeat but in some stagnant period when boredom is reinforced by discontent. They will not talk about surrender, only about peace; and doubtless they will persuade themselves, and perhaps other people, that they are acting for the best. An army of unemployed led by millionaires quoting the Sermon on the Mount[15] – that is our danger. But it cannot arise when we have once introduced a reasonable degree of social justice. The lady in the Rolls-Royce car is more damaging to morale than a fleet of Göring's bombing-planes.

PART III: THE ENGLISH REVOLUTION

The English revolution started several years ago, and it began to gather momentum when the troops came back from Dunkirk. Like all else in England, it happens in a sleepy unwilling way, but it is happening. The war has speeded it up, but it has also increased, and desperately, the necessity for speed.

Progress and reaction are ceasing to have anything to do with party labels. If one wishes to name a particular moment, one can say that the old distinction between Right and Left broke down when *Picture Post* was first published. What are the politics of *Picture Post*? Or of *Cavalcade*, or Priestley's broadcasts, or the leading articles in the *Evening Standard*?[16] None of the old classifications will fit them. They merely point to the existence of multitudes of unlabelled people who have grasped within the last year or two that something is wrong. But since a classless, ownerless society is generally spoken of as 'Socialism', we can give that name to the society towards which we are now moving. The war and the revolution are inseparable. We cannot establish anything that a Western nation would regard as Socialism without defeating Hitler; on the other hand we cannot defeat Hitler while we remain economically and socially in the nineteenth century. The past is fighting the future, and we have two years, a year, possibly only a few months, to see to it that the future wins.

We cannot look to this or to any similar government to put through the necessary changes of its own accord. The initiative will have to come from below. That means that there will have to arise something that has never yet existed in England, a Socialist movement that actually has the mass of the people behind it. But one must start by recognizing why it is that English Socialism has failed.

In England there is only one Socialist party that has ever seriously mattered, the Labour Party. It has never been able to achieve any major change, because except in purely domestic matters it has never possessed a genuinely independent policy. It was and is primarily a party of the Trade Unions, devoted to raising wages and improving working conditions. This meant that all through the critical years it was directly interested in the prosperity of British capitalism. In particular it was interested in the maintenance of the British Empire, for the wealth of England was drawn largely from Asia and Africa. The standard of living of the Trade Union workers, whom the Labour Party represented, depended indirectly on the sweating of Indian coolies. At the same time the Labour Party was a Socialist party, using Socialist phraseology, thinking in terms of an old-fashioned anti-imperialism and more or less pledged to make restitution to the coloured races. It had to stand for the 'independence' of India, just as it had to stand for disarmament and 'progress' generally. Nevertheless everyone was aware that this was nonsense. In the age of the tank and the bombing plane, backward agricultural countries like India and the African colonies can no more be independent than can a cat or a dog. Had any Labour Government come into office with a clear majority and then proceeded to grant India anything that could truly be called independence, India would simply have been absorbed by Japan, or divided between Japan and Russia.

To a Labour Government in power, three imperial policies would have been open. One was to continue administering the Empire exactly as before, which meant dropping all pretensions to Socialism. Another was to set the subject peoples 'free', which meant in practice handing them over to Japan, Italy and other predatory powers, and incidentally causing a catastrophic drop in the British standard of living. The third was to develop a *positive* imperial policy, and aim at transforming the Empire into a federation of Socialist states, like a looser and freer version of the Union of Soviet Republics. But the Labour Party's history and background made this impossible. It was a party of the Trade Unions, hopelessly parochial in outlook, with little interest in imperial affairs and no contacts among the men who actually held the Empire together. It would have had to hand over the administration of India and Africa and the whole job of imperial defence to men drawn from a different class and traditionally hostile to Socialism. Overshadowing everything was the doubt whether a Labour Government which meant business could make itself obeyed. For all the size of its following, the Labour Party had no footing in the navy, little or none in the army or Air Force, none whatever in the colonial services, and not even a sure footing in the Home civil service. In England its position was strong but not unchallengeable, and outside England all the key points were in the hands of its enemies. Once in power, the same dilemma would always have faced it: carry out your promises, and risk revolt, or continue with the same policy as the Conservatives, and stop talking about Socialism. The Labour leaders never found a solution, and from 1935 onwards it was very doubtful whether they had any wish to take office. They had degenerated into a Permanent Opposition.

Outside the Labour Party there existed several extremist parties, of whom the Communists were the strongest. The Communists had considerable influence in the Labour Party in the years 1920–26 and 1935–9. Their chief importance, and that of the whole left wing of the Labour movement, was the part they played in alienating the middle classes from Socialism.

The history of the past seven years has made it perfectly clear that Communism has no chance in Western Europe. The appeal of Fascism is enormously greater. In one country after another the Communists have been rooted out by their more up-to-date enemies, the Nazis. In the English-speaking countries they never had a serious footing. The creed they were spreading could appeal only to a rather rare type of person, found chiefly in the middle-class intelligentsia, the type who has ceased to love his own country but still feels the need of patriotism, and therefore develops patriotic sentiments towards Russia. By 1940, after working for twenty years and spending a great deal of money, the British Communists had barely 20,000 members, actually a smaller number than they had started out with in 1920. The other Marxist parties were of even less importance. They had not the Russian money and prestige behind them, and even more than the Communists they were tied to the nineteenth-century doctrine of the class war. They continued year after year to preach this out-of-date gospel, and never drew any inference from the fact that it got them no followers.

Nor did any strong native Fascist movement grow up. Material conditions were not bad enough, and no leader who could be taken seriously was forthcoming. One would have had to look a long time to find a man more barren of ideas than Sir Oswald Mosley. He was as hollow as a jug. Even the elementary fact that Fascism must not offend national sentiment had escaped him. His entire movement was imitated slavishly from abroad, the uniform and the party programme from Italy and the salute from Germany, with the Jew-baiting tacked on as an afterthought, Mosley having actually started his movement with Jews among his most prominent followers. A man of the stamp of Bottomley[17] or Lloyd George could perhaps have brought a real British Fascist movement into existence. But such leaders only appear when the psychological need for them exists.

After twenty years of stagnation and unemployment, the entire English Socialist movement was unable to produce a version of Socialism which the mass of the people could even find desirable. The Labour Party stood for a timid reformism, the Marxists were looking at the modern world through nineteenth-century spectacles. Both ignored agriculture and imperial problems, and both antagonized the middle classes. The suffocating stupidity of left-wing propaganda had frightened away whole classes of necessary people, factory managers, airmen, naval officers, farmers, white-collar workers, shopkeepers, policemen. All of these people had been taught to think of Socialism as something which menaced their livelihood, or as something seditious, alien, 'anti-British' as they would have called it. Only the intellectuals, the least useful section of the middle class, gravitated towards the movement.

A Socialist Party which genuinely wished to achieve anything would have started by facing several facts which to this day are considered unmentionable in left-wing circles. It would have recognized that England is more united than most countries, that the British workers have a great deal to lose besides their chains, and that the differences in outlook and habits between class and class are rapidly diminishing. In general, it would have recognized that the old-fashioned 'proletarian revolution' is an impossibility. But all through the between-war years no Socialist programme that was both revolutionary and workable ever appeared; basically, no doubt, because no one genuinely wanted any major change to happen. The Labour leaders wanted to go on and on, drawing their salaries and periodically swapping jobs with the Conservatives. The Communists wanted to go on and on, suffering a comfortable martyrdom, meeting with endless defeats and afterwards putting the blame on other people. The left-wing intelligentsia wanted to go on and on, sniggering at the Blimps, sapping away at middle-class morale, but still keeping their favoured position as hangers-on of the dividend-drawers. Labour Party politics had become a variant of Conservatism, 'revolutionary' politics had become a game of make-believe.

Now, however, the circumstances have changed, the drowsy years have ended. Being a Socialist no longer means kicking theoretically against a system which in practice you are fairly well satisfied with. This time our predicament is real. It is 'the Philistines be upon thee, Samson'.[18] We have got to make our words take physical shape, or perish. We know very well that with its present social structure England cannot survive, and we have got to make other people see that fact and act upon it. We cannot win the war without introducing Socialism, nor establish Socialism without winning the war. At such a time it is possible, as it was not in the peaceful years, to be both revolutionary and realistic. A Socialist movement which can swing the mass of the people behind it, drive the pro-Fascists out of positions of control, wipe out the grosser injustices and let the working class see that they have something to fight for, win over the middle classes instead of antagonizing them, produce a workable imperial policy instead of a mixture of humbug and Utopianism, bring patriotism and intelligence into partnership – for the first time, a movement of such a kind becomes possible.

II

The fact that we are at war has turned Socialism from a textbook word into a realizable policy.

The inefficiency of private capitalism has been proved all over Europe. Its injustice has been proved in the East End of London. Patriotism, against which the Socialists fought so long, has become a tremendous lever in their hands. People who at any other time would cling like glue to their miserable scraps of privilege, will surrender them fast enough when their country is in danger. War is the greatest of all agents of change. It speeds up all processes, wipes out minor distinctions, brings realities to the surface. Above all, war brings it home to the individual that he is *not* altogether an individual. It is only because they are aware of this that men will die on the field of battle. At this moment it is not so much a question of surrendering life as of surrendering leisure, comfort, economic liberty, social prestige. There are very few people in England who really want to see their country conquered by Germany. If it can be made clear that defeating Hitler means wiping out class privilege, the great mass of middling people, the £6 a week to £2000 a year class, will probably be on our side. These people are quite indispensable, because they include most of the technical experts. Obviously the snobbishness and political ignorance of people like airmen and naval officers will be a very great difficulty. But without those airmen, destroyer commanders, etc., etc., we could not survive for a week. The only approach to them is through their patriotism. An intelligent Socialist movement will *use* their patriotism, instead of merely insulting it, as hitherto.

But do I mean that there will be no opposition? Of course not. It would be childish to expect anything of the kind.

There will be a bitter political struggle, and there will be unconscious and half-conscious sabotage everywhere. At some point or other it may be necessary to use violence. It is easy to imagine a pro-Fascist rebellion breaking out in, for instance, India. We shall have to fight against bribery, ignorance and snobbery. The bankers and the larger businessmen, the landowners and dividend-drawers, the officials with their prehensile bottoms, will obstruct for all they are worth. Even the middle classes will writhe when their accustomed way of life is menaced. But just because the English sense of national unity has never disintegrated, because patriotism is finally stronger than class-hatred, the chances are that the will of the majority will prevail. It is no use imagining that one can make fundamental changes without causing a split in the nation; but the treacherous minority will be far smaller in time of war than it would be at any other time.

The swing of opinion is visibly happening, but it cannot be counted on to happen fast enough of its own accord. This war is a race between the consolidation of Hitler's empire and the growth of democratic consciousness. Everywhere in England you can see a ding-dong battle raging to and fro – in Parliament and in the Government, in the factories and the armed forces, in the pubs and the air-raid shelters, in the newspapers and on the radio. Every day there are tiny defeats, tiny victories. Morrison for Home Security[19] – a few yards forward. Priestley shoved off the air – a few yards back. It is a struggle between the groping and the unteachable, between the young and the old, between the living and the dead. But it is very necessary that the discontent which undoubtedly exists should take a purposeful and not merely obstructive form. It is time for *the people* to define their war-aims. What is wanted is a simple, concrete programme of action, which can be given all possible publicity, and round which public opinion can group itself.

I suggest that the following six-point programme is the kind of thing we need. The first three points deal with England's internal policy, the other three with the Empire and the world: –

I. Nationalization of land, mines, railways, banks and major industries.

II. Limitation of incomes, on such a scale that the highest tax-free income in Britain does not exceed the lowest by more than ten to one.

III. Reform of the educational system along democratic lines.

IV. Immediate Dominion status for India, with power to secede when the war is over.

V. Formation of an Imperial General Council, in which the coloured peoples are to be represented.

VI. Declaration of formal alliance with China, Abyssinia and all other victims of the Fascist powers.

The general tendency of this programme is unmistakable. It aims quite frankly at turning this war into a revolutionary war and England into a Socialist democracy. I have deliberately included in it nothing that the simplest person could not understand and see the reason for. In the form in which I have put it, it could be printed on the front page of the *Daily Mirror*. But for the purposes of this book a certain amount of amplification is needed.

I. *Nationalization*. One can 'nationalize' industry by the stroke of a pen, but the actual process is slow and complicated. What is needed is that the ownership of all major industry shall be formally vested in the State, representing the common people. Once that is done it becomes possible to eliminate the class of mere *owners* who live not by virtue of anything they produce but by the possession of title-deeds and share-certificates. State ownership implies, therefore, that nobody shall live without working. How sudden a change in the conduct of industry it implies is less certain. In a country like England we cannot rip down the whole structure and build again from the bottom, least of all in time of war. Inevitably the majority of industrial concerns will continue with much the same personnel as before, the one-time owners or managing directors carrying on with their jobs as State-employees. There is reason to think that many of the smaller capitalists would actually welcome some such arrangement. The resistance will come from the big capitalists, the bankers, the landlords and the idle rich, roughly speaking the class with over £2000 a year – and even if one counts in all their dependants there are not more than half a million of these people in England. Nationalization of agricultural land implies cutting out the landlord and the tithe-drawer, but not necessarily interfering with the farmer. It is difficult to imagine any reorganization of English agriculture that would not retain most of the existing farms as units, at any rate at the beginning. The farmer, when he is competent, will continue as a salaried manager. He is virtually that already, with the added disadvantage of having to make a profit and being permanently in debt to the bank. With certain kinds of petty trading, and even the small-scale ownership of land, the State will probably not interfere at all. It would be a great mistake to start by victimizing the smallholder class, for instance. These people are necessary, on the whole they are competent, and the amount of work they do depends on the feeling that they are 'their own masters'. But the State will certainly impose an upward limit to the ownership of land (probably fifteen acres at the very most), and will never permit any ownership of land in town areas.

From the moment that all productive goods have been declared the property of the State, the common people will feel, as they cannot feel now, that the State *is themselves*. They will be ready then to endure the sacrifices that are ahead of us, war or no war. And even if the face of England hardly seems to change, on the day that our main industries are formally nationalized the dominance of a single class will have been broken. From then onwards the emphasis will be shifted from ownership to management, from privilege to competence. It is quite possible that State-ownership will in itself bring about less social change than will be forced upon us by the common hardships of war. But it is the necessary first step without which any *real* reconstruction is impossible.

II. *Incomes.* Limitation of incomes implies the fixing of a minimum wage, which implies a managed internal currency based simply on the amount of consumption-goods available. And this again implies a stricter rationing-scheme than is now in operation. It is no use at this stage of the world's history to suggest that all human beings should have *exactly* equal incomes. It has been shown over and over again that without some kind of money reward there is no incentive to undertake certain jobs. On the other hand the money reward need not be very large. In practice it is impossible that earnings should be limited quite as rigidly as I have suggested. There will always be anomalies and evasions. But there is no reason why ten to one should not be the maximum normal variation. And within those limits some sense of equality is possible. A man with £3 a week and a man with £1500 a year can feel themselves fellow-creatures, which the Duke of Westminster[20] and the sleepers on the Embankment benches cannot.

III. *Education.* In wartime, educational reform must necessarily be promise rather than performance. At the moment we are not in a position to raise the school-leaving age or increase the teaching staffs of the Elementary Schools. But there are certain immediate steps that we could take towards a democratic educational system. We could start by abolishing the autonomy of the public schools and the older universities and flooding them with State-aided pupils chosen simply on grounds of ability. At present, public-school education is partly a training in class prejudice and partly a sort of tax that the middle classes pay to the upper class in return for the right to enter certain professions. It is true that that state of affairs is altering. The middle classes have begun to rebel against the expensiveness of education, and the war will bankrupt the majority of the public schools if it continues for another year or two. The evacuation is also producing certain minor changes. But there is a danger that some of the older schools, which will be able to weather the financial storm longest, will survive in some form or another as festering centres of snobbery. As for the 10,000 'private' schools that England possesses, the vast majority of them deserve nothing except suppression. They are simply commercial undertakings, and in many cases their educational level is actually lower than that of the Elementary Schools. They merely exist because of a widespread idea that there is something disgraceful in being educated by the public authorities. The State could quell this idea by declaring itself responsible for *all* education, even if at the start this were no more than a gesture. We need gestures, as well as actions. It is all too obvious that our talk of 'defending democracy' is nonsense while it is a mere accident of birth that decides whether a gifted child shall or shall not get the education it deserves.

IV. *India.* What we must offer India is not 'freedom', which, as I have said earlier, is impossible, but alliance, partnership – in a word, equality. But we must also tell the Indians that they are free to secede, if they want to. Without that there can be no equality of partnership, and our claim to be defending the coloured peoples against Fascism will never be believed. But it is a mistake to imagine that if the Indians were free to cut themselves adrift they would immediately do so. When a British government *offers* them unconditional independence, they will refuse it. For as soon as they have the power to secede the chief reasons for doing so will have disappeared.

A complete severance of the two countries would be a disaster for India no less than for England. Intelligent Indians know this. As things are at present, India not only cannot defend itself, it is hardly even capable of feeding itself. The whole administration of the country depends on a framework of experts (engineers, forest officers, railwaymen, soldiers, doctors) who are predominantly English and could not be replaced within five or ten years. Moreover, English is the chief lingua franca and nearly the whole of the Indian intelligentsia is deeply anglicized. Any transference to foreign rule – for if the British marched out of India the Japanese and other powers would immediately march in – would mean an immense dislocation. Neither the Japanese, the Russians, the Germans nor the Italians would be capable of administering India even at the low level of efficiency that is attained by the British. They do not possess the necessary supplies of technical experts or the knowledge of languages and local conditions, and they probably could not win the confidence of indispensable go-betweens such as the Eurasians. If India were simply 'liberated', i.e. deprived of British military protection, the first result would be a fresh foreign conquest, and the second a series of enormous famines which would kill millions of people within a few years.

What India needs is the power to work out its own constitution without British interference, but in some kind of partnership that ensures it military protection and technical advice. This is unthinkable until there is a Socialist government in England. For at least eighty years England has artificially prevented the development of India, partly from fear of trade competition if Indian industries were too highly developed, partly because backward peoples are more easily governed than civilized ones. It is a commonplace that the average Indian suffers far more from his own countrymen than from the British. The petty Indian capitalist exploits the town worker with the utmost ruthlessness, the peasant lives from birth to death in the grip of the moneylender. But all this is an indirect result of the British rule, which aims half-consciously at keeping India as backward as possible. The classes most loyal to Britain are the princes, the landowners and the business community – in general, the reactionary classes who are doing fairly well out of the *status quo*. The moment that England ceased to stand towards India in the relation of an exploiter, the balance of forces would be altered. No need then for the British to flatter the ridiculous Indian princes, with their gilded elephants and cardboard armies, to prevent the growth of the Indian Trade Unions, to play off Moslem against Hindu, to protect the worthless life of the moneylender, to receive the salaams of toadying minor officials, to prefer the half-barbarous Gurkha to the educated Bengali. Once check that stream of dividends that flows from the bodies of Indian coolies to the banking accounts of old ladies in Cheltenham, and the whole sahib-native nexus, with its haughty ignorance on one side and envy and servility on the other, can come to an end. Englishmen and Indians can work side by side for the development of India, and for the training of Indians in all the arts which, so far, they have been systematically prevented from learning. How many of the existing British personnel in India, commercial or official, would fall in with such an arrangement – which would mean ceasing once and for all to be 'sahibs' – is a different question. But, broadly speaking, more is to be hoped from the younger men and from those officials (civil engineers, forestry and agricultural experts, doctors, educationists) who have been scientifically educated. The higher officials, the provincial governors, commissioners, judges, etc., are hopeless; but they are also the most easily replaceable.

That, roughly, is what would be meant by Dominion status if it were offered to India by a Socialist government. It is an offer of partnership on equal terms until such time as the world has ceased to be ruled by bombing planes. But we must add to it the unconditional right to secede. It is the only way of proving that we mean what we say. And what applies to India applies, *mutatis mutandis*, to Burma, Malaya and most of our African possessions.

V and VI explain themselves. They are the necessary preliminary to any claim that we are fighting this war for the protection of peaceful peoples against Fascist aggression.

Is it impossibly hopeful to think that such a policy as this could get a following in England? A year ago, even six months ago, it would have been, but not now. Moreover – and this is the peculiar opportunity of this moment – it could be given the necessary publicity. There is now a considerable weekly press, with a circulation of millions, which would be ready to popularize – if not *exactly* the programme I have sketched above, at any rate *some* policy along those lines. There are even three or four daily papers which would be prepared to give it a sympathetic hearing. That is the distance we have travelled in the last six months.

But is such a policy realizable? That depends entirely on ourselves.

Some of the points I have suggested are of the kind that could be carried out immediately, others would take years or decades and even then would not be perfectly achieved. No political programme is ever carried out in its entirety. But what matters is that that or something like it should be our declared policy. It is always the *direction* that counts. It is of course quite hopeless to expect the present government to pledge itself to any policy that implies turning this war into a revolutionary war. It is at best a government of compromise, with Churchill riding two horses like a circus acrobat. Before such measures as limitation of incomes become even thinkable, there will have to be a complete shift of power away from the old ruling class. If during this winter the war settles into another stagnant period, we ought in my opinion to agitate for a General Election, a thing which the Tory Party machine will make frantic efforts to prevent. But even without an election we can get the government we want, provided that we want it urgently enough. A real shove from below will accomplish it. As to who will be in that government when it comes, I make no guess. I only know that the right men will be there when the people really want them, for it is movements that make leaders and not leaders movements.

Within a year, perhaps even within six months, if we are still unconquered, we shall see the rise of something that has never existed before, a specifically *English* Socialist movement. Hitherto there has been only the Labour Party, which was the creation of the working class but did not aim at any fundamental change, and Marxism, which was a German theory interpreted by Russians and unsuccessfully transplanted to England. There was nothing that really touched the heart of the English people. Throughout its entire history the English Socialist movement has never produced a song with a catchy tune – nothing like *La Marseillaise* or *La Cucuracha*, for instance. When a Socialist movement native to England appears, the Marxists, like all others with a vested interest in the past, will be its bitter enemies. Inevitably they will denounce it as 'Fascism'. Already it is customary among the more soft-boiled intellectuals of the Left to declare that if we fight against the Nazis we shall 'go Nazi' ourselves. They might almost equally well say that if we fight against Negroes we shall turn black. To 'go Nazi' we should have to have the history of Germany behind us. Nations do not escape from their past merely by making a revolution. An English Socialist government will transform the nation from top to bottom, but it will still bear all over it the unmistakable marks of our own civilization, the peculiar civilization which I discussed earlier in this book.

It will not be doctrinaire, nor even logical. It will abolish the House of Lords, but quite probably will not abolish the Monarchy. It will leave anachronisms and loose ends everywhere, the judge in his ridiculous horsehair wig and the lion and the unicorn on the soldier's cap-buttons. It will not set up any explicit class dictatorship. It will group itself round the old Labour Party and its mass following will be in the Trade Unions, but it will draw into it most of the middle class and many of the younger sons of the bourgeoisie. Most of its directing brains will come from the new indeterminate class of skilled workers, technical experts, airmen, scientists, architects and journalists, the people who feel at home in the radio and ferro-concrete age. But it will never lose touch with the tradition of compromise and the belief in a law that is above the State. It will shoot traitors, but it will give them a solemn trial beforehand, and occasionally it will acquit them. It will crush any open revolt promptly and cruelly, but it will interfere very little with the spoken and written word. Political parties with different names will still exist, revolutionary sects will still be publishing their newspapers and making as little impression as ever. It will disestablish the Church, but will not persecute religion. It will retain a vague reverence for the Christian moral code, and from time to time will refer to England as 'a Christian country'. The Catholic Church will war against it, but the Nonconformist sects and the bulk of the Anglican Church will be able to come to terms with it. It will show a power of assimilating the past which will shock foreign observers and sometimes make them doubt whether any revolution has happened.

But all the same it will have done the essential thing. It will have nationalized industry, scaled down incomes, set up a classless educational system. Its real nature will be apparent from the hatred which the surviving rich men of the world will feel for it. It will aim not at disintegrating the Empire but at turning it into a federation of Socialist states, freed not so much from the British flag as from the moneylender, the dividend-drawer and the wooden-headed British official. Its war-strategy will be totally different from that of any property-ruled state, because it will not be afraid of the revolutionary after-effects when any existing régime is brought down. It will not have the smallest scruple about attacking hostile neutrals or stirring up native rebellions in enemy colonies. It will fight in such a way that even if it is beaten its memory will be dangerous to the victor, as the memory of the French Revolution was dangerous to Metternich's Europe. The dictators will fear it as they could not fear the existing British régime, even if its military strength were ten times what it is.

But at this moment, when the drowsy life of England has barely altered, and the offensive contrast of wealth and poverty still exists everywhere, even amid the bombs, why do I dare to say that all these things 'will' happen?

Because the time has come when one can predict the future in terms of an 'either–or'. Either we turn this war into a revolutionary war (I do not say that our policy will be *exactly* what I have indicated above – merely that it will be along those general lines) or we lose it, and much more besides. Quite soon it will be possible to say definitely that our feet are set upon one path or the other. But at any rate it is certain that with our present social structure we cannot win. Our real forces, physical, moral or intellectual, cannot be mobilized.

III

Patriotism has nothing to do with Conservatism. It is actually the opposite of Conservatism, since it is a devotion to something that is always changing and yet is felt to be mystically the same. It is the bridge between the future and the past. No real revolutionary has ever been an internationalist.

During the past twenty years the negative, *fainéant* outlook which has been fashionable among English left-wingers, the sniggering of the intellectuals at patriotism and physical courage, the persistent effort to chip away English morale and spread a hedonistic, what-do-I-get-out-of-it attitude to life, has done nothing but harm. It would have been harmful even if we had been living in the squashy League of Nations universe that these people imagined. In an age of Führers and bombing planes it was a disaster. However little we may like it, toughness is the price of survival. A nation trained to think hedonistically cannot survive amid peoples who work like slaves and breed like rabbits, and whose chief national industry is war. English Socialists of nearly all colours have wanted to make a stand against Fascism, but at the same time they have aimed at making their own countrymen unwarlike. They have failed, because in England traditional loyalties are stronger than new ones. But in spite of all the 'anti-Fascist' heroics of the left-wing press, what chance should we have stood when the real struggle with Fascism came, if the average Englishman had been the kind of creature that the *New Statesman*, the *Daily Worker* or even the *News Chronicle* wished to make him?

Up to 1935 virtually all English left-wingers were vaguely pacifist. After 1935 the more vocal of them flung themselves eagerly into the Popular Front movement, which was simply an evasion of the whole problem posed by Fascism. It set out to be 'anti-Fascist' in a purely negative way – 'against' Fascism without being 'for' any discoverable policy – and underneath it lay the flabby idea that when the time came the Russians would do our fighting for us. It is astonishing how this illusion fails to die. Every week sees its spate of letters to the press, pointing out that if we had a government with no Tories in it the Russians could hardly avoid coming round to our side. Or we are to publish high-sounding war-aims (*vide* books like *Unser Kampf, A Hundred Million Allies – If We Choose*,[21] etc.), whereupon the European populations will infallibly rise on our behalf. It is the same idea all the time – look abroad for your inspiration, get someone else to do your fighting for you. Underneath it lies the frightful inferiority complex of the English intellectual, the belief that the English are no longer a martial race, no longer capable of enduring.

In truth there is no reason to think that anyone will do our fighting for us yet awhile, except the Chinese, who have been doing it for three years already.* The Russians may be driven to fight on our side by the fact of a direct attack, but they have made it clear enough that they will not stand up to the German army if there is any way of avoiding it. In any case they are not likely to be attracted by the spectacle of a left-wing government in England. The present Russian régime must almost certainly be hostile to any revolution in the West. The subject peoples of Europe will rebel when Hitler begins to totter, but not earlier. Our potential allies are not the Europeans but on the one hand the Americans, who will need a year to mobilize their resources even if Big Business can be brought to

* Written before the outbreak of the war in Greece [Orwell's note].[22]

heel, and on the other hand the coloured peoples, who cannot be even sentimentally on our side till our own revolution has started. For a long time, a year, two years, possibly three years, England has got to be the shock-absorber of the world. We have got to face bombing, hunger, overwork, influenza, boredom and treacherous peace offers. Manifestly it is a time to stiffen morale, not to weaken it. Instead of taking the mechanically anti-British attitude which is usual on the Left, it is better to consider what the world would really be like if the English-speaking culture perished. For it is childish to suppose that the other English-speaking countries, even the U.S.A., will be unaffected if Britain is conquered.

Lord Halifax, and all his tribe, believe that when the war is over things will be exactly as they were before. Back to the crazy pavement of Versailles,[23] back to 'democracy', i.e. capitalism, back to the dole-queues and the Rolls-Royce cars, back to the grey top hats and the sponge-bag trousers, *in saecula saeculorum.*[24] It is of course obvious that nothing of the kind is going to happen. A feeble imitation of it might just possibly happen in the case of a negotiated peace, but only for a short while. *Laissez-faire* capitalism is dead.* The choice lies between the kind of collective society that Hitler will set up and the kind that can arise if he is defeated.

If Hitler wins this war he will consolidate his rule over Europe, Africa and the Middle East, and if his armies have not been too greatly exhausted beforehand, he will wrench vast territories from Soviet Russia. He will set up a graded caste-society in which the German *Herrenvolk* ('master race' or 'aristocratic race') will rule over Slavs and other lesser peoples whose job will be to produce low-priced agricultural products. He will reduce the coloured peoples once and for all to outright slavery. The real quarrel of the Fascist powers with British imperialism is that they know that it is disintegrating. Another twenty years along the present line of development, and India will be a peasant republic linked with England only by voluntary alliance. The 'semi-apes' of whom Hitler

---

* It is interesting to notice that Mr. Kennedy, U.S.A. Ambassador in London,[25] remarked on his return to New York in October, 1940, that as a result of the war, 'democracy is finished'. By 'democracy', of course, he meant private capitalism [Orwell's footnote].

speaks with such loathing will be flying aeroplanes and manufacturing machine guns. The Fascist dream of a slave empire will be at an end. On the other hand, if we are defeated we simply hand over our own victims to new masters who come fresh to the job and have not developed any scruples.

But more is involved than the fate of the coloured peoples. Two incompatible visions of life are fighting one another. 'Between democracy and totalitarianism', says Mussolini, 'there can be no compromise.' The two creeds cannot even, for any length of time, live side by side. So long as democracy exists, even in its very imperfect English form, totalitarianism is in deadly danger. The whole English-speaking world is haunted by the idea of human equality, and though it would be simply a lie to say that either we or the Americans have ever acted up to our professions, still, the *idea* is there, and it is capable of one day becoming a reality. From the English-speaking culture, if it does not perish, a society of free and equal human beings will ultimately arise. But it is precisely the idea of human equality – the 'Jewish' or 'Judaeo-Christian' idea of equality – that Hitler came into the world to destroy. He has, heaven knows, said so often enough. The thought of a world in which black men would be as good as white men and Jews treated as human beings brings him the same horror and despair as the thought of endless slavery brings to us.

It is important to keep in mind how irreconcilable these two viewpoints are. Some time within the next year a pro-Hitler reaction within the left-wing intelligentsia is likely enough. There are premonitory signs of it already. Hitler's positive achievement appeals to the emptiness of these people, and, in the case of those with pacifist leanings, to their masochism. One knows in advance more or less what they will say. They will start by refusing to admit that British capitalism is evolving into something different, or that the defeat of Hitler can mean any more than a victory for the British and American millionaires. And from that they will proceed to argue that, after all, democracy is 'just the same as' or 'just as bad as' totalitarianism. There is *not much* freedom of speech in England; therefore there is *no more* than exists in Germany. To be on the dole is a horrible experience; therefore it is *no worse* to be in the torture-chambers of the Gestapo. In general, two blacks make a white, half a loaf is the same as no bread.

But in reality, whatever may be true about democracy and totalitarianism, it is not true that they are the same. It would not be true, even if British democracy were incapable of evolving beyond its present stage. The whole conception of the militarized continental state, with its secret police, its censored literature and its conscript labour, is utterly different from that of the loose maritime democracy, with its slums and unemployment, its strikes and party politics. It is the difference between land power and sea power, between cruelty and inefficiency, between lying and self-deception, between the S.S.-man[26] and the rent-collector. And in choosing between them one chooses not so much on the strength of what they now are as of what they are capable of becoming. But in a sense it is irrelevant whether democracy, at its highest or at its lowest, is 'better' than totalitarianism. To decide that one would have to have access to absolute standards. The only question that matters is where one's real sympathies will lie when the pinch comes. The intellectuals who are so fond of balancing democracy against totalitarianism and 'proving' that one is as bad as the other are simply frivolous people who have never been shoved up against realities. They show the same shallow misunderstanding of Fascism now, when they are beginning to flirt with it, as a year or two ago, when they were squealing against it. The question is not, 'Can you make out a debating-society "case" in favour of Hitler?' The question is, 'Do you genuinely accept that case? Are you willing to submit to Hitler's rule? Do you want to see England conquered, or don't you?' It would be better to be sure on that point before frivolously siding with the enemy. For there is no such thing as neutrality in war; in practice one must help one side or the other.

When the pinch comes, no one bred in the Western tradition can accept the Fascist vision of life. It is important to realize that *now*, and to grasp what it entails. With all its sloth, hypocrisy and injustice, the English-speaking civilization is the only large obstacle in Hitler's path. It is a living contradiction of all the 'infallible' dogmas of Fascism. That is why all Fascist writers for years past have agreed that England's power must be destroyed. England must be 'exterminated', must be 'annihilated', must 'cease to exist'. Strategically it would be possible for this war to end with Hitler in secure possession of Europe, and with the British Empire intact and British sea-power barely affected. But ideologically it is not possible; were Hitler to make an offer along those lines, it could only be treacherously, with a view to conquering England indirectly or renewing the attack at some more favourable moment. England cannot possibly be allowed to remain as a sort of funnel through which deadly ideas from beyond the Atlantic flow into the police-states of Europe. And turning it round to our own point of view, we see the vastness of the issue before us, the all-importance of preserving our democracy more or less as we have known it. But to *preserve* is always to *extend*. The choice before us is not so much between victory and defeat as between revolution and apathy. If the thing we are fighting for is altogether destroyed, it will have been destroyed partly by our own act.

It could happen that England should introduce the beginnings of Socialism, turn this war into a revolutionary war, and still be defeated. That is at any rate thinkable. But, terrible as it would be for anyone who is now adult, it would be far less deadly than the 'compromise peace' which a few rich men and their hired liars are hoping for. The final ruin of England could only be accomplished by an English government acting under orders from Berlin. But that cannot happen if England has awakened beforehand. For in that case the defeat would be unmistakable, the struggle would continue, the *idea* would survive. The difference between going down fighting, and surrendering without a fight, is by no means a question of 'honour' and schoolboy heroics. Hitler said once that to *accept* defeat destroys the soul of a nation. This sounds like a piece of claptrap, but it is strictly true. The defeat of 1870 did not lessen the world-influence of France. The Third Republic had more influence, intellectually, than the France of Napoleon III. But the sort of peace that Pétain, Laval & Co.[27] have accepted can only be purchased by deliberately wiping out the national culture. The Vichy government will enjoy a spurious independence only on condition that it destroys the distinctive marks of French culture: republicanism, secularism, respect for the intellect, absence of colour prejudice. We cannot be *utterly* defeated if we have made our revolution beforehand. We may see German troops marching down Whitehall, but another process, ultimately deadly to the German power-dream, will have been started. The Spanish people were defeated, but the things they learned during those two and a half memorable years will one day come back upon the Spanish Fascists like a boomerang.

A piece of Shakespearean bombast was much quoted at the beginning of the war. Even Mr. Chamberlain quoted it once, if my memory does not deceive me:

> Come the three corners of the world in arms
> And we shall shock them. Naught shall make us rue
> If England to herself do rest but true.[28]

It is right enough, if you interpret it rightly. But England has got to be true to herself. She is not being true to herself while the refugees who have sought our shores are penned up in concentration camps, and company directors work out subtle schemes to dodge their Excess Profits Tax.[29] It is good-bye to the *Tatler* and the *Bystander*, and farewell to the lady in the Rolls-Royce car. The heirs of Nelson and of Cromwell are not in the House of Lords. They are in the fields and the streets, in the factories and the armed forces, in the four-ale bar[30] and the suburban back garden; and at present they are still kept under by a generation of ghosts. Compared with the task of bringing the real England to the surface, even the winning of the war, necessary though it is, is secondary. By revolution we become more ourselves, not less. There is no question of stopping short, striking a compromise, salvaging 'democracy', standing still. Nothing ever stands still. We must add to our heritage or lose it, we must grow greater or grow less, we must go forward or go backward. I believe in England, and I believe that we shall go forward.

THE END[31]

1. Fredric Warburg (1898–1980) joined Martin Secker in 1936 to form Martin Secker & Warburg, becoming Orwell's second (and continuing) publisher. He served as an officer on the Somme in the First World War and as a Corporal in Orwell's Home Guard platoon in the Second World War. He, and his wife, Pamela, were very good to Orwell, especially in his final illness. See also n. 1 to 'Publication of *Animal Farm*', below. Tosco Fyvel (1907–85) was Jewish and an active Zionist. He was to work with Golda Meir, Prime Minister of Israel, 1969–74. Although Orwell did not agree with Zionism (because it was a form of nationalism), he and Fyvel remained close friends. See Fyvel's *George Orwell: A Personal Memoir* (1982).

2. Orwell refers to the successful German advance through Belgium in 1940, leading to Dunkirk, and the German invasion of Norway, also in 1940, and the British withdrawal (see p. 92, n. 16, above).

3. When *The Lion and the Unicorn* was published, Germany and the USSR were allies; only the United Kingdom opposed Germany in Europe. Orwell expected Germany to attack

Russia but that assault did not start for another four months (22 June 1941). On 12 July 1941, an Anglo-Soviet pact was signed.

4. See p. 31 above, n. 2.

5. Right-wing papers owned by Lord Beaverbrook (1879–1964). These included the *Daily Express*, *Sunday Express* and London *Evening Standard*. Beaverbrook, a Canadian, formerly Max Aitken, was for a time a successful, if controversial, Minister of Aircraft Production.

6. Viscount Rothermere (1868–1940), with his brother, Alfred Harmsworth (later Lord Northcliffe), built up a newspaper empire that included the *Daily Mail*, *Daily Mirror*, *Sunday Pictorial* and London *Evening News*. Although he advocated rearmament, he was for a time sympathetic to Hitler and Mussolini.

7. Ian Hay (John Hay Beith, 1876–1952), novelist and dramatist. He wrote such successful plays as *A Safety Match* (1911), *The Middle Watch* (1931) and *The Housemaster* (1936), histories of World War I. Hilaire Belloc (1870–1953), essayist, novelist, historian and writer of comic verse. He was a military commentator in both World Wars. He was an active propagandist for Roman Catholicism and was a Liberal MP, 1906–10. André Maurois (1885–1967) was a French writer popular in English translation. His *Ariel, or the Life of Shelley* was the first Penguin book. Among his other works were *Aspects of Biography* and *A History of England*. Charles Bruce Bairnsfather (1888–1959), cartoonist, was the creator of Old Bill, an indomitable Cockney soldier of World War I. His most famous cartoon, showing two soldiers in a shell-hole during a heavy barrage, with the caption 'Well, if you knows of a better 'ole, go to it', was published in *The Bystander*, 24 November 1915. From 1942 to 1944 he was an official cartoonist for the United States Army in Europe.

8. Ernest Bevin (1881–1951), trade union leader, was instrumental in the amalgamation of fourteen unions to form the Transport and General Workers' Union in 1922. He grasped the need for popular communication – hence his role in converting the *Daily Herald* from a Labour Party mouthpiece to a reasonably effective and successful popular newspaper. He was vigorously opposed to pacifism and early recognized the dangers of Nazism. A member of the War Cabinet from October 1940, he served as Minister of Labour and National Service, 1940–45, and Foreign Minister, 1945–50. Much credit for the establishment of NATO falls to him. He steadfastly refused honours.

9. Lord Halifax (1881–1959), Edward Frederick Lindley Wood (Lord Irwin, 1925; 3rd Viscount Halifax, 1934; Earl of Halifax, 1944), was a Conservative politician; Viceroy of India, 1926–31; Foreign Secretary, 1938–40. Although some leaders of the Labour Party preferred Halifax to Churchill as Chamberlain's successor, the question was not formally put to the party and the matter was resolved by Halifax himself. He thought it would be difficult for him to discharge his duties as prime minister because, as a peer, he served in the House of Lords and could not directly respond to members of the House of Commons.

10. See p. 80 above, n. 2. Chamberlain fell on May 8, Paris on June 14.

11. The last two lines of W. H. Auden's 'Spain', 1937 (revd edn, *Another Time*, June 1940). Orwell quoted it incorrectly: 'History to the defeated / May say Alas! but cannot alter or pardon.'

12. The phrase 'the Fifth Column' has a closer, more specific significance for Orwell than it has now in its generalized, uncapitalized use. General Emilio Mola (1887–1937), commander of Franco's northern army, said, in a broadcast in 1936, that while four columns of Franco's Nationalists were advancing on Madrid, there was within the city a Fifth Column working secretly to undermine its defences. For a note on his nightly broadcasts, see Thomas, 283–4.

adopted by the cartoonist, David Low, for over-large, choleric, bumbling, very traditional, senior Army officers resistant to change. The character is featured (not unsympathetically) in Michael Powell and Emeric Pressburger's fine film, *The Life and Death of Colonel Blimp* (1943).

14. Sir Oswald Mosley, Bt. (1896–1980), politician, successively Conservative, Independent and Labour MP. In 1931 he broke away from the Labour Party to form the New Party. He became a fanatical supporter of Hitler and his party became the British Union of Fascists, the uniformed members of which were known as Blackshirts. He was interned during the war.

15. See Matthew 5, especially verses 3–14. Orwell may have had particularly in mind verse 5: 'Blessed are the meek: for they [not millionaires] shall inherit the earth', and verse 13: 'Ye are the salt of the earth: but if the salt have lost his savour, wherewith shall it be salted?' Orwell knew well the Bible and the Book of Common Prayer.

16. *Picture Post*, founded by Edward Hulton, 1 October 1938, ran until 1 June 1957. Its marriage of illustrations, captions and text, coupled with its social and political concerns, especially in its early days, showed how effectively popular interest could be aroused. *Cavalcade* here is a news magazine, first published in February 1936. The *Evening Standard*, first published in 1827, is the sole surviving London evening newspaper. It was part of the Beaverbrook press empire; see n. 5 above. J. B. Priestley (1894–1984) was a prolific and popular novelist, dramatist and man of letters. His plays, especially the 'Time' plays, still draw large audiences. He was active in working for a democratic and egalitarian society, for example through his play *They Came to a City* (1943), which, though now seeming stilted, at the time effectively dramatized hope for a better society after the war. In 1940 he gave a series of morale-boosting broadcasts, urging the nation to unite to fight Hitler, but these were regarded as 'by implication Socialist propaganda' (Orwell's words) and he was 'shoved off the air, evidently at the insistence of the Conservative party' (War-time Diary, 21 October 1940, XII/*698*; and see p. 122, above).

17. Horatio Bottomley (1860–1933), politician, swindler and entrepreneur. He founded, and initially edited, a popular weekly, *John Bull*, in 1906, specializing in sensationalism and competitions for relatively large prizes. Publication ceased in 1960. During World War I he described himself as 'The Soldier's Friend', and he campaigned for Ramsay MacDonald (later to be Labour Prime Minister) to be imprisoned, but it was Bottomley who was imprisoned, for fraud.

18. When Delilah (of whom Samson, champion of the Israelites, was enamoured) had deceived him into allowing her to bind him and, eventually, cutting off his hair, so that she might be paid for delivering him to the Philistines, she called out, 'The Philistines be upon thee, Samson' (Judges 16:9, 12, 14 and 20). Matthew Arnold adapted Philistine from a German word (*Philister*, for someone not of the university) to stand for 'the enemy of the children of light or servants of the idea'. He applied it to the middle class, devoted as it was to a 'dismal and illiberal life', and to aristocrats, for whom 'worldly splendour, security, power and pleasure' are 'irresistible charms'. See Ch. 3 of his *Culture and Anarchy*, 'Barbarians, Philistines, Populace' (1869 and 1875).

19. Herbert Morrison (1888–1965; Baron Morrison of Lambeth), Labour MP from 1923, was leader of the London County Council, 1933–40; Home Secretary and Minister of Home

Security, 1940–45. He joined the War Cabinet in 1942. He was Leader of the House of Commons and Deputy Prime Minister in Attlee's two administrations, 1945–51.

20. The 5th Duke of Westminster (1910–79), in contrast to the propertyless sleepers on the Embankment benches, owned a very valuable portion of London. He served in the Royal Artillery, 1939–45.

21. *Unser Kampf* by Sir Richard Acland was a Penguin Special published in February 1940. *A Hundred Million Allies – If We Choose* has not been traced.

22. The Italians had invaded on 28 October 1940 but had been ignominiously driven back by the Greeks.

23. Orwell probably refers to the patchwork of new nations created by the Treaty of Versailles (1919) and the consequent redrawing of Europe's national boundaries.

24. *in saecula saeculorum*: from one generation unto another – for ever (Latin).

25. Joseph Kennedy (1888–1969), US businessman, born in Boston, Mass.; American Ambassador in London, 1938–40. Father of President John Kennedy and of Robert Kennedy (assassinated 1963 and 1968 respectively).

26. A member of the *Schutzstaffel*, an élite Nazi guard detachment, which included the Waffen SS and the Death's Head units, and which had a thoroughly evil reputation; the latter provided guards for death and concentration camps.

27. Henri Philippe Pétain (1856–1951), successful defender of Verdun in 1916, which led to his becoming a national hero; created Marshal of France in 1918. He became Premier in 1940 and presided over the defeat and dismemberment of France by the Germans. From Vichy (hence 'the Vichy Government') he led the government of unoccupied France until the end of the war. He was tried for collaboration with the Nazis and sentenced to death. President de Gaulle commuted his sentence to solitary confinement for life. Pierre Laval (1883–1945) served variously as French Minister of Public Works, Justice, Labour, Colonies and Foreign Affairs, and as Prime Minister, 1931–2, 1935–6. He left the Socialist Party in 1920 and moved to the extreme right. On 7 January 1935, as Foreign Minister, he signed an agreement with Mussolini backing Italian claims to Abyssinia (Ethiopia). After the Fall of France he became a prominent member of the Vichy government and provided French labour for work in German war production. His name became synonymous with treacherous collaboration. After the war, he tried to commit suicide but was tried and executed.

28. Last three lines of Shakespeare's *King John*. Orwell had 'Come the four corners of the world' – a common error. Shakespeare, taking England to be one corner, has 'three corners', as given in this edition.

29. A wartime tax designed to limit profiteering.

30. The term derives from a public house where, long ago, beer was sold at four old pence a quart (less than one new penny a pint).

31. As so often, Orwell's longer works, in print and typescript, conclude with THE END, even books of essays and *Inside the Whale* (1940). This was not a mere printer's or publisher's convention; indeed, though the typescript of *Animal Farm* concluded with THE END, it was, until the *Complete Works* edition, omitted by English and US publishers, and hence from translations.

[787]

Extract from London Letter [Support for Labour leaders; preservation of democracy in wartime], 15 April 1941
Partisan Review, *July–August 1941*

> *The editors of* Partisan Review *wrote to Orwell on 15 March 1941 telling*
> *him they had liked his first Letter (3 January 1941) very much, even though*
> *'Most of us didn't agree with your political line'. They sent him ten questions,*
> *all of which he answered, with a postscript dated 15 May. That referred to*
> *the British defeats in North Africa and Greece, the worsening situation in*
> *the Middle East, 'Stalin evidently preparing to go into closer partnership*
> *with Hitler', and, within the last two days, the mysterious arrival of Hess*
> *'which caused much amusement and speculation'.*[1] *Orwell's answers to two*
> *questions are directly relevant to* The Lion and the Unicorn; *for Bevin*
> *and Morrison, see pp. 137 and 138 and notes 8 and 19 above. For the whole*
> *Letter, see* XII/787.

6. Would you say that Bevin and Morrison still command the support of the British
working class? Are there any other Labour Party politicians who have taken on
new dimensions in the course of the war – assuming those two have? Is the shop
steward movement still growing?

I know very little of industrial matters. I should say that Bevin does
command working-class support and Morrison probably not. There is a
widespread feeling that the Labour Party as a whole has simply abdicated.
The only other Labour man whose reputation has grown is Cripps.[2] If
Churchill should go, Cripps and Bevin are tipped as the likeliest men for
the premiership, with Bevin evidently favourite.

7. How do you explain what, over here, seems to be the remarkable amount of
democracy and civil liberties preserved during the war? Labour pressure? British
tradition? Weakness of the upper classes?

'British tradition' is a vague phrase, but I think it is the nearest answer.
I suppose I shall seem to be giving myself a free advert., but may I draw
attention to a recent book of mine, *The Lion and the Unicorn* (I believe
copies have reached the U.S.A.)? In it I pointed out that there is in England
a certain feeling of family loyalty which cuts across the class system (also
makes it easier for the class system to survive, I am afraid) and checks the

growth of political hatred. There *could*, I suppose, be a civil war in England, but I have never met any English person able to imagine one. At the same time one ought not to overrate the amount of freedom of the intellect existing here. The position is that in England there is a great respect for freedom of speech but very little for freedom of the press. During the past twenty years there has been much tampering, direct and indirect, with the freedom of the press, and this has never raised a flicker of popular protest. This is a lowbrow country and it is felt that the printed word doesn't matter greatly and that writers and such people don't deserve much sympathy. On the other hand the sort of atmosphere in which you daren't talk politics for fear that the Gestapo may be listening isn't thinkable in England. Any attempt to produce it would be broken not so much by conscious resistance as by the inability of ordinary people to grasp what was wanted of them. With the working classes, in particular, grumbling is so habitual that they don't know when they are grumbling. Where unemployment can be used as a screw, men are often afraid of expressing 'red' opinions which might get round to the overseer or the boss, but hardly anyone would bother, for instance, about being overheard by a policeman. I believe that an organisation now exists for political espionage in factories, pubs, etc., and of course in the army, but I doubt whether it can do more than report on the state of public opinion and occasionally victimise some individual held to be dangerous. A foolish law was passed some time back making it a punishable offence to say anything 'likely to cause alarm and despondency' (or words to that effect). There have been prosecutions under it, a few score I should say, but it is practically a dead letter and probably the majority of people don't know of its existence. You can hardly go into a pub or railway carriage without hearing it technically infringed, for obviously one can't discuss the war seriously without making statements which *might* cause alarm. Possibly at some time a law will be passed forbidding people to listen-in to foreign radio stations, but it will never be enforcible.

The British ruling class believe in democracy and civil liberty in a narrow and partly hypocritical way. At any rate they believe in the letter of the law and will sometimes keep to it when it is not to their advantage. They show no sign of developing a genuinely Fascist mentality. Liberty of every kind must obviously decline as a result of war, but given the present structure of society and social atmosphere there is a point beyond which the decline cannot go. Britain may be fascised° from without or as a result of some internal revolution, but the old ruling class can't, in my opinion, produce a genuine totalitarianism of their own. Not to put it on any other grounds, they are too stupid. It is largely because they have been unable to grasp the first thing about the nature of Fascism that we are in this mess at all . . .

1. Rudolf Hess (1894–1987), Nazi Deputy Führer and close friend of Hitler, flew a Messerschmitt-110 to Scotland on 10 May 1941. He was captured by the Home Guard. He claimed he had come to negotiate a peace settlement. Churchill did not want peace discussed when things were going so badly and wished Hess's arrival could be kept quiet. However, the Germans broke the news on 13 May, declaring Hess to be insane. He was sentenced to life imprisonment at the Nuremberg Trials and died in Spandau prison. Allegations have been made that the man posing as Hess was an imposter.
2. Sir Stafford Cripps (1889–1952), lawyer (in 1927 becoming the youngest King's Counsel) and Labour politician, entered Parliament in 1931, but was expelled from the Labour Party from 1939 to 1945. He was Ambassador to the Soviet Union, 1940–42; Minister of Aircraft Production, 1942–5 and Chancellor of the Exchequer in the Labour government, 1947–50. See Orwell's War-time Diary, XII/*637*, *8.6.40*, regarding his appointment as ambassador. Cripps was widely recognized as a politician of integrity. See below, pp. 150–51.

[843]

Extract from London Letter, 17 August 1941
Partisan Review, *November–December 1941*

> *Germany attacked the Soviet Union early on Sunday, 22 June 1941, along a front of 1,800 miles from the Baltic to the Black Sea. The Soviets, despite warnings to Stalin from Churchill, were taken by surprise. On 12 July 1941, an Anglo-USSR pact to prosecute the war against Germany was signed.*

THE ANGLO-SOVIET ALLIANCE

The most striking thing about the Anglo-Soviet alliance has been its failure to cause any split in the country or any serious political repercussion whatever. It is true that Hitler's invasion of the U.S.S.R. took everyone here very much by surprise. If the alliance had come about in 1938 or 1939, as it might have done, after long and bitter controversies, with the

Popular Fronters shouting on one side and the Tory press playing Red Russia for all it was worth on the other, there would have been a first-rate political crisis, probably a general election and certainly the growth of an openly pro-Nazi party in Parliament, the Army, etc. But by June 1941 Stalin had come to appear as a very small bogey compared with Hitler, the pro-Fascists had mostly discredited themselves, and the attack happened so suddenly that the advantages and disadvantages of a Russian alliance had not even had time to be discussed.

One fact that this new turn of the war has brought out is that there are now great numbers of English people who have no special reaction towards the U.S.S.R. Russia, like China or Mexico, is simply a mysterious country a long way away, which once had a revolution, the nature of which has been forgotten. All the hideous controversies about the purges, the Five Year Plans, the Ukraine famine, etc., have simply passed over the average newspaper-reader's head. But as for the rest, the people who have some definite pro-Russian or anti-Russian slant, they are split up into several sharply-defined blocks, of which the following are the ones that matter:

The rich. The real bourgeoisie are subjectively anti-Russian, and cannot possibly become otherwise. The existence of large numbers of wealthy parlour Bolsheviks does not alter this fact, because these people invariably belong to the decadent third-generation rentier class. Those who are *of* the capitalist class would regard the destruction of the Soviet Union by Hitler with, at best, mixed feelings. But it is an error to suppose that they are plotting direct treachery or that the handful capable of doing so are likely to gain control of the State. Churchill's continuance in office is a guarantee against that.

The working class. All the more thoughtful members of the British working class are mildly and vaguely pro-Russian. The shock caused by the Russian war against Finland was real enough, but it depended on the fact that nothing was happening at that time in the major war, and it has been completely forgotten. But it would probably be a mistake to imagine that the fact of Russia being in the war will in itself stimulate the British working class to greater efforts and greater sacrifices. In so far as strikes and wage disputes during the past two years have been due to deliberate trouble-making by the Communists, they will of course cease, but it is doubtful whether the Communists have ever been able to do more than magnify legitimate grievances. The grievances will still be there, and fraternal messages from *Pravda* will not make much difference to the feelings of the dock-worker unloading during an air-raid or the tired munition-worker who has missed the last tram home. At one point or another the question of working-class loyalty to Russia is likely to come up in some such form as this: if the Government show signs of letting the Russians down, will the working class take steps to force a more active policy upon them? In that moment I believe it will be found that though a sort of loyalty to the Soviet Union still exists – must exist, so long as Russia is the only country even *pretending* to be a workers' State – it is no longer a positive force. The very fact that Hitler dares to make war on Russia is proof of this. Fifteen years ago such a war would have been impossible for any country except perhaps Japan, because the common soldiers could not have been trusted to use their weapons against the Socialist Fatherland. But that kind of loyalty has been gradually wasted by the nationalistic selfishness of Russian policy. Old-fashioned patriotism is now a far stronger force than any kind of internationalism, or any ideas about the Socialist Fatherland, and this fact also will be reflected in the strategy of the war.

The Communists. I do not need to tell you anything about the shifts of official Communist policy during the past two years, but I am not certain whether the mentality of the Communist intelligentsia is quite the same in the U.S.A. as here. In England the Communists whom it is possible to respect are factory workers, but they are not very numerous, and precisely because they are usually skilled workmen and loyal comrades they cannot always be rigidly faithful to the 'line'. Between September 1939 and June 1941 they do not seem to have attempted any definite sabotage of arms production, although the logic of Communist policy demanded this. The middle-class Communists, however, are a different proposition. They include most of the official and unofficial leaders of the party, and with them must be lumped the greater part of the younger literary intelligentsia, especially in the universities. As I have pointed out elsewhere, the 'Communism' of these people amounts simply to nationalism and leader-worship in their most vulgar forms, transferred to the U.S.S.R. Their importance at this moment is that with the entry of Russia into the war they may regain the influence in the press which they had between 1935 and 1939 and lost during the last two years. The *News Chronicle*, after the [*Daily*] *Herald* the leading leftwing daily (circulation about 1,400,000), is already busy whitewashing the men whom it was denouncing as traitors a little while back. The so-called People's Convention, led by D. N. Pritt[1] (Pritt is a Labour M.P. but is always claimed by Communists as an 'underground' member of their party, evidently with truth), is still in existence but has abruptly reversed its policy. If the Communists are allowed the kind of publicity that they were getting in 1938, they will both consciously and unconsciously sow discord between Britain and the U.S.S.R. What they wish for is not the destruction of Hitler and the resettlement of Europe, but a vulgar military triumph for their adopted Fatherland, and they will do their best to insult public opinion here by transferring as much as possible of the prestige of the war to Russia, and by constantly casting doubts on Britain's good faith. The danger of this kind of thing ought not to be underrated. The Russians themselves, however, probably grasp how the land lies and will act accordingly. If we have a long war ahead of us it is not to their advantage that there should be disaffection in this country. But in so far as they can get a hearing, the British Communists must be regarded as one of the forces acting against Anglo-Russian unity.

The Catholics. There are supposed to be some two million Catholics in this country, the bulk of them very poor Irish labourers. They vote Labour and act as a sort of silent drag on Labour Party policy, but are not sufficiently under the thumb of their priests to be Fascist in sympathy. The importance of the middle- and upper-class Catholics is that they are extremely numerous in the Foreign Office and the Consular Service, and also have a good deal of influence in the press, though less than formerly. The 'born' Catholics of the old Catholic families are less ultra-montane and more ordinarily patriotic than the converted intellectuals (Ronald Knox, Arnold Lunn,[2] etc., etc.), who have very much the same mentality, *mutatis mutandis*, as the British Communists. I suppose I need not repeat the history of their pro-Fascist activities in the past. Since the outbreak of war they have not dared to be openly pro-Hitler, but have done their propaganda indirectly by fulsome praises of Pétain and Franco. Cardinal Hinsley,[3] founder of the Sword of the Spirit Movement (Catholic democracy), seems to be sincerely anti-Nazi according to his lights, but represents only one section of Catholic opinion. As soon as Hitler invaded the U.S.S.R., the Catholic press announced that we must take advantage of the respite that this gave us, but 'no alliance with godless Russia'. Significantly, the Catholic papers became much more anti-Russian when it became apparent that the Russians were resisting successfully. No one who has studied Catholic literature during the past ten years can doubt that the bulk of the hierarchy and the intelligentsia would side with Germany as against Russia if they had a quarter of a chance. Their hatred of Russia is really venomous, enough even to disgust an anti-Stalinist like myself, though their propaganda is necessarily old-fashioned (Bolshevik atrocities, nationalisation of women, etc.) and does not make much impression on working-class people. When the Russian campaign is settled one way or the other, i.e. when Hitler is in Moscow or the Russians show signs of invading Europe, they will come out openly on Hitler's side, and they will certainly be to the fore if any plausible terms are suggested for a compromise peace. If anything corresponding to a Pétain government were established here, it would have to lean largely on the Catholics. They are the only really conscious, logical, intelligent enemies that democracy has got in England, and it is a mistake to despise them.

So much for the various currents of opinion. I began this letter some days ago, and since then the feeling that we are not doing enough to help the Russians has noticeably intensified. The favourite quip now is that what we are giving Russia is 'all aid short of war'. Even the Beaverbrook press repeats this. Also, since Russia entered the war there has been a cooling-off in people's feelings towards the U.S.A. The Churchill-Roosevelt declaration caused, I believe, a good deal of disappointment. Where Churchill had gone was an official secret but seems to have been widely known, and most people expected the outcome to be America's entry into the war, or at least the occupation of some more strategic points on the Atlantic. People are saying now that the Russians are fighting and the Americans are talking, and the saying that was current last year, 'sympathy to China, oil to Japan', begins to be repeated.

1. D. N. Pritt (1887–1972), barrister, and Labour MP, 1935–40, when he was expelled from the Party, becoming an Independent Socialist MP until 1950. He was a fervent supporter of left-wing causes and the Soviet Union. Among other books, he published *Light on Moscow* (1939) and *Must the War Spread?* (1940). Orwell included him in his private list of crypto-

communists (XX/3732), remarking, 'Almost certainly underground member [of Communist Party]. Said to handle more money than is accounted for by his job. Good M.P. (i.e. locally). Very able & courageous'. See p. 506, below.

2. Monsignor Ronald Knox (1888–1957), Roman Catholic priest, essayist, author of many religious books and translator of the Vulgate text of the Bible (completed 1955). His *Broadcast Minds* (1932) was a critique of such writers and thinkers as H. G. Wells, Bertrand Russell and Julian Huxley. *Difficulties* (1932) prints his and Arnold Lunn's correspondence about Roman Catholicism. He was a convert to Catholicism and seemed to many people an unofficial spokesman for his Church. Arnold Lunn (1888–1974; Kt., 1952) incurred Orwell's wrath because he supported Franco: see Orwell's review of his *Spanish Rehearsal*, 11 December 1937 (reprinted in *Orwell in Spain* in this series). He was an authority on skiing and did much to foster travel abroad.

3. Cardinal Arthur Hinsley (1865–1943), Archbishop of Westminster from 1935. He attempted to organize opposition to totalitarianism. He was critical of the passivity of Pope Pius XI over the Italian invasion of Abyssinia (Ethiopia) in 1935. In October 1940 he formed the Sword of the Spirit, a political and religious group which brought together Protestant and Roman Catholic churchmen to promote the fight against Fascism.

[908]

Review of Men and Politics *by Louis Fischer*
Now and Then, *Christmas 1941*

The 'political book' – part reportage and part political criticism, usually with a little autobiography thrown in – is a growth of the troubled years from 1933 onwards, and the value of individual books in this genre has depended a good deal upon the orthodoxy of the moment. In periods like that between 1936 and 1939, when fierce controversies were raging and nobody was telling the whole of the truth, it was not easy to write a good political book, even if you knew the facts. Mr. Fischer's book, which is largely about the U.S.S.R., comes at a more fortunate moment. So far as the U.S.S.R. is concerned he evidently *does* know the facts, as far as an outsider can know them, and time itself has done the necessary debunking. After the Russo-German pact the Popular Front orthodoxy of the preceding years became impossible, and on the other hand the German attack on Russia has thrown the whole subject of Russo-German relations into better proportion and wiped out the bitterness caused by the pact itself and by the Finnish episode. Mr. Fischer is left with the conclusion that Stalin is a disgusting tyrant who is nevertheless objectively on our side and must be supported – not a comforting conclusion, perhaps, but more realistic and more likely to produce an interesting book than any that was possible two years ago.

What the majority of readers will probably find most interesting are Mr. Fischer's chapters on the Russian sabotage trials. He saw some of them at close quarters, and in any case in his capacity as newspaper correspondent he had known various of the principal actors in them. The Russian purges are the greatest puzzle of modern times and we can hardly have too many opinions on them. Various explanations are possible, even the explanation that all the charges were true, though this involves accepting certain known contradictions. Mr. Fischer is inclined to think that the confessions of Bukharin, Rakovsky[1] and the rest were obtained by promising them that if they confessed they would not be shot; he even thinks that in some cases the promise may have been kept and the accused men may be still alive. The weakness of this explanation seems to be that the old Bolsheviks, considering the lives they had led, were not the men to care very greatly about being shot or to make incredible confessions which would blacken their names for ever merely for the sake of saving their skins. But it is a fact that any explanation one puts forward can be met by similar objections, and Mr. Fischer's opinion should be treated with respect. One of the great weaknesses of British and American political thought during the past decade has been that people who have lived all their lives in democratic or quasi-democratic countries find it very difficult to imagine the totalitarian atmosphere and tend to translate all that happens abroad into terms of their own experience. This tendency has vitiated most of what has been written about the U.S.S.R., about the Spanish civil war, even about Nazism. Mr. Fischer, who has seen totalitarianism from the inside for many years and still remained a fairly ordinary American with mildly left-wing opinions and a profound belief in democracy, makes a valuable corrective to the parlour Bolsheviks on one side and writers like Eugene Lyons[2] on the other.

He has also been everywhere and met everybody. Negrín, Senator Borah, Bernard Shaw, Colonel Lindbergh, Litvinov, Cordell Hull, Bonnet, Bullitt, Churchill and scores of other celebrities, good and evil, move across his pages.[3] The writing of this book has called for considerable intellectual courage, for it has involved admitting that in the past Mr.

Fischer held opinions which he now thinks false and also that he engaged in propaganda campaigns which even at the time he could see to be misleading. But that kind of admission is a necessary part of the political reorientation which is now going on. Few journalists of our time can speak from wider knowledge than Mr. Fischer, and no book of political reminiscence written since the outbreak of war is of greater value than this one.

1. Nicolai Bukharin (1888–1938), leading theoretician of the Soviet Communist Party following the death of Lenin. Lenin described him as 'the darling of the Party' but that did not save his being charged in the third show trial of the Great Purge and being executed. He supported the New Economic Policy and opposed Stalin's collectivization. He was rehabilitated posthumously in 1987. Khristian Rakovsky (b. 1873; d. after 1938), Bulgarian revolutionary who became a member of Lenin's Bolshevik Party after the October Revolution, 1917. Appointed Soviet chargé d'affaires in London and then Soviet Ambassador to France, 1926. Expelled from the Communist Party, 1927–35. With Bukharin and eighteen others he was tried in the Great Purge on trumped up charges in 1938 and sentenced to twenty years hard labour; he is assumed to have died in a labour camp.

2. Eugene Lyons (1898–1985), American journalist and editor born in Russia, who wrote many books on the USSR, including *Assignment in Utopia* (1937), in which the formula 2 + 2 = 5 appears prominently. Orwell reviewed it, 9 June 1938; see above.

3. Dr Juan Negrín (1889–1956) was the Socialist Prime Minister of Spain during the civil war. William E. Borah (1865–1940), US Senator from Idaho, 1907–1940, chairman of the Senate Foreign Relations Committee from 1924, was an opponent of the League of Nations and progressive legislation, but supporter of Roosevelt's New Deal. Charles A. Lindbergh (1902–74), who became a hero after making the first solo non-stop flight across the Atlantic in 1927, was active in opposing US entanglement in World War II before the Japanese attack on Pearl Harbor, but later helped in the war effort and saw active duty in the Pacific. Maxim Litvinov (1876–1951) was the Soviet Union's Commissar of Foreign Affairs, 1930–39, and Ambassador to the United States, 1941–3. Cordell Hull (1871–1955), US statesman, judge, 1903–7, member of Congress, 1907–21, 1923–31, and the Senate, 1931–3, Secretary of State, 1933–44, pursued enlightened foreign and economic policies which led to the award of the Nobel Peace Prize in 1945. Georges Bonnet (1889–1973), French Ambassador to the United States, 1937, Foreign Minister, 1938–9, wanted, in 1939, to repudiate the alliance with Poland. William C. Bullitt (1891–1967), US diplomat, was the first US Ambassador to the Soviet Union, 1933–6, Ambassador to France, 1936–41, and special assistant to the Secretary of the Navy, 1942.

Sir Stafford Cripps's Mission to India, March–April 1942

Orwell was strongly in favour of independence for India. He had high hopes that Sir Stafford Cripps's Mission to India would lead to a constitutional settlement. The following extracts from his BBC Weekly News Reviews (broadcast to India) and from his War-time Diary, trace, in outline, his reactions to events. Although the Mission failed, the India Independence Act was passed by Parliament in 1947.

[1022]

Extract from BBC Weekly News Review for India, 14
14 March 1942

The most important event this week is not military but political. It is the appointment of Sir Stafford Cripps to proceed to India by air and there lay before the leaders of the Indian political parties the scheme which has been worked out by the British Government.

The Government has not yet announced what its plans are and it would be unwise to make a guess at them, but it is at least certain that no one now alive in Britain is more suited to conduct the negotiations. Sir Stafford Cripps has long been recognised as the ablest man in the British Socialist movement, and he is respected for his absolute integrity even by those who are at the opposite pole from him politically. He has had a varied career, and possesses knowledge and experience of a kind not often shared by professional politicians. During the last war he managed an explosives factory on behalf of the Government. After that, for some years he practised as a barrister, and won for himself an enormous reputation for his skill in dealing with intricate civil cases. In spite of this, he has always lived with extreme simplicity and has given away most of his earnings at the Bar to the cause of Socialism and to the support of his weekly Socialist paper, *The Tribune*. He is a man of great personal austerity, a vegetarian, a teetotaller and a devout practising Christian. So simple are his manners that he is to be seen every morning having his breakfast in a cheap London eating house, among working men and office employees. In the last few years he has given up practising at the Bar in order to devote himself wholly to politics.

The outstanding thing about Sir Stafford Cripps, however, has always been his utter unwillingness to compromise his political principles. He has sometimes made mistakes, but his worst enemy has never suggested that he cared anything for money, popularity or personal power. About seven years ago, he became dissatisfied with the too cautious policy of the Labour Party, and founded the Socialist League, an organisation within the Labour Party, aiming at a more radical Socialist policy, and a firmer front against the Fascist aggression. Its main objectives were to form a Popular Front Government of the same type as then existed in France and Spain, and to bring Great Britain and the other peace-loving nations into closer association with Soviet Russia. This brought him into conflict with the official heads of the Labour Party, who did not at that time grasp the full menace of Fascism. Whereas a lesser man would have given way in order to keep his pre-eminent position within the Labour Party, Cripps preferred to resign, and for several years he was in a very isolated position, only a few members in the House of Commons and a small following in the country at large realising that his policy was the correct one. However, when the Churchill Government was formed in 1940, it was recognised on all sides that no one was so suitable as Sir Stafford Cripps for the British Ambassadorship in Moscow. He discharged his office brilliantly, and undoubtedly did a great deal to make possible a firm alliance between the British and the Russian peoples. Since his return to England, he has followed this up by a series of speeches and broadcasts, by which he has brought home to the ordinary people in Britain the enormous effort which their Russian allies are making, and the necessity of supporting them by every means in our power. Everyone in Britain is delighted to see such an important mission as the one which Cripps is now undertaking, conferred upon a man whom even his critics admit to be gifted, trustworthy and self-sacrificing.

Extracts from War-time Diary

[1075]

1.4.42: Greatly depressed by the apparent failure of the Cripps Mission. Most of the Indians seem down in the mouth about it too. Even the ones who hate England want a solution, I think. I believe, however, that in spite of the 'take it or leave it' with which our government started off, the terms will actually be modified, perhaps in response to pressure at this end. Some think the Russians are behind the Cripps plan and that this accounts for Cripps's confidence in putting forward something so apparently uninviting. Since they are not in the war against Japan the Russians cannot have any official attitude about the Indian affair, but they may serve out a directive to their followers, from whom it will get round to other pro-Russians. But then not many Indians are reliably pro-Russian. No sign yet from the English Communist party, whose behaviour might give a clue to the Russian attitude. It is on this kind of guesswork that we have to frame our propaganda, no clear or useful directive ever being handed out from above.

Connolly[1] wanted yesterday to quote a passage from *Homage to Catalonia* in his broadcast. I opened the book and came on these sentences:

'One of the most horrible features of war is that all the war-propaganda, all the screaming and lies and hatred, comes invariably from people who are not fighting ... It is the same in all wars; the soldiers do the fighting, the journalists do the shouting, and no true patriot ever gets near a front-line trench, except on the briefest of propaganda tours. Sometimes it is a comfort to me to think that the aeroplane is altering the conditions of war. Perhaps when the next great war comes we may see that sight unprecedented in all history, a jingo with a bullet-hole in him.'[2]

Here I am in the BBC, less than 5 years after writing that. I suppose sooner or later we all write our own epitaphs.

1. Cyril Connolly (1903–74) was with Orwell at St Cyprian's Preparatory School, Eastbourne, and at Eton, where he also was a King's Scholar, a year behind Orwell. They met again in 1935. Connolly founded and edited the literary journal *Horizon*, 1940–50, which published

several of Orwell's essays. His *Enemies of Promise* (1938) in part inspired Orwell's 'Such, Such Were the Joys' (see *Orwell's England* in this series). Orwell's second wife, Sonia Brownell, worked for *Horizon*. See Michael Shelden, *Friends of Promise: Cyril Connolly and the World of 'Horizon'* (1989).

2. *Homage to Catalonia, CW*, VI, Appendix I, 208 and 209.

[1080]

3.4.42: Cripps's decision to stay an extra week in India is taken as a good omen. Otherwise not much to be hopeful about. Gandhi[1] is deliberately making trouble, sending telegrams of condolence to Bose's[2] family on the report of his death, then telegrams of congratulation when it turned out that the report was untrue. Also urging Indians not to adopt the scorched earth policy if India is invaded. Impossible to be quite sure what his game is. Those who are anti-Gandhi allege that he has the worst kind of (Indian) capitalist interests behind him, and it is a fact that he usually seems to be staying at the mansion of some kind of millionaire or other. This is not necessarily incompatible with his alleged saintliness. His pacifism may be genuine, however. In the bad period of 1940 he also urged non-resistance in England, should England be invaded. I do not know whether Gandhi or Buchman[3] is the nearest equivalent to Rasputin[4] in our time.

Anand[5] says the morale among the exile Indians here is very low. They are still inclined to think that Japan has no evil designs on India and are all talking of a separate peace with Japan. So much for their declarations of loyalty towards Russia and China. I said to A. that the basic fact about nearly all Indian intellectuals is that they don't expect independence, can't imagine it and at heart don't want it. They want to be permanently in opposition, suffering a painless martyrdom, and are foolish enough to imagine that they could play the same schoolboy games with Japan or Germany as they can with Britain. Somewhat to my surprise he agreed. He says that 'opposition mentality' is general among them, especially among the Communists, and that Krishna Menon[6] is 'longing for the moment when negotiations will break down'. At the same moment as they are coolly talking of betraying China by making a separate peace, they are shouting that the Chinese troops in Burma are not getting proper air support. I remarked that this was childish. A: 'You cannot overestimate their childishness, George. It is fathomless.' The question is how far the

Indians here reflect the viewpoint of the intellectuals in India. They are further from the danger and have probably, like the rest of us, been infected by the peaceful atmosphere of the last 10 months, but on the other hand nearly all who remain here long become tinged with a western Socialist outlook, so that the Indian intellectuals proper are probably far worse. A. himself has not got these vices. He is genuinely anti-Fascist, and has done violence to his feelings, and probably to his reputation, by backing Britain up because he recognizes that Britain is objectively on the anti-Fascist side.

1. Mohandas Gandhi (the Mahatma – 'great soul'; 1869–1948), Indian nationalist leader. He studied law in England and worked for over twenty years in South Africa opposing discrimination against Indians there. He returned to India in 1914. He initiated civil disobedience campaigns, was jailed, and in 1931 attended the Round Table Conference on constitutional reform for India in London. He played a role in the negotiations for independence after the war and, when independence came, endeavoured to stop violence between Hindus and Muslims in Bengal. He was assassinated in Delhi. Orwell had an ambivalent attitude to him. See his 'Reflections on Gandhi', below.

2. Subhas Chandra Bose (1897–1945?) was an Indian nationalist leader and left-wing member of the Indian National Congress. Fiercely anti-British, he organized an Indian National Army to support the Japanese. This he led, unsuccessfully, against the British. He believed that when the INA faced Indian troops led by the British, the latter would not fight but be converted. 'Instead, the revolutionary had reverted to his comfortable mercenary status. INA soldiers took to looting from local tribes' (Mihir Bose, *The Lost Hero* (1982), 236). Bose escaped from India, with German help, via Afghanistan, in the winter of 1940–41. When he reached Moscow, the Russians 'were extremely hospitable but determinedly evasive about helping him. In Berlin the Germans were more receptive' (162). He was in Germany until 8 February 1943, when he sailed from Kiel in a U-boat (205). His followers long believed him to be still alive (despite two Indian government inquiries), but it seems certain he died following a plane crash on 19 August 1945 (251–2). Documents released by the War Office in November 1993 show that a substantial number of Indian prisoners of war defected to the Italians, the first 3,000 arriving in Italy in August 1942. A British Intelligence report stated, 'We have by our policy towards India, bred up a new class of officer who may be loyal to India, and perhaps to Congress, but is not necessarily loyal to us' (*Daily Telegraph*, 5 December 1993).

3. Frank Nathan Daniel Buchman (1878–1961), evangelist and propagandist, founded, in 1921, the Moral Re-Armament Movement, also known, from its place of foundation, as the Oxford Group Movement, and sometimes as Buchmanism.

4. Grigoriy Rasputin (1871?–1916), member of a sect of flagellants (Khlysty) who, despite being a lecher and drunkard, ingratiated himself into the Tsarist family because of his ability to limit the haemophiliac bleeding of the Tsarevich, Alexei. His murder required 'killing' by several means before he succumbed. His name has been loosely applied to those thought to wield evil, even satanic, influence.

5. Mulk Raj Anand (1905–), novelist, short-story writer, essayist and critic, was born in India, fought for the Republicans in the Spanish Civil War, though he did not meet Orwell there, taught literature and philosophy to London County Council adult-education classes and wrote scripts and broadcast for the BBC, 1939–45. After the war he lectured in various Indian universities and was made professor of fine arts, University of Punjab, in 1963. He was awarded an International Peace Prize from the World Council of Peace in 1952. Orwell criticized a review of Anand's *The Sword and the Sickle* by Ranjee Shahne in *The Times Literary Supplement*, 23 May 1942, and reviewed the book in *Horizon*, July 1942; see *1189* and *1257*. In a letter of 29 September 1983, Anand wrote this of Orwell: 'In his life his voice was restrained. He talked in furtive whispers. Often he dismissed the ugly realities with cynical good humour. And I seldom saw him show anger on his face, though the two deep lines on his cheeks and the furrowed brow signified permanent despair. He smiled at tea time and he was a good companion in a pub. But he delivered his shafts in a very mellow voice, something peculiarly English deriving from the Cockney sense of humour'; see Abha Sharma Rodrigues, 'George Orwell, the BBC and India: A Critical Study' (Edinburgh University, Ph.D., 1994); this analyses the relationship between Anand and Orwell. See 173–7, below.
6. V. K. Krishna Menon (1897–1974), Indian statesman, lawyer, author and journalist, who was then living in England. He was active in British left-wing politics and was spokesman of the Indian Congress Party in England in the struggle for independence. In 1947, when India had become independent, he was High Commissioner for India and he represented India at the United Nations, 1952–61. On 31 January 1943, he was one of six speakers at the 'India Demonstration' at the London Coliseum (*Tribune*, 29 January 1943, 20).

10.4.42: British naval losses in the last 3 or 4 days: 2 cruisers and an aircraft carrier sunk, 1 destroyer wrecked.[1] Axis losses: 1 cruiser sunk.

From Nehru's[2] speech today: 'Who dies if India live?' How impressed the pinks will be – and how they would snigger at 'Who dies if England live?'[3]

1. On 5 April, the heavy cruisers *Dorsetshire* and *Cornwall*, the destroyer *Tenedos* and the armed merchant-ship *Hector* were sunk by Japanese aircraft operating from carriers in the Indian Ocean. On 9 April (the day 64,000 Filipinos and 12,000 Americans surrendered at Bataan), the aircraft carrier *Hermes* and the destroyer *Vampire* were among a further group of ships sunk by the Japanese in the Indian Ocean, including 135,000 tons of merchant and troop ships.
2. Jawaharlal Nehru (Pandit – 'teacher'; 1889–1964), leading Indian politician who, after years of struggle and opposition to British rule in India, suffering imprisonment on a number of occasions, became India's first Prime Minister (1947–64) on independence.
3. 'Who dies if England live?' comes from Kipling's 'For All We Have and Are' (1914); it also has the line, 'The Hun is at the gate!'

[1105]

Extract from BBC Weekly News Review for India, 18
18 April 1942

Sir Stafford Cripps is expected to reach Britain *shortly*. Now that a week has gone by since the breakdown of negotiations between Sir Stafford Cripps and the Indian political leaders, it is possible to see his mission in clearer perspective and to say something about the reactions to it in various parts of the world.

It is clear from the reports that have come in from many countries that only the supporters of Fascism are pleased by the failure of Sir Stafford Cripps's mission. On the other hand, there is a general feeling that the failure was not complete, in so much that the negotiations have clarified the issue and did not end in such a way as to make further advances impossible. However deep the disagreement, there was no ill-feeling on either side, and no suggestion that either Sir Stafford Cripps or the Indian political leaders were acting other than in good faith. In Britain and the United States Sir Stafford has actually enhanced his already high reputation. He undertook a difficult job in which he risked being personally discredited, and his obvious sincerity has impressed the whole world. The Axis propagandists are attempting to represent the breakdown as a refusal on the part of India to defend herself, and an actual Indian desire to pass under Japanese rule. This is a direct lie, and the Axis broadcasters are only able to support it by deliberately not quoting from the speeches of Mr. Nehru and the other political leaders. Even Mr. Gandhi, though remaining faithful to his programme of non-violence, has not suggested that he wishes to see the Japanese in India, merely that he believes that they should be resisted by spiritual rather than material weapons. Mr. Nehru has not ceased to be anti-British, but he is even more emphatically anti-Japanese. He has asserted in the most vigorous terms possible that Indian resistance will continue and that the Congress party will do nothing to hamper the British war effort, although the failure to alter the political *status quo* will prevent their taking a very direct part in it. He has said, as on many other occasions, that however deep his own objections to the British Government may be, the fact remains that the cause of Britain, of Soviet Russia and China, represents progress, while the cause of Germany and Japan represents re-action, barbarism and oppression. In spite of the difficulty, therefore, of collaborating directly with the British forces, he will do all in his power to raise popular Indian feeling against the aggressor and to make Indians realise that their liberty is inextricably bound up with an Allied victory. For even at the worst, India *may* get its independence from Britain, whereas the idea of India or any other subject nation winning its liberty in a Fascist-ruled world is laughable.

Extracts from War-time Diary

[1106]

18.4.42: No question that Cripps's speeches etc. have caused a lot of offence, ie. in India. Outside India I doubt whether many people blame the British government for the breakdown. One trouble at the moment is the tactless utterances of Americans who for years have been blahing about 'Indian freedom' and British imperialism, and have suddenly had their eyes opened to the fact that the Indian intelligentsia don't want independence, ie. responsibility. Nehru is making provocative speeches to the effect that all the English are the same, of whatever political party, and also trying to make trouble between Britain and the USA by alleging that the USA has done all the real fighting. At the same time he reiterates at intervals that he is not pro-Japanese and Congress will defend India to the last. The BBC thereupon picks out these passages from his speeches and broadcasts them without mentioning the anti-British passages, whereat Nehru complains (quite justly) that he has been misrepresented. A recent directive tells us that when one of his speeches contains both anti-British and anti-Japanese passages, we had better ignore it altogether. What a mess it all is. But I think on balance the Cripps mission has done good, because without discrediting Cripps in this country (as it so easily might have done) it has clarified the issue. Whatever is said officially, the inference the whole world will draw is that (a) the British ruling class doesn't intend to abdicate and (b) India doesn't want independence and therefore won't get it, whatever the outcome of the war.

Talking to Wintringham[1] about the possible Russian attitude towards the Cripps negotiations (of course, not being in the war against Japan, they can't have an official attitude) I said it might make things easier if as many as possible of the military instructors etc. who will later have to be sent to India were Russians. One possible outcome is that India will ultimately be taken over by the USSR, and though I have never believed that the Russians would behave better in India than ourselves, they might behave differently, owing to the different economic set-up. Wintringham said that even in Spain some of the Russian delegates tended to treat the Spaniards as 'natives', and would no doubt do likewise in India. It's very hard not to, seeing that in practice the majority of Indians *are* inferior to Europeans and one can't help feeling this and, after a little while, acting accordingly.

American opinion will soon swing back and begin putting all the blame for the Indian situation on the British, as before. It is clear from what American papers one can get hold of that anti-British feeling is in full cry and that all the Isolationists, after a momentary retirement, have re-emerged with the same slogans as before. Father Coughlin's paper,[2] however, has just been excluded from the mails. What always horrifies me about American anti-British sentiment is its appalling ignorance. Ditto presumably with anti-American feeling in England.

1. Thomas Henry (Tom) Wintringham, writer and soldier, had commanded the British Battalion of the International Brigade in the Spanish Civil War. He later founded Osterley Park Training Centre for the Home Guard. His books include *New Ways of War*, *Politics of Victory* and *People's War*. See David Fernbach, 'Tom Wintringham and Socialist Defense Strategy', *History Workshop*, 14 (1982), 63–91.

2. Father Charles E. Coughlin (1891–1979), born and educated in Canada, became a Roman Catholic priest and achieved prominence through use of the radio in the United States in the 1930s. As early as 1934, when he founded the National Union for Social Justice, he argued that the US was being manipulated by Britain into involvement in a new European war; 'I raise my voice,' he said, 'to keep America out of war.' Orwell refers to his magazine, *Social Justice*, in which he expressed near-Fascist views. Its circulation through the mail was forbidden in the US because it contravened the Espionage Act. It ceased publication in 1942, the year Coughlin was silenced by his ecclesiastical superiors.

[1130]

29.4.42: Yesterday to the House to hear the India debate. A poor show except for Cripps's speech. They are now sitting in the House of Lords.[1] During Cripps's speech one had the impression that the house was full,

all except the interested minority would accept nationalisation without a blink if they were told authoritatively that you can't have efficient war-production otherwise. The fact is that 'Socialism', called by that name, isn't by itself an effective rallying cry. To the mass of the people 'Socialism' just means the discredited Parliamentary Labour Party, and one feature of the time is the widespread disgust with all the old political parties. But what then do people want? I should say that what they articulately want is more social equality, a complete clean-out of the political leadership, an aggressive war strategy and a tighter alliance with the U.S.S.R. But one has to consider the background of these desires before trying to predict what political development is now possible.

The war has brought the class nature of their society very sharply home to English people, in two ways. First of all there is the unmistakable fact that all real power depends on class privilege. You can only get certain jobs if you have been to one of the right schools, and if you fail and have to be sacked, then somebody else from one of the right schools takes over, and so it continues. This may go unnoticed when things are prospering, but becomes obvious in moments of disaster. Secondly there are the hardships of war, which are, to put it mildly, tempered for anyone with over £2000 a year. I don't want to bore you with a detailed account of the way in which the food rationing is evaded, but you can take it that whereas ordinary people have to live on an uninteresting diet and do without many luxuries they are accustomed to, the rich go short of absolutely nothing except, perhaps, wines, fruit and sugar. You can be almost unaffected by food rationing without even breaking the law, though there is also a lively Black Market. Then there is bootleg petrol and, quite obviously, widespread evasion of Income Tax. This does not go unnoticed, but nothing happens because the will to crack down on it is not there while money and political power more or less coincide. To give just one example. At long last, and against much opposition in high places, the Ministry of Food is about to cut down 'luxury feeding' by limiting the sum of money that can be spent on a meal in a hotel or restaurant. Already, before the law is even passed, ways of evading it have been thought out, and these are discussed almost undisguisedly in the newspapers.

There are other tensions which the war has brought out but which are somewhat less obvious than the jealousy caused by the Black Market or the discontent of soldiers blancoing their gasmasks under the orders of twerps of officers. One is the growing resentment felt by the underpaid armed forces (at any rate the Army) against the high wages of the munition workers. If this were dealt with by raising the soldier's pay to the munition-worker's level the result would be either inflation or the diversion of labour from war-production to consumption goods. The only real remedy is to cut down the civilian worker's wages as well, which could only be made acceptable by the most drastic income cuts all round – briefly, 'war communism'. And apart from the class struggle in its ordinary sense there are deeper jealousies within the bourgeoisie than foreigners sometimes realise. If you talk with a B.B.C. accent you can get jobs that a proletarian couldn't get, but it is almost impossible to get beyond a certain point unless you belong socially to the Upper Crust. Everywhere able men feel themselves bottled down by incompetent idiots from the county families. Bound up with this is the crushing feeling we have all had in England these last twenty years that if you have brains 'they' (the Upper Crust) will see to it that you are kept out of any really important job. During the years of investment capital we produced like a belt of fat the huge blimpocracy which monopolises official and military power and has an instinctive hatred of intelligence. This is probably a more important factor in England than in a 'new' country like the U.S.A. It means that our military weakness goes beyond the inherent weakness of a capitalist state. When in England you find a gifted man in a really commanding position it is usually because he happens to have been born into an aristocratic family (examples are Churchill, Cripps, Mountbatten[2]), and even so he only gets there in moments of disaster when others don't want to take responsibility. Aristocrats apart, those who are branded as 'clever' can't get their hands on the real levers of power, and they know it. Of course 'clever' individuals do occur in the upper strata, but basically it is a class issue, middle class against upper class.

The statement in the March–April *PR* that 'the reins of power are still firmly in the hands of Churchill' is an error. Churchill's position is very shaky. Up to the fall of Singapore it would have been true to say that the mass of the people liked Churchill while disliking the rest of his government, but in recent months his popularity has slumped heavily. In addition he has the right-wing Tories against him (the Tories on the whole have always hated Churchill, though they had to pipe down for a long period), and Beaverbrook is up to some game which I do not fully understand but which must have the object of bringing himself into power. I wouldn't give Churchill many more months of power, but whether he will be replaced by Cripps, Beaverbrook or somebody like Sir John Anderson is still uncertain.

The reason why nearly everyone who was anti-Nazi supported Churchill from the collapse of France onwards was that there was nobody else – i.e., nobody who was already well enough known to be able to step into power and who at the same time could be trusted not to surrender. It is idle to say that in 1940 we ought to have set up a Socialist government; the mass basis for such a thing probably existed, but not the leadership. The Labour party had no guts, the pinks were defeatist, the Communists effectively pro-Nazi, and in any case there did not exist on the Left one single man of really nation-wide reputation. In the months that followed what was wanted was chiefly obstinacy, of which Churchill had plenty. Now, however, the situation has altered. The strategic situation is probably far better than it was in 1940, but the mass of the people don't think so, they are disgusted by defeats some of which they realise were unnecessary, and they have been gradually disillusioned by perceiving that in spite of Churchill's speeches the old gang stays in power and nothing really alters. For the first time since Churchill came to power the government has begun losing by-elections. Of the five most recent it has lost three, and in the two which it didn't lose one opposition candidate was anti-war (I.L.P.[3]) and the other was regarded as a defeatist. In all these elections the polls were extremely low, in one case reaching the depth-record of 24 per cent of the electorate. (Most wartime polls have been low, but one has to write off something for the considerable shift of population.) There is a most obvious loss of the faith in the old parties, and there is a new factor in the presence of Cripps, who enjoys at any rate for the moment a considerable personal reputation. Just at the moment when things were going very badly he came back from Russia in a blaze of undeserved glory. People had by this time forgotten the circumstances in which the Russo-German war broke out and credited Cripps with having 'got Russia in on our side'. He was, however, cashing in on his earlier political history and on having never sold out his political opinions. There is good reason to think that at that moment, with no party machine under his control, he did not realise how commanding his personal position was. Had he appealed directly to the public, through the channels open to him, he could probably then and there have forced a more radical policy on the government, particularly in the direction of a generous settlement with India. Instead he made the mistake of entering the government and the almost equally bad one of going to India with an offer which was certain to be turned down. I can't put in print the little I know about the inner history of the Cripps-Nehru negotiations, and in any case the story is too complex to be written about in a letter of this length. The important thing is to what extent this failure has discredited Cripps. The people most interested in ditching the negotiations were the pro-Japanese faction in the Indian Congress party, and the British right-wing Tories. Halifax's speech made in New York at the time was interpreted here as an effort to tread on as many Indian toes as possible and thus make a get-together between Cripps and Nehru more difficult. Similar efforts are being made from the opposite end at this moment. The upshot is that Cripps's reputation is damaged in India but not in this country – or, if damaged, then by his entry into the government rather than by the failure in Delhi.

I can't yet give you a worthwhile opinion as to whether Cripps is the man the big public think him, or are half-inclined to think him. He is an enigmatic man who has been politically unstable, and those who know him only agree upon the fact that he is personally honest. His position rests purely upon the popular belief in him, for he has the Labour party machine more or less against him, and the Tories are only temporarily supporting him because they want to use him against Churchill and Beaverbrook and imagine that they can make him into another tame cat like Attlee.[4] Some of the factory workers are inclined to be suspicious of him (one comment reported to me was 'Too like Mosley' – meaning too much the man of family who 'goes to the people') and the Communists hate him because he is suspected of being anti-Stalin. Beaverbrook already appears to be instituting an attack on Cripps and his newspapers are making use of anti-Stalinist remarks dropped by Cripps in the past. I note that the Germans, to judge from their wireless, would be willing to see Cripps in power if at that price they could get rid of Churchill. They probably calculate that since Cripps has no party machine to rely on he would soon be levered out by the right-wing Tories and make way for Sir John Anderson, Lord Londonderry or someone of that kind. I can't yet say with certainty that Cripps is not merely a second-rate figure to whom the public have tied their hopes, a sort of bubble blown by popular discontent. But at any rate, the way people talked about him when he came back from Moscow was symptomatically important.

There is endless talk about a second front, those who are for and those who are against being divided roughly along political lines. Much that is said is extremely ignorant, but even people with little military knowledge are able to see that in the last few months we have lost by useless defensive actions a force which, if grouped in one place and used offensively, might have achieved something. Public opinion often seems to be ahead of the so-called experts in matters of grand strategy, sometimes even tactics and weapons. I don't myself know whether the opening of a second front is feasible, because I don't know the real facts about the shipping situation; the only clue I have to the latter is that the food situation hasn't altered during the past year. Official policy seems to be to discountenance the idea of a second front, but just possibly that is only military deception. The right-wing papers make much play with our bombing raids on Germany and suggest that we can tie down a million troops along the coast of Europe by continuous commando raids. The latter is nonsense as the commandos can't do much when the nights get short, and after our own experiences few people here believe that bombing can settle anything. In general the big public is offensive-minded and is always pleased when the government shows by violating international law (eg. Oran, Syria, Madagascar) that it is taking the war seriously. Nevertheless the idea of attacking Spain or Spanish Morocco (much the most hopeful area for a second front in my opinion) is seldom raised. It is agreed by all observers that the Army, ie. rank and file and a lot of the junior officers, is exceedingly browned off, but this does not seem to be the case with the Navy and R.A.F., and it is easy to get recruits for the dangerous corps such as the commandos and parachute troops. An anonymous pamphlet attacking the blimpocracy, button-polishing, etc., recently sold enormously, and this line is also run by the *Daily Mirror*, the soldiers' favourite paper, which was nearly suppressed a few weeks back for its criticisms of the higher command. On the other hand the pamphlets which used to appear earlier in the war, complaining about the hardships of army life, seem to have faded out. Perhaps symptomatically important is the story now widely circulated, that the real reason why the higher-ups have stuck out against adopting dive bombers is that these are cheap to manufacture and don't represent much profit. I know nothing as to the truth of this story, but I record the fact that many people believe it. Churchill's speech a few days back in which he referred to possible use of poison gas by the Germans was interpreted as a warning that gas warfare will begin soon. Usual comment: 'I hope we start using it first.' People seem to me to have got tougher in their attitude, in spite of general discontent and the lack of positive war aims. It is hard to assess how much the man in the street cared about the Singapore disaster. Working-class people seemed to me to be more impressed by the escape of the German warships from Brest.[5] The opinion seems general that Germany is the real enemy, and newspaper efforts to work up a hate over Japanese atrocities failed. My impression is that people will go on fighting indefinitely so long as Germany is in the field, but that if Germany should be knocked out they would not continue the war against Japan unless a real and intelligible war aim were produced.

I have referred in earlier letters to the great growth of pro-Russian feeling. It is difficult, however, to be sure how deep this goes. A Trotskyist said to me recently that he thought that by their successful resistance the Russians had won back all the credit they lost by the Hitler-Stalin pact and the Finnish war. I don't believe this is so. What has happened is that the U.S.S.R. has gained a lot of admirers it did not previously have, but many who used to be its uncritical adherents have grown cannier. One notices here a gulf between what is said publicly and privately. In public nobody says a word against the U.S.S.R., but in private, apart from the 'disillusioned' Stalinists that one is always meeting, I notice a more sceptical attitude among thinking people. One sees this especially in conversations about the second front. The official attitude of the pinks is that if we open up a second front the Russians will be so grateful that they will be our comrades to the last. In reality, to open a second front without a clear agreement beforehand would simply give the Russians the opportunity to make a separate peace; for if we succeeded in drawing the Germans away from their territories, what reason would they have for going on fighting? Another theory favoured in left-wing papers is that the more fighting we do the more say we shall have in the post-war settlement. This again is an illusion; those who dictate the peace treaties are those who have remained strongest, which usually means those who have managed to avoid fighting (eg. the U.S.A. in the last war). Considerations of this kind seldom find their way into print but are admitted readily enough in private. I think people have not altogether forgotten the Russo-German pact and that fear of another doublecross partly explains their desire for a closer alliance. But there is also much sentimental boosting of Russia, based on ignorance and played up by all kinds of crooks who are utterly anti-Socialist but see that the Red Army is a popular line. I must take back some of the favourable references I made in earlier letters to the Beaverbrook press. After giving his journalists a free hand for a year or more, during which some of them did good work in enlightening the big public, Beaverbrook has again cracked the whip and is setting his team at work to attack Churchill and, more directly, Cripps. He is simultaneously yapping against fuel-rationing, petrol-rationing and other restrictions on private capitalism, and posing as more Stalinist than the Stalinists. Most of the right-wing press adopts the more cautious line of praising 'the great Russian people' (historic parallels with Napoleon, etc.) while keeping silent about the nature of the Russian régime. The 'Internationale' is at last being played on the wireless. Molotov's speech on the German atrocities was issued as a White Paper, but in deference to somebody's feelings (I don't know whether Stalin's or the King's) the royal arms were omitted[6] from the cover. People in general want to think well of Russia, though still vaguely hostile to Communism. They would welcome a joint declaration of war aims and a close co-ordination of strategy. I think many people realise that a firm alliance with Russia is difficult while the Munich crew are still more or less in power, but much fewer grasp that the comparative political backwardness of the U.S.A. presents another difficulty.

Well, that is the set-up as I see it. It seems to me that we are back to the 'revolutionary situation' which existed but was not utilised after Dunkirk. From that time until quite recently one's thoughts necessarily moved in some such progression as this:

We can't win the war with our present social and economic structure.

The structure won't change unless there is a rapid growth in popular consciousness.

The only thing that promotes this growth is military disasters.

One more disaster and we shall lose the war.

In the circumstances all one could do was to 'support' the war, which involved supporting Churchill, and hope that in some way it would all come right on the night – ie., that the mere necessities of war, the inevitable drift towards a centralised economy and a more equal standard of living, would force the régime gradually to the left and allow the worst reactionaries to be levered out. No one in his senses supposed that the British ruling classes would legislate themselves out of existence, but they might be manoeuvred into a position where their continuance in power was quite obviously in the Nazi interest. In that case the mass of the nation would swing against them and it would be possible to get rid of them with little or no violence. Before writing this off as a hopeless 'reformist' strategy it is worth remembering that England is literally within gunshot of the continent. Revolutionary defeatism, or anything approaching it, is nonsense in our geographical situation. If there were even a week's serious disorganisation in the armed forces the Nazis would be here, after which one might as well stop talking about revolution.

To some small extent things have happened as I foresaw. One can after all discern the outlines of a revolutionary world war. Britain has been forced into alliance with Russia and China and into restoring Abyssinia and making fairly generous treaties with the Middle Eastern countries, and because of, among other things, the need to raise a huge air force a serious breach has been made in the class system. The defeats in the Far East have gone a long way towards killing the old conception of imperialism. But there was a sort of gap in the ladder which we never got over and which it was perhaps impossible to get over while no revolutionary party and no able left-wing leadership existed. This may or may not have been altered by the emergence of Cripps. I think it is certain that a new political party will have to arise if anything is to be changed, and the obvious bankruptcy of the old parties may hasten this. Maybe Cripps will lose his lustre quite quickly if he does not get out of the government. But at present, in his peculiar isolated position, he is the likeliest man for any new movement to crystallise round. If he fails, God save us from the other probable alternatives to Churchill.

I suppose as usual I have written too much. There is not much change in our everyday lives here. The nation went onto brown bread[7] a few weeks back. The basic petrol ration stops next month, which in theory means the end of private motoring. The new luxury taxes are terrific. Cigarettes now cost a shilling for ten and the cheapest beer tenpence a pint (fourpence in 1936). Everyone seems to be working longer and longer hours. Now and again at intervals of weeks one gets one's head above water for a moment and notices with surprise that the earth is still going round the sun. One day I noticed crocuses in the parks, another day pear blossom, another day hawthorn. One seems to catch vague glimpses of these things through a mist of war news.

1. The article was given this title by the staff of *Partisan Review*, as Orwell notes in his London Letter for March–April 1943; see *1797*. When published, it was given five subheadings, almost certainly by *PR*; they have therefore been omitted.

2. Lord Louis Mountbatten (1900–1979), son of Prince Louis Francis of Battenberg, who relinquished that title in 1917 and assumed the surname Mountbatten, had already achieved fame in command of HMS *Kelly*, in 1939, and later in command of the aircraft-carrier *Illustrious*. He was Commodore and then Chief of Combined Operations, 1941–3; Supreme Allied Commander, Southeast Asia, 1943–6; March to August 1947 the last Viceroy of India; Governor-General of India after partition, August 1947–June 1948. He and members of his family were murdered by the Irish Republican Army in August 1979.

3. Independent Labour Party, of which Orwell had been a member from June 1938 until he resigned shortly after the outbreak of war.

4. Clement Attlee (1883–1967; 1955, Earl Attlee of Walthamstow), called to the Bar, 1905; served in the First World War and thereafter pursued a career in politics, becoming an MP in 1922. Leader of the Labour Party from 1935. Joined the War Cabinet and was Deputy Prime Minister to Churchill, 1942–5. Prime Minister 1945–51; his government was responsible, at a time of great post-war economic difficulty, for, among other things, the establishment of the National Health Service, much nationalization, and giving India and Burma their independence (1947 and 1948). His apparent 'tameness' concealed a steely determination.

5. The battle-cruisers *Scharnhorst* and *Gneisenau*, with the heavy cruiser *Prinz Eugen*, sailed from Brest on 11 February 1942, passed through the Channel, and reached Wilhelmshaven two days later. Despite being warned in advance of their departure by the French Resistance, and notwithstanding individually courageous attempts, the navy and RAF failed to sink them, though *Gneisenau* was damaged. The RAF lost 42 aircraft; the navy, 6 slow Swordfish torpedo-planes. The effect on the public was dismay and anger.

6. 'omitted' was set in the original as 'admitted'.

7. The 'National Loaf', for economy and health reasons, was darker than the standard white loaf. It was off-white, and never very popular. No more white bread could be sold after 6 April.

Extracts from War-time Diary

[1211]

7.6.42: ... Last Tuesday[1] spent a long evening with Cripps (who had expressed a desire to meet some literary people) together with Empson, Jack Common, David Owen, Norman Cameron, Guy Burgess[2] and another man (an official) whose name I didn't get. About 2½ hours of it, with nothing to drink. The usual inconclusive discussion. Cripps, however, very human and willing to listen. The person who stood up to him most successfully was Jack Common. Cripps said several things that amazed and slightly horrified me. One was that many people whose opinion was worth considering believed that the war would be over by October – ie. that Germany would be flat out by that time. When I said that I should look on that as a disaster pure and simple (because if the war were won as easily as that there would have been no real upheaval here and the American millionaires would still be in situ) he appeared not to understand. He said that once the war was won the surviving great powers would in any case have to administer the world as a unit, and seemed not to feel that it made much difference whether the great powers were capitalist or socialist.* Both David Owen and the man whose name I don't know supported him. I saw that I was up against the official mind, which sees everything as a problem in administration and does not grasp that at a certain point, ie. when certain economic interests are menaced, public spirit ceases to function. The basic assumption of such people is that everyone wants the world to function properly and will do his best to keep the wheels running. They don't realise that most of those who have the power don't care a damn about the world as a whole and are only intent on feathering their own nests. I can't help feeling a strong impression that Cripps has already been got at. Not with money or anything of that

---

* Very interesting but perhaps rather hard on Cripps to report an impression like this from a private interview [Orwell's handwritten footnote on typescript].

kind of course, nor even by flattery and the sense of power, which in all probability he genuinely doesn't care about: but simply by responsibility, which automatically makes a man timid. Besides, as soon as you are in power your perspectives are foreshortened. Perhaps a bird's eye view is as distorted as a worm's eye view . . .

1. 2 June 1942.

2. William Empson (1906–84; Kt., 1979), poet, scholar and critic; Professor of English Literature, Tokyo University, 1931–4, and at Peking, 1937–9 and 1947–53. He joined the BBC with Orwell and they worked together. Jack Common (1903–68) worked in a solicitor's office, a shoe shop and as a mechanic. He was co-editor of *The Adelphi*, 1935–6. Crick calls him 'one of the few authentic English proletarian writers', and describes Common's first meeting with Orwell (204). Though there was a certain tension between the two men, they remained friends. Common's books include *The Freedom of the Streets* (1938), described by Crick as 'straight-talking or garrulous polemic' (354), *Kiddar's Luck* (1951) and *The Ampersand* (1954). See *Orwell Remembered*, 139–43. Arthur David Kemp Owen (1904–70), personal assistant to Sir Stafford Cripps, 19 February to 21 November 1942. The poet Norman Cameron (1905–53) was a friend and disciple of Robert Graves, with whom he and Alan Hodge edited *Work in Hand* (1942). His *The Winter House and Other Poems* was published in 1935. He also translated from French and German. Guy Burgess (1911–63) was a communist educated at Eton and Cambridge. He worked for the British security services and the BBC in liaison with the Foreign Office and then joined the Foreign Office. His pro-Soviet activities were unsuspected until, in May 1951, he suddenly fled to Moscow with Donald Maclean, where he remained until his death.

[1380]

12.8.42: Appalling policy handout this morning about affairs in India. The riots are of no significance – situation is well in hand – after all the number of deaths is not large, etc., etc. As to the participation of students in the riots, this is explained along 'boys will be boys' lines. 'We all know that students everywhere are only too glad to join in any kind of rag', etc., etc. Almost everyone utterly disgusted. Some of the Indians when they hear this kind of stuff turn quite pale, a strange sight.

Most of the press taking a tough line, the Rothermere press disgustingly so. If these repressive measures in India are seemingly successful for the time being, the effects in this country will be very bad. All seems set for a big come-back of the reactionaries, and it almost begins to appear as though leaving Russia in the lurch were part of the manoeuvre. This afternoon shown in strict confidence by David Owen Amery's[1] statement

[on] postwar policy towards Burma, based on Dorman-Smith's[2] report. It envisages a return to 'direct rule' for a period of 5–7 years, Burma's reconstruction to be financed by Britain and the big British firms to be re-established on much the same terms as before. Please God no document of this kind gets into enemy hands. I did however get from Owen and from the confidential document one useful piece of information – that, so far as is known, the scorched earth policy was really carried out with extreme thoroughness.

1. Leopold Stennett Amery (1873–1955), Conservative MP, opposed disarmament and supported the Hoare–Laval proposals for resolving the Abyssinian crisis in 1935. In May 1940, after the fall of Norway to the Germans, he directed, at Chamberlain, Cromwell's words to the Long Parliament (1640–53): 'You have sat too long here for any good you may be doing . . . In the name of God, go!' His *My Political Life* (1953–5) gives an account of political events of the thirties.

2. Sir Reginald Hugh Dorman-Smith (1899–1977) was Governor of Burma in 1941 and during the British withdrawal in 1942.

[1391]

To Tom Wintringham
17 August 1942

Dear Wintringham,

I am in general agreement with the document you sent me,[1] and so are most of the people I know, but I think that from the point of view of propaganda approach it is all wrong. In effect, it demands two separate things which the average reader will get mixed up, first, the setting up of a committee, and secondly, the programme which that committee is to use as a basis for discussion. I should start by putting forward boldly and above all with an eye to intelligibility a programme for India coupled with the statement that this is what the Indian political leaders would accept. I would *not* start with any talk about setting up committees; in the first place because it depresses people merely to hear about committees, and in any case because the procedure you suggest would take months to carry through, and would probably lead to an inconclusive announcement. I should head my leaflet or whatever it is RELEASE NEHRU – REOPEN NEGOTIATIONS and then set forth the plan for India in six simple clauses, viz:

1). India to be declared independent immediately.

2). An interim national government from the leading political parties on a proportional basis.

3). India to enter into full alliance with the United Nations.

4). The leading political parties to co-operate in the war effort to their utmost capacity.

5). The existing administration to be disturbed as little as possible during the war period.

6). Some kind of trade agreement allowing for a reasonable safe-guarding of British interests.

Those are the six points. They should be accompanied by an authoritative statement from the Congress Party that they are willing to accept those terms – as they would be – and that if granted these terms they would co-operate in crushing the pro-Japanese faction. Point 6 should carry with it a rider to the effect that the British and Indian Governments will jointly guarantee the pensions of British officials in India. In this way at small cost one could neutralise a not unimportant source of opposition in this country.

All I have said could be got on to a leaflet of a page or two pages, and I think might get a hearing. It is most important to make this matter simple and arresting as it has been so horribly misrepresented in the press and the big public is thoroughly bored by India and only half aware of its strategic significance. Ditto with America.

Yours,

[No name]

1. Tom Wintringham sent Orwell a copy of the press release issued by the Common Wealth National Committee on 15 August 1942. This was issued over the names of J. B. Priestley (Chairman), Richard Acland (Vice-Chairman) and Tom Wintringham (Vice-Chairman). Sir Richard Acland (1906–90; Bt.) was elected a Liberal MP in 1935. From 1936 he was active in the campaign for a Popular Front (see p. 27, n. 2). At the outbreak of war he announced his conversion to socialism, or, as he called it, 'Common Ownership'. In February 1940 he published *Unser Kampf*, one of the most successful of the Penguin Specials. At a meeting in the House of Commons on 12 March 1940, some 150 readers who supported his programme agreed on a 'Manifesto for the Common Man'. From 1942 he represented the Common Wealth Party in Parliament, but the Party was unsuccessful at the polls. He served as a Labour MP, 1947–55, but was later expelled from the party. He then became a Senior Lecturer at St Luke's College of Education, Exeter, 1959–74. He gave his family home,

Killerton, near Exeter, with its beautiful gardens, to the nation. For Orwell's *Profile* of Acland, see XV/2095.

[1964]

Review of Letters on India *by Mulk Raj Anand*
Tribune, *19 March 1943*

Dear Mulk, – I write this review in the form of a letter since your book is itself written in the form of letters answering somebody else's letters, and has provoked yet another letter from Mr. Leonard Woolf,[1] a rather angry one this time, which is printed as a foreword.

On strictly political grounds I can't whack up any serious disagreement with you. I could point to statements in which you have probably been unfair to Britain, but it doesn't seem to me that you misrepresent the essential relationship between your country and mine. For a hundred and fifty years we have been exploiting you, and for at least thirty years we have been artificially holding back your development. I should never think of disputing that. I prefer to start with the policy that we do agree upon, and then point to some of the difficulties that lie in its way – difficulties which it seems to me no one has yet faced up to. You and I both know that there can be no real solution of the Indian problem which does not also benefit Britain. Either we all live in a decent world, or nobody does. It is so obvious, is it not, that the British worker as well as the Indian peasant stands to gain by the ending of capitalist exploitation, and that Indian independence is a lost cause if the Fascist nations are allowed to dominate the world. Quite manifestly the battle against Amery and the battle against Hitler are the same. But if this is obvious, why do so few people grasp it? Well, here are some of the things that stand in the way, and since this must be a short letter I will simply tabulate them instead of trying to weave them into one picture: –

Nationalism. – 'Enlightened' people everywhere refuse to take this seriously. Because of this refusal the huge European Fascist movement grew up under their noses, not merely unfeared but almost unnoticed. You know as well as I do, though you don't emphasise, the element of mere nationalism, even colour-hatred, that enters into the Indian independence movements. Most Indians who are politically conscious hate Britain so much that they have ceased to bother about the consequences of an Axis victory. Here in London young Indians have assured me that Japan is 'civilising' China and has no ill intentions towards India. An Indian friend in Delhi, himself a Communist or ex-Communist, writes to me that the Indian masses are 'whole-heartedly for Germany against Russia'; he describes the newsboys shouting in Urdu, 'Germany smashes Russia at the first battle', etc., etc.; and you know how hard colour-prejudice dies in this country also. A *News Chronicle* despatch from North Africa informs me that the British soldiers' nickname for an Arab village is a 'woggery' – that is, a place inhabited by Wogs, i.e. golliwogs, the most offensive of all the English nicknames for coloured people: this in 1943, when we are fighting a war which is said to be and actually *is* for Democracy against Fascism. Don't let's underrate the danger of this kind of thing.

Differential standard of living. – You put your finger on the difficulty when you said that for a century or two Britain had been almost 'a middle-class country'. One mightn't think it when one looks round the back streets of Sheffield, but the average British income is to the Indian as twelve to one. How can one get anti-Fascist and anti-capitalist solidarity in such circumstances? The normal Socialist arguments fall on deaf ears when they are addressed to India, because Indians refuse to believe that any class-struggle exists in Europe. In their eyes the underpaid, downtrodden English worker is himself an exploiter. And so long as Socialism teaches people to think in terms of material benefit, how would the British worker himself behave if told that he had to choose between keeping India in bondage and lowering his own wages?

Sentimentalism of the Left. – Why did your book annoy Mr. Leonard Woolf so much when the views it uttered were less 'extreme' than those that the *New Statesman* utters every week? At bottom, no doubt, because it gave him the impression that Indian nationalism is a force actually *hostile* to Britain and not merely a pleasant little game of blimp-baiting. You will have noticed that the causes favoured by the English Left in the past have, as often as not, ended by turning into some form of Fascism. Look back the necessary years or decades, and you find 'enlightened' British opinion supporting Japan as against Russia and China, the Boers and Sinn Feiners as against Britain, and the Germans as against the Poles and French. In each case the left-wing orthodoxy of the moment was accepted without any attempt to think out its full implications, because of the false world-view which assumes that all 'enlightened' people think more or less alike. At this moment nearly every English left-winger is pro-Jew as regards Palestine and pro-Congress as regards India. How many of them even know that many, if not most, Congress Indians are violently anti-Jew? And how pained and surprised the Left was when that well-known anti-Fascist Subhas Chandra Bose began broadcasting from Berlin! You see, Mr. Woolf was annoyed by your book because he had expected you to be anti-British in *his* way, whereas *your* way involved a condemnation of Mr. Woolf himself. You were right, of course, we are all nearer to the blimp than we are to the Indian peasant, but don't expect people to like being told so. Opinions sentimentally held are always liable to be suddenly reversed. I know more than one intellectual who has started out with a burning zeal to 'free India' and ending up by feeling that there is a lot to be said for General Dyer.[2] One shouldn't underrate the danger of that either.

Well, I could go on, but I haven't space. There at least are three of the difficulties that lie in the way of a juster and saner relationship between Britain and India. What arises from this? Only that one must work to make people realise that long-term and short-term interests don't necessarily coincide. The Englishman must see that his domination in India is indefensible; the Indian must see that to side with the Fascists for the sake of revenge against Britain would do him no good. It is largely a question of letting each know that the other's viewpoint exists. That brings me back to what I have often said before, that the best bridge between Europe and Asia, better than trade or battleships or aeroplanes, is the English language; and I hope that you and Ahmed Ali[3] and the others will continue to write in it, even if it sometimes leads you to be called a 'babu'[4] (as you were recently) at one end of the map and a renegade at the other.[5]

Yours ever
GEORGE ORWELL

1. Leonard Woolf (1880–1969), author, editor and publisher, served in the Ceylon Civil Service, 1904–11, and one of his novels was based on his time in Ceylon. He and his wife,

Virginia, daughter of Sir Leslie Stephen, founded the Hogarth Press in 1917, which published early works by, among others, E. M. Forster and T. S. Eliot. He was literary editor of the *Nation*, 1923–30, and joint editor of *Political Quarterly*, 1931–59. Among his political and social books were *Socialism and Co-operation* (1921), *Imperialism and Civilization* (1928) and *After the Deluge: A Study of Communal Psychology* (2 vols., 1931, 1939). He also wrote five volumes of autobiography (1960–69), and published them and the diaries of his time in Ceylon.

2. On 13 April 1919, General R. E. H. Dyer (1864–1927) ordered troops under his command to open fire on unarmed protestors, of whom 379 were killed. Although condemned generally and by court martial, the Guardians of the Golden Temple of Amritsar invested him as a Sikh in gratitude for his action and a London newspaper, the *Morning Post*, raised £26,000 for him by public subscription (*DNB*). On 13 March 1940, at the Caxton Hall, London, one of the survivors of the massacre, Udham Singh, assassinated the man who had been Lt. Gov. of the Punjab at the time and General Dyer's superior, Sir Michael O'Dwyer. Udham Singh was hanged on 31 July 1940. His remains were returned to India in 1974, where he is revered to this day.

3. Ahmed Ali (b. *c.* 1908), Pakistani writer and Professor of English in Bengal. In 1940, in his review of *Folios of New Writing*, Orwell wrote that the editor, John Lehmann, 'had made a real find in Ahmed Ali, whose "Morning in Delhi" is an exquisite piece of work' (XII/ 623). He worked as Listener Research Director for the BBC in New Delhi, 1942–5, and he and Orwell were often in contact. He was co-editor of *Indian Writing* (London, 1940–45) and *Tomorrow Bombay* (India, 1942–4). From 1949 to 1960 he worked for the government of Pakistan. He published in Urdu and English and among his publications in English are the novels *Twilight in Delhi* (1940, 1967) and *Ocean of Night* (1964), which reflect on the Muslim heritage in India. Translations into English of Urdu poetry are in his *The Falcon and the Hunted Bird* (1950).

4. 'babu' (or baboo) is properly the Bengali and Hindi equivalent of the English 'Mr' and was a term of respect. However, it came to be used pejoratively, especially of Bengali clerks, with a superficial knowledge of English, as 'a babu'. By 1880 it was being used of de-Europeanized English officers: *Hobson-Jobson: The Anglo-Indian Dictionary* (1886, 1996).

5. Leonard Woolf took up Orwell's reference to his 'rather angry' letter in *Tribune*, 2 April 1943, and on the 9th Anand replied. Orwell had, Woolf wrote, completely misrepresented the facts and his attitude, 'no doubt unintentionally'. He said he had been asked to write a foreword by the publishers and Mr Anand, and that Anand had suggested it be in the form of a letter. The book had not annoyed him and he thought there was no anger in what he wrote. He said that he had written that Anand and he were both Socialists and therefore he agreed with all the 'socialist interpretation' of the history of India Anand had given. For years he had been in favour of the British giving India independence. He hated imperialism for the harm it does both to the imperialist and the subject peoples. He disagreed with Anand on probably not more than 20 per cent of his statements and arguments. His most important disagreement was with Anand's and Congress's attitude to the Muslim minority. He had pointed out that pretending the Muslim problem did not exist played into the hands of British imperialists. In conclusion he asked if Orwell was justified in implying that after starting out with a burning zeal to free India, Woolf had ended up feeling there was a lot to be said for General Dyer. Anand, in his letter, denied that he had ever asked Woolf to

write a foreword, though he had suggested the letter-form. They had met in order to tease out their differences 'on certain vital points'. Anand disagreed with a great deal of Woolf's foreword and had insisted that the Labour Book Service include a reply by Anand to Woolf; further, Anand had refused to allow Woolf's foreword to be included in the trade edition of his book.

[2096]

London Letter [Dissolution of the Comintern; growth of the Common Wealth Party: c. 23 May 1943]
Partisan Review, *July–August 1943*

I begin my letter just after the dissolution of the Comintern,[1] and before the full effects of this have become clear. Of course the immediate results in Britain are easy to foretell. Obviously the Communists will make fresh efforts to affiliate with the Labour Party (this has already been refused by the LP Executive), obviously they will be told that they must dissolve and join as individuals, and obviously, once inside the Labour Party, they will try to act as an organised faction,[2] whatever promises they may have given beforehand. The real interest lies in trying to foresee the long-term effects of the dissolution on a Communist party of the British type.

Weighing up the probabilities, I think the Russian gesture should be taken at its face-value – that is, Stalin is genuinely aiming at a closer tie-up with the U.S.A. and Britain and not merely 'deceiving the bourgeoisie' as his followers like to believe. But that would not of itself alter the behaviour of the British Communists. For after all, their subservience to Moscow during the last fifteen years did not rest on any real authority. The British Communists could not be shot or exiled if they chose to disobey, and so far as I know they have not even had any money from Moscow in recent years. Moreover the Russians made it reasonably clear that they despised them. Their obedience depended on the mystique of the Revolution, which had gradually changed itself into a nationalistic loyalty to the Russian state. The English left-wing intelligentsia worship Stalin because they have lost their patriotism and their religious belief without losing the need for a god and a Fatherland. I have always held that many of them would transfer their allegiance to Hitler if Germany won. So long as 'Communism' merely means furthering the interests of the Russian

Foreign Office, it is hard to see that the disappearance of the Comintern makes any difference. Nearly always one can see at a glance what policy is needed, even if there is no central organisation to hand out directives.

However, one has got to consider the effect on the working-class membership, who have a different outlook from the salaried hacks at the top of the party. To these people the open declaration that the International is dead must make a difference, although it was in fact a ghost already. And even in the central committee of the party there are differences in outlook which might widen if after a while the British Communist Party came to think of itself as an independent party. One must allow here for the effects of self-deception. Even long-term Communists often won't admit to themselves that they are merely Russian agents, and therefore don't necessarily see what move is required until the instructions arrive from Moscow. Thus, as soon as the Franco-Russian military pact was signed, it was obvious that the French and British Communists must go all patriotic, but to my knowledge some of them failed to grasp this. Or again, after the signing of the Russo-German pact several leading members refused to accept the anti-war line and had to do some belly-crawling before their mutiny was forgiven. In the months that followed the two chief publicists of the party became extemely sympathetic to the Nazi *weltanschauung*, evidently to the dismay of some of the others. The line of division is between deracinated intellectuals like Palme Dutt and trade union men like Pollitt and Hannington.[3] After all the years they have had on the job none of these men can imagine any occupation except boosting Soviet Russia, but they might differ as to the best way of doing it if Russian leadership has really been withdrawn. All in all, I should expect the dissolution of the Comintern to produce appreciable results, but not immediately. I should say that for six months, perhaps more, the British Communists will carry on as always, but that thereafter rifts will appear and the party will either wither away or develop into a looser, less Russophile organisation under more up-to-date leadership.

There remains the bigger puzzle of why the Comintern was dissolved. If I am right and the Russians did it to inspire confidence, one must assume that the rulers of Britain and the U.S.A. wanted the dissolution and perhaps demanded it as part of the price of a second front. But in Britain at any rate there has been little sign in the past dozen years that the ruling class seriously objected to the existence of the Communist Party. Even during the People's Convention period they showed it an astonishing amount of tolerance. At all other times from 1935 onwards it has had powerful support from one or other section of the capitalist press. A thing that it is difficult to be sure about is where the Communists get their money from. It is not likely that they get all of it from their declared supporters, and I believe they tell the truth in saying that they get nothing from Moscow. The difference is that they are 'helped' from time to time by wealthy English people who see the value of an organisation which acts as an eel-trap for active Socialists. Beaverbrook for instance is credited, rightly or wrongly, with having financed the Communist Party during the past year or two. This is perhaps not less significant as a rumour than it would be as a fact. When one thinks of the history of the past twenty years it is hard not to feel that the Comintern has been one of the worst enemies the working class has had. Yet the Upper Crust is evidently pleased to see it disappear – a fact which I record but cannot readily explain.

The other important political development during these past months has been the growth of Common Wealth, Sir Richard Acland's party. I mentioned this in earlier letters but underrated its importance. It is now a movement to be seriously reckoned with and is hated by all the other parties alike.

Acland's programme, which is set forth almost in baby language in many leaflets and pamphlets, could be described as Socialism minus the class war and with the emphasis on the moral instead of the economic motive. It calls for nationalisation of all major resources, immediate independence (not Dominion status) for India, pooling of raw materials as between 'have' and 'have not' countries, international administration of backward areas, and a composite army drawn from as many countries as possible to keep the peace after the war is done. All in all this programme is not less drastic than that of the extremist parties of the Left, but it has some unusual features which are worth noticing, since they explain the advance Common Wealth has made during the past few months.

In the first place the whole class war ideology is scrapped. Though all property-owners are to be expropriated, they are to receive fractional compensation – in effect, the bourgeois is to be given a small life-pension

instead of a firing squad. The idea of 'proletarian dictatorship' is specifically condemned; the middle class and the working class are to amalgamate
instead of fighting one another. The party's literature is aimed chiefly at
winning over the middle class, both the technical middle class and the
'little man' (farmers, shopkeepers etc.). Secondly, the economic side of
the programme lays the emphasis on increasing production rather than
equalising consumption. Thirdly, an effort is made to synthesise patriotism
with an internationalist outlook. Stress is laid on the importance of
following British tradition and 'doing things in our own way'. Parliament,
apparently, is to be preserved in much its present form, and nothing is
said against the Monarchy. Fourthly, Common Wealth does not describe
itself as 'Socialist' and carefully avoids Marxist phraseology. It declares
itself willing to collaborate with any other party whose aims are sufficiently
similar. (With the Labour Party the test is that the L.P. shall break the
electoral truce.) Fifthly – and perhaps most important of all – Common
Wealth propaganda has a strong ethical tinge. Its best-known poster
consists simply of the words 'Is it expedient?' crossed out and replaced by
'Is it right?'. Anglican priests are much to the fore in the movement though
the Catholics seem to be opposing it.

Whether this movement has a future I am still uncertain, but its growth
since I last wrote to you has been very striking. Acland's candidates are
fighting by-elections all over the country. Although they have only won
two so far, they have effected a big turn-over of votes against Government
candidates, and what is perhaps more significant, the whole poll seems to
rise wherever a Common Wealth candidate appears. The I.L.P. has been
conducting a distant flirtation with Common Wealth, but the other Left
parties are hostile and perhaps frightened. The usual criticism is that
Common Wealth is only making progress because of the electoral truce
– in other words, because the Labour Party is what it is. In addition it is
said that the membership of the party is wholly middle class. Acland
himself claims to have a good nucleus of followers in the factories and
still more in the Forces. The Communists, of course, have labelled
Common Wealth as Fascist. They and the Conservatives now work
together at by-elections.

The programme I have roughly outlined has elements both of dem-
agogy and of Utopianism, but it takes very much better account of the

actual balance of forces than any of the older Left parties have done. It might have a chance of power if another revolutionary situation arises, either through military disaster or at the end of the war. Some who know Acland declare that he has a 'führer complex' and that if he saw the movement growing beyond his control he would split it sooner than share authority. I don't believe this to be so, but neither do I believe that Acland by himself could bring a nation-wide movement into being. He is not a big enough figure, and not in any way a man of the people. Although of aristocratic and agricultural background (he is a fifteenth baronet) he has the manners and appearance of a civil servant, with a typical upper-class accent. For a popular leader in England it is a serious disability to be a gentleman, which Churchill, for instance, is not. Cripps is a gentleman, but to offset this he has his notorious 'austerity', the Gandhi touch, which Acland just misses, in spite of his ethical and religious slant. I think this movement should be watched with attention. It might develop into the new Socialist party we have all been hoping for, or into something very sinister: it has some rather doubtful followers already.

Finally a word about anti-semitism, which could now be said to have reached the stature of a 'problem'. I said in my last letter that it was not increasing, but I now think it is. The danger signal, which is also a safeguard, is that everyone is very conscious of it and it is discussed interminably in the press.

Although Jews in England have always been socially looked down on and debarred from a few professions (I doubt whether a Jew would be accepted as an officer in the Navy, for instance), anti-semitism is primarily a working-class thing, and strongest among Irish labourers. I have had some glimpses of working-class anti-semitism through being three years in the Home Guard – which gives a good cross-section of society – in a district where there are a lot of Jews. My experience is that middle-class people will laugh at Jews and discriminate against them to some extent, but only among working people do you find the full-blown belief in the Jews as a cunning and sinister race who live by exploiting the Gentiles. After all that has happened in the last ten years it is a fearful thing to hear a workingman saying 'Well, I reckon 'Itler done a good job when 'e turned 'em all out', but I have heard just that, and more than once. These people never seem to be aware that Hitler has done anything to the Jews except 'turned 'em all out'; the pogroms, the deportations etc. have simply escaped their notice. It is questionable, however, whether the Jew is objected to as a Jew or simply as a foreigner. No religious consideration enters. The English Jew, who is often strictly orthodox but entirely anglicised in his habits, is less disliked than the European refugee who has probably not been near a synagogue for thirty years. Some people actually object to the Jews on the ground that Jews are Germans!

But in somewhat different forms anti-semitism is now spreading among the middle class as well. The usual formula is 'of course I don't want you to think I'm anti-semitic, but —' – and here follows a catalogue of Jewish misdeeds. Jews are accused of evading military service, infringing the food laws, pushing their way to the front of queues, etc., etc. More thoughtful people point out that the Jewish refugees use this country as a temporary asylum but show no loyalty towards it. Objectively this is true, and the tactlessness of some of the refugees is almost incredible. (For example, a remark by a German Jewess overheard during the Battle of France: 'These English police are not nearly so smart as our S.S. Men.') But arguments of this kind are obviously rationalisations of prejudice. People dislike the Jews so much that they do not want to remember their sufferings, and when you mention the horrors that are happening in Germany or Poland, the answer is always 'Oh yes, of course that's dreadful, but —' – and out comes the familiar list of grievances. Not all of the intelligentsia are immune from this kind of thing. Here the get-out is usually that the refugees are all 'petty bourgeois'; and so the abuse of Jews can proceed under a respectable disguise. Pacifists and others who are anti-war sometimes find themselves forced into anti-semitism.

One should not exaggerate the danger of this kind of thing. To begin with, there is probably less anti-semitism in England now than there was thirty years ago. In the minor novels of that date you find it taken for granted far oftener than you would nowadays that a Jew is an inferior or a figure of fun. The 'Jew joke' has disappeared from the stage, the radio and the comic papers since 1934. Secondly, there is a great awareness of the prevalence of anti-semitism and a conscious effort to struggle against it. But the thing remains, and perhaps it is one of the inevitable neuroses of war. I am not particularly impressed by the fact that it does not take violent forms. It is true that no one wants to have pogroms and throw elderly Jewish professors into cesspools, but then there is very little crime or violence in England anyway. The milder form of anti-semitism prevailing here can be just as cruel in an indirect way, because it causes people to avert their eyes from the whole refugee problem and remain uninterested in the fate of the surviving Jews of Europe. Because two days ago a fat Jewess grabbed your place on the bus, you switch off the wireless when the announcer begins talking about the ghettoes of Warsaw;[4] that is how people's minds work nowadays.

That is all the political news I have. Life goes on much as before. I don't notice that our food is any different, but the food situation is generally considered to be worse. The war hits one a succession of blows in unexpected places. For a long time razor blades were unobtainable, now it is boot polish. Books are being printed on the most villainous paper and in tiny print, very trying to the eyes. A few people are wearing wooden-soled shoes. There is an alarming amount of drunkenness in London. The American soldiers seem to be getting on better terms with the locals, perhaps having become more resigned to the climate etc. Air raids continue, but on a pitiful scale. I notice that many people feel sympathy for the Germans now that it is they who are being bombed – a change from 1940, when people saw their houses tumbling about them and wanted to see Berlin scraped off the map.

1. The Comintern (Communist International) was established in Moscow in 1919 to promote revolution by workers against capitalist governments. It was dissolved on 15 May 1943 by Stalin. For a sympathetic interpretation of this 'gesture', see the correspondence arising from Orwell's Malay Newsletter of 28 May, representing the official British government line, *2102*.
2. 'faction' printed as 'fraction' – a possible but unlikely reading.
3. Rajani Palme Dutt (1896–1974) was Vice-Chairman of the Communist Party and member of the Executive Committee from 1922. Harry Pollitt (1890–1960) was a founder of the British Communist Party and its General Secretary from 1929. Walter Hannington (b. 1895) was author of *The Problem of the Distressed Areas*, published by the Left Book Club (November 1937), and *Ten Lean Years* (1940), an account of the 1930s.
4. The massacre of Jews in the Warsaw ghetto began on 20 April 1943 and ended on 16 May. At least 56,000 people were killed and those left alive were transported to concentration camps.

[2120]
'Literature and the Left'
Tribune, *4 June 1943*

'When a man of true Genius appears in the World, you may know him by this infallible Sign, that all the Dunces are in Conspiracy against him.' So wrote Jonathan Swift,[1] 200 years before the publication of *Ulysses*.

If you consult any sporting manual or year book you will find many pages devoted to the hunting of the fox and the hare, but not a word about the hunting of the highbrow. Yet this, more than any other, is the characteristic British sport, in season all the year round and enjoyed by rich and poor alike, with no complications from either class-feeling or political alignment.

For it should be noted that in its attitude towards 'highbrows' – that is, towards any writer or artist who makes experiments in technique – the Left is no friendlier than the Right. Not only is 'highbrow' almost as much a word of abuse in the *Daily Worker* as in *Punch*, but it is exactly those writers whose work shows both originality and the power to endure that Marxist doctrinaires single out for attack. I could name a long list of examples, but I am thinking especially of Joyce, Yeats, Lawrence and Eliot. Eliot, in particular, is damned in the left-wing press almost as automatically and perfunctorily as Kipling – and that by critics who only a few years back were going into raptures over the already forgotten masterpieces of the Left Book Club.

If you ask a 'good party man' (and this goes for almost any party of the Left) what he objects to in Eliot, you get an answer that ultimately reduces to this. Eliot is a reactionary (he has declared himself a royalist, an Anglo-Catholic, etc.), and he is also a 'bourgeois intellectual', out of touch with the common man: therefore he is a bad writer. Contained in this statement is a half-conscious confusion of ideas which vitiates nearly all politico-literary criticism.

To dislike a writer's politics is one thing. To dislike him because he forces you to think is another, not necessarily incompatible with the first. But as soon as you start talking about 'good' and 'bad' writers you are tacitly appealing to literary tradition and thus dragging in a totally different set of values. For what is a 'good' writer? Was Shakespeare 'good'? Most people would agree that he was. Yet Shakespeare is, and perhaps was even by the standards of his own time, reactionary in tendency;[2] and he is also a difficult writer, only doubtfully accessible to the common man. What, then, becomes of the notion that Eliot is disqualified, as it were, by being an Anglo-Catholic royalist who is given to quoting Latin?

Left-wing literary criticism has not been wrong in insisting on the importance of subject-matter. It may not even have been wrong, considering the age we live in, in demanding that literature shall be first and foremost propaganda. Where it has been wrong is in making what are ostensibly literary judgments for political ends. To take a crude example, what Communist would dare to admit in public that Trotsky is a better writer than Stalin – as he is, of course? To say 'X is a gifted writer, but he is a political enemy and I shall do my best to silence him' is harmless enough. Even if you end by silencing him with a tommy-gun you are not really sinning against the intellect. The deadly sin is to say 'X is a political enemy: therefore he is a bad writer'. And if anyone says that this kind of thing doesn't happen, I answer merely: look up the literary pages of the left-wing press, from the *News Chronicle* to the *Labour Monthly*, and see what you find.

There is no knowing just how much the Socialist movement has lost by alienating the literary intelligentsia. But it has alienated them, partly by confusing tracts with literature, and partly by having no room in it for a humanistic culture. A writer can vote Labour as easily as anyone else, but it is very difficult for him to take part in the Socialist movement *as a writer*. Both the book-trained doctrinaire and the practical politician will despise him as a 'bourgeois intellectual', and will lose no opportunity of telling him so. They will have much the same attitude towards his work as a golfing stockbroker would have. The illiteracy of politicians is a special feature of our age – as G. M. Trevelyan[3] put it, 'In the seventeenth century Members of Parliament quoted the Bible, in the eighteenth and nineteenth centuries, the classics, and in the twentieth century nothing' – and its corollary is the literary impotence of writers. In the years following the last war the best English writers were reactionary in tendency, though most of them took no direct part in politics. After them, about 1930, there came a generation of writers who tried very hard to be actively useful in the left-wing movement. Numbers of them joined the Communist Party, and got there exactly the same reception as they would have got in the Conservative Party. That is, they were first regarded with patronage and suspicion, and then, when it was found that they would not or could not turn themselves into gramophone records, they were thrown out on their ears. Most of them retreated into individualism. No doubt they still vote Labour but their talents are lost to the movement; and – a more sinister development – after them there comes a new generation of writers who, without being strictly non-political, are outside the Socialist movement from the start. Of the very young writers who are now beginning their careers, the most gifted are pacifists; a few may even have a leaning towards Fascism. There is hardly one to whom the mystique of the Socialist movement appears to mean anything. The ten-year-long struggle against Fascism seems to them meaningless and uninteresting, and they say so frankly. One could explain this in a number of ways, but the contemptuous attitude of the Left towards 'bourgeois intellectuals' is likely to be part of the reason.

Gilbert Murray[4] relates somewhere or other that he once lectured on Shakespeare to a Socialist debating society. At the end he called for questions in the usual way, to receive as the sole question asked: 'Was Shakespeare a capitalist?' The depressing thing about this story is that it might well be true. Follow up its implications, and you perhaps get a glimpse of the reason why Céline wrote *Mea Culpa*[5] and Auden is watching his navel in America.

1. 'When a true Genius appears in the World, you may know him by this Sign, that the Dunces are all in confederacy against him'. *Thoughts on Various Subjects* in Swift's *Miscellanies*, vol. 1 (1728). Orwell, as so often, is probably quoting from memory.

2. Kenneth Muir (1907–96), Shakespearean scholar, later King Alfred Professor of English Literature at the University of Liverpool, wrote to *Tribune* arguing against Orwell's statement that Shakespeare was 'reactionary in tendency'.

3. G. M. Trevelyan (1876–1962), historian whose *History of England* (first published 1926) was often republished in different forms. Among his other notable works was *English Social History: A Survey of Six Centuries, Chaucer to Queen Victoria*, 4 vols. (1942), also published as *An Illustrated Social History* (1949–52).

4. Gilbert Murray (1866–1957), scholar of Greek literature and culture, noted particularly for his editions of Euripides and Aeschylus.

5. Céline (pseud. of Louis-Ferdinand Destouches, 1894–1961), French physician and author, severely wounded in World War I. He worked in a poor area of Paris from 1928 and wrote

two significant novels, *Voyage au bout de la nuit* (1932; *Journey to the End of the Night*), a bitter satire on the society of his time, and *Mort à crédit* (1936; *Death on the Instalment Plan*), and also anti-Semitic pamphlets. *Mea Culpa* (1936) was written following a visit to the Soviet Union and reflected his abhorrence at what he found there. He was rejected when he tried to enlist for war service in 1939. In 1942 he visited Berlin and, in 1944, fearing retribution for his collaboration with the Nazis, tried to flee to Denmark. He was imprisoned in Berlin and practised medicine among Vichy expatriates. He succeeded in escaping to Denmark in 1945, where he was imprisoned for fourteen months for collaboration. In 1950, a French court condemned him to imprisonment for a year, a heavy fine and the confiscation of half his property. The following year, a military court exonerated him. He then set up a medical practice for the poor of Meudon, near Paris.

[2257]

Review of Beggar My Neighbour *by Lionel Fielden*

Horizon, *September 1943;* Partisan Review, *Winter 1944*

GANDHI IN MAYFAIR

If you compare commercial advertising with political propaganda, one thing that strikes you is its relative intellectual honesty. The advertiser at least knows what he is aiming at – that is, money – whereas the propagandist, when he is not a lifeless hack, is often a neurotic working off some private grudge and actually desirous of the exact opposite of the thing he advocates. The ostensible purpose of Mr. Fielden's book is to further the cause of Indian independence. It will not have that effect, and I do not see much reason for thinking that he himself wishes for anything of the kind. For if someone is genuinely working for Indian independence, what is he likely to do? Obviously he will start by deciding what forces are potentially on his side, and then, as cold-bloodedly as any toothpaste advertiser, he will think out the best method of appealing to them. This is not Mr. Fielden's manner of approach. A number of motives are discernible in his book, but the immediately obvious one is a desire to work off various quarrels with the Indian Government, All-India Radio and various sections of the British Press. He does indeed marshal a number of facts about India, and towards the end he even produces a couple of pages of constructive suggestions, but for the most part his book is simply a nagging, irrelevant attack on British rule, mixed up with tourist-like gush about the superiority of Indian civilization. On the fly-leaf, just to induce that matey atmosphere which all propagandists aim at, he signs his dedicatory letter 'among the European barbarians', and then a few pages later introduces an imaginary Indian who denounces Western civilization with all the shrillness of a spinster of thirty-nine denouncing the male sex:

. . . an Indian who is intensely proud of his own traditions, and regards Europeans as barbarians who are continually fighting, who use force to dominate other peaceful peoples, who think chiefly in terms of big business, whisky, and bridge; as people of comparatively recent growth, who, while they put an exaggerated value on plumbing, have managed to spread tuberculosis and venereal disease all over the world . . . he will say that to sit in the water in which you have washed, instead of bathing yourself in running water, is not clean, but dirty and disgusting; he will show, and I shall agree with him absolutely, that the English are a dirty and even a smelly nation compared with the Indians; he will assert, and I am not at all sure that he is wrong, that the use of half-washed forks, spoons and knives by different people for food is revoltingly barbaric when compared with the exquisite manipulation of food by Indian fingers; he will be confident that the Indian room, with its bare walls and beautiful carpets, is infinitely superior to the European clutter of uncomfortable chairs and tables,

etc. etc. etc.

The whole book is written in this vein, more or less. The same nagging, hysterical note crops up every few pages, and where a comparison can be dragged in it is dragged in, the upshot always being that the East is Good and the West is Bad. Now before stopping to inquire what service this kind of thing really does to the cause of Indian freedom, it is worth trying an experiment. Let me rewrite this passage as it might be uttered by an Englishman speaking up for his own civilization as shrilly as Mr. Fielden's Indian. It is important to notice that what he says is not more dishonest or more irrelevant than what I have quoted above:

. . . an Englishman who is intensely proud of his own traditions, and regards Indians as an unmanly race who gesticulate like monkeys, are cruel to women and talk incessantly about money; as a people who take it upon themselves to despise Western science and hence are rotten with malaria and hookworm . . . he will say that in a hot climate washing in running water has its points, but that in cold climates all Orientals either wash as we do or as in the case of many Indian hill tribes – not at all; he will show, and I shall agree with him absolutely, that no Western European can walk through an Indian village without wishing that his smell organs had been removed beforehand; he will assert, and I am not at all sure that he is wrong, that eating with your fingers is a barbarous habit since it cannot be done without making disgusting noises; he will be confident that the English room, with its comfortable armchairs and friendly bookshelves, is infinitely superior to the bare Indian interior where the mere effort of sitting with no support to your back makes for vacuity of mind, etc. etc. etc.

Two points emerge here. To begin with, no English person would now write like that. No doubt many people think such thoughts, and even utter them behind closed doors, but to find anything of the kind in print you would have to go back ten years or so. Secondly, it is worth asking, what would be the effect of this passage on an Indian who happened to take it seriously? He would be offended, and very rightly. Well then, isn't it just possible that passages like the one I quoted from Mr. Fielden might have the same effect on a British reader? No one likes hearing his own habits and customs abused. This is not a trivial consideration, because at this moment books about India have, or could have, a special importance. There is no political solution in sight, the Indians cannot win their freedom and the British Government will not give it, and all one can for the moment do is to push public opinion in this country and America in the right direction. But that will not be done by any propaganda that is merely anti-European. A year ago, soon after the Cripps mission had failed, I saw a well-known Indian nationalist address a small meeting at which he was to explain why the Cripps offer had been refused. It was a valuable opportunity, because there were present a number of American newspaper correspondents who, if handled tactfully, might cable to America a sympathetic account of the Congress Party's[1] case. They had come there with fairly open minds. Within about ten minutes the Indian had converted all of them into ardent supporters of the British Government, because instead of sticking to his subject he launched into an anti-British tirade quite obviously founded on spite and inferiority complex. That is just the mistake that a toothpaste advertiser would not make. But then the toothpaste advertiser is trying to sell toothpaste and not to get his own back on that Blimp who turned him out of a first-class carriage fifteen years ago.

However, Mr. Fielden's book raises wider issues than the immediate political problem. He upholds the East against the West on the ground that the East is religious, artistic and indifferent to 'progress', while the West is materialistic, scientific, vulgar and warlike. The great crime of Britain is to have forced industrialization on India. (Actually, the real crime of Britain during the last thirty years has been to do the opposite.) The West looks on work as an end in itself, but at the same time is obsessed with a 'high standard of living' (it is worth noticing that Mr. Fielden is anti-Socialist, Russophobe and somewhat contemptuous of the English working class), while India wants only to live in ancestral simplicity in a world freed from the machine. India must be independent, and at the same time must be de-industrialized. It is also suggested a number of times, though not in very clear terms, that India ought to be neutral in the present war. Needless to say, Mr. Fielden's hero is Gandhi, about whose financial background he says nothing.

I have a notion that the legend of Gandhi may yet be a flaming inspiration to the millions of the East, and perhaps to those of the West. But it is, for the time being, the East which provides the fruitful soil, because the East has not yet fallen prone before the Golden Calf. And it may be for the East, once again, to show mankind that human happiness does not depend on that particular form of worship, and that the conquest of materialism is also the conquest of war.

Gandhi makes many appearances in the book, playing rather the same part as 'Frank' in the literature of the Buchmanites.[2]

Now, I do not know whether or not Gandhi will be a 'flaming inspiration' in years to come. When one thinks of the creatures who *are* venerated by humanity it does not seem particularly unlikely. But the statement that India 'ought' to be independent, *and* de-industrialized, *and* neutral in the present war, is an absurdity. If one forgets the details of the political struggle and looks at the strategic realities, one sees two facts which are in seeming conflict. The first is that whatever the 'ought' of the question may be, India is very unlikely ever to be independent in the sense in which Britain or Germany is now independent. The second is that India's *desire* for independence is a reality and cannot be talked out of existence.

In a world in which national sovereignty exists, India cannot be a sovereign State, because she is unable to defend herself. And the more she is the cow and spinning-wheel paradise imagined by Mr. Fielden, the more this is true. What is now called independence means the power to manufacture aeroplanes in large numbers. Already there are only five genuinely independent States in the world, and if present trends continue there will in the end be only three. On a long-term view it is clear that India has little chance in a world of power politics, while on a short-term view it is clear that the necessary first step towards Indian freedom is an Allied victory. Even that would only be a short and uncertain step, but the alternatives must lead to India's continued subjection. If we are defeated, Japan or Germany takes over India and that is the end of the story. If there is a compromise peace (Mr. Fielden seems to hint at times that this is desirable), India's chances are no better, because in such circumstances we should inevitably cling to any territories we had captured or not lost. A compromise peace is always a peace of 'grab what you can'. Mr. Fielden brings forward his imaginary Indian to suggest that if India were neutral Japan might leave her alone; I doubt whether any responsible Indian nationalist has said anything quite so stupid as that. The other idea, more popular in left-wing circles, that India could defend herself better on her own than with our help, is a sentimentality. If the Indians were militarily superior to ourselves they would have driven us out long ago. The much-quoted example of China is very misleading here. India is a far easier country to conquer than China, if only because of its better communications, and in any case Chinese resistance depends on help from the highly-industrialized states and would collapse without it. One must conclude that for the next few years India's destiny is linked with that of Britain and the U.S.A. It might be different if the Russians could get their hands free in the West or if China were a great military power; but that again implies a complete defeat of the Axis, and points away from the neutrality which Mr. Fielden seems to think desirable. The idea put forward by Gandhi himself, that if the Japanese came they could be dealt with by sabotage and 'non-co-operation', is a delusion, nor does Gandhi show any very strong signs of believing in it. Those methods have never seriously embarrassed the British and would make no impression on the Japanese. After all, where is the Korean Gandhi?

But against this is the *fact* of Indian nationalism, which is not to be exorcized by the humbug of White Papers or by a few phrases out of Marx. And it is nationalism of an emotional, romantic, even chauvinistic kind. Phrases like 'the sacred soil of the Motherland', which now seem merely ludicrous in Britain, come naturally enough to an Indian intellectual. When the Japanese appeared to be on the point of invading India, Nehru actually used the phrase 'Who dies if India live?'. So the wheel comes full circle and the Indian rebel quotes Kipling.³ And nationalism at this level works indirectly in favour of Fascism. Extremely few Indians are at all attracted by the idea of a federated world, the only kind of world in which India could actually be free. Even those who pay lip-service to federalism usually want only an Eastern federation, thought of as a military alliance against the West. The idea of the class struggle has little appeal anywhere in Asia, nor do Russia and China evoke much loyalty in India. As for the Nazi domination of Europe, only a handful of Indians are able to see that it affects their own destiny in any way. In some of the smaller Asiatic countries the 'my country right or wrong' nationalists were exactly the ones who went over to the Japanese – a step which may not have been wholly due to ignorance.

But here there arises a point which Mr. Fielden hardly touches on, and that is: we don't know to what extent Asiatic nationalism is simply the product of our own oppression. For a century all the major Oriental nations except Japan have been more or less in subjection, and the hysteria and shortsightedness of the various nationalist movements may be the result simply of that. To realize that national sovereignty is the enemy of national freedom may be a great deal easier when you are not being ruled by foreigners. It is not certain that this is so, since the most nationalist of the Oriental nations, Japan, is also the one that has never been conquered, but at least one can say that if the solution is not along these lines, then there *is* no solution. Either power politics must yield to common decency, or the world must go spiralling down into a nightmare of which we can already catch some dim glimpses. And the necessary first step, before we can make our talk about world federation sound even credible, is that

Britain shall get off India's back. This is the only large scale decent action that is possible in the world at this moment. The immediate preliminaries would be: abolish the Viceroyalty and the India Office, release the Congress prisoners, and declare India formally independent. The rest is detail.*

But how are we to bring any such thing about? If it is done at this time, it can only be a voluntary act. Indian independence has no asset except public opinion in Britain and America, which is only a potential asset. Japan, Germany and the British Government are all on the other side, and India's possible friends, China and the U.S.S.R., are fighting for their lives and have little bargaining power. There remain the peoples of Britain and America, who are in a position to put pressure on their own Governments if they see a reason for doing so. At the time of the Cripps mission, for instance, it would have been quite easy for public opinion in this country to force the Government into making a proper offer, and similar opportunities may recur. Mr. Fielden, by the way, does his best to throw doubt on Cripps' personal honesty, and also lets it appear that the Congress Working Committee were unanimously against accepting the Cripps proposals, which was not the case. In fact, Cripps extorted the best terms he could get from the Government; to get better ones he would have had to have public opinion actively and intelligently behind him. Therefore the first job is – win over the ordinary people of this country. Make them see that India matters, and that India has been shamefully treated and deserves restitution. But you are not going to do that by insulting them. Indians, on the whole, grasp this better than their English apologists. After all, what is the probable effect of a book which irrelevantly abuses every English institution, rapturizes over the 'wisdom of the East' like an American schoolmarm on a conducted tour, and mixes up pleas for Indian freedom with pleas for surrender to Hitler? At best it can only convert the converted, and it may de-convert a few of those. The net effect must be to strengthen British imperialism, though its motives are probably more complex than this may seem to imply.

On the surface, Mr. Fielden's book is primarily a plea for 'spirituality'

---

* Of course the necessary corollary would be a military alliance for the duration of the war. But it is not likely that there would be any difficulty in securing this. Extremely few Indians really want to be ruled by Japan or Germany [Orwell's footnote].

as against 'materialism'. On the one hand an uncritical reverence for everything Oriental; on the other a hatred of the West generally, and of Britain in particular, hatred of science and the machine, suspicion of Russia, contempt for the working-class conception of Socialism. The whole adds up to Parlour Anarchism – a plea for the simple life, based on dividends. Rejection of the machine is, of course, always founded on tacit acceptance of the machine, a fact symbolized by Gandhi as he plays with his spinning-wheel in the mansion of some cotton millionaire. But Gandhi also comes into the picture in another way. It is noticeable that both Gandhi and Mr. Fielden have an exceedingly equivocal attitude towards the present war. Although variously credited in this country with being a 'pure' pacifist and a Japanese agent, Gandhi has, in fact, made so many conflicting pronouncements on the war that it is difficult to keep track of them. At one moment his 'moral support' is with the Allies, at another it is withdrawn, at one moment he thinks it best to come to terms with the Japanese, at another he wishes to oppose them by non-violent means – at the cost, he thinks, of several million lives – at another he urges Britain to give battle in the west and leave India to be invaded, at another he 'has no wish to harm the Allied cause' and declares that he does not want the Allied troops to leave India. Mr. Fielden's views on the war are less complicated, but equally ambiguous. In no place does he state whether or not he wishes the Axis to be defeated. Over and over again he urges that an Allied victory can lead to no possible good result, but at the same time he disclaims 'defeatism' and even argues that Indian neutrality would be useful to us in a *military* sense, i.e. that we could fight better if India were not a liability. Now, if this means anything, it means that he wants a compromise, a negotiated peace; and though he fails to say so, I do not doubt that that is what he does want. But curiously enough, this is the *imperialist* solution. The appeasers have always wanted neither defeat nor victory but a compromise with the other imperialist powers; and they too have known how to use the manifest folly of war as an argument.

For years past the more intelligent imperialists have been in favour of compromising with the Fascists, even if they had to give away a good deal in order to do so, because they have seen that only thus could imperialism be salvaged. Some of them are not afraid to hint this fairly broadly even now. If we carry the war to a destructive conclusion, the

British Empire will either be lost, or democratized, or pawned to America. On the other hand it could and probably would survive in something like its present form if there were other sated imperialist powers which had an interest in preserving the existing world system. If we came to an understanding with Germany and Japan we might diminish our possessions (even that isn't certain: it is a little-noticed fact that *in territory* Britain and the U.S.A. have gained more than they have lost in this war), but we should at least be confirmed in what we had already. The world would be split up between three or four great imperial powers who, for the time being, would have no motive for quarrelling. Germany would be there to neutralize Russia, Japan would be there to prevent the development of China. Given such a world system, India could be kept in subjection almost indefinitely. And more than this, it is doubtful whether a compromise peace *could* follow any other lines. So it would seem that Parlour Anarchism is something very innocuous after all. Objectively it only demands what the worst of the appeasers want, subjectively it is of a kind to irritate the possible friends of India in this country. And does not this bear a sort of resemblance to the career of Gandhi, who has alienated the British public by his extremism and aided the British Government by his moderation? Impossibilism and reaction are usually in alliance, though not, of course, conscious alliance.

Hypocrisy is a very rare thing, true villainy is perhaps [as] difficult as virtue. We live in a lunatic world in which opposites are constantly changing into one another, in which pacifists find themselves worshipping Hitler, Socialists become nationalists, patriots become quislings, Buddhists pray for the success of the Japanese army, and the Stock Market takes an upward turn when the Russians stage an offensive. But though these people's motives are often obvious enough when seen from the outside, they are not obvious to themselves. The scenes imagined by Marxists, in which wicked rich men sit in little secret rooms and hatch schemes for robbing the workers, don't happen in real life. The robbery takes place, but it is committed by sleepwalkers. Now, one of the finest weapons that the rich have ever evolved for use against the poor is 'spirituality'. If you can induce the working-man to believe that his desire for a decent standard of living is 'materialism', you have got him where you want him. Also, if you can induce the Indian to remain 'spiritual' instead of taking up with vulgar things like trade unions, you can ensure that he will always remain a coolie. Mr. Fielden is indignant with the 'materialism' of the Western working class, whom he accuses of being even worse in this respect than the rich and of wanting not only radios but even motor-cars and fur coats. The obvious answer is that these sentiments don't come well from someone who is in a comfortable and privileged position himself. But that is only an answer, not a diagnosis, for the problem of the disaffected intelligentsia would be hardly a problem at all if ordinary dishonesty were involved.

In the last twenty years Western civilization has given the intellectual security without responsibility, and in England, in particular, it has educated him in scepticism while anchoring him almost immovably in the privileged class. He has been in the position of a young man living on an allowance from a father whom he hates. The result is a deep feeling of guilt and resentment, not combined with any genuine desire to escape. But some psychological escape, some form of self-justification there must be, and one of the most satisfactory is transferred nationalism. During the nineteen-thirties the normal transference was to Soviet Russia, but there are other alternatives, and it is noticeable that pacifism and Anarchism, rather than Stalinism, are now gaining ground among the young. These creeds have the advantage that they aim at the impossible and therefore in effect demand very little. If you throw in a touch of Oriental mysticism and Buchmanite raptures over Gandhi, you have everything that a disaffected intellectual needs. The life of an English gentleman and the moral attitude of a saint can be enjoyed simultaneously. By merely transferring your allegiance from England to India (it used to be Russia), you can indulge to the full in all the chauvinistic sentiments which would be totally impossible if you recognized them for what they were. In the name of pacifism you can compromise with Hitler, and in the name of 'spirituality' you can keep your money. It is no accident that those who wish for an inconclusive ending to the war tend to extol the East as against the West. The actual facts don't matter very much. The fact that the Eastern nations have shown themselves at least as warlike and bloodthirsty as the Western ones, that so far from rejecting industrialism, the East is adopting it as swiftly as it can – this is irrelevant, since what is wanted is the mythos of the peaceful, religious and patriarchal East to set against the greedy and materialistic West. As soon as you have 'rejected' industrialism, and hence Socialism, you are in that strange no man's land where the Fascist and the pacifist join forces. There is indeed a sort of apocalyptic truth in the statement of the German radio that the teachings of Hitler and Gandhi are the same. One realizes this when one sees Middleton Murry praising the Japanese invasion of China and Gerald Heard[4] proposing to institute the Hindu caste system in Europe at the same time as the Hindus themselves are abandoning it. We shall be hearing a lot about the superiority of Eastern civilization in the next few years. Meanwhile this is a mischievous book, which will be acclaimed in the left-wing Press and welcomed for quite different reasons by the more intelligent Right.[5]

1. The Congress Party of India, of course, not the US Congress.
2. Buchmanites were followers of Frank Nathan Daniel Buchman, the 'Frank' to whom Orwell refers (1878–1961). Buchman was an evangelist and propagandist who, in 1921, founded the Moral Re-Armament Movement, also known, from the place of its foundation, as the Oxford Group Movement, and sometimes as Buchmanism.
3. 'Who stands if Freedom fall?/Who dies if England live?' ('For All We Have and Are', 1914).
4. John Middleton Murry (1889–1957) was nominally editor of *The (New) Adelphi* for some fourteen years but was intimately associated with the journal throughout its life. In the main, it reflected his interests, which were, in 1923, independent of the then dominant Bloomsbury group. He was successively a fervent disciple of D. H. Lawrence, an unorthodox Marxist, a pacifist and a back-to-the-land farmer, all of which were proclaimed in editorials and articles. He also edited *Peace News* from July 1940 to April 1946. Despite his deeply entrenched pacifism (over which he and Orwell disagreed, see pp. 337–8, below), they remained on good terms. Gerald Heard (1889–1971), whom Orwell seems to be linking with Auden and Isherwood as 'the yogis of California' in 'Looking Back on the Spanish War'; see *Orwell in Spain* in this series.
5. Orwell's review brought a long reply, 'Toothpaste in Bloomsbury', from Lionel Fielden (1896–1974). Orwell, he claimed, had produced a 'dialectical house of cards'. He suspected that Orwell, 'who agrees exactly, and says so, with my conclusions about India, hates my methods of approach to those conclusions and is infuriated because he cannot find better ones'. The response, published in *Horizon*, November 1943, is reprinted in *CW*, XV/2258. Fielden, after serving in World War I (including Gallipoli), worked for the League of Nations and the High Commission for Refugees in Greece and the Levant before joining the BBC in 1927. He was Head of the General Talks Department, 1930–35, and Controller of Broadcasting in India, 1935–40. On his return from India he was Indian Editor for the BBC for seven months and then worked for government ministries. He served as a staff officer in Italy in 1943 and from 1944 to 1945 was Director of Public Relations for the Allied Control Commission in Italy. He gave all his royalties from *Beggar My Neighbour* to support the Indian Freedom Campaign.

[2259]
Letter from Roy Walker to Orwell
28 September 1943

One of those who objected to the tenor of Orwell's review of Fielden's book,
and especially to his attitude to Gandhi, was Roy Walker¹ of the Peace
Pledge Union. This important letter from him survives – important because
it quotes from a lost letter Orwell had written to him, and also because what
Walker said may have played a part in the later development of Orwell's
interpretation of Gandhi's character and role in Anglo-Indian affairs (as
expressed, for example, in 'Reflections on Gandhi', January 1949; see
pp. 491–9, below). Orwell and Walker continued to correspond in 1943
but none of Orwell's letters have been traced.

Dear Mr. Orwell,
So what you've got against Gandhi is that some 'big capitalists' show
'veneration' for him! It seems to me that you might just as well speak
slightingly of Stalin's 'financial background' because his present policy
happens to coincide with the immediate interests of the capitalist countries
in the West. By this criterion Stalin went wrong the moment *The Times*
started to call him 'Mr. Stalin'.

Moreover you strangely leave out of account the veneration of the
masses for Gandhi, which he has earned by fighting for them for nearly
half a century with a devotion that puts most socialists to shame. Nehru
has protested vigorously about the slanders of 'parlour socialists' against
Gandhi, and himself does not exactly look on the Mahatma as a pawn in
the capitalist game. From the time when he led the Ahmedabad mill-
workers in their strike in 1917 Gandhi has fought on the side of the
people. He does not accept all the socialist party cries, truly. But that
doesn't put him in the fascist-imperialist camp.

Of course the British officials think Gandhi is useful in some ways, and
he is. At first they thought he was merely simple-minded in preaching
non-violence and that this was equivalent to giving them no trouble. Later
not a few of them have literally prayed that he might fail, that the
violent elements (Bose & Co) might triumph, because of the disastrous
consequences of applying oppression to people who did not hit back,

which had made our name mud in America and a good many other places. Also, the apparently innocuous hand-spinning campaign gave Lancashire a nasty shock in the thirties, and the Government did a lot of propaganda against it.

My own very wobbly *ahimsa*² almost gives way altogether when you say cheerfully that 'one length of railway line torn up achieves more than a lot of soul-force'. If this isn't just back-chat it means that if the Indian nationalists had resorted to violence during the last thirty years, instead of *Satyagraha*,³ they would have achieved, or would be nearer achieving, real independence. You may think so. I don't. If Amritsar had been answered by a counter-massacre, everyone would cheerfully have supported Dyerism without end, and Gandhi would have been hung out of hand.

Your summary of Gandhi's pronouncements since the outbreak of this war is full of mistakes and inaccuracies. (1) He said at first he gave moral support to the British cause and held Hitler responsible for the war *because he had refused arbitration*. (2) He advocated attempting to reach agreement with Japan by negotiation, just as he advised Britain to negotiate with Hitler, and had himself negotiated with boundless patience with Britain. This is not inconsistent at all. Negotiation does not mean surrender. Gandhi contended that if honourable terms could not be got there must be struggle; only if he could influence India it must be non-violent struggle. (3) So far from being willing to 'support the war again tomorrow' if certain concessions were made, he has set his face against such bargaining, which is why he retired from the field during the negotiations with Cripps. (4) While he himself would try to raise a non-violent force, Congress wished India to be defended by force. He explained that *Congress* would not object to the Anglo-American army remaining. Where Gandhi and Congress agreed was that political power should be handed over to a representative Indian Cabinet. (5) Gandhi has said repeatedly that 'cowardice is worse than violence'. Therefore he always admires bravery, and in this sense has praised the Poles and others. He would rather India fought by military means than surrendered. But he would still say, quite consistently, that in all of these cases the 'higher' alternative of 'non-violence' was open, and that the highest courage would have been to adopt that means of struggle. (6) He said candidly to a Pressman (I think) that the theoretical possibility was that the Japanese might kill the whole population of India in an attempt to subdue the country. If they did so, and the Indians died without returning violence for violence, that would have been the triumph of *Satyagraha*. He then said that it was not in the least likely that that would happen, for the Japanese and other terrorists relied on the panic produced by a few atrocities to smash the morale of the mass. If they failed to do so they would give up terrorism.

The White Paper was published over here. *The Times* said that it showed an unfortunate eagerness to make debating points, and the *New Statesman* which is by no means tender to Gandhi described it as from first to last an indictment of Gandhi. I have read it carefully, and find nothing in it which upsets any of the points I have briefly made above.

You sneer a little at Gandhi's description of Chinese resistance against Japan as 'almost non-violent'. (I knew he said that about Poland, and it is quite likely he did say it of China too, although what comments of his I have seen about China were not quite so magnanimous.) I have partly explained this point already. Resistance to evil is essential, Gandhi believes. Courage and the willingness to suffer for a cause are the backbone of any morality. He can admire these qualities wherever they are found. In some cases, as where the small Polish forces stood up to the overwhelming mass of Nazi machinery, the element of courage is so much greater than the element of violence that, almost, such action must be classed with the ideal *Satyagrahi* who also would stand against the oppressor but would not return violence at all. To tear the phrase from its context and pretend it represents only a confusion of thought is unfair and unconvincing.

Don't you think that you should try to go into the evidence before you circulate dirt about 'the sham austerities of the *ashram*'? And what is it in his whole career that makes you think him 'a bit of a charlatan'?

I don't want to involve you in a correspondence about this, because I expect you are busy, as I am. Also I hear from a friend that you may be in poor health – and at the risk of being thought to practise pacifist technique I send my good wishes for your recovery.

But I do think you were grossly unfair to Gandhi in your review, and that your defence of your attitude in your letter to me only underlines your bias towards him. I would like to think that you will, if you have time, go into the question more thoroughly. You may come back with a more imposing indictment of Gandhi. I prefer to believe that if you are really concerned to find the truth about him you will want to write again in *Horizon* or elsewhere and make him some amends. I don't make the kind of assumption about you that you made about Gandhi; I don't judge you by the fact that your gospel is a White Paper (which I think you have not read) and that your bark belongs to the India Office pack. I think you are just in a muddle and are angry with pacifists. You will be a more formidable critic of pacifism if you do us justice.

Every good wish,
Roy Walker

1. Roy Oliver Walker (1913–92), pacifist and prominent member of the Peace Pledge Union, for which he worked, 1937–46, was a frequent contributor to *Peace News*. He took a special interest in the effects of the food blockade, famine and food relief; he was Secretary of the Food Relief Campaign of the PPU and during and after the war wrote several pamphlets and a book, *Famine Over Europe* (1941), on these topics. He also wrote on PPU meetings (1939 and 1940). He was later dismissed by the Executive from service with the PPU, a statement in *Peace News* for 22 February 1946 stating that a majority had voted that he should no longer be employed at Head Office, partly to reduce expenditure and partly because 'for some time he has not been found an easy person to work with' even though it was recognized that the PPU was much indebted to him for his services over the preceding eight years, particularly in connection with food relief. He was three times prosecuted and twice imprisoned for refusing to be medically examined for national service. His selection called *The Wisdom of Gandhi in His Own Words* was published in 1943, and in 1945 his *Sword of Gold: A Life of Mahatma Gandhi*. He wrote a book on card tricks (1933) and studies of *Hamlet* (1948) and *Macbeth* (1949).

2. *ahimsa* means non-violent creed, often used particularly with respect to sparing animal life.

3. *Satyagraha* is usually interpreted as 'passive resistance', for example, civil disobedience, suffering police charges without responding to physical attack, lying down on the track in front of advancing trains. It was evolved by Gandhi in South Africa. In 'Reflections on Gandhi' (see below), Orwell notes that Gandhi objected to the translation 'passive resistance'. In Gujarati, he said, it seemed that *Satyagraha* meant 'firmness in the truth'; literally it means 'holding on to truth'.

[2309]

Review of Reflections on the Revolution of Our Time
by Harold J. Laski

Observer, *10 October 1943*

This book is an impressive and courageous attempt to disentangle the intellectual muddle in which we are now living. In defining what is meant by Socialism and Fascism, and in proclaiming the ends we ought to aim at and the dangers that lie ahead, Professor Laski[1] avoids mere propaganda as completely, and states unpopular views as boldly, as anyone who is personally involved in politics could well do. He has the advantage that his roots lie deeper than those of the majority of left-wing thinkers; he does not ignore the past, and he does not despise his own countrymen. But the position of someone who is a Socialist by allegiance and a Liberal by temperament is not easy, and though he never states it in those words, Professor Laski's book really revolves round this problem.

This is most apparent in his chapter on the Russian Revolution, and in the long chapter towards the end, entitled 'The Threat of Counter-revolution'. Professor Laski is rightly concerned with the danger that totalitarianism may soon extend itself to the countries which now call themselves democracies. He sees clearly enough that the war has made no structural change in Britain or the U.S.A., that the old economic problems will recur in more pressing forms the moment that the fighting stops, and that the inroads on privilege that might have been accepted in the moment of national danger will be resisted when there is no enemy at the gate. He is probably right, therefore, in saying that if we do not put through the necessary reforms during the war, when general consent is at any rate thinkable, we shall soon have them imposed on us by violence and at the cost of a long period of dictatorship. Professor Laski knows pretty well what reforms he wants, and few thinking men will disagree with him: he wants centralised ownership, planned production, social equality and the 'positive state'. Much too readily, however – indeed with an almost Nineteenth Century optimism – he assumes that these things not only can but certainly will be combined with democracy and freedom of thought.

All through his book there is apparent an unwillingness to admit that

Socialism has totalitarian possibilities. He dismisses Fascism as simply monopoly capitalism in its last phase. This is the habitual left-wing diagnosis, but it seems to have been adopted on the principle of *extra ecclesiam nulla salus*,[2] and a false inference has followed from it. Since Fascism was evidently not Socialism, it followed that it must be a form of capitalism. But capitalism, by definition, cannot 'work'; therefore Fascism cannot 'work' – or at best it can only, like any capitalist economy, solve the problem of surplus production by going to war.

Fascist states, it has been assumed, are inherently and inevitably warlike. Professor Laski repeats this over and over again – 'the counter-revolution', he says, 'is bound to make war'. In reality one has only to look at the map to see that most counter-revolutions don't make war and avoid it at almost any cost. Germany, Italy, and Japan bear out Professor Laski's thesis; for the rest, one country after another, in Europe and America, has gone through a counter-revolutionary process and adopted a Fascist economy, without engaging in foreign war. Does General Franco want war, for instance, or Marshal Pétain, or Dr. Salazar,[3] or half a dozen petty South American dictators? It would seem that the essential point about Fascism is not that it solves its problems by war but that it solves them non-democratically and without abolishing private property. The assumption that every totalitarian system must finally wreck itself in meaningless wars is therefore unjustified.

Needless to say, Professor Laski is very unwilling to admit a resemblance between the German and Russian systems. There is much in the Soviet régime that he does not like, and he says so with a boldness that will get him into serious trouble with the Left. He is, perhaps, even too hard on the 'oriental' worship accorded to Marshal Stalin – for, after all, Stalin is not praised more slavishly than a king or a millionaire. But he does defend the purges, the G.P.U.,[4] and the crushing of intellectual liberty by saying that they result from the U.S.S.R.'s backwardness and insecurity. Let Russia be really safe from foreign aggression, he says, and the dictatorship will relax. This is a poor answer, because the Russian dictatorship has evidently grown tighter as the U.S.S.R. grew stronger, militarily and economically.

What the Soviet régime has demonstrated is what the Fascist states have demonstrated in a different fashion: that the 'contradictions' of capitalism can be got rid of non-democratically and without any increase in individual liberty. Economic insecurity can be abolished at the price of handing society over to a new race of oligarchs. This is not in itself an argument against the Soviet system, for it may well be that the Western conceptions of liberty and democracy are worthless. But if they are not worthless, then certain features in Russian policy are not defensible. One cannot have it both ways. Professor Laski does show signs of wanting to have it both ways, and therein is the chief weakness of his book.

Clearly his own instincts are all for liberty, and even for an old-fashioned version of liberty. His remarks on education point to an individualist outlook hardly compatible with any kind of 'positive state'. All the more ought he to realize that Socialism, if it means only centralised ownership and planned production, is not of its nature either democratic or equalitarian. A hierarchical version of Socialism (Hilaire Belloc's *Servile State*[2]) is probably just as workable as the other, and at this moment is much likelier to arrive. Times beyond number Professor Laski repeats that victory in the present war will achieve nothing if it leaves us with the old economic problems unsolved, and without doubt he is right. But it is a pity he did not say more forcibly that to solve our economic problems will settle nothing either, since that, like the defeat of Hitler, is only one step towards the society of free and equal human beings which he himself so obviously desires.

1. Harold Joseph Laski (1893–1950), political scientist at LSE, Marxist, and leading member of the Labour Party. He tried to establish a popular front against Fascism during the Spanish Civil War. Among his many books were *Authority in the Modern State* (1919), *The State in Theory and Practice* (1935) and *The American Democracy: A Commentary and Interpretation* (1948). Orwell reviewed Laski's *Faith, Reason and Civilisation* for the *Manchester Evening News*, but that newspaper rejected the review and he was not paid; a typescript survived and is printed in XVI/ *2434*. Laski was one of the three selectors for the Left Book Club when *Road to Wigan Pier* was chosen.

2. *Salus extra ecclesiam non est*: No salvation exists outside the Church (St Augustine).

3. António de Oliviera Salazar (1889–1970), as Prime Minister of Portugal, 1932–68, acted as a dictator through the *Estado Novo* ('New State'). He was also Minister of War, 1936–44, and Foreign Minister, 1936–47.

4. The GPU was one stage in the evolution of the Soviet security and intelligence service which began with the Cheka in December 1917 and ended with the KGB, March 1954 to December 1991. In the intervening years the service was known as the NKVD, GPU, OGPU, GUGB, NKGB, MGB and MVD at various times. The OGPU ran from July 1923 to July 1934, the GPU preceding it in February 1922 when the Cheka was incorporated in

the NKVD as GPU. The evolution of the KGB is clearly set out on pp. ix–x of *The Mitrokhin Archive*, by Christopher Andrew and Vasili Mitrokhin (1999). The various sets of initials were rather loosely used by many writers to indicate the Soviet secret service.

5. Hilaire Belloc (1870–1953), humorist, essayist, Roman Catholic apologist; Liberal MP 1906–10. *The Servile State* was first published in 1912, and republished in 1913 and 1927 with new prefaces. It was published in New York in 1946, introduced by C. Gauss. It is concerned with, among other things, the price the individual must pay in terms of personal freedom for social security.

[2328]

Review of The Trial of Mussolini *by 'Cassius'*

Tribune, *22 October 1943*

WHO ARE THE WAR CRIMINALS?

On the face of it, Mussolini's collapse was a story straight out of Victorian melodrama. At long last Righteousness had triumphed, the wicked man was discomfited, the mills of God[1] were doing their stuff. On second thoughts, however, this moral tale is less simple and less edifying. To begin with, what crime, if any, has Mussolini committed? In power politics there are no crimes, because there are no laws. And, on the other hand, is there any feature in Mussolini's *internal* régime that could be seriously objected to by any body of people likely to sit in judgment on him? For, as the author of this book abundantly shows – and this in fact is the main purpose of the book – there is not one scoundrelism committed by Mussolini between 1922 and 1940 that has not been lauded to the skies by the very people who are now promising to bring him to trial.

For the purposes of his allegory 'Cassius'[2] imagines Mussolini indicted before a British court, with the Attorney-General as prosecutor. The list of charges is an impressive one, and the main facts – from the murder of Matteotti[3] to the invasion of Greece, and from the destruction of the peasants' co-operatives to the bombing of Addis Ababa – are not denied. Concentration camps, broken treaties, rubber truncheons, castor oil – everything is admitted. The only troublesome question is: How can something that was praiseworthy at the time when you did it – ten years ago, say – suddenly become reprehensible now? Mussolini is allowed to call witnesses, both living and dead, and to show by their own printed words that from the very first the responsible leaders of British opinion have encouraged him in everything that he did. For instance, here is Lord Rothermere in 1928:

In his own country [Mussolini] was the antidote to a deadly poison. For the rest of Europe he has been a tonic which has done to all incalculable good. I can claim with sincere satisfaction to have been the first man in a position of public influence to put Mussolini's splendid achievement in its right light ... He is the greatest figure of our age.

Here is Winston Churchill in 1927:

If I had been an Italian I am sure I should have been wholeheartedly with you in your triumphant struggle against the bestial appetites and passions of Leninism ... [Italy] has provided the necessary antidote to the Russian poison. Hereafter no great nation will be unprovided with an ultimate means of protection against the cancerous growth of Bolshevism.

Here is Lord Mottistone[4] in 1935:

I did not oppose [the Italian action in Abyssinia]. I wanted to dispel the ridiculous illusion that it was a nice thing to sympathise with the underdog ... I said it was a wicked thing to send arms or connive to send arms to these cruel, brutal Abyssinians and still to deny them to others who are playing an honourable part.

Here is Mr. Duff Cooper in 1938:

Concerning the Abyssinian episode, the less said now the better. When old friends are reconciled after a quarrel, it is always dangerous for them to discuss its original causes.

Here is Mr. Ward Price, of the *Daily Mail*, in 1932:

Ignorant and prejudiced people talk of Italian affairs as if that nation were subject to some tyranny which it would willingly throw off. With that rather morbid commiseration for fanatical minorities which is the rule with certain imperfectly informed sections of British public opinion, this country long shut its eyes to the magnificent work that the Fascist régime was doing. I have several times heard Mussolini himself express his gratitude to the *Daily Mail* as having been the first British newspaper to put his aims fairly before the world.

And so on, and so on, and so on. Hoare, [Sir John] Simon, Halifax, Neville Chamberlain, Austen Chamberlain, Hore-Belisha, Amery, Lord Lloyd and various others enter the witness-box, all of them ready to testify that, whether Mussolini was crushing the Italian trade unions, non-intervening in Spain, pouring mustard gas on the Abyssinians, throwing Arabs out of aeroplanes or building up a navy for use against Britain, the British Government and its official spokesmen supported him through thick and thin. We are shown Lady (Austen) Chamberlain shaking hands with Mussolini in 1924, Chamberlain and Halifax banqueting with him and toasting 'the Emperor of Abyssinia' in 1939, Lord Lloyd⁵ buttering up the Fascist régime in an official pamphlet as late as 1940. The net impression left by this part of the trial is quite simply that Mussolini is not guilty. Only later, when an Abyssinian, a Spaniard and an Italian anti-Fascist give their evidence, does the real case against him begin to appear.

Now, the book is a fanciful one, but this conclusion is realistic. It is immensely unlikely that the British Tories will ever put Mussolini on trial. There is nothing that they could accuse him of except his declaration of war in 1940. If the 'trial of war criminals' that some people enjoy dreaming about ever happens, it can only happen after revolutions in the Allied countries. But the whole notion of finding scapegoats, of blaming individuals, or parties, or nations for the calamities that have happened to us, raises other trains of thought, some of them rather disconcerting.

The history of British relations with Mussolini illustrates the structural weakness of a capitalist state. Granting that power politics are not moral, to attempt to buy Italy out of the Axis – and clearly this idea underlay British policy from 1934 onwards – was a natural strategic move. But it was not a move which Baldwin, Chamberlain and the rest of them were capable of carrying out. It could only have been done by being so strong that Mussolini would not dare to side with Hitler. This was impossible, because an economy ruled by the profit motive is simply not equal to re-arming on a modern scale.

Britain only began to arm when the Germans were in Calais. Before that, fairly large sums had, indeed, been voted for armaments, but they slid peaceably into the pockets of the shareholders and the weapons did not appear. Since they had no real intention of curtailing their own privileges, it was inevitable that the British ruling class should carry out every policy half-heartedly and blind themselves to the coming danger. But the moral collapse which this entailed was something new in British politics. In the nineteenth and early twentieth centuries, British politicians might be hypocritical, but hypocrisy implies a moral code. It was something new when Tory M.P.s cheered the news that British ships had been bombed by Italian aeroplanes, or when members of the House of Lords lent themselves to organised libel campaigns against the Basque children who had been brought here as refugees.

When one thinks of the lies and betrayals of those years, the cynical abandonment of one ally after another, the imbecile optimism of the Tory press, the flat refusal to believe that the Dictators meant war, even when they shouted it from the housetops, the inability of the moneyed class to see anything wrong whatever in concentration camps, ghettoes, massacres and undeclared wars, one is driven to feel that moral decadence played its part as well as mere stupidity. By 1937 or thereabouts it was not possible to be in doubt about the nature of the Fascist régimes. But the lords of property had decided that Fascism was on their side and they were willing to swallow the most stinking evils so long as their property remained secure. In their clumsy way they were playing the game of Macchiavelli, of 'political realism', of 'anything is right which advances the cause of the Party' – the Party in this case, of course, being the Conservative Party.

All this 'Cassius' brings out, but he does shirk its corollary. Throughout his book it is implied that only Tories are immoral. 'Yet there was still another England,' he says. 'This other England detested Fascism from the day of its birth . . . This was the England of the Left, the England of Labour.' True, but only part of the truth. The actual behaviour of the Left has been more honourable than its theories. It has fought against Fascism, but its representative thinkers have entered just as deeply as their opponents into the evil world of 'realism' and power politics.

'Realism' (it used to be called dishonesty) is part of the general political atmosphere of our time.[6] It is a sign of the weakness of 'Cassius''s position that one could compile a quite similar book entitled *The Trial of Winston Churchill*, or *The Trial of Chiang Kai-Shek*, or even *The Trial of Ramsay MacDonald*. In each case you would find the leaders of the Left contradicting themselves almost as grossly as the Tory leaders quoted by 'Cassius'. For the Left has also been willing to shut its eyes to a great deal and to accept some very doubtful allies. We laugh now to hear the Tories abusing Mussolini when they were flattering him five years ago, but who would have foretold in 1927 that the Left would one day take Chiang Kai-Shek to its bosom? Who would have foretold just after the General Strike that ten years later Winston Churchill would be the darling of the *Daily Worker*? In the years 1935–39, when almost any ally against Fascism seemed acceptable, left-wingers found themselves praising Mustapha Kemal and then developing a tenderness for Carol of Rumania.

Although it was in every way more pardonable, the attitude of the Left towards the Russian régime has been distinctly similar to the attitude of the Tories towards Fascism. There has been the same tendency to excuse almost anything 'because they're on our side'. It is all very well to talk about Lady Chamberlain photographed shaking hands with Mussolini; the photograph of Stalin shaking hands with Ribbentrop is much more recent. On the whole, the intellectuals of the Left defended the Russo-German pact. It was 'realistic', like Chamberlain's appeasement policy, and with similar consequences. If there is a way out of the moral pig-sty we are living in, the first step towards it is probably to grasp that 'realism' does *not* pay, and that to sell out your friends and sit rubbing your hands while they are destroyed is *not* the last word in political wisdom.

This fact is demonstrable in any city between Cardiff and Stalingrad, but not many people can see it. Meanwhile it is a pamphleteer's duty to attack the Right, but not to flatter the Left. It is partly because the Left have been too easily satisfied with themselves that they are where they are now.

Mussolini, in 'Cassius''s book, after calling his witnesses, enters the box himself. He sticks to his Macchiavellian creed: Might is Right, *vae victis!*[7] He is guilty of the only crime that matters, the crime of failure, and he admits that his adversaries have a right to kill him – but not, he insists, a right to blame him. Their conduct has been similar to his own, and their moral condemnations are all hypocrisy. But thereafter come the other three witnesses, the Abyssinian, the Spaniard and the Italian, who are morally upon a different plane, since they have never temporised with

Fascism nor had a chance to play at power politics; and all three of them demand the death penalty.

Would they demand it in real life? Will any such thing ever happen? It is not very likely, even if the people who have a real right to try Mussolini should somehow get him into their hands. The Tories, of course, though they would shrink from a real inquest into the origins of the war, are not sorry to have the chance of pushing the whole blame on to a few notorious individuals like Mussolini and Hitler. In this way the Darlan-Badoglio[8] manoeuvre is made easier. Mussolini is a good scapegoat while he is at large, though he would be an awkward one in captivity. But how about the common people? Would they kill their tyrants, in cold blood and with the forms of law, if they had the chance?

It is a fact that there have been very few such executions in history. At the end of the last war an election was won partly on the slogan 'Hang the Kaiser', and yet if any such thing had been attempted the conscience of the nation would probably have revolted. When tyrants are put to death, it should be by their own subjects; those who are punished by a foreign authority, like Napoleon, are simply made into martyrs and legends.

What is important is not that these political gangsters should be made to suffer, but that they should be made to discredit themselves. Fortunately they do do so in many cases, for to a surprising extent the war-lords in shining armour, the apostles of the martial virtues, tend not to die fighting when the time comes. History is full of ignominious getaways by the great and famous. Napoleon surrendered to the English in order to get protection from the Prussians, the Empress Eugenie fled in a hansom cab with an American dentist, Ludendorff resorted to blue spectacles, one of the more unprintable[9] Roman emperors tried to escape assassination by locking himself in the lavatory, and during the early days of the Spanish Civil War one leading Fascist made his escape from Barcelona, with exquisite fitness, through a sewer.

It is some such exit that one would wish for Mussolini, and if he is left to himself perhaps he will achieve it. Possibly Hitler also. It used to be said of Hitler that when his time came he would never fly or surrender, but would perish in some operatic manner, by suicide at the very least.[10] But that was when Hitler was successful; during the last year, since things began to go wrong, it is difficult to feel that he has behaved with dignity or courage. 'Cassius' ends his book with the judge's summing-up, and leaves the verdict open, seeming to invite a decision from his readers. Well, if it were left to me, my verdict on both Hitler and Mussolini would be: not death, unless it is inflicted in some hurried unspectacular way. If the Germans and Italians feel like giving them a summary court-martial and then a firing-squad, let them do it. Or better still, let the pair of them escape with a suitcase-full of bearer securities and settle down as the accredited bores of some Swiss pension. But no martyrising, no St. Helena business. And, above all, no solemn hypocritical 'trial of war criminals', with all the slow cruel pageantry of the law, which after a lapse of time has so strange a way of focusing a romantic light on the accused and turning a scoundrel into a hero.

1. 'Though the mills of God grind slowly, yet they grind exceeding small', H. W. Longfellow (1807–82), 'Retribution' (a translation from the *Sinngedichte* of Friedrich von Logau).

2. 'Cassius' was a pen-name for Michael Foot (1913–), politician, journalist and author. He entered Parliament in 1945; Leader of the Labour Party 1980–83. He was Assistant Editor of *Tribune*, 1937–8, Editor, 1948–52 and 1955–60, Managing Director, 1945–74. From 1944 to 1964 he was a political columnist for the *Daily Herald.* He has always been a strong advocate of Orwell and his writing.

3. Giacomo Matteotti (1885–1924), Italian socialist and an outspoken opponent of the Fascists. His murder effectively marked the start of Mussolini's dictatorship.

4. Lord Mottistone (General John Edward Bernard Seely, 1868–1947), Liberal War Minister, 1912–24. In 1930 he wrote to *The Times* stating that 'Britain is confronted with a grave emergency'; an election on party lines would not resolve it; and he accused Labour of 'failing to cure unemployment and grapple with abuses of the dole' (Robert Graves and Alan Hodge, *The Long Week-End*, 1940, 253).

5. Lord George Ambrose Lloyd (1879–1941) was High Commissioner in Egypt when an Anglo-Egyptian Treaty was being negotiated in 1930. He disapproved of the Treaty and resigned. Malcolm Muggeridge (1903–90, a friend of Orwell's, whose *The Thirties* Orwell reviewed (XII/*615*), and who was at this time serving with distinction in the Second World War) commented in *The Thirties* (89): 'Such a display of integrity was ruinous for Lord Lloyd's career . . . If Lord Lloyd . . . had pretended to himself and to others that he believed in the possibility of appeasing conflicts by assuming they did not exist, his promising career would have proceeded without interruption, leading, perhaps, to the Viceroyalty instead of the British Council for Cultural Relations with Foreign Countries.'

6. Orwell, as so often, was ahead of his time. Fifty years later, such weighted trials, affecting a 'realism' that Orwell glossed as dishonesty, had become fashionable television programmes.

7. 'Woe to the vanquished!', Livy, *History*, V.xlviii.9.

8. Admiral François Darlan (1881–1942) was Commander-in-Chief of the French navy from 1939, and Vice-Premier and Foreign Minister in the Vichy French Government, February

1941–April 1942. When the Allies invaded Morocco and Tunisia (then French territories) in November 1942, a deal (much criticized in Britain and America) was negotiated with him in order to reduce casualties that would otherwise occur when those countries were occupied. He was assassinated on 24 December 1942 by a French patriot, Bonnier de la Chapelle, who was rapidly tried and executed two days later. Marshal Pietro Badoglio (1871–1956) was C-in-C of the Italian army when Italy entered the war with Germany in 1940. He resigned after his army was humiliated in Greece and Albania. After Mussolini fell in July 1943, he formed a non-Fascist government of which he was Prime Minister until 1944. He negotiated a peace with the Allies and declared war on Germany. Orwell links the two because they both made deals with those whom they had formerly opposed, a 'manoeuvre' more successful personally for Badoglio than it was for Darlan.

9. Possibly 'unprincipled' was intended.

10. In 1945 Mussolini was shot by Italian partisans and Hitler committed suicide.

[2365]

Review of Subject India *by Henry Noel Brailsford*
Nation, *20 November 1943*

If there is one point in the Indian problem that cannot be disputed – or, at any rate, is not disputed, outside the ranks of the British Conservative Party – it is that Britain ought to stop ruling India as early as possible. But this is a smaller basis of agreement than it sounds, and the answers to literally every other question are always coloured by subjective feelings. Mr. Brailsford[1] is better equipped than the majority of writers on India in that he is not only aware of his own prejudices but possesses enough background knowledge to be unafraid of the 'experts'. Probably he has not been very long in India, perhaps he does not even speak any Indian language, but he differs from the vast majority of English left-wingers in having bothered to visit India at all, and in being more interested in the peasants than in the politicians.

As he rightly says, the great, central fact about India is its poverty. From birth to death, generation after generation, the peasant lives his life in the grip of the landlord or the money-lender – they are frequently the same person – tilling his tiny patch of soil with the tools and methods of the Bronze Age. Over great areas the children barely taste milk after they are weaned, and the average physique is so wretched that ninety-eight pounds is a normal weight for a full-grown man. The last detailed survey to be taken showed that the average Indian income was Rs.62 (about £4 13s. od.) per annum: in the same period the average British income was £94. In spite of the drift to the towns that is occurring in India as elsewhere, the condition of the industrial workers is hardly better than that of the peasants. Brailsford describes them in the slums of Bombay, sleeping eight to a tiny room, with three water taps among four hundred people, and working a twelve-hour day, three hundred and sixty five days a year, for wages of around seven and sixpence a week. These conditions will not be cured simply by the removal of British rule, but neither can they be seriously improved while the British remain, because British policy, largely unconscious, is to hamper industrialisation and preserve the status quo. The worst barbarities from which Indians suffer are inflicted on them not by Europeans but by other Indians – the landlords and money-lenders, the bribe-taking minor officials, and the Indian capitalists who exploit their working people with a ruthlessness quite impossible in the West since the rise of trade unionism. But although the business community, at any rate, tends to be anti-British and is involved in the Nationalist movement, the privileged classes really depend on British arms. Only when the British have gone will what Brailsford calls the latent class war be able to develop.

Brailsford is attempting exposition rather than moral judgment, and he gives no very definite answer to the difficult question of whether, in balance, the British have done India more good than harm. As he points out, they have made possible an increase of population without making it possible for that population to be properly fed. They have saved India from war, internal and external, at the expense of destroying political liberty. Probably their greatest gift to India has been the railway. If one studies a railway map of Asia, India looks like a piece of fishing-net in the middle of a white tablecloth. And this network of communications has not only made it possible to check famines by bringing food to the afflicted areas – the famine now raging in India would hardly have been a famine at all by the standards of a hundred years ago – but to administer India as a unit, with a common system of law, internal free trade and freedom of movement, and even, for the educated minority, a lingua franca in the English language. India is potentially a nation, as Europe, with its smaller population and great racial homogeneity°, is not. But since 1910 or thereabouts the British power has acted as a dead hand. Often loosely denounced as 'fascist', the British régime in India is almost the exact opposite of Fascism, since it has never developed the notion of positive government at all. It has remained an old fashioned despotism, keeping the peace, collecting its taxes, and for the rest letting things slide, with hardly the faintest interest in how its subjects lived or what they thought, so long as they were outwardly obedient. As a result – to pick just one fact out of the thousands one could choose – the whole subcontinent, in this year of 1943, is incapable of manufacturing an automobile engine. In spite of all that can be said on the other side, this fact alone would justify Brailsford in his final conclusion: 'Our day in India is over; we have no creative part to play.'

Brailsford is justifiably bleak about the future. He sees that the handing over of power is a complicated process which cannot be achieved quickly, especially in the middle of a war, and that it will solve nothing in itself. There is still the problem of India's poverty and ignorance to be solved, and the struggle between the landlords, big business and the labour movement to be fought out. And there is also the question of how, if at all, a backward agricultural country like India is to remain independent in a world of power politics. Brailsford gives a good account of the current political situation, in which he struggles very hard not to be engulfed by the prevailing left-wing orthodoxy. He writes judiciously about the tortuous character of Gandhi; comes nearer to being fair to Cripps than most English commentators have been – Cripps, indeed, has been the whipping-boy of the left, both British and Indian – and rightly emphasises the importance of the Indian princes, who are often forgotten and who present a much more serious difficulty than the faked-up quarrel between Hindus and Moslems. At this moment India is such a painful subject that it is hardly possible to write a really good book about it. English books are either dishonest or irresponsible; American books are ignorant and self-righteous; Indian books are coloured by spite and an inferiority complex. Well aware of the gaps in his knowledge and the injustices he is bound to commit, Brailsford has produced not only a transparently honest but – what is much rarer in this context – a good-tempered book. Nearly all books written about the British Empire in these days have the air of being written *at* somebody – either a Blimp, or a Communist, or an

American, as the case may be. Brailsford is writing primarily for the ordinary British public, the people who before all others have the power and the duty to do something about India, and whose conscience it is first necessary to move. But it is a book that the American public might find useful too. Perhaps it is worth uttering the warning that – owing to war-time conditions – there are many misprints, and as some of them have crept into the statistics these are apt to be misleading.

1. Henry Noel Brailsford (1873–1959), socialist intellectual, author, political journalist and leader-writer for the *Manchester Guardian* (predecessor of the *Guardian*), *Daily News* and the *Nation*; he edited the *New Leader*, the weekly organ of the Independent Labour Party, 1922– 36. For Orwell's letters to him over the suppression of the POUM (in whose ranks Orwell fought) by the Communists in the Spanish Civil War, see *Orwell in Spain* in this series.

[2396]

Extract from 'As I Please', 4 [On dissociating Socialism from Utopianism]

Tribune, *24 December 1943*

Orwell contributed to Tribune *on a couple of dozen occasions from 8 March 1940, but from 29 November 1943 to 4 April 1947 he was a regular contributor (with some breaks in order to concentrate on other activities). Initially, from 1943, Orwell served as literary editor. One of his principal contributions was a series of personal columns, 'As I Please', of which he wrote eighty. The title had been used briefly by Raymond Postgate (1896– 1971, editor of* Tribune, *1940–41, an economist, and a writer on food and wine) for a short series in the journal* Controversy *in 1939. The use of this title was suggested to Orwell by his friend Jon Kimche (1909–94). Kimche and Orwell worked together at Booklovers' Corner in Hampstead (see X/ 212), he went to Spain to meet Orwell, and he became acting editor and editor of* Tribune, *1942–6. See* Remembering Orwell, *54–6, 88–9, 94–5, 139–41, 215.*

Reading Michael Roberts's book on T. E. Hulme,[1] I was reminded once again of the dangerous mistake that the Socialist movement makes in ignoring what one might call the neo-reactionary school of writers.

There is a considerable number of these writers: they are intellectually distinguished, they are influential in a quiet way, and their criticisms of the Left are much more damaging than anything that issues from the Individualist League or Conservative Central Office.

T. E. Hulme[2] was killed in the last war and left little completed work behind him, but the ideas that he had roughly formulated had great influence, especially on the numerous writers who were grouped round the *Criterion* in the 'twenties and 'thirties. Wyndham Lewis, T. S. Eliot, Aldous Huxley, Malcolm Muggeridge, Evelyn Waugh and Graham Greene all probably owe something to him. But more important than the extent of his personal influence is the general intellectual movement to which he belonged, a movement which could fairly be described as the revival of pessimism. Perhaps its best-known living exponent is Marshal Pétain. But the new pessimism has queerer affiliations than that. It links up not only with Catholicism, Conservatism and Fascism, but also with pacifism (California brand especially) and Anarchism. It is worth noting that T. E. Hulme, the upper-middle-class English Conservative in a bowler hat, was an admirer and to some extent a follower of the Anarcho-Syndicalist, Georges Sorel.[3]

The thing that is common to all these people, whether it is Pétain mournfully preaching 'the discipline of defeat', or Sorel denouncing liberalism, or Berdyaev shaking his head over the Russian Revolution, or 'Beachcomber' delivering side-kicks at Beveridge in the *Express*, or Huxley advocating non-resistance behind the guns of the American Fleet, is their refusal to believe that human society can be fundamentally improved. Man is non-perfectible, merely political changes can effect nothing, progress is an illusion. The connection between this belief and political reaction is, of course, obvious. Other-worldliness is the best alibi a rich man can have. 'Men cannot be made better by act of Parliament; therefore I may as well go on drawing my dividends.' No one puts it quite so coarsely as that, but the thought of all these people is along those lines: even of those who, like Michael Roberts and Hulme himself, admit that a little, just a *little*, improvement in earthly society may be thinkable.

The danger of ignoring the neo-pessimists lies in the fact that up to a point they are right. So long as one thinks in short periods it is wise not to be hopeful about the future. Plans for human betterment do normally come unstuck, and the pessimist has many more opportunities of saying 'I told you so' than the optimist. By and large the prophets of doom have been righter than those who imagined that a real step forward would be achieved by universal education, female suffrage, the League of Nations, or what-not.

The real answer is to dissociate Socialism from Utopianism. Nearly all neo-pessimist apologetics consists in putting up a man of straw and knocking him down again. The man of straw is called Human Perfectibility. Socialists are accused of believing that society can be – and indeed, after the establishment of Socialism, will be – completely perfect; also that progress is *inevitable*. Debunking such beliefs is money for jam, of course.

The answer, which ought to be uttered more loudly than it usually is, is that Socialism is not perfectionist, perhaps not even hedonistic. Socialists don't claim to be able to make the world perfect: they claim to be able to make it better. And any thinking Socialist will concede to the Catholic that when economic injustice has been righted, the fundamental problem of man's place in the universe will still remain. But what the Socialist does claim is that that problem cannot be dealt with while the average human being's preoccupations are necessarily economic. It is all summed up in Marx's saying that after Socialism has arrived, human history can begin. Meanwhile the neo-pessimists are there, well entrenched in the press of every country in the world, and they have more influence and make more converts among the young than we sometimes care to admit.

1. Michael Roberts (pen-name for W. E. Roberts), *T. E. Hulme* (1938). Orwell had a copy of this book in his library when he died (*3734*, XX/296).

2. Thomas Ernest Hulme (1883–1917), poet, philosopher and literary critic. His works include a translation of Georges Sorel's *Réflexions sur la violence* (1908) as *Reflections on Violence* (1914) and *Speculations: Essays on Humanism and the Philosophy of Art*, edited by Herbert Read (1924). A war poem, 'Trenches: St Eloi', has these lines: 'My mind is a corridor. The minds about me are corridors./Nothing suggests itself. There is nothing to do but keep on.' He was killed at Nieuport, 28 September 1917.

3. Georges Sorel (1847–1922), French philosopher who advocated Direct Action – radical industrial action outside the parliamentary or constitutional framework. He supported Syndicalism, not Anarchism, as Orwell thought. See James Joll, *The Anarchists* (2nd edn, 1980, 192–5).

[2405]

Extract from London Letter, 15 January 1944
Partisan Review, *Spring 1944*

Well, now a word or two about our ancient institutions.

PARLIAMENT

When I was working with the B.B.C. I sometimes had to go and listen to a debate in the Commons.[1] The last time I had been there was about ten years previously, and I was very much struck by the deterioration that seemed to have taken place. The whole thing now has a mangy, forgotten look. Even the ushers' shirt fronts are grimy. And it is noticeable now that, except from the places they sit in (the opposition always sits on the Speaker's left), you can't tell one party from another. It is just a collection of mediocre-looking men in dingy, dark suits, nearly all speaking in the same accent and all laughing at the same jokes. I may say, however, that they don't look such a set of crooks as the French Deputies used to look. The most striking thing of all is the lack of attendance. It would be very rare indeed for 400 members out of the 640 to turn up. The House of Lords, where they are now sitting, only has seating accommodation for about 250, and the old House of Commons (it was blitzed) cannot have been much larger. I attended the big debate on India after Cripps came back. At the start there were a little over 200 members present, which rapidly shrank to about 45. It seems to be the custom to clear out, presumably to the bar, as soon as any important speech begins, but the House fills up again when there are questions or anything else that promises a bit of fun. There is a marked family atmosphere. Everyone shouts with laughter over jokes and allusions which are unintelligible to anyone not an M.P., nicknames are used freely, violent political opponents pal up over drinks. Nearly any member of long standing is corrupted by this kind of thing sooner or later. Maxton,[2] the I.L.P. M.P., twenty years ago an inflammatory orator whom the ruling classes hated like poison, is now the pet of the House, and Gallacher,[3] the Communist M.P., is going the same road. Each time I have been in the House recently I have found myself thinking the same thought – that the Roman Senate still existed under the later Empire.

I don't need [to] indicate to you the various features of capitalism that make democracy unworkable. But apart from these, and apart from the dwindling prestige of representative institutions, there are special reasons why it is difficult for able men to find their way into Parliament. To begin with, the out-of-date electoral system grossly favors the Conservative Party. The rural areas, where, on the whole, people vote as the landlords tell them to, are so much over-represented, and the industrial areas so much under-represented that the Conservatives consistently win a far higher proportion of seats than their share in the total vote entitles them to. Secondly, the electorate seldom have a chance to vote for anyone except the nominees of the party machines. In the Conservative Party safe seats are peddled round to men rich enough to 'keep up' the seat (contributions to local charities, etc.), and no doubt to pay an agreed sum into the party funds as well. Labour Party candidates are selected for their political docility, and a proportion of the Labour M.P.s are always elderly trade-union officials who have been allotted a seat as a kind of pension. Naturally, these men are even more slavishly obedient to the party machine than the Tories. To any M.P. who shows signs of independent thought the same threat is always applied – 'We won't support you at the next election.' In practice a candidate cannot win an election against the opposition of his own party machine, unless the inhabitants of that locality have some special reason for admiring him personally. But the party system has destroyed the territorial basis of politics. Few M.P.s have any connection with their constituency, even to the extent of living there: many have never seen it till they go down to fight their first election. At this moment Parliament is more than usually unrepresentative because, owing to the war, literally millions of people are disenfranchised. There has been no register of voters since 1939, which means that no one under 25, and no one who has changed his place of residence, now has a vote; for practical purposes the men in the forces are disenfranchised as well. On the whole, the people who have lost their votes are those who would vote against the Government. It is fair to add that in the general mechanics of an election in England there is no dirty work – no intimidation, no miscounting of votes or direct bribery, and the ballot is genuinely secret.

The feeling that Parliament has lost its importance is very widespread. The electorate are conscious of having no control over their M.P.s; the

M.P.s are conscious that it is not they who are directing affairs. All major decisions, whether to go to war, whether to open a second front, and where, which power to go into alliance with, and so forth, are taken by an Inner Cabinet which acts first and announces the *fait accompli* afterwards. Theoretically, Parliament has the power to overthrow the Government if it wishes, but the party machines can usually prevent this. The average M.P., or even a minor member of the Government, has no more information about what is going on than any reader of *The Times*. There is an extra hurdle for any progressive policy in the House of Lords, which has supposedly been shorn of its powers but still has the power of obstruction. In all, only two or three bills thrown out by the Lords have ever been forced through by the Commons. Seeing all this, people of every political color simply lose interest in Parliament, which they refer to as 'the talking shop'. One cannot judge from wartime, but for years before the war the percentage of the electorate voting had been going down. Sixty percent was considered a high vote. In the big towns many people do not know the name of their M.P. or which constituency they live in. A social survey at a recent election showed that many adults now don't know the first facts about British electoral procedures – e.g., don't know that the ballot is secret.

Nevertheless, I myself feel that Parliament has justified its existence during the war, and I even think that its prestige has risen slightly in the last two or three years. While losing most of its original powers it has retained its power of criticism, and it is the only remaining place in which one is free, theoretically as well as practically, to utter literally any opinion. Except for sheer personal abuse (and even that has to be something fairly extreme), any remark made in Parliament is privileged. The Government has, of course, devices for dodging awkward questions, but can't dodge all of them. However, the importance of Parliamentary criticism is not so much its direct effect on the Government as its effect on public opinion. For what is said in Parliament cannot go altogether unreported. The newspapers, even *The Times*, and the B.B.C. probably do tend to play down the speeches of opposition members, but cannot do so very grossly because of the existence of Hansard, which publishes the Parliamentary debates verbatim. The effective circulation of Hansard is small (2 or 3 thousand), but so long as it is available to anyone who wants it, a lot of things that the Government would like to suppress get across to the public. This critical function of Parliament is all the more noticeable because intellectually this must be one of the worst Parliaments we have ever had. Outside the Government, I do not think there can be thirty able men in the House, but that small handful have managed to give every subject from dive bombers to 18B[4] an airing. As a legislative body Parliament has become relatively unimportant, and it has even less control over the executive than over the Government. But it still functions as a kind of uncensored supplement to the radio – which, after all, is something worth preserving.

THE MONARCHY

Nothing is harder than to be sure whether royalist sentiment is still a reality in England. All that is said on either side is colored by wish-thinking. My own opinion is that royalism, i.e., popular royalism, was a strong factor in English life up to the death of George V, who had been there so long that he was accepted as 'the' King (as Victoria had been 'the' Queen), a sort of father figure and projection of the English domestic virtues. The 1935 Silver Jubilee, at any rate in the south of England, was a pathetic outburst of popular affection, genuinely spontaneous. The authorities were taken by surprise and the celebrations were prolonged for an extra week while the poor old man, patched up after pneumonia, and in fact dying, was hauled to and fro through slum streets where the people had hung out flags of their own accord and chalked 'Long Live the King. Down with the Landlord' across the roadway.[5]

I think, however, that the abdication of Edward VIII must have dealt royalism a blow from which it may not recover. The row over the abdication, which was very violent while it lasted, cut across existing political divisions, as can be seen from the fact that Edward's loudest champions were Churchill, Mosley and H. G. Wells; but broadly speaking, the rich were anti-Edward and the working classes were sympathetic to him. He had promised the unemployed miners that he would do something on their behalf, which was an offense in the eyes of the rich; on the other hand, the miners and other unemployed probably felt that he had let them down by abdicating for the sake of a woman. Some continental observers believed that Edward had been got rid of because of his association with leading Nazis and were rather impressed by this exhibition of Cromwellism. But the net effect of the whole business was probably to weaken the feeling of royal sanctity which had been so carefully built up from 1880 onwards. It brought home to people the personal powerlessness of the King, and it showed that the much-advertised royalist sentiment of the upper classes was humbug. At the least I should say it would need another long reign, and a monarch with some kind of charm, to put the royal family back where it was in George V's day.

The function of the King in promoting stability and acting as a sort of keystone in a non-democratic society is, of course, obvious. But he also has, or can have, the function of acting as an escape-valve for dangerous emotions. A French journalist said to me once that the monarchy was one of the things that have saved Britain from fascism. What he meant was that modern people can't, apparently, get along without drums, flags and loyalty parades, and that it is better that they should tie their leader-worship onto some figure who has no real power. In a dictatorship the power and the glory belong to the same person. In England the real power belongs to unprepossessing men in bowler hats: the creature who rides in a gilded coach behind soldiers in steel breastplates is really a waxwork. It is at any rate possible that while this division of function exists a Hitler or a Stalin cannot come to power. On the whole the European countries which have most successfully avoided fascism have been constitutional monarchies. The conditions seemingly are that the royal family shall be long-established and taken for granted, shall understand its own position and shall not produce strong characters with political ambitions. These have been fulfilled in Britain, the Low Countries and Scandinavia, but not in, say, Spain or Rumania. If you point these facts out to the average left-winger he gets very angry, but only because he has not examined the nature of his own feelings toward Stalin. I do not defend the institution of monarchy in an absolute sense, but I think that in an age like our own it may have an innoculating effect, and certainly it does far less harm than the existence of our so-called aristocracy. I have often advocated that a Labour government, i.e., one that meant business, would abolish titles while retaining the royal family. But such a move would only have meaning if royal sentiment exists, and so far as I can judge it is much weakened. I am told that the royal visits to war factories are looked on as time-wasting ballyhoo. Nor did the news that the King had caused a black line to be painted round all the baths in Buckingham Palace do much to popularize the five-inch bath.[6]

Well, no more news. I am afraid I have written rather a lot already. It is a foul winter, not at all cold, but with endless fogs, almost like the famous 'London fogs' of my childhood. The blackout seems to get less and not more tolerable as the war goes on. Food is much as usual, but wine has almost vanished and whisky can only be bought by the nip, unless you have influential pals. There are air-raid alarms almost every night, but hardly any bombs. There is much talk about the rocket guns[7] with which the Germans are supposedly going to bombard London. A little while before the talk was of a four-hundred ton bomb which was to be made in the form of an enormous glider and towed across by fleets of German airplanes. Rumors of this kind have followed one another since the beginning of the war, and are always firmly believed in by numbers of people, evidently fulfilling some obscure psychological need.

1. Presumably in connection with the programme 'The Debate Continues' for the BBC's service to India.

2. James Maxton (1885–1946), Independent Labour MP, 1922–46; Chairman of the Independent Labour Party (ILP), 1926–31, 1934–39.

3. William Gallacher (1881–1965), Communist MP, 1935–50, was the sole representative of his party in Parliament, 1935–45, but was then joined by Phil Piratin (who also lost his seat in 1950). Gallacher was Chairman of the Clyde Workers' Committee during World War I and a member of the Communist International from 1920.

4. Regulation 18b, under the Emergency Powers (Defence) Act, enabled aliens to be imprisoned on grounds that they might give aid and comfort to the enemy.

5. Orwell wrote to his friend Brenda Salkeld, on 7 May 1935, about the crowds celebrating the Jubilee of King George V. See *Orwell's England* in this series.

6. As an economy measure, people were encouraged not to fill baths with more than five inches of water. In the editor's experience, it was more widely observed than Orwell suggests, but how widely it is impossible to tell.

7. The rumours were to be proved true. V-1 'flying bombs' were launched on London on the night of 13–14 June 1944, a week after D-Day. The first V-2 rockets were launched against Paris on 6 September 1944 and on London on 8 September.

[2407]

Review of The Machiavellians *by James Burnham*
Manchester Evening News, *20 January 1944*

It is notorious that certain sins, crimes, and vices would lack attraction if they were not forbidden. Mr. Gandhi has described the shuddering joy with which, as a child, he sneaked down to some secret haunt in the bazaar and ate a plate of beef, and our grandfathers derived acute pleasure from drinking champagne out of the satin slippers of actresses.

So also with political theories. Any theory which is obviously dishonest and immoral ('realistic' is the favourite word at this moment) will find adherents who accept it just for that reason. Whether the theory works, whether it attains the result aimed at will hardly be questioned. The mere fact that it throws ordinary decency overboard will be accepted as proof of its grown-upness and consequently of its efficacy.

Mr. Burnham, whose managerial revolution[1] won a large if rather short-lived renown by telling American business-men what they wanted to hear, has now set forth the political doctrine which he derives from Machiavelli and Machiavelli's modern followers, Mosca, Pareto, Michels,[2] and – though it is doubtful whether he really belongs in this school – Georges Sorel.

The world-picture which Mr. Burnham has built up from the teachings of these writers is something like this:

Progress is largely an illusion. Democracy is impossible, though useful as a myth to deceive the masses.

Society is inevitably ruled by oligarchies who hold their position by means of force and fraud, and whose sole objective is power and still more power for themselves. No revolution means more than a change of rulers.

Man, as a political animal, is moved solely by selfish motives, except so far as he is under the influence of myths.

Conscious, planned action for the good of the community is impossible, since each group is simply trying to secure its own advantage.

Politics is, and can be, nothing except a struggle for power. Human equality, human fraternity are empty phrases.

All moral codes, all 'idealistic' conceptions of politics, all visions of a better society in the future are simply lies, conscious or unconscious, covering the naked struggle for power.

Having set forth this thesis Mr. Burnham contradicts it to some extent by adding that various checks on the exercise of power are desirable, in particular, freedom of speech. He also, following Pareto, points out that a ruling caste decays if it is not renewed from time to time by able recruits from the masses.

In one place he even finds himself admitting that the Anglo-Saxon version of democracy has some survival value, and that the Germans might have avoided some of their strategic mistakes if they had not crushed internal opposition.

However, the sudden outburst in favour of freedom of speech, which occupies a chapter or two, is probably only a part of Mr. Burnham's quarrel with the Roosevelt Administration. He ends by looking forward to the emergence of a new ruling class, who will rule 'scientifically' by the conscious use of force and fraud, but who will to some small extent serve the common good because they will recognise that it is to their own interest to do so.

Now, when one examines a political theory of this kind, the first thing one notices is that it is no more scientific than the idealistic creeds it professes to debunk. The premise from which Mr. Burnham starts out is that a relatively decent society, a society, for instance, in which everyone has enough to eat and wars are a thing of the past, is impossible. He puts this forward as an axiom.

Why is such a thing impossible? How is it 'scientific' to make this quite arbitrary assumption?

The argument implied all the way through the book is that a peaceful and prosperous society cannot exist in the future because it has never existed in the past. By the same argument one could have proved the impossibility of aeroplanes in 1900, while only a few centuries earlier one could have 'proved' that civilisation is impossible except on a basis of chattel slavery.

The fact is that much of Machiavelli's teaching has been invalidated by the rise of modern technology.

When Machiavelli wrote, human equality was, if not impossible, certainly undesirable. In the general poverty of the world a privileged class was needed to keep the arts of civilisation alive. In the modern world, where there is no material reason why every human being should not enjoy a fairly high standard of living, this need disappears.

Human equality is technically possible whatever the psychological difficulties may be, and of course the philosophies of Pareto, Mr. Burnham, and the rest are simply efforts to avoid this unwelcome fact.

The scientific approach to Machiavelli's teachings would have to find out what statesmen had modelled themselves upon Machiavelli, and how successful they had been. Mr. Burnham hardly makes this test. He does remark, as an illustration of Machiavelli's prestige, that Thomas Cromwell, Henry VIII's Chancellor, always carried a copy of *The Prince*[3] in his pocket. He does not add that Cromwell ended on the block.

In our own day, Mussolini, the conscious pupil of Machiavelli and Pareto, does not seem to have made a very brilliant success of things. And the Nazi régime, based on essentially Machiavellian principles, is being smashed to pieces by the forces which its own lack of scruple conjured up.

It would seem that the theory that there is no such thing as a 'good' motive in politics, that nothing counts except force and fraud, has a hole in it somewhere, and that the Machiavellian system fails even by its own test of material success.

In the managerial revolution Mr. Burnham foretold that Britain would be swiftly conquered, that Germany would not attack Russia till the war with Britain was over, and that Russia would then be torn to pieces. These prophecies, obviously based on wish-thinking, were falsified almost as soon as made.

In the present book he has wisely refrained from foretelling anything so concrete, but assumes the same air of omniscience. It is doubtful whether he and the many others like him have done more than turn a copybook maxim on its head.

'Dishonesty is the best policy' is the sum of their wisdom. The fact that this shallow piece of naughtiness can – just because it sounds 'realistic' and grown-up – be accepted without any examination does not speak well for the Anglo-American intelligentsia.

1. James Burnham (1905–87) was a Professor of Philosophy at New York University, 1932–54. His *The Managerial Revolution* (1941, revd 1972) created a considerable stir and was discussed by Orwell in 'As I Please', 7, 14 January 1944 (XVI/*2404*). According to Orwell, 'Shortly, Burnham's thesis is this. *Laissez-faire* capitalism is finished and Socialism, at any

rate in the present period of history, is impossible. What is now happening is the appearance of a new ruling class, named by Burnham the "managers". These are represented in Germany and the USSR by the Nazis and the Bolsheviks, and in the USA by the business executives.' Although Orwell thought there was 'a great deal in what Burnham says', he took issue with him – and Burnham responded (see XVI/62–4). Burnham was associated with the Trotskyist Fourth International group from 1933 to about 1939. He then broke with Trotskyism and pursued what his obituary in *The Times* (4 August 1987) described as a 'career of political prophecy and right-wing exaltation which brought him fame'. He was a founder editor with William Buckley, Jun., of *The National Review* in 1955 and was associated with the journal until his death.

2. Gaetano Mosca (1858–1941), Italian jurist, Vilfredo Pareto (1848–1923), Italian economist and sociologist, and Robert Michels (1876–1936), German sociologist and economist, were all concerned with defining the nature and functions of political élites. Perhaps the most important work emanating from these theorists was Pareto's *Trattato di sociologia generale* (1916), translated as *Mind and Society* (1935). Italian Fascism drew on Pareto's theories.

3. Niccolò Machiavelli (1469–1527), Italian politician and theorist. His most famous work is *Il Principe* (The Prince; 1532), though he also wrote other works, including plays. The book is a practical guide to politicians whose chief aim is exerting authority and remaining in power, whatever treachery is needed to achieve those ends. It was condemned by the Pope but its author's name was adopted to describe whatever is treacherous – 'machiavellian'. The Machiavel became familiar to Elizabethans from plays of the period. Thus, 'Machevil' appears as the Prologue to *The Jew of Malta* by Christopher Marlowe, and Shakespeare's Richard III, when still Duke of Gloucester, boasts (with justice) that he can 'set the murderous Machiavel to school' (*3 Henry* VI, III.ii).

Completion of Animal Farm

On 19 March 1944, Orwell wrote to his literary agent, Leonard Moore, and to his then chief publisher, Victor Gollancz, to tell them that he would be posting the typescript of his new book in a few days' time (XVI/2436, 2437). It was, he told Gollancz, 'a little fairy story'. There was much difficulty finding a publisher for Animal Farm, *chiefly because it was critical of the Soviet Union. That was Gollancz's objection. To Nicholson & Watson it was 'bad taste to attack the head of an allied government in that manner'. André Deutsch (1917–2000), not then a publisher in his own right but seeking to become one, was twice offered the book, but though keen felt he could not risk capital he did not have (and lost the chance to make a small fortune). T. S. Eliot turned down the book for Faber & Faber. Jonathan Cape took the advice of 'an important official in the Ministry of Information' that it would be 'highly ill-advised to publish [it] at the present*

*time'. This official was almost certainly Peter Smollett (or Smolka), an
Austrian who had come to England in the 1930s and worked for a time with
the traitor Kim Philby. From 1941 he was head of the Russian section of the
Ministry of Information and was awarded the OBE for his services. He was,
however, (as Orwell suspected) a Soviet spy, codenamed 'ABO'. Indeed, he
was so incredibly successful that the Soviets came to believe his success was
'a cunning plot by British intelligence to hoodwink the NKVD' and so,
necessarily, 'a plant' (Christopher Andrew and Vasili Mitrokhin,* The
Mitrokhin Archive: The KGB in Europe and the West, *1999, 158).
At last, in August 1944, Fredric Warburg,[1] who had risked publishing*
Homage to Catalonia *when Gollancz turned it down, because it exposed
Communist attacks on the POUM, agreed to publish the book – provided
he could get paper, then very severely rationed, except for government
purposes. He hoped to publish in March 1945 but it was not until August
1945, seventeen months after the submission of the typescript, that publication
took place. See* XVI / 2442, 2443, 2448 *(especially n. 1), 2453, 2461, 2494,
2505, 2533 and 2539.*

1. Fredric Warburg (1898–1980), Orwell's second publisher, began his career with George
Routledge & Sons in 1922 on coming down from Oxford, 'fit for practically nothing or,
perhaps more accurately, for nothing practical' (see his *An Occupation for Gentlemen*, 77–83).
He joined Martin Secker in 1936 to form Martin Secker & Warburg, so ensuring that this
distinguished publishing house did not go out of business. When Gollancz turned down
Homage to Catalonia, he took it, and when, later, Gollancz and several other publishers
declined to publish *Animal Farm*, he brought it out. From then on, Martin Secker & Warburg
published all Orwell's books in England. Warburg devotes considerable attention to Orwell
in his autobiographies, *An Occupation for Gentlemen* (1959) and *All Authors are Equal* (1973),
the title of which is derived from Orwell, who is one of its dedicatees. See also *Orwell
Remembered*, 193–9.

Publication of Animal Farm
London, 17 August 1945; New York, 26 August 1946

Animal Farm *was published in London by Martin Secker & Warburg on
17 August 1945 and in New York by Harcourt, Brace on 26 August 1946.
The first English edition was of 4,500 copies. A second impression, of
10,000 copies, was published in November 1945; and a third, of 6,000*

copies, in October 1946. These all sold at 6s per copy. The first cheap edition – 5,000 copies at 3s 6d – was published by Secker & Warburg in May 1949. Thus, by the time Orwell died, 25,500 copies of Animal Farm *had been issued in Britain. The first American edition comprised 50,000 copies; two impressions, of 430,000 and 110,000 copies, were issued as Book-of-the-Month Club editions; and a separate Canadian edition of 2,000 copies appeared in November 1946. According to Ian Willison's thesis (1953), the copy in the American Library in London has an additional imprint (Kingsport Press, Kingsport, Tenn.), suggesting a second impression, but Harcourt, Brace, the publishers, advised Willison that they issued only one impression. Willison records translations into Portuguese, Swedish, Norwegian, German (in one Swiss and two German-national versions), Polish, Persian (via the British Central Office of Information), Dutch, French, Italian, Ukrainian, Danish, Estonian, Spanish, Korean, Japanese, Telugu, Icelandic and Russian by the time Orwell died. Many editions and translations have followed, of which the Penguin edition is probably the most commonly available. The first Penguin edition, of 60,000 copies, was published on 27 July 1951, and a second impression, of 40,000 copies, was issued on 24 October 1952. These sold at 1s 6d and 2s respectively. Secker & Warburg published a corrected edition in the* Complete Works *series, as Volume VIII, in 1987; a Penguin reprint of that edition was published in 1989.*

Despite its great success, Orwell's earnings from Animal Farm *were not as great as these long runs might suggest. On 23 January 1950, shortly after Orwell died, the* Evening Standard *stated: 'Animal Farm made for him at least £12,000. This may seem a low figure, but the majority of the sales were at the low prices of the American Book of the Month Club.' It is not now possible to check the reliability of the figure given by the* Evening Standard*. Orwell stipulated that he should not receive payment for translations of this or any book made by or for refugee groups, students and working-class organizations (3728, XX/227).*

There was to have been a Preface, 'The Freedom of the Press', and space was left for it in the page proofs, but it was not included. The typescript was found many years later by Ian Angus and first published in 1972. It is given here as Appendix I; as Appendix II is the Preface Orwell wrote for the Ukrainian edition. For Orwell's correspondence with Ihor Szewczenko *leading to the writing of this Preface, see especially* XVIII / 2969. *Szewczenko (1921–) was, in April 1946, a Soviet-Ukrainian refugee in Germany, working for a newspaper for the Second Polish (the Maczek) Division and was responsible for surveying the British Press and especially* Tribune. *(He later emigrated to the USA and became Professor of Byzantine Studies at Harvard University.) The edition was distributed through the Displaced Persons' bookshop in Munich, but unfortunately, in a misguided attempt at co-operation with the Soviets, the American Military Government in Germany seized about half the print run of 5,000 copies and handed it over to the Soviets (3728,* XX / 226–7).*

The sub-title to Animal Farm, *'A Fairy Story', appears on all editions published by Secker & Warburg but almost all other publishers in Orwell's lifetime either dropped that sub-title (as did the first US edition), or changed it to 'A Satire', 'A Contemporary Satire', or something to indicate that it was a fable or tale. Only the Telugu translation of those made by 1950 has 'A Fairy Story' included. The significance of the sub-title for what Orwell was saying is now more obvious than it evidently was in the late 1940s.*

On 2 December 1946, the American scholar, literary critic and editor of Politics, *Dwight Macdonald (1906–82), wrote to Orwell about the way US intellectuals were puzzled by the book. He thought it applied 'solely to Russia and [was] not making any larger statement about the philosophy of revolution'. Orwell replied on 5 December (*XVIII / 3128):

Re. your query about Animal Farm. *Of course I intended it primarily as a satire on the Russian revolution. But I did mean it to have a wider application in so much that I meant that that kind of revolution (violent conspiratorial revolution, led by unconsciously power-hungry people) can only lead to a change of masters. I meant the moral to be that revolutions only effect a radical improvement when the masses are alert and know how to chuck out their leaders as soon as the latter have done their job. The turning-point of the story was supposed to be when the pigs kept the milk and apples for themselves (Kronstadt[1]). If the other animals had had the sense to put their foot down then, it would have been all right. If people think I am defending the status quo, that is, I think, because they have grown pessimistic and assume that there is no alternative except dictatorship or laissez-faire capitalism . . . What I was trying to say was, 'You can't have a revolution unless you make it for yourself; there is no such thing as a benevolent dictatorship.'*

Because the significance of the 'turning-point' of the book had been missed,
Orwell strengthened this moment in his adaptation for a BBC radio broadcast,
the script of which he was to deliver a week or so later to Rayner Heppenstall.
See the lines (259 and 260–62) printed at the end of A Note on the Text
(p. 233). Unfortunately, Heppenstall cut these lines from the broadcast.

1. Kronstadt, a naval base guarding the approach to St Petersburg, a few miles from Finland, was established by Peter the Great in 1704. The turning-point in *Animal Farm* is related to events that took place there early in 1921. Food shortages and a harsh regime prompted a series of strikes in Petrograd; in March, the strikers were supported by sailors at the Kronstadt naval base. This was the first serious uprising not only by supporters of the Revolution against their government but by a city and by naval personnel particularly associated with ensuring the success of the 1917 Revolution. Trotsky and Mikhail Tukhachevsky (1893–1937) put down the rebellion, but the losses sustained by the rebels were not in vain. A New Economic Policy was enunciated shortly after which recognized the need for reforms. Tukhachevsky was made a Marshal of the Soviet Union in 1935, but two years later he was executed in one of Stalin's purges.

Animal Farm

A NOTE ON THE TEXT

Animal Farm was published in England on 17 August 1945 and one year
later in the United States. Until Animal Farm *the total print-run of Orwell's*
nine books (including Inside the Whale *and* The Lion and the Unicorn*)*
in Britain and America amounted to some 195,500 copies. Of these, 47,079
were of The Road to Wigan Pier *and 115,000 were Penguin editions of*
Down and Out in Paris and London *(1940) and* Burmese Days
(1944). Shortage of paper after World War II restricted the number of
copies of Animal Farm *printed in Britain, but 25,500 copies had been*
issued by the time Orwell died in January 1950, and 590,000 in America.
These figures give quantitative support to the enormous and immediate
success of Animal Farm, *and they are backed up by the range and variety*
of the translations made during the few remaining years of Orwell's life –
translations into all the principal European languages, as well as Persian,
Telugu, Icelandic and Ukrainian. But what genre of book was being offered
to these different publics? The most important textual variant of Animal

Farm *affects its title-page.* Orwell called his book, Animal Farm: A Fairy Story. *This is the description given in all editions published by Secker &* Warburg and Penguin Books *but the Americans dropped* A Fairy Story *from the outset. (One of the many publishers who declined to publish* Animal Farm *in Britain and America did so because he considered there was no market for children's books.) Only in Telugu, of all the translations made in Orwell's lifetime, was* A Fairy Story *retained. In other translations the subtitle was dropped or became* A Satire, A Contemporary Satire, *or was described as an adventure or tale. This is not the place to discuss the significance of the original subtitle, except, perhaps, to point out that it stems from Orwell's abiding fascination for fairy stories and the like encountered during early childhood, in his work as a teacher and his time at the BBC.*

Typescripts of two of Orwell's books have survived – Animal Farm *and* Nineteen Eighty-Four *– in addition to an author's proof for* Animal Farm. *The number of textual variants is relatively few. When the text was prepared for the English printer, variations in capitalization and spelling were smoothed out (so that Orwell's 'hay field', 'hay-field' and 'hayfield' all became one word) and, on average, the punctuation was changed twice on each page. For this edition Orwell's punctuation has been preferred and what may be a subtle shift from 'seven commandments' (page 245, line 24) to 'Seven Commandments' (e.g., page 249, line 32), after they have become sacrosanct, is restored. In 1945 the pigeons were not permitted to drop dung on Mr Jones and his men (page 254, line 2), but were required, obscurely, to 'mute' upon them instead to avoid offending readers' susceptibilities.*

Of the two most interesting textual characteristics of Animal Farm, *apart from its genre subtitle, one is a change made just in time for the first edition and the other is an afterthought that cannot properly be incorporated.*

In March 1945 Orwell was in Paris working as a war correspondent for the Observer *and the* Manchester Evening News. *He there met Joseph Czapski, a survivor of Soviet concentration camps who had missed the Katyn Massacre. Despite the latter's experiences and his opposition to the Soviet regime, he explained to Orwell (as Orwell wrote to Arthur Koestler) that 'it was the . . . character of Stalin . . . the greatness of Stalin' that saved Russia from the German invasion. 'He stayed in Moscow when the Germans nearly took it, and his courage was what saved the situation.' In* Animal Farm, *although parallels to historical personages are not exact, Stalin is certainly* represented by Napoleon.[1] *A few days after meeting Czapski, Orwell wrote to Roger Senhouse at his publishers asking for the text to be changed in chapter VIII (in this edition page 285, line 26). Instead of 'all the animals, including Napoleon', falling to the ground, he wanted 'all the animals, except Napoleon'. This alteration, he wrote, 'would be fair to Stalin, as he did stay in Moscow during the German advance'.*

At the end of 1946, Orwell prepared an adaptation of Animal Farm *for the BBC Third Programme. On 2 December Dwight Macdonald, editor of the American journal* Politics, *and a friend of Orwell's, wrote saying he assumed* Animal Farm *applied only to Russia and that Orwell was 'not making any larger statement about the philosophy of revolution'. Orwell replied that though* Animal Farm *was 'primarily . . . a satire on the Russian revolution' it was intended to have 'a wider application'. That kind of revolution, which he defined as 'violent conspiratorial revolution, led by unconsciously power-hungry people', could only lead to a change of masters. He went on: 'I meant the moral to be that revolutions only effect a radical improvement when the masses are alert and know how to chuck out their leaders as soon as the latter have done their job. The turning-point of the story was supposed to be when the pigs kept the milk and apples for themselves', and he referred to the naval mutiny at Kronstadt in 1921 when the sailors supported those striking in Petrograd against the Soviet regime. Realizing that the turning-point in the novel was not clear enough, he added these lines of dialogue to the radio adaptation he was just then completing:*

CLOVER: *Do you think that is quite fair to appropriate the apples?*
MOLLY: *What, keep all the apples for themselves?*
MURIEL: *Aren't we to have any?*
COW: *I thought they were going to be shared out equally.*

The significance of these lines was lost on the BBC producer, Rayner Heppenstall, who cut them out. As Orwell did not revise Animal Farm, *it is beyond an editor's remit to add them to the book, but they do highlight what Orwell told Geoffrey Gorer was the 'key passage' of* Animal Farm *(Crick, 490).*

1. In a letter to Yvonne Davet, Orwell described *Animal Farm* as his novel 'contre Stalin'. He suggested as a title for the French translation, 'Union des républiques socialistes animales' –

URSA (the BEAR; XVIII/3063). For the French edition Napoleon was renamed César. Davet (born c. 1895) was for many years secretary to André Gide. She and Orwell corresponded before and after World War II. She translated some of his books into French and some of the footnotes she elicited from him have been included (translated into English) in the Penguin Twentieth-Century Classics editions. She thought so highly of Orwell's work that she began her translation of *Homage to Catalonia* in the summer of 1938 before a publisher was found for it. They exchanged left-wing journals but never met. She also translated novels by Jean Rhys, Graham Greene and Iris Murdoch into French.

CHAPTER I

MR JONES, of the Manor Farm, had locked the hen-houses for the night, but was too drunk to remember to shut the pop-holes. With the ring of light from his lantern dancing from side to side he lurched across the yard, kicked off his boots at the back door, drew himself a last glass of beer from the barrel in the scullery, and made his way up to bed, where Mrs Jones was already snoring.

As soon as the light in the bedroom went out there was a stirring and a fluttering all through the farm buildings. Word had gone round during the day that old Major, the prize Middle White boar, had had a strange dream on the previous night and wished to communicate it to the other animals. It had been agreed that they should all meet in the big barn as soon as Mr Jones was safely out of the way. Old Major (so he was always called, though the name under which he had been exhibited was Willingdon Beauty) was so highly regarded on the farm that everyone was quite ready to lose an hour's sleep in order to hear what he had to say.

At one end of the big barn, on a sort of raised platform, Major was already ensconced on his bed of straw, under a lantern which hung from a beam. He was twelve years old and had lately grown rather stout, but he was still a majestic-looking pig, with a wise and benevolent appearance in spite of the fact that his tushes had never been cut. Before long the other animals began to arrive and make themselves comfortable after their different fashions. First came the three dogs, Bluebell, Jessie and Pincher, and then the pigs, who settled down in the straw immediately in front of the platform. The hens perched themselves on the window-sills, the pigeons fluttered up to the rafters, the sheep and cows lay down behind the pigs and began to chew the cud. The two cart-horses, Boxer and Clover, came in together, walking very slowly and setting down their vast hairy hoofs with great care lest there should be some small animal concealed in the straw. Clover was a stout motherly mare approaching middle life, who had never quite got her figure back after her fourth foal. Boxer was an enormous beast, nearly eighteen hands high, and as strong as any two ordinary horses put together. A white stripe down his nose gave him a somewhat stupid appearance, and in fact he was not of first-rate intelligence, but he was universally respected for his steadiness of character and tremendous powers of work. After the horses came Muriel, the white goat, and Benjamin the donkey. Benjamin was the oldest animal on the farm, and the worst tempered. He seldom talked, and when he did it was usually to make some cynical remark – for instance he would say that God had given him a tail to keep the flies off, but that he would sooner have had no tail and no flies. Alone among the animals on the farm he never laughed. If asked why, he would say that he saw nothing to laugh at. Nevertheless, without openly admitting it, he was devoted to Boxer; the two of them usually spent their Sundays together in the small paddock beyond the orchard, grazing side by side and never speaking.

The two horses had just lain down when a brood of ducklings which had lost their mother filed into the barn, cheeping feebly and wandering from side to side to find some place where they would not be trodden on. Clover made a sort of wall round them with her great foreleg, and the ducklings nestled down inside it and promptly fell asleep. At the last moment Mollie, the foolish, pretty white mare who drew Mr Jones's trap, came mincing daintily in, chewing at a lump of sugar. She took a place near the front and began flirting her white mane, hoping to draw attention to the red ribbons it was plaited with. Last of all came the cat, who looked round, as usual, for the warmest place, and finally squeezed herself in between Boxer and Clover; there she purred contentedly throughout Major's speech without listening to a word of what he was saying.

All the animals were now present except Moses, the tame raven, who slept on a perch behind the back door. When Major saw that they had all made themselves comfortable and were waiting attentively he cleared his throat and began:

'Comrades, you have heard already about the strange dream that I had last night. But I will come to the dream later. I have something else to say first. I do not think, comrades, that I shall be with you for many months longer, and before I die I feel it my duty to pass on to you such wisdom as I have acquired. I have had a long life, I have had much time for thought as I lay alone in my stall, and I think I may say that I understand the nature of life on this earth as well as any animal now living. It is about this that I wish to speak to you.

'Now, comrades, what is the nature of this life of ours? Let us face it, our lives are miserable, laborious and short. We are born, we are given just so much food as will keep the breath in our bodies, and those of us who are capable of it are forced to work to the last atom of our strength; and the very instant that our usefulness has come to an end we are slaughtered with hideous cruelty. No animal in England knows the meaning of happiness or leisure after he is a year old. No animal in England is free. The life of an animal is misery and slavery: that is the plain truth.

'But is this simply part of the order of Nature? Is it because this land of ours is so poor that it cannot afford a decent life to those who dwell upon it? No, comrades, a thousand times no! The soil of England is fertile, its climate is good, it is capable of affording food in abundance to an enormously greater number of animals than now inhabit it. This single farm of ours would support a dozen horses, twenty cows, hundreds of sheep – and all of them living in a comfort and a dignity that are now almost beyond our imagining. Why then do we continue in this miserable condition? Because nearly the whole of the produce of our labour is stolen from us by human beings. There, comrades, is the answer to all our problems. It is summed up in a single word – Man. Man is the only real enemy we have. Remove Man from the scene, and the root cause of hunger and overwork is abolished for ever.

'Man is the only creature that consumes without producing. He does not give milk, he does not lay eggs, he is too weak to pull the plough, he cannot run fast enough to catch rabbits. Yet he is lord of all the animals. He sets them to work, he gives back to them the bare minimum that will prevent them from starving, and the rest he keeps for himself. Our labour tills the soil, our dung fertilises it, and yet there is not one of us that owns more than his bare skin. You cows that I see before me, how many thousands of gallons of milk have you given during this last year? And what has happened to that milk which should have been breeding up sturdy calves? Every drop of it has gone down the throats of our enemies. And you hens, how many eggs have you laid in this last year, and how many of those eggs ever hatched into chickens? The rest have all gone to market to bring in money for Jones and his men. And you, Clover, where are those four foals you bore, who should have been the support and pleasure of your old age? Each was sold at a year old – you will never see one of them again. In return for your four confinements and all your labour in the fields, what have you ever had except your bare rations and a stall?

'And even the miserable lives we lead are not allowed to reach their natural span. For myself I do not grumble, for I am one of the lucky ones. I am twelve years old and have had over four hundred children. Such is the natural life of a pig. But no animal escapes the cruel knife in the end. You young porkers who are sitting in front of me, every one of you will scream your lives out at the block within a year. To that horror we all must come – cows, pigs, hens, sheep, everyone. Even the horses and the dogs have no better fate. You, Boxer, the very day that those great muscles of yours lose their power, Jones will sell you to the knacker, who will cut your throat and boil you down for the foxhounds. As for the dogs, when they grow old and toothless Jones ties a brick round their necks and drowns them in the nearest pond.

'Is it not crystal clear, then, comrades, that all the evils of this life of ours spring from the tyranny of human beings? Only get rid of Man, and the produce of our labour would be our own. Almost overnight we could become rich and free. What then must we do? Why, work night and day, body and soul, for the overthrow of the human race! That is my message to you, comrades: Rebellion! I do not know when that Rebellion will come, it might be in a week or in a hundred years, but I know, as surely as I see this straw beneath my feet, that sooner or later justice will be done. Fix your eyes on that, comrades, throughout the short remainder of your lives! And above all, pass on this message of mine to those who come after you, so that future generations shall carry on the struggle until it is victorious.

'And remember, comrades, your resolution must never falter. No argument must lead you astray. Never listen when they tell you that Man and the animals have a common interest, that the prosperity of the one is the prosperity of the others. It is all lies. Man serves the interests of no creature except himself. And among us animals let there be perfect unity, perfect comradeship in the struggle. All men are enemies. All animals are comrades.'

At this moment there was a tremendous uproar. While Major was speaking four large rats had crept out of their holes and were sitting on their hindquarters, listening to him. The dogs had suddenly caught sight of them, and it was only by a swift dash for their holes that the rats saved their lives. Major raised his trotter for silence:

'Comrades,' he said, 'here is a point that must be settled. The wild creatures, such as rats and rabbits – are they our friends or our enemies? Let us put it to the vote. I propose this question to the meeting: Are rats comrades?'

The vote was taken at once, and it was agreed by an overwhelming majority that rats were comrades. There were only four dissentients, the three dogs and the cat, who was afterwards discovered to have voted on both sides. Major continued:

'I have little more to say. I merely repeat, remember always your duty of enmity towards Man and all his ways. Whatever goes upon two legs is an enemy. Whatever goes upon four legs, or has wings, is a friend. And remember also that in fighting against Man, we must not come to resemble him. Even when you have conquered him, do not adopt his vices. No animal must ever live in a house, or sleep in a bed, or wear clothes, or drink alcohol, or smoke tobacco, or touch money, or engage in trade. All the habits of Man are evil. And above all, no animal must ever tyrannise over his own kind. Weak or strong, clever or simple, we are all brothers. No animal must ever kill any other animal. All animals are equal.

'And now, comrades, I will tell you about my dream of last night. I cannot describe that dream to you. It was a dream of the earth as it will be when Man has vanished. But it reminded me of something that I had long forgotten. Many years ago, when I was a little pig, my mother and the other sows used to sing an old song of which they knew only the tune and the first three words. I had known that tune in my infancy, but it had long since passed out of my mind. Last night, however, it came back to me in my dream. And what is more, the words of the song also came back – words, I am certain, which were sung by the animals of long ago and have been lost to memory for generations. I will sing you that song now, comrades. I am old and my voice is hoarse, but when I have taught you the tune you can sing it better for yourselves. It is called "Beasts of England".'

Old Major cleared his throat and began to sing. As he had said, his voice was hoarse, but he sang well enough, and it was a stirring tune, something between 'Clementine' and 'La Cucuracha'. The words ran:

> *Beasts of England, beasts of Ireland,*
> *Beasts of every land and clime,*
> *Hearken to my joyful tidings*
> *Of the golden future time.*
>
> *Soon or late the day is coming,*
> *Tyrant Man shall be o'erthrown,*
> *And the fruitful fields of England*
> *Shall be trod by beasts alone.*
>
> *Rings shall vanish from our noses,*
> *And the harness from our back,*
> *Bit and spur shall rust forever,*
> *Cruel whips no more shall crack.*
>
> *Riches more than mind can picture,*
> *Wheat and barley, oats and hay,*
> *Clover, beans and mangel-wurzels*
> *Shall be ours upon that day.*
>
> *Bright will shine the fields of England,*
> *Purer shall its waters be,*
> *Sweeter yet shall blow its breezes*
> *On the day that sets us free.*
>
> *For that day we all must labour,*
> *Though we die before it break;*
> *Cows and horses, geese and turkeys,*
> *All must toil for freedom's sake.*

> *Beasts of England, beasts of Ireland,*
> *Beasts of every land and clime,*
> *Hearken well and spread my tidings*
> *Of the golden future time.*

The singing of this song threw the animals into the wildest excitement. Almost before Major had reached the end, they had begun singing it for themselves. Even the stupidest of them had already picked up the tune and a few of the words, and as for the clever ones, such as the pigs and dogs, they had the entire song by heart within a few minutes. And then, after a few preliminary tries, the whole farm burst out into 'Beasts of England' in tremendous unison. The cows lowed it, the dogs whined it, the sheep bleated it, the horses whinnied it, the ducks quacked it. They were so delighted with the song that they sang it right through five times in succession, and might have continued singing it all night if they had not been interrupted.

Unfortunately the uproar awoke Mr Jones, who sprang out of bed, making sure that there was a fox in the yard. He seized the gun which always stood in a corner of his bedroom, and let fly a charge of Number 6 shot into the darkness. The pellets buried themselves in the wall of the barn and the meeting broke up hurriedly. Everyone fled to his own sleeping-place. The birds jumped onto their perches, the animals settled down in the straw, and the whole farm was asleep in a moment.

CHAPTER II

THREE NIGHTS LATER old Major died peacefully in his sleep. His body was buried at the foot of the orchard.

This was early in March. During the next three months there was much secret activity. Major's speech had given to the more intelligent animals on the farm a completely new outlook on life. They did not know when the Rebellion predicted by Major would take place, they had no reason for thinking that it would be within their own lifetime, but they saw clearly that it was their duty to prepare for it. The work of teaching and organising the others fell naturally upon the pigs, who were generally recognised as being the cleverest of the animals. Pre-eminent among the pigs were two young boars named Snowball and Napoleon, whom Mr

Jones was breeding up for sale. Napoleon was a large, rather fierce-looking Berkshire boar, the only Berkshire on the farm, not much of a talker but with a reputation for getting his own way. Snowball was a more vivacious pig than Napoleon, quicker in speech and more inventive, but was not considered to have the same depth of character. All the other male pigs on the farm were porkers. The best known among them was a small fat pig named Squealer, with very round cheeks, twinkling eyes, nimble movements and a shrill voice. He was a brilliant talker, and when he was arguing some difficult point he had a way of skipping from side to side and whisking his tail which was somehow very persuasive. The others said of Squealer that he could turn black into white.

These three had elaborated old Major's teachings into a complete system of thought, to which they gave the name of Animalism. Several nights a week, after Mr Jones was asleep, they held secret meetings in the barn and expounded the principles of Animalism to the others. At the beginning they met with much stupidity and apathy. Some of the animals talked of the duty of loyalty to Mr Jones, whom they referred to as 'Master', or made elementary remarks such as 'Mr Jones feeds us. If he were gone we should starve to death.' Others asked such questions as 'Why should we care what happens after we are dead?' or 'If this Rebellion is to happen anyway, what difference does it make whether we work for it or not?', and the pigs had great difficulty in making them see that this was contrary to the spirit of Animalism. The stupidest questions of all were asked by Mollie, the white mare. The very first question she asked Snowball was: 'Will there still be sugar after the Rebellion?'

'No,' said Snowball firmly. 'We have no means of making sugar on this farm. Besides, you do not need sugar. You will have all the oats and hay you want.'

'And shall I still be allowed to wear ribbons in my mane?' asked Mollie.

'Comrade,' said Snowball, 'those ribbons that you are so devoted to are the badge of slavery. Can you not understand that liberty is worth more than ribbons?'

Mollie agreed, but she did not sound very convinced.

The pigs had an even harder struggle to counteract the lies put about by Moses, the tame raven. Moses, who was Mr Jones's especial pet, was a spy and a tale-bearer, but he was also a clever talker. He claimed to know of the existence of a mysterious country called Sugarcandy Mountain, to which all animals went when they died. It was situated somewhere up in the sky, a little distance beyond the clouds, Moses said. In Sugarcandy Mountain it was Sunday seven days a week, clover was in season all the year round, and lump sugar and linseed cake grew on the hedges. The animals hated Moses because he told tales and did no work, but some of them believed in Sugarcandy Mountain, and the pigs had to argue very hard to persuade them that there was no such place.

Their most faithful disciples were the two cart-horses, Boxer and Clover. These two had great difficulty in thinking anything out for themselves, but having once accepted the pigs as their teachers they absorbed everything that they were told, and passed it on to the other animals by simple arguments. They were unfailing in their attendance at the secret meetings in the barn, and led the singing of 'Beasts of England' with which the meetings always ended.

Now, as it turned out, the Rebellion was achieved much earlier and more easily than anyone had expected. In past years Mr Jones, although a hard master, had been a capable farmer, but of late he had fallen on evil days. He had become much disheartened after losing money in a lawsuit, and had taken to drinking more than was good for him. For whole days at a time he would lounge in his windsor chair in the kitchen, reading the newspapers, drinking, and occasionally feeding Moses on crusts of bread soaked in beer. His men were idle and dishonest, the fields were full of weeds, the buildings wanted roofing, the hedges were neglected and the animals were underfed.

June came and the hay was almost ready for cutting. On Midsummer's Eve, which was a Saturday, Mr Jones went into Willingdon and got so drunk at the Red Lion that he did not come back till midday on Sunday. The men had milked the cows in the early morning and then had gone out rabbiting, without bothering to feed the animals. When Mr Jones got back he immediately went to sleep on the drawing-room sofa with the *News of the World* over his face, so that when evening came the animals were still unfed. At last they could stand it no longer. One of the cows broke in the door of the store-shed with her horn and all the animals began to help themselves from the bins. It was just then that Mr Jones

woke up. The next moment he and his four men were in the store-shed
with whips in their hands, lashing out in all directions. This was more
than the hungry animals could bear. With one accord, though nothing of
the kind had been planned beforehand, they flung themselves upon their
tormentors. Jones and his men suddenly found themselves being butted
and kicked from all sides. The situation was quite out of their control.
They had never seen animals behave like this before, and this sudden
uprising of creatures whom they were used to thrashing and maltreating
just as they chose, frightened them almost out of their wits. After only a
moment or two they gave up trying to defend themselves and took to
their heels. A minute later all five of them were in full flight down the
cart-track that led to the main road, with the animals pursuing them in
triumph.

Mrs Jones looked out of the bedroom window, saw what was happening, hurriedly flung a few possessions into a carpet bag and slipped out
of the farm by another way. Moses sprang off his perch and flapped after
her, croaking loudly. Meanwhile the animals had chased Jones and his
men out onto the road and slammed the five-barred gate behind them.
And so, almost before they knew what was happening, the Rebellion had
been successfully carried through; Jones was expelled, and the Manor
Farm was theirs.

For the first few minutes the animals could hardly believe in their good
fortune. Their first act was to gallop in a body right round the boundaries
of the farm, as though to make quite sure that no human being was hiding
anywhere upon it; then they raced back to the farm buildings to wipe out
the last traces of Jones's hated reign. The harness-room at the end of the
stables was broken open; the bits, the nose-rings, the dog-chains, the
cruel knives with which Mr Jones had been used to castrate the pigs and
lambs, were all flung down the well. The reins, the halters, the blinkers,
the degrading nosebags, were thrown onto the rubbish fire which was
burning in the yard. So were the whips. All the animals capered with joy
when they saw the whips going up in flames. Snowball also threw onto
the fire the ribbons with which the horses' manes and tails had usually
been decorated on market days.

'Ribbons,' he said, 'should be considered as clothes, which are the mark
of a human being. All animals should go naked.'

When Boxer heard this he fetched the small straw hat which he wore in summer to keep the flies out of his ears, and flung it onto the fire with the rest.

In a very little while the animals had destroyed everything that reminded them of Mr Jones. Napoleon then led them back to the store-shed and served out a double ration of corn to everybody, with two biscuits for each dog. Then they sang 'Beasts of England' from end to end seven times running, and after that they settled down for the night and slept as they had never slept before.

But they woke at dawn as usual, and suddenly remembering the glorious thing that had happened they all raced out into the pasture together. A little way down the pasture there was a knoll that commanded a view of most of the farm. The animals rushed to the top of it and gazed round them in the clear morning light. Yes, it was theirs – everything that they could see was theirs! In the ecstasy of that thought they gambolled round and round, they hurled themselves into the air in great leaps of excitement. They rolled in the dew, they cropped mouthfuls of the sweet summer grass, they kicked up clods of the black earth and snuffed its rich scent. Then they made a tour of inspection of the whole farm and surveyed with speechless admiration the ploughland, the hayfield, the orchard, the pool, the spinney. It was as though they had never seen these things before, and even now they could hardly believe that it was all their own.

Then they filed back to the farm buildings and halted in silence outside the door of the farmhouse. That was theirs too, but they were frightened to go inside. After a moment, however, Snowball and Napoleon butted the door open with their shoulders and the animals entered in single file, walking with the utmost care for fear of disturbing anything. They tiptoed from room to room, afraid to speak above a whisper and gazing with a kind of awe at the unbelievable luxury, at the beds with their feather mattresses, the looking-glasses, the horsehair sofa, the Brussels carpet, the lithograph of Queen Victoria over the drawing-room mantelpiece. They were just coming down the stairs when Mollie was discovered to be missing. Going back, the others found that she had remained behind in the best bedroom. She had taken a piece of blue ribbon from Mrs Jones's dressing-table, and was holding it against her shoulder and admiring herself in the glass in a very foolish manner. The others reproached her sharply, and they went outside. Some hams hanging in the kitchen were taken out for burial, and the barrel of beer in the scullery was stove in with a kick from Boxer's hoof, otherwise nothing in the house was touched. A unanimous resolution was passed on the spot that the farmhouse should be preserved as a museum. All were agreed that no animal must ever live there.

The animals had their breakfast, and then Snowball and Napoleon called them together again.

'Comrades,' said Snowball, 'it is half-past six and we have a long day before us. Today we begin the hay harvest. But there is another matter that must be attended to first.'

The pigs now revealed that during the past three months they had taught themselves to read and write from an old spelling book which had belonged to Mr Jones's children and which had been thrown on the rubbish heap. Napoleon sent for pots of black and white paint and led the way down to the five-barred gate that gave on the main road. Then Snowball (for it was Snowball who was best at writing) took a brush between the two knuckles of his trotter, painted out MANOR FARM from the top bar of the gate and in its place painted ANIMAL FARM. This was to be the name of the farm from now onwards. After this they went back to the farm buildings, where Snowball and Napoleon sent for a ladder which they caused to be set against the end wall of the big barn. They explained that by their studies of the past three months the pigs had succeeded in reducing the principles of Animalism to seven commandments. These seven commandments would now be inscribed on the wall; they would form an unalterable law by which all the animals on Animal Farm must live for ever after. With some difficulty (for it is not easy for a pig to balance himself on a ladder) Snowball climbed up and set to work, with Squealer a few rungs below him holding the paint-pot. The commandments were written on the tarred wall in great white letters that could be read thirty yards away. They ran thus:

THE SEVEN COMMANDMENTS

1. *Whatever goes upon two legs is an enemy.*
2. *Whatever goes upon four legs, or has wings, is a friend.*
3. *No animal shall wear clothes.*

4. *No animal shall sleep in a bed.*
5. *No animal shall drink alcohol.*
6. *No animal shall kill any other animal.*
7. *All animals are equal.*

It was very neatly written, and except that 'friend' was written 'freind' and one of the S's was the wrong way round, the spelling was correct all the way through. Snowball read it aloud for the benefit of the others. All the animals nodded in complete agreement, and the cleverer ones at once began to learn the commandments by heart.

'Now, comrades,' cried Snowball, throwing down the paint-brush, 'to the hayfield! Let us make it a point of honour to get in the harvest more quickly than Jones and his men could do.'

But at this moment the three cows, who had seemed uneasy for some time past, set up a loud lowing. They had not been milked for twenty-four hours, and their udders were almost bursting. After a little thought the pigs sent for buckets and milked the cows fairly successfully, their trotters being well adapted to this task. Soon there were five buckets of frothing creamy milk at which many of the animals looked with considerable interest.

'What is going to happen to all that milk?' said someone.

'Jones used sometimes to mix some of it in our mash,' said one of the hens.

'Never mind the milk, comrades!' cried Napoleon, placing himself in front of the buckets. 'That will be attended to. The harvest is more important. Comrade Snowball will lead the way. I shall follow in a few minutes. Forward, comrades! The hay is waiting.'

So the animals trooped down to the hayfield to begin the harvest, and when they came back in the evening it was noticed that the milk had disappeared.

CHAPTER III

HOW THEY TOILED AND SWEATED to get the hay in! But their efforts were rewarded, for the harvest was an even bigger success than they had hoped.

Sometimes the work was hard; the implements had been designed for human beings and not for animals, and it was a great drawback that no animal was able to use any tool that involved standing on his hind legs. But the pigs were so clever that they could think of a way round every difficulty. As for the horses, they knew every inch of the field, and in fact understood the business of mowing and raking far better than Jones and his men had ever done. The pigs did not actually work, but directed and supervised the others. With their superior knowledge it was natural that they should assume the leadership. Boxer and Clover would harness themselves to the cutter or the horse-rake (no bits or reins were needed in these days, of course) and tramp steadily round and round the field with a pig walking behind and calling out 'Gee up, comrade!' or 'Whoa back, comrade!' as the case might be. And every animal down to the humblest worked at turning the hay and gathering it. Even the ducks and hens toiled to and fro all day in the sun, carrying tiny wisps of hay in their beaks. In the end they finished the harvest in two days less time than it had usually taken Jones and his men. Moreover it was the biggest harvest that the farm had ever seen. There was no wastage whatever; the hens and ducks with their sharp eyes had gathered up the very last stalk. And not an animal on the farm had stolen so much as a mouthful.

All through that summer the work of the farm went like clockwork. The animals were happy as they had never conceived it possible to be. Every mouthful of food was an acute positive pleasure, now that it was truly their own food, produced by themselves and for themselves, not doled out to them by a grudging master. With the worthless parasitical human beings gone, there was more for everyone to eat. There was more leisure too, inexperienced though the animals were. They met with many difficulties – for instance, later in the year, when they harvested the corn, they had to tread it out in the ancient style and blow away the chaff with their breath, since the farm possessed no threshing machine – but the pigs with their cleverness and Boxer with his tremendous muscles always pulled them through. Boxer was the admiration of everybody. He had been a hard worker even in Jones's time, but now he seemed more like three horses than one; there were days when the entire work of the farm seemed to rest upon his mighty shoulders. From morning to night he was pushing and pulling, always at the spot where the work was hardest. He had made an arrangement with one of the cockerels to call him in the mornings half an hour earlier than anyone else, and would put in some volunteer labour at whatever seemed to be most needed, before the regular day's work began. His answer to every problem, every setback, was 'I will work harder!' – which he had adopted as his personal motto.

But everyone worked according to his capacity. The hens and ducks, for instance, saved five bushels of corn at the harvest by gathering up the stray grains. Nobody stole, nobody grumbled over his rations, the quarrelling and biting and jealousy which had been normal features of life in the old days had almost disappeared. Nobody shirked – or almost nobody. Mollie, it was true, was not good at getting up in the mornings, and had a way of leaving work early on the ground that there was a stone in her hoof. And the behaviour of the cat was somewhat peculiar. It was soon noticed that when there was work to be done the cat could never be found. She would vanish for hours on end, and then reappear at meal-times, or in the evening after work was over, as though nothing had happened. But she always made such excellent excuses, and purred so affectionately, that it was impossible not to believe in her good intentions. Old Benjamin, the donkey, seemed quite unchanged since the Rebellion. He did his work in the same slow obstinate way as he had done it in Jones's time, never shirking and never volunteering for extra work either. About the Rebellion and its results he would express no opinion. When asked whether he was not happier now that Jones was gone, he would say only 'Donkeys live a long time. None of you has ever seen a dead donkey,' and the others had to be content with this cryptic answer.

On Sundays there was no work. Breakfast was an hour later than usual, and after breakfast there was a ceremony which was observed every week without fail. First came the hoisting of the flag. Snowball had found in the harness-room an old green tablecloth of Mrs Jones's and had painted on it a hoof and a horn in white. This was run up the flagstaff in the farmhouse garden every Sunday morning. The flag was green, Snowball explained, to represent the green fields of England, while the hoof and horn signified the future Republic of the Animals which would arise when the human race had been finally overthrown. After the hoisting of the flag all the animals trooped into the big barn for a general assembly which was known as the Meeting. Here the work of the coming week was planned out and resolutions were put forward and debated. It was always the pigs who put forward the resolutions. The other animals understood how to vote, but could never think of any resolutions of their own. Snowball and Napoleon were by far the most active in the debates. But it was noticed that these two were never in agreement: whatever suggestion either of them made, the other could be counted on to oppose it. Even when it was resolved – a thing no one could object to in itself – to set aside the small paddock behind the orchard as a home of rest for animals who were past work, there was a stormy debate over the correct retiring age for each class of animal. The Meeting always ended with the singing of 'Beasts of England', and the afternoon was given up to recreation.

The pigs had set aside the harness-room as a headquarters for themselves. Here, in the evenings, they studied blacksmithing, carpentering and other necessary arts from books which they had brought out of the farmhouse. Snowball also busied himself with organising the other animals into what he called Animal Committees. He was indefatigable at this. He formed the Egg Production Committee for the hens, the Clean Tails League for the cows, the Wild Comrades' Re-education Committee (the object of this was to tame the rats and rabbits), the Whiter Wool Movement for the sheep, and various others, besides instituting classes in reading and writing. On the whole these projects were a failure. The attempt to tame the wild creatures, for instance, broke down almost immediately. They continued to behave very much as before, and when treated with generosity simply took advantage of it. The cat joined the Re-education Committee and was very active in it for some days. She was seen one day sitting on a roof and talking to some sparrows who were just out of her reach. She was telling them that all animals were now comrades and that any sparrow who chose could come and perch on her paw; but the sparrows kept their distance.

The reading and writing classes, however, were a great success. By the autumn almost every animal on the farm was literate in some degree.

As for the pigs, they could already read and write perfectly. The dogs learned to read fairly well, but were not interested in reading anything except the Seven Commandments. Muriel, the goat, could read somewhat better than the dogs, and sometimes used to read to the others in the evenings from scraps of newspaper which she found on the rubbish heap. Benjamin could read as well as any pig, but never exercised his faculty. So far as he knew, he said, there was nothing worth reading. Clover learnt the whole alphabet, but could not put words together. Boxer could not get beyond the letter D. He would trace out A, B, C, D in the dust with his great hoof, and then would stand staring at the letters with his ears back, sometimes shaking his forelock, trying with all his might to remember what came next and never succeeding. On several occasions, indeed, he did learn E, F, G, H, but by the time he knew them it was always discovered that he had forgotten A, B, C and D. Finally he decided to be content with the first four letters, and used to write them out once or twice every day to refresh his memory. Mollie refused to learn any but the five letters which spelt her own name. She would form these very neatly out of pieces of twig, and would then decorate them with a flower or two and walk round them admiring them.

None of the other animals on the farm could get further than the letter A. It was also found that the stupider animals such as the sheep, hens and ducks, were unable to learn the Seven Commandments by heart. After much thought Snowball declared that the Seven Commandments could in effect be reduced to a single maxim, namely: 'Four legs good, two legs bad'. This, he said, contained the essential principle of Animalism. Whoever had thoroughly grasped it would be safe from human influences. The birds at first objected, since it seemed to them that they also had two legs, but Snowball proved to them that this was not so.

'A bird's wing, comrades,' he said, 'is an organ of propulsion and not of manipulation. It should therefore be regarded as a leg. The distinguishing mark of Man is the *hand*, the instrument with which he does all his mischief.'

The birds did not understand Snowball's long words, but they accepted his explanation, and all the humbler animals set to work to learn the new maxim by heart. FOUR LEGS GOOD, TWO LEGS BAD, was inscribed on the end wall of the barn, above the Seven Commandments and in bigger letters. When they had once got it by heart the sheep developed a great liking for this maxim, and often as they lay in the field they would all start bleating 'Four legs good, two legs bad! Four legs good, two legs bad!' and keep it up for hours on end, never growing tired of it.

Napoleon took no interest in Snowball's committees. He said that the education of the young was more important than anything that could be done for those who were already grown up. It happened that Jessie and

Bluebell had both whelped soon after the hay harvest, giving birth between them to nine sturdy puppies. As soon as they were weaned Napoleon took them away from their mothers, saying that he would make himself responsible for their education. He took them up into a loft which could only be reached by a ladder from the harness-room, and there kept them in such seclusion that the rest of the farm soon forgot their existence.

The mystery of where the milk went to was soon cleared up. It was mixed every day into the pigs' mash. The early apples were now ripening, and the grass of the orchard was littered with windfalls. The animals had assumed as a matter of course that these would be shared out equally; one day, however, the order went forth that all the windfalls were to be collected and brought to the harness-room for the use of the pigs. At this some of the other animals murmured, but it was no use. All the pigs were in full agreement on this point, even Snowball and Napoleon. Squealer was sent to make the necessary explanations to the others.

'Comrades!' he cried. 'You do not imagine, I hope, that we pigs are doing this in a spirit of selfishness and privilege? Many of us actually dislike milk and apples. I dislike them myself. Our sole object in taking these things is to preserve our health. Milk and apples (this has been proved by Science, comrades) contain substances absolutely necessary to the well-being of a pig. We pigs are brainworkers. The whole management and organisation of this farm depend on us. Day and night we are watching over your welfare. It is for *your* sake that we drink that milk and eat those apples. Do you know what would happen if we pigs failed in our duty? Jones would come back! Yes, Jones would come back! Surely, comrades,' cried Squealer almost pleadingly, skipping from side to side and whisking his tail, 'surely there is no one among you who wants to see Jones come back?'

Now if there was one thing that the animals were completely certain of, it was that they did not want Jones back. When it was put to them in this light, they had no more to say. The importance of keeping the pigs in good health was all too obvious. So it was agreed without further argument that the milk and the windfall apples (and also the main crop of apples when they ripened) should be reserved for the pigs alone.

CHAPTER IV

BY THE LATE SUMMER the news of what had happened on Animal Farm had spread across half the county. Every day Snowball and Napoleon sent out flights of pigeons whose instructions were to mingle with the animals on neighbouring farms, tell them the story of the Rebellion, and teach them the tune of 'Beasts of England'.

Most of this time Mr Jones had spent sitting in the taproom of the Red Lion at Willingdon, complaining to anyone who would listen of the monstrous injustice he had suffered in being turned out of his property by a pack of good-for-nothing animals. The other farmers sympathised in principle, but they did not at first give him much help. At heart, each of them was secretly wondering whether he could not somehow turn Jones's misfortune to his own advantage. It was lucky that the owners of the two farms which adjoined Animal Farm were on permanently bad terms. One of them, which was named Foxwood, was a large, neglected, old-fashioned farm, much overgrown by woodland, with all its pastures worn out and its hedges in a disgraceful condition. Its owner, Mr Pilkington, was an easy-going gentleman-farmer who spent most of his time in fishing or hunting according to the season. The other farm, which was called Pinchfield, was smaller and better kept. Its owner was a Mr Frederick, a tough, shrewd man, perpetually involved in lawsuits and with a name for driving hard bargains. These two disliked each other so much that it was difficult for them to come to any agreement, even in defence of their own interests.

Nevertheless they were both thoroughly frightened by the rebellion on Animal Farm, and very anxious to prevent their own animals from learning too much about it. At first they pretended to laugh to scorn the idea of animals managing a farm for themselves. The whole thing would be over in a fortnight, they said. They put it about that the animals on the Manor Farm (they insisted on calling it the Manor Farm; they would not tolerate the name 'Animal Farm') were perpetually fighting among themselves and were also rapidly starving to death. When time passed and the animals had evidently not starved to death, Frederick and Pilkington changed their tune and began to talk of the terrible wickedness that now flourished on Animal Farm. It was given out that the animals there practised cannibalism, tortured one another with red-hot horseshoes and had their females in common. This was what came of rebelling against the laws of Nature, Frederick and Pilkington said.

However, these stories were never fully believed. Rumours of a wonderful farm, where the human beings had been turned out and the animals managed their own affairs, continued to circulate in vague and distorted forms, and throughout that year a wave of rebelliousness ran through the countryside. Bulls which had always been tractable suddenly turned savage, sheep broke down hedges and devoured the clover, cows kicked the pail over, hunters refused their fences and shot their riders on to the other side. Above all, the tune and even the words of 'Beasts of England' were known everywhere. It had spread with astonishing speed. The human beings could not contain their rage when they heard this song, though they pretended to think it merely ridiculous. They could not understand, they said, how even animals could bring themselves to sing such contemptible rubbish. Any animal caught singing it was given a flogging on the spot. And yet the song was irrepressible. The blackbirds whistled it in the hedges, the pigeons cooed it in the elms, it got into the din of the smithies and the tune of the church bells. And when the human beings listened to it they secretly trembled, hearing in it a prophecy of their future doom.

Early in October, when the corn was cut and stacked and some of it was already threshed, a flight of pigeons came whirling through the air and alighted in the yard of Animal Farm in the wildest excitement. Jones and all his men, with half a dozen others from Foxwood and Pinchfield, had entered the five-barred gate and were coming up the cart-track that led to the farm. They were all carrying sticks, except Jones, who was marching ahead with a gun in his hands. Obviously they were going to attempt the recapture of the farm.

This had long been expected, and all preparations had been made. Snowball, who had studied an old book of Julius Caesar's campaigns which he had found in the farmhouse, was in charge of the defensive operations. He gave his orders quickly, and in a couple of minutes every animal was at his post.

As the human beings approached the farm buildings, Snowball

launched his first attack. All the pigeons, to the number of thirty-five, flew to and fro over the men's heads and dropped their dung on them from mid-air; and while the men were dealing with this, the geese, who had been hiding behind the hedge, rushed out and pecked viciously at the calves of their legs. However, this was only a light skirmishing manoeuvre, intended to create a little disorder, and the men easily drove the geese off with their sticks. Snowball now launched his second line of attack. Muriel, Benjamin, and all the sheep, with Snowball at the head of them, rushed forward and prodded and butted the men from every side, while Benjamin turned round and lashed at them with his small hoofs. But once again the men, with their sticks and their hobnailed boots, were too strong for them; and suddenly, at a squeal from Snowball, which was the signal for retreat, all the animals turned and fled through the gateway into the yard.

The men gave a shout of triumph. They saw, as they imagined, their enemies in flight, and they rushed after them in disorder. This was just what Snowball had intended. As soon as they were well inside the yard, the three horses, the three cows and the rest of the pigs, who had been lying in ambush in the cowshed, suddenly emerged in their rear, cutting them off. Snowball now gave the signal for the charge. He himself dashed straight for Jones. Jones saw him coming, raised his gun and fired. The pellets scored bloody streaks along Snowball's back, and a sheep dropped dead. Without halting for an instant Snowball flung his fifteen stone against Jones's legs. Jones was hurled into a pile of dung and his gun flew out of his hands. But the most terrifying spectacle of all was Boxer, rearing up on his hind legs and striking out with his great iron-shod hoofs like a stallion. His very first blow took a stable-lad from Foxwood on the skull and stretched him lifeless in the mud. At the sight, several men dropped their sticks and tried to run. Panic overtook them, and the next moment all the animals together were chasing them round and round the yard. They were gored, kicked, bitten, trampled on. There was not an animal on the farm that did not take vengeance on them after his own fashion. Even the cat suddenly leapt off a roof onto a cowman's shoulders and sank her claws in his neck, at which he yelled horribly. At a moment when the opening was clear the men were glad enough to rush out of the yard and make a bolt for the main road. And so within five minutes of their invasion they were in ignominious retreat by the same way as they had come, with a flock of geese hissing after them and pecking at their calves all the way.

All the men were gone except one. Back in the yard Boxer was pawing with his hoof at the stable-lad who lay face down in the mud, trying to turn him over. The boy did not stir.

'He is dead,' said Boxer sorrowfully. 'I had no intention of doing that. I forgot that I was wearing iron shoes. Who will believe that I did not do this on purpose?'

'No sentimentality, comrade!' cried Snowball, from whose wounds the blood was still dripping. 'War is war. The only good human being is a dead one.'

'I have no wish to take life, not even human life,' repeated Boxer, and his eyes were full of tears.

'Where is Mollie?' exclaimed somebody.

Mollie in fact was missing. For a moment there was great alarm; it was feared that the men might have harmed her in some way, or even carried her off with them. In the end, however, she was found hiding in her stall with her head buried among the hay in the manger. She had taken to flight as soon as the gun went off. And when the others came back from looking for her it was to find that the stable-lad, who in fact was only stunned, had already recovered and made off.

The animals had now reassembled in the wildest excitement, each recounting his own exploits in the battle at the top of his voice. An impromptu celebration of the victory was held immediately. The flag was run up and 'Beasts of England' was sung a number of times, then the sheep who had been killed was given a solemn funeral, a hawthorn bush being planted on her grave. At the graveside Snowball made a little speech, emphasising the need for all animals to be ready to die for Animal Farm if need be.

The animals decided unanimously to create a military decoration, 'Animal Hero, First Class', which was conferred there and then on Snowball and Boxer. It consisted of a brass medal (they were really some old horse-brasses which had been found in the harness-room), to be worn on Sundays and holidays. There was also 'Animal Hero, Second Class', which was conferred posthumously on the dead sheep.

There was much discussion as to what the battle should be called. In the end it was named the Battle of the Cowshed, since that was where the ambush had been sprung. Mr Jones's gun had been found lying in the mud, and it was known that there was a supply of cartridges in the farmhouse. It was decided to set the gun up at the foot of the flagstaff, like a piece of artillery, and to fire it twice a year – once on October the twelfth, the anniversary of the Battle of the Cowshed, and once on Midsummer Day, the anniversary of the Rebellion.

CHAPTER V

AS WINTER DREW ON Mollie became more and more troublesome. She was late for work every morning and excused herself by saying that she had overslept, and she complained of mysterious pains, although her appetite was excellent. On every kind of pretext she would run away from work and go to the drinking pool, where she would stand foolishly gazing at her own reflection in the water. But there were also rumours of something more serious. One day as Mollie strolled blithely into the yard, flirting her long tail and chewing at a stalk of hay, Clover took her aside.

'Mollie,' she said, 'I have something very serious to say to you. This morning I saw you looking over the hedge that divides Animal Farm from Foxwood. One of Mr Pilkington's men was standing on the other side of the hedge. And – I was a long way away, but I am almost certain I saw this – he was talking to you and you were allowing him to stroke your nose. What does that mean, Mollie?'

'He didn't! I wasn't! It isn't true!' cried Mollie, beginning to prance about and paw the ground.

'Mollie! Look me in the face. Do you give me your word of honour that that man was not stroking your nose?'

'It isn't true!' repeated Mollie, but she could not look Clover in the face, and the next moment she took to her heels and galloped away into the field.

A thought struck Clover. Without saying anything to the others she went to Mollie's stall and turned over the straw with her hoof. Hidden under the straw was a little pile of lump sugar and several bunches of ribbon of different colours.

Three days later Mollie disappeared. For some weeks nothing was known of her whereabouts, then the pigeons reported that they had seen her on the other side of Willingdon. She was between the shafts of a smart dogcart painted red and black, which was standing outside a public-house. A fat red-faced man in check breeches and gaiters, who looked like a publican, was stroking her nose and feeding her with sugar. Her coat was newly clipped and she wore a scarlet ribbon round her forelock. She appeared to be enjoying herself, so the pigeons said. None of the animals ever mentioned Mollie again.

In January there came bitterly hard weather. The earth was like iron, and nothing could be done in the fields. Many meetings were held in the big barn, and the pigs occupied themselves with planning out the work of the coming season. It had come to be accepted that the pigs, who were manifestly cleverer than the other animals, should decide all questions of farm policy, though their decisions had to be ratified by a majority vote. This arrangement would have worked well enough if it had not been for the disputes between Snowball and Napoleon. These two disagreed at every point where disagreement was possible. If one of them suggested sowing a bigger acreage with barley the other was certain to demand a bigger acreage of oats, and if one of them said that such and such a field was just right for cabbages, the other would declare that it was useless for anything except roots. Each had his own following, and there were some violent debates. At the Meetings Snowball often won over the majority by his brilliant speeches, but Napoleon was better at canvassing support for himself in between times. He was especially successful with the sheep. Of late the sheep had taken to bleating 'Four legs good, two legs bad' both in and out of season, and they often interrupted the Meeting with this. It was noticed that they were especially liable to break into 'Four legs good, two legs bad' at crucial moments in Snowball's speeches. Snowball had made a close study of some back numbers of the *Farmer and Stockbreeder* which he had found in the farmhouse, and was full of plans for innovations and improvements. He talked learnedly about field-drains, silage and basic slag, and had worked out a complicated scheme for all the animals to drop their dung directly in the fields, at a different spot every day, to save the labour of cartage. Napoleon produced no schemes of his own, but said quietly that Snowball's would come to nothing, and seemed to be biding his time. But of all their controversies, none was so bitter as the one that took place over the windmill.

In the long pasture, not far from the farm buildings, there was a small knoll which was the highest point on the farm. After surveying the ground Snowball declared that this was just the place for a windmill, which could be made to operate a dynamo and supply the farm with electrical power. This would light the stalls and warm them in winter, and would also run a circular saw, a chaff-cutter, a mangel-slicer and an electric milking machine. The animals had never heard of anything of this kind before (for the farm was an old-fashioned one and had only the most primitive machinery), and they listened in astonishment while Snowball conjured up pictures of fantastic machines which would do their work for them while they grazed at their ease in the fields or improved their minds with reading and conversation.

Within a few weeks Snowball's plans for the windmill were fully worked out. The mechanical details came mostly from three books which had belonged to Mr Jones – *One Thousand Useful Things to Do About the House*, *Every Man His Own Bricklayer*, and *Electricity for Beginners*. Snowball used as his study a shed which had once been used for incubators and had a smooth wooden floor, suitable for drawing on. He was closeted there for hours at a time. With his books held open by a stone, and with a piece of chalk gripped between the knuckles of his trotter, he would move rapidly to and fro, drawing in line after line and uttering little whimpers of excitement. Gradually the plans grew into a complicated mass of cranks and cog-wheels, covering more than half the floor, which the other animals found completely unintelligible but very impressive. All of them came to look at Snowball's drawings at least once a day. Even the hens and ducks came, and were at pains not to tread on the chalk marks. Only Napoleon held aloof. He had declared himself against the windmill from the start. One day, however, he arrived unexpectedly to examine the plans. He walked heavily round the shed, looked closely at every detail of the plans and snuffed at them once or twice, then stood for a little while contemplating them out of the corner of his eye; then suddenly he lifted his leg, urinated over the plans and walked out without uttering a word.

The whole farm was deeply divided on the subject of the windmill.

Snowball did not deny that to build it would be a difficult business. Stone would have to be quarried and built up into walls, then the sails would have to be made and after that there would be need for dynamos and cables. (How these were to be procured Snowball did not say.) But he maintained that it could all be done in a year. And thereafter, he declared, so much labour would be saved that the animals would only need to work three days a week. Napoleon, on the other hand, argued that the great need of the moment was to increase food production, and that if they wasted time on the windmill they would all starve to death. The animals formed themselves into two factions under the slogans, 'Vote for Snowball and the three-day week' and 'Vote for Napoleon and the full manger'. Benjamin was the only animal who did not side with either faction. He refused to believe either that food would become more plentiful or that the windmill would save work. Windmill or no windmill, he said, life would go on as it had always gone on – that is, badly.

Apart from the disputes over the windmill, there was the question of the defence of the farm. It was fully realised that though the human beings had been defeated in the Battle of the Cowshed they might make another and more determined attempt to recapture the farm and reinstate Mr Jones. They had all the more reason for doing so because the news of their defeat had spread across the countryside and made the animals on the neighbouring farms more restive than ever. As usual, Snowball and Napoleon were in disagreement. According to Napoleon, what the animals must do was to procure firearms and train themselves in the use of them. According to Snowball, they must send out more and more pigeons and stir up rebellion among the animals on the other farms. The one argued that if they could not defend themselves they were bound to be conquered, the other argued that if rebellions happened everywhere they would have no need to defend themselves. The animals listened first to Napoleon, then to Snowball, and could not make up their minds which was right; indeed they always found themselves in agreement with the one who was speaking at the moment.

At last the day came when Snowball's plans were completed. At the Meeting on the following Sunday the question of whether or not to begin work on the windmill was to be put to the vote. When the animals had assembled in the big barn, Snowball stood up and, though occasionally interrupted by bleating from the sheep, set forth his reasons for advocating the building of the windmill. Then Napoleon stood up to reply. He said very quietly that the windmill was nonsense and that he advised nobody to vote for it, and promptly sat down again; he had spoken for barely thirty seconds, and seemed almost indifferent as to the effect he produced. At this Snowball sprang to his feet, and shouting down the sheep, who had begun bleating again, broke into a passionate appeal in favour of the windmill. Until now the animals had been about equally divided in their sympathies, but in a moment Snowball's eloquence had carried them away. In glowing sentences he painted a picture of Animal Farm as it might be when sordid labour was lifted from the animals' backs. His imagination had now run far beyond chaff-cutters and turnip-slicers. Electricity, he said, could operate threshing-machines, ploughs, harrows, rollers and reapers and binders, besides supplying every stall with its own electric light, hot and cold water and an electric heater. By the time he had finished speaking there was no doubt as to which way the vote would go. But just at this moment Napoleon stood up and, casting a peculiar sidelong look at Snowball, uttered a high-pitched whimper of a kind no one had ever heard him utter before.

At this there was a terrible baying sound outside, and nine enormous dogs wearing brass-studded collars came bounding into the barn. They dashed straight for Snowball, who only sprang from his place just in time to escape their snapping jaws. In a moment he was out of the door and they were after him. Too amazed and frightened to speak, all the animals crowded through the door to watch the chase. Snowball was racing across the long pasture that led to the road. He was running as only a pig can run, but the dogs were close on his heels. Suddenly he slipped and it seemed certain that they had him. Then he was up again, running faster than ever, then the dogs were gaining on him again. One of them all but closed his jaws on Snowball's tail, but Snowball whisked it free just in time. Then he put on an extra spurt and, with a few inches to spare, slipped through a hole in the hedge and was seen no more.

Silent and terrified, the animals crept back into the barn. In a moment the dogs came bounding back. At first no one had been able to imagine where these creatures came from, but the problem was soon solved: they were the puppies whom Napoleon had taken away from their mothers and reared privately. Though not yet full-grown they were huge dogs, and as fierce-looking as wolves. They kept close to Napoleon. It was noticed that they wagged their tails to him in the same way as the other dogs had been used to do to Mr Jones.

Napoleon, with the dogs following him, now mounted onto the raised portion of the floor where Major had previously stood to deliver his speech. He announced that from now on the Sunday-morning Meetings would come to an end. They were unnecessary, he said, and wasted time. In future all questions relating to the working of the farm would be settled by a special committee of pigs, presided over by himself. These would meet in private and afterwards communicate their decisions to the others. The animals would still assemble on Sunday mornings to salute the flag, sing 'Beasts of England' and receive their orders for the week; but there would be no more debates.

In spite of the shock that Snowball's expulsion had given them, the animals were dismayed by this announcement. Several of them would have protested if they could have found the right arguments. Even Boxer was vaguely troubled. He set his ears back, shook his forelock several times, and tried hard to marshal his thoughts; but in the end he could not think of anything to say. Some of the pigs themselves, however, were more articulate. Four young porkers in the front row uttered shrill squeals of disapproval, and all four of them sprang to their feet and began speaking at once. But suddenly the dogs sitting round Napoleon let out deep, menacing growls, and the pigs fell silent and sat down again. Then the sheep broke out into a tremendous bleating of 'Four legs good, two legs bad!' which went on for nearly a quarter of an hour and put an end to any chance of discussion.

Afterwards Squealer was sent round the farm to explain the new arrangement to the others.

'Comrades,' he said, 'I trust that every animal here appreciates the sacrifice that Comrade Napoleon has made in taking this extra labour upon himself. Do not imagine, comrades, that leadership is a pleasure! On the contrary, it is a deep and heavy responsibility. No one believes more firmly than Comrade Napoleon that all animals are equal. He would be only too happy to let you make your decisions for yourselves. But sometimes you might make the wrong decisions, comrades, and then where should we be? Suppose you had decided to follow Snowball, with his moonshine of windmills – Snowball, who, as we now know, was no better than a criminal?'

'He fought bravely at the Battle of the Cowshed,' said somebody.

'Bravery is not enough,' said Squealer. 'Loyalty and obedience are more important. And as to the Battle of the Cowshed, I believe the time will come when we shall find that Snowball's part in it was much exaggerated. Discipline, comrades, iron discipline! That is the watchword for today. One false step, and our enemies would be upon us. Surely, comrades, you do not want Jones back?'

Once again this argument was unanswerable. Certainly the animals did not want Jones back; if the holding of debates on Sunday mornings was liable to bring him back, then the debates must stop. Boxer, who had now had time to think things over, voiced the general feeling by saying: 'If Comrade Napoleon says it, it must be right.' And from then on he adopted the maxim, 'Napoleon is always right', in addition to his private motto of 'I will work harder'.

By this time the weather had broken and the spring ploughing had begun. The shed where Snowball had drawn his plans of the windmill had been shut up and it was assumed that the plans had been rubbed off the floor. Every Sunday morning at ten o'clock the animals assembled in the big barn to receive their orders for the week. The skull of old Major, now clean of flesh, had been disinterred from the orchard and set up on a stump at the foot of the flagstaff, beside the gun. After the hoisting of the flag the animals were required to file past the skull in a reverent manner before entering the barn. Nowadays they did not sit all together as they had done in the past. Napoleon, with Squealer and another pig named Minimus, who had a remarkable gift for composing songs and poems, sat on the front of the raised platform, with the nine young dogs forming a semicircle round them, and the other pigs sitting behind. The rest of the animals sat facing them in the main body of the barn. Napoleon read out the orders for the week in a gruff soldierly style, and after a single singing of 'Beasts of England' all the animals dispersed.

On the third Sunday after Snowball's expulsion, the animals were somewhat surprised to hear Napoleon announce that the windmill was to be built after all. He did not give any reason for having changed his mind, but merely warned the animals that this extra task would mean very hard work; it might even be necessary to reduce their rations. The plans, however, had all been prepared, down to the last detail. A special committee of pigs had been at work upon them for the past three weeks. The building of the windmill, with various other improvements, was expected to take two years.

That evening Squealer explained privately to the other animals that Napoleon had never in reality been opposed to the windmill. On the contrary, it was he who had advocated it in the beginning, and the plan which Snowball had drawn on the floor of the incubator shed had actually been stolen from among Napoleon's papers. The windmill was, in fact, Napoleon's own creation. Why, then, asked somebody, had he spoken so strongly against it? Here Squealer looked very sly. That, he said, was Comrade Napoleon's cunning. He had *seemed* to oppose the windmill, simply as a manoeuvre to get rid of Snowball, who was a dangerous character and a bad influence. Now that Snowball was out of the way the plan could go forward without his interference. This, said Squealer, was something called tactics. He repeated a number of times, 'Tactics, comrades, tactics!', skipping round and whisking his tail with a merry laugh. The animals were not certain what the word meant, but Squealer spoke so persuasively, and the three dogs who happened to be with him growled so threateningly, that they accepted his explanation without further questions.

CHAPTER VI

ALL THAT YEAR the animals worked like slaves. But they were happy in their work; they grudged no effort or sacrifice, well aware that everything that they did was for the benefit of themselves and those of their kind who would come after them, and not for a pack of idle thieving human beings.

Throughout the spring and summer they worked a sixty-hour week, and in August Napoleon announced that there would be work on Sunday afternoons as well. This work was strictly voluntary, but any animal who absented himself from it would have his rations reduced by half. Even so it was found necessary to leave certain tasks undone. The harvest was a little less successful than in the previous year, and two fields which should have been sown with roots in the early summer were not sown because the ploughing had not been completed early enough. It was possible to foresee that the coming winter would be a hard one.

The windmill presented unexpected difficulties. There was a good quarry of limestone on the farm, and plenty of sand and cement had been found in one of the outhouses, so that all the materials for building were at hand. But the problem the animals could not at first solve was how to break up the stone into pieces of suitable size. There seemed no way of doing this except with picks and crowbars, which no animal could use, because no animal could stand on his hind legs. Only after weeks of vain effort did the right idea occur to somebody – namely, to utilise the force of gravity. Huge boulders, far too big to be used as they were, were lying all over the bed of the quarry. The animals lashed ropes round these, and then all together, cows, horses, sheep, any animal that could lay hold of the rope – even the pigs sometimes joined in at critical moments – they dragged them with desperate slowness up the slope to the top of the quarry, where they were toppled over the edge, to shatter to pieces below. Transporting the stone when it was once broken was comparatively simple. The horses carried it off in cartloads, the sheep dragged single blocks, even Muriel and Benjamin yoked themselves into an old governess-cart and did their share. By late summer a sufficient store of stone had accumulated, and then the building began, under the superintendence of the pigs.

But it was a slow, laborious process. Frequently it took a whole day of exhausting effort to drag a single boulder to the top of the quarry, and sometimes when it was pushed over the edge it failed to break. Nothing could have been achieved without Boxer, whose strength seemed equal to that of all the rest of the animals put together. When the boulder began to slip and the animals cried out in despair at finding themselves dragged down the hill, it was always Boxer who strained himself against the rope and brought the boulder to a stop. To see him toiling up the slope inch by inch, his breath coming fast, the tips of his hoofs clawing at the ground and his great sides matted with sweat, filled everyone with admiration. Clover warned him sometimes to be careful not to overstrain himself, but Boxer would never listen to her. His two slogans, 'I will work harder' and

'Napoleon is always right', seemed to him a sufficient answer to all problems. He had made arrangements with the cockerel to call him three-quarters of an hour earlier in the mornings instead of half an hour. And in his spare moments, of which there were not many nowadays, he would go alone to the quarry, collect a load of broken stone and drag it down to the site of the windmill unassisted.

The animals were not badly off throughout that summer, in spite of the hardness of their work. If they had no more food than they had had in Jones's day, at least they did not have less. The advantage of only having to feed themselves, and not having to support five extravagant human beings as well, was so great that it would have taken a lot of failures to outweigh it. And in many ways the animal method of doing things was more efficient and saved labour. Such jobs as weeding, for instance, could be done with a thoroughness impossible to human beings. And again, since no animal now stole it was unnecessary to fence off pasture from arable land, which saved a lot of labour on the upkeep of hedges and gates. Nevertheless as the summer wore on various unforeseen shortages began to make themselves felt. There was need of paraffin oil, nails, string, dog biscuits and iron for the horses' shoes, none of which could be produced on the farm. Later there would also be need for seeds and artificial manures, besides various tools and, finally, the machinery for the windmill. How these were to be procured no one was able to imagine.

One Sunday morning when the animals assembled to receive their orders Napoleon announced that he had decided upon a new policy. From now onwards Animal Farm would engage in trade with the neighbouring farms: not, of course, for any commercial purpose but simply in order to obtain certain materials which were urgently necessary. The needs of the windmill must override everything else, he said. He was therefore making arrangements to sell a stack of hay and part of the current year's wheat crop, and later on, if more money were needed, it would have to be made up by the sale of eggs, for which there was always a market in Willingdon. The hens, said Napoleon, should welcome this sacrifice as their own special contribution towards the building of the windmill.

Once again the animals were conscious of a vague uneasiness. Never to have any dealings with human beings, never to engage in trade, never to make use of money – had not these been among the earliest resolutions passed at that first triumphant Meeting after Jones was expelled? All the animals remembered passing such resolutions: or at least they thought that they remembered it. The four young pigs who had protested when Napoleon abolished the Meetings raised their voices timidly, but they were promptly silenced by a tremendous growling from the dogs. Then, as usual, the sheep broke into 'Four legs good, two legs bad!' and the momentary awkwardness was smoothed over. Finally Napoleon raised his trotter for silence and announced that he had already made all the arrangements. There would be no need for any of the animals to come in contact with human beings, which would clearly be most undesirable. He intended to take the whole burden upon his own shoulders. A Mr Whymper, a solicitor living in Willingdon, had agreed to act as intermediary between Animal Farm and the outside world, and would visit the farm every Monday morning to receive his instructions. Napoleon ended his speech with his usual cry of 'Long live Animal Farm!', and after the singing of 'Beasts of England' the animals were dismissed.

Afterwards Squealer made a round of the farm and set the animals' minds at rest. He assured them that the resolution against engaging in trade and using money had never been passed, or even suggested. It was pure imagination, probably traceable in the beginning to lies circulated by Snowball. A few animals still felt faintly doubtful, but Squealer asked them shrewdly, 'Are you certain that this is not something that you have dreamed, comrades? Have you any record of such a resolution? Is it written down anywhere?' And since it was certainly true that nothing of the kind existed in writing, the animals were satisfied that they had been mistaken.

Every Monday Mr Whymper visited the farm as had been arranged. He was a sly-looking little man with side whiskers, a solicitor in a very small way of business, but sharp enough to have realised earlier than anyone else that Animal Farm would need a broker and that the commissions would be worth having. The animals watched his coming and going with a kind of dread, and avoided him as much as possible. Nevertheless, the sight of Napoleon, on all fours, delivering orders to Whymper, who stood on two legs, roused their pride and partly reconciled them to the new arrangement. Their relations with the human race were now not quite the same as they had been before. The human beings did not hate Animal Farm any less now that it was prospering, indeed they hated it more than ever. Every human being held it as an article of faith that the farm would go bankrupt sooner or later, and, above all, that the windmill would be a failure. They would meet in the public-houses and prove to one another by means of diagrams that the windmill was bound to fall down, or that if it did stand up, then that it would never work. And yet, against their will, they had developed a certain respect for the efficiency with which the animals were managing their own affairs. One symptom of this was that they had begun to call Animal Farm by its proper name and ceased to pretend that it was called the Manor Farm. They had also dropped their championship of Jones, who had given up hope of getting his farm back and gone to live in another part of the county. Except through Whymper there was as yet no contact between Animal Farm and the outside world, but there were constant rumours that Napoleon was about to enter into a definite business agreement either with Mr Pilkington of Foxwood or with Mr Frederick of Pinchfield – but never, it was noticed, with both simultaneously.

It was about this time that the pigs suddenly moved into the farmhouse and took up their residence there. Again the animals seemed to remember that a resolution against this had been passed in the early days, and again Squealer was able to convince them that this was not the case. It was absolutely necessary, he said, that the pigs, who were the brains of the farm, should have a quiet place to work in. It was also more suited to the dignity of the Leader (for of late he had taken to speaking of Napoleon under the title of 'Leader') to live in a house than in a mere sty. Nevertheless some of the animals were disturbed when they heard that the pigs not only took their meals in the kitchen and used the drawing-room as a recreation room, but also slept in the beds. Boxer passed it off as usual with 'Napoleon is always right!', but Clover, who thought she remembered a definite ruling against beds, went to the end of the barn and tried to puzzle out the Seven Commandments which were inscribed there. Finding herself unable to read more than individual letters, she fetched Muriel.

'Muriel,' she said, 'read me the Fourth Commandment. Does it not say something about never sleeping in a bed?'

With some difficulty Muriel spelt it out.

'It says, "No animal shall sleep in a bed *with sheets*",' she announced finally.

Curiously enough, Clover had not remembered that the Fourth Commandment mentioned sheets; but as it was there on the wall, it must have done so. And Squealer, who happened to be passing at this moment, attended by two or three dogs, was able to put the whole matter in its proper perspective.

'You have heard, then, comrades,' he said, 'that we pigs now sleep in the beds of the farmhouse? And why not? You did not suppose, surely, that there was ever a ruling against *beds*? A bed merely means a place to sleep in. A pile of straw in a stall is a bed, properly regarded. The rule was against *sheets*, which are a human invention. We have removed the sheets from the farmhouse beds, and sleep between blankets. And very comfortable beds they are too! But not more comfortable than we need, I can tell you, comrades, with all the brainwork we have to do nowadays. You would not rob us of our repose, would you, comrades? You would not have us too tired to carry out our duties? Surely none of you wishes to see Jones back?'

The animals reassured him on this point immediately, and no more was said about the pigs sleeping in the farmhouse beds. And when, some days afterwards, it was announced that from now on the pigs would get up an hour later in the mornings than the other animals, no complaint was made about that either.

By the autumn the animals were tired but happy. They had had a hard year, and after the sale of part of the hay and corn the stores of food for the winter were none too plentiful, but the windmill compensated for everything. It was almost half built now. After the harvest there was a stretch of clear dry weather, and the animals toiled harder than ever, thinking it well worth while to plod to and fro all day with blocks of stone if by doing so they could raise the walls another foot. Boxer would even come out at nights and work for an hour or two on his own by the light of the harvest moon. In their spare moments the animals would walk round and round the half-finished mill, admiring the strength and perpendicularity of its walls and marvelling that they should ever have been able to build anything so imposing. Only old Benjamin refused to grow enthusiastic about the windmill, though, as usual, he would utter nothing beyond the cryptic remark that donkeys live a long time.

November came, with raging south-west winds. Building had to stop because it was now too wet to mix the cement. Finally there came a night when the gale was so violent that the farm buildings rocked on their foundations and several tiles were blown off the roof of the barn. The hens woke up squawking with terror because they had all dreamed simultaneously of hearing a gun go off in the distance. In the morning the animals came out of their stalls to find that the flagstaff had been blown down and an elm tree at the foot of the orchard had been plucked up like a radish. They had just noticed this when a cry of despair broke from every animal's throat. A terrible sight had met their eyes. The windmill was in ruins.

With one accord they dashed down to the spot. Napoleon, who seldom moved out of a walk, raced ahead of them all. Yes, there it lay, the fruit of all their struggles, levelled to its foundations, the stones they had broken and carried so laboriously scattered all around. Unable at first to speak, they stood gazing mournfully at the litter of fallen stone. Napoleon paced to and fro in silence, occasionally snuffing at the ground. His tail had grown rigid and twitched sharply from side to side, a sign in him of intense mental activity. Suddenly he halted as though his mind were made up.

'Comrades,' he said quietly, 'do you know who is responsible for this? Do you know the enemy who has come in the night and overthrown our windmill? SNOWBALL!' he suddenly roared in a voice of thunder, 'Snowball has done this thing! In sheer malignity, thinking to set back our plans and avenge himself for his ignominious expulsion, this traitor has crept here under cover of night and destroyed our work of nearly a year. Comrades, here and now I pronounce the death sentence upon Snowball. "Animal Hero, Second Class", and half a bushel of apples to any animal who brings him to justice. A full bushel to anyone who captures him alive!'

The animals were shocked beyond measure to learn that even Snowball could be guilty of such an action. There was a cry of indignation, and everyone began thinking out ways of catching Snowball if he should ever come back. Almost immediately the footprints of a pig were discovered in the grass at a little distance from the knoll. They could only be traced for a few yards, but appeared to lead to a hole in the hedge. Napoleon snuffed deeply at them and pronounced them to be Snowball's. He gave it as his opinion that Snowball had probably come from the direction of Foxwood Farm.

'No more delays, comrades!' cried Napoleon when the footprints had been examined. 'There is work to be done. This very morning we begin rebuilding the windmill, and we will build all through the winter, rain or shine. We will teach this miserable traitor that he cannot undo our work so easily. Remember, comrades, there must be no alteration in our plans: they shall be carried out to the day. Forward, comrades! Long live the windmill! Long live Animal Farm!'

CHAPTER VII

It was a bitter winter. The stormy weather was followed by sleet and snow, and then by a hard frost which did not break till well into February. The animals carried on as best they could with the rebuilding of the windmill, well knowing that the outside world was watching them and that the envious human beings would rejoice and triumph if the mill were not finished on time.

Out of spite, the human beings pretended not to believe that it was Snowball who had destroyed the windmill: they said that it had fallen down because the walls were too thin. The animals knew that this was not the case. Still, it had been decided to build the walls three feet thick this time instead of eighteen inches as before, which meant collecting much larger quantities of stone. For a long time the quarry was full of snowdrifts and nothing could be done. Some progress was made in the dry frosty weather that followed, but it was cruel work, and the animals could not feel so hopeful about it as they had felt before. They were always cold, and usually hungry as well. Only Boxer and Clover never lost heart. Squealer made excellent speeches on the joy of service and the dignity of labour, but the other animals found more inspiration in Boxer's strength and his never-failing cry of 'I will work harder!'.

In January food fell short. The corn ration was drastically reduced, and it was announced that an extra potato ration would be issued to make up for it. Then it was discovered that the greater part of the potato crop had been frosted in the clamps, which had not been covered thickly enough.

The potatoes had become soft and discoloured, and only a few were edible. For days at a time the animals had nothing to eat but chaff and mangels. Starvation seemed to stare them in the face.

It was vitally necessary to conceal this fact from the outside world. Emboldened by the collapse of the windmill, the human beings were inventing fresh lies about Animal Farm. Once again it was being put about that all the animals were dying of famine and disease, and that they were continually fighting among themselves and had resorted to cannibalism and infanticide. Napoleon was well aware of the bad results that might follow if the real facts of the food situation were known, and he decided to make use of Mr Whymper to spread a contrary impression. Hitherto the animals had had little or no contact with Whymper on his weekly visits: now, however, a few selected animals, mostly sheep, were instructed to remark casually in his hearing that rations had been increased. In addition, Napoleon ordered the almost empty bins in the store-shed to be filled nearly to the brim with sand, which was then covered up with what remained of the grain and meal. On some suitable pretext Whymper was led through the store-shed and allowed to catch a glimpse of the bins. He was deceived, and continued to report to the outside world that there was no food shortage on Animal Farm.

Nevertheless, towards the end of January it became obvious that it would be necessary to procure some more grain from somewhere. In these days Napoleon rarely appeared in public, but spent all his time in the farmhouse, which was guarded at each door by fierce-looking dogs. When he did emerge it was in a ceremonial manner, with an escort of six dogs who closely surrounded him and growled if anyone came too near. Frequently he did not even appear on Sunday mornings, but issued his orders through one of the other pigs, usually Squealer.

One Sunday morning Squealer announced that the hens, who had just come in to lay again, must surrender their eggs. Napoleon had accepted, through Whymper, a contract for four hundred eggs a week. The price of these would pay for enough grain and meal to keep the farm going till summer came on and conditions were easier.

When the hens heard this they raised a terrible outcry. They had been warned earlier that this sacrifice might be necessary, but had not believed that it would really happen. They were just getting their clutches ready for the spring sitting, and they protested that to take the eggs away now was murder. For the first time since the expulsion of Jones there was something resembling a rebellion. Led by three young Black Minorca pullets, the hens made a determined effort to thwart Napoleon's wishes. Their method was to fly up to the rafters and there lay their eggs, which smashed to pieces on the floor. Napoleon acted swiftly and ruthlessly. He ordered the hens' rations to be stopped, and decreed that any animal giving so much as a grain of corn to a hen should be punished by death. The dogs saw to it that these orders were carried out. For five days the hens held out, then they capitulated and went back to their nesting boxes. Nine hens had died in the meantime. Their bodies were buried in the orchard, and it was given out that they had died of coccidiosis. Whymper heard nothing of this affair, and the eggs were duly delivered, a grocer's van driving up to the farm once a week to take them away.

All this while no more had been seen of Snowball. He was rumoured to be hiding on one of the neighbouring farms, either Foxwood or Pinchfield. Napoleon was by this time on slightly better terms with the other farmers than before. It happened that there was in the yard a pile of timber which had been stacked there ten years earlier when a beech spinney was cleared. It was well seasoned, and Whymper had advised Napoleon to sell it; both Mr Pilkington and Mr Frederick were anxious to buy it. Napoleon was hesitating between the two, unable to make up his mind. It was noticed that whenever he seemed on the point of coming to an agreement with Frederick, Snowball was declared to be in hiding at Foxwood, while when he inclined towards Pilkington, Snowball was said to be at Pinchfield.

Suddenly, early in the spring, an alarming thing was discovered. Snowball was secretly frequenting the farm by night! The animals were so disturbed that they could hardly sleep in their stalls. Every night, it was said, he came creeping in under cover of darkness and performed all kinds of mischief. He stole the corn, he upset the milk-pails, he broke the eggs, he trampled the seed-beds, he gnawed the bark off the fruit trees. Whenever anything went wrong it became usual to attribute it to Snowball. If a window was broken or a drain was blocked up, someone was certain to say that Snowball had come in the night and done it, and when the key of the store-shed was lost the whole farm was convinced that Snowball had thrown it down the well. Curiously enough they went on believing this even after the mislaid key was found under a sack of meal. The cows declared unanimously that Snowball crept into their stalls and milked them in their sleep. The rats, which had been troublesome that winter, were also said to be in league with Snowball.

Napoleon decreed that there should be a full investigation into Snowball's activities. With his dogs in attendance he set out and made a careful tour of inspection of the farm buildings, the other animals following at a respectful distance. At every few steps Napoleon stopped and snuffed the ground for traces of Snowball's footsteps, which, he said, he could detect by the smell. He snuffed in every corner, in the barn, in the cowshed, in the henhouses, in the vegetable garden, and found traces of Snowball almost everywhere. He would put his snout to the ground, give several deep sniffs and exclaim in a terrible voice, 'Snowball! He has been here! I can smell him distinctly!', and at the word 'Snowball' all the dogs let out blood-curdling growls and showed their side teeth.

The animals were thoroughly frightened. It seemed to them as though Snowball were some kind of invisible influence, pervading the air about them and menacing them with all kinds of dangers. In the evening Squealer called them together, and with an alarmed expression on his face told them that he had some serious news to report.

'Comrades!' cried Squealer, making little nervous skips, 'a most terrible thing has been discovered. Snowball has sold himself to Frederick of Pinchfield Farm, who is even now plotting to attack us and take our farm away from us! Snowball is to act as his guide when the attack begins. But there is worse than that. We had thought that Snowball's rebellion was caused simply by his vanity and ambition. But we were wrong, comrades. Do you know what the real reason was? Snowball was in league with Jones from the very start! He was Jones's secret agent all the time. It has all been proved by documents which he left behind him and which we have only just discovered. To my mind this explains a great deal, comrades. Did we not see for ourselves how he attempted – fortunately without success – to get us defeated and destroyed at the Battle of the Cowshed?'

The animals were stupefied. This was a wickedness far outdoing Snowball's destruction of the windmill. But it was some minutes before they could fully take it in. They all remembered, or thought they remembered, how they had seen Snowball charging ahead of them at the Battle of the Cowshed, how he had rallied and encouraged them at every turn, and how he had not paused for an instant even when the pellets from Jones's gun had wounded his back. At first it was a little difficult to see how this fitted in with his being on Jones's side. Even Boxer, who seldom asked questions, was puzzled. He lay down, tucked his fore hoofs beneath him, shut his eyes, and with a hard effort managed to formulate his thoughts.

'I do not believe that,' he said. 'Snowball fought bravely at the Battle of the Cowshed. I saw him myself. Did we not give him "Animal Hero, First Class" immediately afterwards?'

'That was our mistake, comrade. For we know now – it is all written down in the secret documents that we have found – that in reality he was trying to lure us to our doom.'

'But he was wounded,' said Boxer. 'We all saw him running with blood.'

'That was part of the arrangement!' cried Squealer. 'Jones's shot only grazed him. I could show you this in his own writing, if you were able to read it. The plot was for Snowball, at the critical moment, to give the signal for flight and leave the field to the enemy. And he very nearly succeeded – I will even say, comrades, he *would* have succeeded if it had not been for our heroic Leader, Comrade Napoleon. Do you not remember how, just at the moment when Jones and his men had got inside the yard, Snowball suddenly turned and fled, and many animals followed him? And do you not remember, too, that it was just at that moment, when panic was spreading and all seemed lost, that Comrade Napoleon sprang forward with a cry of "Death to Humanity!" and sank his teeth in Jones's leg? Surely you remember *that*, comrades?' exclaimed Squealer, frisking from side to side.

Now when Squealer described the scene so graphically, it seemed to the animals that they did remember it. At any rate, they remembered that at the critical moment of the battle Snowball had turned to flee. But Boxer was still a little uneasy.

'I do not believe that Snowball was a traitor at the beginning,' he said finally. 'What he has done since is different. But I believe that at the Battle of the Cowshed he was a good comrade.'

'Our Leader, Comrade Napoleon,' announced Squealer, speaking very slowly and firmly, 'has stated categorically – categorically, comrade – that Snowball was Jones's agent from the very beginning – yes, and from long before the Rebellion was ever thought of.'

'Ah, that is different!' said Boxer. 'If Comrade Napoleon says it, it must be right.'

'That is the true spirit, comrade!' cried Squealer, but it was noticed he cast a very ugly look at Boxer with his little twinkling eyes. He turned to go, then paused and added impressively: 'I warn every animal on this farm to keep his eyes very wide open. For we have reason to think that some of Snowball's secret agents are lurking among us at this moment!'

Four days later, in the late afternoon, Napoleon ordered all the animals to assemble in the yard. When they were all gathered together Napoleon emerged from the farmhouse, wearing both his medals (for he had recently awarded himself 'Animal Hero, First Class' and 'Animal Hero, Second Class'), with his nine huge dogs frisking round him and uttering growls that sent shivers down all the animals' spines. They all cowered silently in their places, seeming to know in advance that some terrible thing was about to happen.

Napoleon stood sternly surveying his audience; then he uttered a high-pitched whimper. Immediately the dogs bounded forward, seized four of the pigs by the ear and dragged them, squealing with pain and terror, to Napoleon's feet. The pigs' ears were bleeding, the dogs had tasted blood, and for a few moments they appeared to go quite mad. To the amazement of everybody three of them flung themselves upon Boxer. Boxer saw them coming and put out his great hoof, caught a dog in mid-air and pinned him to the ground. The dog shrieked for mercy and the other two fled with their tails between their legs. Boxer looked at Napoleon to know whether he should crush the dog to death or let it go. Napoleon appeared to change countenance, and sharply ordered Boxer to let the dog go, whereat Boxer lifted his hoof, and the dog slunk away, bruised and howling.

Presently the tumult died down. The four pigs waited, trembling, with guilt written on every line of their countenances. Napoleon now called upon them to confess their crimes. They were the same four pigs as had protested when Napoleon abolished the Sunday Meetings. Without any further prompting they confessed that they had been secretly in touch with Snowball ever since his expulsion, that they had collaborated with him in destroying the windmill, and that they had entered into an agreement with him to hand over Animal Farm to Mr Frederick. They added that Snowball had privately admitted to them that he had been Jones's secret agent for years past. When they had finished their confession the dogs promptly tore their throats out, and in a terrible voice Napoleon demanded whether any other animal had anything to confess.

The three hens who had been the ringleaders in the attempted rebellion over the eggs now came forward and stated that Snowball had appeared to them in a dream and incited them to disobey Napoleon's orders. They too were slaughtered. Then a goose came forward and confessed to having secreted six ears of corn during the last year's harvest and eaten them in the night. Then a sheep confessed to having urinated in the drinking pool – urged to do this, so she said, by Snowball – and two other sheep confessed to having murdered an old ram, an especially devoted follower of Napoleon, by chasing him round and round a bonfire when he was suffering from a cough. They were all slain on the spot. And so the tale of confessions and executions went on, until there was a pile of corpses lying before Napoleon's feet and the air was heavy with the smell of blood, which had been unknown there since the expulsion of Jones.

When it was all over, the remaining animals, except for the pigs and dogs, crept away in a body. They were shaken and miserable. They did not know which was more shocking – the treachery of the animals who had leagued themselves with Snowball, or the cruel retribution they had just witnessed. In the old days there had often been scenes of bloodshed equally terrible, but it seemed to all of them that it was far worse now that it was happening among themselves. Since Jones had left the farm, until today, no animal had killed another animal. Not even a rat had been killed. They had made their way onto the little knoll where the half-finished windmill stood, and with one accord they all lay down as though huddling together for warmth – Clover, Muriel, Benjamin, the cows, the sheep and a whole flock of geese and hens – everyone, indeed, except the cat, who had suddenly disappeared just before Napoleon ordered the animals to assemble. For some time nobody spoke. Only

Boxer remained on his feet. He fidgeted to and fro, swishing his long black tail against his sides and occasionally uttering a little whinny of surprise. Finally he said:

'I do not understand it. I would not have believed that such things could happen on our farm. It must be due to some fault in ourselves. The solution, as I see it, is to work harder. From now onwards I shall get up a full hour earlier in the mornings.'

And he moved off at his lumbering trot and made for the quarry. Having got there he collected two successive loads of stone and dragged them down to the windmill before retiring for the night.

The animals huddled about Clover, not speaking. The knoll where they were lying gave them a wide prospect across the countryside. Most of Animal Farm was within their view – the long pasture stretching down to the main road, the hayfield, the spinney, the drinking pool, the ploughed fields where the young wheat was thick and green, and the red roofs of the farm buildings with the smoke curling from the chimneys. It was a clear spring evening. The grass and the bursting hedges were gilded by the level rays of the sun. Never had the farm – and with a kind of surprise they remembered that it was their own farm, every inch of it their own property – appeared to the animals so desirable a place. As Clover looked down the hillside her eyes filled with tears. If she could have spoken her thoughts, it would have been to say that this was not what they had aimed at when they had set themselves years ago to work for the overthrow of the human race. These scenes of terror and slaughter were not what they had looked forward to on that night when old Major first stirred them to rebellion. If she herself had had any picture of the future, it had been of a society of animals set free from hunger and the whip, all equal, each working according to his capacity, the strong protecting the weak, as she had protected the lost brood of ducklings with her foreleg on the night of Major's speech. Instead – she did not know why – they had come to a time when no one dared speak his mind, when fierce, growling dogs roamed everywhere, and when you had to watch your comrades torn to pieces after confessing to shocking crimes. There was no thought of rebellion or disobedience in her mind. She knew that even as things were they were far better off than they had been in the days of Jones, and that before all else it was needful to prevent the return of the human beings. Whatever happened she would remain faithful, work hard, carry out the orders that were given to her, and accept the leadership of Napoleon. But still, it was not for this that she and all the other animals had hoped and toiled. It was not for this that they had built the windmill and faced the pellets of Jones's gun. Such were her thoughts, though she lacked the words to express them.

At last, feeling this to be in some way a substitute for the words she was unable to find, she began to sing 'Beasts of England'. The other animals sitting round her took it up, and they sang it three times over – very tunefully, but slowly and mournfully, in a way they had never sung it before.

They had just finished singing it for the third time when Squealer, attended by two dogs, approached them with the air of having something important to say. He announced that, by a special decree of Comrade Napoleon, 'Beasts of England' had been abolished. From now onwards it was forbidden to sing it.

The animals were taken aback.

'Why?' cried Muriel.

'It is no longer needed, comrade,' said Squealer stiffly. ' "Beasts of England" was the song of the Rebellion. But the Rebellion is now completed. The execution of the traitors this afternoon was the final act. The enemy both external and internal has been defeated. In "Beasts of England" we expressed our longing for a better society in days to come. But that society has now been established. Clearly this song has no longer any purpose.'

Frightened though they were, some of the animals might possibly have protested, but at this moment the sheep set up their usual bleating of 'Four legs good, two legs bad', which went on for several minutes and put an end to the discussion.

So 'Beasts of England' was heard no more. In its place Minimus, the poet, had composed another song which began:

> *Animal Farm, Animal Farm,*
> *Never through me shalt thou come to harm!*

and this was sung every Sunday morning after the hoisting of the flag. But somehow neither the words nor the tune ever seemed to the animals to come up to 'Beasts of England'.

CHAPTER VIII

A FEW DAYS LATER, when the terror caused by the executions had died down, some of the animals remembered – or thought they remembered – that the Sixth Commandment decreed: 'No animal shall kill any other animal.' And though no one cared to mention it in the hearing of the pigs or the dogs, it was felt that the killings which had taken place did not square with this. Clover asked Benjamin to read her the Sixth Commandment, and when Benjamin, as usual, said that he refused to meddle in such matters, she fetched Muriel. Muriel read the Commandment for her. It ran: 'No animal shall kill any other animal *without cause.*' Somehow or other the last two words had slipped out of the animals' memory. But they saw now that the Commandment had not been violated; for clearly there was good reason for killing the traitors who had leagued themselves with Snowball.

Throughout that year the animals worked even harder than they had worked in the previous year. To rebuild the windmill, with walls twice as thick as before, and to finish it by the appointed date, together with the regular work of the farm, was a tremendous labour. There were times when it seemed to the animals that they worked longer hours and fed no better than they had done in Jones's day. On Sunday mornings Squealer, holding down a long strip of paper with his trotter, would read out to them lists of figures proving that the production of every class of foodstuff had increased by two hundred per cent, three hundred per cent, or five hundred per cent, as the case might be. The animals saw no reason to disbelieve him, especially as they could no longer remember very clearly what conditions had been like before the Rebellion. All the same, there were days when they felt that they would sooner have had less figures and more food.

All orders were now issued through Squealer or one of the other pigs. Napoleon himself was not seen in public as often as once in a fortnight. When he did appear he was attended not only by his retinue of dogs but by a black cockerel who marched in front of him and acted as a kind of trumpeter, letting out a loud 'cock-a-doodle-doo' before Napoleon spoke. Even in the farmhouse, it was said, Napoleon inhabited separate apartments from the others. He took his meals alone, with two dogs to wait upon him, and always ate from the Crown Derby dinner service which had been in the glass cupboard in the drawing-room. It was also announced that the gun would be fired every year on Napoleon's birthday, as well as on the other two anniversaries.

Napoleon was now never spoken of simply as 'Napoleon'. He was always referred to in formal style as 'our Leader, Comrade Napoleon', and the pigs liked to invent for him such titles as Father of All Animals, Terror of Mankind, Protector of the Sheepfold, Ducklings' Friend, and the like. In his speeches Squealer would talk with the tears rolling down his cheeks of Napoleon's wisdom, the goodness of his heart, and the deep love he bore to all animals everywhere, even and especially the unhappy animals who still lived in ignorance and slavery on other farms. It had become usual to give Napoleon the credit for every successful achievement and every stroke of good fortune. You would often hear one hen remark to another, 'Under the guidance of our Leader, Comrade Napoleon, I have laid five eggs in six days'; or two cows, enjoying a drink at the pool, would exclaim, 'Thanks to the leadership of Comrade Napoleon, how excellent this water tastes!' The general feeling on the farm was expressed in a poem entitled 'Comrade Napoleon', which was composed by Minimus and which ran as follows:

> *Friend of the fatherless!*
> *Fountain of happiness!*
> *Lord of the swill-bucket! Oh, how my soul is on*
> *Fire when I gaze at thy*
> *Calm and commanding eye,*
> *Like the sun in the sky,*
> *Comrade Napoleon!*
>
> *Thou art the giver of*
> *All that thy creatures love,*
> *Full belly twice a day, clean straw to roll upon;*
> *Every beast great or small*
> *Sleeps at peace in his stall,*
> *Thou watchest over all,*
> *Comrade Napoleon!*

> *Had I a sucking-pig,*
> *Ere he had grown as big*
> *Even as a pint bottle or as a rolling-pin,*
> *He should have learned to be*
> *Faithful and true to thee,*
> *Yes, his first squeak should be*
> *'Comrade Napoleon!'*

Napoleon approved of this poem and caused it to be inscribed on the wall of the big barn, at the opposite end from the Seven Commandments. It was surmounted by a portrait of Napoleon, in profile, executed by Squealer in white paint.

Meanwhile, through the agency of Whymper, Napoleon was engaged in complicated negotiations with Frederick and Pilkington. The pile of timber was still unsold. Of the two, Frederick was the more anxious to get hold of it, but he would not offer a reasonable price. At the same time there were renewed rumours that Frederick and his men were plotting to attack Animal Farm and to destroy the windmill, the building of which had aroused furious jealousy in him. Snowball was known to be still skulking on Pinchfield Farm. In the middle of the summer the animals were alarmed to hear that three hens had come forward and confessed that, inspired by Snowball, they had entered into a plot to murder Napoleon. They were executed immediately, and fresh precautions for Napoleon's safety were taken. Four dogs guarded his bed at night, one at each corner, and a young pig named Pinkeye was given the task of tasting all his food before he ate it, lest it should be poisoned.

At about the same time it was given out that Napoleon had arranged to sell the pile of timber to Mr Pilkington; he was also going to enter into a regular agreement for the exchange of certain products between Animal Farm and Foxwood. The relations between Napoleon and Pilkington, though they were only conducted through Whymper, were now almost friendly. The animals distrusted Pilkington, as a human being, but greatly preferred him to Frederick, whom they both feared and hated. As the summer wore on, and the windmill neared completion, the rumours of an impending treacherous attack grew stronger and stronger. Frederick, it was said, intended to bring against them twenty men all armed with guns, and he had already bribed the magistrates and police, so that if he could once get hold of the title-deeds of Animal Farm they would ask no questions. Moreover terrible stories were leaking out from Pinchfield about the cruelties that Frederick practised upon his animals. He had flogged an old horse to death, he starved his cows, he had killed a dog by throwing it into the furnace, he amused himself in the evenings by making cocks fight with splinters of razor-blade tied to their spurs. The animals' blood boiled with rage when they heard of these things being done to their comrades, and sometimes they clamoured to be allowed to go out in a body and attack Pinchfield Farm, drive out the humans and set the animals free. But Squealer counselled them to avoid rash actions and trust in Comrade Napoleon's strategy.

Nevertheless feeling against Frederick continued to run high. One Sunday morning Napoleon appeared in the barn and explained that he had never at any time contemplated selling the pile of timber to Frederick; he considered it beneath his dignity, he said, to have dealings with scoundrels of that description. The pigeons who were still sent out to spread tidings of the Rebellion were forbidden to set foot anywhere on Foxwood, and were also ordered to drop their former slogan of 'Death to Humanity' in favour of 'Death to Frederick'. In the late summer yet another of Snowball's machinations was laid bare. The wheat crop was full of weeds, and it was discovered that on one of his nocturnal visits Snowball had mixed weed seeds with the seed corn. A gander who had been privy to the plot had confessed his guilt to Squealer and immediately committed suicide by swallowing deadly nightshade berries. The animals now also learned that Snowball had never – as many of them had believed hitherto – received the order of 'Animal Hero, First Class'. This was merely a legend which had been spread some time after the Battle of the Cowshed by Snowball himself. So far from being decorated he had been censured for showing cowardice in the battle. Once again some of the animals heard this with a certain bewilderment, but Squealer was soon able to convince them that their memories had been at fault.

In the autumn, by a tremendous, exhausting effort – for the harvest had to be gathered at almost the same time – the windmill was finished. The machinery had still to be installed, and Whymper was negotiating the purchase of it, but the structure was completed. In the teeth of every difficulty, in spite of inexperience, of primitive implements, of bad luck and of Snowball's treachery, the work had been finished punctually to the very day! Tired out but proud, the animals walked round and round their masterpiece, which appeared even more beautiful in their eyes than when it had been built the first time. Moreover the walls were twice as thick as before. Nothing short of explosives would lay them low this time! And when they thought of how they had laboured, what discouragements they had overcome, and the enormous difference that would be made in their lives when the sails were turning and the dynamos running – when they thought of all this their tiredness forsook them and they gambolled round and round the windmill, uttering cries of triumph. Napoleon himself, attended by his dogs and his cockerel, came down to inspect the completed work; he personally congratulated the animals on their achievement, and announced that the mill would be named Napoleon Mill.

Two days later the animals were called together for a special meeting in the barn. They were struck dumb with surprise when Napoleon announced that he had sold the pile of timber to Frederick. Tomorrow Frederick's wagons would arrive and begin carting it away. Throughout the whole period of his seeming friendship with Pilkington, Napoleon had really been in secret agreement with Frederick.

All relations with Foxwood had been broken off; insulting messages had been sent to Pilkington. The pigeons had been told to avoid Pinchfield Farm and to alter their slogan from 'Death to Frederick' to 'Death to Pilkington'. At the same time Napoleon assured the animals that the stories of an impending attack on Animal Farm were completely untrue, and that the tales about Frederick's cruelty to his own animals had been greatly exaggerated. All these rumours had probably originated with Snowball and his agents. It now appeared that Snowball was not, after all, hiding on Pinchfield Farm, and in fact had never been there in his life: he was living – in considerable luxury, so it was said – at Foxwood, and had in reality been a pensioner of Pilkington for years past.

The pigs were in ecstasies over Napoleon's cunning. By seeming to be friendly with Pilkington he had forced Frederick to raise his price by twelve pounds. But the superior quality of Napoleon's mind, said Squealer, was shown in the fact that he trusted nobody, not even Frederick.

Frederick had wanted to pay for the timber with something called a cheque, which it seemed was a piece of paper with a promise to pay written upon it. But Napoleon was too clever for him. He had demanded payment in real five-pound notes, which were to be handed over before the timber was removed. Already Frederick had paid up; and the sum he had paid was just enough to buy the machinery for the windmill.

Meanwhile the timber was being carted away at high speed. When it was all gone another special meeting was held in the barn for the animals to inspect Frederick's bank-notes. Smiling beatifically, and wearing both his decorations, Napoleon reposed on a bed of straw on the platform, with the money at his side, neatly piled on a china dish from the farmhouse kitchen. The animals filed slowly past, and each gazed his fill. And Boxer put out his nose to sniff at the bank-notes, and the flimsy white things stirred and rustled in his breath.

Three days later there was a terrible hullabaloo. Whymper, his face deadly pale, came racing up the path on his bicycle, flung it down in the yard and rushed straight into the farmhouse. The next moment a choking roar of rage sounded from Napoleon's apartments. The news of what had happened sped round the farm like wildfire. The bank-notes were forgeries! Frederick had got the timber for nothing!

Napoleon called the animals together immediately and in a terrible voice pronounced the death sentence upon Frederick. When captured, he said, Frederick should be boiled alive. At the same time he warned them that after this treacherous deed the worst was to be expected. Frederick and his men might make their long-expected attack at any moment. Sentinels were placed at all the approaches to the farm. In addition, four pigeons were sent to Foxwood with a conciliatory message, which it was hoped might re-establish good relations with Pilkington.

The very next morning the attack came. The animals were at breakfast when the look-outs came racing in with the news that Frederick and his followers had already come through the five-barred gate. Boldly enough the animals sallied forth to meet them, but this time they did not have the easy victory that they had had in the Battle of the Cowshed. There were fifteen men, with half a dozen guns between them, and they opened fire as soon as they got within fifty yards. The animals could not face the terrible explosions and the stinging pellets, and in spite of the efforts of

Napoleon and Boxer to rally them they were soon driven back. A number of them were already wounded. They took refuge in the farm buildings and peeped cautiously out from chinks and knot-holes. The whole of the big pasture, including the windmill, was in the hands of the enemy. For the moment even Napoleon seemed at a loss. He paced up and down without a word, his tail rigid and twitching. Wistful glances were sent in the direction of Foxwood. If Pilkington and his men would help them, the day might yet be won. But at this moment the four pigeons who had been sent out on the day before returned, one of them bearing a scrap of paper from Pilkington. On it was pencilled the words: 'Serves you right.'

Meanwhile Frederick and his men had halted about the windmill. The animals watched them, and a murmur of dismay went round. Two of the men had produced a crowbar and a sledge hammer. They were going to knock the windmill down.

'Impossible!' cried Napoleon. 'We have built the walls far too thick for that. They could not knock it down in a week. Courage, comrades!'

But Benjamin was watching the movements of the men intently. The two with the hammer and the crowbar were drilling a hole near the base of the windmill. Slowly, and with an air almost of amusement, Benjamin nodded his long muzzle.

'I thought so,' he said. 'Do you not see what they are doing? In another moment they are going to pack blasting powder into that hole.'

Terrified, the animals waited. It was impossible now to venture out of the shelter of the buildings. After a few minutes the men were seen to be running in all directions. Then there was a deafening roar. The pigeons swirled into the air, and all the animals, except Napoleon, flung themselves flat on their bellies and hid their faces. When they got up again a huge cloud of black smoke was hanging where the windmill had been. Slowly the breeze drifted it away. The windmill had ceased to exist!

At this sight the animals' courage returned to them. The fear and despair they had felt a moment earlier were drowned in their rage against this vile, contemptible act. A mighty cry for vengeance went up, and without waiting for further orders they charged forth in a body and made straight for the enemy. This time they did not heed the cruel pellets that swept over them like hail. It was a savage, bitter battle. The men fired again and again, and, when the animals got to close quarters, lashed out with their sticks and their heavy boots. A cow, three sheep and two geese were killed, and nearly everyone was wounded. Even Napoleon, who was directing operations from the rear, had the tip of his tail chipped by a pellet. But the men did not go unscathed either. Three of them had their heads broken by blows from Boxer's hoofs, another was gored in the belly by a cow's horn, another had his trousers nearly torn off by Jessie and Bluebell. And when the nine dogs of Napoleon's own bodyguard, whom he had instructed to make a detour under cover of the hedge, suddenly appeared on the men's flank, baying ferociously, panic overtook them. They saw that they were in danger of being surrounded. Frederick shouted to his men to get out while the going was good, and the next moment the cowardly enemy was running for dear life. The animals chased them right down to the bottom of the field, and got in some last kicks at them as they forced their way through the thorn hedge.

They had won, but they were weary and bleeding. Slowly they began to limp back towards the farm. The sight of their dead comrades stretched upon the grass moved some of them to tears. And for a little while they halted in sorrowful silence at the place where the windmill had once stood. Yes, it was gone, almost the last trace of their labour was gone! Even the foundations were partially destroyed. And in rebuilding it they could not this time, as before, make use of the fallen stones. This time the stones had vanished too. The force of the explosion had flung them to distances of hundreds of yards. It was as though the windmill had never been.

As they approached the farm Squealer, who had unaccountably been absent during the fighting, came skipping towards them, whisking his tail and beaming with satisfaction. And the animals heard, from the direction of the farm buildings, the solemn booming of a gun.

'What is that gun firing for?' said Boxer.

'To celebrate our victory!' cried Squealer.

'What victory?' said Boxer. His knees were bleeding, he had lost a shoe and split his hoof, and a dozen pellets had lodged themselves in his hind leg.

'What victory, comrade? Have we not driven the enemy off our soil – the sacred soil of Animal Farm?'

'But they have destroyed the windmill. And we had worked on it for two years!'

'What matter? We will build another windmill. We will build six windmills if we feel like it. You do not appreciate, comrade, the mighty thing that we have done. The enemy was in occupation of this very ground that we stand upon. And now – thanks to the leadership of Comrade Napoleon – we have won every inch of it back again!'

'Then we have won back what we had before,' said Boxer.

'That is our victory,' said Squealer.

They limped into the yard. The pellets under the skin of Boxer's leg smarted painfully. He saw ahead of him the heavy labour of rebuilding the windmill from the foundations, and already in imagination he braced himself for the task. But for the first time it occurred to him that he was eleven years old and that perhaps his great muscles were not quite what they had once been.

But when the animals saw the green flag flying, and heard the gun firing again – seven times it was fired in all – and heard the speech that Napoleon made, congratulating them on their conduct, it did seem to them after all that they had won a great victory. The animals slain in the battle were given a solemn funeral. Boxer and Clover pulled the wagon which served as a hearse, and Napoleon himself walked at the head of the procession. Two whole days were given over to celebrations. There were songs, speeches and more firing of the gun, and a special gift of an apple was bestowed on every animal, with two ounces of corn for each bird and three biscuits for each dog. It was announced that the battle would be called the Battle of the Windmill, and that Napoleon had created a new decoration, the Order of the Green Banner, which he had conferred upon himself. In the general rejoicings the unfortunate affair of the bank-notes was forgotten.

It was a few days later than this that the pigs came upon a case of whisky in the cellars of the farmhouse. It had been overlooked at the time when the house was first occupied. That night there came from the farmhouse the sound of loud singing, in which, to everyone's surprise, the strains of 'Beasts of England' were mixed up. At about half-past nine Napoleon, wearing an old bowler hat of Mr Jones's, was distinctly seen to emerge from the back door, gallop rapidly round the yard and disappear indoors again. But in the morning a deep silence hung over the farmhouse. Not a pig appeared to be stirring. It was nearly nine o'clock when Squealer made his appearance, walking slowly and dejectedly, his eyes dull, his tail hanging limply behind him, and with every appearance of being seriously ill. He called the animals together and told them that he had a terrible piece of news to impart. Comrade Napoleon was dying!

A cry of lamentation went up. Straw was laid down outside the doors of the farmhouse, and the animals walked on tiptoe. With tears in their eyes they asked one another what they should do if their Leader were taken away from them. A rumour went round that Snowball had after all contrived to introduce poison into Napoleon's food. At eleven o'clock Squealer came out to make another announcement. As his last act upon earth, Comrade Napoleon had pronounced a solemn decree: the drinking of alcohol was to be punished by death.

By the evening, however, Napoleon appeared to be somewhat better, and the following morning Squealer was able to tell them that he was well on the way to recovery. By the evening of that day Napoleon was back at work, and on the next day it was learned that he had instructed Whymper to purchase in Willingdon some booklets on brewing and distilling. A week later Napoleon gave orders that the small paddock beyond the orchard, which it had previously been intended to set aside as a grazing-ground for animals who were past work, was to be ploughed up. It was given out that the pasture was exhausted and needed re-seeding: but it soon became known that Napoleon intended to sow it with barley.

About this time there occurred a strange incident which hardly anyone was able to understand. One night at about twelve o'clock there was a loud crash in the yard, and the animals rushed out of their stalls. It was a moonlit night. At the foot of the end wall of the big barn, where the Seven Commandments were written, there lay a ladder broken in two pieces. Squealer, temporarily stunned, was sprawling beside it, and near at hand there lay a lantern, a paintbrush and an overturned pot of white paint. The dogs immediately made a ring round Squealer, and escorted him back to the farmhouse as soon as he was able to walk. None of the animals could form any idea as to what this meant, except old Benjamin, who nodded his muzzle with a knowing air, and seemed to understand, but would say nothing.

But a few days later Muriel, reading over the Seven Commandments to herself, noticed that there was yet another of them which the animals had remembered wrong. They had thought that the Fifth Commandment was 'No animal shall drink alcohol', but there were two words that they had forgotten. Actually the Commandment read: 'No animal shall drink alcohol *to excess*.'

CHAPTER IX

BOXER'S SPLIT HOOF was a long time in healing. They had started the rebuilding of the windmill the day after the victory celebrations were ended. Boxer refused to take even a day off work, and made it a point of honour not to let it be seen that he was in pain. In the evenings he would admit privately to Clover that the hoof troubled him a great deal. Clover treated the hoof with poultices of herbs which she prepared by chewing them, and both she and Benjamin urged Boxer to work less hard. 'A horse's lungs do not last for ever,' she said to him. But Boxer would not listen. He had, he said, only one real ambition left – to see the windmill well under way before he reached the age for retirement.

At the beginning, when the laws of Animal Farm were first formulated, the retiring age had been fixed for horses and pigs at twelve, for cows at fourteen, for dogs at nine, for sheep at seven and for hens and geese at five. Liberal old-age pensions had been agreed upon. As yet no animal had actually retired on pension, but of late the subject had been discussed more and more. Now that the small field beyond the orchard had been set aside for barley, it was rumoured that a corner of the large pasture was to be fenced off and turned into a grazing-ground for superannuated animals. For a horse, it was said, the pension would be five pounds of corn a day and, in winter, fifteen pounds of hay, with a carrot or possibly an apple on public holidays. Boxer's twelfth birthday was due in the late summer of the following year.

Meanwhile life was hard. The winter was as cold as the last one had been, and food was even shorter. Once again all rations were reduced except those of the pigs and the dogs. A too-rigid equality in rations, Squealer explained, would have been contrary to the principles of Animalism. In any case he had no difficulty in proving to the other animals that they were *not* in reality short of food, whatever the appearances might be. For the time being, certainly, it had been found necessary to make a readjustment of rations (Squealer always spoke of it as a 'readjustment', never as a 'reduction'), but in comparison with the days of Jones the improvement was enormous. Reading out the figures in a shrill rapid voice, he proved to them in detail that they had more oats, more hay, more turnips than they had had in Jones's day, that they worked shorter hours, that their drinking water was of better quality, that they lived longer, that a larger proportion of their young ones survived infancy, and that they had more straw in their stalls and suffered less from fleas. The animals believed every word of it. Truth to tell, Jones and all he stood for had almost faded out of their memories. They knew that life nowadays was harsh and bare, that they were often hungry and often cold, and that they were usually working when they were not asleep. But doubtless it had been worse in the old days. They were glad to believe so. Besides, in those days they had been slaves and now they were free, and that made all the difference, as Squealer did not fail to point out.

There were many more mouths to feed now. In the autumn the four sows had all littered about simultaneously, producing thirty-one young pigs between them. The young pigs were piebald, and as Napoleon was the only boar on the farm it was possible to guess at their parentage. It was announced that later, when bricks and timber had been purchased, a schoolroom would be built in the farmhouse garden. For the time being the young pigs were given their instruction by Napoleon himself in the farmhouse kitchen. They took their exercise in the garden, and were discouraged from playing with the other young animals. About this time, too, it was laid down as a rule that when a pig and any other animal met on the path, the other animal must stand aside: and also that all pigs, of whatever degree, were to have the privilege of wearing green ribbons on their tails on Sundays.

The farm had had a fairly successful year, but was still short of money. There were the bricks, sand and lime for the schoolroom to be purchased, and it would also be necessary to begin saving up again for the machinery for the windmill. Then there were lamp oil and candles for the house, sugar for Napoleon's own table (he forbade this to the other pigs, on the ground that it made them fat), and all the usual replacements such as tools, nails, string, coal, wire, scrap-iron and dog biscuits. A stump of hay and part of the potato crop were sold off, and the contract for eggs was increased to six hundred a week, so that that year the hens barely hatched enough chicks to keep their numbers at the same level. Rations, reduced in December, were reduced again in February, and lanterns in the stalls were forbidden to save oil. But the pigs seemed comfortable enough, and in fact were putting on weight if anything. One afternoon in late February a warm, rich, appetising scent, such as the animals had never smelt before, wafted itself across the yard from the little brew-house, which had been disused in Jones's time, and which stood beyond the kitchen. Someone said it was the smell of cooking barley. The animals sniffed the air hungrily and wondered whether a warm mash was being prepared for their supper. But no warm mash appeared, and on the following Sunday it was announced that from now onwards all barley would be reserved for the pigs. The field beyond the orchard had already been sown with barley. And the news soon leaked out that every pig was now receiving a ration of a pint of beer daily, with half a gallon for Napoleon himself, which was always served to him in the Crown Derby soup tureen.

But if there were hardships to be borne, they were partly offset by the fact that life nowadays had a greater dignity than it had had before. There were more songs, more speeches, more processions. Napoleon had commanded that once a week there should be held something called a Spontaneous Demonstration, the object of which was to celebrate the struggles and triumphs of Animal Farm. At the appointed time the animals would leave their work and march round the precincts of the farm in military formation, with the pigs leading, then the horses, then the cows, then the sheep, and then the poultry. The dogs flanked the procession and at the head of all marched Napoleon's black cockerel. Boxer and Clover always carried between them a green banner marked with the hoof and the horn and the caption, 'Long live Comrade Napoleon!' Afterwards there were recitations of poems composed in Napoleon's honour, and a speech by Squealer giving particulars of the latest increases in the production of foodstuffs, and on occasion a shot was fired from the gun. The sheep were the greatest devotees of the Spontaneous Demonstrations, and if anyone complained (as a few animals sometimes did, when no pigs or dogs were near) that they wasted time and meant a lot of standing about in the cold, the sheep were sure to silence him with a tremendous bleating of 'Four legs good, two legs bad!' But by and large the animals enjoyed these celebrations. They found it comforting to be reminded that, after all, they were truly their own masters and that the work they did was for their own benefit. So that what with the songs, the processions, Squealer's lists of figures, the thunder of the gun, the crowing of the cockerel and the fluttering of the flag, they were able to forget that their bellies were empty, at least part of the time.

In April Animal Farm was proclaimed a Republic, and it became necessary to elect a President. There was only one candidate, Napoleon, who was elected unanimously. On the same day it was given out that fresh documents had been discovered which revealed further details about Snowball's complicity with Jones. It now appeared that Snowball had not, as the animals had previously imagined, merely attempted to lose the Battle of the Cowshed by means of a stratagem, but had been openly fighting on Jones's side. In fact it was he who had actually been the leader of the human forces, and had charged into battle with the words 'Long live Humanity!' on his lips. The wounds on Snowball's back, which a few of the animals still remembered to have seen, had been inflicted by Napoleon's teeth.

In the middle of the summer Moses the raven suddenly reappeared on the farm, after an absence of several years. He was quite unchanged, still did no work, and talked in the same strain as ever about Sugarcandy Mountain. He would perch on a stump, flap his black wings, and talk by the hour to anyone who would listen. 'Up there, comrades,' he would say solemnly, pointing to the sky with his large beak – 'up there, just on the other side of that dark cloud that you can see – there it lies, Sugarcandy Mountain, that happy country where we poor animals shall rest for ever from our labours!' He even claimed to have been there on one of his higher flights, and to have seen the everlasting fields of clover and the linseed cake and lump sugar growing on the hedges. Many of the animals believed him. Their lives now, they reasoned, were hungry and laborious; was it not right and just that a better world should exist somewhere else? A thing that was difficult to determine was the attitude of the pigs towards Moses. They all declared contemptuously that his stories about Sugarcandy Mountain were lies, and yet they allowed him to remain on the farm, not working, with an allowance of a gill of beer a day.

After his hoof had healed up Boxer worked harder than ever. Indeed all the animals worked like slaves that year. Apart from the regular work of the farm, and the rebuilding of the windmill, there was the schoolhouse for the young pigs, which was started in March. Sometimes the long hours on insufficient food were hard to bear, but Boxer never faltered. In nothing that he said or did was there any sign that his strength was not what it had been. It was only his appearance that was a little altered; his hide was less shiny than it had used to be, and his great haunches seemed to have shrunken. The others said, 'Boxer will pick up when the spring grass comes on'; but the spring grass came and Boxer grew no fatter. Sometimes on the slope leading to the top of the quarry, when he braced his muscles against the weight of some vast boulder, it seemed that nothing kept him on his feet except the will to continue. At such times his lips were seen to form the words 'I will work harder'; he had no voice left. Once again Clover and Benjamin warned him to take care of his health, but Boxer paid no attention. His twelfth birthday was approaching. He did not care what happened so long as a good store of stone was accumulated before he went on pension.

Late one evening, in the summer, a sudden rumour ran round the farm that something had happened to Boxer. He had gone out alone to drag a load of stone down to the windmill. And sure enough, the rumour was true. A few minutes later two pigeons came racing in with the news: 'Boxer has fallen! He is lying on his side and can't get up!'

About half the animals on the farm rushed out to the knoll where the windmill stood. There lay Boxer, between the shafts of the cart, his neck stretched out, unable even to raise his head. His eyes were glazed, his sides matted with sweat. A thin stream of blood had trickled out of his mouth. Clover dropped to her knees at his side.

'Boxer!' she cried, 'how are you?'

'It is my lung,' said Boxer in a weak voice. 'It does not matter. I think you will be able to finish the windmill without me. There is a pretty good store of stone accumulated. I had only another month to go in any case. To tell you the truth I had been looking forward to my retirement. And perhaps, as Benjamin is growing old too, they will let him retire at the same time and be a companion to me.'

'We must get help at once,' said Clover. 'Run, somebody, and tell Squealer what has happened.'

All the other animals immediately raced back to the farmhouse to give Squealer the news. Only Clover remained, and Benjamin, who lay down at Boxer's side, and, without speaking, kept the flies off him with his long tail. After about a quarter of an hour Squealer appeared, full of sympathy and concern. He said that Comrade Napoleon had learned with the very deepest distress of this misfortune to one of the most loyal workers on the farm, and was already making arrangements to send Boxer to be treated in the hospital at Willingdon. The animals felt a little uneasy at this. Except for Mollie and Snowball no other animal had ever left the farm, and they did not like to think of their sick comrade in the hands of human beings. However, Squealer easily convinced them that the veterinary surgeon in Willingdon could treat Boxer's case more satisfactorily than could be done on the farm. And about half an hour later, when Boxer had somewhat recovered, he was with difficulty got onto his feet, and managed to limp back to his stall, where Clover and Benjamin had prepared a good bed of straw for him.

For the next two days Boxer remained in his stall. The pigs had sent out a large bottle of pink medicine which they had found in the medicine chest in the bathroom, and Clover administered it to Boxer twice a day after meals. In the evenings she lay in his stall and talked to him, while Benjamin kept the flies off him. Boxer professed not to be sorry for what had happened. If he made a good recovery he might expect to live another three years, and he looked forward to the peaceful days that he would spend in the corner of the big pasture. It would be the first time that he had had leisure to study and improve his mind. He intended, he said, to devote the rest of his life to learning the remaining twenty-two letters of the alphabet.

However, Benjamin and Clover could only be with Boxer after working hours, and it was in the middle of the day when the van came to take him away. The animals were all at work weeding turnips under the supervision of a pig, when they were astonished to see Benjamin come galloping from the direction of the farm buildings, braying at the top of his voice. It was the first time that they had ever seen Benjamin excited – indeed, it was the first time that anyone had ever seen him gallop. 'Quick, quick!' he shouted. 'Come at once! They're taking Boxer away!' Without waiting for orders from the pig, the animals broke off work and raced back to the farm buildings. Sure enough, there in the yard was a large closed van, drawn by two horses, with lettering on its side and a sly-looking man in a low-crowned bowler hat sitting on the driver's seat. And Boxer's stall was empty.

The animals crowded round the van. 'Good-bye, Boxer!' they chorused, 'good-bye!'

'Fools! Fools!' shouted Benjamin, prancing round them and stamping the earth with his small hoofs. 'Fools! Do you not see what is written on the side of that van?'

That gave the animals pause, and there was a hush. Muriel began to spell out the words. But Benjamin pushed her aside and in the midst of a deadly silence he read:

'"Alfred Simmonds, Horse Slaughterer and Glue Boiler, Willingdon. Dealer in Hides and Bone-Meal. Kennels Supplied." Do you not understand what that means? They are taking Boxer to the knacker's!'

A cry of horror burst from all the animals. At this moment the man on the box whipped up his horses and the van moved out of the yard at a smart trot. All the animals followed, crying out at the tops of their voices. Clover forced her way to the front. The van began to gather speed. Clover tried to stir her stout limbs to a gallop, and achieved a canter. 'Boxer!' she cried. 'Boxer! Boxer! Boxer!' And just at this moment, as though he had heard the uproar outside, Boxer's face, with the white stripe down his nose, appeared at the small window at the back of the van.

'Boxer!' cried Clover in a terrible voice. 'Boxer! Get out! Get out quickly! They are taking you to your death!'

All the animals took up the cry of 'Get out, Boxer, get out!'. But the van was already gathering speed and drawing away from them. It was uncertain whether Boxer had understood what Clover had said. But a moment later his face disappeared from the window and there was the sound of a tremendous drumming of hoofs inside the van. He was trying to kick his way out. The time had been when a few kicks from Boxer's hoofs would have smashed the van to matchwood. But alas! his strength had left him; and in a few moments the sound of drumming hoofs grew fainter and died away. In desperation the animals began appealing to the two horses which drew the van to stop. 'Comrades, comrades!' they shouted. 'Don't take your own brother to his death!' But the stupid brutes, too ignorant to realise what was happening, merely set back their ears and quickened their pace. Boxer's face did not reappear at the window. Too late, someone thought of racing ahead and shutting the five-barred gate; but in another moment the van was through it and rapidly disappearing down the road. Boxer was never seen again.

Three days later it was announced that he had died in the hospital at Willingdon, in spite of receiving every attention a horse could have. Squealer came to announce the news to the others. He had, he said, been present during Boxer's last hours.

'It was the most affecting sight I have ever seen!' said Squealer, lifting his trotter and wiping away a tear. 'I was at his bedside at the very last. And at the end, almost too weak to speak, he whispered in my ear that his sole sorrow was to have passed on before the windmill was finished. "Forward, comrades!" he whispered. "Forward in the name of the Rebellion. Long live Animal Farm! Long live Comrade Napoleon! Napoleon is always right." Those were his very last words, comrades.'

Here Squealer's demeanour suddenly changed. He fell silent for a moment, and his little eyes darted suspicious glances from side to side before he proceeded.

It had come to his knowledge, he said, that a foolish and wicked rumour had been circulated at the time of Boxer's removal. Some of the animals had noticed that the van which took Boxer away was marked 'Horse Slaughterer', and had actually jumped to the conclusion that Boxer was being sent to the knacker's. It was almost unbelievable, said Squealer, that any animal could be so stupid. Surely, he cried indignantly, whisking his tail and skipping from side to side, surely they knew their beloved Leader, Comrade Napoleon, better than that? But the explanation was really very simple. The van had previously been the property of the knacker, and had been bought by the veterinary surgeon, who had not yet painted the old name out. That was how the mistake had arisen.

The animals were enormously relieved to hear this. And when Squealer went on to give further graphic details of Boxer's death-bed, the admirable care he had received and the expensive medicines for which Napoleon had paid without a thought as to the cost, their last doubts disappeared and the sorrow that they felt for their comrade's death was tempered by the thought that at least he had died happy.

Napoleon himself appeared at the meeting on the following Sunday morning and pronounced a short oration in Boxer's honour. It had not been possible, he said, to bring back their lamented comrade's remains for interment on the farm, but he had ordered a large wreath to be made from the laurels in the farmhouse garden and sent down to be placed on Boxer's grave. And in a few days' time the pigs intended to hold a memorial banquet in Boxer's honour. Napoleon ended his speech with a reminder of Boxer's two favourite maxims, 'I will work harder' and 'Comrade Napoleon is always right' – maxims, he said, which every animal would do well to adopt as his own.

On the day appointed for the banquet a grocer's van drove up from Willingdon and delivered a large wooden crate at the farmhouse. That night there was the sound of uproarious singing, which was followed by what sounded like a violent quarrel and ended at about eleven o'clock with a tremendous crash of glass. No one stirred in the farmhouse before noon on the following day. And the word went round that from somewhere or other the pigs had acquired the money to buy themselves another case of whisky.

CHAPTER X

YEARS PASSED. The seasons came and went, the short animal lives fled by. A time came when there was no one who remembered the old days before the Rebellion, except Clover, Benjamin, Moses the raven, and a number of the pigs.

Muriel was dead, Bluebell, Jessie and Pincher were dead. Jones too was dead – he had died in an inebriates' home in another part of the county. Snowball was forgotten. Boxer was forgotten, except by the few who had known him. Clover was an old stout mare now, stiff in the joints and with a tendency to rheumy eyes. She was two years past the retiring age, but in fact no animal had ever actually retired. The talk of setting aside a corner of the pasture for superannuated animals had long since been dropped. Napoleon was now a mature boar of twenty-four stone. Squealer was so fat that he could with difficulty see out of his eyes. Only old Benjamin was much the same as ever, except for being a little greyer about the muzzle, and, since Boxer's death, more morose and taciturn than ever.

There were many more creatures on the farm now, though the increase was not so great as had been expected in earlier years. Many animals had been born to whom the Rebellion was only a dim tradition, passed on by word of mouth, and others had been bought who had never heard mention of such a thing before their arrival. The farm possessed three horses now besides Clover. They were fine upstanding beasts, willing workers and good comrades, but very stupid. None of them proved able to learn the alphabet beyond the letter B. They accepted everything that they were told about the Rebellion and the principles of Animalism, especially from Clover, for whom they had an almost filial respect; but it was doubtful whether they understood very much of it.

The farm was more prosperous now, and better organised; it had even been enlarged by two fields which had been bought from Mr Pilkington. The windmill had been successfully completed at last, and the farm possessed a threshing machine and a hay elevator of its own, and various new buildings had been added to it. Whymper had bought himself a dogcart. The windmill, however, had not after all been used for generating electrical power. It was used for milling corn, and brought in a handsome money profit. The animals were hard at work building yet another windmill: when that one was finished, so it was said, the dynamos would be installed. But the luxuries of which Snowball had once taught the animals to dream, the stalls with electric light and hot and cold water, and the three-day week, were no longer talked about. Napoleon had denounced such ideas as contrary to the spirit of Animalism. The truest happiness, he said, lay in working hard and living frugally.

Somehow it seemed as though the farm had grown richer without making the animals themselves any richer – except, of course, for the pigs and the dogs. Perhaps this was partly because there were so many pigs and so many dogs. It was not that these creatures did not work, after their fashion. There was, as Squealer was never tired of explaining, endless work in the supervision and organisation of the farm. Much of this work was of a kind that the other animals were too ignorant to understand. For example, Squealer told them that the pigs had to expend enormous labours every day upon mysterious things called 'files', 'reports', 'minutes' and 'memoranda'. These were large sheets of paper which had to be closely covered with writing, and as soon as they were so covered they were burnt in the furnace. This was of the highest importance for the welfare of the farm, Squealer said. But still, neither pigs nor dogs produced any food by their own labour; and there were very many of them, and their appetites were always good.

As for the others, their life, so far as they knew, was as it had always been. They were generally hungry, they slept on straw, they drank from the pool, they laboured in the fields; in winter they were troubled by the cold, and in summer by the flies. Sometimes the older ones among them racked their dim memories and tried to determine whether in the early days of the Rebellion, when Jones's expulsion was still recent, things had been better or worse than now. They could not remember. There was nothing with which they could compare their present lives: they had nothing to go upon except Squealer's lists of figures, which invariably demonstrated that everything was getting better and better. The animals found the problem insoluble; in any case they had little time for speculating on such things now. Only old Benjamin professed to remember every detail of his long life and to know that things never had been, nor ever could be, much better or much worse – hunger, hardship and disappointment being, so he said, the unalterable law of life.

And yet the animals never gave up hope. More, they never lost, even for an instant, their sense of honour and privilege in being members of Animal Farm. They were still the only farm in the whole country – in all England! – owned and operated by animals. Not one of them, not even the youngest, not even the newcomers who had been brought from farms ten or twenty miles away, ever ceased to marvel at that. And when they heard the gun booming and saw the green flag fluttering at the masthead, their hearts swelled with imperishable pride, and the talk turned always towards the old heroic days, the expulsion of Jones, the writing of the Seven Commandments, the great battles in which the human invaders had been defeated. None of the old dreams had been abandoned. The Republic of the Animals which Major had foretold, when the green fields of England should be untrodden by human feet, was still believed in. Some day it was coming: it might not be soon, it might not be within the lifetime of any animal now living, but still it was coming. Even the tune of 'Beasts of England' was perhaps hummed secretly here and there: at any rate it was a fact that every animal on the farm knew it, though no one would have dared to sing it aloud. It might be that their lives were hard and that not all of their hopes had been fulfilled; but they were conscious that they were not as other animals. If they went hungry, it was not from feeding tyrannical human beings; if they worked hard, at least they worked for themselves. No creature among them went upon two legs. No creature called any other creature 'Master'. All animals were equal.

One day in early summer Squealer ordered the sheep to follow him and led them out to a piece of waste ground at the other end of the farm, which had become overgrown with birch saplings. The sheep spent the whole day there browsing at the leaves under Squealer's supervision. In the evening he returned to the farmhouse himself, but, as it was warm weather, told the sheep to stay where they were. It ended by their remaining there for a whole week, during which time the other animals saw nothing of them. Squealer was with them for the greater part of every day. He was, he said, teaching them to sing a new song, for which privacy was needed.

It was just after the sheep had returned, on a pleasant evening when the animals had finished work and were making their way back to the farm buildings, that the terrified neighing of a horse sounded from the yard. Startled, the animals stopped in their tracks. It was Clover's voice. She neighed again, and all the animals broke into a gallop and rushed into the yard. Then they saw what Clover had seen.

It was a pig walking on his hind legs.

Yes, it was Squealer. A little awkwardly, as though not quite used to supporting his considerable bulk in that position, but with perfect balance, he was strolling across the yard. And a moment later, out from the door of the farmhouse came a long file of pigs, all walking on their hind legs. Some did it better than others, one or two were even a trifle unsteady and looked as though they would have liked the support of a stick, but every one of them made his way right round the yard successfully. And finally there was a tremendous baying of dogs and a shrill crowing from the black cockerel, and out came Napoleon himself, majestically upright, casting haughty glances from side to side, and with his dogs gambolling round him.

He carried a whip in his trotter.

There was a deadly silence. Amazed, terrified, huddling together, the animals watched the long line of pigs march slowly round the yard. It was as though the world had turned upside-down. Then there came a moment when the first shock had worn off and when in spite of everything – in spite of their terror of the dogs, and of the habit, developed through long years, of never complaining, never criticising, no matter what happened – they might have uttered some word of protest. But just at that moment, as though at a signal, all the sheep burst out into a tremendous bleating of –

'Four legs good, two legs *better*! Four legs good, two legs *better*! Four legs good, two legs *better*!'

It went on for five minutes without stopping. And by the time the sheep had quieted down the chance to utter any protest had passed, for the pigs had marched back into the farmhouse.

Benjamin felt a nose nuzzling at his shoulder. He looked round. It was Clover. Her old eyes looked dimmer than ever. Without saying anything she tugged gently at his mane and led him round to the end of the big barn, where the Seven Commandments were written. For a minute or two they stood gazing at the tarred wall with its white lettering.

'My sight is failing,' she said finally. 'Even when I was young I could not have read what was written there. But it appears to me that that wall looks different. Are the Seven Commandments the same as they used to be, Benjamin?'

For once Benjamin consented to break his rule, and he read out to her what was written on the wall. There was nothing there now except a single Commandment. It ran:

ALL ANIMALS ARE EQUAL
BUT SOME ANIMALS ARE MORE EQUAL THAN OTHERS.

After that it did not seem strange when next day the pigs who were supervising the work of the farm all carried whips in their trotters. It did not seem strange to learn that the pigs had bought themselves a wireless set, were arranging to install a telephone, and had taken out subscriptions to *John Bull*, *Tit-Bits* and the *Daily Mirror*. It did not seem strange when Napoleon was seen strolling in the farmhouse garden with a pipe in his mouth – no, not even when the pigs took Mr Jones's clothes out of the wardrobes and put them on, Napoleon himself appearing in a black coat, ratcatcher breeches and leather leggings, while his favourite sow appeared in the watered silk dress which Mrs Jones had been used to wear on Sundays.

A week later, in the afternoon, a number of dogcarts drove up to the farm. A deputation of neighbouring farmers had been invited to make a tour of inspection. They were shown all over the farm, and expressed great admiration for everything they saw, especially the windmill. The animals were weeding the turnip field. They worked diligently, hardly raising their faces from the ground, and not knowing whether to be more frightened of the pigs or of the human visitors.

That evening loud laughter and bursts of singing came from the farmhouse. And suddenly, at the sound of the mingled voices, the animals were stricken with curiosity. What could be happening in there, now that for the first time animals and human beings were meeting on terms of equality? With one accord they began to creep as quietly as possible into the farmhouse garden.

At the gate they paused, half frightened to go on, but Clover led the way in. They tiptoed up to the house, and such animals as were tall enough peered in at the dining-room window. There, round the long table, sat half a dozen farmers and half a dozen of the more eminent pigs, Napoleon himself occupying the seat of honour at the head of the table. The pigs appeared completely at ease in their chairs. The company had been enjoying a game of cards, but had broken off for the moment, evidently in order to drink a toast. A large jug was circulating, and the mugs were being refilled with beer. No one noticed the wondering faces of the animals that gazed in at the window.

Mr Pilkington, of Foxwood, had stood up, his mug in his hand. In a moment, he said, he would ask the present company to drink a toast. But before doing so there were a few words that he felt it incumbent upon him to say.

It was a source of great satisfaction to him, he said – and, he was sure, to all others present – to feel that a long period of mistrust and misunderstanding had now come to an end. There had been a time – not that he, or any of the present company, had shared such sentiments – but there had been a time when the respected proprietors of Animal Farm had been regarded, he would not say with hostility, but perhaps with a certain measure of misgiving, by their human neighbours. Unfortunate incidents had occurred, mistaken ideas had been current. It had been felt that the existence of a farm owned and operated by pigs was somehow abnormal and was liable to have an unsettling effect in the neighbourhood. Too many farmers had assumed, without due enquiry, that on such a farm a spirit of licence and indiscipline would prevail. They had been nervous about the effects upon their own animals, or even upon their human employees. But all such doubts were now dispelled. Today he and his friends had visited Animal Farm and inspected every inch of it with their own eyes, and what did they find? Not only the most up-to-date methods, but a discipline and an orderliness which should be an example to all farmers everywhere. He believed that he was right in saying that the lower animals on Animal Farm did more work and received less food than any animals in the county. Indeed he and his fellow-visitors today had observed many features which they intended to introduce on their own farms immediately.

He would end his remarks, he said, by emphasising once again the friendly feelings that subsisted, and ought to subsist, between Animal Farm and its neighbours. Between pigs and human beings there was not and there need not be any clash of interests whatever. Their struggles and their difficulties were one. Was not the labour problem the same everywhere? Here it became apparent that Mr Pilkington was about to spring some carefully-prepared witticism on the company, but for a moment he was too overcome by amusement to be able to utter it. After much choking, during which his various chins turned purple, he managed to get it out: 'If you have your lower animals to contend with,' he said, 'we have our lower classes!' This *bon mot* set the table in a roar; and Mr Pilkington once again congratulated the pigs on the low rations, the long working-hours and the general absence of pampering which he had observed on Animal Farm.

And now, he said finally, he would ask the company to rise to their feet and make certain that their glasses were full. 'Gentlemen,' concluded Mr Pilkington, 'gentlemen, I give you a toast: To the prosperity of Animal Farm!'

There was enthusiastic cheering and stamping of feet. Napoleon was so gratified that he left his place and came round the table to clink his mug against Mr Pilkington's before emptying it. When the cheering had died down, Napoleon, who had remained on his feet, intimated that he too had a few words to say.

Like all of Napoleon's speeches, it was short and to the point. He too, he said, was happy that the period of misunderstanding was at an end. For a long time there had been rumours – circulated, he had reason to think, by some malignant enemy – that there was something subversive and even revolutionary in the outlook of himself and his colleagues. They had been credited with attempting to stir up rebellion among the animals on neighbouring farms. Nothing could be further from the truth! Their sole wish, now and in the past, was to live at peace and in normal business relations with their neighbours. This farm which he had the honour to control, he added, was a co-operative enterprise. The title-deeds, which were in his own possession, were owned by the pigs jointly.

He did not believe, he said, that any of the old suspicions still lingered, but certain changes had been made recently in the routine of the farm which should have the effect of promoting confidence still further. Hitherto the animals on the farm had had a rather foolish custom of addressing one another as 'Comrade'. This was to be suppressed. There had also been a very strange custom, whose origin was unknown, of marching every Sunday morning past a boar's skull which was nailed to a post in the garden. This too would be suppressed, and the skull had already been buried. His visitors might have observed, too, the green flag which flew from the masthead. If so, they would perhaps have noted that the white hoof and horn with which it had previously been marked had now been removed. It would be a plain green flag from now onwards.

He had only one criticism, he said, to make of Mr Pilkington's excellent and neighbourly speech. Mr Pilkington had referred throughout to 'Animal Farm'. He could not of course know – for he, Napoleon, was only now for the first time announcing it – that the name 'Animal Farm' had been abolished. Henceforward the farm was to be known as 'The Manor Farm' – which, he believed, was its correct and original name.

'Gentlemen,' concluded Napoleon, 'I will give you the same toast as before, but in a different form. Fill your glasses to the brim. Gentlemen, here is my toast: To the prosperity of The Manor Farm!'

There was the same hearty cheering as before, and the mugs were emptied to the dregs. But as the animals outside gazed at the scene, it seemed to them that some strange thing was happening. What was it that had altered in the faces of the pigs? Clover's old dim eyes flitted from one face to another. Some of them had five chins, some had four, some had three. But what was it that seemed to be melting and changing? Then, the applause having come to an end, the company took up their cards and continued the game that had been interrupted, and the animals crept silently away.

But they had not gone twenty yards when they stopped short. An uproar of voices was coming from the farmhouse. They rushed back and looked through the window again. Yes, a violent quarrel was in progress. There were shoutings, bangings on the table, sharp suspicious glances, furious denials. The source of the trouble appeared to be that Napoleon and Mr Pilkington had each played an ace of spades simultaneously.

Twelve voices were shouting in anger, and they were all alike. No question, now, what had happened to the faces of the pigs. The creatures outside looked from pig to man, and from man to pig, and from pig to man again: but already it was impossible to say which was which.

November 1943–February 1944

THE END

APPENDIX I

Orwell's Proposed Preface to Animal Farm

Space was allowed in the first edition of Animal Farm *for a preface by Orwell, as the pagination of the author's proof indicates. This preface was not included and the typescript was only found years later by Ian Angus. It was published, with an introduction by Professor Bernard Crick entitled 'How the essay came to be written', in* The Times Literary Supplement, *15 September 1972.*

The Freedom of the Press

This book was first thought of, so far as the central idea goes, in 1937, but was not written down until about the end of 1943. By the time when it came to be written it was obvious that there would be great difficulty in getting it published (in spite of the present book shortage which ensures that anything describable as a book will 'sell'), and in the event it was refused by four publishers. Only one of these had any ideological motive. Two had been publishing anti-Russian books for years, and the other had no noticeable political colour. One publisher actually started by accepting the book, but after making the preliminary arrangements he decided to consult the Ministry of Information, who appear to have warned him, or at any rate strongly advised him, against publishing it. Here is an extract from his letter:

I mentioned the reaction I had had from an important official in the Ministry of Information[1] with regard to *Animal Farm.* I must confess that this expression of opinion has given me seriously to think. . . . I can see now that it might be regarded as something which it was highly ill-advised to publish at the present time. If the fable were addressed generally to dictators and dictatorships at large then publication would be all right, but the fable does follow, as I see now, so completely the progress of the Russian Soviets and their two dictators, that it can apply only to Russia, to the exclusion of the other dictatorships. Another thing: it would be less offensive if the predominant caste in the fable were not pigs.* I think the choice of pigs as the ruling caste will no doubt give offence to many people, and particularly to anyone who is a bit touchy, as undoubtedly the Russians are.

This kind of thing is not a good symptom. Obviously it is not desirable that a government department should have any power of censorship (except security censorship, which no one objects to in war time) over books which are not officially sponsored. But the chief danger to freedom of thought and speech at this moment is not the direct interference of the

---

* It is not quite clear whether this suggested modification is Mr . . .'s own idea, or originated with the Ministry of Information; but it seems to have the official ring about it [Orwell's note].

MOI or any official body. If publishers and editors exert themselves to keep certain topics out of print, it is not because they are frightened of prosecution but because they are frightened of public opinion. In this country intellectual cowardice is the worst enemy a writer or journalist has to face, and that fact does not seem to me to have had the discussion it deserves.

Any fairminded person with journalistic experience will admit that during this war *official* censorship has not been particularly irksome. We have not been subjected to the kind of totalitarian 'co-ordination' that it might have been reasonable to expect. The press has some justified grievances, but on the whole the Government has behaved well and has been surprisingly tolerant of minority opinions. The sinister fact about literary censorship in England is that it is largely voluntary. Unpopular ideas can be silenced, and inconvenient facts kept dark, without the need for any official ban. Anyone who has lived long in a foreign country will know of instances of sensational items of news – things which on their own merits would get the big headlines – being kept right out of the British press, not because the Government intervened but because of a general tacit agreement that 'it wouldn't do' to mention that particular fact. So far as the daily newspapers go, this is easy to understand. The British press is extremely centralised, and most of it is owned by wealthy men who have every motive to be dishonest on certain important topics. But the same kind of veiled censorship also operates in books and periodicals, as well as in plays, films and radio. At any given moment there is an orthodoxy, a body of ideas which it is assumed that all right-thinking people will accept without question. It is not exactly forbidden to say this, that or the other, but it is 'not done' to say it, just as in mid-Victorian times it was 'not done' to mention trousers in the presence of a lady. Anyone who challenges the prevailing orthodoxy finds himself silenced with surprising effectiveness. A genuinely unfashionable opinion is almost never given a fair hearing, either in the popular press or in the highbrow periodicals.

At this moment what is demanded by the prevailing orthodoxy is an uncritical admiration of Soviet Russia. Everyone knows this, nearly everyone acts on it. Any serious criticism of the Soviet régime, any disclosure of facts which the Soviet government would prefer to keep hidden, is next door to unprintable. And this nation-wide conspiracy to flatter our ally takes place, curiously enough, against a background of genuine intellectual tolerance. For though you are not allowed to criticise the Soviet government, at least you are reasonably free to criticise our own. Hardly anyone will print an attack on Stalin, but it is quite safe to attack Churchill, at any rate in books and periodicals. And throughout five years of war, during two or three of which we were fighting for national survival, countless books, pamphlets and articles advocating a compromise peace have been published without interference. More, they have been published without exciting much disapproval. So long as the prestige of the USSR is not involved, the principle of free speech has been reasonably well upheld. There are other forbidden topics, and I shall mention some of them presently, but the prevailing attitude towards the USSR is much the most serious symptom. It is, as it were, spontaneous, and is not due to the action of any pressure group.

The servility with which the greater part of the English intelligentsia have swallowed and repeated Russian propaganda from 1941 onwards would be quite astounding if it were not that they have behaved similarly on several earlier occasions. On one controversial issue after another the Russian viewpoint has been accepted without examination and then publicised with complete disregard to historical truth or intellectual decency. To name only one instance, the BBC celebrated the twenty-fifth anniversary of the Red Army without mentioning Trotsky. This was about as accurate as commemorating the battle of Trafalgar without mentioning Nelson, but it evoked no protest from the English intelligentsia. In the internal struggles in the various occupied countries, the British press has in almost all cases sided with the faction favoured by the Russians and libelled the opposing faction, sometimes suppressing material evidence in order to do so. A particularly glaring case was that of Colonel Mihailovich, the Jugoslav Chetnik leader.[2] The Russians, who had their own Jugoslav protégé in Marshal Tito, accused Mihailovich of collaborating with the Germans. This accusation was promptly taken up by the British press: Mihailovich's supporters were given no chance of answering it, and facts contradicting it were simply kept out of print. In July of 1943 the Germans offered a reward of 100,000 gold crowns for the capture of Tito, and a similar reward for the capture of Mihailovich. The British press 'splashed' the reward for Tito, but only one paper mentioned (in small print) the reward for Mihailovich: and the charges of collaborating with the Germans continued. Very similar things happened during the Spanish civil war. Then, too, the factions on the Republican side which the Russians were determined to crush were recklessly libelled in the English leftwing [*sic*] press, and any statement in their defence even in letter form, was refused publication. At present, not only is serious criticism of the USSR considered reprehensible, but even the fact of the existence of such criticism is kept secret in some cases. For example, shortly before his death Trotsky had written a biography of Stalin. One may assume that it was not an altogether unbiased book, but obviously it was saleable. An American publisher had arranged to issue it and the book was in print – I believe the review copies had been sent out – when the USSR entered the war. The book was immediately withdrawn. Not a word about this has ever appeared in the British press, though clearly the existence of such a book, and its suppression, was a news item worth a few paragraphs.

It is important to distinguish between the kind of censorship that the English literary intelligentsia voluntarily impose upon themselves, and the censorship that can sometimes be enforced by pressure groups. Notoriously, certain topics cannot be discussed because of 'vested interests'. The best-known case is the patent medicine racket. Again, the Catholic Church has considerable influence in the press and can silence criticism of itself to some extent. A scandal involving a Catholic priest is almost never given publicity, whereas an Anglican priest who gets into trouble (e.g. the Rector of Stiffkey[3]) is headline news. It is very rare for anything of an anti-Catholic tendency to appear on the stage or in a film. Any actor can tell you that a play or film which attacks or makes fun of the Catholic Church is liable to be boycotted in the press and will probably be a failure. But this kind of thing is harmless, or at least it is understandable. Any large organisation will look after its own interests as best it can, and overt propaganda is not a thing to object to. One would no more expect the *Daily Worker* to publicise unfavourable facts about the USSR than one would expect the *Catholic Herald* to denounce the Pope. But then every thinking person knows the *Daily Worker* and the *Catholic Herald* for what they are. What is disquieting is that where the USSR and its policies are concerned one cannot expect intelligent criticism or even, in many cases, plain honesty from Liberal [*sic* – and throughout as typescript] writers and journalists who are under no direct pressure to falsify their opinions. Stalin is sacrosanct and certain aspects of his policy must not be seriously discussed. This rule has been almost universally observed since 1941, but it had operated, to a greater extent than is sometimes realised, for ten years earlier than that. Throughout that time, criticism of the Soviet régime *from the left* could only obtain a hearing with difficulty. There was a huge output of anti-Russian literature, but nearly all of it was from the Conservative angle and manifestly dishonest, out of date and actuated by sordid motives. On the other side there was an equally huge and almost equally dishonest stream of pro-Russian propaganda, and what amounted to a boycott on anyone who tried to discuss all-important questions in a grown-up manner. You could, indeed, publish anti-Russian books, but to do so was to make sure of being ignored or misrepresented by nearly the whole of the highbrow press. Both publicly and privately you were warned that it was 'not done'. What you said might possibly be true, but it was 'inopportune' and 'played into the hands of' this or that reactionary interest. This attitude was usually defended on the ground that the international situation, and the urgent need for an Anglo-Russian alliance, demanded it; but it was clear that this was a rationalisation. The English intelligentsia, or a great part of it, had developed a nationalistic loyalty towards the USSR, and in their hearts they felt that to cast any doubt on the wisdom of Stalin was a kind of blasphemy. Events in Russia and events elsewhere were to be judged by different standards. The endless executions in the purges of 1936–8 were applauded by life-long opponents of capital punishment, and it was considered equally proper to publicise famines when they happened in India and to conceal them when they happened in the Ukraine. And if this was true before the war, the intellectual atmosphere is certainly no better now.

But now to come back to this book of mine. The reaction towards it of most English intellectuals will be quite simple: 'It oughtn't to have been published.' Naturally, those reviewers who understand the art of denigration will not attack it on political grounds but on literary ones. They will say that it is a dull, silly book and a disgraceful waste of paper. This may well be true, but it is obviously not the whole of the story. One does not say that a book 'ought not to have been published' merely because it is a bad book. After all, acres of rubbish are printed daily and no one bothers. The English intelligentsia, or most of them, will object to this book because it traduces their Leader and (as they see it) does harm to the cause of progress. If it did the opposite they would have nothing to say against it, even if its literary faults were ten times as glaring as they are. The success of, for instance, the Left Book Club over a period of four or five years shows how willing they are to tolerate both scurrility and slipshod writing, provided that it tells them what they want to hear.

The issue involved here is quite a simple one: Is every opinion, however unpopular – however foolish, even – entitled to a hearing? Put it in that form and nearly any English intellectual will feel that he ought to say 'Yes'. But give it a concrete shape, and ask, 'How about an attack on Stalin? Is *that* entitled to a hearing?', and the answer more often than not will be 'No'. In that case the current orthodoxy happens to be challenged, and so the principle of free speech lapses. Now, when one demands liberty of speech and of the press, one is not demanding absolute liberty. There always must be, or at any rate there always will be, some degree of censorship, so long as organised societies endure. But freedom, as Rosa Luxembourg [sic] said, is 'freedom for the other fellow'. The same principle is contained in the famous words of Voltaire: 'I detest what you say; I will defend to the death your right to say it.'[4] If the intellectual liberty which without a doubt has been one of the distinguishing marks of western civilisation means anything at all, it means that everyone shall have the right to say and to print what he believes to be the truth, provided only that it does not harm the rest of the community in some quite unmistakable way. Both capitalist democracy and the western versions of Socialism have till recently taken that principle for granted. Our Government, as I have already pointed out, still makes some show of respecting it. The ordinary people in the street – partly, perhaps, because they are not sufficiently interested in ideas to be intolerant about them – still vaguely hold that 'I suppose everyone's got a right to their own opinion.' It is only, or at any rate it is chiefly, the literary and scientific intelligentsia, the very people who ought to be the guardians of liberty, who are beginning to despise it, in theory as well as in practice.

One of the peculiar phenomena of our time is the renegade Liberal. Over and above the familiar Marxist claim that 'bourgeois liberty' is an illusion, there is now a widespread tendency to argue that one can only defend democracy by totalitarian methods. If one loves democracy, the argument runs, one must crush its enemies by no matter what means. And who are its enemies? It always appears that they are not only those who attack it openly and consciously, but those who 'objectively' endanger it by spreading mistaken doctrines. In other words, defending democracy involves destroying all independence of thought. This argument was used, for instance, to justify the Russian purges. The most ardent Russophile hardly believed that all of the victims were guilty of all the things they were accused of: but by holding heretical opinions they 'objectively' harmed the régime, and therefore it was quite right not only to massacre them but to discredit them by false accusations. The same argument was used to justify the quite conscious lying that went on in the leftwing press about the Trotskyists and other Republican minorities in the Spanish civil war. And it was used again as a reason for yelping against *habeas corpus* when Mosley was released in 1943.

These people don't see that if you encourage totalitarian methods, the time may come when they will be used against you instead of for you. Make a habit of imprisoning Fascists without trial, and perhaps the process won't stop at Fascists. Soon after the suppressed *Daily Worker* had been reinstated, I was lecturing to a workingmen's college in South London. The audience were working-class and lower-middle-class intellectuals – the same sort of audience that one used to meet at Left Book Club branches. The lecture had touched on the freedom of the press, and at the end, to my astonishment, several questioners stood up and asked me: Did I not think that the lifting of the ban on the *Daily Worker* was a great mistake? When asked why, they said that it was a paper of doubtful loyalty and ought not to be tolerated in war time. I found myself defending the *Daily Worker*, which has gone out of its way to libel me more than once. But where had these people learned this essentially totalitarian outlook? Pretty certainly they had learned it from the Communists them-selves! Tolerance and decency are deeply rooted in England, but they are not indestructible, and they have to be kept alive partly by conscious effort. The result of preaching totalitarian doctrines is to weaken the instinct by means of which free peoples know what is or is not dangerous. The case of Mosley illustrates this. In 1940 it was perfectly right to intern

Mosley, whether or not he had committed any technical crime. We were fighting for our lives and could not allow a possible quisling to go free. To keep him shut up, without trial, in 1943 was an outrage. The general failure to see this was a bad symptom, though it is true that the agitation against Mosley's release was partly factitious and partly a rationalisation of other discontents. But how much of the present slide towards Fascist ways of thought is traceable to the 'anti-Fascism' of the past ten years and the unscrupulousness it has entailed?

It is important to realise that the current Russomania is only a symptom of the general weakening of the western liberal tradition. Had the MOI chipped in and definitely vetoed the publication of this book, the bulk of the English intelligentsia would have seen nothing disquieting in this. Uncritical loyalty to the USSR happens to be the current orthodoxy, and where the supposed interests of the USSR are involved they are willing to tolerate not only censorship but the deliberate falsification of history. To name one instance. At the death of John Reed, the author of *Ten Days that Shook the World* – a first-hand account of the early days of the Russian Revolution – the copyright of the book passed into the hands of the British Communist Party, to whom I believe Reed had bequeathed it. Some years later the British Communists, having destroyed the original edition of the book as completely as they could, issued a garbled version from which they had eliminated mentions of Trotsky and also omitted the introduction written by Lenin.[5] If a radical intelligentsia had still existed in Britain, this act of forgery would have been exposed and denounced in every literary paper in the country. As it was there was little or no protest. To many English intellectuals it seemed quite a natural thing to do. And this tolerance or [*sic* = of?] plain dishonesty means much more than that admiration for Russia happens to be fashionable at this moment. Quite possibly that particular fashion will not last. For all I know, by the time this book is published my view of the Soviet régime may be the generally-accepted one. But what use would that be in itself? To exchange one orthodoxy for another is not necessarily an advance. The enemy is the gramophone mind, whether or not one agrees with the record that is being played at the moment.

I am well acquainted with all the arguments against freedom of thought and speech – the arguments which claim that it cannot exist, and the arguments which claim that it ought not to. I answer simply that they don't convince me and that our civilisation over a period of four hundred years has been founded on the opposite notice.[6] For quite a decade past I have believed that the existing Russian régime is a mainly evil thing, and I claim the right to say so, in spite of the fact that we are allies with the USSR in a war which I want to see won. If I had to choose a text to justify myself, I should choose the line from Milton:

By the known rules of ancient liberty.[7]

The word *ancient* emphasises the fact that intellectual freedom is a deep-rooted tradition without which our characteristic western culture could only doubtfully exist. From that tradition many of our intellectuals are visibly turning away. They have accepted the principle that a book should be published or suppressed, praised or damned, not on its merits but according to political expediency. And others who do not actually hold this view assent to it from sheer cowardice. An example of this is the failure of the numerous and vocal English pacifists to raise their voices against the prevalent worship of Russian militarism. According to those pacifists, all violence is evil, and they have urged us at every stage of the war to give in or at least to make a compromise peace. But how many of them have ever suggested that war is also evil when it is waged by the Red Army? Apparently the Russians have a right to defend themselves, whereas for us to do [so] is a deadly sin. One can only explain this contradiction in one way: that is, by a cowardly desire to keep in with the bulk of the intelligentsia, whose patriotism is directed towards the USSR rather than towards Britain. I know that the English intelligentsia have plenty of reason for their timidity and dishonesty, indeed I know by heart the arguments by which they justify themselves. But at least let us have no more nonsense about defending liberty against Fascism. If liberty means anything at all it means the right to tell people what they do not want to hear. The common people still vaguely subscribe to that doctrine and act on it. In our country – it is not the same in all countries: it was not so in republican France, and it is not so in the USA today – it is the liberals who fear liberty and the intellectuals who want to do dirt on the intellect: it is to draw attention to that fact that I have written this preface.

1. This was almost certainly Peter Smollett (real name Smolka; 1912–80), author, journalist and Soviet agent: see the headnote on the completion of *Animal Farm*, above.

2. General Draža Mihailović (1893?–1946) led the Chetnik guerrillas against the Axis during World War II. He and Tito failed to agree, and Tito won Allied support. After the war, Mihaílović was tried for treason and executed. See also *1579, n. 2.*

3. The Reverend Harold Davidson, when Rector of Stiffkey, Norfolk, though commended by the Bishop of London for his missionary work, was defrocked by Norwich Consistory Court for immoral practices. The case proved a field-day for the popular press. Davidson thereafter made a living by entertaining cinema audiences and then appearing in a barrel as an attraction at Blackpool Pleasure Beach. 'In the end, like the early Christians, he was thrown to the lions' (*The Thirties*, 172). He was exhibited in 1937 in a circus cage of lions but was mauled and killed.

4. Attributed to Voltaire by S. G. Tallentyre, *The Friends of Voltaire* (1907).

5. There is no evidence that such a 'garbled' edition was issued by the British Communist Party or anyone else. Orwell may be confusing the attempt by the *News Chronicle* to serialize *Ten Days that Shook the World* in 1937 to mark the twentieth anniversary of the Russian Revolution. This the Party would only permit if all references to Trotsky were removed. See *New Leader*, 19 November 1937 and *Evening Standard*, 12 November 1937. (Information from Clive Fleay and Mike Sanders.) See also Orwell's fourth annotation to Randall Swingler's 'The Right to Free Expression', *Polemic*, 5, Sept.–Oct. 1946, XVIII/*3090.*

6. notice: Orwell possibly intended 'notion'.

7. Compare the first two lines of the epigram from Euripides' *The Suppliants* on the title-page of Milton's *Areopagitica* (1644): 'This is true Liberty when free born men / Having to advise the public may speak free.'

APPENDIX II

Orwell's Preface to the Ukrainian Edition of Animal Farm

21 March 1947 (XIX/3197)

The Ukrainian translation of Animal Farm *was intended for Ukrainians living in the camps for Displaced Persons in Germany under British and American administration after World War II. These, as indicated in a letter from the man who organized the translation and distribution, Ihor Szewczenko, were people who supported the October Revolution and who were determined to defend what had been won, but who had turned against 'the counter-revolutionary Bonapartism of Stalin' and the 'Russian nationalistic exploitation of the Ukrainian people'. They were simple people, peasants and workers, some half-educated, but all of whom read eagerly. For these people he asked Orwell to write a special introduction. The English original has been lost and the version reproduced here is a recasting back into English*

of the Ukrainian version. Orwell insisted that he receive no royalties for this
edition, nor for other translations intended for those too poor to buy them
(e.g., editions in Persian and Telugu). Orwell himself paid the production
costs of a Russian-language edition printed on thin paper, which was
intended for soldiers and others behind the Iron Curtain.

I have been asked to write a preface to the Ukrainian translation of *Animal Farm*. I am aware that I write for readers about whom I know nothing, but also that they too have probably never had the slightest opportunity to know anything about me.

In this preface they will most likely expect me to say something of how *Animal Farm* originated but first I would like to say something about myself and the experiences by which I arrived at my political position.

I was born in India in 1903. My father was an official in the English administration there, and my family was one of those ordinary middle-class families of soldiers, clergymen, government officials, teachers, lawyers, doctors, etc. I was educated at Eton, the most costly and snobbish of the English Public Schools.* But I had only got in there by means of a scholarship; otherwise my father could not have afforded to send me to a school of this type.

Shortly after I left school (I wasn't quite twenty years old then) I went to Burma and joined the Indian Imperial Police. This was an armed police, a sort of *gendarmerie* very similar to the Spanish *Guardia Civil* or the *Garde Mobile* in France. I stayed five years in the service. It did not suit me and made me hate imperialism, although at that time nationalist feelings in Burma were not very marked, and relations between the English and the Burmese were not particularly unfriendly. When on leave in England in

---

* These are not public 'national schools', but something quite the opposite: exclusive and expensive residential secondary schools, scattered far apart. Until recently they admitted almost no one but the sons of rich aristocratic families. It was the dream of *nouveau riche* bankers of the nineteenth century to push their sons into a Public School. At such schools the greatest stress is laid on sport, which forms, so to speak, a lordly, tough and gentlemanly outlook. Among these schools, Eton is particularly famous. Wellington is reported to have said that the victory of Waterloo was decided on the playing fields of Eton. It is not so very long ago that an overwhelming majority of the people who in one way or another ruled England came from the Public Schools [Orwell's note].

1927, I resigned from the service and decided to become a writer: at first without any especial success. In 1928–9 I lived in Paris and wrote short stories and novels that nobody would print (I have since destroyed them all). In the following years I lived mostly from hand to mouth, and went hungry on several occasions. It was only from 1934 onwards that I was able to live on what I earned from my writing. In the meantime I sometimes lived for months on end amongst the poor and half-criminal elements who inhabit the worst parts of the poorer quarters, or take to the streets, begging and stealing. At that time I associated with them through lack of money, but later their way of life interested me very much for its own sake. I spent many months (more systematically this time) studying the conditions of the miners in the north of England. Up to 1930 I did not on the whole look upon myself as a Socialist. In fact I had as yet no clearly defined political views. I became pro-Socialist more out of disgust with the way the poorer section of the industrial workers were oppressed and neglected than out of any theoretical admiration for a planned society.

In 1936 I got married. In almost the same week the civil war broke out in Spain. My wife and I both wanted to go to Spain and fight for the Spanish Government. We were ready in six months, as soon as I had finished the book I was writing. In Spain I spent almost six months on the Aragón front until, at Huesca, a Fascist sniper shot me through the throat.

In the early stages of the war foreigners were on the whole unaware of the inner struggles between the various political parties supporting the Government. Through a series of accidents I joined not the International Brigade like the majority of foreigners, but the POUM militia – i.e. the Spanish Trotskyists.

So in the middle of 1937, when the Communists gained control (or partial control) of the Spanish Government and began to hunt down the Trotskyists, we both found ourselves amongst the victims. We were very lucky to get out of Spain alive, and not even to have been arrested once. Many of our friends were shot, and others spent a long time in prison or simply disappeared.

These man-hunts in Spain went on at the same time as the great purges in the USSR and were a sort of supplement to them. In Spain as well as in Russia the nature of the accusations (namely, conspiracy with the Fascists) was the same and as far as Spain was concerned I had every reason to believe that the accusations were false. To experience all this was a valuable object lesson: it taught me how easily totalitarian propaganda can control the opinion of enlightened people in democratic countries.

My wife and I both saw innocent people being thrown into prison merely because they were suspected of unorthodoxy. Yet on our return to England we found numerous sensible and well-informed observers believing the most fantastic accounts of conspiracy, treachery and sabotage which the press reported from the Moscow trials.

And so I understood, more clearly than ever, the negative influence of the Soviet myth upon the western Socialist movement.

And here I must pause to describe my attitude to the Soviet régime.

I have never visited Russia and my knowledge of it consists only of what can be learned by reading books and newspapers. Even if I had the power, I would not wish to interfere in Soviet domestic affairs: I would not condemn Stalin and his associates merely for their barbaric and undemocratic methods. It is quite possible that, even with the best intentions, they could not have acted otherwise under the conditions prevailing there.

But on the other hand it was of the utmost importance to me that people in western Europe should see the Soviet régime for what it really was. Since 1930 I had seen little evidence that the USSR was progressing towards anything that one could truly call Socialism. On the contrary, I was struck by clear signs of its transformation into a hierarchical society, in which the rulers have no more reason to give up their power than any other ruling class. Moreover, the workers and intelligentsia in a country like England cannot understand that the USSR of today is altogether different from what it was in 1917. It is partly that they do not want to understand (i.e. they want to believe that, somewhere, a really Socialist country does actually exist), and partly that, being accustomed to comparative freedom and moderation in public life, totalitarianism is completely incomprehensible to them.

Yet one must remember that England is not completely democratic. It is also a capitalist country with great class privileges and (even now, after a war that has tended to equalise everybody) with great differences in wealth. But nevertheless it is a country in which people have lived together for several hundred years without major conflict, in which the laws are relatively just and official news and statistics can almost invariably be believed, and, last but not least, in which to hold and to voice minority views does not involve any mortal danger. In such an atmosphere the man in the street has no real understanding of things like concentration camps, mass deportations, arrests without trial, press censorship, etc. Everything he reads about a country like the USSR is automatically translated into English terms, and he quite innocently accepts the lies of totalitarian propaganda. Up to 1939, and even later, the majority of English people were incapable of assessing the true nature of the Nazi régime in Germany, and now, with the Soviet régime, they are still to a large extent under the same sort of illusion.

This has caused great harm to the Socialist movement in England, and had serious consequences for English foreign policy. Indeed, in my opinion, nothing has contributed so much to the corruption of the original idea of Socialism as the belief that Russia is a Socialist country and that every act of its rulers must be excused, if not imitated.

And so for the past ten years I have been convinced that the destruction of the Soviet myth was essential if we wanted a revival of the Socialist movement.

On my return from Spain I thought of exposing the Soviet myth in a story that could be easily understood by almost anyone and which could be easily translated into other languages. However, the actual details of the story did not come to me for some time until one day (I was then living in a small village) I saw a little boy, perhaps ten years old, driving a huge cart-horse along a narrow path, whipping it whenever it tried to turn. It struck me that if only such animals became aware of their strength we should have no power over them, and that men exploit animals in much the same way as the rich exploit the proletariat.

I proceeded to analyse Marx's theory from the animals' point of view. To them it was clear that the concept of a class struggle between humans was pure illusion, since whenever it was necessary to exploit animals, all humans united against them: the true struggle is between animals and humans. From this point of departure, it was not difficult to elaborate the story. I did not write it out till 1943, for I was always engaged on other work which gave me no time; and in the end I included some events, for example the Teheran Conference,[1] which were taking place while I was writing. Thus the main outlines of the story were in my mind over a period of six years before it was actually written.

I do not wish to comment on the work; if it does not speak for itself, it is a failure. But I should like to emphasise two points: first, that although the various episodes are taken from the actual history of the Russian Revolution, they are dealt with schematically and their chronological order is changed; this was necessary for the symmetry of the story. The second point has been missed by most critics, possibly because I did not emphasise it sufficiently. A number of readers may finish the book with the impression that it ends in the complete reconciliation of the pigs and the humans. That was not my intention; on the contrary I meant it to end on a loud note of discord, for I wrote it immediately after the Teheran Conference which everybody thought had established the best possible relations between the USSR and the West. I personally did not believe that such good relations would last long; and, as events have shown, I wasn't far wrong.

I don't know what more I need add. If anyone is interested in personal details, I should add that I am a widower with a son almost three years old, that by profession I am a writer, and that since the beginning of the war I have worked mainly as a journalist.

The periodical to which I contribute most regularly is *Tribune*, a socio-political weekly which represents, generally speaking, the left wing of the Labour Party. The following of my books might most interest the ordinary reader (should any reader of this translation find copies of them): *Burmese Days* (a story about Burma), *Homage to Catalonia* (arising from my experiences in the Spanish Civil War), and *Critical Essays* (essays mainly about contemporary popular English literature and instructive more from the sociological than from the literary point of view).

1. The Teheran Conference, 28 November to 1 December 1943, was the first of three conferences held by the leaders of Britain, the USA and the USSR. It was attended by Churchill, Roosevelt and Stalin. At Teheran agreement was reached on a date for the invasion of Western Europe by Britain and the USA. The same three leaders attended a conference at Yalta, 4–12 February 1945, which discussed plans for dealing with a defeated

Germany and a liberated Europe. The third conference, at Potsdam, 17 July to 2 August 1945, was attended by Stalin, Truman for Roosevelt (who had died), and at first Churchill, but he was replaced by Attlee when the result of the British General Election was announced. This conference led to the agreement on dividing Germany into four zones, reparations and new borders for Poland.

[2441]

'As I Please', 17 [What is Fascism?]
Tribune, 24 March 1944

Of all the unanswered questions of our time, perhaps the most important is: 'What is Fascism?'

One of the social survey organisations in America recently asked this question of a hundred different people, and got answers ranging from 'pure democracy' to 'pure diabolism'. In this country if you ask the average thinking person to define Fascism, he usually answers by pointing to the German and Italian régimes. But this is very unsatisfactory, because even the major Fascist states differ from one another a good deal in structure and ideology.

It is not easy, for instance, to fit Germany and Japan into the same framework, and it is even harder with some of the small states which are describable as Fascist. It is usually assumed, for instance, that Fascism is inherently warlike, that it thrives in an atmosphere of war hysteria and can only solve its economic problems by means of war-preparation or foreign conquests. But clearly this is not true of, say, Portugal or the various South American dictatorships. Or again, anti-Semitism is supposed to be one of the distinguishing marks of Fascism; but some Fascist movements are not anti-Semitic. Learned controversies, reverberating for years on end in American magazines, have not even been able to determine whether or not Fascism is a form of Capitalism. But still, when we apply the term 'Fascism' to Germany or Japan or Mussolini's Italy, we know broadly what we mean. It is in internal politics that this word has lost the last vestige of meaning. For if you examine the Press you will find that there is almost no set of people – certainly no political party or organised body of any kind – which has not been denounced as Fascist during the past ten years.

Here I am not speaking of the verbal use of the term 'Fascist'. I am speaking of what I have seen in print. I have seen the words 'Fascist in sympathy', or 'of Fascist tendency', or just plain 'Fascist', applied in all seriousness to the following bodies of people:

Conservatives: All Conservatives, appeasers or anti-appeasers, are held to be subjectively pro-Fascist. British rule in India and the Colonies is held to be indistinguishable from Nazism. Organisations of what one might call a patriotic and traditional type are labelled crypto-Fascist or 'Fascist-minded'. Examples are the Boy Scouts, the Metropolitan Police, M.I.5,[1] the British Legion. Key phrase: 'The public schools are breeding-grounds of Fascism.'

Socialists: Defenders of old-style capitalism (example, Sir Ernest Benn)[2] maintain that Socialism and Fascism are the same thing. Some Catholic journalists maintain that Socialists have been the principal collaborators in the Nazi-occupied countries. The same accusation is made from a different angle by the Communist Party during its ultra-Left phases. In the period 1930–5 the *Daily Worker* habitually referred to the Labour Party as the Labour Fascists. This is echoed by other Left extremists such as Anarchists. Some Indian Nationalists consider the British trade unions to be Fascist organisations.

Communists: A considerable school of thought (examples, Rauschning,[3] Peter Drucker,[4] James Burnham, F. A. Voigt[5]) refuses to recognise a difference between the Nazi and Soviet régimes; and holds that all Fascists and Communists are aiming at approximately the same thing and are even to some extent the same people. Leaders in *The Times* (pre-war) have referred to the U.S.S.R. as a 'Fascist country'. Again from a different angle this is echoed by Anarchists and Trotskyists.

Trotskyists: Communists charge the Trotskyists proper, i.e., Trotsky's own organisation, with being a crypto-Fascist organisation in Nazi pay. This was widely believed on the Left during the Popular Front period. In their ultra-Right phases the Communists tend to apply the same accusation to all fractions[6] to the Left of themselves, e.g., Common Wealth or the I.L.P.

Catholics: Outside its own ranks, the Catholic Church is almost universally regarded as pro-Fascist, both objectively and subjectively.

War-resisters: Pacifists and others who are anti-war are frequently accused not only of making things easier for the Axis, but of becoming tinged with pro-Fascist feeling.

Supporters of the war: War-resisters usually base their case on the claim that British Imperialism is worse than Nazism, and tend to apply the term 'Fascist' to anyone who wishes for a military victory. The supporters of the People's Convention came near to claiming that willingness to resist a Nazi invasion was a sign of Fascist sympathies. The Home Guard was denounced as a Fascist organisation as soon as it appeared. In addition, the whole of the Left tends to equate militarism with Fascism. Politically conscious private soldiers nearly always refer to their officers as 'Fascist-minded' or 'natural Fascists'. Battle schools, spit and polish, saluting of officers are all considered conducive to Fascism. Before the war, joining the Territorials was regarded as a sign of Fascist tendencies. Conscription and a professional army are both denounced as Fascist phenomena.

Nationalists: Nationalism is universally regarded as inherently Fascist, but this is held only to apply to such national movements as the speaker happens to disapprove of. Arab nationalism, Polish nationalism, Finnish nationalism, the Indian Congress Party, the Muslim League, Zionism, and the I.R.A. are all described as Fascist – but not by the same people.

It will be seen that, as used, the word 'Fascism' is almost entirely meaningless. In conversation, of course, it is used even more wildly than in print. I have heard it applied to farmers, shopkeepers, Social Credit, corporal punishment, foxhunting, bullfighting, the 1922 Committee, the 1941 Committee, Kipling, Gandhi, Chiang Kai-Shek, homosexuality, Priestley's broadcasts, Youth Hostels, astrology, women, dogs and I do not know what else.

Yet underneath all this mess there does lie a kind of buried meaning. To begin with, it is clear that there are very great differences, some of them easy to point out and not easy to explain away, between the régimes called Fascist and those called democratic. Secondly, if 'Fascist' means 'in sympathy with Hitler', some of the accusations I have listed above are obviously very much more justified than others. Thirdly, even the people who recklessly fling the word 'Fascist' in every direction attach at any rate an emotional significance to it. By 'Fascism' they mean, roughly speaking, something cruel, unscrupulous, arrogant, obscurantist, anti-liberal and anti-working-class. Except for the relatively small number of

Fascist sympathisers, almost any English person would accept 'bully' as a synonym for 'Fascist'. That is about as near to a definition as this much-abused word has come.

But Fascism is also a political and economic system. Why, then, cannot we have a clear and generally accepted definition of it? Alas! we shall not get one – not yet, anyway. To say why would take too long, but basically it is because it is impossible to define Fascism satisfactorily without making admissions which neither the Fascists themselves, nor the Conservatives, nor Socialists of any colour, are willing to make. All one can do for the moment is to use the word with a certain amount of circumspection and not, as is usually done, degrade it to the level of a swearword.

1. Military Intelligence [Section] 5: the British internal security service answerable for many years only to the Prime Minister through the Home Secretary. MI6, the Secret Intelligence Service, operated outside the United Kingdom and was answerable to the Foreign Secretary.
2. Sir Ernest Benn (1875–1954) was founder of Benn's Sixpenny Library and Sixpenny Poets, and publisher of the Blue Guides (travel books). Among his own publications were *Confessions of a Capitalist* (1925), which espoused an 'austere Victorian *laisser-faire*' philosophy (*DNB*), and *Governed to Death* (a pamphlet, 1948). In August 1942 he had a main finger in drafting a manifesto on British liberty and three months later in founding the Society of Individualists.
3. Hermann Rauschning (1887–1982) was described by Orwell in 'Wells, Hitler and the World State' (see *837*) as among the best authors of the 'political book'. Orwell equated him in this respect with Trotsky, Silone, Borkenau and Koestler, among others. William Steinhoff, in *George Orwell and the Origins of 1984* (1975), arguing that 'Orwell understood totalitarianism', states that the long dialogue between O'Brien and Winston Smith in *Nineteen Eighty-Four* 'demonstrates Orwell's awareness that implicit in totalitarianism is a desire for expansion – physical, intellectual, spiritual – that, as Rauschning said, recognizes no limits' (208); Steinhoff lists Rauschning's *The Revolution of Nihilism* (London and New York, 1939) in his bibliography. Rauschning also published (in several language versions) *Hitler Speaks: A Series of Political Conversations with Adolf Hitler on His Real Aims* (1939) and *The Conservative Revolution* (New York, 1941). From 1948 until his death he lived as a farmer in Oregon.
4. Peter Drucker (1909–), author and university teacher. He was born in Vienna and emigrated to the USA in 1937. He wrote over thirty books. Those in the early thirties are in German. His *The End of Economic Man: A Study of the New Totalitarianism* was published in 1939 and *The Future of Industrial Man: A Conservative Approach* in 1942 in New York, and the next year in London. Orwell recommended the latter to readers of the *Manchester Evening News* on 3 January 1946; see 'The Intellectual Revolt', below.
5. F. A. Voigt (1892–1957) was an outstanding foreign correspondent. He was one of the first to draw attention to the dangers of National Socialism, through his columns in the *Manchester Guardian*. So effective was his analysis of the rise of Nazism that he was unable to work in Germany after Hitler came to power in 1933. He reported from Barcelona during the Spanish Civil War. His *Unto Caesar* was published in 1938. Orwell grouped him with

Anglophobes who suddenly became violently pro-British, in his 'Notes on Nationalism', and among 'The Pessimists', in his essay 'The Intellectual Revolt'; see below. He edited *The Nineteenth Century and After* from 1938 to 1946.
6. 'factions' may be intended.

[2468]

Review of Empire *by Louis Fischer*
Nation *(New York), 13 May 1944*

Imperialism means India, and in so short and 'popular' a book Mr. Fischer is quite right to ignore the more complex colonial problems that exist in Africa and the Pacific. He is not trying to stimulate anti-British prejudice, and the uninformed reader would come away from this book with a true general picture as well as some quotable facts and figures.

As he perceives, the uninformed reader is the one most worth aiming at. No enlightened person needs any longer to be told that imperialism is an evil. The point Mr. Fischer is at pains to make clear is that it not only breeds war but impoverishes the world as a whole by preventing the development of backward areas. The 'owner' of a colony usually does its best to exclude foreign trade; it strangles local industries – the British, to take only one instance, have deliberately prevented the growth of an automobile industry in India; and in self-protection it not only goes on the principle of 'divide and rule' but more or less consciously fosters ignorance and superstition. In the long run it is not to the advantage, even in crude cash terms, of the ordinary Briton or American that India should remain in the Middle Ages; and the common people of both countries ought to realize this, for they are the only ones who are likely to do anything about it. No one in his senses imagines that the British ruling class will relinquish India voluntarily. The only hope lies in British and American public opinion, which at the time of the Cripps mission, for instance, could have forced a more generous offer upon the British government if it had understood the issues.

At the same time Mr. Fischer does oversimplify the Indian problem, even in terms of the very general picture that he is trying to give. To begin with, he does not say often enough or emphatically enough that

India has no chance of freedom until some sort of international authority is established. In a world of national sovereignties and power politics it is improbable that even a British government of the left would willingly grant genuine independence to India. To do so would simply be to hand India over to some other power, which from either a selfish or an altruistic point of view is no solution. Secondly, in his anxiety to sound reasonable Mr. Fischer overplays the economic motive. It is not certain that increased prosperity for India would benefit the rest of the world *immediately*. Just suppose, he says, that 400,000,000 Indians all took to wearing shoes. Would not that mean a wonderful market for British and American shoe manufacturers? The Indians, however, might prefer to make their shoes for themselves, and as the Indian capitalist's idea of a living wage is two cents an hour, the effect of Indian competition on the Western standard of living might be disastrous. At present the West as a whole is exploiting Asia as a whole, and to right the balance may mean considerable sacrifices over a number of years. It is better to warn people of this and not lead them to imagine that honesty always pays in the financial sense.

The direct, assessable money profit that Britain draws from India is not enormous. If one divided it up amongst the British population it would only amount to a few pounds a year. But as Mr. Fischer rightly emphasizes, it is not divided among the population; it flows into the pockets of a few thousand persons who also control government policy and incidentally own all the newspapers. Up to date these people have been uniformly successful in keeping the truth about India from the British public. To enlighten the American public may perhaps be a little easier, since American interests are not so directly involved, and Mr. Fischer's book is not bad as a start. But he ought to supplement it by warning his readers of the difficult transition period that lies ahead, and also of the sinister forces, political and economic, that exist within India itself.

[2481]

'Benefit of Clergy: Some Notes on Salvador Dali'
Intended for The Saturday Book, *4, 1944*

Although not directly 'political', 'Benefit of Clergy' is important in this context as a revelation of the moral stance underlying Orwell's approach to people and politics. See especially the last sentences of the final two paragraphs and note 9. Before The Saturday Book *in which it first appeared was distributed, the publishers took fright and, fearing it was obscene, had the essay sliced out of the bound copies (though the contents page still listed the title). A few copies escaped the razor, hence this text. When Evelyn Waugh reviewed Orwell's* Critical Essays *(in which this essay was printed) in the Roman Catholic journal,* The Tablet, *in 1946, he noted the essay had originally been suppressed, and commented: 'there is nothing in [Orwell's] writing that is inconsistent with high moral principles' (2898, XVIII/107). The essay was prompted by Dali's autobiography,* The Secret Life of Salvador Dali *(New York, 1942).*

Autobiography is only to be trusted when it reveals something disgraceful. A man who gives a good account of himself is probably lying, since any life when viewed from the inside is simply a series of defeats. However, even the most flagrantly dishonest book (Frank Harris's autobiographical writings are an example) can without intending it give a true picture of its author. Dali's recently-published *Life* comes under this heading. Some of the incidents in it are flatly incredible, others have been re-arranged and romanticised, and not merely the humiliation but the persistent *ordinariness* of everyday life has been cut out. Dali is even by his own diagnosis narcissistic, and his autobiography is simply a strip-tease act conducted in pink limelight. But as a record of fantasy, of the perversion of instinct that has been made possible by the machine age, it has great value.

Here then are some of the episodes in Dali's life, from his earliest years onward. Which of them are true and which are imaginary hardly matters: the point is that this is the kind of thing that Dali would have *liked* to do.

When he is six years old there is some excitement over the appearance of Halley's comet:

Suddenly one of my father's office clerks appeared in the drawing-room doorway and announced that the comet could be seen from the terrace . . . While crossing the hall I caught sight of my little three-year-old sister crawling unobtrusively through a doorway. I stopped, hesitated a second, then gave her a terrible kick in the head as though it had been a ball, and continued running carried away with a 'delirious joy' induced by this savage act. But my father, who was behind me, caught me and led me down into his office, where I remained as a punishment till dinner time.

A year earlier than this Dali had 'suddenly, as most of my ideas occur' flung another little boy off a suspension bridge. Several other incidents of the same kind are recorded, including (this was when he was twenty-nine years old) knocking down and trampling on a girl 'until they had to tear her, bleeding, out of my reach'.

When he is about five he gets hold of a wounded bat which he puts into a tin pail. Next morning he finds that the bat is almost dead and is covered with ants which are devouring it. He puts it in his mouth, ants and all, and bites it almost in half.

When he is adolescent a girl falls desperately in love with him. He kisses and caresses her so as to excite her as much as possible, but refuses to go further. He resolves to keep this up for five years (he calls it his 'five year plan'), enjoying her humiliation and the sense of power it gives him. He frequently tells her that at the end of five years he will desert her, and when the time comes he does so.

Till well into adult life he keeps up the practice of masturbation, and likes to do this, apparently, in front of a looking-glass. For ordinary purposes he is impotent, it appears, till the age of thirty or so. When he first meets his future wife, Gala, he is greatly tempted to push her off a precipice. He is aware that there is something that she wants him to do to her, and after their first kiss the confession is made:

I threw back Gala's head, pulling it by the hair, and, trembling with complete hysteria, I commanded,

'Now tell me what you want me to do with you! But tell me slowly, looking me in the eye, with the crudest, the most ferociously erotic words that can make both of us feel the greatest shame!'

... Then, Gala, transforming the last glimmer of her expression of pleasure into the hard light of her own tyranny, answered,

'I want you to kill me!'

He is somewhat disappointed by this demand, since it is merely what he wanted to do already. He contemplates throwing her off the bell-tower of the Cathedral of Toledo, but refrains from doing so.

During the Spanish Civil War he astutely avoids taking sides and makes a trip to Italy. He feels himself more and more drawn towards the aristocracy, frequents smart salons, finds himself wealthy patrons, and is photographed with the plump Vicomte de Noailles, whom he describes as his 'Maecenas'. When the European war approaches he has one preoccupation only: how to find a place which has good cookery and from which he can make a quick bolt if danger comes too near. He fixes on Bordeaux, and duly flees to Spain during the Battle of France. He stays in Spain long enough to pick up a few anti-Red atrocity stories, then makes for America. The story ends in a blaze of respectability. Dali, at thirty-seven, has become a devoted husband, is cured of his aberrations, or some of them, and is completely reconciled to the Catholic Church. He is also, one gathers, making a good deal of money.

However, he has by no means ceased to take pride in the pictures of his Surrealist period, with titles like *The Great Masturbator*, *Sodomy of a Skull with a Grand Piano*, etc. There are reproductions of these all the way through the book. Many of Dali's drawings are simply representational and have a characteristic to be noted later. But from his Surrealist paintings and photographs the two things that stand out are sexual perversity and necrophilia. Sexual objects and symbols – some of them well-known, like our old friend the high-heeled slipper, others, like the crutch and the cup of warm milk, patented by Dali himself – recur over and over again, and there is a fairly well-marked excretory motif as well. In his painting *Le Jeu Lugubre*, he says, 'the drawers bespattered with excrement were painted with such minute and realistic complacency that the whole little surrealist group was anguished by the question: Is he coprophagic or not?' Dali adds firmly that he is *not*, and that he regards this aberration as repulsive, but it seems to be only at that point that his interest in excrement stops. Even when he recounts the experience of watching a woman urinate standing up, he has to add the detail that she misses her aim and dirties her shoes. It is not given to any one person to have all the vices, and Dali also boasts that he is not homosexual, but otherwise he seems to have as good an outfit of perversions as anyone could wish for.

However, his most notable characteristic is his necrophilia. He himself freely admits to this, and claims to have been cured of it. Dead faces, skulls, corpses of animals occur fairly frequently in his pictures, and the ants which devoured the dying bat make countless reappearances. One photograph shows an exhumed corpse, far gone in decomposition. Another shows the dead donkeys putrefying on top of grand pianos which formed part of the Surrealist film *Le Chien Andalou*.[1] Dali still looks back on these donkeys with great enthusiasm:

> I 'made up' the putrefaction of the donkeys with great pots of sticky glue which I poured over them. Also I emptied their eye sockets and made them larger by hacking them out with scissors. In the same way I furiously cut their mouths open to make the white rows of their teeth show to better advantage, and I added several jaws to each mouth so that it would appear that although the donkeys were already rotting they were vomiting up a little more of their own death, above those other rows of teeth formed by the keys of the black pianos.

And finally there is the picture – apparently some kind of faked photograph – of *Mannequin rotting in a taxicab*. Over the already somewhat bloated face and breast of the apparently dead girl, huge snails are crawling. In the caption below the picture Dali notes that these are Burgundy snails – that is, the edible kind.

Of course, in this long book of 400 quarto pages there is more than I have indicated, but I do not think that I have given an unfair account of its moral atmosphere and mental scenery. It is a book that stinks. If it were possible for a book to give a physical stink off its pages, this one would – a thought that might please Dali, who before wooing his future wife for the first time rubbed himself all over with an ointment made of goat's dung boiled up in fish glue. But against this has to be set the fact that Dali is a draughtsman of very exceptional gifts. He is also, to judge by the minuteness and the sureness of his drawings, a very hard worker. He is an exhibitionist and a careerist, but he is not a fraud. He has fifty times more talent than most of the people who would denounce his morals and jeer at his paintings. And these two sets of facts, taken together, raise a question which for lack of any basis of agreement seldom gets a real discussion.

The point is that you have here a direct, unmistakable assault on sanity and decency: and even – since some of Dali's pictures would tend to poison the imagination like a pornographic postcard – on life itself. What Dali has done and what he has imagined is debatable, but in his outlook, his character, the bedrock decency of a human being does not exist. He is as anti-social as a flea. Clearly, such people are undesirable, and a society in which they can flourish has something wrong with it.

Now, if you showed this book, with its illustrations, to Lord Elton,[2] to Mr Alfred Noyes,[3] to *The Times* leader-writers who exult over the 'eclipse of the highbrow', in fact to any 'sensible' art-hating English person, it is easy to imagine what kind of response you would get. They would flatly refuse to see any merit in Dali whatever. Such people are not only unable to admit that what is morally degraded can be aesthetically right, but their real demand of every artist is that he shall pat them on the back and tell them that thought is unnecessary. And they can be especially dangerous at a time like the present, when the Ministry of Information and the British Council put power into their hands. For their impulse is not only to crush every new talent as it appears, but to castrate the past as well. Witness the renewed highbrow-baiting that is now going on in this country and America, with its outcry not only against Joyce, Proust, and Lawrence, but even against T. S. Eliot.

But if you talk to the kind of person who *can* see Dali's merits, the response that you get is not as a rule very much better. If you say that Dali, though a brilliant draughtsman, is a dirty little scoundrel, you are looked upon as a savage. If you say that you don't like rotting corpses, and that people who do like rotting corpses are mentally diseased, it is assumed that you lack the aesthetic sense. Since *Mannequin rotting in a taxicab* is a good composition (as it undoubtedly is), it cannot be a disgusting, degrading picture: whereas Noyes, Elton, etc., would tell you that because it is disgusting it cannot be a good composition. And between these two fallacies there is no middle position: or rather, there is a middle position, but we seldom hear much about it. On the one side, *Kulturbolschevismus*: on the other (though the phrase itself is out of fashion)

'Art for Art's sake'. Obscenity is a very difficult question to discuss honestly. People are too frightened either of seeming to be shocked, or of seeming not to be shocked, to be able to define the relationship between art and morals.

It will be seen that what the defenders of Dali are claiming is a kind of *benefit of clergy*.[4] The artist is to be exempt from the moral laws that are binding on ordinary people. Just pronounce the magic word 'Art', and everything is O.K. Rotting corpses with snails crawling over them are O.K.; kicking little girls on the head is O.K.; even a film like *L'Age d'Or*[5] is O.K.* It is also O.K. that Dali should batten on France for years and then scuttle off like a rat as soon as France is in danger. So long as you can paint well enough to pass the test, all shall be forgiven you.

One can see how false this is if one extends it to cover ordinary crime. In an age like our own, when the artist is an altogether exceptional person, he must be allowed a certain amount of irresponsibility, just as a pregnant woman is. Still, no one would say that a pregnant woman should be allowed to commit murder, nor would anyone make such a claim for the artist, however gifted. If Shakespeare returned to the earth tomorrow, and if it were found that his favourite recreation was raping little girls in railway carriages, we should not tell him to go ahead with it on the ground that he might write another *King Lear*. And after all, the worst crimes are not always the punishable ones. By encouraging necrophilic reveries one probably does quite as much harm as by, say, picking pockets at the races. One ought to be able to hold in one's head simultaneously the two facts that Dali is a good draughtsman and a disgusting human being. The one does not invalidate or, in a sense, affect the other. The first thing that we demand of a wall is that it shall stand up. If it stands up it is a good wall, and the question of what purpose it serves is separable from that. And yet even the best wall in the world deserves to be pulled down if it surrounds a concentration camp. In the same way it should be possible to say, 'This is a good book or a good picture, and it ought to

---

* Dali mentions *L'Age d'Or* and adds that its first public showing was broken up by hooligans, but he does not say in detail what it was about. According to Henry Miller's account of it, it showed among other things some fairly detailed shots of a woman defaecating [Orwell's footnote].

be burned by the public hangman.' Unless one can say that, at least in imagination, one is shirking the implications of the fact that an artist is also a citizen and a human being.

Not, of course, that Dali's autobiography, or his pictures, ought to be suppressed. Short of the dirty postcards that used to be sold in Mediterranean seaport towns, it is doubtful policy to suppress anything, and Dali's fantasies probably cast useful light on the decay of capitalist civilisation. But what he clearly needs is diagnosis. The question is not so much *what* he is as *why* he is like that. It ought not to be in doubt that he is a diseased intelligence, probably not much altered by his alleged conversion, since genuine penitents, or people who have returned to sanity, do not flaunt their past vices in that complacent way. He is a symptom of the world's illness. The important thing is not to denounce him as a cad who ought to be horsewhipped, or to defend him as a genius who ought not to be questioned, but to find out *why* he exhibits that particular set of aberrations.

The answer is probably discoverable in his pictures, and those I myself am not competent to examine. But I can point to one clue which perhaps takes one part of the distance. This is the old-fashioned, over-ornate, Edwardian style of drawing to which Dali tends to return when he is not being Surrealist. Some of Dali's drawings are reminiscent of Dürer, one (p. 113) seems to show the influence of Beardsley, another (p. 269) seems to borrow something from Blake. But the most persistent strain is the Edwardian one. When I opened this book for the first time and looked at its innumerable marginal illustrations, I was haunted by a resemblance which I could not immediately pin down. I fetched up at the ornamental candlestick at the beginning of Part I (p. 7). What did this thing remind me of? Finally I tracked it down. It reminded me of a large, vulgar, expensively got-up edition of Anatole France (in translation) which must have been published about 1913. That had ornamental chapter headings and tailpieces after this style. Dali's candlestick displays at one end a curly fish-like creature that looks curiously familiar (it seems to be based on the conventional dolphin), and at the other is the burning candle. This candle, which recurs in one picture after another, is a very old friend. You will find it, with the same picturesque gouts of wax arranged on its sides, in those phoney electric lights done up as candlesticks which are popular in sham-Tudor country hotels. This candle, and the design beneath it, convey at once an intense feeling of sentimentality. As though to counteract this Dali has spattered a quill-ful of ink all over the page, but without avail. The same impression keeps popping up on page after page. The design at the bottom of page 62, for instance, would nearly go into *Peter Pan*. The figure on page 224, in spite of having her cranium elongated into an immense sausage-like shape, is the witch of the fairy-tale books. The horse on page 234 and the unicorn on page 218 might be illustrations to James Branch Cabell.[6] The rather pansified drawings of youths on pages 97, 100, and elsewhere convey the same impression. Picturesqueness keeps breaking in. Take away the skulls, ants, lobsters, telephones, and other paraphernalia, and every now and again you are back in the world of Barrie, Rackham, Dunsany and *Where the Rainbow Ends*.[7]

Curiously enough, some of the naughty-naughty touches in Dali's autobiography tie up with the same period. When I read the passage I quoted at the beginning, about the kicking of the little sister's head, I was aware of another phantom resemblance. What was it? Of course! *Ruthless Rhymes for Heartless Homes* by Harry Graham.[8] Such rhymes were very popular round about 1912, and one that ran:

> Poor little Willy is crying so sore,
> A sad little boy is he,
> For he's broken his little sister's neck
> And he'll have no jam for tea.

might almost have been founded on Dali's anecdote. Dali, of course, is aware of his Edwardian leanings, and makes capital out of them, more or less in a spirit of pastiche. He professes an especial affection for the year 1900, and claims that every ornamental object of 1900 is full of mystery, poetry, eroticism, madness, perversity, etc. Pastiche, however, usually implies a real affection for the thing parodied. It seems to be, if not the rule, at any rate distinctly common for an intellectual bent to be accompanied by a non-rational, even childish urge in the same direction. A sculptor, for instance, is interested in planes and curves, but he is also a person who enjoys the physical act of mucking about with clay or stone. An engineer is a person who enjoys the feel of tools, the noise of dynamos and the smell of oil. A psychiatrist usually has a leaning towards some sexual aberration himself. Darwin became a biologist partly because he was a country gentleman and fond of animals. It may be, therefore, that Dali's seemingly perverse cult of Edwardian things (for example his 'discovery of the 1900 subway entrances') is merely the symptom of a much deeper, less conscious affection. The innumerable, beautifully executed copies of textbook illustrations, solemnly labelled 'le rossignol', 'une montre' and so on, which he scatters all over his margins, may be meant partly as a joke. The little boy in knickerbockers playing with a diabolo on page 103 is a perfect period piece. But perhaps these things are also there because Dali can't help drawing that kind of thing, because it is to that period and that style of drawing that he really belongs.

If so, his aberrations are partly explicable. Perhaps they are a way of assuring himself that he is not commonplace. The two qualities that Dali unquestionably possesses are a gift for drawing and an atrocious egoism. 'At seven,' he says in the first paragraph of his book, 'I wanted to be Napoleon. And my ambition has been growing steadily ever since.' This is worded in a deliberately startling way, but no doubt it is substantially true. Such feelings are common enough. 'I knew I was a genius,' somebody once said to me, 'long before I knew what I was going to be a genius *about*.' And suppose that you have nothing in you except your egoism and a dexterity that goes no higher than the elbow: suppose that your real gift is for a detailed, academic, representational style of drawing, your real *métier* to be an illustrator of scientific textbooks. How then do you become Napoleon?

There is always one escape: *into wickedness*. Always do the thing that will shock and wound people. At five, throw a little boy off a bridge, strike an old doctor across the face with a whip and break his spectacles – or, at any rate, dream about doing such things. Twenty years later, gouge the eyes out of dead donkeys with a pair of scissors. Along those lines you can always feel yourself original. And after all, it pays! It is much less dangerous than crime. Making all allowance for the probable suppressions in Dali's autobiography, it is clear that he has not had to suffer for his eccentricities as he would have done in an earlier age. He grew up into the corrupt world of the nineteen-twenties, when sophistication was immensely widespread and every European capital swarmed with aristocrats and rentiers who had given up sport and politics and taken to patronising the arts. If you threw dead donkeys at people they threw money back. A phobia for grasshoppers – which a few decades back would merely have provoked a snigger – was now an interesting 'complex' which could be profitably exploited. And when that particular world collapsed before the German Army, America was waiting. You could even top it all up with religious conversion, moving at one hop and without a shadow of repentance from the fashionable salons of Paris to Abraham's bosom.[9]

That, perhaps, is the essential outline of Dali's history. But why his aberrations should be the particular ones they were, and why it should be so easy to 'sell' such horrors as rotting corpses to a sophisticated public – those are questions for the psychologist and the sociological critic. Marxist criticism has a short way with such phenomena as Surrealism. They are 'bourgeois decadence' (much play is made with the phrases 'corpse poisons' and 'decaying rentier class'), and that is that. But though this probably states a fact, it does not establish a connection. One would still like to know *why* Dali's leaning was towards necrophilia (and not, say, homosexuality), and *why* the rentiers and the aristocrats should buy his pictures instead of hunting and making love like their grandfathers. Mere moral disapproval does not get one any further. But neither ought one to pretend, in the name of 'detachment', that such pictures as *Mannequin rotting in a taxicab* are morally neutral. They are diseased and disgusting, and any investigation ought to start out from that fact.

1. *Un Chien Andalou* (Orwell has *Le* for *Un*) has been claimed as the first Surrealist film and was made by Luis Buñuel and Salvador Dali in 1929. Plate 143 of *Surrealism* by Patrick Waldberg (1978) illustrates a still from the film. Maurice Nadeau, in his *The History of Surrealism* (New York, 1965), lists five earlier such films, from 1925 on, including Antonin Artaud's *La coquille et le clergyman* (1928).

2. Godfrey, Lord Elton (1892–1973), historian and author. His books include *England Arise!* (1931) and *Towards the New Labour Party* (1932). Only the first volume of his *The Life of James Ramsay MacDonald* (1939) was published. Malcolm Muggeridge, writing of how 'every bubbling trend and fashion' would empty into the BBC in the 1930s, included as one strand 'a domestic chat from Lord Elton' (*The Thirties*, 59).

3. Alfred Noyes (1880–1958), poet, novelist and dramatist, now out of fashion. Nevertheless, his poem 'Spring and the Blind Children' still has a power to move. Orwell reviewed his *The Edge of the Abyss* on 27 February 1944 (XVI/2425). Noyes's thesis 'is that western civilisation is in danger of actual destruction' by economic maladjustments and 'the decay of the belief in absolute good and evil'. Noyes attacks highbrows, 'our pseudo-intellectuals', as he calls them, as largely responsible for this. Orwell begins: 'Incoherent and, in places, silly though it is, this book raises a real problem and will set its readers thinking, even if

their thinking only starts to be useful at about the place where Mr Noyes leaves off.' He also wrote for children (*The Secret of Pooduck Island*, New York, 1943).

4. The clergy were once exempted from trial by a secular court if charged with a felony. In time, 'clergy' meant little more than those who could read and write and who might, therefore, be capable of becoming ordained. It was abolished in 1827.

5. *L'Age d'Or* was made by Luis Buñuel and Salvador Dali in 1930. Plate 144 of *Surrealism* by Patrick Waldberg (1978) illustrates a still from the film.

6. James Branch Cabell (1879–1958), American novelist, many of his novels being set in a world of medieval myth (Poictesme), in which the hero strives for ideals which he realizes are unattainable.

7. *Where the Rainbow Ends* was a very successful fairy play which ran for many Christmas seasons from 1911. It was written by Clifford Mills and John Ramsey (= Reginald Owen) and had music by Roger Quilter.

8. Harry Graham (1874–1936), writer for children. He is still fun for his *Ruthless Rhymes for Heartless Homes* (1899) and its successor, *More Ruthless Rhymes* (1930).

9. With 'fashionable salons of Paris to Abraham's bosom', Orwell alludes to 'There is no leaping from Delilah's lap into Abraham's bosom', that is, if one lives in sin and corruption, one cannot expect heavenly repose after death. The source is Luke 16:19–31. The beggar, Lazarus, is 'carried by the angels into Abraham's bosom' while the rich man, who had neglected him on earth, is tormented in the fires of hell; there is a great gulf between them which none can traverse (v. 26).

[2527]

Conclusion to letter to John Middleton Murry
5 August 1944

On 21 July 1944 (XVI/2516), Orwell, responding to Murry, explained he objected to 'the circumspect kind of pacifism which denounces one kind of violence while endorsing or avoiding mention of another'. He referred specifically to Murry's 'failure to make a clear statement about the Russo-German war'. On 2 August Murry replied, admitting that he had 'failed to make a clear statement on the Russo-German war', but thought the charge of 'a circumspect kind of pacifism' of the kind Orwell defined was unwarranted. In his response of 5 August, Orwell said he could not 'escape the impression' that Murry avoided or glozed over the whole subject of Russian militarism and internal totalitarianism, in part because it would involve him 'in the only kind of unpopularity an intellectual cares about'. He concluded:

Of course, fanatical Communists and Russophiles generally can be respected, even if they are mistaken. But for people like ourselves, who suspect that something has gone very wrong with the Soviet Union, I consider that willingness to criticise Russia and Stalin is *the* test of intellectual honesty. It is the only thing that from a literary intellectual's point of view is really dangerous. If one is over military age or physically unfit, and if one lives one's life inside the intelligentsia, it seems to me nonsense to say that it needs any courage to refuse military service or to express any kind of antinomian opinions. To do so only gets one into trouble with the blimps, and who cares what they say? In any case the blimps hardly interfere. The thing that needs courage is to attack Russia, the only thing that the greater part of the British intelligentsia now believe in. The very tender way in which you have handled Stalin and his régime, compared with your denunciations of, say, Churchill, seems to me to justify the word 'circumspect'. If you are genuinely anti-violence you ought to be anti-Russian at least as much as you are anti-British. But to be anti-Russian makes enemies, whereas the other doesn't – ie. not such enemies as people like us would care about.

I don't agree with pacifism, but I judge the sincerity of pacifists by the subjects they avoid. Most pacifists talk as though the war were a meaningless bombing match between Britain and Germany, with no other countries involved. A courageous pacifist would not simply say 'Britain ought not to bomb Germany'. Anyone can say that. He would say, 'The Russians should let the Germans have the Ukraine, the Chinese should not defend themselves against Japan, the European peoples should submit to the Nazis, the Indians should not try to drive out the British.' Real pacifism would involve all of that: but one can't say that kind of thing and also keep on good terms with the rest of the intelligentsia. It is because they consistently avoid mentioning such issues as these, while continuing to squeal against obliteration bombing etc., that I find the majority of English pacifists so difficult to respect.

[2542]

Review of Selections from the Works of Gerrard
Winstanley, *edited by Leonard Hamilton, with an
Introduction by Christopher Hill*
Observer, *3 September 1944*

Every successful revolution has its June Purge. A moment always comes
when the party which has seized power crushes its own Left Wing and
then proceeds to disappoint the hopes with which the revolution started
out. The dictators of the past, however, lacked modern thoroughness in
silencing their opponents, and the defeated minorities of one revolution
after another have left behind residues of thought which have gradually
coalesced into the modern Socialist movement. Even the poor, humble
English Diggers, as these pamphlets show, were able in their few years of
activity to disseminate ideas which may have contributed to Spanish
Anarchism and may even have remotely influenced such thinkers as
Gandhi.

Winstanley,[1] who it seems was not the originator of the Digger movement but was its chief publicist, was born in Wigan in 1609 and was for
a while a cloth merchant in London. He was ruined by the Civil War. In
1649 he and twenty or thirty others took over and began cultivating some
waste land on St. George's Hill, near Cobham, forming themselves into a
self-supporting community on what would now be called Communist-
Anarchist lines. In this community there was to be no money, no trade,
no inequality, no idle persons, no priests, and as far as possible no law. As
Winstanley saw it, the land of England had once belonged to the common
people and had been unjustly taken from them, and the best way to get it
back was for bodies of landless men to form colonies which would act as
an example to the mass of the nation. At the beginning he was simple
enough to imagine that even the landlords could ultimately be won over
to the Anarchist programme. But ideas similar to his own were evidently
widespread, as other colonies of Diggers were started in various parts of
the country at about the same time.

Needless to say, the Diggers were swiftly crushed. The parvenu gentry
who had won the civil war were willing enough to divide the lands of
the Royalists among themselves, but they had no intention of setting up

an egalitarian society, and they saw the danger of allowing such experiments as Winstanley's to succeed. The Diggers were beaten up, their crops were trampled on, their stock was taken away from them by means of law suits in which packed juries imposed impossible damages. Troops of soldiers sent to deal with them tended to be sympathetic – this was the period of the revolt of the Levellers in the army – but the gentry won and the Digger movement was effectively finished by 1652. Winstanley vanishes from history about 1660.

It is clear from these pamphlets that, though a visionary, Winstanley was by no means a fool. He did not expect his ideas to be accepted immediately, and he was ready to modify them at need. After his experiment had failed he submitted to Cromwell a quite detailed and practical programme from which the earlier extravagances had been eliminated. This makes provision for laws, magistrates and foreign trade, even, in spite of his pacifist tinge, for a standing army and the death penalty for certain offences. But the central idea is still the same – a society founded on brotherhood and co-operation, with no profit-making, and, for internal purposes, no money. 'Everyone shall put to their hands to till the earth and bring up cattle, and the blessing of the earth shall be common to all; when a man hath need of any corn or cattle, take from the next store-house he meets with. *Acts, iv, 32.*'²

Winstanley's thought links up with Anarchism rather than Socialism because he thinks in terms of a purely agricultural community living at a low level of comfort, lower than was even then strictly necessary. Not foreseeing the machine, he states that a man cannot be rich except by exploiting others, but it is evident that, like Mr. Gandhi, he also values simplicity for its own sake. Moreover, he clings to a belief which seems to haunt all thinkers of the Anarchist type – the belief that the wished-for Utopia has already existed in the past. The land did once belong to the common people, but has been taken away from them. According to Winstanley, this happened at the Norman Conquest, which in his eyes is the cardinal fact in English history. The essential struggle is the struggle of the Saxon common people against the Frenchified upper class. In every pamphlet, almost in every paragraph, he refers to the defeated Royalists as 'Normans'. But alas! he could see only too clearly that the victors of the civil war were themselves developing 'Norman' characteristics:

And you zealous preachers and professors of the City of London, and you great officers and soldiery of the army, where are all your victories over the Cavaliers, that you made such a blaze in the land, in giving God thanks for, and which you begged in your fasting days and morning exercises? Are they all sunk into the Norman power again, and must the old prerogative laws stand? What freedom did you then give thanks for? Surely that you had killed him that rode upon you, that you may get up into his saddle to ride upon others. Oh, thou City, thou hypocritical City! Thou blindfold, drowsy England, that sleeps and snorts in the bed of covetousness, awake, awake! The enemy is upon thy back, he is ready to scale the walls and enter possession, and wilt not look out?

If only our modern Trotskyists and Anarchists – who in effect are saying the same thing – could write prose like that! This is not a book that can be read through at one sitting, but it is a book to buy and keep. Mr. Hill's short introduction is useful and interesting.

> *In the* New Leader, *16 September 1944, Reg Groves*[3] *took issue with Orwell's review, in particular for Orwell's 'apparent indifference to the visionary side of Winstanley's writings'. Orwell was evidently upset by the criticism and wrote to Groves. On 28 October, the journal published a letter from Groves which said he had now been informed that the passages on this aspect had been omitted owing to lack of space (paper was then in very short supply) and saying that in stressing that criticism he had been 'unintentionally unfair to Mr Orwell'. In passing, it is important to bear in mind that reviews and articles were frequently cut, often without Orwell's knowledge.*

1. Gerrard Winstanley (1609?–after 1660), political pamphleteer. In 1649–50, he led a group of agrarian communists who set about cultivating land in two areas of Surrey in the belief that land should be provided for the poor. They were dispersed by force.

2. Acts 4:32 reads: 'And the multitude of them that believed were of one heart and of one soul: neither said any of them that ought of the things which he possessed was his own; but they had all things common.'

3. Reg Groves (1908–c. 1985) is described by Crick as an agitator and author and personally abrasive. He was one of the first British Trotskyists and had immediately preceded Orwell at the Westropes' bookshop. They had met but did not know each other well. Groves described *Homage to Catalonia* as 'the best thing that ever happened to us' (Crick, 270, 363, 611).

[2570]

Review *of* Verdict on India *by Beverley Nichols*
Observer, *29 October 1944*

It is fair to say that this book does not read as though it were intended to make mischief, but that is the effect it will probably have. Mr. Nichols[1] spent about a year in India – as an unofficial visitor, he insists – travelling all over the country and interviewing Indians of every description, from maharajahs to naked mendicants. When he got there the menace of a Japanese invasion still loomed large and the 'Quit India' campaign was in full swing. A little later there was the Bengal famine, of which he records some horrifying details. In a slapdash way he has obviously tried very hard to get at the truth, and his willingness to disclose scandals, together with frank, even violent, partisanship in Indian internal affairs, will cause much offence among Indians. It would not even be surprising if this book, like *Mother India*,[2] provoked a whole series of counterblasts.

Mr. Nichols's essential quarrel is with Hinduism. He detests the Hindu religion itself – its cow-worship, the obscene carvings in the temples, its caste-system, and the endless superstitions which war against science and enlightenment – but above all he is politically anti-Hindu. He is an advocate of Pakistan, which he believes will certainly be established by one means or another, and his favourite Indian politician is Mr. Jinnah.[3] Much of what he says is true, but his way of saying it, and the things he leaves out, may mislead some people and will certainly antagonise countless others.

The thing Mr. Nichols never really gets round to admitting is that India's major grievance against Britain is justified. The British are still in India long after the Indians have ceased to want them there. If one keeps that in mind, much of Mr. Nichols's indictment of the Congress politicians can be accepted. India's immediate problems will not be solved by the disappearance of the British, and the Nationalist propaganda which declares every existing evil to be a direct result of British rule is dishonest as well as hysterical. As Mr. Nichols is aware – indeed, too much aware – this propaganda is lapped up by well-meaning Liberals in this country and America who are all the readier to accept what Indian apologists tell them because they have no real interest in Indian problems. Many of Mr.

Nichols's points would have been well worth making if only he could have made them in a better-tempered way.

It is quite true that Hindu-Moslem antagonism is played down in Nationalist propaganda and that the Moslem end of the case seldom gets a fair hearing outside India. Again, it is true that the Congress Party is not the idealistic left-wing organisation which western Liberals imagine it to be, but has considerable resemblances to the Nazi Party and is backed by sinister business men with pro-Japanese leanings. Again, it is true that pro-Indian and anti-British propaganda habitually skates over huge problems such as Untouchability and ignores or misrepresents the positive achievements of the British in India. One could make a whole list of similar points on which Mr. Nichols is probably in the right. But he does not see that the appalling atmosphere of Indian politics, the hysteria, the lies, the pathological hatred, suspicion, and credulity, is itself the result of wounded national pride. He observes with some acuteness the mentality of a subject people, but talks of it as though it were innate or simply the product of the Hindu religion.

For instance, he has an undisguised contempt for the army of half-educated youths, picking up a precarious living from journalism and litigation, who are the noise-makers of the Nationalist movement. He barely admits that the existence of this huge unemployed intelligentsia is a commentary on British educational methods, or that these people might develop a more grown-up mentality if they had real responsibilities to face.

A more serious mistake is that he repeatedly attacks Mr. Gandhi, for whom he has an unconquerable aversion. Mr. Gandhi is an enigmatic character, but he is obviously not a plain crook, which is what Mr. Nichols seems to imply, and even his endless self-contradictions may be simply a form of sincerity. Throughout nearly the whole of Mr. Nichols's book, indeed, there is an air of prejudice and irritation which weakens even his justified criticisms.

Mr. Nichols is not unwilling to admit that the British in India have faults, especially social faults (he says, exaggerating slightly, that no European ever says 'Thank you' to an Indian), and towards the end he makes some constructive suggestions. The British, he considers, both should, and will, quit India in the fairly near future. It would have created a very much better impression if he had said this on the first page of the book. Morally, he says, there is no case for our remaining there after the war is won, though it was, as he rightly emphasises, an absurdity to ask Britain simply to hand India over to the Japanese. His formula is 'Divide and Quit' – that is, we are to recognise Indian independence, but make sure that Pakistan is established first. This is perhaps a thinkable solution, and if the Moslem League has the following that Mr. Nichols claims for it, it might help to avert civil war after the British power is withdrawn.

1. John Beverley Nichols (1899–1983), prolific author, travel writer, journalist and broadcaster. Malcolm Muggeridge described him as 'notably susceptible to the contemporary mood's fluctuations ... In 1930, he was still praising the delights of rural retirement; ... in 1936 God was his preoccupation, and in 1938, England'. He mocked his own sentimentality, for example, in having picture-postcards of his dog sold, inscribed 'I just want him to be his own woolly self'. He was, however, influential in setting a mood, hence the attention Orwell paid this book. (See *The Thirties*, 33–4.)

2. *Mother India* by Katherine Mayo, an American, was published in New York and London in 1927. It exposed, with great frankness, 'the worst plague spots in the social customs and practices that still prevail behind the purdah', in particular the way women were treated in India, economic waste, 'cruelty to animals involved in the worship of the cow', and 'poisonously insanitary conditions ... in the most sacred shrines and cities' (*Times Literary Supplement*, 28 July 1927). Books by at least ten authors were published in reply. In its review of *Unhappy India*, by Lajpat Rai (Calcutta), and *India: Its Character*, by J. A. Chapman (Oxford), the *TLS* said that Miss Mayo's 'facts were largely true, but their presentation was sometimes distorted' (23 August 1928).

3. Muhammad Ali Jinnah (1876–1948), founder of Pakistan. He led the Indian Muslim League, founded to protect the interests of Muslims in British India and supported Hindu–Muslim unity until 1930 when he opposed Gandhi's policy of civil disobedience and demanded, successfully, a separate state for Muslims. He was the first Governor-General of Pakistan but died soon after independence had been achieved.

[2597]

Review of Der Führer *by Conrad Heiden*
Manchester Evening News, *4 January 1945*

About eight years ago, from the same publishing house as has just produced *Der Führer*,[1] there appeared another fat and imposing book about Hitler, entitled, significantly, *Hitler, the Pawn*. Its thesis, then a widely accepted one, was that Hitler was a nonentity, a mere puppet of German big business.

Later events have made that incredible, and Mr. Heiden's long detailed but very readable book is an attempt to disentangle the extremely complex causes – causes which are intellectual and religious as well as economic and political – that have allowed a semi-lunatic to gain control of a great nation and cause the death of some tens of millions of human beings.

Mr. Heiden ends his story with the June purge of 1934 – which, as he points out, is not altogether an arbitrary stopping-point, because with that atrocious deed there began a new historical phase which has not yet ended.

The story starts some time before Hitler's birth. It starts, to be precise, in 1864, with an illegal and now forgotten pamphlet attacking Napoleon III.

Somewhat later the Czarist secret police were to get hold of this pamphlet and concoct out of it that celebrated forgery, *The Protocols of the Elders of Zion*.[2] Their object was to frighten the Czar with tales of a Jewish conspiracy and thus provoke him into violent measures against the Russian Revolutionaries.

Rosenberg, the racial theorist,[3] a Baltic Russian, and at the time of the revolution a student in Moscow, brought a copy of the protocols with him when he fled to Germany: and it was from this source that Hitler derived the anti-Semitism that was to be both a cherished delusion and a cunning political device.

Mr. Heiden follows up Hitler's early history with great minuteness, plugging the gaps in *Mein Kampf* with the statements of a painter named Hanisch, who shared Hitler's poverty for several years in Vienna.

It appears from Mr. Heiden's researches that the autobiographical part of *Mein Kampf* is reasonably truthful. Even on his own showing, Hitler was a complete failure, even a ne'er-do-well, until the outbreak of war in 1914. His main characteristics were laziness, an inability to make friends, a hatred of the society which had failed to give him a decent livelihood, and a vague leaning towards painting.

(Many dictators, it is worth noticing, are failed artists – Henry VIII and Frederick the Great both wrote bad verse, and Napoleon and Mussolini wrote plays which nobody would produce.)

The war was Hitler's great opportunity. He loved every moment of it, and it appears to be true, though it has often been denied, that he served with distinction and was decorated for bravery. He says himself that he wept when the war stopped, and from then onwards to restore the atmosphere of war was his main aim.

In the chaotic Germany of 1918 it was natural for a man of Hitler's temperament to plunge into conspiratorial politics. He joined the German Workers' party – later to become the National Socialist party – which at that date consisted of six members and had as its entire equipment a single briefcase and a cigar-box which was used as a cash-box.

The disbanded Reichswehr officers, who were already planning to rebuild the German Army in defiance of the Versailles Treaty, were on the look-out for a political party which could act as a cover for their aims, and the German Workers' party, with its sham-Socialist programme, seemed to them to have possibilities.

Hitler, therefore, had a measure of support almost from the start, but it was not until some time later, when he was already a political force to be counted with, that the industrialists began to finance him in a big way.

As a politician he had three great assets. One was his complete lack of pity, affection, or human ties of any kind. Another was his bottomless belief in himself and contempt for everybody else. And the third was his powerful and impressive voice, which within a few minutes could make any audience forget his Charlie Chaplin-like appearance.

Within a few years he had talked a formidable movement into existence, pouring out on platform after platform a message – anti-Jewish, anti-Capitalist, anti-Bolshevik, and anti-French – which appealed equally to the unemployed workers, the ruined middle-class, and the officers who were pining for another war.

However, to win supreme power was another matter, and for years the history of the National Socialist party was one of ups and downs. Broadly speaking, when things went badly, Hitler's star rose; when they went well, it sank. In the prosperous period of the middle twenties, the period of the Dawes Plan,[4] the economic recovery in Britain and the U.S.A. and the N.E.P.[5] in Russia, the National Socialist party seemed likely to disappear.

Then came the great depression, and Hitler rose again like a rocket. We shall never know whether even at that late date he might have been defeated, but at any rate it is a fact that his only real enemies inside Germany, the Communists and the Social Democrats, persisted in fighting one another instead of combining against the common enemy.

Having made use of their dissensions, Hitler destroyed both of them, and finally made quite sure of his position by massacring the Left Wing of his own party. The rest of the story is only too well known.

This book gives useful background information about others besides Hitler – in particular, Hess, Goering, Roehm,[6] and Houston Chamberlain[7] the strange renegade Englishman who was one of the founders of the Pan-German Movement. It is a valuable book because it neither underrates Hitler nor overrates him. It does not, that is to say, explain him away in narrow economic terms, nor does it pretend that the major problems of the world will be solved by his disappearance. To quote Mr. Heiden's own words –

Hitler was able to enslave his own people because he was able to give them something that even the traditional religions could no longer provide – the belief in a meaning to existence beyond the narrowest self-interest. The real degradation began when people realised that they were in league with the devil, but felt that even the devil was preferable to the emptiness of an existence which lacked a larger significance.

The problem to-day is to give that larger significance and dignity to a life that has been dwarfed by the world of material things. Until that problem is solved, the annihilation of Nazism will be no more than the removal of one symptom of the world's unrest.

1. Victor Gollancz Ltd.
2. *The Protocols of the Elders of Zion* was a particularly vicious fraud purporting to show how Judaism should spread throughout the world subverting liberalism and Christian societies. Its origins are expertly described by Nicolas Barker in the British Library's *Fake? The Art of Deception*, edited by Mark Jones (1990, 70–72), from which these notes are extracted. The fraud is based on two works: an attack on the French Third Empire by a lawyer, Maurice Joly, *Dialogue aux enfers entre Montesquieu et Machiavel* (Brussels, 1864), and a virulent anti-Semitic tract by the Serb, Osman Bey, *Die Eroberung der Welt durch die Juden* (Wiesbaden, 1875). The two were (according to Mikhail Lepekhine, *Daily Telegraph*, 19 November 1999) written by Mathieu Golovinski in the anti-Semitic newspaper *Znamya* (St Petersburg, 1903). Joly's text was manipulated, and a measure of the work's preposterous nature can be gauged from its proposal that underground railways should join capital cities so that the Elders could quell opposition by using them to blow up the cities if the need arose. This fraudulent work was printed many times in Russia, and after 1917 spread abroad. It was reported in *The Times*, 8 May 1920, but exposed in August 1921. Nevertheless it is still in print, and Barker reports that it was 'printed recently in Los Angeles by a body called the Christian Nationalist Crusade'.

3. Alfred Rosenberg (1893–1946), born in Estonia; his *Der Mythus des 20 Jahrhunderts* (The Myth of the Twentieth Century; 1930) served as a quasi-scientific basis for Hitler's racial policy. He was hanged following conviction at Nuremberg as a war criminal.

4. The Dawes Plan was devised in 1924 by a commission headed by Charles Gates Dawes (1865–1961), American lawyer, financier, statesman, who was the first director of the US Bureau of the Budget, 1921. The plan sought to reduce the amount of reparations payable by Germany following her defeat in World War I and attempted to stabilize the country's finances. Dawes, later, was US Vice-President, 1925–9, Ambassador to Great Britain, 1929–32, and co-recipient, with Sir Austen Chamberlain, of the Nobel Peace Prize, 1925.

5. The New Economic Policy was introduced by Lenin in March 1921 following the Tenth Congress of the Bolshevik Party. It was designed to restore levels of production by allowing some private business to develop. Though opposed by hard-line Communists, it proved effective, and by 1927 production in the Soviet Union had reached the level achieved in 1913. The policy came to an end under Stalin in 1929.

6. Ernst Roehm (1887–1934), leader of the Nazi 'Brownshirts' (SA), was executed, along with more than eighty others, by Himmler's 'Blackshirts' (SS) during the weekend of 29 June–2 July 1934 ('The Night of the Long Knives').

7. Houston Stewart Chamberlain (1855–1927), British political philosopher and racial ideologist, exemplified by his *Foundations of the Nineteenth Century* (1899). In the summer of 1923 – before Hitler's attempted *putsch* in Munich, November 1923 – Hitler visited Wahnfried, the home of the Wagner family in Bayreuth. Alan Bullock writes of this occasion that Hitler 'impressed Winnifried Wagner and captivated the aged Chamberlain, who had married one of Wagner's daughters, and who wrote to him afterwards: "My faith in the Germans had never wavered for a moment, but my hope, I must own, had sunk to a low ebb. At one stroke you have transformed the state of my soul" ' (*Hitler: A Study in Tyranny*, revised edition, 1962); the passage quoted by Bullock is from Konrad Heiden, *Der Führer* (1944, 198).

[2609]

Extract from 'As I Please', 56 [On European freedom]
Tribune, *26 January 1945*

The other night I attended a mass meeting of an organisation called the League for European Freedom. Although officially an all-party organisation – there was one Labour M.P. on the platform – it is, I think it is safe to say, dominated by the anti-Russian wing of the Tory Party.

I am all in favour of European freedom, but I feel happier when it is coupled with freedom elsewhere – in India, for example. The people on the platform were concerned with the Russian actions in Poland, the Baltic countries, etc., and the scrapping of the principles of the Atlantic Charter that those actions imply. More than half of what they said was justified, but curiously enough they were almost as anxious to defend our own coercion of Greece as to condemn the Russian coercion of Poland.[1] Victor Raikes,[2] the Tory M.P., who is an able and outspoken reactionary, made a speech which I should have considered a good one if it had referred only to Poland and Yugoslavia. But after dealing with those two countries he went on to speak about Greece, and then suddenly black became white, and white black. There was no booing, no interjections from the quite large audience – no one there, apparently, who could see that the forcing of quisling governments upon unwilling peoples is equally undesirable whoever does it.

It is very hard to believe that people like this are really interested in political liberty as such. They are merely concerned because Britain did not get a big enough cut in the sordid bargain that appears to have been driven at Teheran.[3] After the meeting I talked with a journalist whose contacts among influential people are much more extensive than mine. He said he thought it probable that British policy will shortly take a violent anti-Russian swing, and that it would be quite easy to manipulate public opinion in that direction if necessary. For a number of reasons I don't believe he was right, but if he does turn out to be right, then ultimately it is *our* fault and not that of our adversaries.

No one expects the Tory Party and its press to spread enlightenment. The trouble is that for years past it has been impossible to extract a grown-up picture of foreign politics from the left-wing press either. When it comes to such issues as Poland, the Baltic countries, Yugoslavia or Greece, what difference is there between the Russophile press and the extreme Tory press? The one is simply the other standing on its head. The *News Chronicle* gives the big headlines to the fighting in Greece but tucks away the news that 'force has had to be used' against the Polish Home Army in small print at the bottom of a column. The *Daily Worker* disapproves of dictatorship in Athens, the *Catholic Herald* disapproves of dictatorship in Belgrade. There is no one who is able to say – at least, no one who has the chance to say in a newspaper of big circulation – that this whole dirty game of spheres of influence, quislings, purges, deportations, one-party elections and hundred per cent plebiscites is morally the same whether it is done by ourselves, the Russians or the Nazis. Even in the case of such frank returns to barbarism as the use of hostages, disapproval is only felt when it happens to be the enemy and not ourselves who is doing it.

And with what result? Well, one result is that it becomes much easier to mislead public opinion. The Tories are able to precipitate scandals when they want to, partly because on certain subjects the Left refuses to talk in a grown-up manner. An example was the Russo-Finnish war of 1940. I do not defend the Russian action in Finland, but it was not especially wicked. It was merely the same kind of thing as we ourselves did when we seized Madagascar. The public could be shocked by it, and indeed worked up into a dangerous fury about it, because for years they had been falsely taught that Russian foreign policy was morally different from that of other countries. And it struck me as I listened to Mr. Raikes the other night that if the Tories do choose to start spilling the beans about the Lublin Committee,[4] Marshal Tito and kindred subjects, there will be – thanks to prolonged self-censorship on the Left – plenty of beans for them to spill.

But political dishonesty has its comic side. Presiding over that meeting of the League for European Freedom was no less a person than the Duchess of Atholl.[5] It is only about seven years since the Duchess – 'the red duchess' as she was affectionately nicknamed – was the pet of the *Daily Worker* and lent the considerable weight of her authority to every lie that the Communists happened to be uttering at the moment. Now she is fighting against the monster that she helped to create. I am sure that neither she nor her Communist ex-friends see any moral in this.

1. For a later comment by Orwell on the Russian/Polish and the British/Greek relationships, see his unpublished letter to *Tribune*, 26? June 1945, below.

2. H. Victor Raikes (1901–86; Kt., 1953), barrister, first elected to Parliament in 1931, served in the RAF during the war and was elected for Wavertree, Liverpool in 1945, and, when that constituency disappeared under redistribution, for Garston, 1950–57. By 1957 he had become an Independent Conservative.

3. The Teheran Conference, 28 November–1 December 1943, was attended by Churchill, Roosevelt and Stalin in order to co-ordinate the Allied landings in France and a renewed Soviet offensive against Germany. It failed to agree on the post-war government of Poland.

4. On 18 January 1945, a Soviet-backed puppet government of Poland was installed in Lublin under President Boleslaw Bierut. Its first actions were to demand the rounding-up of what it called irresponsible members of the Home Army and those following the London Polish government in exile. It condemned General Bór-Komorowski, who had led the Warsaw uprising, and maintained that that rising was 'provocative', and the surrender of

those who had fought the Germans against desperate odds had actually aided the Germans. The purge of all non-Communists followed.

5. Katharine Stewart-Murray, Duchess of Atholl (1874–1960), devoted her life to public service, becoming the second woman, and first Conservative woman, to hold ministerial office. Orwell reviewed her *Searchlight on Spain* (1938) twice; see *Orwell in Spain* in this series and XI/*469*.

[2623]

Extract from 'As I Please', 59 [Future of Burma]
Tribune, *16 February 1945*

Last week I received a copy of a statement on the future of Burma, issued by the Burma Association, an organisation which includes most of the Burmese resident in this country. How representative this organisation is I am not certain, but probably it voices the wishes of a majority of politically-conscious Burmese. For reasons I shall try to make clear presently, the statement just issued is an important document. Summarised as shortly as possible, it makes the following demands: –

(i) An amnesty for Burmese who have collaborated with the Japs during the occupation. (ii) Statement by the British Government of a definite date at which Burma shall attain Dominion status. The period, if possible, to be less than six years. The Burmese people to summon a Constituent Assembly in the meantime. (iii) No interim of 'direct rule'. (iv) The Burmese people to have a greater share in the economic development of their own country. (v) The British Government to make an immediate unequivocal statement of its intentions towards Burma.

The striking thing about these demands is how moderate they are. No political party with any tinge of nationalism, or any hope of getting a mass following, could possibly ask for less. But why do these people pitch their claims so low? Well, I think one can guess at two reasons. To begin with, the experience of Japanese occupation has probably made Dominion status seem a more tempting goal than it seemed three years ago. But – much more important – if they demand so little it is probably because they expect to be offered even less. And I should guess that they expect right. Indeed, of the very modest suggestions listed above, only the first is likely to be carried out.

The Government has never made any clear statement about the future of Burma, but there have been persistent rumours that when the Japs are driven out there is to be a return to 'direct rule', which is a polite name for military dictatorship. And what is happening, politically, in Burma at this moment? We simply don't know: nowhere have I seen in any newspaper one word about the way in which the reconquered territories are being administered. To grasp the significance of this one has to look at the map of Burma. A year ago Burma proper was in Japanese hands and the Allies were fighting in wild territories thinly populated by rather primitive tribes who have never been much interfered with and are traditionally pro-British. Now they are penetrating into the heart of Burma, and some fairly important towns, centres of administration, have fallen into their hands. Several million Burmese must be once again under the British flag. Yet we are told nothing whatever about the form of administration that is being set up. Is it surprising if every thinking Burmese fears the worst?

It is vitally important to interest the British public in this matter, if possible. Our eyes are fixed on Europe, we forget that at the other end of the world there is a whole string of countries awaiting liberation and in nearly every case hoping for something better than a mere change of conquerors. Burma will probably be the first British territory to be reconquered, and it will be a test case: a more important test than Greece or Belgium, not only because more people are involved, but because it will be almost wholly a British responsibility. It will be a fearful disaster if through apathy and ignorance we let Churchill, Amery[1] and Co. put across some reactionary settlement which will lose us the friendship of the Burmese people for good.

For a year or two after the Japanese have gone, Burma will be in a receptive mood and more pro-British than it has been for a dozen years past. Then is the moment to make a generous gesture. I don't know whether Dominion status is the best possible solution. But if the politically conscious section of the Burmese ask for Dominion status, it would be monstrous to let the Tories refuse it in a hopeless effort to bring back the past. And there must be a date attached to it, a not too distant date. Whether these people remain inside the British Commonwealth or outside it, what matters in the long run is that we should have their friendship –

and we *can* have it if we do not play them false at the moment of crisis. When the moment comes for Burma's future to be settled, thinking Burmese will not turn their eyes towards Churchill. They will be looking at *us*, the Labour movement, to see whether our talk about democracy, self-determination, racial equality and what-not has any truth in it. I do not know whether it will be in our power to force a decent settlement upon the Government; but I do know that we shall harm ourselves irreparably if we do not make at least as much row about it as we did in the case of Greece.

1. L. S. (Leo) Amery (1873–1955), Conservative politician, was particularly associated in office with British colonies and dominions: Colonial Secretary, 1924–9; Dominions Secretary, 1925–9; Secretary of State for India and for Burma, 1940–45. He had supported Italy in its attack on Abyssinia, 1935, and denounced the League of Nations. After the failure of the Norwegian campaign in 1940, he was among those who opposed Chamberlain, concluding a speech against him with Cromwell's words addressed to the Rump of the Long Parliament in April 1653: 'Depart, I say, and let us have done with you. In the name of God, go!'

[2631]

Extract from 'Occupation's Effect on French Outlook' [Post-liberation killings in France], Paris, March 3
Observer, *4 March 1945*

No matter to whom you talk in this country, you are soon brought up against the same fact – that Britain has not known what it is like to be occupied.

It is impossible to discuss the 'purge', for instance, without being reminded of this.

The people who would like to see the 'purge' in full swing – and some of them say freely that they believe several thousand executions to be necessary – are not reactionaries and not necessarily Communists: they may be thoughtful, sensitive people whose antecedents are Liberal, Socialist, or non-political.[1]

Your objections always get much the same answer: 'It's different for you in England. You can do things peacefully because there is no real division within the nation. Here we have to deal with actual traitors. It's not safe to let them remain alive.' So also with the attitude towards Germany. A highly intelligent Frenchman, brushing aside my suggestion that a Democratic Germany might arise when Hitler is gone, said to me:

It's not a question of wanting revenge. It's merely that after having had them here for four years, I have great difficulty in believing that the Germans are the same kind of people as ourselves.

Some observers think that the present rather Chauvinist cast of French thought is a superficial symptom, and that quite other tendencies will show themselves when the war is safely won.

Meanwhile, whatever divergencies there may be either in high policy or in public opinion, there appears to be no anti-British feeling in France.

If one may judge by Paris, France has never been more Anglophile, and one is paid quite embarrassing compliments on the subject of Britain's lonely struggle in 1940 and on the 'très correct' bearing of the comparatively few British soldiers who are to be seen in the streets.

1. The taking of revenge by French men and women on their own people after the Occupation was particularly savage. David Pryce-Jones in his *Paris in the Third Reich: A History of the German Occupation, 1940–1944* (1981) quotes Raymond Aron's conservative estimate that after the liberation there were between 30,000 and 40,000 summary executions; but Adrien Tixier, the post-war Minister of Justice, stated that there were 105,000 such executions between June 1944 and February 1945 throughout France; the journal *Historia* (No. 41) records apparently one million arrests, of which 100,000 were in the Paris area, between 21 August and 1 October 1944 (Pryce-Jones, 206). The Germans deported 75,721 Jews from France, though this must be taken as 'the minimum number'; about one-third were French nationals; about 3,000 survived (144). Pryce-Jones concludes: 'the number of Frenchmen killed by other Frenchmen, whether through summary execution or rigged tribunals akin to lynch mobs or court-martials and High Court trials, equalled or even exceeded the number of those sent to their death by the Germans as hostages, deportees, and slave laborers' (207). These figures exaggerate and underestimate. Officially, some 10,000 people were 'executed', although Professor M. R. D. Foot has suggested to the editor that that number should be about 20,000. The Mémorial des Martyrs et de la Déportation in Paris commemorates 200,000 French men, women and children deported to their deaths in Germany.

[2668]
'Notes on Nationalism'
Polemic: A Magazine of Philosophy, Psychology & Aesthetics,
No. 1, [October] 1945[1]

Somewhere or other Byron makes use of the French word *longueur*, and remarks in passing that though in England we happen not to have the *word*, we have the *thing* in considerable profusion. In the same way, there is a habit of mind which is now so widespread that it affects our thinking on nearly every subject, but which has not yet been given a name. As the nearest existing equivalent I have chosen the word 'nationalism', but it will be seen in a moment that I am not using it in quite the ordinary sense, if only because the emotion I am speaking about does not always attach itself to what is called a nation – that is, a single race or a geographical area. It can attach itself to a church or a class, or it may work in a merely negative sense, *against* something or other and without the need for any positive object of loyalty.

By 'nationalism' I mean first of all the habit of assuming that human beings can be classified like insects and that whole blocks of millions or tens of millions of people can be confidently labelled 'good' or 'bad'.* But secondly – and this is much more important – I mean the habit of identifying oneself with a single nation or other unit, placing it beyond good and evil and recognising no other duty than that of advancing its interests. Nationalism is not to be confused with patriotism. Both words are normally used in so vague a way that any definition is liable to be challenged, but one must draw a distinction between them, since two different and even opposing ideas are involved. By 'patriotism' I mean devotion to a particular place and a particular way of life, which one

---

* Nations, and even vaguer entities such as the Catholic Church or the proletariat, are commonly thought of as individuals and often referred to as 'she'. Patently absurd remarks such as 'Germany is naturally treacherous' are to be found in any newspaper one opens, and reckless generalisations about national character ('The Spaniard is a natural aristocrat' or 'Every Englishman is a hypocrite') are uttered by almost everyone. Intermittently these generalisations are seen to be unfounded, but the habit of making them persists, and people of professedly international outlook, *e.g.* Tolstoy or Bernard Shaw, are often guilty of them [Orwell's footnote].

believes to be the best in the world but has no wish to force upon other people. Patriotism is of its nature defensive, both militarily and culturally. Nationalism, on the other hand, is inseparable from the desire for power. The abiding purpose of every nationalist is to secure more power and more prestige, *not* for himself but for the nation or other unit in which he has chosen to sink his own individuality.

So long as it is applied merely to the more notorious and identifiable nationalist movements in Germany, Japan and other countries, all this is obvious enough. Confronted with a phenomenon like Nazism, which we can observe from the outside, nearly all of us would say much the same things about it. But here I must repeat what I said above, that I am only using the word 'nationalism' for lack of a better. Nationalism, in the extended sense in which I am using the word, includes such movements and tendencies as Communism, political Catholicism, Zionism, anti-Semitism, Trotskyism and Pacifism. It does not necessarily mean loyalty to a government or a country, still less to *one's own* country, and it is not even strictly necessary that the units in which it deals should actually exist. To name a few obvious examples, Jewry, Islam, Christendom, the Proletariat and the White Race are all of them the objects of passionate nationalistic feeling: but their existence can be seriously questioned, and there is no definition of any one of them that would be universally accepted.

It is also worth emphasising once again that nationalist feeling can be purely negative. There are, for example, Trotskyists who have become simply the enemies of the U.S.S.R. without developing a corresponding loyalty to any other unit. When one grasps the implications of this, the nature of what I mean by nationalism becomes a good deal clearer. A nationalist is one who thinks solely, or mainly, in terms of competitive prestige. He may be a positive or a negative nationalist – that is, he may use his mental energy either in boosting or in denigrating – but at any rate his thoughts always turn on victories, defeats, triumphs and humiliations. He sees history, especially contemporary history, as the endless rise and decline of great power units, and every event that happens seems to him a demonstration that his own side is on the up grade and some hated rival on the down grade. But finally, it is important not to confuse nationalism with mere worship of success. The nationalist does not go on the principle of simply ganging up with the strongest side. On the contrary, having picked his side, he persuades himself that it *is* the strongest, and is able to stick to his belief even when the facts are overwhelmingly against him. Nationalism is power-hunger tempered by self-deception. Every nationalist is capable of the most flagrant dishonesty, but he is also – since he is conscious of serving something bigger than himself – unshakeably certain of being in the right.

Now that I have given this lengthy definition, I think it will be admitted that the habit of mind I am talking about is widespread among the English intelligentsia, and more widespread there than among the mass of the people. For those who feel deeply about contemporary politics, certain topics have become so infected by considerations of prestige that a genuinely rational approach to them is almost impossible. Out of the hundreds of examples that one might choose, take this question: Which of the three great allies, the U.S.S.R., Britain and the U.S.A., has contributed most to the defeat of Germany? In theory it should be possible to give a reasoned and perhaps even a conclusive answer to this question. In practice, however, the necessary calculations cannot be made, because anyone likely to bother his head about such a question would inevitably see it in terms of competitive prestige. He would therefore *start* by deciding in favour of Russia, Britain or America as the case might be, and only *after* this would begin searching for arguments that seemed to support his case. And there are whole strings of kindred questions to which you can only get an honest answer from someone who is indifferent to the whole subject involved, and whose opinion on it is probably worthless in any case. Hence, partly, the remarkable failure in our time of political and military prediction. It is curious to reflect that out of all the 'experts' of all the schools, there was not a single one who was able to foresee so likely an event as the Russo-German Pact of 1939.* And when the news of the Pact broke, the most wildly divergent explanations of it were given, and predictions were made which were falsified almost immediately, being

---

* A few writers of conservative tendency, such as Peter Drucker, foretold an agreement between Germany and Russia, but they expected an actual alliance or amalgamation which would be permanent. No Marxist or other left-wing writer, of whatever colour, came anywhere near foretelling the Pact [Orwell's footnote].

based in nearly every case not on a study of probabilities but on a desire to make the U.S.S.R. seem good or bad, strong or weak. Political or military commentators, like astrologers, can survive almost any mistake, because their more devoted followers do not look to them for an appraisal of the facts but for the stimulation of nationalistic loyalties.* And aesthetic judgements, especially literary judgements, are often corrupted in the same way as political ones. It would be difficult for an Indian Nationalist to enjoy reading Kipling or for a Conservative to see merit in Mayakovsky,[3] and there is always a temptation to claim that any book whose tendency one disagrees with must be a bad book from a *literary* point of view. People of strongly nationalistic outlook often perform this sleight of hand without being conscious of dishonesty.

In England, if one simply considers the number of people involved, it is probable that the dominant form of nationalism is old-fashioned British jingoism. It is certain that this is still widespread, and much more so than most observers would have believed a dozen years ago. However, in this essay I am concerned chiefly with the reactions of the intelligentsia, among whom jingoism and even patriotism of the old kind are almost dead, though they now seem to be reviving among a minority. Among the intelligentsia, it hardly needs saying that the dominant form of nationalism is Communism – using this word in a very loose sense, to include not merely Communist Party members but 'fellow travellers' and Russophiles generally. A Communist, for my purpose here, is one who looks upon the U.S.S.R. as his Fatherland and feels it his duty to justify Russian policy and advance Russian interests at all costs. Obviously such people abound in England today, and their direct and indirect influence is very great. But many other forms of nationalism also flourish, and it is by

---

* The military commentators of the popular press can mostly be classified as pro-Russian or anti-Russian, pro-blimp or anti-blimp. Such errors as believing the Maginot Line impregnable, or predicting that Russia would conquer Germany in three months, have failed to shake their reputation, because they were always saying what their own particular audience wanted to hear. The two military critics most favoured by the intelligentsia are Captain Liddell Hart and Major-General Fuller,[2] the first of whom teaches that the defence is stronger than the attack, and the second that the attack is stronger than the defence. This contradiction has not prevented both of them from being accepted as authorities by the same public. The secret reason for their vogue in left-wing circles is that both of them are at odds with the War Office [Orwell's footnote].

noticing the points of resemblance between different and even seemingly opposed currents of thought that one can best get the matter into perspective.

Ten or twenty years ago, the form of nationalism most closely corresponding to Communism today was political Catholicism. Its most outstanding exponent – though he was perhaps an extreme case rather than a typical one – was G. K. Chesterton.[4] Chesterton was a writer of considerable talent who chose to suppress both his sensibilities and his intellectual honesty in the cause of Roman Catholic propaganda. During the last twenty years or so of his life, his entire output was in reality an endless repetition of the same thing, under its laboured cleverness as simple and boring as 'Great is Diana of the Ephesians'.[5] Every book that he wrote, every paragraph, every sentence, every incident in every story, every scrap of dialogue, had to demonstrate beyond possibility of mistake the superiority of the Catholic over the Protestant or the pagan. But Chesterton was not content to think of this superiority as merely intellectual or spiritual: it had to be translated into terms of national prestige and military power, which entailed an ignorant idealisation of the Latin countries, especially France. Chesterton had not lived long in France, and his picture of it – as a land of Catholic peasants incessantly singing the *Marseillaise* over glasses of red wine – had about as much relation to reality as *Chu Chin Chow* has to every-day life in Baghdad. And with this went not only an enormous over-estimation of French military power (both before and after 1914–18 he maintained that France, by itself, was stronger than Germany), but a silly and vulgar glorification of the actual process of war. Chesterton's battle poems, such as *Lepanto* or *The Ballad of Saint Barbara*, make *The Charge of the Light Brigade* read like a pacifist tract: they are perhaps the most tawdry bits of bombast to be found in our language. The interesting thing is that had the romantic rubbish which he habitually wrote about France and the French army been written by somebody else about Britain and the British army, he would have been the first to jeer. In home politics he was a Little Englander, a true hater of jingoism and imperialism, and according to his lights a true friend of democracy. Yet when he looked outwards into the international field, he could forsake his principles without even noticing that he was doing so. Thus, his almost mystical belief in the virtues of democracy did not prevent him from admiring Mussolini. Mussolini had destroyed the representative government and the freedom of the press for which Chesterton had struggled so hard at home, but Mussolini was an Italian and had made Italy strong, and that settled the matter. Nor did Chesterton ever find a word to say against imperialism and the conquest of coloured races when they were practised by Italians or Frenchmen. His hold on reality, his literary taste, and even to some extent his moral sense, were dislocated as soon as his nationalistic loyalties were involved.

Obviously there are considerable resemblances between political Catholicism as exemplified by Chesterton, and Communism. So there are between either of these and, for instance, Scottish Nationalism, Zionism, Anti-semitism or Trotskyism. It would be an over-simplification to say that all forms of nationalism are the same, even in their mental atmosphere, but there are certain rules that hold good in all cases. The following are the principal characteristics of nationalist thought: —

OBSESSION. As nearly as possible, no nationalist ever thinks, talks or writes about anything except the superiority of his own power unit. It is difficult if not impossible for any nationalist to conceal his allegiance. The smallest slur upon his own unit, or any implied praise of a rival organisation, fills him with uneasiness which he can only relieve by making some sharp retort. If the chosen unit is an actual country, such as Ireland or India, he will generally claim superiority for it not only in military power and political virtue, but in art, literature, sport, the structure of the language, the physical beauty of the inhabitants, and perhaps even in climate, scenery and cooking. He will show great sensitiveness about such things as the correct display of flags, relative size of headlines and the order in which different countries are named.* Nomenclature plays a very important part in nationalist thought. Countries which have won their independence or gone through a nationalist revolution usually change their names, and any country or other unit round which strong feelings revolve is likely to have several names, each of them carrying a different implication. The two sides in the Spanish Civil War had between them

---

* Certain Americans have expressed dissatisfaction because 'Anglo-American' is the normal form of combination for these two words. It has been proposed to substitute 'Americo-British' [Orwell's footnote].

nine or ten names expressing different degrees of love and hatred. Some of these names (*e.g.* 'Patriots' for Franco-supporters, or 'Loyalists' for Government-supporters) were frankly question-begging, and there was no single one of them which the two rival factions could have agreed to use. All nationalists consider it a duty to spread their own language to the detriment of rival languages, and among English-speakers this struggle reappears in subtler form as a struggle between dialects. Anglophobe Americans will refuse to use a slang phrase if they know it to be of British origin, and the conflict between Latinisers and Germanisers often has nationalist motives behind it. Scottish nationalists insist on the superiority of Lowland Scots, and Socialists whose nationalism takes the form of class hatred tirade against the B.B.C. accent and even the broad 'A'. One could multiply instances. Nationalist thought often gives the impression of being tinged by belief in sympathetic magic – a belief which probably comes out in the widespread custom of burning political enemies in effigy, or using pictures of them as targets in shooting galleries.

INSTABILITY. The intensity with which they are held does not prevent nationalist loyalties from being transferable. To begin with, as I have pointed out already, they can be and often are fastened upon some foreign country. One quite commonly finds that great national leaders, or the founders of nationalist movements, do not even belong to the country they have glorified. Sometimes they are outright foreigners, or more often they come from peripheral areas where nationality is doubtful. Examples are Stalin, Hitler, Napoleon, de Valera, D'Israeli, Poincaré, Beaverbrook.[6] The Pan-German movement was in part the creation of an Englishman, Houston Chamberlain. For the past fifty or a hundred years, transferred nationalism has been a common phenomenon among literary intellectuals. With Lafcadio Hearn[7] the transference was to Japan, with [Thomas] Carlyle and many others of his time to Germany, and in our own age it is usually Russia. But the peculiarly interesting fact is that *re*-transference is also possible. A country or other unit which has been worshipped for years may suddenly become detestable, and some other object of affection may take its place with almost no interval. In the first version of H. G. Wells's *Outline of History*,[8] and others of his writings about that time, one finds the United States praised almost as extravagantly as Russia is praised by Communists today: yet within a few years this uncritical admiration had turned into hostility. The bigoted Communist who changes in a space of weeks, or even days, into an equally bigoted Trotskyist is a common spectacle. In continental Europe Fascist movements were largely recruited from among Communists, and the opposite process may well happen within the next few years. What remains constant in the nationalist is his own state of mind: the object of his feelings is changeable, and may be imaginary.

But for an intellectual, transference has an important function which I have already mentioned shortly in connection with Chesterton. It makes it possible for him to be much *more* nationalistic – more vulgar, more silly, more malignant, more dishonest – than he could ever be on behalf of his native country, or any unit of which he had real knowledge. When one sees the slavish or boastful rubbish that is written about Stalin, the Red Army, etc. by fairly intelligent and sensitive people, one realises that this is only possible because some kind of dislocation has taken place. In societies such as ours, it is unusual for anyone describable as an intellectual to feel a very deep attachment to his own country. Public opinion – that is, the section of public opinion of which he as an intellectual is aware – will not allow him to do so. Most of the people surrounding him are sceptical and disaffected, and he may adopt the same attitude from imitativeness or sheer cowardice: in that case he will have abandoned the form of nationalism that lies nearest to hand without getting any closer to a genuinely internationalist outlook. He still feels the need for a Fatherland, and it is natural to look for one somewhere abroad. Having found it, he can wallow unrestrainedly in exactly those emotions from which he believes that he has emancipated himself. God, the King, the Empire, the Union Jack – all the overthrown idols can reappear under different names, and because they are not recognised for what they are they can be worshipped with a good conscience. Transferred nationalism, like the use of scapegoats, is a way of attaining salvation without altering one's conduct.

INDIFFERENCE TO REALITY. All nationalists have the power of not seeing resemblances between similar sets of facts. A British Tory will defend self-determination in Europe and oppose it in India with no feeling of inconsistency. Actions are held to be good or bad, not on their own merits but according to who does them, and there is almost no kind of outrage – torture, the use of hostages, forced labour, mass deportations, imprisonment without trial, forgery, assassination, the bombing of civilians – which does not change its moral colour when it is committed by 'our' side. The Liberal *News Chronicle* published, as an example of shocking barbarity, photographs of Russians hanged by the Germans, and then a year or two later published with warm approval almost exactly similar photographs of Germans hanged by the Russians.* It is the same with historical events. History is thought of largely in nationalist terms, and such things as the Inquisition, the tortures of the Star Chamber, the exploits of the English buccaneers (Sir Francis Drake, for instance, who was given to sinking Spanish prisoners alive), the Reign of Terror, the heroes of the Mutiny blowing hundreds of Indians from the guns, or Cromwell's soldiers slashing Irishwomen's faces with razors, become morally neutral or even meritorious when it is felt that they were done in 'the right' cause. If one looks back over the past quarter of a century, one finds that there was hardly a single year when atrocity stories were not being reported from some part of the world: and yet in not one single case were these atrocities – in Spain, Russia, China, Hungary, Mexico, Amritsar, Smyrna – believed in and disapproved of by the English intelligentsia as a whole.[9] Whether such deeds were reprehensible, or even whether they happened, was always decided according to political predilection.

The nationalist not only does not disapprove of atrocities committed by his own side, but has a remarkable capacity for not even hearing about them. For quite six years the English admirers of Hitler contrived not to learn of the existence of Dachau and Buchenwald. And those who are loudest in denouncing the German concentration camps are often quite unaware, or only very dimly aware, that there are also concentration camps in Russia. Huge events like the Ukraine famine of 1933, involving the deaths of millions of people, have actually escaped the attention of the majority of English Russophiles. Many English people have heard

---

* The *News Chronicle* advised its readers to visit the news film at which the entire execution could be witnessed, with close-ups. The *Star* published with seeming approval photographs of nearly naked female collaborationists being baited by the Paris mob. These photographs had a marked resemblance to the Nazi photographs of Jews being baited by the Berlin mob [Orwell's footnote].

almost nothing about the extermination of German and Polish Jews during the present war. Their own anti-semitism has caused this vast crime to bounce off their consciousness. In nationalist thought there are facts which are both true and untrue, known and unknown. A known fact may be so unbearable that it is habitually pushed aside and not allowed to enter into logical processes, or on the other hand it may enter into every calculation and yet never be admitted as a fact, even in one's own mind.

Every nationalist is haunted by the belief that the past can be altered. He spends part of his time in a fantasy world in which things happen as they should – in which, for example, the Spanish Armada was a success or the Russian Revolution was crushed in 1918 – and he will transfer fragments of this world to the history books whenever possible. Much of the propagandist writing of our time amounts to plain forgery. Material facts are suppressed, dates altered, quotations removed from their context and doctored so as to change their meaning. Events which, it is felt, ought not to have happened are left unmentioned and ultimately denied.* In 1927 Chiang Kai-Shek boiled hundreds of Communists alive, and yet within ten years he had become one of the heroes of the Left. The realignment of world politics had brought him into the anti-Fascist camp, and so it was felt that the boiling of the Communists 'didn't count', or perhaps had not happened. The primary aim of propaganda is, of course, to influence contemporary opinion, but those who rewrite history do probably believe with part of their minds that they are actually thrusting facts into the past. When one considers the elaborate forgeries that have been committed in order to show that Trotsky did not play a valuable part in the Russian civil war, it is difficult to feel that the people responsible are merely lying. More probably they feel that their own version *was* what happened in the sight of God, and that one is justified in rearranging the records accordingly.

Indifference to objective truth is encouraged by the sealing-off of one part of the world from another, which makes it harder and harder to

---

* An example is the Russo-German Pact, which is being effaced as quickly as possible from public memory. A Russian correspondent[10] informs me that mention of the Pact is already being omitted from Russian year books which table recent political events [Orwell's footnote].

discover what is actually happening. There can often be a genuine doubt about the most enormous events. For example, it is impossible to calculate within millions, perhaps even tens of millions, the number of deaths caused by the present war. The calamities that are constantly being reported – battles, massacres, famines, revolutions – tend to inspire in the average person a feeling of unreality. One has no way of verifying the facts, one is not even fully certain that they have happened, and one is always presented with totally different interpretations from different sources. What were the rights and wrongs of the Warsaw rising of August 1944? Is it true about the German gas ovens in Poland? Who was really to blame for the Bengal famine? Probably the truth is discoverable, but the facts will be so dishonestly set forth in almost any newspaper that the ordinary reader can be forgiven either for swallowing lies or for failing to form an opinion. The general uncertainty as to what is really happening makes it easier to cling to lunatic beliefs. Since nothing is ever quite proved or disproved, the most unmistakable fact can be impudently denied. Moreover, although endlessly brooding on power, victory, defeat, revenge, the nationalist is often somewhat uninterested in what happens in the real world. What he wants is to *feel* that his own unit is getting the better of some other unit, and he can more easily do this by scoring off an adversary than by examining the facts to see whether they support him. All nationalist controversy is at the debating-society level. It is always entirely inconclusive, since each contestant invariably believes himself to have won the victory. Some nationalists are not far from schizophrenia, living quite happily amid dreams of power and conquest which have no connection with the physical world.

I have examined as best I can the mental habits which are common to all forms of nationalism. The next thing is to classify those forms, but obviously this cannot be done comprehensively. Nationalism is an enormous subject. The world is tormented by innumerable delusions and hatreds which cut across one another in an extremely complex way, and some of the most sinister of them have not yet even impinged on the European consciousness. In this essay I am concerned with nationalism as it occurs among the English intelligentsia. In them, much more often than in ordinary English people, it is unmixed with patriotism and can therefore be studied pure. Below are listed the varieties of nationalism now flourishing among English intellectuals, with such comments as seem to be needed. It is convenient to use three headings, Positive, Transferred and Negative, though some varieties will fit into more than one category: –

POSITIVE NATIONALISM

(i.) NEO-TORYISM. Exemplified by such people as Lord Elton, A. P. Herbert, G. M. Young, Professor Pickthorne, by the literature of the Tory Reform Committee, and by such magazines as the *New English Review* and the *Nineteenth Century and After*. The real motive force of Neo-Toryism, giving it its nationalistic character and differentiating it from ordinary Conservatism, is the desire not to recognise that British power and influence have declined. Even those who are realistic enough to see that Britain's military position is not what it was, tend to claim that 'English ideas' (usually left undefined) must dominate the world. All Neo-Tories are anti-Russian, but sometimes the main emphasis is anti-American. The significant thing is that this school of thought seems to be gaining ground among youngish intellectuals, sometimes ex-Communists, who have passed through the usual process of disillusionment and become disillusioned with that. The Anglophobe who suddenly becomes violently pro-British is a fairly common figure. Writers who illustrate this tendency are F. A. Voigt, Malcolm Muggeridge, Evelyn Waugh, Hugh Kingsmill, and a psychologically similar development can be observed in T. S. Eliot, Wyndham Lewis and various of their followers.

(ii.) CELTIC NATIONALISM. Welsh, Irish and Scottish nationalism have points of difference but are alike in their anti-English orientation. Members of all three movements have opposed the war while continuing to describe themselves as pro-Russian, and the lunatic fringe has even contrived to be simultaneously pro-Russian and pro-Nazi. But Celtic nationalism is not the same thing as Anglophobia. Its motive force is a belief in the past and future greatness of the Celtic peoples, and it has a strong tinge of racialism. The Celt is supposed to be spiritually superior to the Saxon – simpler, more creative, less vulgar, less snobbish, etc. – but the usual power-hunger is there under the surface. One symptom of it is the delusion that Eire, Scotland or even Wales could preserve its independence unaided and owes nothing to British protection. Among writers, good examples of this school of thought are Hugh MacDiarmid and Sean O'Casey. No modern Irish writer, even of the stature of Yeats or Joyce, is completely free from traces of nationalism.

(iii.) ZIONISM. This has the usual characteristics of a nationalist movement, but the American variant of it seems to be more violent and malignant than the British. I classify it under Direct and not Transferred nationalism because it flourishes almost exclusively among the Jews themselves. In England, for several rather incongruous reasons, the intelligentsia are mostly pro-Jew on the Palestine issue, but they do not feel strongly about it. All English people of good will are also pro-Jew in the sense of disapproving of Nazi persecution. But any actual nationalistic loyalty, or belief in the innate superiority of Jews, is hardly to be found among Gentiles.

TRANSFERRED NATIONALISM

(i.) COMMUNISM.

(ii.) POLITICAL CATHOLICISM.

(iii.) COLOUR FEELING. The old-style contemptuous attitude towards 'natives' has been much weakened in England, and various pseudo-scientific theories emphasising the superiority of the white race have been abandoned.* Among the intelligentsia, colour feeling only occurs in the transposed form, that is, as a belief in the innate superiority of the coloured races. This is now increasingly common among English intellectuals, probably resulting more often from masochism and sexual frustration than from contact with the Oriental and Negro nationalist movements. Even among those who do not feel strongly on the colour question, snobbery and imitation have a powerful influence. Almost any English intellectual

---

* A good example is the sunstroke superstition. Until recently it was believed that the white races were much more liable to sunstroke than the coloured, and that a white man could not safely walk about in tropical sunshine without a pith helmet. There was no evidence whatever for this theory, but it served the purpose of accentuating the difference between 'natives' and Europeans. During the present war the theory has been quietly dropped and whole armies manoeuvre in the tropics without pith helmets. So long as the sunstroke superstition survived, English doctors in India appear to have believed in it as firmly as laymen [Orwell's footnote].

would be scandalised by the claim that the white races are superior to the coloured, whereas the opposite claim would seem to him unexceptionable even if he disagreed with it. Nationalistic attachment to the coloured races is usually mixed up with the belief that their sex lives are superior, and there is a large underground mythology about the sexual prowess of Negroes.

(iv.) CLASS FEELING. Among upper-class and middle-class intellectuals, only in the transposed form – *i.e.* as a belief in the superiority of the proletariat. Here again, inside the intelligentsia, the pressure of public opinion is overwhelming. Nationalistic loyalty towards the proletariat, and most vicious theoretical hatred of the bourgeoisie, can and often do co-exist with ordinary snobbishness in every-day life.

(v.) PACIFISM. The majority of pacifists either belong to obscure religious sects or are simply humanitarians who object to taking life and prefer not to follow their thoughts beyond that point. But there is a minority of intellectual pacifists whose real though unadmitted motive appears to be hatred of western democracy and admiration for totalitarianism. Pacifist propaganda usually boils down to saying that one side is as bad as the other, but if one looks closely at the writings of the younger intellectual pacifists, one finds that they do not by any means express impartial disapproval but are directed almost entirely against Britain and the United States. Moreover they do not as a rule condemn violence as such, but only violence used in defence of the western countries. The Russians, unlike the British, are not blamed for defending themselves by warlike means, and indeed all pacifist propaganda of this type avoids mention of Russia or China. It is not claimed, again, that the Indians should abjure violence in their struggle against the British. Pacifist literature abounds with equivocal remarks which, if they mean anything, appear to mean that statesmen of the type of Hitler are preferable to those of the type of Churchill, and that violence is perhaps excusable if it is violent enough. After the fall of France, the French pacifists, faced by a real choice which their English colleagues have not had to make, mostly went over to the Nazis, and in England there appears to have been some small overlap of membership between the Peace Pledge Union and the Blackshirts. Pacifist writers have written in praise of Carlyle, one of the intellectual fathers of Fascism. All in all it is difficult not to feel that pacifism, as it appears among a section of the intelligentsia, is secretly inspired by an admiration for power and successful cruelty. The mistake was made of pinning this emotion to Hitler, but it could easily be re-transferred.

NEGATIVE NATIONALISM

(i.) ANGLOPHOBIA. Within the intelligentsia, a derisive and mildly hostile attitude towards Britain is more or less compulsory, but it is an unfaked emotion in many cases. During the war it was manifested in the defeatism of the intelligentsia, which persisted long after it had become clear that the Axis powers could not win. Many people were undisguisedly pleased when Singapore fell or when the British were driven out of Greece, and there was a remarkable unwillingness to believe in good news, *e.g.* el Alamein, or the number of German planes shot down in the Battle of Britain. English left-wing intellectuals did not, of course, actually want the Germans or Japanese to win the war, but many of them could not help getting a certain kick out of seeing their own country humiliated, and wanted to feel that the final victory would be due to Russia, or perhaps America, and not to Britain. In foreign politics many intellectuals follow the principle that any faction backed by Britain must be in the wrong. As a result, 'enlightened' opinion is quite largely a mirror-image of Conservative policy. Anglophobia is always liable to reversal, hence that fairly common spectacle, the pacifist of one war who is a bellicist in the next.

(ii.) ANTI-SEMITISM. There is little evidence about this at present, because the Nazi persecutions have made it necessary for any thinking person to side with the Jews against their oppressors. Anyone educated enough to have heard the word 'anti-semitism' claims as a matter of course to be free of it, and anti-Jewish remarks are carefully eliminated from all classes of literature. Actually anti-semitism appears to be widespread, even among intellectuals, and the general conspiracy of silence probably helps to exacerbate it. People of Left opinions are not immune to it, and their attitude is sometimes affected by the fact that Trotskyists and Anarchists tend to be Jews. But anti-semitism comes more naturally to people of Conservative tendency, who suspect the Jews of weakening national morale and diluting the national culture. Neo-Tories and political Catholics are always liable to succumb to anti-semitism, at least intermittently.

(iii.) TROTSKYISM.[11] This word is used so loosely as to include anarchists, democratic Socialists and even Liberals. I use it here to mean a doctrinaire Marxist whose main motive is hostility to the Stalin régime. Trotskyism can be better studied in obscure pamphlets or in papers like the *Socialist Appeal* than in the works of Trotsky himself, who was by no means a man of one idea. Although in some places, for instance in the United States, Trotskyism is able to attract a fairly large number of adherents and develop into an organised movement with a petty fuehrer of its own, its inspiration is essentially negative. The Trotskyist is *against* Stalin just as the Communist is *for* him, and, like the majority of Communists, he wants not so much to alter the external world as to feel that the battle for prestige is going in his own favour. In each case there is the same obsessive fixation on a single subject, the same inability to form a genuinely rational opinion based on probabilities. The fact that Trotskyists are everywhere a persecuted minority, and that the accusation usually made against them, *i.e.* of collaborating with the Fascists, is obviously false, creates an impression that Trotskyism is intellectually and morally superior to Communism; but it is doubtful whether there is much difference. The most typical Trotskyists, in any case, are ex-Communists, and no one arrives at Trotskyism except *via* one of the left-wing movements. No Communist, unless tethered to his party by years of habit, is secure against a sudden lapse into Trotskyism. The opposite process does not seem to happen equally often, though there is no clear reason why it should not.

In the classification I have attempted above, it will seem that I have often exaggerated, oversimplified, made unwarranted assumptions and left out of account the existence of ordinarily decent motives. This was inevitable, because in this essay I am trying to isolate and identify tendencies which exist in all our minds and pervert our thinking, without necessarily occurring in a pure state or operating continuously. It is important at this point to correct the oversimplified picture which I have been obliged to make. To begin with, one has no right to assume that *everyone*, or even every intellectual, is infected by nationalism; secondly, nationalism can be intermittent and limited. An intelligent man may half-succumb to a belief which attracts him but which he knows to be absurd, and he may keep it out of his mind for long periods, only reverting to it in moments of anger or sentimentality, or when he is certain that no important issue is involved. Thirdly, a nationalistic creed may be adopted in good faith from non-nationalist motives. Fourthly, several kinds of nationalism, even kinds that cancel out, can co-exist in the same person.

All the way through I have said 'the nationalist does this' or 'the nationalist does that', using for purposes of illustration the extreme, barely sane type of nationalist who has no neutral areas in his mind and no interest in anything except the struggle for power. Actually such people are fairly common, but they are not worth powder and shot. In real life Lord Elton, D. N. Pritt, Lady Houston, Ezra Pound, Lord Vansittart, Father Coughlin[12] and all the rest of their dreary tribe have to be fought against, but their intellectual deficiencies hardly need pointing out. Monomania is not interesting, and the fact that no nationalist of the more bigoted kind can write a book which still seems worth reading after a lapse of years has a certain deodorising effect. But when one has admitted that nationalism has not triumphed everywhere, that there are still people whose judgements are not at the mercy of their desires, the fact does remain that the nationalistic habit of thought is widespread, so much so that various large and pressing problems – India, Poland, Palestine, the Spanish Civil War, the Moscow trials, the American Negroes, the Russo-German pact or what-have-you – cannot be, or at least never are, discussed upon a reasonable level. The Eltons and Pritts and Coughlins, each of them simply an enormous mouth bellowing the same lie over and over again, are obviously extreme cases, but we deceive ourselves if we do not realise that we can all resemble them in unguarded moments. Let a certain note be struck, let this or that corn be trodden on – and it may be a corn whose very existence has been unsuspected hitherto – and the most fair-minded and sweet-tempered person may suddenly be transformed into a vicious partisan, anxious only to 'score' over his adversary and indifferent as to how many lies he tells or how many logical errors he commits in doing so. When Lloyd George, who was an opponent of the Boer War, announced in the House of Commons that the British communiques, if one added them together, claimed the killing of more Boers than the whole Boer nation contained, it is recorded that Arthur Balfour[13] rose to his feet and shouted 'Cad!'. Very few people are proof against lapses of this type. The Negro snubbed by a white woman, the Englishman who hears England ignorantly criticised by an American, the Catholic apologist reminded of the Spanish Armada, will all react in much the same way. One prod to the nerve of nationalism, and the intellectual decencies can vanish, the past can be altered, and the plainest facts can be denied.

If one harbours anywhere in one's mind a nationalistic loyalty or hatred, certain facts, although in a sense known to be true, are inadmissible. Here are just a few examples. I list below five types of nationalist, and against each I append a fact which it is impossible for that type of nationalist to accept, even in his secret thoughts: —

BRITISH TORY. Britain will come out of this war with reduced power and prestige.

COMMUNIST. If she had not been aided by Britain and America, Russia would have been defeated by Germany.

IRISH NATIONALIST. Eire can only remain independent because of British protection.

TROTSKYIST. The Stalin régime is accepted by the Russian masses.

PACIFIST. Those who 'abjure' violence can only do so because others are committing violence on their behalf.

All of these facts are grossly obvious if one's emotions do not happen to be involved: but to the kind of person named in each case they are also *intolerable*, and so they have to be denied, and false theories constructed upon their denial. I come back to the astonishing failure of military prediction in the present war. It is, I think, true to say that the intelligentsia have been more wrong about the progress of the war than the common people, and that they were wrong precisely because they were more swayed by partisan feelings. The average intellectual of the Left believed, for instance, that the war was lost in 1940, that the Germans were bound to overrun Egypt in 1942, that the Japanese would never be driven out of the lands they had conquered, and that the Anglo-American bombing offensive was making no impression on Germany. He could believe these things because his hatred of the British ruling class forbade him to admit that British plans could succeed. There is no limit to the follies that can be swallowed if one is under the influence of feelings of this kind. I have heard it confidently stated, for instance, that the American troops had been brought to Europe not to fight the Germans but to crush an English revolution. One has to belong to the intelligentsia to believe things like that: no ordinary man could be such a fool. When Hitler invaded Russia, the officials of the M.O.I.[14] issued 'as background' a warning that Russia might be expected to collapse in six weeks. On the other hand the Communists regarded every phase of the war as a Russian victory, even when the Russians were driven back almost to the Caspian sea and had lost several million prisoners. There is no need to multiply instances. The point is that as soon as fear, hatred, jealousy and power-worship are involved, the sense of reality becomes unhinged. And, as I have pointed out already, the sense of right and wrong becomes unhinged also. There is no crime, absolutely none, that cannot be condoned when 'our' side commits it. Even if one does not deny that the crime has happened, even if one knows that it is exactly the same crime as one has condemned in some other case, even if one admits in an intellectual sense that it is unjustified – still one cannot *feel* that it is wrong. Loyalty is involved, and so pity ceases to function.

The reason for the rise and spread of nationalism is far too big a question to be raised here. It is enough to say that, in the forms in which it appears among English intellectuals, it is a distorted reflection of the frightful battles actually happening in the external world, and that its worst follies have been made possible by the break-down of patriotism and religious belief. If one follows up this train of thought, one is in danger of being led into a species of Conservatism, or into political quietism. It can be plausibly argued, for instance—it is even probably true—that patriotism is an inoculation against nationalism, that monarchy is a guard against dictatorship, and that organised religion is a guard against superstition. Or again it can be argued that *no* unbiassed outlook is possible, that *all* creeds and causes involve the same lies, follies and barbarities; and this is often advanced as a reason for keeping out of politics altogether. I do not accept this argument, if only because in the modern world no one describable as an intellectual *can* keep out of politics in the sense of not caring about them. I think one must engage in politics

– using the word in a wide sense – and that one must have preferences:
that is, one must recognise that some causes are objectively better than
others, even if they are advanced by equally bad means. As for the
nationalistic loves and hatreds that I have spoken of, they are part of the
make-up of most of us, whether we like it or not. Whether it is possible
to get rid of them I do not know, but I do believe that it is possible to
struggle against them, and that this is essentially a *moral* effort. It is a
question first of all of discovering what one really is, what one's own
feelings really are, and then of making allowance for the inevitable bias.
If you hate and fear Russia, if you are jealous of the wealth and power of
America, if you despise Jews, if you have a sentiment of inferiority towards
the British ruling class, you cannot get rid of those feelings simply by
taking thought. But you can at least recognise that you have them, and
prevent them from contaminating your mental processes. The emotional
urges which are inescapable, and are perhaps even necessary to political
action, should be able to exist side by side with an acceptance of reality.
But this, I repeat, needs a *moral* effort, and contemporary English literature,
so far as it is alive at all to the major issues of our time, shows how few
of us are prepared to make it.

*The Ministry of Information arranged for abridgements of this article to be
published in periodicals it published in French, Dutch, Italian and Finnish
in 1946; see* XVII/155–6.

1. Nos. 1–8 of *Polemic*, 1945–7, were edited by Humphrey Slater. Orwell's Payments Book
indicates that this essay was completed on 15 May 1945, and that he was paid a fee of £25.
2. Captain Sir Basil Henry Liddell Hart (1895–1970), military historian and commentator,
and author of infantry training manuals. Major-General J. F. C. Fuller (1878–1966; CB,
DSO), soldier and author; served with distinction in the South African war and World War
I. He published many books on military history and future developments. In January 1993,
Fuller's name appeared in a list of eighty-two suspected potential German collaborators
released by the Public Record Office. Fuller headed the list of those to be immediately
arrested if German forces landed in Britain in 1940–41. In the *DNB*, Field-Marshal Lord
Carver described Fuller as believing in 'an idealised form of fascism' in the 1930s.
3. Vladimir Mayakovsky (1893–1930, by suicide), Russian (Georgian) Futurist poet and
satirical playwright. During the 1917 Revolution he was the spokesman for Bolshevik
propaganda.
4. Gilbert Keith Chesterton (1874–1936), essayist, biographer, novelist and poet; remem-

bered particularly for his comic verse, the Father Brown detective stories (1911–35) and *The Man Who Was Thursday* (1908). He was converted to Roman Catholicism in 1922. He founded *G.K.'s Weekly* in 1925 and edited it until his death. He published Orwell's first 'commercial' article in English, 'A Farthing Newspaper', in December 1928; see *Orwell and the Dispossessed* in this series.

5. The Statue of Ephesus was either a wooden statue or a cone, said to have fallen from heaven (so, a meteorite), covered with breasts. Acts 19:24–8 describes how silversmiths at Ephesus made 'silver shrines for Diana' which 'brought no small gain unto the craftsmen'. One such, Demetrius, raised the wrath of his fellows because St Paul 'hath persuaded and turned away much people, saying that they be no gods, which are made with hands'. Thus the silversmiths feared the loss of business and, in their anger, they 'cried out, saying, Great is Diana of the Ephesians'. This came to signify the power of self-interest over truth.

6. Orwell's Second Literary Notebook, 1948 (XIX/*3515*), lists 'Nationalist leaders & romantics of foreign origin'. Stalin is listed as Georgian; Hitler, Austrian; Napoleon, Corsican; Eamon de Valera (1882–1975; three times Prime Minister of Eire and its President, 1959–73), is queried as Portuguese and Jewish; D'Israeli (Benjamin Disraeli, 1804–81; twice Prime Minister, statesman and novelist; son of an Anglicized Jew), as 'Jewish (Spanish)'; Raymond Poincaré (1860–1934; three times Prime Minister of France, and President, 1913–20; he urged severe punishment of Germany after World War I), as 'Alsatian?'; Lord Beaverbrook, Canadian.

7. Lafcadio Hearn (1850–1904), writer, translator, university teacher, born in the Ionian Islands of Irish–Maltese parents. He lived in the United States, 1869–90, and then in Japan, becoming a citizen of that country. He wrote several books on Japanese life and customs and three of his ghost stories were made into a Japanese film, *Kwaidon* (1965).

8. First published in twenty-four fortnightly parts, 1919–20. There were numerous revised editions thereafter.

9. Following the assassination of Reinhard Heydrich (1904–42), head of the Gestapo in Occupied Czechoslovakia, the Germans wiped out the village of Lidice, shooting all the men and sending women and children to concentration camps. Of some 2,000 inhabitants, very few survived. The Crown Film Unit made a film setting this event in Ystradgynlais, South Wales (*The Silent Village*, directed by Humphrey Jennings, 1943). In his War-time Diary for 11 June 1942 (XIII/*1218*), Orwell reported this atrocity and then made a list of atrocities believed by the politically Right and Left. One, the Turkish massacre of Armenians in Smyrna in 1920, was, he wrote, believed by Right and Left. He does not list atrocities in Hungary and Mexico; for Amritsar, see above, p. 176, n. 2 (General Dyer); China is included because of Japanese atrocities (believed by the Left – e.g. Nanking); Bolshevik atrocities, inflicted on their own people in 1920, 1933 and 1937 (the purges), are said to be believed by the Right; the Right believed 'Red atrocities in Spain', and the Left, Fascist atrocities there, 1937–9. Among other atrocities, Orwell lists the Left believing British atrocities in 1939 in the 'Isle of Man etc', referring to those who had come to Britain as refugees (mainly Jewish) being interned there at the outbreak of war. The 'etc' might refer to the shipping of Jews to Australia on the SS *Dunera*. Both, though misconceived, were stupid rather than cruel on the scale of other atrocities listed.

10. Orwell's correspondent was Gleb Struve (1898–1985), born in St Petersburg, who taught at the School of Slavonic and East European Studies, London University, 1932–47, and then

at the University of California, Berkeley, 1947–65. He was the author of *Soviet Literature, 1917–50* (1951), reissued as *Soviet Literature under Lenin and Stalin* (1973).

11. Trotskyism was a theory of permanent revolution enunciated by Leon Trotsky (1879–1940), and brought him into sharp conflict with Stalin. He played an important part in bringing into effect the 1917 Revolution and is credited with the creation of the Red Army. He was sent into internal exile in 1927, expelled from the USSR in 1929 and in photographs showing him in action in 1917 he was airbrushed out. He was sentenced to death in his absence in 1937. He was assassinated on Stalin's orders in Mexico, where he had taken refuge.

12. For Lord Elton, see n. 2 to 'Benefit of Clergy: Some Notes on Salvador Dali'; D. N. Pritt, see n. 1 to London Letter, 17 August 1941; Father Coughlin, see p. 158, n. 2 to War-time Diary: all above. Lady (Dame Fanny Lucy) Houston (1857–1936) owned and edited the *Saturday Review*, 1933–6 and 1934–6 respectively. She was fiercely patriotic and anti-Communist, and denounced most politicians except the Fascist, Oswald Mosley. She was a supporter of King Edward VIII at the time of his abdication. Ezra Pound (1885–1972), American poet and critic. He was an active supporter of Mussolini. At the end of the war he was charged with treason by the US and declared insane. Orwell wrote in support of the award of the Bollingen Prize for Poetry to him in 1949 (XX/*3612*). Robert Vansittart (1881–1957; Kt., 1929; created Baron, 1941), diplomat and Permanent Under-Secretary of State for Foreign Affairs, 1930–38, and chief adviser to the Foreign Secretary, 1938–41. He was an outspoken critic of Germany and the Germans.

13. David Lloyd George (1863–1945; 1st Earl Lloyd George of Dwyfor, 1945) was Liberal Prime Minister, 1916–22. He was unsuccessful in advocating a reasonable peace settlement with Germany after the First World War. When Chancellor of the Exchequer, 1908–15, he introduced old-age pensions and national insurance, the precursors to the Welfare State. Arthur James Balfour (1848–1930; created 1st Earl Balfour, 1922), Conservative Prime Minister, 1902–5. His policy when Chief Secretary for Ireland (1887–91) led to his gaining the soubriquet 'Bloody Balfour'. He set out what came to be called the Balfour Declaration in 1917; this promised Zionists a Palestinian homeland.

14. Ministry of Information (i.e., Propaganda); later COI, Central Office of Information. During the war, the MOI's main building was the Senate House of the University of London. This served as the model for Minitrue in *Nineteen Eighty-Four*.

[2685]

Unpublished letter to Tribune *[Trial of sixteen Poles in Moscow]*
26? June 1945

This letter was set up in type but, according to Orwell's marginal note on the galley slip, 'withdrawn because Tribune *altered attitude in following week'.*

POLISH TRIAL

I read with some disappointment your comment on the trial of the sixteen Poles in Moscow,[1] in which you seemed to imply that they had behaved in a discreditable manner and deserved punishment.

Early in the proceedings I formed the opinion that the accused were technically guilty: only, just what were they guilty of? Apparently it was merely of doing what everyone thinks it right to do when his country is occupied by a foreign power – that is, of trying to keep a military force in being, of maintaining communication with the outside world, of committing acts of sabotage and occasionally killing people. In other words, they were accused of trying to preserve the independence of their country against an unelected puppet government, and of remaining obedient to a government which at that time was recognised by the whole world except the U.S.S.R. The Germans during their period of occupation could have brought exactly the same indictment against them, and they would have been equally guilty.

It will not do to say that the efforts of the Poles to remain independent 'objectively' aided the Nazis, and leave it at that. Many actions which Left-wingers do not disapprove of have 'objectively' aided the Germans. How about E.A.M., for instance?[2] They also tried to keep their military force in being, and they, too, killed Allied soldiers – British in this case – and they were not even acting under the orders of a government which was recognised by anyone as legal. But what of it? We do not disapprove of their action, and if sixteen E.A.M. leaders were now brought to London and sentenced to long terms of imprisonment we should rightly protest.

To be anti-Polish and pro-Greek is only possible if one sets up a double standard of political morality, one for the U.S.S.R. and the other for the rest of the world. Before these sixteen Poles went to Moscow they were described in the Press as political delegates, and it was stated that they had been summoned there to take part in discussions on the formation of a new government. After their arrest all mention of their status as political delegates was dropped from the British Press – an example of the kind of censorship that is necessary if this double standard is to be made acceptable to the big public. Any well-informed person is aware of similar instances. To name just one: at this moment speakers up and down the country are justifying the Russian purges on the ground that Russia 'had no quislings', at the same time as any mention of the considerable numbers of Russian troops, including several generals, who changed sides and fought for the Germans is being suppressed by cautious editors. This kind of white-washing may be due to a number of different motives, some of them respectable ones, but its effect on the Socialist movement can be deadly if it is long continued.

When I wrote in your columns I repeatedly said that if one criticises this or that Russian action one is not obliged to put on airs of moral superiority. Their behaviour is not worse than that of capitalist governments, and its actual results may often be better. Nor is it likely that we shall alter the behaviour of the rulers of the U.S.S.R. by telling them that we disapprove of them. The whole point is the effect of the Russian mythos on the Socialist movement *here*. At present we are all but openly applying the double standard of morality. With one side of our mouths we cry out that mass deportations, concentration camps, forced labour and suppression of freedom of speech are appalling crimes, while with the other we proclaim that these things are perfectly all right if done by the U.S.S.R. or its satellite states: and where necessary we make this plausible by doctoring the news and cutting out unpalatable facts. One cannot possibly build up a healthy Socialist movement if one is obliged to condone no matter what crime when the U.S.S.R. commits it. No one knows better than I do that it is unpopular to say anything anti-Russian *at this moment*. But what of it? I am only 42, and I can remember the time when it was as dangerous to say anything pro-Russian as it is to say anything anti-Russian now. Indeed, I am old enough to have seen work-ing-class audiences booing and jeering at speakers who had used the

word Socialism. These fashions pass away, but they can't be depended on
to do so unless thinking people are willing to raise their voices against
the fallacy of the moment. It is only because over the past hundred years
small groups and lonely individuals have been willing to face unpopularity
that the Socialist movement exists at all.

1. The British had called for a meeting of the leaders of the Polish underground to discuss
the implementation of the Yalta decisions on the formation of a Polish Government of
National Unity. The preliminary meeting was to be held in Moscow and a further meeting
was planned for London. However, when the Poles reached Moscow they were put on trial.
2. EAM (Ethnikon Apeleftherotikon Metopon), the National Liberation Front, was formed
in Greece in 1941 after the German invasion. It started as a true resistance movement with
nearly the whole population as members. By early 1942 it was discovered that it was in fact
a Communist-organized movement. A national guerrilla army was then formed to fight the
Germans, but found itself also fighting the EAM. When the British returned to Greece in
1945, they also found themselves fighting the EAM.

[2792]
'The Prevention of Literature'
Polemic, *January 1946*; Atlantic Monthly, *March 1947*

About a year ago I attended a meeting of the P.E.N. Club,[1] the occasion
being the tercentenary of Milton's *Areopagitica* – a pamphlet, it may be
remembered, in defence of freedom of the Press. Milton's famous phrase
about the sin of 'killing' a book[2] was printed on the leaflets advertising
the meeting which had been circulated beforehand.

There were four speakers on the platform. One of them delivered a
speech which did deal with the freedom of the Press, but only in relation
to India; another said, hesitantly, and in very general terms, that liberty
was a good thing; a third delivered an attack on the laws relating to
obscenity in literature. The fourth devoted most of his speech to a defence
of the Russian purges. Of the speeches from the body of the hall, some
reverted to the question of obscenity and the laws that deal with it, others
were simply eulogies of Soviet Russia. Moral liberty – the liberty to
discuss sex questions frankly in print – seemed to be generally approved,
but political liberty was not mentioned. Out of this concourse of several
hundred people, perhaps half of whom were directly connected with the

writing trade, there was not a single one who could point out that freedom
of the Press, if it means anything at all, means the freedom to criticise and
oppose. Significantly, no speaker quoted from the pamphlet which was
ostensibly being commemorated. Nor was there any mention of the
various books that have been 'killed' in this country and the United States
during the war. In its net effect the meeting was a demonstration in favour
of censorship.*

There was nothing particularly surprising in this. In our age, the idea
of intellectual liberty is under attack from two directions. On the one side
are its theoretical enemies, the apologists of totalitarianism, and on the
other its immediate, practical enemies, monopoly and bureaucracy. Any
writer or journalist who wants to retain his integrity finds himself thwarted
by the general drift of society rather than by active persecution. The sort
of things that are working against him are the concentration of the Press
in the hands of a few rich men, the grip of monopoly on radio and the
films, the unwillingness of the public to spend money on books, making
it necessary for nearly every writer to earn part of his living by hackwork,
the encroachment of official bodies like the M.O.I. and the British
Council, which help the writer to keep alive but also waste his time and
dictate his opinions, and the continuous war atmosphere of the past ten
years, whose distorting effects no one has been able to escape. Everything
in our age conspires to turn the writer, and every other kind of artist as
well, into a minor official, working on themes handed to him from above
and never telling what seems to him the whole of the truth. But in
struggling against this fate he gets no help from his own side: that is,
there is no large body of opinion which will assure him that he is in the
right. In the past, at any rate throughout the Protestant centuries, the idea
of rebellion and the idea of intellectual integrity were mixed up. A heretic
– political, moral, religious, or aesthetic – was one who refused to outrage

---

* It is fair to say that the P.E.N. Club celebrations, which lasted a week or more, did not
always stick at quite the same level. I happened to strike a bad day. But an examination of
the speeches (printed under the title *Freedom of Expression* [see XVII/ *2764*]) shows that almost
nobody in our own day is able to speak out as roundly in favour of intellectual liberty as
Milton could do 300 years ago – and this in spite of the fact Milton was writing in a period
of civil war [Orwell's footnote].

his own conscience. His outlook was summed up in the words of the Revivalist hymn:

> Dare to be a Daniel,
> Dare to stand alone;
> Dare to have a purpose firm,
> Dare to make it known.

To bring this hymn up to date one would have to add a 'Don't' at the beginning of each line. For it is the peculiarity of our age that the rebels against the existing order, at any rate the most numerous and characteristic of them, are also rebelling against the idea of individual integrity. 'Daring to stand alone' is ideologically criminal as well as practically dangerous. The independence of the writer and the artist is eaten away by vague economic forces, and at the same time it is undermined by those who should be its defenders. It is with the second process that I am concerned here.

Freedom of speech and of the Press are usually attacked by arguments which are not worth bothering about. Anyone who has experience in lecturing and debating knows them backwards. Here I am not trying to deal with the familiar claim that freedom is an illusion, or with the claim that there is more freedom in totalitarian countries than in democratic ones, but with the much more tenable and dangerous proposition that freedom is undesirable and that intellectual honesty is a form of anti-social selfishness. Although other aspects of the question are usually in the foreground, the controversy over freedom of speech and of the Press is at bottom a controversy over the desirability, or otherwise, of telling lies. What is really at issue is the right to report contemporary events truthfully, or as truthfully as is consistent with the ignorance, bias and self-deception from which every observer necessarily suffers. In saying this I may seem to be saying that straightforward 'reportage' is the only branch of literature that matters: but I will try to show later that at every literary level, and probably in every one of the arts, the same issue arises in more or less subtilised forms. Meanwhile, it is necessary to strip away the irrelevancies in which this controversy is usually wrapped up.

The enemies of intellectual liberty always try to present their case as a plea for discipline versus individualism. The issue truth-versus-untruth is as far as possible kept in the background. Although the point of emphasis may vary, the writer who refuses to sell his opinions is always branded as a mere egoist. He is accused, that is, either of wanting to shut himself up in an ivory tower, or of making an exhibitionist display of his own personality, or of resisting the inevitable current of history in an attempt to cling to unjustified privileges. The Catholic and the Communist are alike in assuming that an opponent cannot be both honest and intelligent. Each of them tacitly claims that 'the truth' has already been revealed, and that the heretic, if he is not simply a fool, is secretly aware of 'the truth' and merely resists it out of selfish motives. In Communist literature the attack on intellectual liberty is usually masked by oratory about 'petty-bourgeois individualism', 'the illusions of nineteenth-century liberalism', etc., and backed up by words of abuse such as 'romantic' and 'sentimental', which, since they do not have any agreed meaning, are difficult to answer. In this way the controversy is manoeuvred away from its real issue. One can accept, and most enlightened people would accept, the Communist thesis that pure freedom will only exist in a classless society, and that one is most nearly free when one is working to bring about such a society. But slipped in with this is the quite unfounded claim that the Communist party is itself aiming at the establishment of the classless society, and that in the U.S.S.R. this aim is actually on the way to being realised. If the first claim is allowed to entail the second, there is almost no assault on common sense and common decency that cannot be justified. But meanwhile, the real point has been dodged. Freedom of the intellect means the freedom to report what one has seen, heard, and felt, and not to be obliged to fabricate imaginary facts and feelings. The familiar tirades against 'escapism', 'individualism', 'romanticism' and so forth, are merely a forensic device, the aim of which is to make the perversion of history seem respectable.

Fifteen years ago, when one defended the freedom of the intellect, one had to defend it against Conservatives, against Catholics, and to some extent – for in England they were not of great importance – against Fascists. Today one has to defend it against Communists and 'fellow travellers'. One ought not to exaggerate the direct influence of the small English Communist party, but there can be no question about the poisonous effect of the Russian *mythos* on English intellectual life. Because of it, known facts are suppressed and distorted to such an extent as to make it doubtful whether a true history of our times can ever be written. Let me give just one instance out of the hundreds that could be cited. When Germany collapsed, it was found that very large numbers of Soviet Russians – mostly, no doubt, from non-political motives – had changed sides and were fighting for the Germans. Also, a small but not negligible proportion of the Russian prisoners and Displaced Persons refused to go back to the U.S.S.R., and some of them, at least, were repatriated against their will. These facts, known to many journalists on the spot, went almost unmentioned in the British Press, while at the same time Russophile publicists in England continued to justify the purges and deportations of 1936–38 by claiming that the U.S.S.R. 'had no quislings'. The fog of lies and misinformation that surrounds such subjects as the Ukraine famine, the Spanish Civil War, Russian policy in Poland, and so forth, is not due entirely to conscious dishonesty, but any writer or journalist who is fully sympathetic to the U.S.S.R. – sympathetic, that is, in the way the Russians themselves would want him to be – does have to acquiesce in deliberate falsification on important issues. I have before me what must be a very rare pamphlet, written by Maxim Litvinoff[3] in 1918 and outlining the recent events in the Russian Revolution. It makes no mention of Stalin, but gives high praise to Trotsky, and also to Zinoviev,[4] Kamenev,[5] and others. What could be the attitude of even the most intellectually scrupulous Communist towards such a pamphlet? At best, he would take the obscurantist attitude that it is an undesirable document and better suppressed. And if for some reason it should be decided to issue a garbled version of the pamphlet, denigrating Trotsky and inserting references to Stalin, no Communist who remained faithful to his party could protest. Forgeries almost as gross as this have been committed in recent years. But the significant thing is not that they happen, but that even when they are known, they provoke no reaction from the left-wing intelligentsia as a whole. The argument that to tell the truth would be 'inopportune' or would 'play into the hands of' somebody or other is felt to be unanswerable, and few people are bothered by the prospect that the lies which they condone will get out of the newspapers and into the history books.

The organised lying practised by totalitarian states is not, as is sometimes claimed, a temporary expedient of the same nature as military deception. It is something integral to totalitarianism, something that would still continue even if concentration camps and secret police forces had ceased to be necessary. Among intelligent Communists there is an underground legend to the effect that although the Russian government is obliged now to deal in lying propaganda, frame-up trials, and so forth, it is secretly recording the facts and will publish them at some future time. We can, I believe, be quite certain that this is not the case, because the mentality implied by such an action is that of a liberal historian who believes that the past cannot be altered and that a correct knowledge of history is valuable as a matter of course. From the totalitarian point of view history is something to be created rather than learned. A totalitarian state is in effect a theocracy, and its ruling caste, in order to keep its position, has to be thought of as infallible. But since, in practice, no one is infallible, it is frequently necessary to rearrange past events in order to show that this or that mistake was not made, or that this or that imaginary triumph actually happened. Then, again, every major change in policy demands a corresponding change of doctrine and a revaluation of prominent historical figures. This kind of thing happens everywhere, but clearly it is likelier to lead to outright falsification in societies where only one opinion is permissible at any given moment. Totalitarianism demands, in fact, the continuous alteration of the past, and in the long run probably demands a disbelief in the very existence of objective truth. The friends of totalitarianism in this country usually tend to argue that since absolute truth is not attainable, a big lie is no worse than a little lie. It is pointed out that all historical records are biased and inaccurate, or, on the other hand, that modern physics has proved that what seems to us the real world is an illusion, so that to believe in the evidence of one's senses is simply vulgar philistinism. A totalitarian society which succeeded in perpetuating itself would probably set up a schizophrenic system of thought, in which the laws of common sense held good in everyday life and in certain exact sciences, but could be disregarded by the politician, the historian, and the sociologist. Already there are countless people who would think it scandalous to falsify a scientific textbook, but would see nothing wrong in falsifying a historical fact. It is at the point where literature and politics cross that totalitarianism exerts its greatest pressure on the intellectual. The exact sciences are not, at this date, menaced to anything like the same extent. This difference partly accounts for the fact that in all countries it is easier for the scientists than for the writers to line up behind their respective governments.

To keep the matter in perspective, let me repeat what I said at the beginning of this essay: that in England the immediate enemies of truthfulness, and hence of freedom of thought, are the Press lords, the film magnates, and the bureaucrats, but that on a long view the weakening of the desire for liberty among the intellectuals themselves is the most serious symptom of all. It may seem that all this time I have been talking about the effects of censorship, not on literature as a whole, but merely on one department of political journalism. Granted that Soviet Russia constitutes a sort of forbidden area in the British Press, granted that issues like Poland, the Spanish Civil War, the Russo-German pact, and so forth, are debarred from serious discussion, and that if you possess information that conflicts with the prevailing orthodoxy you are expected either to distort it or to keep quiet about it – granted all this, why should literature in the wider sense be affected? Is every writer a politician, and is every book necessarily a work of straightforward 'reportage'? Even under the tightest dictatorship, cannot the individual writer remain free inside his own mind and distil or disguise his unorthodox ideas in such a way that the authorities will be too stupid to recognise them? And if the writer himself is in agreement with the prevailing orthodoxy, why should it have a cramping effect on him? Is not literature, or any of the arts, likeliest to flourish in societies in which there are no major conflicts of opinion and no sharp distinctions between the artist and his audience? Does one have to assume that every writer is a rebel, or even that a writer as such is an exceptional person?

Whenever one attempts to defend intellectual liberty against the claims of totalitarianism, one meets with these arguments in one form or another. They are based on a complete misunderstanding of what literature is, and how – one should perhaps rather say *why* – it comes into being. They assume that a writer is either a mere entertainer or else a venal hack who can switch from one line of propaganda to another as easily as an organ grinder changes tunes. But after all, how is it that books ever come to be written? Above a quite low level, literature is an attempt to influence the views of one's contemporaries by recording experience. And so far as freedom of expression is concerned, there is not much difference between a mere journalist and the most 'unpolitical' imaginative writer. The journalist is unfree, and is conscious of unfreedom, when he is forced to write lies or suppress what seems to him important news: the imaginative writer is unfree when he has to falsify his subjective feelings, which from his point of view are facts. He may distort and caricature reality in order to make his meaning clearer, but he cannot misrepresent the scenery of his own mind: he cannot say with any conviction that he likes what he dislikes, or believes what he disbelieves. If he is forced to do so, the only result is that his creative faculties dry up. Nor can the imaginative writer solve the problem by keeping away from controversial topics. There is no such thing as genuinely non-political literature, and least of all in an age like our own, when fears, hatreds, and loyalties of a directly political kind are near to the surface of everyone's consciousness. Even a single tabu can have an all-round crippling effect upon the mind, because there is always the danger that any thought which is freely followed up may lead to the forbidden thought. It follows that the atmosphere of totalitarianism is deadly to any kind of prose writer, though a poet, at any rate a lyric poet, might possibly find it breathable. And in any totalitarian society that survives for more than a couple of generations, it is probable that prose literature, of the kind that has existed during the past four hundred years, must actually *come to an end*.

Literature has sometimes flourished under despotic régimes, but, as has often been pointed out, the despotisms of the past were not totalitarian. Their repressive apparatus was always inefficient, their ruling classes were usually either corrupt or apathetic or half-liberal in outlook, and the prevailing religious doctrines usually worked against perfectionism and the notion of human infallibility. Even so it is broadly true that prose literature has reached its highest levels in periods of democracy and free speculation. What is new in totalitarianism is that its doctrines are not only unchallengeable but also unstable. They have to be accepted on pain of damnation, but on the other hand they are always liable to be altered at a moment's notice. Consider, for example, the various attitudes, completely incompatible with one another, which an English Communist or 'fellow traveller' has had to adopt towards the war between Britain and Germany. For years before September 1939 he was expected to be in a continuous stew about 'the horrors of Nazism' and to twist everything he wrote into a denunciation of Hitler;[6] after September 1939, for twenty months, he had to believe that Germany was more sinned against than sinning, and the word 'Nazi', at least so far as print went, had to drop right out of his vocabulary. Immediately after hearing the 8 o'clock news bulletin on the morning of June 22, 1941,[7] he had to start believing once again that Nazism was the most hideous evil the world had ever seen. Now, it is easy for a politician to make such changes: for a writer the case is somewhat different. If he is to switch his allegiance at exactly the right moment, he must either tell lies about his subjective feelings, or else suppress them altogether. In either case he has destroyed his dynamo. Not only will ideas refuse to come to him, but the very words he uses will seem to stiffen under his touch. Political writing in our time consists almost entirely of prefabricated phrases bolted together like the pieces of a child's Meccano set. It is the unavoidable result of self-censorship. To write in plain, vigorous language one has to think fearlessly, and if one thinks fearlessly one cannot be politically orthodox. It might be otherwise in an 'age of faith', when the prevailing orthodoxy has been long established and is not taken too seriously. In that case it would be possible, or might be possible, for large areas of one's mind to remain unaffected by what one officially believed. Even so, it is worth noticing that prose literature almost disappeared during the only age of faith that Europe has ever enjoyed. Throughout the whole of the Middle Ages there was almost no imaginative prose literature and very little in the way of historical writing: and the intellectual leaders of society expressed their most serious thoughts in a dead language which barely altered during a thousand years.

Totalitarianism, however, does not so much promise an age of faith as an age of schizophrenia. A society becomes totalitarian when its structure becomes flagrantly artificial: that is, when its ruling class has lost its function but succeeds in clinging to power by force or fraud. Such a society, no matter how long it persists, can never afford to become either tolerant or intellectually stable. It can never permit either the truthful recording of facts, or the emotional sincerity, that literary creation demands. But to be corrupted by totalitarianism one does not have to live in a totalitarian country. The mere prevalence of certain ideas can spread a poison that makes one subject after another impossible for literary purposes. Wherever there is an enforced orthodoxy – or even two orthodoxies, as often happens – good writing stops. This was well illustrated by the Spanish Civil War. To many English intellectuals the war was a deeply moving experience, but not an experience about which they could write sincerely. There were only two things that you were allowed to say, and both of them were palpable lies: as a result, the war produced acres of print but almost nothing worth reading.

It is not certain whether the effects of totalitarianism upon verse need be so deadly as its effects on prose. There is a whole series of converging reasons why it is somewhat easier for a poet than for a prose writer to feel at home in an authoritarian society. To begin with, bureaucrats and other 'practical' men usually despise the poet too deeply to be much interested in what he is saying. Secondly, what the poet is saying – that is, what his poem 'means' if translated into prose – is relatively unimportant even to himself. The thought contained in a poem is always simple, and is no more the primary purpose of the poem than the anecdote is the primary purpose of a picture. A poem is an arrangement of sounds and associations, as a painting is an arrangement of brush-marks. For short snatches, indeed, as in the refrain of a song, poetry can even dispense with meaning altogether. It is therefore fairly easy for a poet to keep away from dangerous subjects and avoid uttering heresies: and even when he does utter them, they may escape notice. But above all, good verse, unlike good prose, is not necessarily an individual product. Certain kinds of poems, such as ballads, or, on the other hand, very artificial verse forms, can be composed co-operatively by groups of people. Whether the ancient English and Scottish ballads were originally produced by individuals, or by the people at large, is disputed; but at any rate they are non-individual in the sense that they constantly change in passing from mouth to mouth. Even in print no two versions of a ballad are ever quite the same. Many primitive peoples compose verse communally. Someone begins to improvise, probably accompanying himself on a musical instrument, somebody else chips in with a line or a rhyme when the first singer breaks down, and so the process continues until there exists a whole song or ballad which has no identifiable author.

In prose, this kind of intimate collaboration is quite impossible. Serious prose, in any case, has to be composed in solitude, whereas the excitement of being part of a group is actually an aid to certain kinds of versification. Verse – and perhaps good verse of its kind, though it would not be the highest kind – might survive under even the most inquisitorial régime. Even in a society where liberty and individuality had been extinguished, there would still be need either for patriotic songs and heroic ballads celebrating victories, or for elaborate exercises in flattery: and these are the kinds of poetry that can be written to order, or composed communally, without necessarily lacking artistic value. Prose is a different matter, since the prose writer cannot narrow the range of his thoughts without killing his inventiveness. But the history of totalitarian societies, or of groups of people who have adopted the totalitarian outlook, suggests that loss of liberty is inimical to *all* forms of literature. German literature almost disappeared during the Hitler régime, and the case was not much better in Italy. Russian literature, so far as one can judge by translations, has deteriorated markedly since the early days of the Revolution, though some of the verse appears to be better than the prose. Few if any Russian novels that it is possible to take seriously have been translated for about fifteen years. In western Europe and America large sections of the literary intelligentsia have either passed through the Communist party or been warmly sympathetic to it, but this whole leftward movement has produced extraordinarily few books worth reading. Orthodox Catholicism, again, seems to have a crushing effect upon certain literary forms, especially the novel. During a period of three hundred years, how many people have been at once good novelists and good Catholics? The fact is that certain themes cannot be celebrated in words, and tyranny is one of them. No one ever wrote a good book in praise of the Inquisition. Poetry *might* survive in a totalitarian age, and certain arts or half-arts, such as architecture, might even find tyranny beneficial, but the prose writer would have no choice between silence and death. Prose literature as we know it is the product of rationalism, of the Protestant centuries, of the autonomous individual. And the destruction of intellectual liberty cripples the journalist, the sociological writer, the historian, the novelist, the critic, and the poet, in that order. In the future it is possible that a new kind of literature, not involving individual feeling or truthful observation, may arise, but no such thing is at present imaginable. It seems much likelier that if the liberal culture that we have lived in since the Renaissance actually comes to an end, the literary art will perish with it.

Of course, print will continue to be used, and it is interesting to speculate what kinds of reading matter would survive in a rigidly totalitarian society. Newspapers will presumably continue until television technique reaches a higher level, but apart from newspapers it is doubtful even now whether the great mass of people in the industrialised countries feel the need for any kind of literature. They are unwilling, at any rate, to spend anywhere near as much on reading matter as they spend on several other recreations. Probably novels and stories will be completely superseded by film and radio productions. Or perhaps some kind of low-grade sensational fiction will survive, produced by a sort of conveyor-belt process that reduces human initiative to the minimum.

It would probably not be beyond human ingenuity to write books by machinery. But a sort of mechanising process can already be seen at work in the film and radio, in publicity and propaganda, and in the lower reaches of journalism. The Disney films, for instance, are produced by what is essentially a factory process, the work being done partly mechanically and partly by teams of artists who have to subordinate their individual style. Radio features are commonly written by tired hacks to whom the subject and the manner of treatment are dictated beforehand: even so, what they write is merely a kind of raw material to be chopped into shape by producers and censors. So also with the innumerable books and pamphlets commissioned by government departments. Even more machine-like is the production of short stories, serials, and poems for the very cheap magazines. Papers such as the *Writer* abound with advertisements of Literary Schools, all of them offering you readymade plots at a few shillings a time. Some, together with the plot, supply the opening and closing sentences of each chapter. Others furnish you with a sort of algebraical formula by the use of which you can construct your plots for yourself. Others offer packs of cards marked with characters and situations, which have only to be shuffled and dealt in order to produce ingenious stories automatically. It is probably in some such way that the literature of a totalitarian society would be produced, if literature were still felt to be necessary. Imagination – even consciousness, so far as possible – would be eliminated from the process of writing. Books would be planned in their broad lines by bureaucrats, and would pass through so many hands that when finished they would be no more an individual product than a Ford car at the end of the assembly line. It goes without saying that anything so produced would be rubbish; but anything that was not rubbish would endanger the structure of the state. As for the surviving literature of the past, it would have to be suppressed or at least elaborately rewritten.

Meanwhile totalitarianism has not fully triumphed anywhere. Our own society is still, broadly speaking, liberal. To exercise your right of free speech you have to fight against economic pressure and against strong sections of public opinion, but not, as yet, against a secret police force. You can say or print almost anything so long as you are willing to do it in a hole-and-corner way. But what is sinister, as I said at the beginning of this essay, is that the conscious enemies of liberty are those to whom liberty ought to mean most. The public do not care about the matter one way or the other. They are not in favour of persecuting the heretic, and they will not exert themselves to defend him. They are at once too sane and too stupid to acquire the totalitarian outlook. The direct, conscious attack on intellectual decency comes from the intellectuals themselves.

It is possible that the Russophile intelligentsia, if they had not succumbed to that particular myth, would have succumbed to another of much the same kind. But at any rate the Russian myth is there, and the corruption it causes stinks. When one sees highly educated men looking on indifferently at oppression and persecution, one wonders which to despise more, their cynicism or their short-sightedness. Many scientists, for example, are uncritical admirers of the U.S.S.R. They appear to think that the destruction of liberty is of no importance so long as their own line of work is for the moment unaffected. The U.S.S.R. is a large, rapidly developing country which has acute need of scientific workers and, consequently, treats them generously. Provided that they steer clear of dangerous subjects such as psychology, scientists are privileged persons. Writers, on the other hand, are viciously persecuted. It is true that literary prostitutes like Ilya Ehrenburg or Alexei Tolstoy are paid huge sums of money, but the only thing which is of any value to the writer as such – his freedom of expression – is taken away from him. Some, at least, of the English scientists who speak so enthusiastically of the opportunities enjoyed by scientists in Russia are capable of understanding this. But their reflection appears to be: 'Writers are persecuted in Russia. So what? I am not a writer.' They do not see that *any* attack on intellectual liberty, and on the concept of objective truth, threatens in the long run every department of thought.

For the moment the totalitarian state tolerates the scientist because it needs him. Even in Nazi Germany, scientists, other than Jews, were relatively well treated, and the German scientific community, as a whole, offered no resistance to Hitler. At this stage of history, even the most autocratic ruler is forced to take account of physical reality, partly because of the lingering-on of liberal habits of thought, partly because of the need to prepare for war. So long as physical reality cannot be altogether ignored, so long as two and two have to make four when you are, for example, drawing the blueprint of an aeroplane, the scientist has his function, and can even be allowed a measure of liberty. His awakening will come later, when the totalitarian state is firmly established. Meanwhile, if he wants to safeguard the integrity of science, it is his job to develop some kind of solidarity with his literary colleagues and not regard it as a matter of indifference when writers are silenced or driven to suicide, and newspapers systematically falsified.

But however it may be with the physical sciences, or with music, painting, and architecture, it is – as I have tried to show – certain that literature is doomed if liberty of thought perishes. Not only is it doomed in any country which retains a totalitarian structure; but any writer who adopts the totalitarian outlook, who finds excuses for persecution and the falsification of reality, thereby destroys himself as a writer. There is no way out of this. No tirades against 'individualism' and 'the ivory tower', no pious platitudes to the effect that 'true individuality is only attained through identification with the community', can get over the fact that a bought mind is a spoiled mind. Unless spontaneity enters at some point or another, literary creation is impossible, and language itself becomes ossified. At some time in the future, if the human mind becomes something totally different from what it now is, we may learn to separate literary creation from intellectual honesty. At present we know only that the imagination, like certain wild animals, will not breed in captivity. Any writer or journalist who denies that fact – and nearly all the current praise of the Soviet Union contains or implies such a denial – is, in effect, demanding his own destruction.[8]

1. Founded in 1921, the International PEN Club was an association of Poets, Playwrights, Editors, Essayists and Novelists. Despite his strictures, Orwell was persuaded to join in January 1948; see XIX/3302 and 3355.

2. Milton's *Areopagitica* was a speech to Parliament 'for the Liberty of Unlicensed Printing' (i.e., for freedom to print without censorship) and was given and published (without licence) in 1644. The Areopagus is a small, rocky hill near the Acropolis in Athens. It was from the seventh to sixth centuries BC the seat of a judicial tribunal. St Paul preached there in the first century AD (Acts 17:19–31). The reference to 'killing a book' runs, 'as good almost kill a Man as kill a good Book; who kills a man kills a reasonable creature, God's image; but he who destroys a good Book, kills reason itself, kills the image of God, as it were in the eye'.

3. Maxim Litvinov (1876–1951) represented the Soviet Union abroad in many capacities from 1917, when he was the unacknowledged Ambassador to Britain, to 1941–3, when he served as Ambassador to the United States. He was a Jew and a prominent anti-Nazi; he recommended collective action against Hitler. Three months before the Soviet–Nazi pact was signed (see n. 6, below), he was dismissed as Commissar of Foreign Affairs (3 May 1939).

4. Gregoriy Zinoviev (1883–1936), Ukrainian-Jewish revolutionary. Made a member of the Politburo in 1924, but he opposed Stalin and was expelled from the Communist Party in 1926. Although reinstated, 1928–32, in 1935 he was arrested, charged with terrorism and executed following the first of the Great Purge trials.

5. Lev Kamenev (1883–1936) was involved in revolutionary activities in Russia from 1901. After the 1917 Revolution he was appointed to the Communist Central Committee. He was expelled for a year from 1927 as a Trotskyist, expelled again in 1932 and shot in 1936.

6. A sub-editor of the *Atlantic Monthly* queried the date of the Soviet–Nazi pact, giving 'August 23' [1939]. Orwell did not follow this suggestion. It was signed in Moscow by Molotov and Ribbentrop on 23 August 1939 and made public on 24/25 August. However, its Secret Protocol, which dealt with the division of Eastern Europe between the Soviet Union and Germany, was kept secret until discovered by the Americans in Nazi archives at the end of the war; it was not officially published until 1948. Soviet judges at the Nuremberg Trials refused to admit as evidence anything that referred to this Secret Protocol. Another Secret Protocol was signed by the Soviet Union and Germany on 28 September 1939; that settled Germany's eastern frontier. The American sub-editor was right to point out that changes in attitudes of western communists and fellow travellers should date from 23 August, but evidently Orwell thought September 1939 more clearly represented to general memory the Communist change of line.

7. Operation Barbarossa, the German invasion of the Soviet Union.

8. Fifty years after Orwell wrote this essay, 'the prevention of literature' at its most extreme was revealed in specific detail in *The KGB's Literary Archive* by Vitaly Shentalinsky, translated by John Crowfoot (1995). Some 1,500 writers perished at the hands of the NKVD and thousands of manuscripts were burnt.

[2813]

'Freedom of the Park'
Tribune, 7 December 1945

A few weeks ago, five people who were selling papers outside Hyde Park were arrested by the police for obstruction. When taken before the magistrate they were all found guilty, four of them being bound over for six months and the other sentenced to forty shillings' fine or a month's imprisonment. He preferred to serve his term, so I suppose he is still in jail at this moment.

The papers these people were selling were *Peace News*, *Forward* and *Freedom*,[1] besides other kindred literature. *Peace News* is the organ of the Peace Pledge Union, *Freedom* (till recently called *War Commentary*) is that of the Anarchists: as for *Forward*, its politics defy definition, but at any rate it is violently Left. The magistrate, in passing sentence, stated that he was not influenced by the nature of the literature that was being sold: he was concerned merely with the fact of obstruction, and that this offence had technically been committed.

This raises several important points. To begin with, how does the law stand on the subject? As far as I can discover, selling newspapers in the street *is* technically obstruction, at any rate if you fail to move on when the police tell you to. So it would be legally possible for any policeman who felt like it to arrest any newsboy for selling the *Evening News*. Obviously this doesn't happen, so that the enforcement of the law depends on the discretion of the police.

And what makes the police decide to arrest one man rather than another? However it may have been with the magistrate, I find it hard to believe that in this case the police were not influenced by political considerations. It is a bit too much of a coincidence that they should have picked on people selling just those papers. If they had also arrested someone who was selling *Truth*, or the *Tablet*, or the *Spectator*, or even the *Church Times*, their impartiality would be easier to believe in.

The British police are not like a continental gendarmerie or Gestapo, but I do not think one maligns them in saying that, in the past, they have been unfriendly to left-wing activities. They have generally shown a tendency to side with those whom they regarded as the defenders of private property. There were some scandalous cases at the time of the Mosley disturbances. At the only big Mosley meeting I ever attended, the police collaborated with the Blackshirts in 'keeping order', in a way in which they certainly would not have collaborated with Socialists or Communists. Till quite recently 'red' and 'illegal' were almost synonymous, and it was always the seller of, say, the *Daily Worker*, never the seller of, say, the *Daily Telegraph*, who was moved on and generally harassed. Apparently it can be the same, at any rate at moments, under a Labour government.

A thing I would like to know – it is a thing we hear very little about – is what changes are made in the administrative personnel when there has been a change of government. Does the police officer who has a vague notion that 'Socialism' means something against the law carry on just the same when the government itself is Socialist? It is a sound principle that the official should have no party affiliations, should serve successive governments faithfully and should not be victimised for his political opinions. Still, no government can afford to leave its enemies in key positions, and when Labour is in undisputed power for the first time – and therefore when it is taking over an administration formed by Conservatives – it clearly must make sufficient changes to prevent sabotage. The official, even when friendly to the government in power, is all too conscious that he is a permanency and can frustrate the short-lived Ministers whom he is supposed to serve.

When a Labour Government takes over, I wonder what happens to Scotland Yard Special Branch? To Military Intelligence? To the Consular Service? To the various colonial administrations – and so on and so forth? We are not told, but such symptoms as there are do not suggest that any very extensive reshuffling is going on. We are still represented abroad by the same ambassadors, and B.B.C. censorship seems to have the same subtly reactionary colour that it always had. The B.B.C. claims, of course, to be both independent and non-political. I was told once that its 'line', if any, was to represent the Left Wing of the government in power. But that was in the days of the Churchill Government. If it represents the Left Wing of the present Government, I have not noticed the fact.

However, the main point of this episode is that the sellers of newspapers and pamphlets should be interfered with at all. Which particular minority is singled out – whether Pacifists, Communists, Anarchists, Jehovah's Witness or the Legion of Christian Reformers who recently declared Hitler to be Jesus Christ – is a secondary matter. It is of symptomatic importance that these people should have been arrested at that particular spot. You are not allowed to sell literature inside Hyde Park, but for many years past it has been usual for the paper-sellers to station themselves just outside the gates and distribute literature connected with the open-air meetings a hundred yards away. Every kind of publication has been sold there without interference.

As for the meetings inside the Park, they are one of the minor wonders of the world. At different times I have listened there to Indian nationalists, Temperance reformers, Communists, Trotskyists, the S.P.G.B.,[2] the Catholic Evidence Society, Freethinkers, vegetarians, Mormons, the Salvation Army, the Church Army, and a large variety of plain lunatics, all taking their turn at the rostrum in an orderly way and receiving a fairly good-humoured hearing from the crowd. Granted that Hyde Park is a special area, a sort of Alsatia[3] where outlawed opinions are permitted to walk – still, there are very few countries in the world where you can see a similar spectacle. I have known continental Europeans, long before Hitler seized power, come away from Hyde Park astonished and even perturbed by the things they had heard Indian or Irish nationalists saying about the British Empire.

The degree of freedom of the press existing in this country is often overrated. Technically there is great freedom, but the fact that most of the press is owned by a few people operates in much the same way as a State censorship. On the other hand freedom of speech is real. On the platform, or in certain recognised open-air spaces like Hyde Park, you can say almost anything, and, what is perhaps more significant, no one is frightened to utter his true opinions in pubs, on the tops of buses, and so forth.

The point is that the relative freedom which we enjoy depends on public opinion. The law is no protection. Governments make laws, but whether they are carried out, and how the police behave, depends on the general temper of the country. If large numbers of people are interested in freedom of speech, there will be freedom of speech, even if the law forbids it; if public opinion is sluggish, inconvenient minorities will be persecuted, even if laws exist to protect them. The decline in the desire for intellectual liberty has not been so sharp as I would have predicted six years ago, when the war was starting, but still there has been a decline. The notion that certain opinions cannot safely be allowed a hearing is growing. It is given currency by intellectuals who confuse the issue by not distinguishing between democratic opposition and open rebellion, and it is reflected in our growing indifference to tyranny and injustice abroad. And even those who declare themselves to be in favour of freedom of opinion generally drop their claim when it is their own adversaries who are being persecuted.

I am not suggesting that the arrest of five people for selling harmless newspapers is a major calamity. When you see what is happening in the world today, it hardly seems worth squealing about such a tiny incident. All the same, it is not a good symptom that such things should happen when the war is well over, and I should feel happier if this, and the long series of similar episodes that have preceded it, were capable of raising a genuine popular clamour, and not merely a mild flutter in sections of the minority press.

1. *Forward* was published by the Glasgow Labour Party. *Freedom*'s full title was *Freedom – through Anarchism.*

2. The Socialist Party of Great Britain, a Marxist organization having no connection with the Labour Party.

3. The French edition of *Down and Out in Paris and London* (1935) had a footnote by Orwell explaining Alsatia. This read (translated into English): 'A name once given to the district of Whitefriars, which was, in the seventeenth century, a regular refuge for all kinds of wrongdoers by virtue of a right of sanctuary which was finally abolished in 1697.' See I/171 and 228, note to that page.

[2815]

'Politics and the English Language'
Payments Book, 11 December 1945; Horizon, April 1946[1]

Most people who bother with the matter at all would admit that the English language is in a bad way, but it is generally assumed that we cannot by conscious action do anything about it. Our civilization is decadent, and our language – so the argument runs – must inevitably share in the general collapse. It follows that any struggle against the abuse of language is a sentimental archaism, like preferring candles to electric light or hansom cabs to aeroplanes. Underneath this lies the half-conscious belief that language is a natural growth and not an instrument which we shape for our own purposes.

Now, it is clear that the decline of a language must ultimately have political and economic causes: it is not due simply to the bad influence of this or that individual writer. But an effect can become a cause, reinforcing the original cause and producing the same effect in an intensified form, and so on indefinitely. A man may take to drink because he feels himself to be a failure, and then fail all the more completely because he drinks. It is rather the same thing that is happening to the English language. It becomes ugly and inaccurate because our thoughts are foolish, but the slovenliness of our language makes it easier for us to have foolish thoughts. The point is that the process is reversible. Modern English, especially written English, is full of bad habits which spread by imitation and which can be avoided if one is willing to take the necessary trouble. If one gets rid of these habits one can think more clearly, and to think clearly is a necessary first step towards political regeneration: so that the fight against bad English is not frivolous and is not the exclusive concern of professional writers. I will come back to this presently, and I hope that by that time the meaning of what I have said here will have become clearer. Meanwhile, here are five specimens of the English language as it is now habitually written.

These five passages have not been picked out because they are especially bad – I could have quoted far worse if I had chosen – but because they illustrate various of the mental vices from which we now suffer. They are a little below the average, but are fairly representative samples. I number them so that I can refer back to them when necessary:

(1) I am not, indeed, sure whether it is not true to say that the Milton who once seemed not unlike a seventeenth-century Shelley had not become, out of an experience ever more bitter in each year, more alien (*sic*) to the founder of that Jesuit sect which nothing could induce him to tolerate.

Professor Harold Laski (Essay in *Freedom of Expression*)

(2) Above all, we cannot play ducks and drakes with a native battery of idioms which prescribes such egregious collocations of vocables as the Basic *put up with* for *tolerate* or *put at a loss* for *bewilder*.

Professor Lancelot Hogben (*Interglossa*)

(3) On the one side we have the free personality: by definition it is not neurotic, for it has neither conflict nor dream. Its desires, such as they are, are transparent, for they are just what institutional approval keeps in the forefront of consciousness; another institutional pattern would alter their number and intensity; there is little in them that is natural, irreducible, or culturally dangerous. But *on the other side*, the social bond itself is nothing but the mutual reflection of these self-secure integrities. Recall the definition of love. Is not this the very picture of a small academic? Where is there a place in this hall of mirrors for either personality or fraternity?

Essay on psychology in *Politics* (New York)

(4) All the 'best people' from the gentlemen's clubs, and all the frantic fascist captains, united in common hatred of Socialism and bestial horror of the rising tide of the mass revolutionary movement, have turned to acts of provocation, to foul incendiarism, to medieval legends of poisoned wells, to legalize their own destruction of proletarian organizations, and rouse the agitated petty-bourgeoisie to chauvinistic fervour on behalf of the fight against the revolutionary way out of the crisis.

Communist pamphlet

(5) If a new spirit *is* to be infused into this old country, there is one thorny and contentious reform which must be tackled, and that is the humanization and galvanization of the B.B.C. Timidity here will bespeak canker and atrophy of the soul. The heart of Britain may be sound and of strong beat, for instance, but the British lion's roar at present is like that of Bottom in Shakespeare's *Midsummer Night's Dream* – as gentle as any sucking dove. A virile new Britain cannot continue indefinitely to be traduced in the eyes, or rather ears, of the world by the effete languors of Langham Place, brazenly masquerading as 'standard English'. When the Voice of Britain is heard at nine o'clock, better far and infinitely less ludicrous to hear aitches honestly dropped than the present priggish, inflated, inhibited, school-ma'amish arch braying of blameless bashful mewing maidens!

Letter in *Tribune*

Each of these passages has faults of its own, but, quite apart from avoidable ugliness, two qualities are common to all of them. The first is staleness of imagery: the other is lack of precision. The writer either has a meaning and cannot express it, or he inadvertently says something else, or he is almost indifferent as to whether his words mean anything or not. This mixture of vagueness and sheer incompetence is the most marked characteristic of modern English prose, and especially of any kind of political writing. As soon as certain topics are raised, the concrete melts into the abstract and no one seems able to think of turns of speech that are not hackneyed: prose consists less and less of *words* chosen for the sake of their meaning, and more and more of *phrases* tacked together like the sections of a prefabricated henhouse. I list below, with notes and examples, various of the tricks by means of which the work of prose-construction is habitually dodged:

Dying metaphors. A newly invented metaphor assists thought by evoking a visual image, while on the other hand a metaphor which is technically 'dead' (e.g. *iron resolution*) has in effect reverted to being an ordinary word and can generally be used without loss of vividness. But in between these two classes there is a huge dump of worn-out metaphors which have lost all evocative power and are merely used because they save people the trouble of inventing phrases for themselves. Examples are: *Ring the changes on, take up the cudgels for, toe the line, ride roughshod over, stand shoulder to shoulder with, play into the hands of, no axe to grind, grist to the mill, fishing in troubled waters, [rift within the lute[2]], on the order of the day, Achilles' heel, swan song, hotbed.* Many of these are used without knowledge of their meaning (what is a 'rift', for instance?), and incompatible metaphors are frequently mixed, a sure sign that the writer is not interested in what he is saying. Some metaphors now current have been twisted out of their original meaning without those who use them even being aware of the fact. For example, *toe the line* is sometimes written *tow the line*. Another example is *the hammer and the anvil*, now always used with the implication that the anvil gets the worst of it. In real life it is always the anvil that breaks the hammer, never the other way about: a writer who stopped to think what he was saying would be aware of this, and would avoid perverting the original phrase.

Operators, or *verbal false limbs.* These save the trouble of picking out appropriate verbs and nouns, and at the same time pad each sentence with extra syllables which give it an appearance of symmetry. Characteristic phrases are: *render inoperative, militate against, prove unacceptable, make contact with, be subjected to, give rise to, give grounds for, have the effect of, play a leading part (role) in, make itself felt, take effect, exhibit a tendency to, serve the purpose of,* etc., etc. The keynote is the elimination of simple verbs. Instead of being a single word, such as *break, stop, spoil, mend, kill,* a verb becomes a *phrase,* made up of a noun or adjective tacked on to some general-purposes verb such as *prove, serve, form, play, render.* In addition, the passive voice is wherever possible used in preference to the active, and noun constructions are used instead of gerunds (*by examination of* instead of *by examining*). The range of verbs is further cut down by means of the *-ize* and *de-* formations, and banal statements are given an appearance of profundity by means of the *not un-*formation. Simple conjunctions and prepositions are replaced by such phrases as *with respect to, having regard to, the fact that, by dint of, in view of, in the interests of, on the hypothesis that*; and the ends of sentences are saved from anticlimax by such resounding commonplaces as *greatly to be desired, cannot be left out of account, a development to be expected in the near future, deserving of serious consideration, brought to a satisfactory conclusion,* and so on and so forth.

Pretentious diction. Words like *phenomenon, element, individual* (as noun), *objective, categorical, effective, virtual, basic, primary, promote, constitute, exhibit, exploit, utilize, eliminate, liquidate,* are used to dress up simple statement[s] and give an air of scientific impartiality to biased judgements. Adjectives like *epoch-making, epic, historic, unforgettable, triumphant, age-old, inevitable, inexorable, veritable,* are used to dignify the sordid processes of international politics, while writing that aims at glorifying war usually takes on an archaic colour, its characteristic words being: *realm, throne, chariot, mailed fist, trident, sword, shield, buckler, banner, jackboot, clarion.* Foreign words and expressions such as *cul de sac, ancien régime, deus ex machina, mutatis mutandis, status quo, gleichschallung, weltanschauung,* are used to give an air of culture and elegance. Except for the useful abbreviations *i.e., e.g.,* and *etc.,* there is no real need for any of the hundreds of foreign phrases now current in English. Bad writers, and especially scientific, political and sociological writers, are nearly always haunted by the notion that Latin or Greek words are grander than Saxon ones, and unnecessary words like *expedite, ameliorate, predict, extraneous, deracinated, clandestine, subaqueous* and hundreds of others constantly gain ground from their Anglo-Saxon opposite numbers.* The jargon peculiar to Marxist writing (*hyena, hangman, cannibal, petty bourgeois, these gentry, lacquey, flunkey, mad dog, White Guard*, etc.) consists largely of words and phrases translated from Russian, German or French; but the normal way of coining a new word is to use a Latin or Greek root with the appropriate affix and, where necessary, the *-ize* formation. It is often easier to make up words of this kind (*deregionalize, impermissible, extramarital, non-fragmentary*[3] and so forth) than to think up the English words that will cover one's meaning. The result, in general, is an increase in slovenliness and vagueness.

Meaningless words. In certain kinds of writing, particularly in art criticism and literary criticism, it is normal to come across long passages which are almost completely lacking in meaning.† Words like *romantic, plastic, values, human, dead, sentimental, natural, vitality*, as used in art criticism, are strictly meaningless, in the sense that they not only do not point to any discoverable object, but are hardly even expected to do so by the reader. When one critic writes, 'The outstanding feature of Mr. X's work is its living quality', while another writes, 'The immediately striking thing about Mr. X's work is its peculiar deadness', the reader accepts this as a simple difference of opinion. If words like *black* and *white* were involved, instead of the jargon words dead and living, he would see at once that language was being used in an improper way. Many political words are similarly abused. The word *Fascism* has now no meaning except in so far as it signifies 'something not desirable'. The words *democracy, socialism, freedom, patriotic, realistic, justice*, have each of them several different mean-

---

* An interesting illustration of this is the way in which the English flower names which were in use till very recently are being ousted by Greek ones, *snapdragon* becoming *antirrhinum, forget-me-not* becoming *myosotis*, etc. It is hard to see any practical reason for this change of fashion: it is probably due to an instinctive turning-away from the more homely word and a vague feeling that the Greek word is scientific [Orwell's footnote].

† Example: 'Comfort's catholicity of perception and image, strangely Whitmanesque in range, almost the exact opposite in aesthetic compulsion, continues to evoke that trembling atmospheric accumulative hinting at a cruel, an inexorably serene timelessness ... Wrey Gardiner scores by aiming at simple bullseyes with precision. Only they are not so simple, and through this contented sadness runs more than the surface bitter-sweet of resignation' (*Poetry Quarterly*) [Orwell's footnote].

ings which cannot be reconciled with one another. In the case of a word like *democracy*, not only is there no agreed definition, but the attempt to make one is resisted from all sides. It is almost universally felt that when we call a country democratic we are praising it: consequently the defenders of every kind of régime claim that it is a democracy, and fear that they might have to stop using the word if it were tied down to any one meaning. Words of this kind are often used in a consciously dishonest way. That is, the person who uses them has his own private definition, but allows his hearer to think he means something quite different. Statements like *Marshal Pétain was a true patriot, The Soviet Press is the freest in the world, The Catholic Church is opposed to persecution*, are almost always made with intent to deceive. Other words used in variable meanings, in most cases more or less dishonestly, are: *class, totalitarian, science, progressive, reactionary, bourgeois, equality*.

Now that I have made this catalogue of swindles and perversions, let me give another example of the kind of writing that they lead to. This time it must of its nature be an imaginary one. I am going to translate a passage of good English into modern English of the worst sort. Here is a well-known verse from *Ecclesiastes*:

I returned, and saw under the sun, that the race is not to the swift, nor the battle to the strong, neither yet bread to the wise, nor yet riches to men of understanding, nor yet favour to men of skill; but time and chance happeneth to them all.[4]

Here it is in modern English:

Objective consideration of contemporary phenomena compels the conclusion that success or failure in competitive activities exhibits no tendency to be commensurate with innate capacity, but that a considerable element of the unpredictable must invariably be taken into account.

This is a parody, but not a very gross one. Exhibit (3), above, for instance, contains several patches of the same kind of English. It will be seen that I have not made a full translation. The beginning and ending of the sentence follow the original meaning fairly closely, but in the middle the concrete illustrations – race, battle, bread – dissolve into the vague phrase 'success or failure in competitive activities'. This had to be so, because no modern writer of the kind I am discussing – no one capable of

using phrases like 'objective consideration of contemporary phenomena' –
would ever tabulate his thoughts in that precise and detailed way. The
whole tendency of modern prose is away from concreteness. Now analyse
these two sentences a little more closely. The first contains 49 words but
only 60 syllables, and all its words are those of everyday life. The second
contains 38 words of 90 syllables: 18 of its words are from Latin roots,
and one from Greek. The first sentence contains six vivid images, and
only one phrase ('time and chance') that could be called vague. The second
contains not a single fresh, arresting phrase, and in spite of its 90 syllables
it gives only a shortened version of the meaning contained in the first.
Yet without a doubt it is the second kind of sentence that is gaining
ground in modern English. I do not want to exaggerate. This kind of
writing is not yet universal, and outcrops of simplicity will occur here and
there in the worst-written page. Still, if you or I were told to write a few
lines on the uncertainty of human fortunes, we should probably come
much nearer to my imaginary sentence than to the one from *Ecclesiastes*.

  As I have tried to show, modern writing at its worst does not consist
in picking out words for the sake of their meaning and inventing images
in order to make the meaning clearer. It consists in gumming together
long strips of words which have already been set in order by someone
else, and making the results presentable by sheer humbug. The attraction
of this way of writing is that it is easy. It is easier – even quicker, once
you have the habit – to say *In my opinion it is a not unjustifiable assumption
that* than to say *I think*. If you use ready-made phrases, you not only don't
have to hunt about for words; you also don't have to bother with the
rhythms of your sentences, since these phrases are generally so arranged
as to be more or less euphonious. When you are composing in a hurry –
when you are dictating to a stenographer, for instance, or making a public
speech – it is natural to fall into a pretentious, Latinized style. Tags like *a
consideration which we should do well to bear in mind* or *a conclusion to which
all of us would readily assent* will save many a sentence from coming down
with a bump. By using stale metaphors, similes and idioms, you save much
mental effort, at the cost of leaving your meaning vague, not only for your
reader but for yourself. This is the significance of mixed metaphors. The
sole aim of a metaphor is to call up a visual image. When these images
clash – as in *The Fascist octopus has sung its swan song, the jackboot is thrown*

into the melting pot – it can be taken as certain that the writer is not seeing a mental image of the objects he is naming; in other words he is not really thinking. Look again at the examples I gave at the beginning of this essay. Professor Laski (1) uses five negatives in 53 words. One of these is superfluous, making nonsense of the whole passage, and in addition there is the slip *alien* for *akin*, making further nonsense, and several avoidable pieces of clumsiness which increase the general vagueness. Professor Hogben (2) plays ducks and drakes with a battery which is able to write prescriptions, and, while disapproving of the everyday phrase *put up with*, is unwilling to look *egregious* up in the dictionary and see what it means. (3), if one takes an uncharitable attitude towards it, is simply meaningless: probably one could work out its intended meaning by reading the whole of the article in which it occurs. In (4), the writer knows more or less what he wants to say, but an accumulation of stale phrases chokes him like tea leaves blocking a sink. In (5), words and meaning have almost parted company. People who write in this manner usually have a general emotional meaning – they dislike one thing and want to express solidarity with another – but they are not interested in the detail of what they are saying. A scrupulous writer, in every sentence that he writes, will ask himself at least four questions, thus: What am I trying to say? What words will express it? What image or idiom will make it clearer? Is this image fresh enough to have an effect? And he will probably ask himself two more: Could I put it more shortly? Have I said anything that is avoidably ugly? But you are not obliged to go to all this trouble. You can shirk it by simply throwing your mind open and letting the ready-made phrases come crowding in. They will construct your sentences for you – even think your thoughts for you, to a certain extent – and at need they will perform the important service of partially concealing your meaning even from yourself. It is at this point that the special connection between politics and the debasement of language becomes clear.

In our time it is broadly true that political writing is bad writing. Where it is not true, it will generally be found that the writer is some kind of rebel, expressing his private opinions and not a 'party line'. Orthodoxy, of whatever colour, seems to demand a lifeless, imitative style. The political dialects to be found in pamphlets, leading articles, manifestos, White Papers and the speeches of under-secretaries do, of course, vary from party to party, but they are all alike in that one almost never finds in them a fresh, vivid, home-made turn of speech. When one watches some tired hack on the platform mechanically repeating the familiar phrases – *bestial atrocities, iron heel, bloodstained tyranny, free peoples of the world, stand shoulder to shoulder* – one often has a curious feeling that one is not watching a live human being but some kind of dummy: a feeling which suddenly becomes stronger at moments when the light catches the speaker's spectacles and turns them into blank discs which seem to have no eyes behind them. And this is not altogether fanciful. A speaker who uses that kind of phraseology has gone some distance towards turning himself into a machine. The appropriate noises are coming out of his larynx, but his brain is not involved as it would be if he were choosing his words for himself. If the speech he is making is one that he is accustomed to make over and over again, he may be almost unconscious of what he is saying, as one is when one utters the responses in church. And this reduced state of consciousness, if not indispensable, is at any rate favourable to political conformity.

In our time, political speech and writing are largely the defence of the indefensible. Things like the continuance of British rule in India, the Russian purges and deportations, the dropping of the atom bombs on Japan, can indeed be defended, but only by arguments which are too brutal for most people to face, and which do not square with the professed aims of political parties. Thus political language has to consist largely of euphemism, question-begging and sheer cloudy vagueness. Defenceless villages are bombarded from the air, the inhabitants driven out into the countryside, the cattle machine-gunned, the huts set on fire with incendiary bullets: this is called *pacification*. Millions of peasants are robbed of their farms and sent trudging along the roads with no more than they can carry: this is called *transfer of population* or *rectification of frontiers*. People are imprisoned for years without trial, or shot in the back of the neck or sent to die of scurvy in Arctic lumber camps: this is called *elimination of unreliable elements*. Such phraseology is needed if one wants to name things without calling up mental pictures of them. Consider for instance some comfortable English professor defending Russian totalitarianism. He cannot say outright, 'I believe in killing off your opponents when you can get good results by doing so.' Probably, therefore, he will say something like this:

While freely conceding that the Soviet régime exhibits certain features which the humanitarian may be inclined to deplore, we must, I think, agree that a certain curtailment of the right to political opposition is an unavoidable concomitant of transitional periods, and that the rigours which the Russian people have been called upon to undergo have been amply justified in the sphere of concrete achievement.

The inflated style is itself a kind of euphemism. A mass of Latin words falls upon the facts like soft snow, blurring the outlines and covering up all the details. The great enemy of clear language is insincerity. When there is a gap between one's real and one's declared aims, one turns as it were instinctively to long words and exhausted idioms, like a cuttlefish squirting out ink. In our age there is no such thing as 'keeping out of politics'. All issues are political issues, and politics itself is a mass of lies, evasions, folly, hatred and schizophrenia. When the general atmosphere is bad, language must suffer. I should expect to find – this is a guess which I have not sufficient knowledge to verify – that the German, Russian and Italian languages have all deteriorated in the last ten or fifteen years, as a result of dictatorship.

But if thought corrupts language, language can also corrupt thought. A bad usage can spread by tradition and imitation, even among people who should and do know better. The debased language that I have been discussing is in some ways very convenient. Phrases like *a not unjustifiable assumption, leaves much to be desired, would serve no good purpose, a consideration which we should do well to bear in mind*, are a continuous temptation, a packet of aspirins always at one's elbow. Look back through this essay, and for certain you will find that I have again and again committed the very faults I am protesting against. By this morning's post I have received a pamphlet dealing with conditions in Germany. The author tells me that he 'felt impelled' to write it. I open it at random, and here is almost the first sentence that I see: '(The Allies) have an opportunity not only of achieving a radical transformation of Germany's social and political structure in such a way as to avoid a nationalistic reaction in Germany itself, but at the same time of laying the foundations of a co-operative and unified Europe.' You see, he 'feels impelled' to write – feels, presumably, that he has something new to say – and yet his words, like cavalry horses answering the bugle, group themselves automatically into the familiar dreary pattern. This invasion of one's mind by ready-made phrases (*lay the foundations, achieve a radical transformation*) can only be prevented if one is constantly on guard against them, and every such phrase anaesthetizes a portion of one's brain.

I said earlier that the decadence of our language is probably curable. Those who deny this would argue, if they produced an argument at all, that language merely reflects existing, social conditions, and that we cannot influence its development by any direct tinkering with words and constructions. So far as the general tone or spirit of a language goes, this may be true, but it is not true in detail. Silly words and expressions have often disappeared, not through any evolutionary process but owing to the conscious action of a minority. Two recent examples were *explore every avenue* and *leave no stone unturned*, which were killed by the jeers of a few journalists. There is a long list of flyblown metaphors which could similarly be got rid of if enough people would interest themselves in the job; and it should also be possible to laugh the *not un-* formation out of existence,* to reduce the amount of Latin and Greek in the average sentence, to drive out foreign phrases and strayed scientific words, and, in general, to make pretentiousness unfashionable. But all these are minor points. The defence of the English language implies more than this, and perhaps it is best to start by saying what it does *not* imply.

To begin with, it has nothing to do with archaism, with the salvaging of obsolete words and turns of speech, or with the setting-up of a 'standard English' which must never be departed from. On the contrary, it is especially concerned with the scrapping of every word or idiom which has outworn its usefulness. It has nothing to do with correct grammar and syntax, which are of no importance so long as one makes one's meaning clear, or with the avoidance of Americanisms, or with having what is called a 'good prose style'. On the other hand it is not concerned with fake simplicity and the attempt to make written English colloquial. Nor does it even imply in every case preferring the Saxon word to the Latin one, though it does imply using the fewest and shortest words that will

---

* One can cure oneself of the *not un-* formation by memorizing this sentence: *A not unblack dog was chasing a not unsmall rabbit across a not ungreen field* [Orwell's footnote].

cover one's meaning. What is above all needed is to let the meaning choose the word, and not the other way about. In prose, the worst thing one can do with words is to surrender to them. When you think of a concrete object, you think wordlessly, and then, if you want to describe the thing you have been visualizing, you probably hunt about till you find the exact words that seem to fit it. When you think of something abstract you are more inclined to use words from the start, and unless you make a conscious effort to prevent it, the existing dialect will come rushing in and do the job for you, at the expense of blurring or even changing your meaning. Probably it is better to put off using words as long as possible and get one's meaning as clear as one can through pictures or sensations. Afterwards one can choose – not simply *accept* – the phrases that will best cover the meaning, and then switch round and decide what impression one's words are likely to make on another person. This last effort of the mind cuts out all stale or mixed images, all prefabricated phrases, needless repetitions, and humbug and vagueness generally. But one can often be in doubt about the effect of a word or a phrase, and one needs rules that one can rely on when instinct fails. I think the following rules will cover most cases:

(i) Never use a metaphor, simile or other figure of speech which you are used to seeing in print.

(ii) Never use a long word where a short one will do.

(iii) If it is possible to cut a word out, always cut it out.

(iv) Never use the passive where you can use the active.

(v) Never use a foreign phrase, a scientific word or a jargon word if you can think of an everyday English equivalent.

(vi) Break any of these rules sooner than say anything outright barbarous.

These rules sound elementary, and so they are, but they demand a deep change of attitude in anyone who has grown used to writing in the style now fashionable. One could keep all of them and still write bad English, but one could not write the kind of stuff that I quoted in those five specimens at the beginning of this article.

I have not here been considering the literary use of language, but merely language as an instrument for expressing and not for concealing or preventing thought. Stuart Chase[5] and others have come near to claiming that all abstract words are meaningless, and have used this as a pretext for advocating a kind of political quietism. Since you don't know what Fascism is, how can you struggle against Fascism? One need not swallow such absurdities as this, but one ought to recognize that the present political chaos is connected with the decay of language, and that one can probably bring about some improvement by starting at the verbal end. If you simplify your English, you are freed from the worst follies of orthodoxy. You cannot speak any of the necessary dialects, and when you make a stupid remark its stupidity will be obvious, even to yourself. Political language – and with variations this is true of all political parties, from Conservatives to Anarchists – is designed to make lies sound truthful and murder respectable, and to give an appearance of solidity to pure wind. One cannot change this all in a moment, but one can at least change one's own habits, and from time to time one can even, if one jeers loudly enough, send some worn-out and useless phrase – some *jackboot, Achilles' heel, hotbed, melting pot, acid test, veritable inferno* or other lump of verbal refuse – into the dustbin where it belongs.

1. Orwell kept lists of his earnings to assist in the preparation of his income-tax return. Only one book has survived, that for July 1943 to December 1945; see XVII/ *2831*. For Orwell's preparatory notes for this essay, see XVII/ *2816*; see also 'Propaganda and Demotic Speech', XVI/ *2523*.

2. '*rift within the lute*' is given after 'fishing in troubled waters' in Orwell's list of Metaphors in his notes; XVII/ *2816*. Not all the metaphors in this list are in the essay, but in his next sentence Orwell asks, 'what is a "rift", for instance?' He must have intended to include this metaphor, since his question does not make sense without it; it has therefore been added here in square brackets. The line comes from Tennyson's *Idylls of the King*, 'Merlin and Vivien'. Vivien sings to Merlin a song she heard Sir Launcelot once sing. It includes these two stanzas, which make the meaning plain:

> It [want of faith] is the little rift within the lute,
> That by and by will make the music mute,
> And ever widening slowly silence all.
>
> The little rift within the lover's lute,
> Or little pitted speck in garner'd fruit,
> That rotting inward slowly moulders all. [Lines 388–93]

3. Neither 'non-fragmentary' nor 'deregionalize' appears in the 1991 edition of the *Oxford English Dictionary*, though 'regionalize' and 'deruralize' do.

4. Ecclesiastes 9:11.

5. Stuart Chase (1888–1985), economist who investigated the US meat-packing industry

and served with the Labor Bureau Inc. Orwell probably refers to his *The Tyranny of Words* (1938). He also wrote *Men and Machines* (1929), *The Economy of Abundance* (1934) and *Rich Land, Poor Land* (1936).

[2841]

'Freedom and Happiness'
Tribune, *4 January 1946*

Several years after hearing of its existence, I have at last got my hands on a copy of Zamyatin's *We*,[1] which is one of the literary curiosities of this book-burning age. Looking it up in Gleb Struve's *25 Years of Soviet Russian Literature*,[2] I find its history to have been this:

Zamyatin, who died in Paris in 1937, was a Russian novelist and critic who published a number of books both before and after the Revolution. *We* was written about 1923, and though it is not about Russia and has no direct connection with contemporary politics – it is a fantasy dealing with the twenty-sixth century A.D. – it was refused publication on the ground that it was ideologically undesirable. A copy of the manuscript found its way out of the country, and the book has appeared in English, French and Czech translations, but never in Russian. The English translation was published in the United States, and I have never been able to procure a copy: but copies of the French translation (the title is *Nous Autres*) do exist, and I have at last succeeded in borrowing one.[3] So far as I can judge it is not a book of the first order, but it is certainly an unusual one, and it is astonishing that no English publisher has been enterprising enough to re-issue it.

The first thing anyone would notice about *We* is the fact – never pointed out, I believe – that Aldous Huxley's *Brave New World*[4] must be partly derived from it. Both books deal with the rebellion of the primitive human spirit against a rationalised, mechanised, painless world, and both stories are supposed to take place about six hundred years hence. The atmosphere of the two books is similar, and it is roughly speaking the same kind of society that is being described, though Huxley's book shows less political awareness and is more influenced by recent biological and psychological theories.

In the twenty-sixth century, in Zamyatin's vision of it, the inhabitants of Utopia have so completely lost their individuality as to be known only by numbers. They live in glass houses (this was written before television was invented), which enables the political police, known as the 'Guardians', to supervise them more easily. They all wear identical uniforms, and a human being is commonly referred to either as 'a number' or 'a unif' (uniform). They live on synthetic food, and their usual recreation is to march in fours while the anthem of the Single State is played through loudspeakers. At stated intervals they are allowed for one hour (known as 'the sex hour') to lower the curtains round their glass apartments. There is, of course, no marriage, though sex life does not appear to be completely promiscuous. For purposes of love-making everyone has a sort of ration book of pink tickets, and the partner with whom he spends one of his allotted sex hours signs the counterfoil. The Single State is ruled over by a personage known as the Benefactor, who is annually re-elected by the entire population, the vote being always unanimous. The guiding principle of the State is that happiness and freedom are incompatible. In the Garden of Eden man was happy, but in his folly he demanded freedom and was driven out into the wilderness. Now the Single State has restored his happiness by removing his freedom.

So far the resemblance with *Brave New World* is striking. But though Zamyatin's book is less well put together – it has a rather weak and episodic plot which is too complex to summarise – it has a political point which the other lacks. In Huxley's book the problem of 'human nature' is in a sense solved, because it assumes that by pre-natal treatment, drugs and hypnotic suggestion the human organism can be specialised in any way that is desired. A first-rate scientific worker is as easily produced as an Epsilon semi-moron, and in either case the vestiges of primitive instincts, such as maternal feeling or the desire for liberty, are easily dealt with. At the same time no clear reason is given why society should be stratified in the elaborate way that is described. The aim is not economic exploitation, but the desire to bully and dominate does not seem to be a motive either. There is no power-hunger, no sadism, no hardness of any kind. Those at the top have no strong motive for staying at the top, and though everyone is happy in a vacuous way, life has become so pointless that it is difficult to believe that such a society could endure.

Zamyatin's book is on the whole more relevant to our own situation. In spite of education and the vigilance of the Guardians, many of the ancient human instincts are still there. The teller of the story, D-503, who, though a gifted engineer, is a poor conventional creature, a sort of Utopian Billy Brown of London Town, is constantly horrified by the atavistic impulses which seize upon him. He falls in love (this is a crime, of course) with a certain I-330 who is a member of an underground resistance movement and succeeds for a while in leading him into rebellion. When the rebellion breaks out it appears that the enemies of the Benefactor are in fact fairly numerous, and these people, apart from plotting the over-throw of the State, even indulge, at the moment when their curtains are down, in such vices as smoking cigarettes and drinking alcohol. D-503 is ultimately saved from the consequences of his own folly. The authorities announce that they have discovered the cause of the recent disorders: it is that some human beings suffer from a disease called imagination. The nerve-centre responsible for imagination has now been located, and the disease can be cured by X-ray treatment. D-503 undergoes the operation, after which it is easy for him to do what he has known all along that he ought to do – that is, betray his confederates to the police. With complete equanimity he watches I-330 tortured by means of compressed air under a glass bell:

She looked at me, her hands clasping the arms of the chair, until her eyes were completely shut. They took her out, brought her to herself by means of an electric shock, and put her under the bell again. This operation was repeated three times, and not a word issued from her lips.

The others who had been brought along with her showed themselves more honest. Many of them confessed after one application. Tomorrow they will all be sent to the Machine of the Benefactor.

The Machine of the Benefactor is the guillotine. There are many executions in Zamyatin's Utopia. They take place publicly, in the presence of the Benefactor, and are accompanied by triumphal odes recited by the official poets. The guillotine, of course, is not the old crude instrument but a much improved model which literally liquidates its victim, reducing him in an instant to a puff of smoke and a pool of clear water. The execution is, in fact, a human sacrifice, and the scene describing it is given deliberately the colour of the sinister slave civilisations of the ancient world. It is this intuitive grasp of the irrational side of totalitarianism – human sacrifice, cruelty as an end in itself, the worship of a Leader who is credited with divine attributes – that makes Zamyatin's book superior to Huxley's.

It is easy to see why the book was refused publication. The following conversation (I abridge it slightly) between D-503 and I-330 would have been quite enough to set the blue pencils working:

Do you realise that what you are suggesting is revolution?'

'Of course, it's revolution. Why not?'

'Because there can't *be* a revolution. *Our* revolution was the last and there can never be another. Everybody knows that.'

'My dear, you're a mathematician: tell me, which is the last number?'

'What do you mean, the last number?'

'Well, then, the biggest number!'

'But that's absurd. Numbers are infinite. There can't be a last one.'

'Then why do you talk about the last revolution?'

There are other similar passages. It may well be, however, that Zamyatin did not intend the Soviet régime to be the special target of his satire. Writing at about the time of Lenin's death, he cannot have had the Stalin dictatorship in mind, and conditions in Russia in 1923 were not such that anyone would revolt against them on the ground that life was becoming too safe and comfortable. What Zamyatin seems to be aiming at is not any particular country but the implied aims of industrial civilisation. I have not read any of his other books, but I learn from Gleb Struve that he had spent several years in England and had written some blistering satires on English life. It is evident from *We* that he had a strong leaning towards primitivism. Imprisoned by the Czarist Government in 1906, and then imprisoned by the Bolsheviks in 1922 in the same corridor of the same prison, he had cause to dislike the political régime he had lived under, but his book is not simply the expression of a grievance. It is in effect a study of the Machine, the genie that man has thoughtlessly let out of its bottle and cannot put back again. This is a book to look out for when an English version appears.[5]

1. Yevgeny Zamyatin (1884–1937), naval engineer and satirical author, was arrested in 1905 following his participation in the unsuccessful revolution against the Russian government; he was exiled but, in 1913, amnestied. *We* was written in 1920 (not 1923), but its publication was forbidden in Soviet Russia. An English translation was published in New York in 1924, with Zamyatin's consent, and it was published outside Russia, in Russian, by a White Russian émigré journal in 1927. For that, Zamyatin was attacked by the Association of Proletarian Writers in 1929. He was allowed to leave Russia in 1931 and settled in Paris, where he died. See the excellent short introduction by Sophie Fuller and Julian Sacchi to their translation of his stories *Islanders* and *The Fisher of Men* (1984), the first of which is set in England, where it was written in 1917 while he supervised the construction of icebreakers for Russia in the northeast of England and Scotland. A recent translation of *We* by Clarence Brown is available in Penguin Modern Classics (1993).

2. This was the first version of Struve's book. See also n. 10 to 'Notes on Nationalism', above.

3. The journalist Alan Moray Williams (1915–) lent Orwell a copy of the French translation of *We* (*Nous Autres*). Williams wrote to Ian Angus on 30 September 1976 to say that he had briefly mentioned *We* in an article, 'What is Socialist Realism?', in *Tribune*, 16 June 1944: 'Genius always breaks rules. Presumably a rebel genius could find a printer or send his manuscript abroad (like Zamyatin with his *We*) even in the U.S.S.R.' Orwell had expressed interest, and Williams lent him his copy a week or two later. He did not discount the possibility that Orwell may have heard of the book before that: he himself might have referred to it, or Orwell could have come across it when he lived in Paris. However, Williams was sure that Orwell had not read *We* in any language until 1944.

4. Aldous Huxley, (1894–1963), novelist, poet and essayist published *Brave New World* in 1932. The title is ironic. The novel presents a nightmare vision of the future. As Huxley wrote in a Preface in 1946, in the future we may have 'either a number of national, militarized totalitarianisms', or else 'one supra-national totalitarianism'.

5. See Gleb Struve's letter to *Tribune*, 4 January 1946 (reprinted in XVIII/16–17). In addition to mentioning Zamyatin's *Islanders*, describing it as 'a bitingly satirical picture of English smugness and philistinism', he refers to Zamyatin's play, *The Fires of St Dominic*, 'generally believed to have been aimed at the Soviet Cheka' (a predecessor of the KGB). *Islanders* and *The Fisher of Men* are still very effective today.

The Intellectual Revolt
Four articles, Manchester Evening News

Although these four articles were published over a period of a month, Orwell apparently conceived of the series as a single entity. He certainly agreed to have them abridged and translated into German as a long essay of some 5,500 words, and added an 'Afterword', which was published in Neue

Auslese. He seems, if mistakenly, to have believed that the four articles were issued in pamphlet form. No such pamphlet has been traced and none was published by the Manchester Evening News. *He may have been confused by one issued by the Socialist Book Centre,* James Burnham and the Managerial Revolution *(see* XVIII/ 2989), *or he may have had in mind the German abridgement of this one in* Neue Auslese.

In his list of reprintable articles, Orwell included this sequence, but he noted that 'The Intellectual Revolt' was not his title; see XIX/ 3323.

[2875]

1. 'THE INTELLECTUAL REVOLT': PESSIMISTS
24 January 1946

During recent years it has become more and more obvious that old-style, laissez-faire capitalism is finished.

Far back in the nineteenth century this fact had been grasped by various clear-sighted individuals, and it was later made apparent to millions by the disaster of the 1914–18 war, by the success of the Russian revolution, and by the rise of the Fascist régimes, which were not strictly capitalist and could solve problems before which the old democracies, such as Britain or the United States, remained helpless.

The events of the last six years have merely underlined the lesson. Unmistakably, the drift everywhere is towards planned economies and away from an individualistic society in which property rights are absolute and money-making is the chief incentive.

However, simultaneously with this development there has happened an intellectual revolt which is not simply the uneasiness of property-owners who see their privileges menaced. If not a majority, at any rate a large proportion of the best minds of our time are dismayed by the turn of events and doubtful whether mere economic security is a worthwhile objective.

There is a widespread disappointment with the Russian form of Social-ism, and, lying deeper than this, a mistrust of the whole machine of civilisation and its implied aims. Naturally, this intellectual revolt takes almost as many forms as there are individual thinkers, but there are certain main tendencies, which can be grouped as follows: –

1. The Pessimists. – Those who deny that a planned society can lead either to happiness or to true progress.

2. The Left-wing Socialists. – Those who accept the principle of planning, but are chiefly concerned to combine it with individual liberty.

3. The Christian Reformers. – Those who wish to combine revolutionary social change with adherence to Christian doctrine.

4. The Pacifists. – Those who wish to get away from the centralised State and from the whole principle of government by coercion.

Of course, there is an overlap between these different schools of thought, and some of them also overlap with ordinary Conservatism on the one side or with orthodox Socialism on the other.

Still, a large number of distinguished and representative thinkers can be accurately grouped under these headings. In the first of these four essays I deal with those I have labelled 'Pessimists'.

Perhaps the best expression of the pessimistic viewpoint, at any rate in English and in recent years, is F. A. Voigt's *Unto Caesar,* which was published about 1938.[1] This heavily documented book is in the main an examination of Communism and Nazism, written round the thesis that societies which set out to establish the 'earthly paradise' always end in tyranny.

Voigt assumes throughout his book that Russian Communism and German Fascism are for practical purposes the same thing and have almost the same objective. This is certainly an over-simplification and is unable to explain all the known facts. Nevertheless Voigt makes out a very strong case for narrowing down the scope of politics and not expecting too much from political action.

His basic argument is quite simple. A statesman who aims at perfection, and thinks that he knows how to reach it, will stop at nothing to drive others along the same road, and his political ideals will be inextricably mixed up with his desire to remain in power. Perfection, in practice, is never attained, and the terrorism used in pursuit of it simply breeds the need for fresh terrorism. Consequently the attempt to establish liberty and equality always ends in the police state: whereas more limited aims, based on the realisation that man's nature is full of evil, may lead to a fairly decent society.

Approximately the same line is taken by the American writer, Peter Drucker, author of *The End of Economic Man* and *The Future of Industrial Man*.[2] Drucker was one of the very small handful of publicists who foretold the Russo-German Pact of 1939. Particularly in the second of the above-named books, he argues the need for what he calls a 'Conservative revolution' meaning not a return of capitalism, but the revival of the idea of a 'mixed society' in which there is a system of checks and balances which make it impossible for any one section of the community to become all-powerful.

This, Drucker argues, was the real aim of the eighteenth-century leaders of the American revolution. Other writers who have advanced rather similar arguments against perfectionism are Michael Roberts (in his book on T. E. Hulme), Malcolm Muggeridge (*The Thirties*)[3] and Hugh Kingsmill in *The Poisoned Crown*.[4] The last-named book consists of four studies of Queen Elizabeth, Cromwell, Napoleon and Abraham Lincoln – it is perhaps a somewhat perverse book, but it contains some penetrating remarks on dictatorship.

The whole problem of Utopian aims, and their tendency to end in tyranny, is discussed by Bertrand Russell in a number of books, particularly *The Scientific Outlook, Freedom and Organisation* and *Power: A New Analysis*.[5] Russell has held very different political views at different periods of his life, but his vision of the future has been almost uniformly pessimistic, and he is inclined to think that liberty and efficiency are of their nature incompatible.

The planned, centralised State has also been attacked on the ground that, even in terms of its own objectives, it does not work. Perhaps the ablest exposition of this viewpoint is Professor Hayek's *The Road to Serfdom*,[6] which was published in 1944 and raised a great deal of discussion, especially in the United States.

Hayek argues that centralism and detailed planning not only destroy liberty but are incapable of affording as high a standard of living as laissez-faire capitalism. He claims that before Hitler came to power his essential work had been done for him by the German Social-Democrats and Communists, who had succeeded in breaking down the average German's desire for liberty and independence.

His main argument is that a centralised economy necessarily gives great power to the bureaucrats at the centre, and that people who want power for its own sake will gravitate towards the key positions. A rather similar line is taken in *Contempt of Freedom*, by Professor Michael Polanyi of Manchester University, who studied conditions in the U.S.S.R. over a number of years and subjected the Webbs' famous book, *Soviet Communism – a New Civilisation?* to some searching criticism. The biologist John R. Baker[7] has also argued (*Science and the Planned State*) that scientific research cannot flourish under the rule of a bureaucracy.

Finally, one can number among the 'pessimists' James Burnham, whose book *The Managerial Revolution* made such a stir when it was published five years ago. More particularly in his next published book, *The Machiavellians*,[8] Burnham argues that neither Socialism nor full democracy are attainable aims, and that the most we can do is to establish safeguards – for example, autonomous trade unions and a free press – against the abuse of power.

He goes much further than the other writers I have named, in that he denies even the possibility of decent political behaviour and merely advocates that we should use political trickery for limited ends instead of extravagant ones; but at many points his world-view coincides with that of the others.

The term 'pessimist' fits all of these writers in so much that they refuse to believe in the possibility of an earthly Utopia, while most of them also do not believe in a 'next world' in which this one will be put right. Except perhaps for Drucker and Burnham, who wish to guide the existing trend rather than oppose it, the weakness of all of them is that they are not advocating any policy likely to get a large following.

Hayek's able defence of capitalism, for instance, is wasted labour, since hardly anyone wishes for the return of old-style capitalism. Faced with the choice between serfdom and economic insecurity the masses everywhere would probably choose outright serfdom, at least if it were called by some other name. Most of the others are putting forward what is in essence a religious view of life without the consolations of orthodox religion.

If one were obliged to give the writers of this school a political label one would have to call them Conservatives – but in most cases theirs is a romantic Conservatism, which fights against irreversible facts. But that is not to deny that they and other writers of kindred tendency have uttered much useful criticism of the folly and wickedness of the Totalitarian age.

1. F. A. Voigt (1892–1957), journalist, early recognized the true nature of Nazism; see n. 5 to 'As I Please', 17, above.

2. *The Future of Industrial Man*, reviewed by Orwell in the *Manchester Evening News*, 3 January 1946; for Peter Drucker, see n. 4 to 'As I Please', 17, above.

3. *The Thirties*, reviewed in 'Notes on the Way', *Time and Tide*, 6 April 1940 (XII/604) and in *New English Weekly*, 25 April 1940 (XII/615).

4. *The Poisoned Crown*, reviewed in the *Observer*, 23 April 1944 (XVI/2458). Hugh Kingsmill (= Hugh K. Lunn, 1889–1944), critic, editor and anthologist.

5. *Power: A New Social Analysis*, reviewed in *The Adelphi*, January 1939 (XI/520).

6. *The Road to Serfdom*, reviewed in the *Observer*, 9 April 1944 (XVI/2451).

7. Orwell wrote 'James Baker' by mistake. It was in fact John R. Baker (1900–84), who wrote a counterblast to Professor J. D. Bernal's *The Social Future of Science*, in the *New Statesman*, 29 July 1939. He was a founder-member of the Society for Freedom in Science in 1941. Gary Wersky described him as a 'conservative, reactionary eugenist' with 'no faith in the democratic process', who believed that High Science should be used against claims by the masses for egalitarianism (*The Visible College*, 1978, 282–4). When Orwell wrote this article he had not read anything by Baker and he may have had a mistaken understanding of what Baker stood for. See XV/2377, Orwell's notes for 'The Last Man in Europe' (which lead to *Nineteen Eighty-Four*), where the term 'Bakerism' appears, though it does not appear in the novel (see n. 2 thereto in *CW*). Professor Bernal (1901–71) was included by Orwell in his list of Crypto-Communists and Fellow-Travellers (XX/243).

8. For Orwell's review of *The Machiavellians*, see above, and n. 1 thereto for James Burnham.

[2876]

2. 'WHAT IS SOCIALISM?'
31 January 1946

Until the twentieth century, and indeed until the nineteen-thirties, all Socialist thought was in some sense Utopian. Socialism had nowhere been tested in the physical world, and in the mind of almost everyone, including its enemies, it was bound up with the idea of liberty and equality.

Only let economic injustice be brought to an end and all other forms of tyranny would vanish also. The age of human brotherhood would begin, and war, crime, disease, poverty and overwork would be things of the past. There were some who disliked this objective, and many who assumed that it would never be reached, but that at least was the objective.

Thinkers as far apart as Karl Marx and William Morris, Anatole France and Jack London, all had a roughly similar picture of the Socialist future, though they might differ violently as to the best way of getting there.

After 1930 an ideological split began to appear in the Socialist movement. By this time 'Socialism' was no longer a mere word evoking a dream. A huge and powerful country, Soviet Russia, had adopted a Socialist economy and was rapidly reconstructing its national life, and in nearly all countries there was an unmistakable swing towards public ownership and large-scale planning. At the same time for the word 'Socialism' [there grew up in Germany the][1] monstrosity of Nazism, which called itself Socialism and did have certain quasi-Socialist features, but embodied them in one of the most cruel and cynical régimes the world has ever seen. Evidently it was time for the word 'Socialism' to be re-defined.

What is Socialism? Can you have Socialism without liberty, without equality, and without internationalism? Are we still aiming at universal human brotherhood, or must we be satisfied with a new kind of caste society in which we surrender our individual rights in return for economic security?

Among recent books, perhaps the best discussion of these questions is to be found in Arthur Koestler's book *The Yogi and the Commissar*,[2] published about a year ago.

According to Koestler, what is now needed is, 'a synthesis of the saint and the revolutionary'. To put it in different words – revolutions have to happen, there can be no moral progress without drastic economic changes, and yet the revolutionary wastes his labour if he loses touch with ordinary human decency. Somehow the dilemma of ends and means must be resolved. We must be able to act, even to use violence, and yet not be corrupted by action. In specific political terms, this means rejection of Russian Communism on the one hand and of Fabian gradualism on the other.

Like most writers of similar tendency, Koestler is an ex-Communist, and inevitably his sharpest reaction is against the developments that have appeared in Soviet policy since about 1930. His best book is a novel, *Darkness at Noon*,[3] dealing with the Moscow sabotage trials.

Other writers who can be placed roughly in the same category are Ignazio Silone, André Malraux and the Americans John Dos Passos and James Farrell.

One might add André Gide, who only arrived at Communism, or

indeed at political consciousness, late in life, but, having done so, passed almost at once into the ranks of the rebels. One can also add the French Trotskyist, Victor Serge, and the Italian, Gaetano Salvemini, the historian of Fascism. Salvemini is a Liberal rather than a Socialist, but he resembles the others in that his main emphasis is anti-totalitarian, and he has been deeply involved in the internal struggles of the Left.

In spite of the superficial resemblance that appears at certain moments, there is no real affinity between dissident Socialists like Koestler or Silone, and enlightened Conservatives like Voigt or Drucker. Silone's book of political dialogues, *The School for Dictators*,[4] may seem on the surface as pessimistic, and as critical of the existing Left Wing parties as *Unto Caesar*, but the underlying world-view is very different.

The point is that a Socialist or Communist, as such – and perhaps this applies most of all to the one who breaks with his own party on a point of doctrine – is a person who believes the 'earthly paradise' to be possible. Socialism is in the last analysis an optimistic creed and not easy to square with the doctrine of original sin.

A Socialist is not obliged to believe that human society can actually be made perfect, but almost any Socialist does believe that it could be a great deal better than it is at present, and that most of the evil that men do results from the warping effects of injustice and inequality. The basis of Socialism is humanism. It can co-exist with religious belief, but not with the belief that man is a limited creature who will always misbehave himself if he gets half a chance.

The emotion behind books like *Darkness at Noon*, or Gide's *Return from the U.S.S.R.*, or Eugene Lyons's *Assignment in Utopia*,[5] or others of similar tendency, is not simply disappointment because the expected paradise has not arrived quickly enough. It is also a fear that the original aims of the Socialist movement are becoming blurred.

It is certainly true that orthodox Socialist thought, either reformist or revolutionary, has lost some of the messianic quality that it had 30 years ago. This results from the growing complexity of industrial life, from the day-to-day needs of the struggle against Fascism, and from the example of Soviet Russia. In order to survive the Russian Communists were forced to abandon, at any rate temporarily, some of the dreams with which they had started out.

Strict economic equality was found to be impracticable; freedom of speech, in a backward country which had passed through civil war, was too dangerous; internationalism was killed by the hostility of the capitalist powers.

From about 1925 onwards Russian policies, internal and external, grew harsher and less idealistic, and the new spirit was carried abroad by the Communist parties of the various countries. The history of these Communist parties can be conveniently studied in Franz Borkenau's book *The Communist International.*[6]

In spite of much courage and devotion the main effect of Communism in Western Europe has been to undermine the belief in democracy and tinge the whole Socialist movement with Machiavellianism. It is not only the writers I have named who are in revolt against these tendencies. There is a whole host of others, great and small, who have gone through a similar development. To name only a few: Freda Utley, Max Eastman, Ralph Bates, Stephen Spender, Philip Toynbee, Louis Fischer.

Except, perhaps, for Max Eastman none of these writers could be said to have reverted towards Conservatism. They are all aware of the need for planned societies and for a high level of industrial development. But they want the older conception of Socialism, which laid its stress on liberty and equality and drew its inspiration from the belief in human brotherhood, to be kept alive.

The viewpoint that they are expressing exists in the Left Wing of the Socialist movement everywhere, or at least in the more advanced countries, where a high standard of living is taken for granted. In more primitive countries political extremism is more likely to take the form of anarchism. Among those who believe in the possibility of human progress a three-cornered struggle is always going on between Machiavellianism, bureaucracy and Utopianism.

At this moment it is difficult for Utopianism to take shape in a definite political movement. The masses everywhere want security much more than they want equality, and do not generally realise that freedom of speech and of the Press are of urgent importance to themselves. But the desire for earthly perfection has a very long history behind it.

If one studied the genealogy of the ideas for which writers like Koestler and Silone stand, one would find it leading back through Utopian dreamers like William Morris and mystical democrats like Walt Whitman, through Rousseau, through the English diggers and levellers, through the peasant revolts of the Middle Ages, and back to the early Christians and the slave rebellions of antiquity.

The pamphlets of Gerrard Winstanley,[7] the digger from Wigan, whose experiment in primitive Communism was crushed by Cromwell, are in some ways strangely close to modern Left Wing literature.

The 'earthly paradise' has never been realised, but as an idea it never seems to perish in spite of the ease with which it can be debunked by practical politicians of all colours.

Underneath it lies the belief that human nature is fairly decent to start with and is capable of indefinite development. This belief has been the main driving force of the Socialist movement, including the underground sects who prepared the way for the Russian revolution, and it could be claimed that the Utopians, at present a scattered minority, are the true upholders of Socialist tradition.

Freda Utley: *The Dream We Lost*;[8] Max Eastman: *Since Lenin Died, Artists in Uniform*; Louis Fischer: *Men and Politics*;[9] Arthur Koestler: *The Gladiators, Scum of the Earth*; Ignazio Silone: *Fontamara, Bread and Wine, The Seed Beneath the Snow*; André Malraux: *Storm Over Shanghai, Days of Hope*; Gaetano Salvemini: *Under the Axe of Fascism*; Gerrard Winstanley: *Selections*.

1. The words within square brackets are not found in the original in the *Manchester Evening News*; they come from the German version: 'Zur gleichen Zeit wuchs in Deutschland eine Massenbewegung an, die sich nationaler Sozialismus nannte und gewisse quasi-sozialistische Zuge aufwies, aber das grausamte und zynischte Regime verkörperte, das die Welt je gesehen hat.' Literally translated, this reads: 'At the same time there grew up in Germany a mass movement which called itself National Socialism and exhibited certain quasi-Socialist features, but embodied them in one of the most cruel and cynical regimes the world has ever seen.'

2. *The Yogi and the Commissar*, reviewed in *C. W. Review*, November 1945 (XVII/2778); see also, and for (the later) *The Gladiators* and *Scum of the Earth*, Orwell's essay 'Arthur Koestler', *Focus*, 2, 1946, and in *Critical Essays* (1946; XVI/2548). Koestler (1905–83), novelist and essayist, was born in Budapest and joined the Communist Party in 1931, leaving in the late thirties. He spent a year in the USSR and worked as a reporter in the Spanish Civil War; he was captured and condemned to death but escaped in an exchange of prisoners. He was interned by the French in 1940 and imprisoned for a time by the British as an alien. He and Orwell were close friends and worked together on the Freedom Defence Committee.

3. *Darkness at Noon*, reviewed in the *New Statesman & Nation*, 4 January 1941 (XII/741).

4. *The School for Dictators*, reviewed in *New English Weekly*, 8 June 1939 (XI/547).

5. *Assignment in Utopia*, reviewed in *New English Weekly*, 9 June 1938, see above.

6. *The Communist International*, reviewed in *New English Weekly*, 22 September 1938, see above.

7. *Selections from the Works of Gerrard Winstanley*, reviewed in the *Observer*, 3 September 1944, see above. In the reading list at the end of the essay, this was said to be edited by Christopher Hill, but Hill provided an introduction; the selection was edited by Leonard Hamilton.

8. Orwell spelt 'Utley' as 'Uttley' on each occasion. *The Dream We Lost: Soviet Russia Then and Now* was published in New York in 1940; copies were evidently not readily available in England: the British and London Libraries have none. She translated V. Astrov, *An Illustrated History of the Russian Revolution* (1928), and described her experiences in Russia in *Lost Illusions* (1949), which had an introduction by Bertrand Russell. Freda Utley also wrote about political events in China and Japan in the 1930s and in particular on the relationship of Lancashire to the Far East.

9. *Men and Politics*, reviewed in *Now and Then*, Christmas 1941, see above.

[2877]

3. 'THE CHRISTIAN REFORMERS'

7 February 1946

The belief in life after death and the desire for earthly happiness are irreconcilable, but they pull in opposite directions. If there is a life beyond the grave our chief purpose must be to prepare for that life, and the necessary spiritual discipline may lie in pain, sorrow, poverty, and all the other things that the social reformer wants to get rid of.

In any case, the idea of submission to the will of God, and the idea of increasing human control over nature, are felt to be inimical. On the whole, therefore, the Christian churches – and especially the Catholic, Orthodox, Anglican and Lutheran churches, each of them bound up with a well-established social order – have been hostile to the idea of progress and have resisted any political theory tending to weaken the institution of private property.

However, one cannot equate Christian belief with Conservatives. Even in the Middle Ages there were already heretical sects which preached revolutionary political doctrines, and after the Reformation there was a close connection between Radicalism and Protestantism. The roots of the English Socialist movement lie partly in Nonconformity.

In our own time, however, there has been a more far-reaching development in the attempt to reconcile orthodox, other-worldly, Christian belief with revolutionary Socialism. Catholic Socialist parties have appeared all over the Continent. The Russian Orthodox Church, or an important part of it, has made its peace with the Soviet Government, and corresponding currents of thought have shown themselves in the Church of England.

There is more than one reason for this development, but it would not have happened if individual Christians, both priests and laymen, had not become more and more convinced of the inherent wickedness of capitalist society. It would not do, as in the past, to preach that God made rich and poor and that what mattered was the saving of souls.

As Pastor Niemöller[1] put it, the conditions of poverty in a great city were such as to make a Christian life impossible. Perhaps the teachings of Christ pointed the way to pure Communism. At any rate, they evidently demanded a radical redistribution of property.

During the last 20 years the most distinguished religious thinkers have not been political reactionaries in the ordinary sense: that is, they have not been defenders of *laissez-faire* capitalism. There are many gradations of opinion among them, but it is possible to sort out three main tendencies.

First, there are those who simply identify Christianity with Communism and lay their main emphasis on the political and economic implications of the Gospel. Some, of whom the Dean of Canterbury[2] is the best known, consider Soviet Russia to be the nearest existing approach to a truly Christian Society.

Professor John Macmurray (*The Clue to History*)[3] goes almost as far along this road as the Dean of Canterbury, and holds that the anti-religious bias of the Soviet régime is simply an error which can and should be rectified. Professor Macmurray, however, rejects the doctrine of personal immortality, so that he can hardly be considered an orthodox believer.

Another Anglican writer who has made utterances more or less in the same sense, though with much more emphasis on the sanctity of the individual, is Sydney Dark (*I Sit and I Think and I Wonder*), the one-time editor of the *Church Times*.[4] In spite of some recent efforts in France, there has never been any sign of a real reconciliation between Russian

Communism and the Catholic Church. Within the Church of England, however, Left Wing sympathies seem to be strongest among the Anglo-Catholics who are doctrinally nearest to Rome.

Secondly, there are those who accept Socialism as the inevitable and even the desirable next step in human history, but are chiefly concerned to Christianise the new Socialist society and prevent it from cutting its spiritual links with the past. The two most distinguished writers in this school are the French Bergsonian writer, Jacques Maritain, and the Russian émigré writer, Nicolai Berdyaev.

Maritain, whose *Christianity and Democracy*[5] was published in this country last year, is a very subtle thinker and deeply respected in the Catholic world, and he has done great service to the cause of Socialism by managing to reconcile the idea of social progress with strict Catholic orthodoxy. During the war he used all the weight of his intellectual authority against the Pétain régime, and during the Spanish Civil War he refused to be stamped into acclaiming Franco as the champion of Christendom.

The Catholic novelist Georges Bernanos (*The Diary of a Country Priest* and *A Diary of My Times*)[6] took a similar stand, but in a more vehement way. As a thinker, however, Bernanos should probably be placed in the third of these groups I am considering. The nearest English equivalent to Maritain is the Catholic historian Christopher Dawson.[7] Berdyaev's case is different from that of the others in that he started as a Marxian Socialist and only later became a religious believer.[8]

He left Russia at the time of the Revolution, but, though extremely hostile to Bolshevism, he has written of it with more understanding and respect than most of its opponents, and his remarks on the connection between the primitive faith of the Russian peasant and the violence of the Revolution are of great interest.

All the writers in this group would admit that if the Church has lost the support of the masses it is largely by tolerating social injustice. The political expression of this new viewpoint is Christian Socialism, which has already reached impressive proportions in France.

Finally — and in a way this is the most interesting group — there are those who admit the injustice of present-day society and are ready for drastic changes but reject Socialism and, by implication, industrialism. As long ago as 1911 Hilaire Belloc wrote his very prescient book *The Servile State*,[9] in which he foretold that capitalist society would soon degenerate into something resembling what afterwards came to be called Fascism.

Belloc's remedy was the splitting-up of large property and a return to a peasant proprietorship. Belloc's friend, G. K. Chesterton, made this idea the basis of a political movement which he called Distributism. Chesterton, a convert to Catholicism, had the mental background of a nineteenth-century radical, and his desire for a simpler form of society was combined with an almost mystical belief in democracy and the virtues of the common man.

His movement never gained a large following, and after his death a few of his disciples drifted into the British Union of Fascists, while others looked for a remedy in currency reform. Nevertheless, his doctrines reappear, essentially unchanged, in T. S. Eliot's idea of a Christian society.[10] The significance of Chesterton is that he expresses in a simplified – indeed, a caricatured – form, certain tendencies that exist in every Christian reformer.

The specifically Christian virtues are likeliest to flourish in small communities, where life is simple and the family is a natural unit. Therefore the tug of Christian thought, even in those who admit the necessity for planning and centralised ownership, is always away from a highly complex, luxurious society, and towards the mediaeval village. Even a writer like Professor Macmurray, who can accept Russian Communism almost without reservations, wants people to live in what he calls 'a workaday world', where life will not be too easy.

Mediaevalism, as it is presented by Chesterton, or even by Eliot, is not serious politics. It is merely a symptom of the malaise which any sensitive person feels before the spectacle of machine civilisation.

But Christian thinkers who are more realistic than Chesterton still have to face an unsolved problem. They claim, rightly, that if our civilisation does not regenerate itself morally it is likely to perish – and they may be right in adding that, at least in Europe, its moral code must be based on Christian principles. But the Christian religion includes, as an integral part of itself, doctrines which large numbers of people can no longer be brought to accept.

The belief in personal immortality, for instance, is almost certainly dwindling. If the Church clings to such doctrines it cannot attract the great mass of the people – but if it abandons them it will have lost its *raison d'être* and may well disappear.

This is merely to say over again, in different words, that Christianity is of its nature 'other-worldly', while Socialism is of its nature 'this worldly'. Nearly all religious discussion, in our time, revolves round this problem, but no satisfying answer has been found.

Meanwhile, the fact that writers and thinkers of the stature of Maritain, Eliot, Reinhold Niebuhr and Christopher Dawson have been forced not only to take an interest in contemporary politics but to come down on what is loosely called the 'progressive' side, helps to counteract the too-easy optimism and the ill-thought-out materialism which are among the weaknesses of the Left Wing movement.

Dean of Canterbury: *Marxism and the Individual* (pamphlet); Jacques Maritain: *True Humanism, Science and Wisdom, The Rights of Man*; Nicolas Berdyaev: *Christianity and Class War, Russian Religious Psychology and Communist Atheism*; E. Lampert: *Nicolas Berdyaev and the New Middle Ages*; Christopher Dawson: *Beyond Politics, The Judgment of the Nations*; Reinhold Niebuhr: *Moral Man and Immoral Society.*

1. Martin Niemöller (1892–1984), German Lutheran pastor who publicly opposed the Nazi regime and was sent to a concentration camp. In the First World War he had commanded a U-Boat. In 1961 he became President of the World Council of Churches.

2. Very Reverend Hewlett Johnson (1874–1966), Dean of Canterbury, 1931–63. His sympathies for the USSR led to his being called 'The Red Dean'. Despite his communist sympathies, it was while he was Dean that T. S. Eliot's play *Murder in the Cathedral* was first performed in the cathedral (1935). Orwell included him in his list of Crypto-Communists and Fellow-Travellers (XX/247).

3. John Macmurray (1891–76), Grote Professor of the Philosophy of Mind and Logic, University of London, 1922–44, and Professor of Moral Philosophy, University of Edinburgh, 1944–58. Awarded the MC in World War I. Orwell invited him to broadcast to India for the BBC on 10 May 1943 on the New Testament, in a series, 'Books that Changed the World', which he did. Orwell reviewed *The Clue to History* in February 1943 (XI/531). He described him as a 'Decayed liberal' in his list of Crypto-Communists and Fellow-Travellers (XX/250).

4. Sydney Dark (1874–1947) edited the *Church Times*, 1924–41. Orwell reviewed *I Sit and I Think and I Wonder*, 7 November 1943 (XV/2347). In his list of Crypto-Communists and Fellow-Travellers, Orwell described him as 'Warm-hearted & stupid' (XX/246).

5. Jacques Maritain (1882–1973), French Roman Catholic philosopher. He wrote more than fifty books. Orwell reviewed his *Christianity and Democracy* on 10 June 1945 (XVII/2676).

He taught at Columbia and Princeton universities, 1941–4; was Ambassador to the Vatican, 1945–8; and Professor of Philosophy, Princeton, 1948–60.

6. Georges Bernanos (1888–1948) was a polemical novelist whose passion was expressed subtly. *Diary of My Times* (*Les grands cimetières sous la lune*, 1938) fiercely condemns atrocities committed in Mallorca by the Fascists in the Spanish Civil War which were sanctioned by his (the Roman Catholic) Church. He is best remembered for *The Diary of a Country Priest* (1937; *Journal d'un curé de campagne*, 1936). Orwell reviewed his *Plea for Liberty*, 21 April 1946 (XVIII/*2980*).

7. Christopher Dawson (1889–1970), in addition to his own books, edited *Essays in Order* (16 vols., 1931–6, with T. F. Burns and B. Wall); the *Dublin Review*, 1940–44; and the *Makers of Christendom* series from 1954. Orwell briefly reviewed his *Medieval Religion*, November 1934 (X/*214*), finding it 'almost entirely lacking in the humbug which we have come to expect as a matter of course from English Roman Catholics'.

8. Nicholas Berdyaev (1874–1948), Russian Orthodox Church religious philosopher, exiled from Russia in 1922. He was at one time a Marxist but came to stress the need for spiritual meaning in personal and public life.

9. Hilaire Belloc (1870–1953): see p. 137, n. 7, above. His *The Servile State* was first published in 1912, above. In 'Notes on the War', 6 April 1940, Orwell remarked that it 'foretold with astonishing accuracy the things that are happening now' (XII/*604*).

10. Anglo-Catholicism was fundamental to the concept of an ordered society held by T. S. Eliot (1888–1965). It was a motivating force for much of his poetry, drama and criticism, either overtly or covertly, for example, in essays and critical works such as *Thoughts After Lambeth* (1931), *The Idea of a Christian Society* (1939) and *Notes Towards the Definition of Culture* (1948); in drama, directly in *Murder in the Cathedral* (1935) and indirectly in *The Cocktail Party* (1949); and in much of his poetry, especially *The Four Quartets* (1935–42), in each of which there is a movement devoted to a specific manifestation of Divinity.

[*2878*]

4. 'PACIFISM AND PROGRESS'

14 February 1946

'Pacifism' is a vague word, since it is usually taken as expressing a mere negative, that is, a refusal to perform military service or rejection of war as an instrument of policy.

This does not of itself carry any definite political implication, nor is there any general agreement as to what activities a war-resister ought to accept or refuse.

The majority of conscientious objectors are merely unwilling to take life and are ready to do some kind of alternative job, such as agricultural work, in which their contribution to the war effort is indirect instead of direct.

On the other hand, the really uncompromising war-resisters, who refuse every form of national service and are ready to face persecution for their beliefs, are often people who have no theoretical objection to violence, but are merely opponents of the Government which happens to be waging the war.

Hence there were many Socialists who opposed the war of 1914–18 and supported that of 1939–45, and, granting their premises, there was no inconsistency in this.

The whole theory of pacifism, if one assumes it to mean outright renunciation of violence, is open to very serious objections. It is obvious that any Government that is unwilling to use force must be at the mercy of any other Government, or even of any individual, that is less scrupulous – so that the refusal to use force simply tends to make civilised life impossible.

However, there are people describable as pacifists who are quite intelligent enough to see and admit this and who still have an answer. And though, of course, there are differences of opinion among them, their answer is something like this:

Of course, civilisation now rests upon force. It rests not only on guns and bombing planes, but on prisons, concentration camps and the policeman's truncheon. And it is quite true that if peaceful people refuse to defend themselves, the immediate effect is to give more power to gangsters like Hitler and Mussolini. But it is also true that the use of force makes real progress impossible. The good society is one in which human beings are equal and in which they co-operate with one another willingly and not because of fear or economic compulsion.

This is what Socialists, Communists and Anarchists, in their different ways, are all aiming at. Obviously it cannot be reached in a moment, but to accept war as an instrument is to take a step away from it.

The waging of war, and the preparation for war, make necessary the centralised modern state, which destroys liberty and perpetuates inequalities. Moreover, every war breeds fresh wars. Even if human life is not wiped out altogether – and this is quite a likely development, considering the destructiveness of present-day weapons – there can be no genuine advance while the process continues.

Probably there will be actual degeneration, because the tendency is for each war to be more brutal and degrading than the last. At some point or another the cycle must be broken. Even at the cost of accepting defeat and foreign domination, we must begin to act pacifically and refuse to return evil for evil.

The seeming result of this, at the start, will be to make evil stronger but that is the price we have to pay for the barbarous history of the past 400 years. Even if it is still necessary to struggle against oppression we must struggle against it by non-violent means. The first step towards sanity is to break the cycle of violence.

Among the writers who can be roughly grouped as pacifists, and who would probably accept what I have said above as a preliminary statement of their views, are Aldous Huxley,[1] John Middleton Murry,[2] the late Max Plowman[3] the anarchist, poet, and critic, Herbert Read,[4] and a number of very young writers such as Alex Comfort[5] and D. S. Savage.[6]

The two thinkers to whom all of these writers are in some degree indebted are Tolstoi and Gandhi. But one can distinguish among them at least two schools of thought – the real point at issue is the acceptance or non-acceptance of the State and of mechanical civilisation.

In his earlier pacifist writings, such as *Ends and Means*, Huxley stressed chiefly the destructive folly of war, and rather overplayed the argument that one cannot bring about a good result by using evil methods. More recently he seems to have arrived at the conclusion that political action is inherently evil, and that, strictly speaking, it is not possible for society to be saved – only individuals can be saved, and then only by means of religious exercises which the ordinary person is hardly in a position to undertake.

In effect this is to despair of human institutions and counsel disobedience to the State, though Huxley has never made any definite political pronouncement. Middleton Murry arrived at pacifism by way of Socialism, and his attitude to the State is somewhat different. He does not demand that it should be simply abolished, and he realises that machine civilisation cannot be scrapped, or at any rate is not going to be scrapped.

In a recent book, *Adam and Eve*, he makes the interesting though disputable point that, if we are to retain the machine, full employment is an objective that should not be aimed at. A highly developed industry, if it is working full time, will produce an unusable surplus of goods, and hence lead to the scramble for markets, and the competition in armaments, whose natural end is war.

What is to be aimed at is a decentralised society, agricultural rather than industrial, and prizing leisure more highly than luxury. Such a society, Murry thinks, would be inherently peaceful, and would not invite attack, even from aggressive neighbours.

Herbert Read, curiously enough, although as an anarchist he regards the State as something to be repudiated utterly, is not hostile to the machine. A high level of industrial development would, he thinks, be compatible with the complete absence of central controls. Some of the younger pacifist writers, such as Comfort and Savage, do not offer any programme for society as a whole, but lay their emphasis on the need to preserve one's own individuality against the encroachment either of the State or of political parties.

It will be seen that the real problem is whether pacifism is compatible with the struggle for material comfort. On the whole, the direction of pacifist thought is towards a kind of primitivism. If you want a high standard of living you must have a complex industrial society – but that implies planning, organisation and coercion – in other words, it implies the State, with its prisons, its police forces and its inevitable wars. The more extreme pacifists would say that the very existence of the State is incompatible with true peace.

It is clear that if one thinks along these lines it is almost impossible to imagine any complete and rapid regeneration of society. The pacifist and anarchist ideal can only be realised piecemeal, if at all. Hence the idea, which has haunted anarchist thought for 100 years past, of self-contained agricultural communities, within which the classless, non-violent society can exist, as it were, in small patches.

At different times such communities have actually existed in various parts of the world – in nineteenth-century Russia and America, in France and Germany during the between-war years, and in Spain for a brief period during the Civil War.

In Britain, also, small groups of conscientious objectors have attempted something of the kind in recent years. The idea is not simply to escape from society – it is rather to create spiritual oases like the monasteries of the dark ages, from which a new attitude towards life can gradually diffuse itself.

The trouble with such communities is that they are never genuinely independent of the outside world, and that they can only exist so long as the State, which they regard as their enemy, chooses to tolerate them. In a wider sense the same criticism applies to the pacifist movement as a whole.

It can only survive where there is some degree of democracy, and in many parts of the world it has never been able to exist at all. There was no pacifist movement in Nazi Germany, for instance.

The tendency of pacifism, therefore, is always to weaken those Governments and social systems that are most favourable to it. During the ten years before the war there is little doubt that the prevalence of pacifist ideas in Britain, France and the U.S.A. encouraged Fascist aggression. And even in their subjective feelings, English and American pacifists often seem to be more hostile to capitalist democracy than to totalitarianism.[7] But in a negative sense their criticism has been useful.

They have rightly insisted that present-day society, even when the guns do not happen to be firing, is not peaceful, and they have kept alive the idea – somewhat neglected since the Russian Revolution – that the aim of progress is to abolish the authority of the State and not to strengthen it.

Aldous Huxley: *Grey Eminence, What Are You Going to Do About It?*, I and II (pamphlets); Max Plowman: *Bridge Into the Future* (letters); Herbert Read: *Poetry and Anarchism*; Alex Comfort: *No Such Liberty*; D. S. Savage: *The Personal Principle*; Leo Tolstoi: *What, Then, Must We Do?*; Wilfred Wellock: *A Mechanistic or a Human Society?* (pamphlet); Roy Walker:[8] *The Wisdom of Gandhi* (pamphlet).

1. Aldous Huxley: see n. 4 to 'Freedom and Happiness', above. Orwell referred many times in his writings to *Brave New World* (1932) and reviewed it on 12 July 1940 (XII/655) with other books of its genre: see above. *Ends and Means: an enquiry into the nature of ideals and into the methods employed in their realization* was published in 1937. *What are You Doing About It?; the case for constructive peace* was published in 1936.

2. John Middleton Murry: see n. 4 to 'Gandhi in Mayfair', above. Orwell reviewed *Adam and Eve* on 19 October 1944 (XVI/*2565*).

3. Max Plowman (1883–1941) worked on *The Adelphi* from 1929 until his death. He was Warden of the Adelphi Centre, 1938–41, an ardent supporter of the Peace Pledge Union from its foundation in 1934 and its General Secretary, 1937–38. His publications include *Introduction to the Study of Blake, A Subaltern on the Somme,* and *The Faith Called Pacifism.* He and his wife, Dorothy, remained friends of Orwell. Orwell reviewed his *Bridge into the Future* on 7 December 1944 (XVI/*2589*).

4. Herbert Read: see n. 1 to Letter to Herbert Read, above.

5. Alex Comfort (1920–2000), poet, novelist and medical biologist. Orwell reviewed his *No Such Liberty* in October 1941 (XIII/*855*). He and Orwell exchanged satirical poems in *Tribune* in 1943. Comfort adopted the *nom de plume* Obadiah Hornbooke; Orwell's poem was headed 'As One Non-Combatant to Another' (XV/*2137* and *2138*). He took part in 'Pacifism and the War: A Controversy' with D. S. Savage, George Woodcock and Orwell, in *Partisan Review,* September–October 1942 (XIII/*1270*); the contributions were written in May 1942. His *The Joy of Sex* (1972) sold over ten million copies.

6. D. S. Savage (1917–), poet and critic. *The Personal Principle: Studies in Modern Poetry* was published in 1944. He worked for the Transport and General Workers' Union, Christian Aid and the Anglican Pacifist Fellowship. See also note 5, above. He contributed a rather hostile chapter on Orwell to *The New Pelican Guide to English Literature,* vol. 8, ed. Boris Ford (1983).

7. An editorial comment in *Peace News,* 1 March 1946, quoted Orwell's statement that English and American pacifists often seemed more hostile to capitalist democracy than to totalitarianism. In refuting him, it claimed that *Peace News* had 'a clean record in this matter' and thought 'it may be that Orwell is deceived by appearances'. It argued that 'totalitarianism is a remedy – worse, indeed, than the disease – for the failure of capitalist democracy. But to understand totalitarianism is not to sympathize with, still less to support it.'

8. Roy Walker: see n. 1 to Letter from Roy Walker to Orwell, above.

[2879]

AFTERWORD

[April 1946]

Orwell wrote this Afterword for the German abridgement of the four articles comprising 'The Intellectual Revolt' published in Neue Auslese. *The English original has not survived. The editor is grateful to all those who assisted in making this translation; their names are given in the headnote to* XVIII/*2879, where the German version will be found.*

What writers, artists, scientists and philosophers say today is indicative of future rather than current developments.

The growing power of the State produces, as we have seen, considerable dismay, particularly amongst those for whom only ten or twenty years ago Socialism was the guarantee of progress. But this idea has so far only gained hold of a section of the public. The magic which concepts like centralisation and planning possess today, and the idea that almost everything else can be sacrificed for economic security, still hold the masses under a spell, and their power will probably increase. It is still considered heresy to reject the materialistic version of Socialism just as thirty years ago Socialism was itself a heresy.

The antitotalitarian tendencies described are not evenly distributed among the intellectuals. Writers and artists reject the centralised State much more decisively than do scientists and engineers. We have eminent scientists who admire Soviet Russia unreservedly and even submit to the discipline of the Communist Party, while writers of both the Right and the Left do not as a rule follow the party line.

They distrust any restriction on their liberty by the State even when they are dependent on the State for economic support. On the other hand, the majority of scientists rely on the State for support of their work, which depends less on the individual and which, moreover, society regards as useful. The fact that authors like Gide, Malraux, Maritain, Koestler and Bertrand Russell, each in his own way remains sceptical about Russian Communism and the values of the Machine Age would not of its own produce a political movement, not even if these authors were agreed among themselves. For a political movement must be not just the expression of an idea, it has also to represent the material interests of part of the population, without which no political organisation can be created. In England, where there are only two parties of any consequence, the Labour Party and the Conservative Party, attempts to found new parties have always failed because they only represented sectional interests. Even the Communist Party has never enjoyed much of a following, despite its Soviet-Russian aura, although it has at times exercised considerable influence.

One must, however, allow for the time factor. Fifty years ago a Socialist was seen here as a follower of a cause which had no chance of success, as an odd man out or a rebel, despised by the leaders of society and almost ignored by the masses. And yet today the principle of public ownership is accepted by almost everyone, including many who call themselves Conservatives. It proved acceptable because it seemed appropriate to the structure of an industrialised country and because it brought advantages for the majority of the people which unrestrained capitalism had denied them. Today the whole world is moving towards a tightly planned society in which personal liberty is being abolished and social equality unrealised. This is what the masses want, for to them security is more important than anything else. But why should this last any longer than the trend established about 1900 when private profit was the thing that mattered most? There will be a change of direction once centralisation and bureaucracy come into conflict with the interests of large groups.

Those intellectuals who today are rebels do not suffer economic hardship because almost every intellectual is better off than before. As soon as his most urgent needs are met he discovers that it is not so much money and status he lacks as liberty and a world not wrecked and made soulless by the machine: those are the things that really matter. In seeking such things, he is of course swimming against the tide. The question is, will the masses ever rebel in this way? Will the man in the street ever feel that freedom of the mind is as important and as much in need of being defended as his daily bread?[1]

No convincing answer springs to mind, but there is one hopeful sign: the modern State, whether it wants it or not, needs constantly to raise the general level of education. Even the totalitarian State needs intelligent citizens to ensure that it is not at a disadvantage in the struggle for military and industrial supremacy. On the other hand they must be loyal and obedient and must not risk contamination by undesirable doctrines. But is it possible to educate people without at the same time exposing them to unorthodox ideas? The more educated people are – assuming that education does not just mean training in technological skills – the more they become aware of their individuality and the less will the structure of society be organised like a beehive.[2]

Which set of ideas will gain the upper hand cannot be discussed here, but all intellectuals, whether they are opposed to centralisation and planning, or approve of a society so ordered, want to give it a more human face[3] – whether they are believers who think genuine reform is only possible on the basis of orthodox Christian teaching or are against the whole machine of government and want only to pursue a simple, natural life – all hold one thing in common: opposition to the tyranny of the State. That so many minds in so many countries agree on this leads one to conclude that centralisation and bureaucratic controls, however much they may thrive today, will not be permitted unlimited growth.[4]

1. Writing to Dr David Jones on 7 June 1944, in the context that the threat from Soviet totalitarianism was as serious as that from the totalitarianism of the Right in the 1930s ('a novel idea in the period 1944–5, when admiration for Uncle Joe and all his works was at its height'), David Astor said: 'Orwell's view on this is that soon all countries will have state planning and therefore a more or less degree of state ownership of property. The old Marxist struggle will thus be played out. The new struggle will be for more or less freedom within the planned state' (Richard Cockett, *David Astor and 'The Observer'*, 114). David Jones (1870–1955) served as deputy secretary to the Cabinet from the end of World War I to 1930 and instigated the setting up of what became the Arts Council of Great Britain.

2. The German word *Bienenstaat* implies to a German reader not simply beehive but a labour-oriented society with strict hierarchies which reflect the allocation of tasks and duties. Whether this summarized what Orwell wrote at greater length in the English original, and whether he used the word 'beehive', cannot be ascertained.

3. For 'give it a more human face', the German has 'sie aber vermenschlichen wollen'; this might be more literally rendered, 'wishing rather to humanize it'.

4. For 'will not be permitted unlimited growth', the German text has 'nicht in den Himmel wachsen werden' – an image of trees not being allowed to grow too tall heavenwards. This is commonly used as an idiom to express the curbing of overweening ambition. 'Himmel' effectively concludes a sequence translated here as heresy, soulless, undesirable doctrines, unorthodox ideas, believers and orthodox Christian teaching. To what extent Orwell's original used such language is not known.

[2919]

Extract from letter to Arthur Koestler
5 March 1946

This letter lacks a strip from its right-hand side and has had to be reconstructed; for details, see CW. *The letter stands here for Orwell's (and Koestler's) deep concern for the fate of Poles, at Katyn and the associated camps (Dergachi and Bologoye), and in the post-war period. Both worked, especially through the Freedom Defence Committee, to assist them, for example, from forced repatriation from the UK. Joseph Czapski[1] was a direct influence on* Animal Farm *(see note 3) and his experiences were an indirect influence on* Nineteen Eighty-Four.

Dear Arthur,

It's funny you should send me Czapski's pamphlet, which I have been trying for some time to get someone to translate and publish. Warburg wouldn't do it because he said it was an awkward length, and latterly I gave it to the Anarchist (Freedom Press) group. I don't know what decision they've come to. I met Czapski in Paris and had lunch with him.[2] There is no doubt that he is not only authentic but a rather exceptional person, though whether he is any good as a painter I don't know. He is the person who made to me a remark which I may or may not have retailed to you – I forget. After telling me something of the privation and his sufferings in the concentration camp, he said something like this: 'For a while in 1941 and 1942 there was much defeatism in Russia, and in fact it was touch and go whether the Germans won the war. Do you know what saved Russia at that time? In my opinion it was the personal character of Stalin – I put it down to the greatness of Stalin. He stayed in Moscow when the Germans nearly took it, and his courage was what saved the situation.[3] Considering what he had been through, this seemed to me sufficient proof of Czapski's reliability. I told him I would do what I could about the pamphlet here. If the Freedom Press people fall through, what about Arthur Ballard, who is now beginning to publish pamphlets? He might take it.[4] Do you want this copy back? The Anarchists [have mine] and it's a rather treasured item of my collection.[5]

1. Joseph Czapski (1896–?), wrote to Orwell on 11 December 1945 at the suggestion of 'mon ami Poznanski' because he thought Orwell could find an English publisher for his pamphlet (a quite sizeable booklet), *Souvenirs de Starobielsk*. This had originally been published in Polish as *Wspomnienia Starobielskia* in 1944; Italian and French translations followed in 1945. Czapski, a Polish painter and author, but born in Prague, studied in St Petersburg, 1912–17, and witnessed the Russian Revolution; in 1920 he returned to Poland and from 1924 to 1931 he studied and worked as a painter in Paris, being shown there and in Geneva. He fought with the 8th Polish Lancers against the Germans and then the Russians in 1939, and was taken prisoner by the Soviets. He was one of seventy-eight of nearly 4,000 prisoners at Starobielsk prison camp transferred to a prison camp at Gryazovets. He spent twenty-three months in these camps. When the Germans invaded Russia, he was allowed to join other Polish prisoners, many of whom had suffered terrible privations, in a Polish Army under

General Anders to fight the Germans. Anders commissioned him to try to discover what had happened to prisoners at Starobielsk and Kozelsk. He spent a year on this with no success. He later graphically described how the news of what had been perpetrated was given to Colonel, later General, Berling, who commanded Polish forces in Russia after Anders. When Berling was told by Beria, head of the Secret Police, and Mierkulov that the Poles, whatever their politics, could serve in this army, Berling said, 'We have an excellent nucleus for this army in the camps of Starobielsk and Kozelsk.' Mierkulov replied, 'No, not those men. In dealing with them we have been guilty of a gross error (*bolshuyu oshibku*).' Czapski so advised Anders, realizing that 'gross error' meant the massacre of these men. Anders, after some reflection, said, as if to himself, 'I think of them all as comrades and friends whom we have lost in action' (Joseph Czapski, *The Inhuman Land*, 1951, 163–4). Czapski died at Maisons Lafitte, France. See also XVIII/*2956, endnote*. It is known that some 15,700 Poles were murdered by the Russians at Katyn and other camps (Czapski's figures, *Souvenirs de Starobielsk*, 1945, 18). A further 7,000 from camps in the Komi Republic were packed into barges which were deliberately sunk in the White Sea, causing their deaths by drowning (*The Inhuman Land*, 35–6).

2. Orwell went to Paris as a war correspondent on 15 February 1945. He must have met Czapski shortly afterwards, for there can be little doubt that he was the source of the change to the text of *Animal Farm* which Orwell sent to Senhouse on 17 March; see n. 3, below.

3. The reference to Stalin staying in Moscow here and in his letter to Koestler link this alteration closely with Orwell's meeting with Czapski in Paris; for this and the change to *Animal Farm* see Note on the Text, pp. 232–3 above, and for the passage in *Animal Farm*, see p. 285 [*CW*, VIII/69]. Orwell explains in this letter to Koestler what convinced him that Czapski was trustworthy; Koestler had accepted Czapski's reliability because he had been vouched for in a letter 'from von Ranke, former commisar° of the Thaelmann Brigade in Spain'. See p. 233, and n. 4 below.

4. Arthur Ballard and Frank Horrabin were the two directors of the Socialist Book Centre in the Strand, London. They published Orwell's pamphlet *James Burnham and the Managerial Revolution*, summer 1946. However, Orwell and Koestler were unsuccessful. Despite the booklet's having what Czapski called 'une certaine actualité' in the light of what was being presented in evidence at the Nuremberg Trial of War Criminals, *Souvenirs de Starobielsk* was not then translated into English and has never been published in Britain. The massacres of Poles at Katyn and other camps by the Russians was attributed for decades to the Nazis. Although a US Congressional investigation of 1951–2 blamed the Russians, European governments continued to connive at this deception. Count Zygmunt Zamoyski claimed that in 1976 the Labour Government 'forbade any serving British officer to attend in uniform [at] the unveiling of the Katyn Memorial at Gunnersbury Cemetery in London' and 'the Church of England authorities would not allow the date [1940] of the massacres to appear on the memorial when an application was first made to them to erect it in a disused Chelsea graveyard' (*The Times*, 8 August 1988). As late as July 1988 a Conservative government was claiming that there was 'no conclusive evidence of the responsibility for these murders', although on 27 July it was finally admitted, in a parliamentary reply, that 'There is indeed substantial evidence pointing to Soviet responsibility for the killings'. Since then, the Russians have admitted their guilt and apologized formally to the Polish people.

5. Koestler told Orwell to keep Czapski's booklet and it remains in his pamphlet collection.

For Poles, Orwell has, understandably, remained a champion of their interests and has been honoured by them. One interesting example is the set of four stamps (blue, red, brown and green) issued by Solidarity for its 'underground' mail service. These bear a fine cartoon-drawing of Orwell and the date '1984'. The editor is grateful to Bartek Zborski for providing him with these.

[2923]
'Do Our Colonies Pay?'
Tribune, *8 March 1946*

I have before me a copy of *Socialist Commentary*, the organ of the Socialist Vanguard Group, and another of *Bulletin*, the organ of the (American) Council on Jewish-Arab Co-operation. From the first I take the following sentences:

The balance sheet between Britain and India gives little support to the hypothesis that Britain is exploiting India . . . A merely 'moral' approach (to colonial problems) is insufficient, so long as many persons are hoodwinked into believing that [the] British economy is largely 'dependent' upon the possession of India and other colonies.

From the second I take the following:

British Governments pledged to maintain the Empire have shown and can show no deviation in foreign policy regardless of political denomination . . . The British standard of living depends on the Empire, and the Empire must have permanent military installations in the Far East.

Here, therefore, you have one writer in a Left-wing paper flatly stating that British living standards *are* dependent on colonial exploitation, and another writer in another Left-wing paper stating equally definitely that they are *not* so dependent. For the moment I am not concerned with the question of which of them is right, but with the fact that they can differ in this way. It is probably not important that one paper is British and the other American, since the writer in the British paper is an American, as it happens.

It should be noticed that the question of whether we are exploiting India, and the question of whether our prosperity depends on India, are separate. It may well be that we *are* exploiting India, but for the profit of a small minority, without benefit to the nation as a whole. And of these two questions, the second is the more immediately important. If it is really true that our comparative comfort is simply a product of imperialism, that such things as the Beveridge Scheme,[1] increased Old Age Pensions, raising of the school-leaving age, slum clearance, improved health services and what-not are luxuries which we can only afford if we have millions of oriental slaves at our command – that, surely, is a serious consideration. For, as Socialists, we want an improved standard of living for our own people, and, again as Socialists, we want justice for the colonial peoples. Are the two things compatible? Whatever the rights and wrongs of the matter may be, one would at least think that this question could be authoritatively answered. The facts, which are chiefly statistical facts, must be ascertainable. Yet no agreed opinion exists. Those two flatly contradictory statements which I quoted above are typical of hundreds of others which I could collect.

I know people who can prove to me with pencil and paper that we should be just as well off, or perhaps better, if all our colonial possessions were lost to us; and I know others who can prove that if we had no colonies to exploit our standard of living would slump catastrophically. And curiously enough this division of opinion cuts right across political parties. Thus, all Tories are imperialists, but whereas some Tories assert that without our empire we should be ruined economically as well as militarily, others assert that the empire is a non-paying concern and that we only maintain it from motives of public spirit. Socialists of the extreme Left, such as the I.L.P., usually take it for granted that Britain would be plunged into the blackest poverty if she stopped looting the coloured peoples, while others not far to the Right of them declare that if only the coloured peoples were liberated, they would develop more rapidly and their productive power would increase, which would be to our own advantage. Among Asiatic nationalists the same division of opinion exists. The most violently anti-British ones declare that when India is lost the British will all starve to death, while others argue that a free and friendly India would be a much better customer for British goods than a hostile and backward dependency. And yet, as I said above, this is quite obviously *not* an insoluble question. The figures that would settle it once and for all must exist, if one knew where to look for them.

However, it is not necessarily the case that either of the two current opinions is the right one. The person who says, 'Yes, Britain depends on India', usually assumes that if India were free, British trade with India would cease forthwith. The person who says, 'No, Britain doesn't depend on India', usually assumes that if India were free, British-Indian trade would proceed as before, with no period of dislocation. My own view has always been (a) that over a long period we have definitely exploited, i.e. robbed, our colonial possessions, (b) that to some extent the whole British nation has benefited from this, in an economic sense, and (c) that we cannot make restitution to the colonial peoples without lowering our own standard of living for several years at the least. The really essential thing, almost never mentioned when this subject is raised, is the time factor. Quite likely it would be to our advantage to make an end of imperialism, but not *immediately*. There might be a long and uncomfortable transition period first. This is a bleak thought, and I believe that it is a half-conscious avoidance of it that makes almost all discussions of this question curiously unreal.

At the General Election, for instance, the avoidance of imperial issues was quite astonishing. When foreign affairs were mentioned at all, the reference was almost invariably to the U.S.S.R. or the United States. I don't think I ever heard any speaker on any platform mention India spontaneously. Once or twice, at Labour meetings, I tried the experiment of asking a question about India, to get an answer which sounded something like this: 'The Labour Party is, of course, in fullest sympathy with the aspiration of the Indian people towards independence, next question, please.' And there the matter dropped, with not a flicker of interest on the part of the audience. The handbook issued to Labour speakers contained 200 pages, out of which one not very informative page was devoted to India. Yet India has nearly ten times the population of Britain! The subjects which, in my experience, roused real passion were housing, full employment and social insurance. Who could have guessed, from the manner in which they were discussed, that these subjects were in any way bound up with our possession of colonies which give us raw materials and assured markets?

In the long run an evasion of the truth is always paid for. One thing that we are gradually paying for now is our failure to make clear to the

British people that their prosperity depends partly on factors outside Britain. Extremists of both Right and Left have grossly exaggerated the advantages of imperialism, while the optimists who stand between them have talked as though military control over your markets and sources of raw material were of no importance. They have assumed that a liberated India would still be our customer, without considering what might happen if India passed under control of a foreign power, or broke up into anarchy, or developed a closed economy, or were ruled over by a Nationalist government which made a policy of boycotting British goods. What we *ought* to have said throughout these last twenty years is something like this: 'It is our duty as Socialists to liberate the subject peoples, and in the long run it will be to our advantage as well. But only in the long run. In the short run we have got to count with the hostility of these peoples, with the chaos into which they will probably fall, and with their frightful poverty, which will compel us to *give* them goods of various kinds in order to put them on their feet. If we are very lucky our standard of living may not suffer by the liberation of the colonies, but the probability is that it will suffer for years, or even for decades. You have got to choose between liberating India and having extra sugar. Which do you prefer?'

What would the average woman in the fish queue say if it were put to her like that? I am not certain. But the point is that it never has been put to her like that, and if she plumps for the extra sugar – as she may – when the moment of crisis comes, it will be because the issues have not been fully discussed beforehand. Instead, we have had such contradictory statements as I quoted above, both in the last analysis untrue, and both, in their different ways, tending to perpetuate imperialism.[2]

1. By the 'Beveridge Scheme' Orwell means what came to be called 'The Beveridge Report', 1942. This was properly the *Report on Social Insurance and Allied Services* by Sir William Beveridge (1879–1963), which laid the foundation of the Welfare State. Beveridge was an economist, Director of the London School of Economics (1919–37), Master of University College, Oxford (1937–44) and a Liberal MP (1944–5; created a Baron 1946). The changes later instituted greatly improved those introduced in the National Insurance Act of 1911 by David Lloyd George; those benefits, especially pensions, were familiarly referred to by the elderly as 'their Lloyd George' in the 1920s and 1930s. It was those that Orwell would have known about when he wrote.

2. *Tribune* published two letters in response to Orwell's article. One, by John Jennings, agreed with Orwell about the choice 'we have to make in regard to Empire liberation', but thought the part played by bank capital had not to be overlooked. The other, by Bankole

Akpata, thought Orwell evasive: 'Of course Colonies pay . . . All we ask is for a chance to manage the Colonies in our own way; maybe we might make them pay.'

[2970]

'Some Thoughts on the Common Toad'
Tribune, *12 April 1946*

> In 'Why I Write', Orwell said that in the preceding ten years what he had
> most wanted to do was 'to make political writing into an art' (see below,
> pp. 461–2). This brief essay, seemingly no more than a light, often witty,
> causerie, is a perfect example of his success; see A Literary Life, 96–8.

Before the swallow, before the daffodil, and not much later than the snow-drop, the common toad salutes the coming of spring after his own fashion, which is to emerge from a hole in the ground, where he has lain buried since the previous autumn, and crawl as rapidly as possible towards the nearest suitable patch of water. Something – some kind of shudder in the earth, or perhaps merely a rise of a few degrees in the temperature – has told him that it is time to wake up: though a few toads appear to sleep the clock round and miss out a year from time to time – at any rate, I have more than once dug them up, alive and apparently well, in the middle of the summer.[1]

At this period, after his long fast, the toad has a very spiritual look, like a strict Anglo-Catholic towards the end of Lent.[2] His movements are languid but purposeful, his body is shrunken, and by contrast his eyes look abnormally large. This allows one to notice, what one might not at another time, that a toad has about the most beautiful eye of any living creature. It is like gold, or more exactly it is like the gold-coloured semi-precious stone which one sometimes sees in signet rings, and which I think is called a chrysoberyl.

For a few days after getting into the water the toad concentrates on building up his strength by eating small insects. Presently he has swollen to his normal size again, and then he goes through a phase of intense sexiness. All he knows, at least if he is a male toad, is that he wants to get his arms round something, and if you offer him a stick, or even your finger, he will cling to it with surprising strength and take a long time to discover that it is not a female toad. Frequently one comes upon shapeless masses of ten or twenty toads rolling over and over in the water, one clinging to another without distinction of sex. By degrees, however, they sort themselves out into couples, with the male duly sitting on the female's back. You can now distinguish males from females, because the male is smaller, darker and sits on top, with his arms tightly clasped round the female's neck. After a day or two the spawn is laid in long strings which wind themselves in and out of the reeds and soon become invisible. A few more weeks, and the water is alive with masses of tiny tadpoles which rapidly grow larger, sprout hind-legs, then fore-legs, then shed their tails: and finally, about the middle of the summer, the new generation of toads, smaller than one's thumb-nail but perfect in every particular, crawl out of the water to begin the game anew.

I mention the spawning of the toads because it is one of the phenomena of Spring which most deeply appeal to me, and because the toad, unlike the skylark and the primrose, has never had much of a boost from the poets. But I am aware that many people do not like reptiles or amphibians, and I am not suggesting that in order to enjoy the Spring you have to take an interest in toads. There are also the crocus, the missel thrush, the cuckoo, the blackthorn, etc. The point is that the pleasures of Spring are available to everybody, and cost nothing. Even in the most sordid street the coming of Spring will register itself by some sign or other, if it is only a brighter blue between the chimney pots or the vivid green of an elder sprouting on a blitzed site. Indeed it is remarkable how Nature goes on existing unofficially, as it were, in the very heart of London. I have seen a kestrel flying over the Deptford gasworks, and I have heard a first-rate performance by a blackbird in the Euston Road. There must be some hundreds of thousands, if not millions, of birds living inside the four-mile radius, and it is rather a pleasing thought that none of them pays a halfpenny of rent.

As for Spring, not even the narrow and gloomy streets round the Bank of England are quite able to exclude it. It comes seeping in everywhere, like one of those new poison gases which pass through all filters. The Spring is commonly referred to as 'a miracle', and during the past five or six years this worn-out figure of speech has taken on a new lease of life. After the sort of winters we have had to endure recently, the Spring does seem miraculous, because it has become gradually harder and harder to believe that it is actually going to happen. Every February since 1940 I have found myself thinking that this time Winter is going to be permanent. But Persephone,[3] like the toads, always rises from the dead at about the same moment. Suddenly, towards the end of March, the miracle happens and the decaying slum in which I live[4] is transfigured. Down in the square the sooty privets have turned bright green, the leaves are thickening on the chestnut trees, the daffodils are out, the wallflowers are budding, the policeman's tunic looks positively a pleasant shade of blue, the fishmonger greets his customers with a smile, and even the sparrows are quite a different colour, having felt the balminess of the air and nerved themselves to take a bath, their first since last September.

Is it wicked to take a pleasure in Spring and other seasonal changes? To put it more precisely, is it politically reprehensible, while we are all groaning, or at any rate ought to be groaning, under the shackles of the capitalist system, to point out that life is frequently more worth living because of a blackbird's song, a yellow elm tree in October, or some other natural phenomenon which does not cost money and does not have what the editors of Left-wing newspapers call a class angle? There is no doubt that many people think so. I know by experience that a favourable reference to 'Nature' in one of my articles is liable to bring me abusive letters, and though the key-word in these letters is usually 'sentimental', two ideas seem to be mixed up in them. One is that any pleasure in the actual process of life encourages a sort of political quietism. People, so the thought runs, ought to be discontented, and it is our job to multiply our wants and not simply to increase our enjoyment of the things we have already. The other idea is that this is the age of machines and that to dislike the machine, or even to want to limit its domination, is backward-looking, reactionary and slightly ridiculous. This is often backed up by the statement that a love of Nature is a foible of urbanised people who have no notion what Nature is really like. Those who really have to deal with the soil, so it is argued, do not love the soil, and do not take the faintest interest in birds or flowers, except from a strictly utilitarian point of view. To love the country one must live in the town, merely taking an occasional week-end ramble at the warmer times of year.

This last idea is demonstrably false. Medieval literature, for instance, including the popular ballads, is full of an almost Georgian enthusiasm for Nature, and the art of agricultural peoples such as the Chinese and Japanese centres always round trees, birds, flowers, rivers, mountains. The other idea seems to me to be wrong in a subtler way. Certainly we ought to be discontented, we ought not simply to find out ways of making the best of a bad job, and yet if we kill all pleasure in the actual process of life, what sort of future are we preparing for ourselves? If a man cannot enjoy the return of Spring, why should he be happy in a labour-saving Utopia? What will he do with the leisure that the machine will give him? I have always suspected that if our economic and political problems are ever really solved, life will become simpler instead of more complex, and that the sort of pleasure one gets from finding the first primrose will loom larger than the sort of pleasure one gets from eating an ice to the tune of a Wurlitzer. I think that by retaining one's childhood love of such things as trees, fishes, butterflies and – to return to my first instance – toads, one makes a peaceful and decent future a little more probable, and that by preaching the doctrine that nothing is to be admired except steel and concrete, one merely makes it a little surer that human beings will have no outlet for their surplus energy except in hatred and leader-worship.

At any rate, Spring is here, even in London N.1, and they can't stop you enjoying it. This is a satisfying reflection. How many a time have I stood watching the toads mating, or a pair of hares having a boxing match in the young corn, and thought of all the important persons who would stop me enjoying this if they could. But luckily they can't. So long as you are not actually ill, hungry, frightened or immured in a prison or a holiday camp, Spring is still Spring. The atom bombs are piling up in the factories, the police are prowling through the cities, the lies are streaming from the loudspeakers, but the earth is still going round the sun, and neither the dictators nor the bureaucrats, deeply as they disapprove of the process, are able to prevent it.

On 18 April 1946, John Betjeman wrote to Orwell to say he thought he was 'one of the best living writers of prose' and he wished him to know how very much he had 'enjoyed & echoed every sentiment' of Orwell's thoughts on the common toad.

1. On 10 August 1946, Orwell records that he accidentally killed a toad when he was digging (XVIII/*3046*).

2. Lent, of course, is not only the period of fasting before Easter but, in Anglo-Saxon, *lencten* meant 'spring'. Hence, in the Book of Common Prayer (with which Orwell was very familiar from his schooldays), the singing of the canticle that rejoices in the natural world, 'Benedicite, omnia opera' ('O all ye works of the Lord, bless ye the Lord'), replaces the 'Te Deum laudamus' ('We praise thee, O God'), which is used throughout the rest of the year at Morning Prayer.

3. Orwell's choice of Persephone is doubly apt: she was a goddess of Hades (resort of the dead), and goddess of the germination of seed. This conjunction of life and death echoes Orwell's earlier simile, 'like one of those new poison gases' which, like spring, seeps in everywhere.

4. Orwell was living at 27B Canonbury Square, Islington – not then a fashionable area.

[2988]

Unsigned editorial [1] *[On defending intellectual decency]*
Polemic, *3 May 1946*

The December number of the *Modern Quarterly* [2] devotes one paragraph of its editorial to an attack upon *Polemic*, which, it seems, is guilty of 'persistent attempts to confuse moral issues, to break down the distinction between right and wrong'. It is perhaps of some significance that *Polemic* – and not, shall we say, *Truth*, the *Tablet* or the *Nineteenth Century and After* – is the only periodical that the Communist-controlled *Modern Quarterly* singles out for attack. But before dealing with this point, it is worth casting a glance at the moral code whose champion the *Modern Quarterly* sets out to be.

The above-quoted statement implies that there are two definite entities called 'right' and 'wrong', which are clearly distinguishable from one another and are of a more or less permanent nature. Without some such assumption, it has no meaning. In the next paragraph of the editorial we find the statement that 'the whole basis of ethics needs re-examination' – which implies, of course, that the distinction between right and wrong is *not* obvious and unchallengeable, and that to break it down, or to define it in a new way, may well be a duty. Later in the same number, in an essay entitled *Belief and Action*, we find Professor J. D. Bernal [3] in effect claiming that almost any moral standard can and should be scrapped when political expediency demands it. Needless to say, Professor Bernal does not put it quite so plainly as that, but if his words mean anything, that is what they mean. Here is one of various passages in which his doctrine is set forth. The emphasis is ours:

A radical change in morality is in any case required by the new social relations which men are already entering into in an organised and planned society. The relative importance of different virtues are bound to be affected. Old virtues may even appear as vices and new virtues instituted [*sic*]. Many of the basic virtues – truthfulness and good fellowship – are, of course, as old as humanity and need no changing, but *those based on excessive concern with individual rectitude need reorienting in the direction of social responsibility.*

Put in plain English, the passage emphasised means that public spirit and common decency pull in opposite directions; while the paragraph as a whole means that we must alter our conception of right and wrong from year to year, and if necessary from minute to minute. And there can be no doubt that Professor Bernal and his fellow-thinkers have shown great alacrity in doing this. During the past five or six years right and wrong have changed into one another at dizzying speed, and it is even probably true that actions which were wrong at one moment have afterwards become retrospectively right, and *vice versa*. Thus, in 1939, the Moscow radio denounced the British naval blockade of Germany as an inhuman measure which struck at women and children, while, in 1945, those who objected to some ten million German peasants being driven out of their homes were denounced by the same radio as pro-Nazis. So that the starvation of German women and children had changed from a bad action into a good one, and probably the earlier starvation had also become good with the passage of time. We may assume that Professor Bernal was in agreement with the Moscow radio on both occasions. Similarly, in 1945, the German invasion of Norway was a treacherous attack upon a defenceless neutral while, in 1940, it was a well-justified counter to a previous invasion by the British. One could multiply such examples indefinitely. But it is evident that from Professor Bernal's point of view any virtue can become a vice, and any vice a virtue, according to the political needs of the moment. When he makes a specific exception of 'truthfulness', he is presumably actuated by mere prudence. The implication of the whole passage is that telling lies might also be a virtue. But that is not the kind of thing that it pays to put in print.

A little later in the essay we read: 'Because collective action in the industrial and political field is the only effective action, it is the only virtuous action.' This contains the doctrine that an action – at any rate in political and industrial affairs – is only right when it is successful. It would be unfair to take this as meaning that every action which is successful is right, but the general tone of the essay does not leave much doubt that power and virtue are inextricably mixed up in Professor Bernal's mind. Right action does not lie in obeying your conscience, or a traditional moral code: right action lies in pushing history in the direction in which it is actually going. And what is that direction? Naturally, the direction of the classless society which all decent people desire. But, though that is where we are going, it needs effort to get there. And precisely what kind of effort? Well, of course, close co-operation with the Soviet Union – which, as any Communist would and must interpret it, means subservience to the Soviet Union. Here are some bits from Professor Bernal's peroration:

The war has been won and the world is about to enter the hard but glorious period of recovery and reconstruction . . . The great alliance of the United Nations which has been achieved through the bitter needs of the war has now become even more important as a guarantee against future wars which might be far worse than that through which we have passed. To maintain that alliance and to guard it against its open enemies and the more subtle disseminators of mutual suspicion will require constant vigilance and continued efforts to reach ever-closer understanding . . . To the degree to which we can see things in the same light we can go forward together in fellowship and hope.

What exactly does Professor Bernal mean by 'fellowship' and 'ever-closer understanding' between Britain and USSR? Does he mean, for instance, that independent British observers in large numbers should be allowed to travel freely through Soviet territory and send home uncensored reports? Or that Soviet citizens should be encouraged to read British newspapers, listen to the BBC and view the institutions of this country with a friendly eye? Obviously he doesn't mean that. All he can mean, therefore, is that Russian propaganda in this country should be intensified, and that critics of the Soviet régime (darkly referred to as 'subtle disseminators of mutual suspicion') should be silenced. He says much the same thing in several other places in his essay. So that, if we reduce his message to its essentials, we get the following propositions:

Apart from 'truthfulness and good fellowship', no quality can be definitely labelled good or bad. Any action which serves the cause of progress is virtuous.

Progress means moving towards a classless and scientifically-planned society.

The quickest way to get there is to co-operate with the Soviet Union.

Co-operation with the Soviet Union means not criticising the Stalin régime.

To put it even more shortly: any thing is right which furthers the aims of Russian foreign policy. Professor Bernal would probably not admit that this is what he means, but it is in effect what he is saying, though it takes him fifteen pages to do so.

A thing that is especially noticeable in Professor Bernal's article is the English, at once pompous and slovenly, in which it is written. It is not pedantic to draw attention to this, because the connection between totalitarian habits of thought and the corruption of language is an important subject which has not been sufficiently studied.[4] Like all writers of his school, Professor Bernal has a strong tendency to drop into Latin when something unpleasant has to be said. It is worth looking again at the passage in the first of the quotations given above. To say, 'party loyalty means doing dirt on your own conscience', would be too crude: to say '(virtues) based on excessive concern with individual rectitude need reorienting in the direction of social responsibility', comes to much the same thing, but far less courage is required in saying it. The long, vague words express the intended meaning and at the same time blur the moral squalor of what is being said. A remark that occurs in F. Anstey's *Vice Versa*, 'Drastic measures is Latin for a whopping',[5] illustrates well enough the essential principle of this style of writing. But there is another characteristic of writers friendly to totalitarianism which has been less noticed. This is a tendency to play tricks with syntax and produce un-buttoned-up or outright meaningless sentences. It will be seen that one of the sentences quoted from Professor Bernal has had to be given a '*sic*' to show that there is no misprint, and there are other and more extreme instances. In the *Partisan Review* for the winter of 1944, the

American critic Edmund Wilson makes some interesting remarks on this subject, apropos of the film *Mission to Moscow*.

Mission to Moscow was founded on a book by Joseph E. Davies,[6] who had been United States ambassador in Moscow during the period of the purges. In the book he expressed grave doubts about the justice of the verdicts in the sabotage trials, whereas in the film (in which he figures as a character) he is represented as feeling no doubts whatever. By the time when the film was made the USA and the USSR were allies, and part of its object was to 'build up' the Russian purges as a fully-justified extermination of traitors. The first version even contained 'shots' of Trotsky engaged in secret negotiations with Ribbentrop: these were afterwards cut out, perhaps in deference to the feelings of the Jewish community, or possibly because they were too like the real photographs of Ribbentrop negotiating with Stalin. Davies gave his imprimatur to the film, which was in effect a falsification of what he had said. Discussing this, Wilson gives some samples of Davies's prose, for the sake of the light that they probably cast on his mentality. Two extracts will do:

The peace of Europe, if maintained, is in imminent danger of being a peace imposed by the dictators, under conditions where all of the smaller countries will speedily rush in to get under the shield of the German aegis, and under conditions where, even though there be a concert of power, as I have predicted to you two years ago, with 'Hitler leading the band'.

Here is Mr. Davies on the subject of *Eugen Onegin*:

Both the opera and the ballet were based on Pushkin's works, and the music was by the great Tchaikovsky. The opera was *Eugen Onegin*, a romantic story of two young men of position whose friendship was broken up over a misunderstanding and lovers' quarrel, which resulted in a duel in which the poet was killed. It was significant of Pushkin's own end and, oddly enough, was written by him.

The confusion in this passage is such that it takes several minutes to sort out the various errors. But here is Professor Bernal:

Our British democracy, from long practice, does enable us to secure without coercion or bloodshed, but clumsily, far too slowly and with a heavy bias on ancient privilege.

What word, or phrase, is missing here? We do not know, and probably Professor Bernal does not either, but at any rate the sentence is meaningless. And curiously enough a rather similar kind of English turns up in the editorial:

> If science has much to teach us which we still have to learn, science must also be aware that it is fiercely assailed to-day by those who fear that man has power at his disposal beyond his moral capacity to control it. This is precisely one of those glib and pretentious ideas that is in need of ruthless criticism.

One non-sequitur, one tautological phrase and two grammatical errors, all in sixty words. And the writing of the editorial nowhere rises far above this level. It is not suggested, of course, that the causes of slovenly or meaningless writing are the same in every case. Sometimes 'Freudian errors' are to blame, sometimes sheer mental incompetence, and sometimes an instinctive feeling that clear thought is dangerous to orthodoxy. But there does seem to be a direct connection between acceptance of totalitarian doctrines and the writing of bad English, and we think it important that this should be pointed out.

To return to the *Modern Quarterly*'s attack on *Polemic*. We have shown that Professor Bernal teaches, and the editorial seems to endorse, the doctrine that nearly anything is right if it is politically expedient. Why then do they simultaneously charge *Polemic* with 'confusing moral issues', as though 'right' and 'wrong' were fixed entities which every decent person knows how to distinguish already? The reason can only be that they are a little nervous about the reactions of their more tender-minded readers, and think that their real aims should not be stated too bluntly. So, also, with their claim that they will give a hearing to all viewpoints, or very many viewpoints.*

> There is (says the editorial) wide scope for differences of opinion within our terms of reference. A certain speculative freedom and adventurousness of presentation is not only allowable but eminently desirable. No one should be deterred by feeling that his views may shock any kind of orthodoxy, left or right, from stating his

* Professor Bernal was asked to write for the first and second *Polemic*s. He is now invited to contribute to the next [Orwell's footnote].[7]

case. On the other hand, if the holiest canons seem to be unwisely and ignorantly challenged, there is always a remedy – instant and effective reply.

It would be interesting to subject this statement to a few tests. Would the *Modern Quarterly*, for instance, print a full history of the arrest and execution of Ehrlich and Alter,[8] the Polish Socialist leaders? Would it reprint any extract from the Communist Party's 'stop the war' pamphlets of 1940? Would it publish articles by Anton Ciliga[9] or Victor Serge?[10] It would not. The above-quoted statement, therefore, is simply a falsehood, the aim of which is to make an impression of broad-mindedness on inexperienced readers.

The reason for the *Modern Quarterly*'s hostility to *Polemic* is not difficult to guess. *Polemic* is attacked because it upholds certain moral and intellectual values whose survival is dangerous from the totalitarian point of view. These are what is loosely called the liberal values – using the word 'liberal' in its old sense of 'liberty-loving'. Its aim, before all else, is to defend the freedom of thought and speech that has been painfully won during the past four hundred years. It is only natural that Professor Bernal and others like him should regard this as a worse offence than the setting-up of some rival form of totalitarianism. According to Professor Bernal:

The liberal, individualistic, almost atomic philosophy started in the Renaissance and grew to full stature with the French Revolution. It is a philosophy of the 'rights of man', of 'liberty, equality, and fraternity', of private property, free enterprise, and free trade. We have known it in such a debased form, so unrelated to the pattern of the needs of the times, that only lip service is paid to it, and honest but ignorant minds have preferred even the bestialities of fascism to its unreal and useless tenets.

We have to contend here with the usual cloudy language and confusion of ideas, but if the last sentence means anything, it means that Professor Bernal considers fascism to be slightly preferable to liberalism. Presumably the editors of the *Modern Quarterly* are in agreement with him about this. So we arrive at the old, true and unpalatable conclusion that a communist and a fascist are somewhat nearer to one another than either is to a democrat. As to the special accusation levelled against us, of 'breaking down the distinction between right and wrong', it arose particularly out of the fact that one of our contributors objected to the disgusting gloating in the British press over the spectacle of dangling corpses. We think we have said enough to show that our real crime, in the eyes of the *Modern Quarterly*, lies in *defending* a conception of right and wrong, and of intellectual decency, which has been responsible for all true progress for centuries past, and without which the very continuance of civilised life is by no means certain.

1. This is unsigned but listed by Orwell among his writings.

2. *Modern Quarterly*, NS, Vols. 1–8, No. 4, December 1945–Autumn 1953, edited by John Lewis.

3. Professor John Desmond Bernal (1901–71), physicist and crystallographer, Marxist and author of books on science and sociology, including *The Freedom of Necessity* (1949). Orwell invited him to contribute to one of his series of BBC talks for India in March 1942; see XIII/*1005*. He at first accepted but later withdrew. Orwell included him in his list of Crypto-Communists and Fellow-Travellers (XX/*243*).

4. But see 'Politics and the English Language', above; the relationship of politics to the decline of the English language is outlined in the first two paragraphs.

5. F. Anstey (pen-name of Thomas Anstey Guthrie, 1856–1934), novelist. In his *Vice Versa* (1882), an Indian charm exchanges the physical characteristics of a father and son although each retains his mental and social characteristics. The father has, therefore, to attend school and, as a father, be treated (and mistreated) as if he were a schoolboy.

6. Joseph E. Davies (1876–1958), Ambassador to the USSR (1937–8) and to Belgium (1938–40). His book, *Mission to Moscow*, was published in 1941 and gave an account of conditions in Russia. The film, *Mission to Moscow*, was released by Warner Brothers on 30 April 1943. It was 'the most extreme example of official attempts to create support [for the Soviet Union] by distorting history'. It was one of a number of Hollywood films instigated by the US Government to dispel 'widespread popular distrust of the Soviet Union' (David Culbert, 'Our Awkward Ally', in *American History/American Film*, ed. John E. O'Connor and Martin A. Jackson, New York, 1979). Culbert devotes his chapter to the 'extreme fabrications' of this 'Frankenstein monster'.

7. Bernal did not accept this invitation.

8. Henryk Erlich (not Ehrlich) and Viktor Alter were Polish-Jewish Socialist leaders. Their fate only came to light during the course of fierce Soviet protestations that the Soviets were *not* responsible for the massacre of Poles at Katyn, Starobielsk, Kozelsk and Ostashkov. The Soviets claimed the Nazis had committed these atrocities and that this 'slanderous campaign hostile to the Soviet Union' was 'taken up by the Polish Government' (in London) and 'fanned in every way by the Polish official press' (also in London). As we now know, it was the Soviets who were guilty of these mass murders. In what is described as a '*Note*' to a very long account of the Soviet accusations, *Keesing's Contemporary Archives* for 24 April to 1 May 1943 (page 5732) states that the two men were arrested in September 1939 when the Soviets invaded Eastern Poland as the Germans were invading from the west. They were held in prison for about 18 months, then tried for 'subversive activities' and sentenced to death, but

that was commuted to ten years' imprisonment. A month after Germany attacked Russia on 22 June 1941, a Russo-Polish Agreement was signed and the men were released. However, they were re-arrested in December 1941, tried for conducting 'propaganda for an immediate peace with Germany', sentenced to death and executed. On the instructions of Vyacheslav Molotov (1890–1986), Soviet Foreign Minister, this information was passed by Maxim Litvinov (1876–1951), Soviet Ambassador to the USA, to William Green (1873–1952), President of the American Federation of Labor.

9. In his review of pamphlet literature, 9 January 1943 (see XIV/*1807*), Orwell described *The Kronstadt Revolt* by Anton Ciliga (b. 1898), published in Paris 1938, and in 1942 by the Freedom Press, as an 'Anarchist pamphlet, largely an attack on Trotsky'; his Classified List of Pamphlets (see below) categorizes it as Trotskyist, not Anarchist; see XX/*3733*. For the significance of Kronstadt to an understanding of *Animal Farm*, see Orwell's letter to Dwight Macdonald, 5 December 1946, XVIII/*3128*, especially n. 4 and p. 230, above. In a letter to Macdonald of 15 April 1947 (see XIX/*3215*), Orwell recommends Ciliga's *The Russian Enigma* as giving a good account of concentration camps.

10. Victor Serge (1890–1947), author and journalist, born in Brussels of exiled Russian parents, French by adoption. He was associated with the anarchist movement in Paris. After the Russian Revolution he worked in Moscow, Leningrad and Berlin (where he ran the newspaper, the *Communist International*). His close association with Trotsky led to his being deported to Siberia in 1933. After his release, he was Paris correspondent for the POUM (the organization with whom Orwell fought in the Spanish Civil War). In 1941 he settled in Mexico. He died there in poverty. Among his books are *From Lenin to Stalin* (1937), *Vie et mort de Trotsky* (Paris, 1951) and *Memoirs of a Revolutionary* (1963).

[3007]

'Why I Write'
Gangrel, *[No. 4, Summer]* 1946[1]

From a very early age, perhaps the age of five or six, I knew that when I grew up I should be a writer. Between the ages of about seventeen and twenty-four I tried to abandon this idea, but I did so with the consciousness that I was outraging my true nature and that sooner or later I should have to settle down and write books.

I was the middle child of three, but there was a gap of five years on either side, and I barely saw my father before I was eight. For this and other reasons I was somewhat lonely, and I soon developed disagreeable mannerisms which made me unpopular throughout my schooldays. I had the lonely child's habit of making up stories and holding conversations with imaginary persons, and I think from the very start my literary ambitions were mixed up with the feeling of being isolated and under-valued. I knew that I had a facility with words and a power of facing unpleasant facts, and I felt that this created a sort of private world in which I could get my own back for my failure in everyday life. Nevertheless the volume of serious – i.e. seriously intended – writing which I produced all through my childhood and boyhood would not amount to half a dozen pages. I wrote my first poem at the age of four or five, my mother taking it down to dictation. I cannot remember anything about it except that it was about a tiger and the tiger had 'chair-like teeth' – a good enough phrase, but I fancy the poem was a plagiarism of Blake's 'Tiger, Tiger'. At eleven, when the war of 1914–18 broke out, I wrote a patriotic poem which was printed in the local newspaper, as was another, two years later, on the death of Kitchener.[2] From time to time, when I was bit older, I wrote bad and usually unfinished 'nature poems' in the Georgian style. I also, about twice, attempted a short story which was a ghastly failure. That was the total of the would-be serious work that I actually set down on paper during all those years.

However, throughout this time I did in a sense engage in literary activities. To begin with there was the made-to-order stuff which I produced quickly, easily and without much pleasure to myself. Apart from school work, I wrote *vers d'occasion*, semi-comic poems which I could turn out at what now seems to me astonishing speed – at fourteen I wrote a whole rhyming play, in imitation of Aristophanes, in about a week – and helped to edit school magazines, both printed and in manuscript. These magazines were the most pitiful burlesque stuff that you could imagine, and I took far less trouble with them than I now would with the cheapest journalism. But side by side with all this, for fifteen years or more, I was carrying out a literary exercise of a quite different kind: this was the making up of a continuous 'story' about myself, a sort of diary existing only in the mind. I believe this is a common habit of children and adolescents. As a very small child I used to imagine that I was, say, Robin Hood and picture myself as the hero of thrilling adventures, but quite soon my 'story' ceased to be narcissistic in a crude way and became more and more a mere description of what I was doing and the things I saw. For minutes at a time this kind of thing would be running through my head: 'He pushed the door open and entered the room. A yellow beam of sunlight, filtering through the muslin curtains, slanted on to the table, where a matchbox, half open, lay beside the inkpot. With his right hand in his pocket he moved across to the window. Down in the street a tortoiseshell cat was chasing a dead leaf,' etc., etc. This habit continued till I was about twenty-five, right through my non-literary years. Although I had to search, and did search, for the right words, I seemed to be making this descriptive effort almost against my will, under a kind of compulsion from outside. The 'story' must, I suppose, have reflected the styles of the various writers I admired at different ages, but so far as I remember it always had the same meticulous descriptive quality.

When I was about sixteen I suddenly discovered the joy of mere words, i.e. the sounds and associations of words. The lines from *Paradise Lost* –

> So hee with difficulty and labour hard
> Moved on: with difficulty and labour hee,[3]

which do not now seem to me so very wonderful, sent shivers down my backbone; and the spelling 'hee' for 'he' was an added pleasure. As for the need to describe things, I knew all about it already. So it is clear what kind of books I wanted to write, in so far as I could be said to want to write books at that time. I wanted to write enormous naturalistic novels with unhappy endings, full of detailed descriptions and arresting similes, and also full of purple passages in which words were used partly for the sake of their sound. And in fact my first completed novel, *Burmese Days*, which I wrote when I was thirty but projected much earlier, is rather that kind of book.

I give all this background information because I do not think one can assess a writer's motives without knowing something of his early development. His subject-matter will be determined by the age he lives in – at least this is true in tumultuous, revolutionary ages like our own – but before he ever begins to write he will have acquired an emotional attitude from which he will never completely escape. It is his job, no doubt, to discipline his temperament and avoid getting stuck at some immature stage, or in some perverse mood: but if he escapes from his early influences altogether, he will have killed his impulse to write. Putting aside the need to earn a living, I think there are four great motives for writing, at any rate for writing prose. They exist in different degrees in every writer, and in any one writer the proportions will vary from time to time, according to the atmosphere in which he is living. They are:

(i) Sheer egoism. Desire to seem clever, to be talked about, to be remembered after death, to get your own back on grown-ups who snubbed you in childhood, etc., etc. It is humbug to pretend that this is not a motive, and a strong one. Writers share this characteristic with scientists, artists, politicians, lawyers, soldiers, successful business men – in short, with the whole top crust of humanity. The great mass of human beings are not acutely selfish. After the age of about thirty they abandon individual ambition – in many cases, indeed, they almost abandon the sense of being individuals at all – and live chiefly for others, or are simply smothered under drudgery. But there is also the minority of gifted, wilful people who are determined to live their own lives to the end, and writers belong in this class. Serious writers, I should say, are on the whole more vain and self-centred than journalists, though less interested in money.

(ii) Aesthetic enthusiasm. Perception of beauty in the external world, or, on the other hand, in words and their right arrangement. Pleasure in the impact of one sound on another, in the firmness of good prose or the rhythm of a good story. Desire to share an experience which one feels is valuable and ought not to be missed. The aesthetic motive is very feeble in a lot of writers, but even a pamphleteer or a writer of textbooks will have pet words and phrases which appeal to him for non-utilitarian reasons; or he may feel strongly about typography, width of margins, etc. Above the level of a railway guide, no book is quite free from aesthetic considerations.

(iii) Historical impulse. Desire to see things as they are, to find out true facts and store them up for the use of posterity.

(iv) Political purpose – using the word 'political' in the widest possible sense. Desire to push the world in a certain direction, to alter other people's idea of the kind of society that they should strive after. Once again, no book is genuinely free from political bias. The opinion that art should have nothing to do with politics is itself a political attitude.

It can be seen how these various impulses must war against one another, and how they must fluctuate from person to person and from time to time. By nature – taking your 'nature' to be the state you have attained when you are first adult – I am a person in whom the first three motives would outweigh the fourth. In a peaceful age I might have written ornate or merely descriptive books, and might have remained almost unaware of my political loyalties. As it is I have been forced into becoming a sort of pamphleteer. First I spent five years in an unsuitable profession (the Indian Imperial Police, in Burma), and then I underwent poverty and the sense of failure. This increased my natural hatred of authority and made me for the first time fully aware of the existence of the working classes, and the job in Burma had given me some understanding of the nature of imperialism: but these experiences were not enough to give me an accurate political orientation. Then came Hitler, the Spanish Civil War, etc. By the end of 1935 I had still failed to reach a firm decision. I remember the last three stanzas of a little poem that I wrote at that date, expressing my dilemma:

> I am the worm who never turned,
> The eunuch without a harem;
> Between the priest and the commissar
> I walk like Eugene Aram;
>
> And the commissar is telling my fortune
> While the radio plays,
> But the priest has promised an Austin Seven,
> For Duggie always pays.
>
> I dreamed I dwelt in marble halls,
> And woke to find it true:
> I wasn't born for an age like this;
> Was Smith? Was Jones? Were you?[4]

The Spanish war and other events in 1936–7 turned the scale and thereafter I knew where I stood. Every line of serious work that I have written since 1936 has been written, directly or indirectly, *against* totalitarianism and *for* democratic Socialism, as I understand it. It seems to me nonsense, in a period like our own, to think that one can avoid writing of such subjects. Everyone writes of them in one guise or another. It is simply a question of which side one takes and what approach one follows. And the more one is conscious of one's political bias, the more chance one has of acting politically without sacrificing one's aesthetic and intellectual integrity.

What I have most wanted to do throughout the past ten years is to make political writing into an art. My starting point is always a feeling of partisanship, a sense of injustice. When I sit down to write a book, I do not say to myself, 'I am going to produce a work of art.' I write it because there is some lie that I want to expose, some fact to which I want to draw attention, and my initial concern is to get a hearing. But I could not do the work of writing a book, or even a long magazine article, if it were not also an aesthetic experience. Anyone who cares to examine my work will see that even when it is downright propaganda it contains much that a full-time politician would consider irrelevant. I am not able, and I do not want, completely to abandon the world-view that I acquired in childhood. So long as I remain alive and well I shall continue to feel strongly about prose style, to love the surface of the earth, and to take a pleasure in solid objects and scraps of useless information. It is no use trying to suppress that side of myself. The job is to reconcile my ingrained likes and dislikes with the essentially public, non-individual activities that this age forces on all of us.

It is not easy. It raises problems of construction and of language, and it raises in a new way the problem of truthfulness. Let me give just one example of the cruder kind of difficulty that arises. My book about the Spanish Civil War, *Homage to Catalonia*, is, of course, a frankly political book, but in the main it is written with a certain detachment and regard for form. I did try very hard in it to tell the whole truth without violating my literary instincts. But among other things it contains a long chapter, full of newspaper quotations and the like, defending the Trotskyists who were accused of plotting with Franco. Clearly such a chapter, which after a year or two would lose its interest for any ordinary reader, must ruin the book.[5] A critic whom I respect read me a lecture about it. 'Why did you put in all that stuff?' he said.[6] 'You've turned what might have been a good book into journalism.' What he said was true, but I could not have done otherwise. I happened to know, what very few people in England had been allowed to know, that innocent men were being falsely accused. If I had not been angry about that I should never have written the book.

In one form or another this problem comes up again. The problem of language is subtler and would take too long to discuss. I will only say that of late years I have tried to write less picturesquely and more exactly. In any case I find that by the time you have perfected any style of writing, you have always outgrown it. *Animal Farm* was the first book in which I tried, with full consciousness of what I was doing, to fuse political purpose and artistic purpose into one whole. I have not written a novel for seven years, but I hope to write another fairly soon. It is bound to be a failure, every book is a failure, but I do know with some clarity what kind of book I want to write.

Looking back through the last page or two, I see that I have made it appear as though my motives in writing were wholly public-spirited. I don't want to leave that as the final impression. All writers are vain, selfish and lazy, and at the very bottom of their motives there lies a mystery. Writing a book is a horrible, exhausting struggle, like a long bout of some painful illness. One would never undertake such a thing if one were not driven on by some demon whom one can neither resist or° understand. For all one knows that demon is simply the same instinct that makes a baby squall for attention. And yet it is also true that one can write nothing readable unless one constantly struggles to efface one's own personality. Good prose is like a window pane. I cannot say with certainty which of my motives are the strongest, but I know which of them deserve to be followed. And looking back through my work, I see that it is invariably where I lacked a *political* purpose that I wrote lifeless books and was betrayed into purple passages, sentences without meaning, decorative adjectives and humbug generally.

1. *Gangrel*, Nos. 1–4, January 1945–6; the editors, J. B. Pick and Charles Neill, asked a number of authors to explain why they wrote. Orwell's response was placed second.
2. These poems, published in *The Henley and South Oxfordshire Standard* on 2 October 1914 and 21 July 1916, were 'Awake! Young Men of England' and 'Kitchener' (drowned when HMS *Hampshire* struck a mine). The first was sent to the newspaper by Mrs Vaughan Wilkes, the headmaster's wife at Orwell's preparatory school, St Cyprian's, Eastbourne; Orwell sent the second himself. The poems, Orwell's first published work, are printed in X/20.
3. Lines 1021–2 of Book II of *Paradise Lost*. 'He' is Satan: 'Sin and Death amain / Following his track.' Orwell gave his copy of *Milton's Poems* to Guinever Buddicom in August 1921. This carried an inscription (see X/36) in which Orwell complained that he had been 'compelled to / Squander three & sixpence / On this nasty little book'.
4. These are the last three stanzas of the nine making up Orwell's poem 'A happy vicar I might have been', *The Adelphi*, December 1936: see X/335; punctuation has been amended here to conform to that version. The first line is drawn from 'The smallest worm will turn, being trodden on', Shakespeare, *3 Henry VI*, II.ii. Eugene Aram was a schoolmaster of some learning and good repute who lived in Knaresborough, Yorkshire. In 1745 he murdered a man named Clark, but the murder was not discovered until 1758. Aram was arrested while

teaching a class, tried, and executed in 1759. Thomas Hood (a favourite of Orwell's) wrote a poem, 'The Dream of Eugene Aram', published in 1829. The Austin Seven was a very successful small family car before World War II; the 'seven' refers to the engine's horsepower. 'Duggie always pays' is a variant of the advertising slogan used by the bookmaker, Douglas Stuart, 'Duggie never owes'. 'I dreamed I dwelled in marble halls' is the first line of a very popular Victorian song by Alfred Bunn (1796?–1860), though that has 'dreamt' for 'dreamed'.

5. Orwell asked that various changes be made to *Homage to Catalonia* and that chapters five and eleven be removed from the body of the book and made into appendixes. About six months before he died, he sent a marked copy of the text to Roger Senhouse and asked him to ensure that the changes were made. Senhouse ignored this request, and the marked book was sold with Senhouse's effects. Some of the changes were made independently by Madame Davet in her French translation, published by Gallimard in 1955. For details of what Orwell required, see the Note on the Text to *Homage to Catalonia* in *Orwell in Spain* in this series.

6. The critic has not been identified. Cyril Connolly springs to mind, but Geoffrey Gorer is also a possibility.

[3115]

Extract from 'As I Please', 61 [Attitudes to immigrants]
Tribune, 15 November 1946

As the clouds, most of them much larger and dirtier than a man's hand, come blowing up over the political horizon, there is one fact that obtrudes itself over and over again. This is that the Government's troubles, present and future, arise quite largely from its failure to publicise itself properly.

People are not told with sufficient clarity what is happening, and why, and what may be expected to happen in the near future. As a result, every calamity, great or small, takes the mass of the public by surprise, and the Government incurs unpopularity by doing things which any government, of whatever colour, would have to do in the same circumstances.

Take one question which has been much in the news lately but has never been properly thrashed out: the immigration of foreign labour into this country. Recently we have seen a tremendous outcry at the T.U.C. conference against allowing Poles to work in the two places where labour is most urgently needed – in the mines and on the land.

It will not do to write this off as something 'got up' by Communist sympathisers, nor on the other hand to justify it by saying that the Polish refugees are all Fascists who 'strut about' wearing monocles and carrying brief-cases.

The question is, would the attitude of the British trade unions be any friendlier if it were a question, not of alleged Fascists but of the admitted victims of Fascism?

For example, hundreds of thousands of homeless Jews are now trying desperately to get to Palestine. No doubt many of them will ultimately succeed, but others will fail. How about inviting, say, 100,000 Jewish refugees to settle in this country? Or what about the Displaced Persons, numbering nearly a million, who are dotted in camps all over Germany, with no future and no place to go, the United States and the British Dominions having already refused to admit them in significant numbers? Why not solve their problem by offering them British citizenship?

It is easy to imagine what the average Briton's answer would be. Even before the war, with the Nazi persecutions in full swing, there was no popular support for the idea of allowing large numbers of Jewish refugees into this country: nor was there any strong move to admit the hundreds of thousands of Spaniards who had fled from Franco to be penned up behind barbed wire in France.

For that matter, there was very little protest against the internment of the wretched German refugees in 1940. The comments I most often overheard at the time were 'What did they want to come here for?' and 'They're only after our jobs'.

The fact is that there is strong popular feeling in this country against foreign immigration. It arises partly from simple xenophobia, partly from fear of undercutting in wages, but above all from the out-of-date notion that Britain is overpopulated and that more population means more unemployment.

Actually, so far from having more workers than jobs, we have a serious labour shortage which will be accentuated by the continuance of conscription, and which will grow worse, not better, because of the ageing of the population.

Meanwhile our birth-rate is still frighteningly low, and several hundred thousand women of marriageable age have no chance of getting husbands. But how widely are these facts known or understood?

In the end it is doubtful whether we can solve our problems without encouraging immigration from Europe. In a tentative way the Government has already tried to do this, only to be met by ignorant hostility, because the public has not been told the relevant facts beforehand. So also with countless other unpopular things that will have to be done from time to time.

But the most necessary step is not to prepare public opinion for particular emergencies, but to raise the general level of political understanding: above all, to drive home the fact, which has never been properly grasped, that British prosperity depends largely on factors outside Britain.

This business of publicising and explaining itself is not easy for a Labour Government, faced by a press which at bottom is mostly hostile. Nevertheless, there are other ways of communicating with the public, and Mr. Attlee and his colleagues might well pay more attention to the radio, a medium which very few politicians in this country have ever taken seriously.

[3146]

Extract from 'As I Please', 68 [Class distinctions]

Tribune, 3 January 1947[1]

Nearly a quarter of a century ago I was travelling on a liner to Burma. Though not a big ship, it was a comfortable and even a luxurious one, and when one was not asleep or playing deck games one usually seemed to be eating. The meals were of that stupendous kind that steamship companies used to vie with one another in producing, and in between times there were snacks such as apples, ices, biscuits and cups of soup, lest anyone should find himself fainting from hunger. Moreover, the bars opened at ten in the morning, and, since we were at sea, alcohol was relatively cheap.

The ships of this line were mostly manned by Indians, but apart from the officers and the stewards they carried four European quartermasters whose job was to take the wheel. One of these quartermasters, though I suppose he was only aged forty or so, was one of those old sailors on whose back you almost expect to see barnacles growing. He was a short, powerful, rather ape-like man, with enormous forearms covered by a mat of golden hair. A blond moustache which might have belonged to Charlemagne completely hid his mouth. I was only twenty years old and very conscious of my parasitic status as a mere passenger, and I looked up to the quartermasters, especially the fair-haired one, as godlike beings on a par with the officers. It would not have occurred to me to speak to one of them without being spoken to first.

One day, for some reason, I came up from lunch early. The deck was empty except for the fair-haired quartermaster, who was scurrying like a rat along the side of the deck-houses, with something partially concealed between his monstrous hands. I had just time to see what it was before he shot past me and vanished into a doorway. It was a pie dish containing a half-eaten baked custard pudding.

At one glance I took in the situation – indeed, the man's air of guilt made it unmistakable. The pudding was a left-over from one of the passengers' tables. It had been illicitly given to him by a steward, and he was carrying it off to the seamen's quarters to devour it at leisure. Across more than twenty years I can still faintly feel the shock of astonishment that I felt at that moment. It took me some time to see the incident in all its bearings: but do I seem to exaggerate when I say that this sudden revelation of the gap between function and reward – the revelation that a highly-skilled craftsman, who might literally hold all our lives in his hands, was glad to steal scraps of food from our table – taught me more than I could have learned from half a dozen Socialist pamphlets?

1. After Orwell had died (Saturday, 21 January 1950), this number of 'As I Please' was chosen to be reprinted in tribute to him in *Tribune*, 27 January 1950. The other items concerned a purge of writers and artists then taking place in Yugoslavia, and reflections on earlier Soviet purges organized by Andrei Zhdanov (1896–1948), Secretary of the Central Committee in charge of ideology, a close associate of Stalin, and an advocate of social realism. Orwell specifically mentions the poet Anna Akhmatova (1889–1966), and the satirist, Mikhail Zoschenko (1895–1957/8). Zoschenko was, among other things, criticized for alleged malicious distortions of popular speech. The final item was a quotation from Marcus Aurelius, starting, 'In the morning when thou risest unwillingly, let this thought be present: I am rising to the work of a human being. Why then am I dissatisfied? . . .'

Extract from 'As I Please', 70 [Attitudes to Poles in Scotland]

Tribune, 24 January 1947

Recently I was listening to a conversation between two small business-men in a Scottish hotel.[1] One of them, an alert-looking, well-dressed man of about forty-five, was something to do with the Federation of Master Builders. The other, a good deal older, with white hair and a broad Scottish accent, was some kind of wholesale tradesman. He said grace before his meals, a thing I had not seen anyone do for many a year. They belonged, I should say, in the £2,000-a-year and the £1,000-a-year income groups respectively.[2]

We were sitting round a rather inadequate peat fire, and the conversation started off with the coal shortage. There was no coal, it appeared, because the British miners refused to dig it out, but on the other hand it was important not to let Poles work in the pits because this would lead to unemployment. There was severe unemployment in Scotland already. The older man then remarked with quiet satisfaction that he was very glad – 'varra glad indeed' – that Labour had won the general election. Any government that had to clean up after the war was in for a bad time, and as a result of five years of rationing, housing shortage, unofficial strikes and so forth, the general public would see through the promises of the Socialists and vote Conservative next time.

They began talking about the housing problem, and almost immediately they were back to the congenial subject of the Poles. The younger man had just sold his flat in Edinburgh at a good profit and was trying to buy a house. He was willing to pay £2,700. The other was trying to sell his house for £1,500 and buy a smaller one. But it seemed that it was impossible to buy houses or flats nowadays. The Poles were buying them all up, and 'where they get the money from is a mystery'. The Poles were also invading the medical profession. They even had their own medical school in Edinburgh or Glasgow (I forget which) and were turning out doctors in great numbers while 'our lads' found it impossible to buy practices. Didn't everyone know that Britain had more doctors than it could use? Let the Poles go back to their own country. There were too many people in this country already. What was needed was emigration.

The younger man remarked that he belonged to several business and civic associations, and that on all of them he made a point of putting forward resolutions that the Poles should be sent back to their own country. The older one added that the Poles were 'very degraded in their morals'. They were responsible for much of the immorality that was prevalent nowadays. 'Their ways are not our ways,' he concluded piously. It was not mentioned that the Poles pushed their way to the head of queues, wore bright-coloured clothes and displayed cowardice during air raids, but if I had put forward a suggestion to this effect I am sure it would have been accepted.

One cannot, of course, do very much about this kind of thing. It is the contemporary equivalent of anti-semitism. By 1947, people of the kind I am describing would have caught up with the fact that anti-semitism is discreditable, and so the scapegoat is sought elsewhere. But the race hatred and mass delusions which are part of the pattern of our time might be somewhat less bad in their effects if they were not reinforced by ignorance. If in the years before the war, for instance, the facts about the persecution of Jews in Germany had been better known, the sub-jective popular feeling against Jews would probably not have been less, but the actual treatment of Jewish refugees might have been better. The refusal to allow refugees in significant numbers into this country would have been branded as disgraceful. The average man would still have felt a grudge against the refugees, but in practice more lives would have been saved.

So also with the Poles. The thing that most depressed me in the above-mentioned conversation was the recurrent phrase, 'let them go back to their own country'. If I had said to those two business-men, 'Most of these people have no country to go back to,' they would have gaped. Not one of the relevant facts would have been known to them. They would never have heard of the various things that have happened to Poland since 1939, any more than they would have known that the over-population of Britain is a fallacy or that local unemployment can co-exist with a general shortage of labour. I think it is a mistake to give such people the excuse of ignorance. You can't actually change their feelings, but you can make them understand what they are saying when they demand that homeless refugees shall be driven from our shores, and the knowledge may make them a little less actively malignant.[3]

1. Presumably this conversation took place on either 30 or 31 December 1946, when Orwell 'had to hang about for 2 days in Glasgow'; see XIX/*3147*.

2. The average wage in 1946 was about £350 a year.

3. Orwell took considerable interest in the fate of Poles living in Scotland; see 'As I Please', 73, 14 February 1947, below. This may have stemmed from his time as a war correspondent in Germany in 1945. It was probably prompted by the debate on this issue when he was in Jura in 1946. For example, from 30 August to 11 October 1946 a fairly vituperative correspondence attacking the presence of Poles in Scotland was published by *John O'Groats Journal*. This, on the Scottish side, sought to require their return to Poland; the semi-official responses from a Polish organization (much more temperately expressed) pointed out the part played by Poles in the Allied forces and stressed the danger they faced if they returned home to a Soviet-dominated society. Orwell seems to have played no part in this correspondence but among his papers at his death was a long letter from John M. Sutherland of Bonar Bridge, Sutherland, dated 16 September 1946. This opens 'Dear Sir' and refers to 'your letter' in the *Journal* of 13 September. The only letter on this subject in that issue was from Z. Nagórski of the Polish Press Agency, 43 Charlotte Square, Edinburgh, which set out the three chief reasons for hostility to the Poles: a minority were Communists; extreme Protestants in Scotland feared an influx of Roman Catholic Poles; and 'Scots of all parties but mainly nationalists . . . see in Polish resettlement an attempt by England to pay her debt to Poland at the expense of Scotland . . . in accord with the historic English tradition of paying her debts out of someone else's pocket'. He believed 'few Scots have any real hostility to the Poles' and if they were at loggerheads it would serve English interests by keeping their minds off more serious problems. Orwell followed up what happened to twenty-six Polish ex-servicemen who had been repatriated from Scotland to Poland. A report dated 15 January 1947 stated that twenty-three were charged with being spies. One was Francisek Kilański. He managed to escape and get into the British Zone of Germany but, because his identification papers had been taken from him in Poland, he could not gain admission to a camp for displaced persons. That would mean he would have no ration card. He was simply wandering about. Orwell and George Woodcock, through the Freedom Defence Committee, argued that repatriated soldiers were being politically persecuted on their return home. On 14 April the Control Office for Germany and Austria advised the Freedom Defence Committee that such Polish nationals would be given the status of German nationals, entitling them to ration cards. See XIX/*3180*.

[3171]

Extract from 'As I Please', 73 [Scottish Nationalism]
Tribune, *14 February 1947*

Here are some excerpts from a letter from a Scottish Nationalist.[1] I have cut out anything likely to reveal the writer's identity. The frequent references to Poland are there because the letter is primarily concerned with the presence of exiled Poles in Scotland:

The Polish forces have now discovered how untrue it is to say 'An Englishman's word is his bond'. We could have told you so hundreds of years ago. The invasion of Poland was only an excuse for these brigands in bowler hats to beat up their rivals the Germans and the Japs, with the help of Americans, Poles, Scots, Frenchmen, etc., etc. Surely no Pole believes any longer in English promises. Now that the war is over you are to be cast aside and dumped in Scotland. If this leads to friction between the Poles and Scots so much the better. Let them slit each other's throats and two problems would be thereupon 'solved'. Dear, kind little England! It is time for all Poles to shed any ideas they may have about England as a champion of freedom. Look at her record in Scotland, for instance. And please don't refer to us as 'Britons'. There is *no* such race. We are Scots and that's good enough for us. The English changed their name to British; but even if a criminal changes his name he can be known by his fingerprints ... Please disregard any anti-Polish statement in the *John O'Groats Journal*.[2] It is a boot-licking pro-English (pro-Moscow you would call it) rag. Scotland experienced her Yalta in 1707 when English gold achieved what English guns could not do. But we will never accept defeat. After more than two hundred years we are still fighting for our country and will never acknowledge defeat whatever the odds.

There is a good deal more in the letter, but this should be enough. It will be noted that the writer is not attacking England from what is called a 'left' standpoint, but on the ground that Scotland and England are enemies *as nations*. I don't know whether it would be fair to read race-theory into this letter, but certainly the writer hates us as bitterly as a devout Nazi would hate a Jew. It is not a hatred of the capitalist class, or anything like that, but *of England*. And though the fact is not sufficiently realised, there is an appreciable amount of this kind of thing knocking about. I have seen almost equally violent statements in print.

Up to date the Scottish Nationalist movement seems to have gone almost unnoticed in England. To take the nearest example to hand, I don't remember having seen it mentioned in *Tribune*, except occasionally in book reviews. It is true that it is a small movement, but it could grow, because there is a basis for it. In this country I don't think it is enough realised – I myself had no idea of it until a few years ago – that Scotland has a case against England. On economic grounds it may not be a very strong case. In the past, certainly, we have plundered Scotland shamefully, but whether it is *now* true that England as a whole exploits Scotland as a whole, and that Scotland would be better off if fully autonomous, is another question. The point is that many Scottish people, often quite moderate in outlook, are beginning to think about autonomy and to feel that they are pushed into an inferior position. They have a good deal of reason. In some areas, at any rate, Scotland is almost an occupied country. You have an English or Anglicised upper-class, and a Scottish working-class which speaks with a markedly different accent, or even, part of the time, in a different language. This is a more dangerous kind of class division than any now existing in England. Given favourable circumstances it might develop in an ugly way, and the fact that there was a progressive Labour Government in London might not make much difference.

No doubt Scotland's major ills will have to be cured along with those of England. But meanwhile there are things that could be done to ease the cultural situation. One small but not negligible point is the language. In the Gaelic-speaking areas, Gaelic is not taught in the schools. I am speaking from limited experience, but I should say that this is beginning to cause resentment. Also, the B.B.C. only broadcasts two or three half-hour Gaelic programmes a week, and they give the impression of being rather amateurish programmes. Even so they are eagerly listened to. How easy it would be to buy a little goodwill by putting on a Gaelic programme at least once daily.

At one time I would have said that it is absurd to keep alive an archaic language like Gaelic, spoken by only a few hundred thousand people. Now I am not so sure. To begin with, if people feel that they have a special culture which ought to be preserved, and that the language is part of it, difficulties should not be put in their way when they want their children to learn it properly. Secondly, it is probable that the effort of being bi-lingual is a valuable education in itself. The Scottish Gaelic-speaking peasants speak beautiful English, partly, I think, because English is an almost foreign language which they sometimes do not use for days together. Probably they benefit intellectually by having to be aware of dictionaries and grammatical rules, as their English opposite numbers would not be.

At any rate, I think we should pay more attention to the small but violent separatist movements which exist within our own island. They may look very unimportant now, but, after all, the Communist Manifesto was once a very obscure document, and the Nazi Party only had six members when Hitler joined it.[3]

1. This letter, from John M. Sutherland, dated 16 September 1946, was sent to Orwell by Z. Nagórski of the Polish Press Agency, Edinburgh, in connection with the case of a Polish soldier which Orwell raised with the Freedom Defence Committee; see XIX/*3180*. See also n. 3 to 'As I Please', 70, 24 January 1947, above.

2. The name of the journal is left as a blank in 'As I Please', but it appears in the original letter, of course. It has been restored here.

3. Orwell's comments on nationalism drew a long letter from Cyril Hughes of 3 March 1947 in which he explained that as he understood nationalism, from a Welsh standpoint, Orwell's 'underlining of economic causes' in defence of nationalism was not the most important issue. What mattered in Wales, he argued, was that 'The tribe, or gwely . . . founded on a limited consanguinity, had evolved a sense of mutual social responsibility superior to any comparable modern practice.' Though he conceded that one could not return to tribalism, which had been 'bloodily rooted out, and an alien [social system] planted in the wound', it was important to recognize that nations had not learned the social lessons exemplified by tribes. For further extracts, see XIX/*3171*, *n. 3*. The argument may be sound but the Welsh is not. The Welsh for 'tribe' is *llwyth*. Mr Hughes may have confused *gwely* and *gwehelyth*. The latter means 'lineage'; *gwely* means 'bed'.

[3244]

'Toward European Unity'
Partisan Review, *July–August 1947*

A socialist today is in the position of a doctor treating an all but hopeless case. As a doctor, it is his duty to keep the patient alive, and therefore to assume that the patient has at least a chance of recovery. As a scientist, it is his duty to face the facts, and therefore to admit that the patient will probably die. Our activities as socialists only have meaning if we assume that socialism *can* be established, but if we stop to consider what probably *will* happen, then we must admit, I think, that the chances are against us. If I were a bookmaker, simply calculating the probabilities and leaving my own wishes out of account, I would give odds against the survival of civilization within the next few hundred years. As far as I can see, there are three possibilities ahead of us:

1. That the Americans will decide to use the atomic bomb while they have it and the Russians haven't. This would solve nothing. It would do away with the particular danger that is now presented by the U.S.S.R., but would lead to the rise of new empires, fresh rivalries, more wars, more atomic bombs, etc. In any case this is, I think, the least likely outcome of the three, because a preventive war is a crime not easily committed by a country that retains any traces of democracy.

2. That the present 'cold war' will continue until the U.S.S.R., and several other countries, have atomic bombs as well. Then there will only be a short breathing-space before whizz! go the rockets, wallop! go the bombs, and the industrial centers of the world are wiped out, probably beyond repair. Even if any one state, or group of states, emerges from such a war as technical victor, it will probably be unable to build up the machine civilization anew. The world, therefore, will once again be inhabited by a few million, or a few hundred million human beings living by subsistence agriculture, and probably, after a couple of generations, retaining no more of the culture of the past than a knowledge of how to smelt metals. Conceivably this is a desirable outcome, but obviously it has nothing to do with socialism.

3. That the fear inspired by the atomic bomb and other weapons yet to come will be so great that everyone will refrain from using them. This seems to me the worst possibility of all. It would mean the division of the world among two or three vast superstates, unable to conquer one another and unable to be overthrown by any internal rebellion. In all probability their structure would be hierarchic, with a semidivine caste at the top and outright slavery at the bottom, and the crushing out of liberty would exceed anything that the world has yet seen. Within each state the necessary psychological atmosphere would be kept up by complete severance from the outer world, and by a continuous phony war against rival states. Civilizations of this type might remain static for thousands of years.

Most of the dangers that I have outlined existed and were foreseeable long before the atomic bomb was invented. The only way of avoiding them that I can imagine is to present somewhere or other, on a large scale, the spectacle of a community where people are relatively free and happy and where the main motive in life is not the pursuit of money or power. In other words, democratic socialism must be made to work throughout some large area. But the only area in which it could conceivably be made to work, in any near future, is western Europe. Apart from Australia and New Zealand, the tradition of democratic socialism can only be said to exist – and even there it only exists precariously – in Scandinavia, Germany, Austria, Czecho-Slovakia, Switzerland, the Low Countries, France, Britain, Spain, and Italy. Only in those countries are there still large numbers of people to whom the word 'socialism' has some appeal and for whom it is bound up with liberty, equality, and internationalism. Elsewhere it either has no foothold or it means something different. In North America the masses are contented with capitalism, and one cannot tell what turn they will take when capitalism begins to collapse. In the U.S.S.R. there prevails a sort of oligarchical collectivism which could only develop into democratic socialism against the will of the ruling minority. Into Asia even the word 'socialism' has barely penetrated. The Asiatic nationalist movements are either fascist in character, or look toward Moscow, or manage to combine both attitudes: and at present all movements among the colored peoples are tinged by racial mysticism. In most of South America the position is essentially similar, so is it in Africa and the Middle East. Socialism does not exist anywhere, but even as an idea it is at present valid only in Europe. Of course, socialism cannot properly be said to be established until it is world-wide, but the process must begin somewhere, and I cannot imagine it beginning except through the federation of the western European states, transformed into socialist republics without colonial dependencies. Therefore a socialist United States of Europe seems to me the only worth-while political objective today. Such a federation would contain about 250 million people, including perhaps half the skilled industrial workers of the world. I do not need to be told that the difficulties of bringing any such thing into being are enormous and terrifying, and I will list some of them in a moment. But we ought not to feel that it is of its nature impossible, or that countries so different from one another would not voluntarily unite. A western European union is in itself a less improbable concatenation than the Soviet Union or the British Empire.

Now as to the difficulties. The greatest difficulty of all is the apathy and conservatism of people everywhere, their unawareness of danger, their inability to imagine anything new – in general, as Bertrand Russell put it recently, the unwillingness of the human race to acquiesce in its own survival. But there are also active malignant forces working against European unity, and there are existing economic relationships on which the European peoples depend for their standard of life and which are not compatible with true socialism. I list what seem to me to be the four main obstacles, explaining each of them as shortly as I can manage:

1. Russian hostility. The Russians cannot but be hostile to any European union not under their own control. The reasons, both the pretended and the real ones, are obvious. One has to count, therefore, with the danger of a preventive war, with the systematic terrorizing of the smaller nations, and with the sabotage of the Communist parties everywhere. Above all there is the danger that the European masses will continue to believe in the Russian myth. As long as they believe it, the idea of a socialist Europe will not be sufficiently magnetic to call forth the necessary effort.

2. American hostility. If the United States remains capitalist, and especially if it needs markets for exports, it cannot regard a socialist Europe with a friendly eye. No doubt it is less likely than the U.S.S.R. to intervene with brute force, but American pressure is an important factor because it can be exerted most easily on Britain, the one country in Europe which is outside the Russian orbit. Since 1940 Britain has kept its feet against the European dictators at the expense of becoming almost a dependency of the U.S.A. Indeed, Britain can only get free of America by dropping the attempt to be an extra-European power. The English-speaking Dominions, the colonial dependencies, except perhaps in Africa, and even Britain's supplies of oil, are all hostages in American hands. Therefore there is always the danger that the United States will break up any European coalition by drawing Britain out of it.

3. Imperialism. The European peoples, and especially the British, have long owed their high standard of life to direct or indirect exploitation of the colored peoples. This relationship has never been made clear by

official socialist propaganda, and the British worker, instead of being told that, by world standards, he is living above his income, has been taught to think of himself as an overworked, down-trodden slave. To the masses everywhere 'socialism' means, or at least is associated with, higher wages, shorter hours, better houses, all-round social insurance, etc., etc. But it is by no means certain that we can afford these things if we throw away the advantages we derive from colonial exploitation. However evenly the national income is divided up, if the income as a whole falls, the working-class standard of living must fall with it. At best there is liable to be a long and uncomfortable reconstruction period for which public opinion has nowhere been prepared. But at the same time the European nations *must* stop being exploiters abroad if they are to build true socialism at home. The first step toward a European socialist federation is for the British to get out of India. But this entails something else. If the United States of Europe is to be self-sufficient and able to hold its own against Russia and America, it must include Africa and the Middle East. But that means that the position of the indigenous peoples in those countries must be changed out of recognition – that Morocco or Nigeria or Abyssinia must cease to be colonies or semicolonies and become autonomous republics on a complete equality with the European peoples. This entails a vast change of outlook and a bitter, complex struggle which is not likely to be settled without bloodshed. When the pinch comes the forces of imperialism will turn out to be extremely strong, and the British worker, if he has been taught to think of socialism in materialistic terms, may ultimately decide that it is better to remain an imperial power at the expense of playing second fiddle to America. In varying degrees all the European peoples, at any rate those who are to form part of the proposed union, will be faced with the same choice.

4. The Catholic Church. As the struggle between East and West becomes more naked, there is danger that democratic socialists and mere reactionaries will be driven into combining in a sort of Popular Front. The Church is the likeliest bridge between them. In any case the Church will make every effort to capture and sterilize any movement aiming at European unity. The dangerous thing about the Church is that it is *not* reactionary in the ordinary sense. It is not tied to laissez-faire capitalism or to the existing class system, and will not necessarily perish with them.

It is perfectly capable of coming to terms with socialism, or appearing to do so, provided that its own position is safeguarded. But if it is allowed to survive as a powerful organization, it will make the establishment of true socialism impossible, because its influence is and always must be against freedom of thought and speech, against human equality, and against any form of society tending to promote earthly happiness.

When I think of these and other difficulties, when I think of the enormous mental readjustment that would have to be made, the appearance of a socialist United States of Europe seems to me a very unlikely event. I don't mean that the bulk of the people are not prepared for it, in a passive way. I mean that I see no person or group of persons with the slightest chance of attaining power and at the same time with the imaginative grasp to see what is needed and to demand the necessary sacrifices from their followers. But I also can't at present see any other hopeful objective. At one time I believed that it might be possible to form the British Empire into a federation of socialist republics, but if that chance ever existed, we lost it by failing to liberate India, and by our attitude toward the colored peoples generally. It may be that Europe is finished and that in the long run some better form of society will arise in India or China. But I believe that it is only in Europe, if anywhere, that democratic socialism could be made a reality in short enough time to prevent the dropping of the atom bombs.

Of course, there are reasons, if not for optimism, at least for suspending judgment on certain points. One thing in our favor is that a major war is not likely to happen immediately. We could, I suppose, have the kind of war that consists in shooting rockets, but not a war involving the mobilization of tens of millions of men. At present any large army would simply melt away, and that may remain true for ten or even twenty years. Within that time some unexpected things might happen. For example, a powerful socialist movement might for the first time arise in the United States. In England it is now the fashion to talk of the United States as 'capitalistic', with the implication that this is something unalterable, a sort of racial characteristic like the color of eyes or hair. But in fact it cannot be unalterable, since capitalism itself has manifestly no future, and we cannot be sure in advance that the next change in the United States will not be a change for the better.

Then, again, we do not know what changes will take place in the

U.S.S.R. if war can be staved off for the next generation or so. In a society of that type, a radical change of outlook always seems unlikely, not only because there can be no open opposition but because the régime, with its complete hold over education, news, etc., deliberately aims at preventing the pendulum swing between generations which seems to occur naturally in liberal societies. But for all we know the tendency of one generation to reject the ideas of the last is an abiding human characteristic which even the N.K.V.D. will be unable to eradicate. In that case there may by 1960 be millions of young Russians who are bored by dictatorship and loyalty parades, eager for more freedom, and friendly in their attitude toward the West.

Or again, it is even possible that if the world falls apart into three unconquerable superstates, the liberal tradition will be strong enough within the Anglo-American section of the world to make life tolerable and even offer some hope of progress. But all this is speculation. The actual outlook, so far as I can calculate the probabilities, is very dark, and any serious thought should start out from that fact.

[3346]

'Marx and Russia'
Observer, *15 February 1948*

This essay was prompted by the publication of What is Communism? *by John Petrov Plamenatz (1912–75),[1] published by National News-Letter, associated with Commander Stephen King-Hall's News-Letter Service (founded in 1936). King-Hall (1893–1966) contributed an introduction.*

The word 'Communism', unlike 'Fascism', has never degenerated into a meaningless term of abuse. Nevertheless, a certain ambiguity does cling to it, and at the least it means two different things, only rather tenuously connected: a political theory, and a political movement which is not in any noticeable way putting the theory into practice. On the face of it, the deeds of the Cominform might seem more important than the prophecies of Marx, but, as Mr. John Plamenatz reminds us in his recently-published booklet, the original vision of Communism must never be forgotten, since it is still the dynamo which supplies millions of adherents with faith and hence with the power to act.

Originally, 'Communism' meant a free and just society based on the principle of 'to each according to his needs'. Marx gave this vision probability by making it part of a seemingly inevitable historical process. Society was to dwindle down to a tiny class of possessors and an enormous class of dispossessed, and one day, almost automatically, the dispossessed were to take over. Only a few decades after Marx's death the Russian Revolution broke out, and the men who guided its course proclaimed themselves, and believed themselves, to be Marx's most faithful disciples. But their success really depended on throwing a good deal of their master's teaching overboard.

Marx had foretold that revolution would happen first in the highly industrialised countries. It is now clear that this was an error, but he was right in this sense, that the kind of revolution that he foresaw could not happen in a backward country like Russia, where the industrial workers were a minority. Marx had envisaged an overwhelmingly powerful proletariat sweeping aside a small group of opponents, and then governing democratically, through elected representatives. What actually happened, in Russia, was the seizure of power by a small body of classless professional revolutionaries, who claimed to represent the common people but were not chosen by them nor genuinely answerable to them.

From Lenin's point of view this was unavoidable. He and his group had to stay in power, since they alone were the true inheritors of the Marxist doctrine, and it was obvious that they could not stay in power democratically. The 'dictatorship of the proletariat' had to mean the dictatorship of a handful of intellectuals, ruling through terrorism. The Revolution was saved, but from then onwards the Russian Communist Party developed in a direction of which Lenin would probably have disapproved if he had lived longer.

Placed as they were, the Russian Communists necessarily developed into a permanent ruling caste, or oligarchy, recruited not by birth but by adoption. Since they could not risk the growth of opposition they could not permit genuine criticism, and since they silenced criticism they often made avoidable mistakes: then, because they could not admit that the mistakes were their own they had to find scapegoats, sometimes on an enormous scale.

The upshot is that the dictatorship has grown tighter as the régime has grown more secure, and that Russia is perhaps farther from egalitarian Socialism today than she was 30 years ago. But, as Mr. Plamenatz rightly warns us, never for one moment should we imagine that the original fervour has faded. The Communists may have perverted their aims, but they have not lost their mystique. The belief that they and they alone are the saviours of humanity is as unquestioning as ever. In the years 1935–39 and 1941–44 it was easy to believe that the U.S.S.R. had abandoned the idea of world revolution, but it is now clear that this was not the case. The idea has never been dropped: it has merely been modified, 'revolution' tending more and more to mean 'conquest'.

No doubt unavoidably in so short a book, Mr. Plamenatz confines himself to one facet of his subject, and says very little about the role and character of the Communist parties outside the U.S.S.R. He also barely touches on the question of whether the Russian régime will, or indeed can, grow more liberal of its own accord. This last question is all-important, but for lack of precedents one can only guess at the answer.

Meanwhile, we are faced with a world-wide political movement which threatens the very existence of Western civilisation, and which has lost none of its vigour because it has become in a sense corrupt. Mr. Plamenatz concludes bleakly that though the U.S.S.R. will not necessarily precipitate an aggressive war against the West, its rulers regard a struggle to the death as inevitable, and will never come to any real agreement with those whom they regard as their natural enemies. Evidently, as Commander Stephen King-Hall says in his Introduction, if we want to combat Communism we must start by understanding it. But beyond understanding there lies the yet more difficult task of being understood, and – a problem that few people seem to have seriously considered as yet – of finding some way of making our point of view known to the Russian people.

1. John Petrov Plamenatz had his first book, *Consent, Freedom and Political Obligation*, published by Oxford University Press in 1938. Also published by him in Orwell's lifetime were *The Case for General Mihailovic* (privately printed, 1944), *What is Communism?* (1947) and *Mill's Utilitarianism* (with *The English Utilitarians*, 1949).

[3364]

'Writers and Leviathan' [1]
Politics and Letters, *Summer 1948*

The position of the writer in an age of State control is a subject that has already been fairly largely discussed, although most of the evidence that might be relevant is not yet available. In this place I do not want to express an opinion either for or against State patronage of the arts, but merely to point out that *what kind* of State rules over us must depend partly on the prevailing intellectual atmosphere: meaning, in this context, partly on the attitude of writers and artists themselves, and on their willingness or otherwise to keep the spirit of Liberalism alive. If we find ourselves in ten years' time cringing before somebody like Zhdanov, [2] it will probably be because that is what we have deserved. Obviously there are strong tendencies towards totalitarianism at work within the English literary intelligentsia already. But here I am not concerned with any organised and conscious movement such as Communism, but merely with the effect, on people of good will, of political thinking and the need to take sides politically.

This is a political age. War, Fascism, concentration camps, rubber truncheons, atomic bombs, etc., are what we daily think about, and therefore to a great extent what we write about, even when we do not name them openly. We cannot help this. When you are on a sinking ship, your thoughts will be about sinking ships. But not only is our subject-matter narrowed, but our whole attitude towards literature is coloured by loyalties which we at least intermittently realise to be non-literary. I often have the feeling that even at the best of times literary criticism is fraudulent, since in the absence of any accepted standards whatever – any *external* reference which can give meaning to the statement that such and such a book is 'good' or 'bad' – every literary judgement consists in trumping up a set of rules to justify an instinctive preference. One's real reaction to a book, when one has a reaction at all, is usually 'I like this book' or 'I don't like it', and what follows is a rationalisation. But 'I like this book' is not, I think, a non-literary reaction; the non-literary reaction is 'This book is on my side, and therefore I must discover merits in it'. Of course, when one praises a book for political reasons one may be emotionally sincere, in the sense that one does feel strong approval of it, but also it often happens that party solidarity demands a plain lie. Anyone used to reviewing books for political periodicals is well aware of this. In general, if you are writing for a paper that you are in agreement with, you sin by commission, and if for a paper of the opposite stamp, by omission. At any rate, innumerable controversial books – books for or against Soviet Russia, for or against Zionism, for or against the Catholic Church, etc. – are judged before they are read, and in effect before they are written. One knows in advance what reception they will get in what papers. And yet, with a dishonesty that sometimes is not even quarter-conscious, the pretence is kept up that genuinely literary standards are being applied.

Of course, the invasion of literature by politics was bound to happen. It must have happened, even if the special problem of totalitarianism had never arisen, because we have developed a sort of compunction which our grandparents did not have, an awareness of the enormous injustice and misery of the world, and a guilt-stricken feeling that one ought to be doing something about it, which makes a purely aesthetic attitude towards life impossible. No one, now, could devote himself to literature as single-mindedly as Joyce or Henry James. But unfortunately, to accept political responsibility now means yielding oneself over to orthodoxies and 'party lines', with all the timidity and dishonesty that that implies. As against the Victorian writers, we have the disadvantage of living among clear-cut political ideologies and of usually knowing at a glance what thoughts are heretical. A modern literary intellectual lives and writes in constant dread – not, indeed, of public opinion in the wider sense, but of public opinion within his own group. As a rule, luckily, there is more than one group, but also at any given moment there is a dominant orthodoxy, to offend against which needs a thick skin and sometimes means cutting one's income in half for years on end. Obviously, for about fifteen years past, the dominant orthodoxy, especially among the young, has been 'left'. The key words are 'progressive', 'democratic' and 'revolutionary', while the labels which you must at all costs avoid having gummed upon you are 'bourgeois', 'reactionary' and 'Fascist'. Almost everyone nowadays, even the majority of Catholics and Conservatives, is 'progressive', or at least wishes to be thought so. No one, so far as I know, ever describes himself

as a 'bourgeois', just as no one literate enough to have heard the word
ever admits to being guilty of anti-semitism. We are all of us good
democrats, anti-Fascist, anti-imperialist, contemptuous of class distinctions, impervious to colour prejudice, and so on and so forth. Nor is there
much doubt that the present-day 'left' orthodoxy is better than the rather
snobbish, pietistic Conservative orthodoxy which prevailed twenty years
ago, when the *Criterion* and (on a lower level) the *London Mercury*[3] were
the dominant literary magazines. For at the least its implied objective is a
viable form of society which large numbers of people actually want. But
it also has its own falsities which, because they cannot be admitted, make
it impossible for certain questions to be seriously discussed.

The whole left-wing ideology, scientific and utopian, was evolved by
people who had no immediate prospect of attaining power. It was,
therefore, an extremist ideology, utterly contemptuous of kings, governments, laws, prisons, police forces, armies, flags, frontiers, patriotism,
religion, conventional morality, and, in fact, the whole existing scheme
of things. Until well within living memory the forces of the left in all
countries were fighting against a tyranny which appeared to be invincible,
and it was easy to assume that if only *that* particular tyranny – capitalism
– could be overthrown, Socialism would follow. Moreover, the left had
inherited from Liberalism certain distinctly questionable beliefs, such as
the belief that the truth will prevail and persecution defeats itself, or that
man is naturally good and is only corrupted by his environment. This
perfectionist ideology has persisted in nearly all of us, and it is in the
name of it that we protest when (for instance) a Labour government
votes huge incomes to the King's daughters[4] or shows hesitation about
nationalising steel. But we have also accumulated in our minds a whole
series of unadmitted contradictions, as a result of successive bumps against
reality.

The first big bump was the Russian Revolution. For somewhat complex
reasons, nearly the whole of the English left has been driven to accept the
Russian régime as 'Socialist', while silently recognising that its spirit and
practice are quite alien to anything that is meant by 'Socialism' in this
country. Hence there has arisen a sort of schizophrenic manner of thinking,
in which words like 'democracy' can bear two irreconcilable meanings,
and such things as concentration camps and mass deportations can be

right and wrong simultaneously. The next blow to the left-wing ideology was the rise of Fascism, which shook the pacifism and internationalism of the left without bringing about a definite restatement of doctrine. The experience of German occupation taught the European peoples something that the colonial peoples knew already, namely, that class antagonisms are not all-important and that there is such a thing as national interest. After Hitler it was difficult to maintain seriously that 'the enemy is in your own country' and that national independence is of no value. But though we all know this and act upon it when necessary, we still feel that to say it aloud would be a kind of treachery. And finally, the greatest difficulty of all, there is the fact that the left is now in power and is obliged to take responsibility and make genuine decisions.

Left governments almost invariably disappoint their supporters because, even when the prosperity which they have promised is achievable, there is always need of an uncomfortable transition period about which little has been said beforehand. At this moment we see our own government, in its desperate economic straits, fighting in effect against its own past propaganda. The crisis that we are now in is not a sudden unexpected calamity, like an earthquake, and it was not caused by the war, but merely hastened by it. Decades ago it could be foreseen that something of this kind was going to happen. Ever since the nineteenth century our national income, dependent partly on interest from foreign investments, and on assured markets and cheap raw materials in colonial countries, had been extremely precarious. It was certain that, sooner or later, something would go wrong and we should be forced to make our exports balance our imports: and when that happened the British standard of living, including the working-class standard, was bound to fall, at least temporarily. Yet the left-wing parties, even when they were vociferously anti-imperialist, never made these facts clear. On occasion they were ready to admit that the British workers had benefited, to some extent, by the looting of Asia and Africa, but they always allowed it to appear that we could give up our loot and yet in some way contrive to remain prosperous. Quite largely, indeed, the workers were won over to Socialism by being told that they were exploited, whereas the brute truth was that, in world terms, they were exploiters. Now, to all appearances, the point has been reached when the working-class living-standard *cannot* be maintained, let alone raised. Even if we squeeze the rich out of existence, the mass of the people must either consume less or produce more. Or am I exaggerating the mess we are in? I may be, and I should be glad to find myself mistaken. But the point I wish to make is that this question, among people who are faithful to the left ideology, cannot be genuinely discussed. The lowering of wages and raising of working hours are felt to be inherently anti-Socialist measures, and must therefore be dismissed in advance, whatever the economic situation may be. To suggest that they may be unavoidable is merely to risk being plastered with those labels that we are all terrified of. It is far safer to evade the issue and pretend that we can put everything right by redistributing the existing national income.

To accept an orthodoxy is always to inherit unresolved contradictions. Take for instance the fact, which came out in Mr. Winkler's essay in this series, that all sensitive people are revolted by industrialism and its products, and yet are aware that the conquest of poverty and the emancipation of the working class demand not less industrialisation, but more and more. Or take the fact that certain jobs are absolutely necessary and yet are never done except under some kind of coercion. Or take the fact that it is impossible to have a positive foreign policy without having powerful armed forces. One could multiply examples. In every such case there is a conclusion which is perfectly plain but which can only be drawn if one is privately disloyal to the official ideology. The normal response is to push the question, unanswered, into a corner of one's mind, and then continue repeating contradictory catchwords. One does not have to search far through the reviews and magazines to discover the effects of this kind of thinking.

I am not, of course, suggesting that mental dishonesty is peculiar to Socialists and left-wingers generally, or is commonest among them. It is merely that acceptance of *any* political discipline seems to be incompatible with literary integrity. This applies equally to movements like Pacifism and Personalism,[5] which claim to be outside the ordinary political struggle. Indeed, the mere sound of words ending in -ism seems to bring with it the smell of propaganda. Group loyalties are necessary, and yet they are poisonous to literature, so long as literature is the product of individuals. As soon as they are allowed to have any influence, even a negative one, on creative writing, the result is not only falsification, but often the actual drying-up of the inventive faculties.

Well, then, what? Do we have to conclude that it is the duty of every writer to 'keep out of politics'? Certainly not! In any case, as I have said already, no thinking person can or does genuinely keep out of politics, in an age like the present one. I only suggest that we should draw a sharper distinction than we do at present between our political and our literary loyalties, and should recognise that a willingness to *do* certain distasteful but necessary things does not carry with it any obligation to swallow the beliefs that usually go with them. When a writer engages in politics he should do so as a citizen, as a human being, but not *as a writer*. I do not think that he has the right, merely on the score of his sensibilities, to shirk the ordinary dirty work of politics. Just as much as anyone else, he should be prepared to deliver lectures in draughty halls, to chalk pavements, to canvass voters, to distribute leaflets, even to fight in civil wars if it seems necessary. But whatever else he does in the service of his party, he should never write for it. He should make it clear that his writing is a thing apart. And he should be able to act co-operatively while, if he chooses, completely rejecting the official ideology. He should never turn back from a train of thought because it may lead to a heresy, and he should not mind very much if his unorthodoxy is smelt out, as it probably will be. Perhaps it is even a bad sign in a writer if he is not suspected of reactionary tendencies today, just as it was a bad sign if he was not suspected of Communist sympathies twenty years ago.

But does all this mean that a writer should not only refuse to be dictated to by political bosses, but also that he should refrain from writing *about* politics? Once again, certainly not! There is no reason why he should not write in the most crudely political way, if he wishes to. Only he should do so as an individual, an outsider, at the most an unwelcome guerrilla on the flank of a regular army. This attitude is quite compatible with ordinary political usefulness. It is reasonable, for example, to be willing to fight in a war because one thinks the war ought to be won, and at the same time to refuse to write war propaganda. Sometimes, if a writer is honest, his writings and his political activities may actually contradict one another. There are occasions when that is plainly undesirable: but then the remedy is not to falsify one's impulses, but to remain silent.

To suggest that a creative writer, in a time of conflict, must split his life into two compartments, may seem defeatist or frivolous: yet in practice I do not see what else he can do. To lock yourself up in the ivory tower is impossible and undesirable. To yield subjectively, not merely to a party machine, but even to a group ideology, is to destroy yourself as writer. We feel this dilemma to be a painful one, because we see the need of engaging in politics while also seeing what a dirty, degrading business it is. And most of us still have a lingering belief that every choice, even every political choice, is between good and evil, and that if a thing is necessary it is also right. We should, I think, get rid of this belief, which belongs to the nursery. In politics one can never do more than decide which of two evils is the less, and there are some situations from which one can only escape by acting like a devil or a lunatic. War, for example, may be necessary, but it is certainly not right or sane. Even a general election is not exactly a pleasant or edifying spectacle. If you have to take part in such things – and I think you do have to, unless you are armoured by old age or stupidity or hypocrisy – then you also have to keep part of yourself inviolate. For most people the problem does not arise in the same form, because their lives are split already. They are truly alive only in their leisure hours, and there is no emotional connection between their work and their political activities. Nor are they generally asked, in the name of political loyalty, to debase themselves as workers. The artist, and especially the writer, is asked just that – in fact, it is the only thing that politicians ever ask of him. If he refuses, that does not mean that he is condemned to inactivity. One half of him, which in a sense is the whole of him, can act as resolutely, even as violently if need be, as anyone else. But his writings, in so far as they have any value, will always be the product of the saner self that stands aside, records the things that are done and admits their necessity, but refuses to be deceived as to their true nature.

1. Leviathan: some form of water monster, as in Psalm 104:26; more fully described in Job, chapter 41, e.g., 'Canst thou draw out [of the water] leviathan with an hook?' (v. 1); 'wilt thou bind him for thy maidens?' (v. 5); 'Who can open the doors of his face? his teeth are terrible round about' (v. 14 – as if leviathan were a crocodile); 'His heart is as firm as a stone' (v. 24); 'When he raiseth up himself, the mighty are afraid' (v. 25); 'he is a king over all the children of pride' (the concluding half of v. 34, the final verse). The name of this creature was taken by Thomas Hobbes (1588–1679) as the title for his treatise on political philosophy, *The Leviathan, or the Matter, Form, and Power of a Commonwealth, Ecclesiastical and Civil* (1651). He describes the life of man in the 'state of nature' as 'solitary, poor, nasty, brutish and short'; to order society in which, for example, a man must only demand as much liberty as

he would allow others against himself, there must be a sovereign, external power responsible to God. Though that power is in itself absolute, it lapses if, for example, it can no longer protect the subject. Here, Orwell uses 'Leviathan' to stand for the State and State control. For the writer, 'acceptance of *any* political discipline seems to be incompatible with literary integrity'. The preparatory notes Orwell made for this article are reproduced as XIX/*3365*.

2. For Zhdanov, see n. 1 to extract from 'As I Please', 68, above.

3. The *Criterion* (briefly as the *New Criterion* and the *Monthly Criterion*) ran from October 1922 to January 1939, mainly as a quarterly. It was edited by T. S. Eliot. The *London Mercury* was a monthly founded in 1919 by John Squire (1884–1958; Kt., 1933), poet, journalist and essayist. Squire edited it from 1919 to 1934. It was incorporated in *Life and Letters Today*, May 1939.

4. The daughters are those of King George VI and Queen Elizabeth, the then Princess Elizabeth (as Queen Elizabeth II from 6 February 1952) and Princess Margaret.

5. Personalism is a form of Idealism in which whatever is 'real' exists in the experience of persons.

[*3485*]

Review of Portrait of the Anti-Semite *by Jean-Paul Sartre; translated by Erik de Mauny*

Observer, 7 November 1948

Anti-Semitism is obviously a subject that needs serious study, but it seems unlikely that it will get it in the near future.[1] The trouble is that so long as anti-Semitism is regarded simply as a disgraceful aberration, almost a crime, anyone literate enough to have heard the word will naturally claim to be immune from it; with the result that books on anti-Semitism tend to be mere exercises in casting motes out of other people's eyes.[2] M. Sartre's book is no exception, and it is probably no better for having been written in 1944, in the uneasy, self-justifying, quisling-hunting period that followed on the Liberation.[3]

At the beginning, M. Sartre[4] informs us that anti-Semitism has no rational basis: at the end, that it will not exist in a classless society, and that in the meantime it can perhaps be combated to some extent by education and propaganda. These conclusions would hardly be worth stating for their own sake, and in between them there is, in spite of much cerebration, little real discussion of the subject, and no factual evidence worth mentioning.

We are solemnly informed that anti-Semitism is almost unknown among the working class. It is a malady of the bourgeoisie, and, above all, of that goat upon whom all our sins are laid, the 'petty bourgeois'. Within the bourgeoisie it is seldom found among scientists and engineers. It is a peculiarity of people who think of nationality in terms of inherited culture and of property in terms of land.

Why these people should pick on Jews rather than some other victim M. Sartre does not discuss, except, in one place, by putting forward the ancient and very dubious theory that the Jews are hated because they are supposed to have been responsible for the Crucifixion. He makes no attempt to relate anti-Semitism to such obviously allied phenomena as, for instance, colour prejudice.

Part of what is wrong with M. Sartre's approach is indicated by his title. 'The' anti-Semite, he seems to imply all through the book, is always the same kind of person, recognisable at a glance and, so to speak, in action the whole time. Actually one has only to use a little observation to see that anti-Semitism is extremely widespread, is not confined to any one class, and, above all, in any but the worst cases, is intermittent.

But these facts would not square with M. Sartre's atomised vision of society. There is, he comes near to saying, no such thing as a human being, there are only different categories of men, such as 'the' worker and 'the' bourgeois, all classifiable in much the same way as insects. Another of these insectlike creatures is 'the' Jew, who, it seems, can usually be distinguished by his physical appearance. It is true that there are two kinds of Jew, the 'Authentic Jew', who wants to remain Jewish, and the 'Inauthentic Jew', who would like to be assimilated; but a Jew, of whichever variety, is not just another human being. He is wrong, at this stage of history, if he tries to assimilate himself, and we are wrong if we try to ignore his racial origin. He should be accepted into the national community, not as an ordinary Englishman, Frenchman, or whatever it may be, but as a Jew.

It will be seen that this position is itself dangerously close to anti-Semitism. Race-prejudice of any kind is a neurosis, and it is doubtful whether argument can either increase or diminish it, but the net effect of books of this kind, if they have an effect, is probably to make anti-Semitism slightly more prevalent than it was before. The first step towards serious study of anti-Semitism is to stop regarding it as a crime. Meanwhile, the less talk there is about 'the' Jew or 'the' anti-Semite, as a species of animal different from ourselves, the better.

1. See Orwell's 'Anti-Semitism in Britain', *Contemporary Jewish Record*, April 1945, XVII/2626. In this he describes anti-Semitism as 'only one manifestation of nationalism, and not everyone will have the disease in that particular form' (70); see also 'Notes on Nationalism', above.
2. Matthew 7:3: 'And why beholdest thou the mote that is in thy brother's eye, but considerest not the beam that is in thine own eye?', referring to v. 1: 'Judge not, that ye be not judged.'
3. See n. 1 to *Extract from* 'Occupation's Effect on French Outlook', above.
4. Jean-Paul Sartre (1905–80), French author, playwright and existentialist philosopher. In Orwell's lifetime he was especially known for *L'Être et le néant* (1943; *Being and Nothingness*, 1956); the plays, *Les Mouches* (1943; *The Flies*, 1947) and *Huis clos* (1944; as, variously, *No Exit, Vicious Circle*, and *In Camera*, 1946); and his trilogy, *Les Chemins de la liberté*, (1945–49; *The Roads to Freedom*, 1947–50). Orwell's opinion of Sartre is summed up in a letter he wrote to Fredric Warburg on receiving this book for review: 'I think Sartre is a bag of wind and I am going to give him a good boot' (XIX/3477).

[3516]

'Reflections on Gandhi'
Partisan Review, *January 1949*

Saints should always be judged guilty until they are proved innocent, but the tests that have to be applied to them are not, of course, the same in all cases. In Gandhi's case the questions one feels inclined to ask are: to what extent was Gandhi moved by vanity – by the consciousness of himself as a humble, naked old man, sitting on a praying-mat and shaking empires by sheer spiritual power – and to what extent did he compromise his own principles by entering into politics, which of their nature are inseparable from coercion and fraud? To give a definite answer one would have to study Gandhi's acts and writings in immense detail, for his whole life was a sort of pilgrimage in which every act was significant. But this partial autobiography,[1] which ends in the nineteen-twenties, is strong evidence in his favor, all the more because it covers what he would have called the unregenerate part of his life and reminds one that inside the saint, or near-saint, there was a very shrewd, able person who could, if he had chosen, have been a brilliant success as a lawyer, an administrator or perhaps even a business man.

At about the time when the autobiography first appeared I remember reading its opening chapters in the ill-printed pages of some Indian newspaper. They made a good impression on me, which Gandhi himself, at that time, did not. The things that one associated with him – homespun cloth, 'soul forces' and vegetarianism – were unappealing, and his medievalist program was obviously not viable in a backward, starving, over-populated country. It was also apparent that the British were making use of him, or thought they were making use of him. Strictly speaking, as a Nationalist, he was an enemy, but since in every crisis he would exert himself to prevent violence – which, from the British point of view, meant preventing any effective action whatever – he could be regarded as 'our man'. In private this was sometimes cynically admitted. The attitude of the Indian millionaires was similar. Gandhi called upon them to repent, and naturally they preferred him to the Socialists and Communists who, given the chance, would actually have taken their money away. How reliable such calculations are in the long run is doubtful; as Gandhi himself says, 'in the end deceivers deceive only themselves'; but at any rate the gentleness with which he was nearly always handled was due partly to the feeling that he was useful. The British Conservatives only became really angry with him when, as in 1942, he was in effect turning his non-violence against a different conqueror.

But I could see even then that the British officials who spoke of him with a mixture of amusement and disapproval also genuinely liked and admired him, after a fashion. Nobody ever suggested that he was corrupt, or ambitious in any vulgar way, or that anything he did was actuated by fear or malice. In judging a man like Gandhi one seems instinctively to apply high standards, so that some of his virtues have passed almost unnoticed. For instance, it is clear even from the autobiography that his natural physical courage was quite outstanding: the manner of his death was a later illustration of this, for a public man who attached any value to his own skin would have been more adequately guarded. Again, he seems to have been quite free from that maniacal suspiciousness which, as E. M. Forster rightly says in *A Passage to India*, is the besetting Indian vice, as hypocrisy is the British vice. Although no doubt he was shrewd enough in detecting dishonesty, he seems wherever possible to have believed that other people were acting in good faith and had a better nature through which they could be approached. And though he came of a poor middle-class family, started life rather unfavorably, and was probably of unimpressive physical appearance, he was not afflicted by envy or by the feeling of inferiority. Color feeling, when he first met it in its worst form in South Africa, seems rather to have astonished him. Even when he was fighting what was in effect a color war, he did not think of people in terms of race or status. The governor of a province, a cotton millionaire, a half-starved Dravidian cooly, a British private soldier, were all equally human beings, to be approached in much the same way. It is noticeable that even in the worst possible circumstances, as in South Africa when he was making himself unpopular as the champion of the Indian community, he did not lack European friends.

Written in short lengths for newspaper serialization, the autobiography is not a literary masterpiece, but it is the more impressive because of the commonplaceness of much of its material. It is well to be reminded that Gandhi started out with the normal ambitions of a young Indian student and only adopted his extremist opinions by degrees and, in some cases, rather unwillingly. There was a time, it is interesting to learn, when he wore a top hat, took dancing lessons, studied French and Latin, went up the Eiffel Tower and even tried to learn the violin – all this with the idea of assimilating European civilization as thoroughly as possible. He was not one of those saints who are marked out by their phenomenal piety from childhood onwards, nor one of the other kind who forsake the world after sensational debaucheries. He makes full confession of the misdeeds of his youth, but in fact there is not much to confess. As a frontispiece to the book there is a photograph of Gandhi's possessions at the time of his death. The whole outfit could be purchased for about £5, and Gandhi's sins, at least his fleshly sins, would make the same sort of appearance if placed all in one heap. A few cigarettes, a few mouthfuls of meat, a few annas pilfered in childhood from the maidservant, two visits to a brothel (on each occasion he got away without 'doing anything'), one narrowly escaped lapse with his landlady in Plymouth, one outburst of temper – that is about the whole collection. Almost from childhood onwards he had a deep earnestness, an attitude ethical rather than religious, but, until he was about thirty, no very definite sense of direction. His first entry into anything describable as public life was made by way of vegetarianism. Underneath his less ordinary qualities one feels all the time the solid middle-class business men who were his ancestors. One feels that even after he had abandoned personal ambition he must have been a resourceful, energetic lawyer and a hardheaded political organizer, careful in keeping down expenses, an adroit handler of committees and an indefatigable chaser of subscriptions. His character was an extraordinarily mixed one, but there was almost nothing in it that you can put your finger on and call bad, and I believe that even Gandhi's worst enemies would admit that he was an interesting and unusual man who enriched the world simply by being alive. Whether he was also a lovable man, and whether his teachings can have much value for those who do not accept the religious beliefs on which they are founded, I have never felt fully certain.

Of late years it has been the fashion to talk about Gandhi as though he were not only sympathetic to the Western leftwing movement, but were even integrally part of it. Anarchists and pacifists, in particular, have claimed him for their own, noticing only that he was opposed to centralism and State violence and ignoring the otherworldly, anti-humanist tendency of his doctrines. But one should, I think, realize that Gandhi's teachings cannot be squared with the belief that Man is the measure of all things, and that our job is to make life worth living on this earth, which is the only earth we have. They make sense only on the assumption that God exists and that the world of solid objects is an illusion to be escaped from. It is worth considering the disciplines which Gandhi imposed on himself and which – though he might not insist on every one of his followers observing every detail – he considered indispensable if one wanted to serve either God or humanity. First of all, no meat-eating, and if possible no animal food in any form. (Gandhi himself, for the sake of his health, had to compromise on milk, but seems to have felt this to be a backsliding.) No alcohol or tobacco, and no spices or condiments, even of a vegetable kind, since food should be taken not for its own sake but solely in order to preserve one's strength. Secondly, if possible, no sexual intercourse. If sexual intercourse must happen, then it should be for the sole purpose of begetting children and presumably at long intervals. Gandhi himself, in his middle thirties, took the vow of *bramahcharya*, which means not only complete chastity but the elimination of sexual desire. This condition, it seems, is difficult to attain without a special diet and frequent fasting. One of the dangers of milk-drinking is that it is apt to arouse sexual desire.

And finally – this is the cardinal point – for the seeker after goodness there must be no close friendships and no exclusive loves whatever.

Close friendships, Gandhi says, are dangerous, because 'friends react on one another' and through loyalty to a friend one can be led into wrong-doing. This is unquestionably true. Moreover, if one is to love God, or to love humanity as a whole, one cannot give one's preference to any individual person. This again is true, and it marks the point at which the humanistic and the religious attitude cease to be reconcilable. To an ordinary human being, love means nothing if it does not mean loving some people more than others. The autobiography leaves it uncertain whether Gandhi behaved in an inconsiderate way to his wife and children, but at any rate it makes clear that on three occasions he was willing to let his wife or a child die rather than administer the animal food prescribed by the doctor. It is true that the threatened death never actually occurred, and also that Gandhi – with, one gathers, a good deal of moral pressure in the opposite direction – always gave the patient the choice of staying alive at the price of committing a sin: still, if the decision had been solely his own, he would have forbidden the animal food, whatever the risks might be. There must, he says, be some limit to what we will do in order to remain alive, and the limit is well on this side of chicken broth. This attitude is perhaps a noble one, but, in the sense which – I think – most people would give to the word, it is inhuman. The essence of being human is that one does not seek perfection, that one *is* sometimes willing to commit sins for the sake of loyalty, that one does not push asceticism to the point where it makes friendly intercourse impossible, and that one is prepared in the end to be defeated and broken up by life, which is the inevitable price of fastening one's love upon other human individuals. No doubt alcohol, tobacco and so forth are things that a saint must avoid, but sainthood is also a thing that human beings must avoid. There is an obvious retort to this, but one should be wary about making it. In this yogi-ridden age, it is too readily assumed that 'non-attachment' is not only better than a full acceptance of earthly life, but that the ordinary man only rejects it because it is too difficult: in other words, that the average human being is a failed saint. It is doubtful whether this is true. Many people genuinely do not wish to be saints, and it is probable that some who achieve or aspire to sainthood have never felt much temptation to be human beings. If one could follow it to its psychological roots, one would, I believe, find that the main motive for 'non-attachment' is a desire to escape from the pain of living, and above all from love, which, sexual or non-sexual, is hard work. But it is not necessary here to argue whether the other-worldly or the humanistic ideal is 'higher'. The point is that they are incompatible. One must choose between God and Man, and all 'radicals' and 'progressives', from the mildest Liberal to the most extreme Anarchist, have in effect chosen Man.

However, Gandhi's pacifism can be separated to some extent from his other teachings. Its motive was religious, but he claimed also for it that it was a definite technique, a method, capable of producing desired political results. Gandhi's attitude was not that of most Western pacifists. *Satyagraha*,[2] first evolved in South Africa, was a sort of non-violent warfare, a way of defeating the enemy without hurting him and without feeling or arousing hatred. It entailed such things as civil disobedience, strikes, lying down in front of railway trains, enduring police charges without running away and without hitting back, and the like. Gandhi objected to 'passive resistance' as a translation of *Satyagraha*: in Gujarati, it seems, the word means 'firmness in the truth'. In his early days Gandhi served as a stretcher-bearer on the British side in the Boer War, and he was prepared to do the same again in the war of 1914–18. Even after he had completely abjured violence he was honest enough to see that in war it is usually necessary to take sides. He did not – indeed, since his whole political life centered round a struggle for national independence, he could not – take the sterile and dishonest line of pretending that in every war both sides are exactly the same and it makes no difference who wins. Nor did he, like most Western pacifists, specialize in avoiding awkward questions. In relation to the late war, one question that every pacifist had a clear obligation to answer was: 'What about the Jews? Are you prepared to see them exterminated? If not, how do you propose to save them without resorting to war?' I must say that I have never heard, from any Western pacifist, an honest answer to this question, though I have heard plenty of evasions, usually of the 'you're another' type. But it so happens that Gandhi was asked a somewhat similar question in 1938 and that his answer is on record in Mr. Louis Fischer's *Gandhi and Stalin*.[3] According to Mr. Fischer, Gandhi's view was that the German Jews ought to commit collective suicide, which 'would have aroused the world and the people of Germany to Hitler's violence'. After the war he justified himself: the Jews had been killed anyway, and might as well have died significantly. One has the impression that this attitude staggered even so warm an admirer as Mr. Fischer, but Gandhi was merely being honest. If you are not prepared to take life, you must often be prepared for lives to be lost in some other way. When, in 1942, he urged non-violent resistance against a Japanese invasion, he was ready to admit that it might cost several million deaths.

At the same time there is reason to think that Gandhi, who after all was born in 1869, did not understand the nature of totalitarianism and saw everything in terms of his own struggle against the British government. The important point here is not so much that the British treated him forbearingly as that he was always able to command publicity. As can be seen from the phrase quoted above, he believed in 'arousing the world', which is only possible if the world gets a chance to hear what you are doing. It is difficult to see how Gandhi's methods could be applied in a country where opponents of the régime disappear in the middle of the night and are never heard of again. Without a free press and the right of assembly, it is impossible not merely to appeal to outside opinion, but to bring a mass movement into being, or even to make your intentions known to your adversary. Is there a Gandhi in Russia at this moment? And if there is, what is he accomplishing? The Russian masses could only practice civil disobedience if the same idea happened to occur to all of them simultaneously, and even then, to judge by the history of the Ukraine famine,[4] it would make no difference. But let it be granted that non-violent resistance can be effective against one's own government, or against an occupying power: even so, how does one put it into practice internationally? Gandhi's various conflicting statements on the late war seem to show that he felt the difficulty of this. Applied to foreign politics, pacifism either stops being pacifist or becomes appeasement. Moreover the assumption, which served Gandhi so well in dealing with individuals, that all human beings are more or less approachable and will respond to a generous gesture, needs to be seriously questioned. It is not necessarily true, for example, when you are dealing with lunatics. Then the question becomes: Who is sane? Was Hitler sane? And is it not possible for one whole culture to be insane by the standards of another? And, so far as one can gauge the feelings of whole nations, is there any apparent connection between a generous deed and a friendly response? Is gratitude a factor in international politics?

These and kindred questions need discussion, and need it urgently, in the few years left to us before somebody presses the button and the rockets begin to fly. It seems doubtful whether civilization can stand another major war, and it is at least thinkable that the way out lies through non-violence. It is Gandhi's virtue that he would have been ready to give honest consideration to the kind of question that I have raised above; and, indeed, he probably did discuss most of these questions somewhere or other in his innumerable newspaper articles. One feels of him that there was much that he did not understand, but not that there was anything that he was frightened of saying or thinking. I have never been able to feel much liking for Gandhi, but I do not feel sure that as a political thinker he was wrong in the main, nor do I believe that his life was a failure. It is curious that when he was assassinated, many of his warmest admirers exclaimed sorrowfully that he had lived just long enough to see his life work in ruins, because India was engaged in a civil war which had always been foreseen as one of the by-products of the transfer of power. But it was not in trying to smoothe down Hindu-Moslem rivalry that Gandhi had spent his life. His main political objective, the peaceful ending of British rule, had after all been attained. As usual, the relevant facts cut across one another. On the one hand, the British did get out of India without fighting, an event which very few observers indeed would have predicted until about a year before it happened. On the other hand, this was done by a Labour government, and it is certain that a Conservative government, especially a government headed by Churchill, would have acted differently. But if, by 1945, there had grown up in Britain a large body of opinion sympathetic to Indian independence, how far was this due to Gandhi's personal influence? And if, as may happen, India and Britain finally settle down into a decent and friendly relationship, will this be partly because Gandhi, by keeping up his struggle obstinately and without hatred, disinfected the political air? That one even thinks of asking such questions indicates his stature. One may feel, as I do, a sort of aesthetic distaste for Gandhi, one may reject the claims of sainthood made on his behalf (he never made any such claim himself, by the way), one may also reject sainthood as an ideal and therefore feel that Gandhi's basic aims were anti-human and reactionary: but regarded simply as a politician, and compared with the other leading political figures of our time, how clean a smell he has managed to leave behind![5]

1. *The Story of my Experiments with Truth*, by M. K. Gandhi; translated from Gujarati by Mahadev Desai, 2 vols. (1927–9).

2. See n. 3 to letter from Roy Walker, above.

3. Orwell reviewed *Gandhi and Stalin* on 10 October 1948; see XIX/3469.

4. See n. 1 to the review of *Assignment in Utopia*, above.

5. It is remarkable that Orwell should have written this article for *Partisan Review* when he was ill and desperately exhausting himself completing the final revision and typing of *Nineteen Eighty-Four*. Perhaps he felt it was 'unfinished business' in the light of his correspondence with Roy Walker (see above). The article was later abridged and modified in *Mirror*, 16, as 'Gandhi: a critical study'. This monthly journal was published by the British government's Central Office of Information. It has no date but was printed in June 1949 and the British Library copy is date-stamped 27 October 1949. Although a few of the changes made, such as 'I must say that' and 'after all', might stem from Orwell, many pretty certainly do not. For example, 'maniacal suspiciousness' as 'the besetting Indian vice' has 'maniacal' omitted, and hypocrisy as the British vice is cut. In general, the article is made overtly propagandist in favour of Gandhi. Thus, Orwell's feeling of 'a sort of aesthetic distaste for Gandhi' is omitted. Full details are given in XX/3516. Coming from Orwell the COI version must have seemed especially telling. There is no way of knowing whether Orwell was party to these changes but, given his state of health, it seems very unlikely he was consulted. To put it crudely, it looks as if Orwell's independence was hijacked by the COI. This was particularly ironical when Minitrue (whose real-life building had housed the COI's predecessor, the Ministry of Information) had not long burst on the literary scene.

[3646]

Orwell's Statement on Nineteen Eighty-Four
July 1949

Orwell completed Nineteen Eighty-Four *at Barnhill, Jura, on 4 December 1948. He entered the Cotswold Sanatorium, Cranham, on 6 January 1949 and transferred from there to University College Hospital on 3 September, where he died on 21 January 1950.* Nineteen Eighty-Four *was published in England on 8 June 1949 and in the United States on 13 June. It was an outstanding success, but it was subject to misunderstanding, especially in the United States. Orwell was distressed that his novel was interpreted as an*

attack on the Labour Party in, for example, the New York Daily News.
The Socialist Call *(on 22 July),* Life *(on 25 July), and the New York*
Times Book Review *(on 31 July) published the following statement by*
Orwell (the NYTBR *omitting the second paragraph):*

My recent novel *Nineteen Eighty-Four* is NOT intended as an attack on
socialism, or on the British Labour Party (of which I am a supporter)
but as a show-up of the perversions to which a centralized economy is
liable and which have already been partly realized in Communism and
Fascism.

I do not believe that the kind of society which I described necessarily
will arrive, but I believe (allowing of course for the fact that the book is
a satire) that something resembling it could arrive. I believe also that
totalitarian ideas have taken root in the minds of intellectuals everywhere,
and I have tried to draw these ideas out to their logical consequences.

The scene of the book is laid in Britain in order to emphasize that the
English speaking races are not innately better than anyone else and that
totalitarianism, **if not fought against**, could triumph anywhere.

On 8 July 1950, Orwell's friend Tosco Fyvel[1] *wrote to Margaret M.*
Goalby in answer to her questions about Orwell's responses to events in the
last months of his life and the meaning of 'Ingsoc':

Orwell believed in the old Liberal principles and the value of truth and ordinary
decency. He was also firmly of the view that these principles demanded a democratic
socialist structure of society. It is true that he was pessimistic about the extent to which
these principles could prevail in most parts of the world. But I know that he was
pleasantly surprised at the firmness with which the Labour Government here at home
continued in office after mitigating the worst harshnesses of British society by means
of the Health Service, the National Social Insurance Act, the nationalisation of the
mines, the development of the depressed areas, and so on. All these measures were steps
in the direction Orwell desired . . . Even during his last weeks in hospital, Orwell was
keenly interested in the coming election and the chances of his various friends among
Labour M.P.s. He also said that one point in 1984 had been misunderstood by the
critics. 'Ingsoc', the totalitarian society, was not represented as arising out of democratic
socialism. On the contrary: his imaginary totalitarians who arose in England after an

atomic war merely adopted the name of 'English Socialism' because they thought it had popular appeal – in the same way as the Nazis, while allying themselves in 1933 with the Ruhr industrialists and smashing the German trade unions and Socialist Party, called themselves 'National-Socialists' to dupe the German working class.

1. See n. 1 to *The Lion and the Unicorn,* above

[3732]

Extracts from Orwell's List of Crypto-Communists and Fellow-Travellers

Orwell compiled a list of those whom he described as 'crypto-communists and fellow-travellers'¹ even though he was strongly opposed to the suppression of the Communist Party 'at any time when it did not unmistakably endanger national survival'. That 'would be calamitous' (XIX/103; and see the article in which that appears: 'Burnham's View of the Contemporary World Struggle', XIX/3204; this discusses crypto-communists and fellow-travellers). Furthermore, in August–September 1947 he wrote 'In Defence of Comrade Zilliacus', a crypto-communist (XIX/3254), an article Tribune *rejected. However, as he told Celia Kirwan,² he thought it was not 'a bad idea to have the people who are probably unreliable listed' (XX/3615). He had suffered from Communism in Spain, he knew how it persecuted others, Russians and Poles especially (see pp. 438–40, above). Gollancz refused to publish* Homage to Catalonia *for fear of offending Communists; Jonathan Cape was persuaded not to publish* Animal Farm *because of Soviet influence, and its French edition had to be published in Monaco by Odile Pathé because it was too politically dangerous to be published in France (XVIII/2950), where there was fear that Communist-dominated unions would stop the book being printed. Mlle Pathé, Orwell told Yvonne Davet (French translator of* Homage to Catalonia*), 'had a lot more courage than most publishers' (XVIII/2963). Kingsley Martin blocked Orwell's attempts to reveal in the* New Statesman *what the Communists were doing in Spain (see XI/119–20). And so on.*

Orwell compiled the list in a quarto notebook with a pale-blue cover. He did so in co-operation with Sir Richard Rees.³ Rees said that although

Orwell took the infiltration of such people very seriously, there was the element of a game about the project – thus, perhaps, the reason for the inclusion of an income-tax inspector's name. Most of the names in this notebook have been transcribed and printed in CW *(XX/3732); the exceptions are the names of those persons who are, or may be, alive and they are withheld solely to avoid the tedium and cost of possible actions for defamation. In due time they will be published but there will be no surprises. This notebook has been seen by only a few people and was* never *sent to the Information Research Department of the Foreign Office, as has been suggested.*[4] *So much for Orwell's private list, a list as private as a conversation in a pub or over dinner, sometimes incorrect, often injudicious, but never intended for publication. This list has been confused with a list of about thirty-five names sent by Orwell to Celia Kirwan at the Information Research Department on 2 May 1949. At present, these names have not been released by the Public Record Office, but the editor has made a guess as to which they might be from markings in the private manuscript book and those names are identified in* CW.

The Information Research Department was set up early in 1948 after much heart-searching by the Labour Government's Foreign Minister, Ernest Bevin. Bevin was concerned that 'the Russian and the Communist Allies are threatening the whole fabric of Western civilization . . . Soviet propaganda has . . . carried on . . . a vicious attack against the British Commonwealth and against Western Democracy'. On 4 February 1948, Bevin signed a Cabinet Minute setting up the IRD. One of its aims was to 'disseminate clear and cogent answers to Russian misrepresentation about Britain . . . we must see to it that our friends in Europe and elsewhere are armed with the facts and the answers to Russian propaganda. If we do not provide this ammunition, they will not get it from any other source.'[5] *Four months after Bevin signed this Minute, the Soviets began to blockade Berlin. When Orwell was asked for help, the blockade was still in force; it only ended on 12 May 1949. With powerful Communist parties in France and Italy, and constant attacks by the Soviets against Britain at the United Nations (a matter of particular concern to Bevin), had the blockade been successful, Stalin's domination would have extended from Russia to the Atlantic. It is indicative of the seriousness of the Soviet threat that, at a prime ministerial meeting in the autumn of 1948, Pandit Nehru and Liaquat Ali Khan, Prime Ministers of newly independent India and Pakistan, asked for the IRD's help to counter Soviet imperialism in their countries.*

Initially the IRD was seeking those who would write articles and briefing notes (e.g. for the UK's representatives at the United Nations) on its behalf. Among those whom Orwell suggested were Franz Borkenau, Gleb Struve and Darsie Gillie, the Manchester Guardian's Paris correspondent. He also suggested books that might usefully be circulated, one of which was Julian Huxley's Genetics and World Science *(to refute the fraudulent policies of the plant physiologist, Trofim Lysenko, 1898–1976⁶). The IRD also circulated 210 copies of each issue of* Tribune *to seventy-four consulates and reading rooms throughout the world because, though consistently championing 'objectives which left-wing sympathizers normally support', it 'often contains fairly trenchant criticisms of His Majesty's Government' – i.e., democratic socialism in action.⁷ Orwell was concerned enough at the danger of Soviet imperialism to send to Celia Kirwan on 2 May 1949 a list of 'about 35 names' of those who were 'probably unreliable', though it was not 'very sensational' and was unlikely to 'tell your friends anything they don't know' (XX/3615). This list did no more than indicate those whom Orwell thought should* not *be invited to write on behalf of the British Government. There are those (with a singular lack of historical perspective) who are quick to condemn Orwell (even if they had been members of a government which had operated the IRD). One of those who defended Orwell from such attacks justly summarizes Orwell's position. Denzil Jacobs (1921–) served with his father in Orwell's Home Guard platoon before joining the RAF. He and his father frequently visited Orwell in his last weeks in University College Hospital. Mr Jacobs responded to an attack in the* Evening Standard *by one such politician. He, wrote Jacobs, 'vilifies a man of high principle whose views were very clear-cut and who, in my opinion, was a great patriot. In 1940 he was well aware that Stalin and Stalinism were no longer tolerable to a man of his ideals. He was of the Left, but detested dictatorship, whether fascist or communist. I had many conversations with him during the nights we were on duty and I can quite see that he regarded it as his patriotic duty to give names of those supporting the Soviet Union to the Secret Service.'⁸ In fact, the names remained within the IRD and were never passed to the Secret Service.*

The notebook has 135 names. CW *contains one hundred names (XX/*

3732 and 3590A, n. 10). Names with asterisks (originally, red and added by hand) were probably those passed to the IRD. Only a few names – those which might be of interest in the light of what is reprinted in this volume – have been selected here. Two kinds of brackets are used: round brackets are Orwell's; square brackets are editorial; struck-through type indicates passages Orwell crossed out. A few brief editorial notes are printed in small type after some names.

NAME	JOBS	REMARKS
Beavan, John [1910–94; Baron Ardwick, 1970]	*Manchester Evening News* (editor) Previously *Observer* (news editor).	Sympathiser only. Anti British C.P. Might change???

Beavan was editor of the *Daily Herald*, 1960–62, and political adviser to the *Daily Mirror* group, 1962–76. He commissioned Orwell to write 'The Intellectual Revolt' and other articles and reviews for the *Manchester Evening News*. He was a Trustee of the Orwell Archive, University College London, from 1960 until his death.

NAME	JOBS	REMARKS
*Bernal, Professor J. D. (Irish extraction) [1901–71]	Scientist (physicist) Birkbeck College, London University. President, Association of Scientific Workers. Scientific staff of Combined Operations during war. ~~Science & Society~~, The Social Function of Science	Qy. open C.P.? Very gifted. Said to have been educated for R.C. priesthood. [in pencil:] I am pretty sure he *is* an open member.

NAME	JOBS	REMARKS
Braddock, Mrs. E. M. [1899–1970]	M.P. (Lab)	??

Bessie Braddock was a much-loved MP for the Liverpool Exchange Division. Orwell was mistaken in thinking her a crypto-communist.

| Driberg, Tom (English Jew) [1905–76] | M.P. (Ind) Malden *Reynolds's News* (Commentator). | Commonly thought to be underground member. Shows signs of independence occasionally. |
| [red* against Driberg crossed out in blue ink] | | Homosexual. *Makes occasional anti-C.P. comments in his column.* |

Driberg *was* a KGB agent; his code-name was LEPAGE. He flaunted his homosexuality when this was illegal and wrote a 'disingenuous study' of the spy Guy Burgess, *Guy Burgess: a Portrait with Background*, the proofs of which seem to have been vetted by the KGB; see *The Mitrokhin Archive*, 522–6.

Orwell's notes that some of those he listed were homosexuals or Jews may, in part, be explained because homosexuals were notoriously easily blackmailed by those who wished to recruit them, and Jews because (as Denzil Jacobs, a Jew, explained to the editor) after the war many Jews lost faith in the West because it had done so little about the Holocaust. Unfortunately, their trust in the Soviets was misplaced because of the rise in official anti-Semitism in the late forties and early fifties (see Vasily Grossman, *Life and Fate*, and Robert Chandler's introduction (1995 edn, 8 and 14–15).

| *Dover, Cedric (Eurasian) [1905–51] | Writer. (*Half Caste*, etc.) Some training as biologist. | Main emphasis anti-white but reliably pro-Russian on all major issues. Dishonest, and a good deal of a careerist. In USA? (1949) |

Although Orwell did not trust Dover in this context, he found work for him at the BBC, lent him money, and twice wrote on his behalf for grants from the Royal Literary Fund in 1943 and 1944 (XV/*2078* and XVI/*2479*).

| *Martin, Kingsley [1897–1969] | *New Statesman* (editor). Pamphlets & books. | Probably no definite organisational connection . . . Decayed liberal. Very dishonest. |

It was Martin who rejected Orwell's review of *The Spanish Cockpit* by Franz Borkenau for fear of offending Communists; see XI/119–20 and *Orwell in Spain* in this series for the review.

[Entry in pencil] Mikardo, Ian (Jewish?) [1908–93]	Labour M.P. (Reading). Column in *Tribune.* [later addition:] (Resigned from editorial board of *Tribune* May 1949. On political grounds.)	?I dont know much about him, but have sometimes wondered Prob. not. Silly.

Ian Mikardo was often thought to be unduly sympathetic to Communism but his passionate Zionism ensured he never forgot or forgave Stalin for his treatment of the Jews.

*Pritt, D. N. [1887–1972]	M.P. (independent – expelled L.P.) for West Hammersmith. Barrister. Author of many books, pamphlets etc. *Choose Your Future* issued 1940, withdrawn 1941.	Almost certainly underground member. Said to handle more money than is accounted for by his job. Good M.P. (ie. locally). Very able & courageous.
Priestley, J. B. [1894–1984] [red* against Priestley crossed out in blue ink with large ? added]	Novelist, broadcaster. Book Club selector. [later note:] Appears to have changed latterly (1949).	Strong sympathiser, possibly has some kind of organisational tie-up. Very anti- USA. Development of last 10 years or less. Might change. Makes huge sums of money in USSR. ?? [large question-

[marks; may refer specifically to making money in USSR]

Orwell admired Priestley but his *Russian Journey* (1946) showed how easily he could be duped by a visit to the USSR. There were, he said, no secret police, 'unless they were disguised as sparrows'.

*Padmore, George (Negro. Qy. African origin?) [Pseudonym of Malcolm Nurse, b. Trinidad, 1903–59; died London but buried in Ghana]	Organiser League against Imperialism & kindred activities. Books, pamphlets.	Expelled C.P. about 1936. Nevertheless reliably pro-Russian. Main emphasis anti-white. Friend (lover?) of Nancy Cunard. [Left C.P. 1934; founded Pan-African Federation 1944]
*Smollet°, Peter (Smolka?) (Austrian) [Harry Peter Smollett = Smolka; 1912–80]	Beaverbrook Press (correspondent). Russian section M.O.I. during war [awarded Order of the British Empire for his services].	Almost certainly agent of some kind. Said to be careerist. Very dishonest.

His success as a secret agent was so outstanding that the NKVD thought he must be an MI5 plant (*The Mitrokhin Archive*, 158). However, he was undetected by British Intelligence.

Spender, Stephen [1909–95]	Poet, critic etc. Literary organisations of various kinds. (UNESCO).	Sentimental sympathiser, & very unreliable. Easily influenced. Tendency towards homosexuality.

Spender (Kt., 1983) was not a Communist agent. Ironically, and unwittingly, the journal he co-edited (1953–67), *Encounter*, proved to be funded surreptitiously by

Orwell and Politics

the US Central Intelligence Agency. He immediately left the editorial board when this was revealed.

| 'Vicky' (name?) [Victor Weisz, [1913–66] | Cartoonist, *News-Chronicle*. | ?? (Don't thinks so.) Yes. |
| *Zilliacus, K. (Finnish? 'Jewish'?) [1894–1967] | M.P. Gateshead (Labour). 'Vigilantes.' Author of many books. Previously League of Nations official. Expelled from L.P. 1949 Made equivocal remark (re Tito) Sept. 1949. Attacked in Moscow press. Continued F.T. activities. | Possibly no organisational connection. Close fellow-traveller only since about 1943. Anti-Russian during Finnish war [1939–40]. Good M.P. (locally.) Refused re-nomination by L.P. 1949. Nominated candidate for E.C. [Labour Party Executive Committee?] by D.L.P. [Democratic Labour Party?] |

1. 'Fellow-travellers' is the English equivalent of the Russian *poputchik*, a word Trotsky used to describe writers sympathetic to the Revolution who were not members of the Communist Party. The *OED* notes the first usage in English in this sense as occurring in the *Nation*, New York, 24 October 1936. In *Comintern Army*, R. Dan Richardson states that Willi Münzenberg, a German political exile living in Paris after 1933, 'invented and made use of the "fellow traveller", a new species which was to have a significant future, especially during the popular front period'. Münzenberg was chief of agitprop for Western Europe for the Comintern. Arthur Koestler worked with him in those days and called him the 'Red Eminence of the international anti-fascist movement'. He 'produced International Committees, Congresses and movements as a conjurer produces rabbits out of his hat', according to Koestler in *The God That Failed*, ed. Richard Crossman (1950), 56, whom Richardson quotes (9–10).

2. Celia Kirwan (now Celia Goodman) was the twin sister of Arthur Koestler's wife, Mamaine. She and Orwell, with his son Richard, spent Christmas 1945 at the Koestlers' house at

Bwylch Ocyn in Wales. She worked as an editorial assistant on *Polemic* (to which Orwell contributed) and when that collapsed in 1947 went to work in Paris for the trilingual magazine *Occident*. She returned to London to work for the Information Research Department in 1948 and visited Orwell at the Cotswold Sanatorium on 29 March 1949 to ask him if he would write articles for the IRD. He declined because he was too ill but suggested names of those who might be suitable. See XX/*3590A* and *3590B*. Orwell proposed marriage to Celia Kirwan after Eileen had died (on 29 March 1945). She declined but they remained friends. See *Remembering Orwell*, 162–5, 215.

3. Sir Richard Rees (1900–1970), artist and editor of *The Adelphi*, October 1930–1937 (1930–32 with Max Plowman), and a good friend of Orwell's from 1930 until Orwell's death; with Sonia Orwell he served as Orwell's literary executor. He had been an attaché at the British Embassy in Berlin, 1922–3, and Honorary Treasurer and Lecturer, London District of the Workers' Educational Association, 1925–7. He gave Orwell much encouragement, and he and Orwell were partners of Barnhill on Jura. Ravelston of *Keep the Aspidistra Flying* owes something to Rees's generous nature. See his *George Orwell: Fugitive from the Camp of Victory* (1961); Crick, 202–5; *Orwell Remembered*, 115–26; S&A, *Unknown Orwell*, 186–7, 248–9; Shelden, 223–4.

4. So claimed by Paul Lashmar and James Oliver, *Britain's Secret Propaganda War: The Foreign Office and the Cold War 1948–1977* (1998), 95–8. Celia Goodman categorically denied that the IRD had ever seen the notebook (letter to the editor, 24 February 1999).

5. Cabinet Papers 48, 6. For details of the IRD, see *History Notes*, 9: *IRD: Origins and Establishment of the Foreign Office Information Research Department, 1946–48* (August 1995); Public Record Office, FO 1110/189, 221, 264 (1634 G, June 1949) and 232; and PR 442, 622/41/G, 1135/11/G and 3361/33/913.

6. Letter from IRD, 4 March 1949, PR 442/33/913.

7. Lysenko declared that the Mendelian laws of heredity, established in 1866, were erroneous, and maintained that heredity could be managed by techniques of husbandry. He won the support of Stalin; leading scientists who pointed to the fallacy of Lysenko's case were dismissed, and the effect of Lysenko's theories on Soviet food production was disastrous.

8. *Evening Standard*, 16 July 1996, responding to an article of 11 July.

Extracts from Orwell's Pamphlet Collection Catalogue

Orwell probably started collecting pamphlets about 1935–7 and carried on until at least March 1947. He thought he had between 1,200 and 2,000 and made more than one attempt to classify and catalogue them. He wished that after his death they should be donated to the British Museum and they are now held by the British Library, call number 1899 ss 1–21, 23–48, item 48 being a typed but incomplete catalogue. Orwell made a handwritten classified list of 364 pamphlets in about 1946–7. He classified the pamphlets in the three categories reproduced here as Anarchist (An), Labour Party (LP) and Trotskyist (Tr). Other abbreviations used are: AF, Anarchist Federation; FP, Freedom Press; FPDC, Freedom Press Defence League; LL, Leninist League; SLP, Socialist Labour Press; WIL, Workers' International League; WIP, Workers' International Press. Some pamphlets appear more than once; item 12 under 'Anarchism' duplicates item 1 and has been omitted here. Orwell's Spanish Civil War pamphlets are listed in Orwell in Spain. *For a full account, see 3733, XX/259–86. Details given here have Orwell's classifications and the boxes in which the pamphlets are to be found; notes within square brackets and in smaller type are editorial.*

ANARCHISM: THEORY & HISTORY

1. The British General Strike (Tom Brown) 3 [FP, 1943]   Box 3 (10)
    The figure 3 indicates the number of copies Orwell had.

2. The Anarchist Revolution (G. Barrett) [FP, 1920]   (An) Box 3 (12)

3. Anarchy (Malatesta) [FP, 1942]   (An) Box 3 (13)
    Errico Malatesta (1850–1932), Italian Anarchist. FP also
    published his *Anarchy*.

4. Objections to Anarchism (G. Barrett) [FP, 1921]   (An) Box 3 (20)

5. Revolutionary Government (Kropotkin) [FP, 1941]   (An) Box 3 (56)

6. What is Anarchism? (Woodcock) [FP, 1945]   (An) Box 4 (1)
    Orwell initially wrote Box 3.

7. The Struggle in the Factory [AF, 1945]   (An) Box 4 (8)

8. Vote For What? (Malatesta) [FP, 1945]   (An) Box 4 (28)

9. Freedom – Is it a Crime? (H. Read) [FPDC, 1945]   (An) Box 4 (29)

10. Selections from Godwin's 'Political Justice' [FP, 1945]   (An) Box 4 (39)

11. Peter Kropotkin – His Federalist Ideas (Berneri)   (An) Box 4 (42)
    [FP, 1942]
    First published in Italian, 1922. Camillo Berneri (1897–1937),
    Italian anarchist. Took refuge in France, 1926, following
    Mussolini's rise to power. Murdered in Barcelona.

13. Socialism versus Anarchism (Daniel de Leon) [SLP,   (An) Box 4 (19)
    pre-war]
    Daniel de Leon, intellectual Marxist initially involved in formation
    in the US of IWW (International Workers of the World); broke
    away in 1908 because committed to political action through the
    Socialist Labour Party. (James Joll, *The Anarchists*, 201–2.)
    Typescript spells name 'D. de Lion'.

Trotskyism: History & Theory

1. The Russian Myth [FP, 1941]   (An) Box 3 (25)
   'An' is overwritten with what looks like 'Tr'; an 'x' has been
   written above.

2. The Kronstadt Revolt (A. Ciliga) [FP, 1942]   (Tr) Box 3 (28)
   In his review of pamphlet literature, 9 January 1943 (XIV/*1807*),
   Orwell describes this as 'Anarchist pamphlet, largely an attack on
   Trotsky'. Anton Ciliga is referred to by Orwell in his Unsigned
   Editorial, *Polemic*, 3, May 1946; see p. 455 above. For a later
   reference to the Kronstadt Revolt, see Orwell's letter to Dwight
   Macdonald regarding the meaning of *Animal Farm*, 5 December
   1946, pp. 230–31, above.

3. The End of Socialism in Russia ([M[ax] Eastman) [Secker   (Tr) Box 3 (30)
   & Warburg, 1937]
   Crick suggests that Orwell might have read this (especially since
   it was published by Secker & Warburg) before writing *Homage
   to Catalonia*, 'and it would have refortified all he meant to
   say' (634).

4. Trotskyism, Left Flank of the Reformist [LL, 1943]   (Tr) Box 3 (43)

5. I Stake My Life! ([L.] Trotsky) [Fourth International, 1937] (Tr) Box 3 (53)

6. Cauchemar en U.R.S.S. ([B.] Souvarine) [Plon, 1937,   (Tr) Box 3 (69)
   2 francs]
   Boris Souvarine, Russian-born, naturalized Frenchman
   (pseudonym of Boris Lifchitz; 1895–1984), had been a founder of
   the Parti Communiste Français, a member of the Executive
   Committee of the Comintern, and editor of the Communist
   newspaper *L'Humanité*. After about 1935 he became highly critical
   of Stalin's Soviet Union. This is expressed in this item, first
   published in *Revue de Paris*, 1 July 1937 – just as Orwell returned
   from Spain. As William Steinhoff shows, it was influential on
   Nineteen Eighty-Four; see *George Orwell and the Origins of 1984*
   (1975), 32–4. In the manuscript, the French form 'URSS' is
   written 'USSR': the typed catalogue has a (typed) note: 'prob,
   rare.'

7. The Case for Socialist Revolution [WIL, Wartime]   (Tr) Box 4 (12)

Four items catalogued under 'U.S.S.R.: Internal Affairs' are of interest here:

2. Why Did They 'Confess'? (U.S.) [Pioneer Publishers,   (Tr) Box 4 (36)
   1937]
   Orwell annotated the typed catalogue that this has an
   Introduction by James Burnham. The subject of the pamphlet is
   the trial in January 1937 of Karl Radek and sixteen alleged
   co-conspirators, of whom thirteen, but not Radek, were executed.
   A chapter is devoted to the trial in Robert Payne, *The Rise and Fall
   of Stalin* (1966).

3. Summary of the Final Report on the Moscow Trials [WIP,   (Tr) Box 4 (46)
   1938?]
   The typed catalogue gives the title as 'Summary of the final report
   of the Commission of Enquiry into the charges made against
   Trotsky in the Moscow Trials'. The date has been added in
   Orwell's hand.

4. How the Russians Live [W. Miller; Socialist Propaganda   (LP) Box 5 (1)
   Committee, 1942]

5. Stalin-Wells Talk (Shaw, Wells etc) 2 [*New Statesman*, 1934]   (LP) Box 5 (7)
   'LP' appears to be written over 'Tr'.

Further Reading

The principal source for this volume is *The Complete Works of George Orwell*, edited by Peter Davison, assisted by Ian Angus and Sheila Davison, 20 vols (1998; paperback edn, from September 2000). Reference might also usefully be made to *The Collected Essays, Journalism and Letters of George Orwell*, edited by Sonia Orwell and Ian Angus, 4 volumes, 1968 (Penguin, 1970). *Orwell in Spain* in this series has most of Orwell's political writing related to Spain, and see *Orwell and the Dispossessed* and *Orwell's England*, also in this series.

Volumes of *CW* in which items will be found are as follows:

X 1–355	XIV 1435–1915	XVIII 2832–3143
XI 355A–582	XV 1916–2377	XIX 3144–3515
XII 583–843	XVI 2378–2596	XX 3516–3715
XIII 844–1434	XVII 2597–2831	

Vol. XX also includes in Appendix 15 the following supplementary items: 2278A, 2278B, 2420A, 2451A, 2563B, 2593A, 2625A, 3351A and 3715A. Each volume is indexed and vol. XX has a Cumulative Index, indexes of topic, and an index of serials in which Orwell's work appeared.

Orwell wrote far more related to politics than could be contained in this volume. The following list gives most of the articles and reviews, and a few of the letters, which can be found in *CW*.

Review of Franz Borkenau, *The Totalitarian Enemy*, 4 May 1940, XII/620
Review of Francis Williams, *War by Revolution*, September 1940, XII/682
'Our Opportunity', January 1941, XII/737
'Fascism and Democracy', February 1941, XII/753
'Will Freedom Die with Capitalism', April 1941, XII/782
Literary Criticism IV: Literature and Totalitarianism, 21 May 1941, XII/804

The following is a highly selective reading list:

Christopher Andrew and Oleg Gordievsky, *KGB: The Inside Story* (1991)

Christopher Andrew and Vasili Mitrokhin, *The Mitrokhin Archive: The KGB in Europe and the West* (1999)

Correlli Barnett, *The Audit of War: The Illusion & Reality of Britain as a Great Nation* (1986)

Audrey Coppard and Bernard Crick, eds., *Orwell Remembered* (1984)

Bernard Crick, *George Orwell: A Life* (1980; 3rd edn 1992)

Andy Croft, *Red Letter Days: British Fiction in the 1930s* (1990)

Valentine Cunningham, *British Writers of the Thirties* (1989)

Peter Davison, *George Orwell: A Literary Life* (1996)

Paul Fussell, *Wartime: Understanding and Behaviour in the Second World War* (1989)

Tosco Fyvel, *George Orwell: A Personal Memoir* (1982)

Charles Garrett, *The Collected George Garrett*, edited by Michael Murphy (1999)

George Orwell at Home (and among the Anarchists): Essays and Photographs [by Vernon Richards] (1998)

Robert Graves and Alan Hodge, *The Long Week-End: A Social History of Great Britian 1918–1939* (1940)

Miriam Gross, ed., *The World of George Orwell* (1971)

Vasily Grossman, *Life and Fate* (1995), with Robert Chandler's introduction

Rayner Heppenstall, *Four Absentees* (1960)

Robert Hewison, *Under Siege: Literary Life in London, 1939–45* (1978)

Graham Holderness, Bryan Loughrey and Nahem Yousaf, *George Orwell* (Contemporary Critical Essays; 1998)

Humphrey Jennings and Charles Madge, eds., *May the Twelfth: Mass-Observation Day-Surveys, 1937* (1937; reprinted with a new Afterword, 1987)

James Joll, *The Anarchists* (2nd edn, 1979)

Robert Kee, *The World We Left Behind: A Chronicle of the Year 1939* (1984)

Peter Lewis, *George Orwell: The Road to 1984* (1981)

Jeffrey Meyers, ed., *George Orwell: The Critical Heritage* (1975)

—, *Orwell: Wintry Conscience of a Generation* (2000)

Janet Montefiore, *Men and Women Writers of the 1930s: The Dangerous Flood of History* (1996)

Malcolm Muggeridge, *The Thirties* (1940); reviewed by Orwell, 25 April 1940 (XII/615)

David Christie Murray, *A Novelist's Note Book* (1887)

John Newsinger, *Orwell's Politics* (1999)

Christopher Norris, ed., *Inside the Myth: Orwell: Views from the Left* (1984)

Alok Rai, *Orwell and the Politics of Despair* (1988)

Sir Richard Rees, *For Love or Money* (1960)

—, *George Orwell: Fugitive from the Camp of Victory* (1961)

Patrick Reilly, *George Orwell: The Age's Adversary* (1986)

John Rodden, *The Politics of Literary Reputation: The Making and Claiming of 'St George Orwell'* (1989)

Michael Shelden, *Orwell: The Authorised Biography* (1991)

Ian Slater, *Orwell: The Road to Airstrip One: The Development of George Orwell's Political and Social Thought from Burmese Days to 1984* (1985)

Peter Stansky and William Abrahams, *The Unknown Orwell* (1974)

—, *Orwell: The Transformation* (1979)

John Thompson, *Orwell's London* (1984)

Richard J. Voorhees, *The Paradox of George Orwell* (1961)

Stephen Wadhams, ed., *Remembering Orwell* (1984)

Eugen Weber, *The Hollow Years: France in the 1930s* (1995)

George Woodcock, *The Crystal Spirit: A Study of George Orwell* (1967)

David Wykes, *A Preface to Orwell* (1987)

Selective Index

This volume is concerned with Orwell's interest in politics and that covers a wide field. To index every reference, direct and indirect, would overwhelm the user. Imperialism, England (often referred to as Britain), the British Empire, Democracy and Fascism are topics that occur on almost every page. To some extent this is true of Anarchism, Trotskyism, Russia (or the USSR), Communism, and some other topics. The first group of topics is therefore not indexed except when, for example, the nature of Fascism is discussed, and other topics are indexed selectively. The references to 'Concentration Camps' may include other forms of repression not separately indexed (e.g., rubber truncheons, castor oil, deportations). Bracketed explanations are sometimes provided after line references to provide additional guidance (e.g., 'rev.' for Orwell's reviews). Sources within footnotes are not usually indexed although there are exceptions if it is thought these would help the user. Authors and titles in Orwell's Pamphlet Collection are not indexed, nor are details of those given in Orwell's List of Crypto-Communists and Fellow-Travellers. The lists of further reading are not indexed nor are the newspaper sources of Orwell's 'Diary of Events Leading Up to the War'. The various forms of the Soviet secret police (e.g., OGPU, KGB) are listed under NKVD. The text of *Animal Farm* has not been indexed. Page numbers for the text are given in roman type (e.g., 57, 168); notes are in italic (e.g., *33, 284*); bold italic is used for biographical and explanatory detail (e.g., ***44, 357***).